About the Author

Steven Price's first collection of poems, *Anatomy of Keys*, won the Gerald Lampert Award for Best First Collection, was shortlisted for the BC Poetry Prize and was named a *Globe and Mail* Book of the Year. His first novel, *Into That Darkness*, was shortlisted for the 2012 BC Fiction Prize. His second collection of poems, *Omens in the Year of the Ox*, won the 2013 ReLit Award. He lives in Victoria, British Columbia, with his family.

Praise for *By Gaslight*

Longlisted for the Giller Prize
A Walter Scott Prize Academy Recommended Read
A *Vanity Fair* Must Read Book of the Fall
A *Chicago Review of Books* 10 Best New Books Pick
A *Huffington Post* Best Fall Book
A *Globe and Mail* Book of the Year

'Steven Price has done a daring thing: taken a long, complex, but utterly fascinating 19th century crime tale and applied to it the rules of modern mystery writing. The result is something unique, but it is his gift for unraveling a terrific yarn, in whatever manner, that shines through. Do not be daunted by length: give this book a try.'

Caleb Carr, author of *The Alienist*

'A dark tale of love, betrayal and murder that reaches from the slums of Victorian London to the diamond mines in South Africa, to the American Civil War and back. Superb storytelling.'

Kurt Palka, author of *The Piano Maker*

'Uniting the literary grace and depth of William Faulkner and Cormac McCarthy with the intrigue and momentum of a Sherlock Holmes story, *By Gaslight* is completely absorbing – an epic, brilliantly written novel to rank with the world's best.'

Jacqueline Baker, author of *The Broken Hours*

'This darkly mesmerizing tale is worthy of the great Victorian thriller writers, but Steven Price brings to his prose a sensibility and dazzling skill all his own.'   Marina Endicott, author of *Close To Hugh*

'A poetic, persuasive pea-souper. Think Dickens with Maigret's whiskers.'
Anakana Schofield, author of *Malarky*

'I found myself returning to passages...because I wanted to revisit the somber music of the telling...Spinning fiction out of fact, Price creates an evocative world, cast not in shades of stark black and white, but rather in morally complex herringbone...raw and beautiful...always expressing the complexities of the human heart... *By Gaslight* can be seen as Arthur Conan Doyle by way of Dickens by way of Faulkner. Intense, London-centric, threaded through with a melancholy brilliance, it is an extravagant novel that takes inspiration from the classics and yet remains wholly itself.'   NPR

'Reads like a resurrected Conan Doyle has created a high-quality thriller for a Sky Atlantic series...breathtakingly atmospheric.'
Peterborough Telegraph

'Price's naturalism is unsentimental, adding verisimilitude to a book already thrumming with emotional and psychological realism. The author's blend of quest, grief, betrayal and the mysteries of identity will appeal to readers of literary crime fiction.'   *Library Journal*

'A postmodern take on noir mysteries...The real highlight of the novel, though, is the mesmerizing writing style, which is difficult to decipher but lyrically rewarding and intensely evocative of setting and character. Intense, frustrating and magical.'   *Booklist*

'Price's elegantly written, vividly evoked second novel marries historical suspense with literary sophistication...With its intricate cat-and-mouse game, array of idiosyncratic characters and brooding atmosphere, *By Gaslight* has much to please fans of both classic suspense and Victorian fiction. Yet Price's novel is entirely contemporary, and assuredly his own: a sweeping tale of hunter and hunted in which the most-dangerous pursuer is always the human heart.'
Publishers Weekly

'Rich in characterization and description as well as evidently well-researched material.'   *Historical Novels Review*

'[An] extraordinary historical novel, finely written and deeply researched...[with] a cast of truly gothic characters, half-mad and all dangerous.'   Alan Furst, author of *The Foreign Correspondent*

'Canadian poet Price turns to fiction with this lively visitation to the foggy streets of Victorian Blighty...the story is utterly Sherlock-ian... Fans of steampunk and Victorian detective fiction alike will enjoy Price's continent-hopping romp in time.'   *Kirkus*

'[*By Gaslight*] magically transports the reader, as if by time machine, to another world.'   *Dallas Morning News*

'A formidable mystery.'   *Buffalo News*

'Utterly compelling...unique. But it is his gift for unraveling this terrific yarn, in a literary style often reminiscent of William Faulkner, that makes this stand out from the ordinary.'   *Crime Review*

'For long winter evenings...*By Gaslight* seems like an excellent choice'.   *New Books*

'Remarkable...*By Gaslight* wears its erudition with flair and admirable lightness. The novel abounds in exhilarating set-pieces – a séance that takes an alarming turn; an untethered balloon ride over a Civil War slaughter; the near-obligatory descent into Bazalgette's sewers – and a supporting cast of vividly conjured grotesques.'   *Globe and Mail*

'For all its panache as a historical thriller, *By Gaslight* is strongest as a war novel...*By Gaslight* is an engrossing read. The twists and turns deepen our understanding of the characters even as they advance multiple plot strands, and Price immerses us in a world of sights and smells so precisely rendered they are nearly tangible.'   *Quill & Quire*

'Price's darkly feverish page-turner is buoyed by inventive cat-meets-mice plotting, brooding, secretive and quicksilver characters, and vivid cinematic tours...there's no resisting its gripping enormity.'   *The Star*

BY
GASLIGHT

STEVEN PRICE

ONEWORLD

A Oneworld Book

First published in Great Britain and Australia by Oneworld Publications, 2C
This paperback edition published 2017
Reprinted, 2017, 2018

ISBN 978-1-78607-102-6
ISBN 978-1-78074-869-6 (ebook)

Printed and bound in Great Britain by Clays Ltd, St Ives plc

Oneworld Publications
10 Bloomsbury Street
London WC1B 3SR
England

for Cleo & Maddox

and in memory of Ellen Seligman

If a man is willing to accept the consequences,
there is nothing that need limit his effectiveness.

All that we remember will one day be forgotten.

Take everything.

ADAM FOOLE

—————————

I really and truly think I can handle this man.
I can make him useful to us.

WILLIAM PINKERTON

The Woman
in the Thames:
Part One

1885

LONDON

ONE

He was the oldest son.

He wore his black moustaches long in the manner of an outlaw and his right thumb hooked at his hip where a Colt Navy should have hung. He was not yet forty but already his left knee went stiff in a damp cold from an exploding Confederate shell at Antietam. He had been sixteen then and the shrapnel had stood out from his knee like a knuckle of extra bone while the dirt heaved and sprayed around him. Since that day he had twice been thought killed and twice come upon his would-be killers like an avenging spectre. He had shot twenty-three men and one boy outlaws all and only the boy's death did not trouble him. He entered banks with his head low, his eyebrows drawn close, his huge menacing hands empty as if fixed for strangling. When he lurched aboard crowded street-cars men instinctively pulled away and women followed him with their eyelashes, bonnets tipped low. He had not been at home more than a month at a stretch for five years now though he loved his wife and daughters, loved them with the fear a powerful man feels who is given to breaking things. He had long yellow teeth, a wide face, sunken eyes, pupils as dark as the twist of a man's intestines.

So.

He loathed London. Its cobbled streets were filthy even to a man whose business was filth, who would take a saddle over a bed and huddle all night in a brothel's privy with his Colt drawn until the right arse stumbled in. Here he had seen nothing green in a month that was not holly or a cut bough carted in from a countryside he could not imagine. On Christmas he had watched the poor swarm a man in daylight, all clutched rags and greed; on New Year's he had seen a lady kick a watercress girl from the step of a carriage, then curse the child's blood spotting her laces. A rot ate its way through London, a wretchedness older and more brutal than any he had known in Chicago.

He was not the law. No matter. In America there was not a thief who did not fear him. By his own measure he feared no man living and only one man dead and that man his father.

It was a bitter January and that father six months buried when he descended at last into Bermondsey in search of an old operative of his father's, an old friend. Wading through the night's fog, another man's blood barnacling his knuckles, his own business in London nearly done.

He was dressed like a gentleman though he had lost his gloves and he clutched his walking stick in one fist like a cudgel. A stain spotted his cuffs that might have been soot or mud but was not either. He had been waiting for what passed for morning in this miserable winter and paused now in a narrow alley at the back of Snow Fields, opera hat collapsed in one hand, frost creaking in the timbers of the shopfronts, not sure it had come. Fog spilled over the cobblestones, foul and yellow and thick with coal fumes and a bitter stink that crusted the nostrils, scalded the back of the throat. That fog was everywhere, always, drifting through the streets and pulling apart low to the ground, a living thing. Some nights it gave off a low hiss, like steam escaping a valve.

Six weeks ago he had come to this city to interrogate a woman who last night after a long pursuit across Blackfriars Bridge had leaped the railing and vanished into the river. He thought of the darkness, the black water foaming outward, the slapping of the Yard sergeants' boots on the granite setts.

He could still feel the wet scrape of the bridge bollards against his wrists.

She had been living lawful in this city as if to pass for respectable and in this way absolve herself of a complicated life but as with anything it had not helped. She had been calling herself LeRoche but her real name was Reckitt and ten years earlier she had been an associate of the notorious cracksman and thief Edward Shade. That man Shade was the one he really hunted and until last night the Reckitt woman had been his one certain lead. She'd had small sharp teeth, long white fingers, a voice low and vicious and lovely.

The night faded, the streets began to fill. In the upper windows of the building across the street a pale sky glinted, reflected the watery silhouettes below, the passing shadows of the early horses hauling their waggons, the huddled cloth caps and woollens of the outsides perched on their sacks. The iron-shod wheels chittering and squeaking in the cold. He coughed and lit a cigar and smoked in silence, his small deep-set eyes predatory as any cutthroat's.

After a time he ground the cigar under one heel and punched out his hat and put it on. He withdrew a revolver from his pocket and clicked it open and dialed through its chambers for something to do and when he could wait no longer he hitched up one shoulder and started across.

If asked he would say he had never met a dead nail didn't want to go straight. He would say no man on the blob met his own shadow and did not flinch. He would run a hand along his unshaved jaw and glower down at whatever reporter swayed in front of him and mutter some unprintable blasphemy in flash dialect and then he would lean over and casually rip that page from the reporter's ring-coil notebook. He would say lack of education is the beginning of the criminal underclass and both rights and laws are failing the country. A man is worth more than a horse any day though you would never guess it to see it.

The cleverest jake he'd ever met was a sharper and the kindest jill a whore and the world takes all types. Only the soft-headed think a thing looks like what it is.

In truth he was about as square as a broken jaw but then he'd never met a cop any different so what was the problem and whose business was it anyway.

He did not go directly in but slipped instead down a side alley. Creatures stirred in the papered windows as he passed. The alley was a river of muck and he walked carefully. In openings in the wooden walls he glimpsed the small crouched shapes of children, all bones and knees, half dressed, their breath pluming out before them in the cold. They met his eyes boldly. The fog was thinner here, the stink more savage and bitter. He ducked under a gate to a narrow passage, descended a crooked wooden staircase, and entered a nondescript door on the left.

In the sudden stillness he could hear the slosh of the river, thickening in the runoffs under the boards. The walls creaked, like the hold of a ship.

That rooming house smelled of old meat, of water-rotted wood. The lined wallpaper was thick with a sooty grime any cinderman might scrape with a blade for half a shilling. He was careful not to touch the railing as he made his way upstairs. On the third floor he stepped out from the unlit stairwell and counted off five doors and at the sixth he stopped. Out of the cold now his bruised knuckles had begun to ache. He did not knock but jigged the handle softly and found it was not locked. He looked back the way he had come and he waited a moment and then he opened the door.

Mr. Porter? he called.

His voice sounded husky to his ears, scoured, the voice of a much older man.

Benjamin Porter? Hello?

As his eyes adjusted he could see a small desk in the gloom, a dresser, what passed for a scullery in a nook beyond the window. A sway-backed cot in one corner, the cheap mattress stuffed with wool flock bursting at one corner, the naked ticking cover neither waxed nor cleaned in some time. All this his eye took in as a force of habit. Then the bed groaned under the weight of something, someone, huddled in a blanket against the wall.

Ben?

Who's that now?

It was a woman's voice. She turned towards him, a grizzled Negro woman, her grey hair shorn very short and her face grooved and thickened. He did not know her. But then she blinked and tilted her face as if to see past his shoulder and he saw the long scar in the shape of a sickle running the length of her face.

Sally, he said softly.

A suspicion flickered in her eyes, burned there a moment. Billy?

He stepped cautiously forward.

You come on over here. Let me get a look at you. Little lantern-box Billy. Goodness.

No one's called me that in a long time.

Well, shoot. Look at how you grown. Ain't no one dare to.

He took off his hat, collapsed it uneasily before him. The air was dense with sweat and smoke and the fishy stench of unemptied chamber pots, making the walls that much closer, the ceiling that much lower. He felt big, awkward, all elbows.

I'm sorry to come round so early, he said. He was smiling a sad smile. She had grown so old.

Rats and molasses, she snorted. It ain't so early as all that.

I was just in the city, thought I'd stop by. See how you're keeping.

There were stacks of papers on the floor around the small desk, the rough chair with its fourth leg shorter than the others. He could see the date stamp from his Chicago office on several of the papers even from where he stood, he could see his father's letterhead and the old familiar signature. The curtains though drawn were thin from long use and the room slowly belled with a grey light. The fireplace was dead, the ashes old, an ancient roasting jack suspended on a cord there. On the mantel a glazed pottery elephant, the paint flecking off its shanks. High in one corner a bubble in the plaster shifted and boiled up and he realized it was a cluster of beetles. He looked away. There was no lamp, only a single candle stub melted into the floor by the bed. He could see her more clearly now. Her hands were very dirty.

Where's Ben? he asked.

Oh he would of wanted to seen you. He always did like you.

Did I miss him?

I guess you did.

He lifted his face. Then her meaning came clear.

Aw, now, she said. It all right.

When?

August. His heart give out on him. Just give right out.

I didn't know.

Sure.

My father always spoke well of him.

She waved a gruff hand, her knuckles thick and scarred.

Why didn't you write us? We would've helped with the expenses. You know it.

Well. You got your own sorrows.

I didn't know if you got my letter, he said quietly. I mean if Ben got it. I sent it to your old address—

I got it.

Ben Porter. I always thought he was indestructible.

I reckon he thought so hisself.

He was surprised at the anger he felt. It seemed to him a generation was passing all as a whole from this earth. That night in Chicago, almost thirty years gone. The rain as it battered down over the waggon, the canvas clattering under its onslaught, the thick waxing cut of the wheels in the deep mud lanes of that city. He had been a boy and sat beside his father up front clutching the lantern box in the rain, struggling to keep it dry and alight as his father cursed under his breath and slapped the reins and peered out into the blackness. They were a group of eleven fugitive slaves led by the furious John Brown and they had hidden for days in his father's house. Each would be loaded like cargo into a boxcar and sent north to Canada. They had journeyed for eight weeks on stolen horses over the winter plains and had lost one man in the going. He had known Benjamin and Sally and two others also but the rest were only bundles of suffering, big men gone thin in the arms from the long trek, women with sallow faces and bloodshot eyes. Their waggon had lurched to a halt in a thick pool of muck just two miles shy of the rail yards and he remembered Ben Porter's strong frame as he leaned into the back corner, squatted, hefted the waggon clear of its pit, the rain running in ropes over his arms, his powerful legs, and the strange low sound of the women singing in the streaming dark.

Sally was watching him with a peculiar expression on her face. You goin to want some tea, she said.

He looked at her modest surroundings. He nodded. Thank you. Tea would be just fine. He made as if to help her but she shooed him down.

I ain't so old as all that. I can still walk on these old hoofs.

She got heavily to her feet, gripping the edge of one bedpost and leaning into it with her twisted forearm, and then she shuffled over to the fireplace. She broke a splint from a near-toothless comb of parlour matches and drew it through a fold of sandpaper. He heard a rasp, smelled a grim whiff of phosphorous, and then she was lighting a twist of paper, bending over the iron grate, the low rack of packing wood stacked there. The bricks he saw were charred as if she had failed to put out whatever fire had burned there last.

How you take it? she asked.

Black.

Well I see you got you lumps already. She gestured to his swollen knuckles.

He smiled.

She was wrestling the cast-iron kettle over the grating. You moved, he said delicately. He did not want to embarrass her. I didn't have your new address.

She turned back to look at him. One eye scrunched shut, her spine humped and malformed under her nightgown. You a detective ain't you?

Maybe not a very good one. What can I do to help?

Aw, it boil in just a minute. Ain't nothin to be done.

I didn't mean with the tea.

I know what you meant.

He nodded.

It ain't much to look at but it keep me out of the soup. An I got my old arms and legs still workin. I ain't like to complain.

He had leaned his walking stick against the brickwork under the mantel and he watched Sally run her rough hands over the silver griffin's claw that crested its tip. Over and over, as if to buff it smooth. When the water had boiled she turned back and poured it out and let it steep and shuffled over to the scullery and upended one fine white china teacup.

You say you been here workin? she called out to him.

That's right.

I allowed maybe you been lookin for that murderer we been readin bout. The one from Leicester.

He shrugged a heavy shoulder. He doubted she was doing any reading at all, given her eyes. I've been tailing a grifter, she had a string of bad luck in Philadelphia. Ben knew her.

Sure.

I caught up with her last night but she jumped into the river. I'd guess she'll wash up in a day or two. I told Shore I was here if he needs me. At least as long as the Agency can spare me.

Who's that now. Inspector Shore?

Chief Inspector Shore.

She snorted. Chief Inspector? That Shore ain't no kind of nothin.

Well. He's a friend.

He's a scoundrel.

He frowned uneasily. I'm surprised Ben talked about him, he said slowly.

Wasn't a secret between us, not in sixty-two years. Specially not to do with no John Shore. Sally carried to him an unsteady cup of tea, leaned in close, gave him a long sad smile as if to make some darker point. You got youself a fine heart, Billy. It just don't always know the cut of a man's cloth.

She sat back on her bed. She had not poured herself a cup and he saw this with some discomfort. She looked abruptly up at him and said, How long you say you been here? Ain't you best be gettin on home?

Well.

You got you wife to think about.

Margaret. Yes. And the girls.

Ain't right, bein apart like that.

No.

Ain't natural.

Well.

You goin to drink that or leave it for the rats?

He took a sip. The delicate bone cup in his big hand.

She nodded to herself. Yes sir. A fine heart.

Not so fine, he said. I'm too good a hater for much. He set his hat on his head, got slowly to his feet. Like my father was, he added.

She regarded him from the wet creases of her eyes. My Mister Porter always tellin me, you got to shoe a horse, best not ask its permission.

I beg your pardon?

You goin to leave without sayin what you come for?

He was standing between the chair and the door. No, he said. Well. I hate to trouble you.

She folded her hands at her stomach, leaned back thin in her grey bedclothes. Trouble, she said, turning the word over in her mouth. You know, I goin to be eighty-three years old this year. Ain't no one left from my life who isn't dead already. Ever mornin I wake up surprised to be seein it at all. But one thing

I am sure of is next time you over this side of the ocean I like to be dead and buried as anythin. Aw, now, dyin is just a thing what happen to folk, it ain't so bad. But you got somethin to ask of me, you best to ask it.

He regarded her a long moment.

Go on. Out with it.

He shook his head. I don't know how much Ben talked to you about his work. About what he did for my father.

I read you letter. If you come wantin them old papers they all still there at his desk. You welcome to them.

Yes. Well. I'll need to take those.

But that ain't it.

He cleared his throat. After my father passed I found a file in his private safe. Hundreds of documents, receipts, reports. There was a note attached to the cover with Ben's name on it, and several numbers, and a date. He withdrew from his inside pocket a folded envelope, opened the complicated flap, slid out a sheet of drafting paper. He handed it across to her. She held the paper but did not read it.

Ben's name goin to be in a lot of them old files.

He nodded. The name on this file was Shade. Edward Shade.

She frowned.

It was in my father's home safe. I thought maybe Ben could help me with it.

A brougham clattered past in the street below.

Sally? he said.

Edward Shade. Shoot.

You've heard of him?

Ain't never *stopped* hearin bout him. She cast her face towards the weak light coming through the window. You father had Ben huntin that Shade over here for years. Never found nothin on him, not in ten years. She looked disgusted. Everyone you ask got they own version of Edward Shade, Billy. I won't pretend what I heard is the true.

I'd like to hear it.

It's a strange story, now.

Tell me.

She crushed her eyes shut, as if they pained her. Nodded. This were some years after the war, she said. Sixty-seven, sixty-eight. Shade or someone callin hisself Shade done a series of thefts in New York an Baltimore. Private houses, big houses. A senator's residence is the one I heard about. Stole paintings, sculptures, suchlike. All them items he mailed to you father's home address in Chicago, along with a letter claimin responsibility an namin the rightful owner. Who was Edward Shade? No one knew. No one ever seen him. It was just a name in a letter far as anyone known. First packages come through, you father he return them on the quiet to they owners an get a heapful of gratitude in turn. But when it keep on happenin, some folk they start to ask questions. All of it lookin mighty suspicious, month after month. Like he was orchestratin the affair to make the Agency look more efficient. Some daily in New York published a piece all about it, kept it goin for weeks. That newspaper was mighty rough on the Agency. It embarrassed you father something awful, it did.

I remember something about that.

Sure. But what else was he goin to do? They was stolen items, ain't no choice for a man like you father but to return them rightfully back.

Yes.

An then the case broke an the whole affair got cleaned up. Turned out Shade weren't no one after all. It were a ring of bad folk had some grudge against you father. They was lookin for some leverage an if that weren't possible they was hopin to embarrass the Agency out of its credibility. Edward Shade, that were just a name they made up.

But he had Ben hunting Shade for years after.

Right up until the end. You father had his notions.

None of that was in the file.

Sally nodded. Worst way to keep a secret is to write it down.

Ben ever mention a Charlotte Reckitt?

Sally touched two fingers to her lips, studied him. Reckitt?

Charlotte Reckitt. In the file on Shade there was a photograph of her. Her measurements were on the back in Ben's handwriting. There was a transcript attached, an interview between Ben and Reckitt from seventy-nine. In it he asks her about some nail she worked with, someone she couldn't remember. Ben claimed there were stories about them in the flash houses in Chicago but she didn't know what he was talking about or claimed she didn't. He left it alone eventually. Diamond heists, bank heists, forgeries circulating through France and the Netherlands, that sort of thing. According to my father's notes, he was certain this nail was Shade. In September I sent out a cable here and to Paris and to our offices in the west with a description of Charlotte Reckitt. Shore got back to me in November, said she was here, in London. Where my father had Ben on the payroll.

Billy.

Before he died, the last time I saw him, he looked me in the eye and he called me Edward.

Billy.

It was almost the last thing he said to me.

She looked saddened. My Mister Porter got mighty confused hisself, at the end, she said. You know I loved you father. You know my Mister Porter an me we owe him our whole lives. But that Edward Shade, now? You take them papers, go on. You read them an you see. It ain't like you father made it out to be. He were obsessed with it. Shade were like a sickness with him.

He studied her in the gloom. I found her, Sally. The woman I was following last night, the woman who took her life. It was Charlotte Reckitt.

Shoot.

I talked to her before she jumped, I asked her about Shade. She knew him.

She told you that?

He was silent a long moment and then he said, quietly, Not in so many words.

Sally opened her hands. Aw, Billy, she said. If you huntin the breath in a man, what is it you huntin?

He said nothing.

My Mister Porter used to say, Ever day you wake up you got to ask youself what is it you huntin for.

Okay.

What is it you huntin for?

He walked to the window and stared out through the frost and soot on the pane at the crooked rooftops of the riverside warehouses feeling her eyes on him. The sound of her breathing in the darkness there. What are you saying? That Shade didn't exist?

She shook her head. There ain't no catchin a ghost, Billy.

When does a life begin its decline.

He thought of the Porters as they had once been and still were in his mind's eye. The glistening rib cage of the one in the orange lantern light and the rain, wool-spun shirt plastered to his skin, his shoulders hoisting that cart up out of the muck. The low plaintive song of the other as she knelt coatless in the waters. He thought of the weeks he had tailed Charlotte Reckitt from her terrace house in Hampstead to the galleries in Piccadilly, trailed her languidly down to the passenger steamers on the Thames, watched in gaslight the curtained windows of her house. Hoping for a glimpse of Edward Shade. She was a small woman with liquid eyes and black hair and he thought suddenly of how she had regarded him from the steps of that theatre in St. Martin's Lane, one gloved wrist bent back. The fear in her eyes. Her small hands. She had leaped a railing into a freezing river and they would find her body in the morning or the day after.

So.

He would be thirty-nine years old this year and he was already famous and already lonely. In Chicago his wife was dying from a tumour the size of a quarter knuckled behind her right eye though neither he nor she knew it yet. It would be another ten years before it killed her. He had held the rope as his father's casket went in and turned the first shovel of earth over the grave. That scrape of dirt would echo in him always. Whether he lived to eighty or no the greater part of his life lay behind him.

When does a life begin its decline? He stared up at the red sky now and thought of the Atlantic crossing and then of his home. The fog thinning around him, the passersby in their ghostly shapes. Then he went down to Tooley Street to catch the rail line back to his hotel.

His name. Yes that.

His name was William Pinkerton.

TWO

Here is another.

His eyes would fill with light even after a light was extinguished, like the eyes of a cat. They were violet and hard as amethysts and they liked the darkness. His side-whiskers he wore fashionably trimmed though the deep black in them had long ago bleached to white. Though it had been a bad crossing even during the roughest weather he had sat in the smoking room of the RMS *Aurania* turning the ironed pages of the *Times* with a wetted finger. He had been seen thus and thus only by men who mattered. His skin a light brown against the starched white collars, his long fingers. Seen in tailored suits and expensive fitted waistcoats as if a jeweller or industrialist just back from Bombay although in truth he had fallen on hard times and when he crossed his legs he would first hitch a pinch of trouser up his thigh with a worry for the thread. But his cuff-links were emeralds set in gold leaf, his tie pin studded with diamonds. Asked if any line existed between how a man looked and what a man was, he would smile a sad knowledgeable smile, as if he had lived a long time and seen too much of the world for certainties to be conceded.

Go on.

No he was no liar. He just was not what he seemed to be. He was travelling with a little girl he would introduce as his daughter. His voice was soft and curiously high. His mother had been born in a narrow house in Calcutta and at thirteen

and still unmarried had made her way along the banks of the
Hooghly River to the sea. Her burnished skin gleamed in his
own face and throat on sunlit days, the shadows around his
eyes were the purple of cold-water anemones. He was small the
way she had been small, with strong narrow shoulders and
thick wrists, and though all his childhood he had heard tales
of his Yorkshire father's great size he had never known anything of it. He had lived among the very poor and the very rich
both and he knew which world he preferred. Despite all this he
lived with a sharp impatience for anything that broke the moral
law for that law he believed was absolute and took the one
measure of all who drew breath on God's earth. No man should
embrace violence. No man had a right to hold any other back.
Those in need must be cared for. If pressed during a round of
whist he might confess that truth in his experience was just a
lie refined into elegance and that nothing in this world was
sacred though all things in the next world might be. In an age
of industrialists and bluebloods he was a self-made man and
not ashamed to say it.

For twenty-three years now he had answered to the name of
Adam Foole. He had already made his fortune and wasted it
several times over. In certain banks along the Eastern Seaboard
his name was now anathema, in others it remained respected,
in still others managers would hurriedly unhook their wire
spectacles and stand at their desks to consider his newest venture. An elegant club in New York held an oak-panelled room
in reserve on weeks when he walked in that city though he had
not settled that bill in three years. His business was multifold
and various and suitably vague in an age of gentlemen investors
and he did not advertise his talents.

He had been away from England only six weeks and it was
a letter in a woman's handwriting that had drawn him back so
soon. On what business. What else.

No wealth is ever sufficient.

———

He stood now at the railing feeling the engines of the ocean liner thrum up through his feet then slowly punch down stage by stage through their gearings. There were others on deck in the cold though not many and all of them stood wind-racked and wrappered in thick scarves or deck blankets emblazoned with the Cunard logo and each huddled with arms at their chests clutching their morning coats closed. He was dressed in last season's fashions, a double-breasted tweed, a lounge coat buttoned fast, a brown bowler lifting in the wind.

He felt his whiskers stir and raised his eyes. The sky was overcast but bright off the white hulls of the lifeboats where they hung in their casings above the deck. To the east he could see Liverpool like a smudge of ink against the grey. The factory chimneys, their brown smoke standing off angular in the wind.

Just then a child came through the saloon doors pulling at the lace of her bonnet, not quite eleven years old.

For god's sake, Molly, he called. Look at you. Your boots.

The soft leather was scuffed with red chalk on the toes and up along the laces as if she had been kicking god knew what. Do I look a sight? she said with a grin.

Come here.

Her cool eyes, her freckled nose. She flounced against the railing, folded her elbows over. The wind pressed her dress crackling against her legs and he could see the boyish shape of her hips through it, he knew her buttoned gloves concealed fingernails ragged and bitten. He reached around, tied her bonnet more firmly.

What's that smell? she asked.

Stop squirming. Creosote.

She mouthed the word.

Did the porter collect the bags? he asked.

I left them in the hallway. Like you told me to.

As I told you to. As. After a moment Foole held out an empty hand and she blinked her dark eyes at it.

What?

You know what.

She frowned and reached into her sleeve and withdrew the five-pound tip he had given her for the porter and she handed it across. I like you better when we're rich, she said.

He took it wordlessly. But as she turned to look out at the river something caught his eye and he reached into the folds of her dress, withdrew a small plaster doll. Where did you get this? he demanded.

She snatched it back, suddenly feral.

Is that the doll the Webster girl was playing with?

It's not.

He turned and studied the crest of foam unfurling away from the hull and then looked at her again. What's got into you?

She don't know it were me.

That's not the point.

The girl was blushing, she would not meet his eye. You want me to give it back?

What do you think?

Then they'll *know* it were me what took it.

He shook his head.

She was silent a moment and studied her boots in the Mersey's silver brightness and then she looked at him. Anyhow, she said sullenly. She got lots of others.

He looked past her. A thin man in a funereal topcoat and black hat had come out and was standing with one hand on the heavy door of the smoking lounge. He squinted into the wind towards them then raised a hand in greeting and let the door swing shut. The whitewashed deck was wide and alcoved with brass spittoons riveted into place and porthole windows gleaming in the grey light and as he approached them his dark reflection passed warpling alongside.

Molly followed Foole's gaze over her shoulder then gave him a look and muttered something and then with a sarcastic curtsy she slid away, beating her gloved hand on the railing as she went. Her other hand clutched the doll at the neck as if to strangle it.

Be at our cabin in ten minutes, he called to her. Molly? I mean it.

She raised an arm in the wind without turning round.

Your daughter? the man said as he approached. A handsome girl, sir. I did not see her on the crossing.

Foole raised his hands in defeat.

The gentleman laughed. I have nieces aplenty myself, sir. One can see the breeding at once in her. Her mother is?

Dead, Foole said quietly. He waved a hand. Time goes on though our hearts may not wish it.

She must have been a great beauty, sir.

Foole cleared his throat.

I mean in her lineaments, the man went on. Certainly your daughter appears to have many advantages. She is an excellent specimen.

Specimen?

The gentleman laughed. Forgive me. I have been so long in my work that I lose the language of the everyday. It is a hazard.

What did you say it was? Phrenology?

He nodded in satisfaction. Phrenology, sir, yes. The science of human potential. Forgive me, what line did you say you were in?

I didn't.

Clearly not whist.

At last Foole smiled too, though ruefully. I'd hoped at some point these past days to win some of it back, he said. I'd hoped at least to get close.

I had been hoping that also for you, sir.

Wasn't in the cards, I guess.

The phrenologist cleared his throat. If I may be so bold—

Foole reached into his vest and unclipped the chain and held it out, weighing it in his palm. It belonged to my father, he said.

It is exquisite.

It was a silver watch built in Philadelphia twenty years past with a single band of copper encircling its face and filigreed with a delicate latticework of gold inlay in the shape of an unblinking eye. At a click the lid lifted and there, etched as if in copperplate, was the inscription: FOR MY SON.

He clicked it shut. If you would be willing, Foole began, I'd be pleased to send you the funds upon my arrival in London—

The phrenologist held up a regretful finger, the joints crooked and swollen. His eyes had scarce lifted from the watch.

I am sure I can depend upon you, sir, the phrenologist said. But it is the principle of it, you understand. A man cannot just sit down at a table and outplay his hand without meeting the consequences. The phrenologist was nodding now, sadly. There are always consequences, he went on. That is the point. That is what I wish to impart to you. It is how we keep our honour, sir, here in England.

Of course. I only just thought, perhaps—

Ah. No.

He was a tall man, though thin, and he stepped forward now and loomed over Foole. There was in his gesture both threat and coiled restraint and Foole felt the railing bite into his ribs and he cleared his throat and then he gave the man the watch. Something sharp and painful turned over inside him as he did so.

The phrenologist held it up to the light, opened it, closed it with a click, then shut his claw-like fist around it and slipped it into his waistcoat in a single smooth motion.

Foole made a pained face. I always clear a debt, he said.

Indeed, sir.

Foole turned and regarded the low roofline of the landing stage at Pierhead, the wide-planked boardwalk just coming visible there, the dock offices looming up behind. Upriver he could see the squat sooty brickwork of the Albert Dock. The air felt cold, grim.

And how long do you mean to stay in Liverpool, sir, if I may be so bold? the phrenologist asked. You'll be staying at the Adelphi, I trust?

We're travelling up to London this evening. On the London North Western.

Excellent, excellent. May I recommend the American Bar, at the Criterion in Piccadilly?

Foole grunted. And you are returning home, I take it.

To my practice, yes. I have been visiting a most fascinating collection of Indian skulls in Boston. Most remarkable. Foole watched the fingers of the man's left hand shift in his waistcoat, turning and turning his watch.

It is an instrument of some personal value, Foole said after a moment. He nodded at the man's pocket. Perhaps we might negotiate it back, at some future date? At interest, of course.

The phrenologist withdrew his hand from his pocket, smoothed his whiskers, peered out at the cranes and tackle swaying on their ropes at the freight docks. I think we might come to some agreement, sir. I would not wish to deprive you of something you value so highly. This is my visiting card. Should you ever have need of a physician in Liverpool, or simply wish to pass an evening in company, I should be delighted.

I fear I couldn't afford it. The evening, that is.

You might win your timepiece back.

I might lose my shirt.

The phrenologist made a show of inspecting the smaller man's collar and cuffs. Mm, he said with a smile. Not likely.

Foole was all at once tired of it. The dark outlines of the ramps, the arcades of the landing pier slid nearer.

The phrenologist regarded him. You do not have the spirit of a gambler, sir.

Foole smiled tightly. No one does, he said.

It was a steel-plated behemoth inclined to roll with a displacement of just over seven thousand tons and a single screw and twin smokestacks that ran hot. The crossing had taken all of eleven days despite the black weather and the hull had lifted and crested the cold slate swells then crashed breaking down out of the roll then lifted again until no man on board had not been sick at least the once and the dining hall had thinned to a man. It was rigged as a barque and bore one mast fore and two aft like a memory of an earlier age but its opulent saloon was all polished brass and riveted leather like the fittings in some modern postwar paddlewheeler off the Mississippi. Every second evening a French magician worked his sleight in top hat and evening dress while a lady accompanied him on the piano. Each night before he slept Foole would take out a small brown envelope and unfold the letter within and reread it in silence with his lips mouthing the words and then he would listen to Molly snoring softly and slip the letter back into the envelope and slide the envelope under his pillow.

Her handwriting had changed in the ten years since he had seen her last and he thought of who she would be now, fearing from her tone that she had fallen onto hard times herself. She wrote with a gentleness that surprised him given their past and made no mention of wrongs done, of betrayals made. Each morning he gripped the polished railing of his bed and felt the vessel's sway and thought how much closer he now must be and something stirred in him that he had not felt in a very long time. Among those who lurched into the breakfast saloon were an American senator he recognized from the newspapers and a burly doctor from Edinburgh who laughed loudly among the men but when ladies were present conducted himself with impeccable politeness. He seemed to know something about everything and would speak at luncheons of bare-knuckle boxing and the rightness of the British Empire and of recent oracular surgeries in France and at nights would posit the possibility of spirits and Foole had liked him immensely from the very first. One evening he complained of detective stories dependent on the foolishness of the criminal rather than the intelligence of the detective and Foole had smiled at the simplicity of it but the doctor only chuckled and said, Deduction, my good man, deduction. He was one among them who had gathered late into the night to play whist and while the drinks shifted elliptically to the swells and the men had smoked and laughed, only the doctor had kept his true self hidden. The doctor that is and Foole. For no man he met kept better counsel. Five days out and Foole had grown used to the bite of the salt air and the plummet and lift of the deck and he would take his evening constitutionals leaning into the wind then come in soaked to the skin and clapping his frozen hands and Molly would shake her head at him in disgust.

None of that mattered now.

The days had passed. England neared.

By late morning the liner had docked and lashed its twin gangways fast and Foole watched the trunks and crates of the saloon passengers twist slowly in their nets above the wharf. Any who leaned over the upper-deck railing would see the steerage boiling up out of the guts of the vessel, a roiling crush of families and workers and drifters dragging suitcases or sacks, some gnawing sticks of sausage, others clutching the necks of bottles, a sea of slouching grey caps and brown bonnets and faded shawls lost and then again visible under the low grey drifts of steam, while the great boilers below decks clocked down.

Foole made his way through the saloon and down the marble staircase to the second level and along the wide gaslit hallway to his and Molly's second-class cabin. There were porters and passengers milling about and some fixing their hats in the hurry and he twisted the heavy latch of his door but he did not see the child.

Molly? he called.

The stateroom was empty, the bedsheets turned back and pressed, the mahogany desk already cleared to a shine. He saw their luggage had been picked up and he cursed himself for having left no tip. He set the five pounds down on the desk then thought better of it and pocketed it again. A crewman knocked at his door and called out the minutes and went on.

He stood studying his face in the small mirror bolted to the wall. The lines at the corners of his eyes like a fine web of craquelure. The white hair, the dark worried forehead. The already thorny eyebrows. When did he get old. What would she say to see him now.

What would she say.

A shudder passed up through the hull. After a moment he set his bowler, sharpened his starched cuffs, took up his cane, and went out on deck. The off-loading had already begun its slow shuffle forward. The saloon class had been nearly full with a list of ninety-six passengers registered and Foole pressed through those who were loitering until he had joined the rear of the disembarkation line on the gangway. He did not see any sign of Molly but knew she would be near, somewhere in the crowd.

He worked his way up until he was standing behind a huge man in a homespun coat, canvas pants, a tattered leather trunk hoisted on one shoulder. He could smell the boiled-sausage reek of the man's skin, the grey rime of filth at his neck. Everywhere around them were the manicured and tailored figures of men of standing.

A customs agent in white was inspecting tickets at the first stage on the pier and he stopped the giant and lifted his paperwork in two fingers, turning it in the light.

You're in the wrong class, sir, the agent said. How did you get up here?

Foole heard the giant mutter some word and then the agent lowered the ticket.

I beg your pardon?

The giant was sullen, silent.

You will exit from down there, sir, the agent said.

He pointed below at the crowd of third-class passengers, crushed together and hollering against the press of unwashed bodies. Foole's eyes followed his gloved finger down.

The giant shrugged one massive meaty shoulder and turned sideways. He might have been a bare-knuckle boxer for all the look of him.

Excuse me, sir, Foole called ahead. Surely you might let the fellow through? We do have engagements to keep, sir.

The agent turned. Are you with him?

The giant gave him a glower.

Foole held up both hands, the cane hooked over a thumb.

He made as if to take a step back and was surprised to find a space had opened at his back.

I will not be dictated to, the agent was saying. Not by you, sir, and not by the likes of this.

The likes of what, now? the giant said.

The agent sniffed and peered past him. Step aside, sir. Next? Me papers are in order.

Next.

No one moved. All at once the giant slid his big trunk onto the ramp and then in a single coiled gesture he enfolded the front of the customs agent's waistcoat in his hand and half hoisted the man into the air.

He was whispering into the man's ear and Foole could see the alarm in the agent's eyes as he looked sideways at the giant, looked away. The whitewashed ramp with its slatted stops just beyond the gate, the roiling crowds exiting from steerage. He felt suddenly very tired.

But he stepped forward all the same. All right now, he said. That'll do.

Feeling something sinking inside him as he did so.

The giant's shirt was open where the collar did not fit his throat and he held a proofed bottle half concealed under one stained sleeve even as he dangled the agent above the decking. The lips under his black beard were red and wet.

Put the man down, Foole said. This is not fit behaviour, sir.

The customs agent spluttered. His pink tongue, whites of his bulging eyes. The brass buttons of his collar glinting in the daylight like coins.

You, the giant snapped. You shut your mouth. It ain't your concern.

Foole nodded unhappily. He could smell the garlic on the man's breath. He had thought some other might step forward with him but he stood alone. He could see Molly's red bonnet dipping and weaving behind the crowds massed there as if she were trying to get closer. He felt something like dread pass through him, very hot, then very cold. He altered his grip on his cane.

Put him down, he said, more firmly.

Everything went still. The vessel at its moorings, the crowd, the gulls swarming the air of the docks below.

The giant took a deep breath, he shook his head. With his free hand he leaned across and before Foole could react he shoved him lazily and the force of it was tremendous and sent Foole staggering back with his arms wheeling to keep his balance.

I said to shut it.

Foole rubbed at his coat. A sudden flare of anger rose in him and he stepped forward, he pushed at the giant as hard as he could, square in the big man's back. The giant dropped the customs agent, and turned, he stared at Foole in astonishment.

An what do you reckon you're doin? he said in a low voice, all at once uncertain. His eyes flicked over the assembled crowd.

There are ladies present, sir, Foole said loudly. There are witnesses. Step down, sir.

A look of confusion slid like a shadow over the giant's face and then it was gone. Foole took a deep breath, he tightened his grip on his walking stick.

And then without warning the giant lurched forward and was upon him. Lifting both fists thick as a block of tackle and swinging them overhand as if to stove in Foole's skull. The man was thick in the waist and leaned his weight in behind him and he moved fast despite his size. But as the fists came down Foole stepped smoothly back and then to the left feeling the whoosh of air in the space where he had stood and then he raised his cane and brought it sharply down on the giant's temple in two quick strikes and the big man went down.

There was a cracking sound, like a rivet punching from an iron boiler. Foole watched a dark blister of blood swell just behind the giant's eye where he lay with his face twisted to one side and then on the decking under his beard a whorl of blood began to seep outward and down through the steel joinings.

A stunned silence passed over the crowd. Then a whirl of voices, shoving elbows, faces drained of blood.

Dear god, man, a porter was shouting. Give them air, give them air.

Foole let himself be jostled aside. After a moment he stepped to the railing with his back to the maelstrom and stood, very silent, very still, as the gulls wheeled and plunged in the air just beyond the ramp. Far below him he could see the yellow waters of the Mersey boiling under the hull.

On the silver head of his cane a small bead of blood glistened like oil and he saw this and withdrew a starched handkerchief and rubbed it thoughtfully away.

It was a woman's letter had brought him back to England. On what business. What else.

He had eyes the colour of irises in bloom and wore his pale whiskers trimmed and said nothing of consequence to anyone. In an interior pocket of his steamer trunk he kept wrapped in an old woollen scarf an ancient daguerreotype framed and battered and long since clouded into grey. A young woman in crinoline and bonnet seated half obliterated in an open door of a studio, his younger self standing behind her, while the sunshine gleamed off a balcony railing beyond them. The heat of that sun long since burned off, her face long since faded, eaten into whiteness, a slash of shadow where her lips and eyes had once frowned out. It did not matter. He knew that visage in its every line and curve. Her throat, he recalled, had smelled of wild raspberries in summer.

That daguerreotype was taken in September of 1874 in the bustling harbour city of Port Elizabeth, South Africa. He had been poor then. The photographer's name was de Hoeck and his studio a dim warren of rooms just north of the public gardens, reeking of fixative and other jars of chemicals standing with lids half unscrewed behind a curtain in a backroom just out of sight. Foole had sat in a corner clutching her shawl in his fists as the man adjusted his lenses and as she sat sorrowful in her beauty and then he had stood and joined her. It had been

her last week in Africa. His last week with her. He understood
she was living somewhere in London and unhappy in that life.
She would be thirty now and no longer as she had been.

Did it matter? It did not matter.

Her name was Charlotte Reckitt and he had loved her once
and loved her still.

THREE

William Pinkerton crossed the narrow lobby of the Grand Metropolitan Hotel without checking in at the front desk for the post. There was a man in a flat-topped bowler reading a broadside under the dwarf palms where the brass railing of the bar met the lobby and he saw the man and how the man looked at him but he did not slow. He felt light-headed, thin in the throat, a shivering in his hands as he went. The gaslights were gleaming in the brass and the mirrors and the marble underfoot and something in all this made him sick. When the gate of the lift folded shut behind him the operator nodded and pulled the lever and the lift creaked under his big weight but the operator did not ask his floor. He could see as they ascended the man near the palms fold his paper, tuck it under one arm, stride out through the lobby doors.

At his room the door opened at a touch. He felt the hairs on his neck prickle.

Hello? he called in.

The air was hushed.

Show yourself, he called, more sharply.

After a moment he grimaced and dropped his walking stick and hat on the pier table in the hall and shut the door. He was making himself crazy, he thought. The papers from Sally Porter were rolled tight under one elbow and he understood he had reached the limit of something. He unrolled the papers and opened the shallow cigar drawer and put them away. Stepped back onto the mat and scraped his shoes wearily on the horn, slipped off his chesterfield, slung it on the oak coat tree. In the small drawing room to the left he could see the dim shapes of sofas, cane chairs, aproned side tables all crouched and waiting. He ran a hand along the back of his neck.

Benjamin Porter was gone.

It did not seem right. He knew the world was not a place of rightness and yet something in his visit to Sally had left him uneasy. He could feel the old melancholy settling in, the slow depressed weariness of an investigation closing. He was this way always after finishing a case, restless and brooding, left wandering room to room in his house in Chicago like a man just risen from a sickbed. Margaret knew not to speak to him at such times, knew to leave him to his loneliness and gloom. But this was different. Since slipping from Sally's room he had been unable to shake the feeling of a figure just ahead of him, exiting each space as he entered, almost visible. *Ain't no catchin a ghost*, Sally had said. Both of them knowing which ghost it was. He had not loved his father in life and he did not love him in death. But grief he knew was a heavier thing than love between the living and the lost.

The maid had been in. He did not know the hour but thought it still early. The mattress had been turned, sheets and bolster changed. The green curtains in the bedroom were open on their brass rods, their folds waterfalling in elegant swags on either side of the big front windows. He walked the length of the room scraping the curtains on their rings shut. The room darkened window by window until only thin stripes of daylight fell aslant the floor where the curtains failed to meet. But when he turned he could still see the wet heel prints his shoes had left on the carpet. He did not care. He thought of Sally Porter's decaying room and felt ashamed.

In the middle of the floor stood an old-fashioned four-poster bed carved from Spanish mahogany and big enough for two. William peeled off his cutaway and withdrew his tie pin and loosened his tie. Then he lay down on top of the bedclothes and closed his eyes. He did not unbutton his waistcoat, did not unloop his starched collar, did not draw the heavy drapery shut around the bed. In the dimness the grey face of his wife stared out at him from her silver frame.

He awoke to a hammering at the door, to a muffled voice calling for him. He rolled over, shut his eyes, pulled a frilled pillow over his face.

When he next awoke, the sound of the knocking had altered. A high, reedy voice was calling to him through the wood.

Mr. Pinkerton, sir? Mr. Pinkerton?

He wet his lips.

Are you awake, sir? Mr. Pinkerton?

He opened one slow eyelid.

Sir? Chief Inspector Shore sent me.

He got groggily to his feet and peered about at the room, recognizing none of it. He could hear the faint clatter of horses in the street outside, the sound of hawkers shouting from the corner of the square. It was still morning.

Sir?

Just a minute, he barked.

When he unlocked the door and opened it he found a boy in corduroy trousers, a heavy jacket, a squashed cap of wet red wool. Not ten years old if a day. His raw-looking nose was slick and he licked at his glistening upper lip and blinked twice and then he took off his cap. His fingernails were black. William did not know him.

He glanced along the corridor in both directions and then glowered down at the boy.

Persistent little devil, aren't you.

Sir?

What time is it?

Half ten, sir.

You weren't knocking earlier?

Sir?

He shook his head. Never mind. What's this about Shore?

The boy straightened. If you'll come with me, sir. It's something you should see.

What is it?

If you please, sir. He said not to tell you.

You're a runner from the Yard?

Yes sir.

Has he recovered the body?

The body, sir?

A door opened across the hallway. A man with red hair and waxed moustaches emerged in his shirt sleeves and there was ink on his fingers and William glared at him, then ran one bruised hand down his face.

For god's sake, he said, steering the boy by one shoulder out of the corridor. This better be about Charlotte Reckitt.

He was not, officially, in London.

He had arrived on the last Friday in November when the Chicago office had slowed for the season and that date now was already six weeks gone. It had been the first Christmas with his father dead and he thought of his daughters guiltily and of his wife's recriminating letters with sadness. His brother had written from the New York offices wondering at his absence but he had not written back.

After their father's funeral they had spoken little but as brothers it had never been their way and it did not mean what it might have. Robert was the second son and could do little right in their father's eyes and William knew this and watched his brother at the cemetery feeling a heaviness in his throat. They had gone over their father's office at the Agency for outstanding business but there had been little for the old man to do in those final months and his desk had been uncommonly tidy. Robert had taken a brass statuette of a racehorse from the bureau, nothing else. All that July William had slept badly and worked long hours while the daylight lingered in an attempt to quiet his heart but nothing it seemed could do so. At last in

September he went alone to their mother's house and ate a quiet dinner with her while the candles blazed in their sconces and when she kissed him good night he followed her heavily upstairs and went into his father's home office. He sat awhile in the dark. Then he lit a fire in the grate and began to go through the old man's things.

It was midnight and he had opened his father's safe and was unpacking its documents when he came across the file marked *Shade*. The green papered walls, the desk gleaming in the window glass. The house creaking around him. He was on his knees amid a storm of papers and he read carefully. That file had included memoranda and notes in his father's cribbed hand and in the papers mentioning Shade's accomplices he found an old photograph of Charlotte Reckitt with her measurements on the back. There was a list of partial aliases also. The file still smelled of his father's cigars and William closed it and sat thinking. Later that week he sent out a circular with Charlotte Reckitt's description but heard nothing back and thought little more of it.

Then in October word reached him of a failed heist in Philadelphia. Such reports were routine and he almost did not read it. Seated in his leather desk chair staring out at the late autumn sunlight while the traffic passed in the street below. Feeling a hollowness coming up in him. He had started to leaf through the pages and then stopped and turned back to the first page and started to read it again, more slowly.

The thief had spooked, had left in a hurry. Although the heist had been aborted the Agency's operatives had canvassed the neighbourhood to collect the details. A Mrs. Eliza LeRoche, widowed, still young, had leased a shopfront on Congress Street in the last week of September ostensibly to promote Dr. Gilliam's Mendicant Oil & Miracle Cure. There were the slender green bottles pyramided into window displays, the illustrated broadsides with testimonials from South America, the daily notices paid in advance in the Boston *Advertiser*. But behind a japanned screen in the rear of the shop a tunnel led through the floor and under a vault of the bank next door. LeRoche's handwriting was on the lease and on the papers she had left amid the complete stock of Dr. Gilliam's Mendicant Oil & Miracle Cure. A pair of clean high-heeled boots with laces tied had been placed neatly at the mouth of the tunnel. Something in all this would not leave him alone and two days later while eating breakfast William remembered where he had heard that name and he set his spoon down in his porridge and stared at his hands and Margaret had stopped eating and watched him.

He was careful, he made inquiries. She had been seen locking up her shop in the early hours of October seventh by sweepers working the crossings. A postman claimed she had spoken with a Continental accent and that she was either Irish or Polish. The high-heeled boots had been cobbled by Smiley & Sons of Glasgow and were sold only in Britain though the company had mailed out several orders directly to customers in Philadelphia during the past six months. In August three pairs had been delivered to a brownstone rented to LeRoche just off Independence Square. Then the two sweepers identified Charlotte Reckitt through her rogues' gallery photograph, hair cut shorter, yes, a little older, aye, but those eyes, it was her.

He sent out another circular, to Toronto, San Francisco, London, Paris. In November the woman was spotted in Piccadilly and William locked up his office and bid his secretary good night and walked quietly down the stairs of his building feeling the eyes of his employees on the back of his neck and knowing what his wife would say and that it would not matter. He purchased a ticket for Liverpool on the Cunard Line that week and sent a telegram to John Shore at Scotland Yard. He would seek out Charlotte Reckitt himself. It was not answers he wanted, but something else.

He found her house in Hampstead on his third night. He had known by the last week of 1884 that he had the woman cornered and she had known it also. She had slept at home on the thirtieth and changed her hairstyle for the New Year's celebrations and William had trailed her home from the opera and watched her drift from window to window all that long, quiet, exhausted night, running her index finger and thumb over the jewels at her throat. He had tipped his hat at each sighting as if to greet her from where he stood, the street lamp casting a crescent of shadow over his eyes. He had wanted to be seen. He had wanted her to know it was finished.

It didn't matter that he liked her well enough. In his world if you turned a blind eye you got cracked overhand with a bottle. You turned the other cheek and you woke up with your pockets turned out and your watch chain gone.

The boy led him down into the street.

The silver curvature of the cobblestones, the glassed dark of the gas lamps. Orange fog in its thick hang.

He had left a hansom waiting in the cold and William noted this but did not remark on it. When he gripped the rail and lurched up he felt the coiled springs shiver and sway under his weight and then the mare lowered its head into a bag of feed and William watched a thick green knot of shit dispel in front of him.

The driver from his perch behind them was already shaking the reins, clicking his tongue, and the cab jounced and started sharply. It did not set off in the direction of Whitehall.

Where are we going?

Pitchcott's, sir.

The mortuary? What's there?

Bodies, sir.

William allowed himself a weary smile. Is it Charlotte Reckitt, son?

The boy grinned back. They don't tell me nothing.

Nuffink, it sounded like. William shook his head.

The cold air smelled of snow though it had not snowed. As they went, the orange fog burned around the horse's hooves, scattered and roiled and reshaped itself while the hansom rattled on through the chill. William knew horses and he regarded the frosted cobblestones with a wariness, thinking of the lack of traction there and how easily the beast could go down.

As they rounded the corner past Long Acre he could see a postman in his scarlet coat trudging through the fog, his breath pluming out before him. The high narrow buildings cast the shopfronts in shadow. Then they were into the traffic and the muffled life of the day. He watched a coal scuttler draw up a heavy iron plate from the footway outside a confectionery, his sleeves rolled and his big fists wielding a hook for the purpose. A roan horse and cart looming silently at the curb. He had known that work himself as a young man and hated the drudgery of it. There were clerks in their black coats and tall hats shoving their way along the footways and others trotting grimly between the slow waggons and omnibuses in the low fog and William leaned back, he closed his eyes.

He could feel the boy at his side bouncing and jostling as the hansom kept on.

What's your name, son?

Ollie, sir.

Oliver?

Just Ollie, sir. I don't go in for nothing fancy.

William smiled and opened one eye. You been doing this a long time, Ollie?

Near six months, sir.

You like it?

The boy shrugged, rubbed at his nose with his jacket cuff. It pays the bills an all.

That sounds sensible.

Ollie nodded. Well it's more of a stepping stone, sir. To get me where I want to be.

And where would that be?

Detective.

William nodded seriously. That's a hard life.

Every life is, sir, when you got a family to support.

Very true.

The boy nodded sagely and watched the street pass. He

twisted all at once around and hammered at the roof of the hansom and hollered up, It's Pitchcott's we're going, driver. Take us down Frith here.

William regarded him, his wet nose, his red lips, his grey skin. After a moment he said, And do you, Ollie? Have a family to support?

The boy grinned. Oh I'm not married yet, sir, if that's what you mean.

No.

Seems like a right lot of trouble, that.

William laughed. You're a wise fellow.

I wouldn't like to say so, sir, Ollie said modestly, then lifted his face and leaned forward scanning the street and all at once the hansom came to a rattling halt.

Pitchcott's here, sir, the boy said.

William glanced out. It was a squat unmarked frontage on the corner between a haberdashery and a decrepit surgeon's offices. The windows above all three looked dark and unlet. As William swung down from the cab he stumbled and half fell and held himself upright by one big hand on the door. He brushed himself off and glanced at the boy but the boy was scrambling down on the far side, holding out the copper tuppence to the driver.

William reached into his pocket and withdrew a white handkerchief. Ollie, he said. You need this more than me. Go on, it's clean.

The boy grinned again. A clean shilling be even better.

I'm sure it would.

That's the chief there, sir.

William nodded but did not for a moment move and then he sighed and glanced at the cold sky, the painful white hole in it where the sun did not burn through.

John Shore was leaning against the brick entrance with his arms folded and one leg crossed at the ankle and when he saw William he pushed off from the step and came towards him. His arm left a smudge on the wall where he had been. He was

ating down hard on a briarwood pipe and his frock coat hung slackly from his shoulders, unbuttoned, parting over his heavy belly. His checked trousers were spattered at the knees with grey mud, his top hat unbrushed. He looked, William thought, deflated and sad.

The chief inspector plunged his hands into his pockets. Sleep well?

William shrugged.

Sorry about the hour.

Where did she wash up?

Who?

Isn't this about Charlotte Reckitt?

Shore's eyes looked rimmed and sore. Well, he said. I wanted you to see it for yourself.

Shore had a florid face and thick red fingers that reminded William of Italian meats. He had liaised with William's father for ten years, fielding requests to the Yard for information, meeting with the elder Pinkerton on his visits to London, soaking up the rough wild stories his father liked to tell. Shore was the son of a butcher and he had spoken once of his lonely childhood going from house to house with a basket of cuttings on one shoulder while the birds flocked and circled overhead. His own father he said would keep a live calf each Christmas tethered in his shop with 6d per lb seared into the shivering thing's chest. There was something in that, he explained, that he thought of when he took a man into custody. How so? William had asked. Does a man have what he's worth marked out on him?

Not what he's worth, Shore had replied. What he'll sell for.

It was a soot-stained door he took him through with no windows and a single ancient lock of iron that William understood would keep no one out but perhaps someone in. The air inside was close, the gas in the fixture turned high. The plaster walls were crumbling from damp to the height of a man's shoulder and the ceiling was not much higher. A stench filled the corridor that was not from the gas and William cleared his throat and squinted and regretted giving the boy his handkerchief.

Your father always brought a pipe, Shore said. I don't imagine you—?

William grimaced. It's not my first time in a mortuary, he said. Withdrawing his pipe from his overcoat pocket even as he spoke, tamping it, lighting it. It was an old cherrywood pipe from Virginia with the scabs of bark left on it and it reminded him of the war. To their left a door stood ajar on an empty filing room, paperwork strewn across the small desk. A single candle was burning there. The dark wainscoting behind it looked water-spotted and old.

Do I need to sign in?

It's not that sort of establishment. You haven't breakfasted yet?

No.

Probably a good thing. How's your hand?

How's it look?

Pretty as a flower. You'd fit right in at Millbank.

William grunted. Let's get this over with, he said.

The mortuary was long, low-ceilinged, badly lit. There were short tables along both walls and a narrow space between each and on the tables were bodies both covered and not. The legs of those dead hung off the ends of the tables suspended there and the smell they gave off was foul, tinged with a peculiar ripe sweetness William knew from transporting the murdered on the railroads of the Midwest. He smoked and smoked.

There was a young constable just inside the doorway slouching in his immaculate blues and he straightened and nodded politely as they approached. He was clean-shaven, already balding, his collar badges glinting in the light as he turned.

Shore looked past him into the gloom. Who is the assistant in post here, Mr. Stone?

Mr. Cruikes, sir.

At the end of the long room a man in a stained apron was swaying between the tables of the dead. Slats of shadow, slats of light. A low soft crooning as he worked.

He's drunk.

It rather goes with the job, Shore said grimly. So long as they get the bodies in and out and mostly tagged as they should be. We won't be needing Mr. Cruikes, Constable.

Yes sir.

William said nothing. Shore led them down between the tables, their footsteps scraping in the quiet, and then the three of them stopped at the foot of a covered table. Shore pulled the oilcloth back and William stepped closer.

It was the severed head of a woman. A torso lay next to it. The legs were missing and looked to have been sawed roughly off judging by the stumps. The skin on the face had greyed and gone soft and the black hair had been shorn. A towel had been folded at the crown to hold it upright. Her eyes were rolled sightlessly up in her head and her lips were parted slightly. The skin on the torso had not greyed in the same way but in the eerie light it glowed as if lit from within. There were puckered slashes where a blade had gone in under the ribs and across the belly.

Shore was watching his reaction. Is it her?

What happened to her hair?

That's the question you ask? She's been carved into pieces.

William unclenched the pipe from his teeth and moved it to one side of his mouth and he said, quietly, It does look like her.

Charlotte Reckitt.

Yes.

I thought so too. We haven't acquired an identification yet from her kin. But we brought the neighbour down from Hampstead and he recognized her also. The shape of her face and so on.

What happened? Was she cut up by a river steamer?

Shore shook his head. Irishman on the docks fished the head out of the river this morning. Mr. Stone was the first one there.

William glanced at the constable and the young man frowned with great seriousness.

His name was Malone, sir. He was working down at the loading piers on a vessel just in from Holland. Carrying bulbs, it was.

Bulbs?

Flowers, sir.

I know what bulbs are, Constable. He leaned in closer, pulled the oilcloth up to her hips, peered at her torso. The mottled skin on her upper arms where she might have been gripped and shaken. Her chiselled rib cage, the soft spill of her breasts, the nipples blue in the cold. Where are the legs?

We don't know that yet, sir.

The head was at the docks? Where was the rest of her?

That's the queer part of it. Shore cleared his throat. A constable found the torso tied in a sack under a piece of masonry on a building site out at Edgware Road. That was five o'clock this morning.

I don't understand. It wasn't in the river?

Shore frowned no. But Mr. Cruikes fit the cut of the neck to the torso. It's a match.

William glanced back at her in interest. That head doesn't look fresh.

Aye. The river will do that.

William walked to the other side of the table. Look at these stab wounds, he said. Is there water in the lungs?

We think she must have been attacked with a knife, sir, the constable said. Then they cut her up. After she died, like.

You don't think she did the violence to herself?

To herself, sir?

He's being rough with you, Constable.

William turned back to Shore. An awful lot of trouble for a drowned woman.

Aye.

Why would anyone do this? Revenge?

I'd guess the head was weighted down in sacking to lose it in the river. To keep her from being identified. Something must have gone wrong, it rolled loose, floated out. Neighbour remembers a man shouting and something heavy being dragged across a floor two weeks back. Says he was walking his dog at the time.

Two weeks back. How does that help with this?

Shore looked tired. He plucked his pipe from his lips and rubbed wearily at the stem. Women like that don't just get murdered for no reason.

Women like that.

Aye.

William said nothing. After a moment he said, There'll be some evidence somewhere. You can't cut up a body and clean up the mess perfectly.

Unless it was done in the river.

Then someone saw it. There's a lot of blood in a body, John.

Aye.

It just doesn't make sense.

You know what these types are like. Maybe an old mark caught up with her. Maybe she tried to sell a job to the wrong customer. Maybe she had something on someone and was going to come to us with it.

After she climbed out of the river you mean?

Maybe someone didn't want her to leave the city. Or maybe it had nothing to do with her, maybe she was just in the wrong place at the wrong time. I don't know, William. Maybe this isn't even her.

You think it isn't?

Maybe she was with child, sir, the constable said.

Shore ran a hand through his thinning hair, looked at the doorway, looked at the girl on the slab. What the devil does that have to do with anything?

Like the Tabitha case in Brighton last summer, sir. The serving girl who was killed by her mistress.

William glanced past the chief inspector at the constable standing with his heavy helmet in one hand. Where's Dr. Breck? he asked. Why don't you have him take the girl apart, see what he can find. If there's water in the lungs you have a different sort of offence here.

Shore scowled. I'll run my own affairs, thank you.

Okay.

Mr. Stone, Shore barked at the young constable. Make

certain Dr. Breck has a look at her. He turned back to William. You don't think she might have been pregnant?

I don't.

If she was pregnant there might be a man involved.

I'd guess so.

What did you think of her? Her character, I mean?

He frowned and turned his glance away. He said, There was nothing wrong with Charlotte Reckitt twenty dollars wouldn't fix. It just wouldn't fix it for very long. He stepped forward, brushed her cold wrist. The flesh was spongelike against his own. He murmured, How does a woman jump from a bridge in the middle of the night and end up cut into pieces in different parts of the city by morning?

Your father would've had a theory.

William ignored this. Where are the legs? he said. What happened to her hair?

Constable Stone cleared his throat. I'd wager she had it cut for a disguise, sir.

Why would she bother with something like that?

The constable frowned.

Why are there no wounds on her hands and arms? If she was attacked she would have tried to fight the assailant off.

Maybe she was asleep, sir.

Wonderful. Where. In her bed?

The constable nodded.

You think she leapt from the bridge, swam to shore, went home to cut her hair, then went to bed and was assaulted and that her killer cut her up and spent the night going from Edgware Road to the river with sacks of remains?

The constable flushed.

Maybe she never fought back, Shore said. Maybe she knew her attacker.

Maybe. William gestured to a blue-green mottling along her forearms, just above the wrists. More likely she was tied up. I'd talk to this Malone again. He turned to the constable. You have an address for him?

Constable Stone blushed and turned the helmet in his hands. Workingmen don't give up their addresses, sir. Not to us. But I know the sight of him. I could describe him to a hair.

All right, Shore said. We'll find him if we need him.

Sure you will. How many Irishmen named Malone work out at the docks? William dipped his chin, massaged his neck wearily. Are we done here, John?

Shore nodded.

William made to turn away but the chief inspector was still studying the girl's swollen mouth. Very slowly he reached forward and drew the oilcloth over her torso, over the head. He looked up and his pouched eyes were very black. Just so you know, he said. No one kills a girl over here because she's pregnant. They just disown them or ship them off to relations in the country. Or else leave the nuggets out in the cold when they're born.

William met the chief inspector's eye. Nuggets? he said.

Aye.

You English, he muttered.

FOUR

nglish? the turnkey scowled.

He was the port officer for the dock cells and he frowned up over the small square lenses of an ancient pair of spectacles.

An Englishman, Foole said again. Just in from Boston, on the *Aurania*. A big man, black beard, heavy-set. They say he assaulted a man at the saloon-class exit.

The turnkey scratched at his grizzled chops. Leaned back on his high drafting stool, the backrest creaking under him. Staring aslant at Foole all the while as if at some savage dressed to pass for white and Foole scraped at the dust of the floor, clasped both hands on his walking stick, leaned irritably upon it.

I believe his head was bleeding, he added.

An why would ye be wanting this particular someone then?

Daylight was filtering in through a long row of leaded windows and the chill from the waterside made its way up the walls and Foole withdrew a pair of pale green gloves and tucked his walking stick under his left arm and slowly pulled on each of the gloves. He understood this shed must be a temporary jail although the low ceiling was long stained with smoke from the lamps and the streaks of rust from the corners of the window frames must have taken some years to leak. A small, dingy, narrow place reeking with the offal from the fish houses just off the ramp. All this time he had not taken his eyes from the

turnkey and that stare was cold and hooded and it warned that
his business was his alone.

After a moment the turnkey shrugged. Suit yourself then,
he grunted. He stood and came around the desk and led Foole
down a corridor to a locked cell. He was smaller even than
Foole and he walked with a hand in the curve of his back as if
he had suffered some injury when young.

When they reached the far cell he curled one fist around a
crossbar. Ye don't mean this one?

The giant sat slumped on a steel bench suspended by chains
and he did not lift his head.

The very man, Foole said.

Go on. Ye ain't in his employ now?

Foole smiled. Hardly. I'm the man he assaulted.

The turnkey frowned, took off his spectacles, wiped them.
I don't know how things is done where ye come from, he said.
But here we works with the law. I can't just be turnin a blind
eye, see. More's the pity, maybe.

It took Foole a moment to understand the man's meaning.
I'm not here to do him harm, he said. I'm here because I don't
wish to see him prosecuted.

You don't mean to press charges? The turnkey glanced dubiously at the giant's cell. With due respect. Ye sayin you would
have us release him?

Yes.

What in the devil for?

Call me a sentimental soul.

There are some as might call ye somethin else. Begging your
pardon.

Foole withdrew a shilling and held it softly in his palm. For
your trouble, he said.

It weren't no trouble, the turnkey replied. Just doin me job.
But his hairy fingers closed over the coin all the same. I can't see
what good keepin him here is like to do, he said. If you don't aim
to pursue the matter. There's the small issue of the fine though.

Foole waited.

Disorderly conduct, drunk in public. Be another shilling, that one.

Foole withdrew the last shilling from his pocket and studied it a moment in his gloved fingers and then he handed it across.

Well, man, he called out over the turnkey's shoulder. We can see past this misunderstanding, can't we?

The giant sat unmoving, buckled forward, his tangled mass of black hair threaded in his hands.

Course ye'll be walkin the same streets as the monster, the turnkey said. Wouldn't ye be needin an escort?

I'll be fine.

Ye don't aim to just walk out with him now?

Walk out with him? Foole smiled at the idea, adjusting each glove at the wrist. I should think not, he said. No, I mean to stand the man a drink.

The giant's name was Japheth Fludd. Foole walked with him in silence up Water Street and past the Cunard Line offices then turned down Castle to Derby Square and the chaos of Lord Street with its buggies and clerks and sailors swaggering on shore leave with hands in pockets and pipes in teeth. At a narrow alley they turned and slipped down a short flight of steps into a dark flash house still without talking and in the corner took the end of a scarred trestle that served as a table. Two whores perched at the far end saw the giant in his battered state and exchanged a glance and stood and moved to a different table. After a moment a small girl in a boy's hat and a blue work coat with the stuffing coming through at the seams of the shoulders got up from where she had been sitting under the room's only window and came over to them with a grin. She was swinging a small suitcase before her.

Took your sweet time, she said. You two have a nice holiday?

Foole winked. Hello Molly.

Damn bugger near stove me head in, Fludd muttered. Look at me face.

She slid along the bench with a teasing sigh. You think you got it rough? O lord I tell you those skirts is awful complicated to get out of.

I reckon our Mr. Adam's took more of them off than you have, kid. An he weren't the one wearin them at the time.

Fludd's cheek was discolouring and there were bruises deepening under his eyes. Foole felt a quiet regret seeing this but knew the big man had taken worse without complaint and that violence to him was a way of being in the world. Fludd's father had been a minister in the prisons in Australia in his childhood and something of the fury of the transported had settled in his blood. He had been in a federal prison outside New York for six years and three months on an attempted-murder charge for stalking and crushing the skull of a crooked policeman and Foole and Molly had gone to America in part to meet him upon his release and bring him back to London. Those six years had grooved the giant's face with new scars and Foole looked at his old friend feeling startled by how the man had aged.

Now he put a hand out on the table. What have you got for us, Molly? he asked.

Pies. And fried taters.

He means the poke, birdie.

Molly's grin faded from her face and when she looked at Fludd her eyes were flat and hard and old for her years. Go on, she said. Say that again.

Say what, birdie?

Japheth, Foole said.

Molly was sucking at her upper lip in anger. She was a gifted pickpocket and had been both ward and accomplice to Foole while Fludd was in prison and the two had only just met for the first time three weeks ago. That was the ninth of December 1884, the morning Fludd trudged out of the prison gates with a sack of clothes over his shoulder and his boot prints filling quietly with snow. Almost her first words to the giant had been to keep his head and to pay attention, as if she and not the giant were the veteran of the flash life. That, and to warn him in a growl never to call her birdie.

Now she was turning to Foole with a plaintive look. He knows he ain't supposed to say that to me, she said. He knows it.

Aw, I'm just bein rough with her, Fludd grinned. She knows it don't mean nothin.

Is that a apology?

Sure.

Molly looked disgusted. Say it. Say it or it don't count.

Say what?

That you apologize, you two-penny bollocking bastard.

All right, that's enough, Foole said, with a weary look. Both of you. I mean it.

Just then the barkeep came out to their table with two greasy plates in the crook of one elbow and three pints between his two fists. A pie swimming in some grey grease. Sausages in a gluey lump. Limp slices of what must have been potato. Fludd reached for his pint.

You know, Molly said. Now that I look at your face, I mean now that I really look at it—

What.

It do look rotten. Where Adam hit you.

Fludd reached up and touched the bruises gingerly.

Like a bit of beef pudding.

Bugger it all, Adam. You an your bloody stick.

Foole turned a mouthful of the pie from side to side in his mouth.

What side he hit you on? Molly asked. The left?

Fludd looked at her a long moment and then he said, It were the right side of me face. Here.

She peered in an exaggerated fashion from side to side. An on your nose too?

You bloody minx, Fludd said. It were me temple.

But Fludd was grinning and so was the girl.

You should thank god I only hit you in the head, Foole said. I might have hurt you.

Molly had pulled out a pack of cards and she split the deck swiftly and dealt two dead man's hands one to Fludd and one to Foole and then she cut out a card for herself and left it lying face down. It was the cleanest way to distribute the poke. They would play out their hands and absorb the winnings Molly had lifted from the passengers on the *Aurania*'s gangplank. Fludd shovelled in a forkful of pie then picked out a string of meat and pushed his plate aside and laid down a clean hand and Molly passed him the first cut of his earnings and then Foole did likewise. He knew it had been a foolish dip despite their straitened finances but some part of him did not care and some other part of him understood it was important to keep Fludd and the kid in the poke.

Fludd laid down a second hand and drained his pint and wiped a hand across his beard. He plucked the sausages one by one from their slime and tossed them onto Foole's plate.

Foole shook his head. What's wrong with them?

Fludd shrugged.

Molly started to laugh. He's still a bloody vegetable eater.

You two thought maybe I'd quit? You thought I weren't able to keep at it, like?

Foole was shaking his head. I thought maybe I'd knocked some sense into you.

Vegetables ain't good for you, Molly laughed. They just ain't healthy. You goin to shrivel right up on us.

Go on, give us another slice of the blunt, Fludd said.

Molly slid a sovereign over to his side. Use that to buy your cabbage.

They played out the hour and cut the pickings and Foole kept one eye on the door but no one entered that he recognized and the barkeep did not ever lay his towel over his left shoulder. That would have been the sign, Foole knew, to scatter.

Fludd had grown restless. He had bottomed three pints already and was rolling an empty glass between his big hands. What time do our train leave?

Half five.

An what kind of time do that give us?

Foole reached instinctively for his pocket watch then remembered the phrenologist and stopped himself.

Molly winked at him.

Slowly she reached around into her waistcoat pocket and withdrew a silver pocket watch with an inlaid gold eye on its front. She flipped the elegant casing open. It was ringed in copper and bore an inscription engraved within. Let me see now, she murmured to herself. If the big hand's pointin at the—

O you beautiful creature, Foole said. You make a fine daughter.

She laughed and clicked the watch shut. An you make a rotten pa. So you goin to tell us what we come back to England for?

Foole lifted his wrists, turned them out as if to show his sleeves empty.

Go on, she said. What's that supposed to mean?

It means you don't be askin, he ain't like to lie to you, Fludd said. You ain't gettin no answer out of him, kid. Is there time for a last bumper or what?

Molly took a deep draw on her bitter and smacked her lips at the giant. Is it to do with that letter? Is that the job?

Foole did not stop smiling but something darkened between them. Which letter would that be? he said pleasantly.

She looked all at once uneasy.

Letter? Fludd asked. He was looking from one to the other in bafflement. Bugger it all. I got time for a pint or not?

You do not, Foole said without looking at him. To Molly he said, An old friend is in some trouble. She's written to ask us back. We are to be of assistance.

Molly had lowered her eyes.

Who's that now? Fludd said. I ain't goin back to the pinch just yet, Mr. Adam.

Foole was still looking at Molly. You'll want to get changed again, he said. My manservants are a little more refined in their dress.

She started to speak and then she bit her tongue and then she could not help herself. What about Japheth? she said. Do he get to wear that?

Never mind him.

After a moment she pulled a bundle of clothes from her small suitcase and got sullenly up and crossed to the bar and the barman said something to her and lifted up the heavy swing counter and she ducked under it and was gone.

She's kind of a scary wee dipper, ain't she, Fludd said. Weren't she never just a kid?

Not since I met her.

Never?

Foole looked at him. You have your answer, Japheth, he said quietly.

Foole had rented her as a gonoph for a delicate job of distraction on some minor heist in Hyde Park in that first year after Fludd's conviction in New York and she had been so clever and so convincing that he had doubted her age. She was living then with seven other waifs in a pickpockets' crew under the care of two half-blind sisters, both cruel, the elder a widow who went by the name of Sharper and who was rumoured to have poisoned her husband. Molly they had called *birdie* in what Foole had believed at first to be affection. Her sole companion during those years had been a four-year-old boy named Peter who fetched wood and emptied the chamber pots and huddled with Molly for warmth at night. She loved him like a brother. Like any of the Sharper dippers she could be rented by the hour or by the fortnight by members of the flash world and Mrs. Sharper asked no questions so long as her merchandise was returned undamaged. Foole bought the child outright on her sixth birthday knowing nothing of the boy Peter and she already knew to dress in rags with her tiny feet bare for better purchase and knew to wipe grease on her fingertips to slip them more surely into a lady's handbag. They were nimble fingers and long for her size and he had admired them from the first. Two weeks after he bought her he gave her her freedom and she had gone at once out into the streets in search of Peter and returned at dawn alone. There had been blood on her sleeves and her face when she came back but it was not hers and he had not asked and she had not spoken of it. She could outrun a beak's whistle the length of a city block and could time a street crossing to pass under the belly of a dray. But she dipped only those marks as instructed and turned over her poke without complaint and kept no fig for herself. She had a talent for accents and speaking as others spoke and was smarter than she was hungry. Foole tutored her in her letters himself and she learned to read quickly as if already understanding the rare gift that would be. She wore boys' clothes always unless a job called for other and even then it was a labour to convince her. Despite their bickering she and Fludd had taken to each other almost at once upon the giant's release and the three of them made already a strange kind of family. Molly the child of none and all. For Foole had seen her wax up a stick of peppermint of a Sunday out of a shopkeeper's very hand and had heard her reciting her alphabet backward in order to fall asleep and watching her small white face as she dreamed he could have sworn a sweetness played at her lips. Could she not be more than she was? Of course she could. Was she never a child? Of course she was. A child she was still.

That is what hurt his heart so.

From the flash house they made their way to the sleek rolling roofline of Lime Street station. It was all iron and glass and seemed a wonder to Foole in its flow like a thing of water fixed in place and a mark of the new age. The dark château of the North Western Hotel loomed up just beyond, its weird new electric lighting just coming on in the afternoon gloom, and across the way he could see the drumlike facade of the Picton Reading Room and he thought of its fluted columns and its carbon-arc lighting within and he understood he was again nearing the centre of a modern empire.

The station was cold, vast, loud with the clash and echo of voices in the huge space. He had last been here on a summer morning eighteen months earlier without a shilling to his name and the station then had been filled with light like a bell and he had wondered at the strange new beauty of it. Now there was a thin layer of coal dust on the counters and railings and crumpled wrappers and old tickets kicked into corners and several stalls along one wall were hawking books and newspapers and savouries. The warm smell of baked goods mingled with the pipe smoke of sailors and the harsh bite of tar coming in from the platforms. The porter he showed their tickets to nodded and pointed where a guard had raised the signal for the London train on the central platform and they could see the carriages were already loading. Molly left to find their luggage, which had been sent on ahead. He watched the girl disappear in the crowds wearing her boy's suit and with her hair tucked up under a cap and he felt something savage and protective rise in him that he swallowed down. Fludd was grimacing and carrying his trunk in both fists out in front of him towards the platform. He too had changed into a black frock coat and grey trousers and had cut back his beard and no man from the *Aurania* would know him to see him, never mind his size. Foole stopped at the mesh telegraph wicket and waited in the line and when he reached the clerk he scrawled out a quick message and had it sent on ahead. Then he bought a copy of the *Times* and adjusted his bowler and his cuffs and folded the newspaper under one arm.

He glimpsed Molly in the crowds arguing with one of the porters and he watched her throw up her arms and shake her head and then turn away. She was biting her lip and she reached into her pocket and threw something into a bin and then she saw him and came towards him.

What's the concern? he asked.

She tipped her cap back on her forehead and made a sour face. No concern, she said. They just want to skim the top of it is all.

The luggage?

All up.

Foole nodded. As she slipped on ahead of him he lingered a moment studying the cold grey light in the station and then as he turned to go he sighted something in the bin. A fold of pink cloth in the shape of a body. A pale edge of porcelain flaring in the light like a burst of phosphorus. It was the doll Molly had stolen from the Webster girl on the ship. Foole frowned and looked across through the drifts of steam on the platform but Molly and Fludd had already boarded and he looked back at the doll. The head had been ripped from the body and thrown in on top of it. It had been painted delicately once with a fine brush but was chipped now and dulled though the yellow hair looked soft still. Its eyes were green cut glass and under their heavy lids they would move when its bearer moved.

Foole stared and the doll stared back and the day felt luminous and sad.

As he came into their compartment an exhaustion poured suddenly through his legs and he sat with a groan, eager for sleep. Fludd was picking at something in his teeth, his big knees crowding the space. Molly leaned against the window facing the door as if she had been watching this long while for him to appear, as if afraid he might vanish even then.

He sat down across from her with a sigh. His leg touched Fludd's and he pulled away.

The benches were a dark polished oak like secular pews but softened with individual velvet cushions held in place by a brass bar and Foole adjusted his and crossed his legs and opened his paper. They had hired foot warmers and he could feel the heat coming up through his shoes. He could hear the banging of boots on the roof above them as the porters lashed fast some baggage or other and then there was a sharp whistle and a rush of steam and the train shuddered and began, slowly, to move. There were still men on the platforms waving and walking alongside the carriages passing packages and handkerchiefs up through the windows and he watched them with a blank face, the paper opened out on his legs.

Molly cleared her throat. Who is she? she said softly.

He looked at her in surprise.

She had lifted her cap and was stuffing a strand of hair back into place and biting her lip as she did so and there was a tightness around her eyes that he understood or believed he did.

Who you on about? Fludd said irritably. He was fussing with his seat. Who is who?

Foole said nothing.

Molly met his gaze. Then she reached into her waistcoat and took out the daguerreotype of himself and Charlotte Reckitt from Port Elizabeth all those years ago in the sunlight and studied it and screwed up one eye in a squint as she did so.

Give it over, Foole said. What are you doing with your eye?

Molly, squinting and squinting. Who is she? she said again. She looks fat. Is she fat? What's wrong with her eye?

What are you talking about?

Her eye. Look at it.

Fludd leaned his bulk over, peered at the daguerreotype. Is that Charlotte Reckitt?

Who's Charlotte Racket?

Her eye do look weird. Fludd screwed his own eye up.

Who's Charlotte Racket? Molly repeated.

Give it over, Foole said again, glaring, uncrossing his legs.

Aw it's a scratch, kid, look. Fludd rubbed a thick fingertip over the woman's face. Right there on her eye.

Charlotte bloody Racket who? Molly said again, as Foole reached across and plucked the daguerreotype from her small hands and leaned irritably back in his seat.

Reckitt, kid, Fludd said, grimacing. Charlotte Reckitt. Mr. Adam's sweetheart, once upon a time. You never told her bout Charlotte Reckitt? A fat lot of trouble, that one.

Where did you find this? he said to Molly.

She shrugged. In the cabin. You dropped it.

He looked at her. He'd be damned if he had.

You never mentioned her, she muttered.

Les sociétés ont les criminaux qu'elles méritent, he said.

Fludd laughed.

Molly's expression turned sullen, suspicious.

It's from Lacassagne, he said, rubbing at his eyes. The carriage rattled and creaked as they pulled slowly through the station, through the cut-away, the high brick walls steaming and wet and glistening in the dying light, and then the sudden flashes of darkness as they accelerated through the short tunnels and rose up out of the earth and were away. He was brooding at the sight of it and then said, to Fludd: Lacassagne is a detective with the Sûreté in Paris. An interesting man. You would like him, Japheth.

Foole could see Molly did not want to ask its meaning and he felt a quiet satisfaction and then under that a distaste at himself for feeling it. She was headstrong but what else did he expect.

It means you get what you deserve, birdie, Fludd said to her.

It means if I travel with a dipper, Foole said with a shrug. He smiled to soften it and smoothed a hand over the newsprint laid out before him and studied the columns there though he was not reading them. Charlotte Reckitt, he said, resigned, has written me a letter. Mrs. Sykes forwarded it to our hotel in New York. Charlotte was one of the flash mob, Molly, untraceable. As light a touch as I ever saw. You wouldn't have even been born when she worked the lay. He met Fludd's eye. She wants to see me.

Fludd grunted. I thought she were retired.

It seems not.

How long I been in the darbie? You ain't forgot what she done to you, Mr. Adam?

I haven't forgotten anything.

Molly had gone very quiet.

Fludd looked across at her uneasily, cleared his throat, rubbed his enormous hands on his knees. Aw now, kid, he said, it were all a long time ago. Back when it were just Mr. Adam an me. Charlotte Reckitt's uncle, Martin, he were almost the only

jake we was all afraid of. You turn your back on a buzzer like
that, well. Used to call him the priest, on account of his bein
thrown out of the priesthood when he were young. He liked to
say he followed a higher callin. You remember what he done to
that lad in Bristol, Mr. Adam? With the bad leg? He looked at
Molly. Carved the boy's nose from his face while he were sleepin one off. Martin Reckitt's hands they was always dry. Dry
like a lizard. We ain't never worked with him much but there
were a job in South Africa Mr. Adam got involved in, Reckitt
gone down there with him to work it. It were there Mr. Adam
met Charlotte. I met her later, once or twice, after that job gone
bad, after Mr. Adam missed his rendezvous in Brindisi. Then
we all had our fallin-out an we tried not to cross paths no more.
I don't think we ever much did. Did we? He turned his huge
shaggy face towards Foole and his eyes were unreadable in the
shadow for a long moment while the tracks rattled past underneath and when Foole said nothing he said, in a low voice, So
what is it she writes then?

Foole traced a reluctant finger along the edge of the newspaper. There's a job, he said. Six months in the planning. She's
being watched by some detective and needs another party in.
She doesn't discuss details—

Course she don't. Is that bastard priest uncle in on it?

Martin's up in Millbank.

Fludd gave him a long appraising look. Still a guest of Her
Majesty?

Apparently so.

He let out a low whistle. An you sure you ain't gettin you
head mixed up with no other bits?

Foole felt the heat rise to his cheeks. I never said we were
going to do anything. I'm considering it, that's all. It might
prove profitable.

Be a nice change, that, Molly muttered.

No other reason? Fludd said.

Everything else is in the past, Japheth.

Char-lotte Reck-itt, Molly said quietly. Char-lotte Reck-itt.

It's exhaustin, that is, Fludd said.

What is?

The past.

You never mentioned her, Adam, Molly said. Why not?

Foole shrugged tiredly.

The locomotive was reaching speed now and the evening opened into darkness. Liverpool felt like an unsettling dream.

Molly was kicking at Fludd's seat, steadily, rhythmically. Whispering in time to her kicks.

Char-lotte, Reck-itt. Char-lotte, Reck-itt.

The hours passed.

They had been travelling through the night for some time when Foole at last folded the *Times* and set it down on the empty seat beside him and stared at his reflection. His eyes like small burning lanterns in the glass. Outside the winter passed and passed. He could feel the ties clattering underneath them, hear the rattle of their carriage adjusting around a curve. Then the weight shifted and the sound altered to a hollow clacking and he understood they were passing over a wooden trestle. A kind of lightness came over him. He thought of the black waters churning far below, he thought of the veer and the plummet. He remembered then that last afternoon with Charlotte in Port Elizabeth and the easy way she greeted him in the hotel lounge. The slant of the sunlight through the big green leaves and the way her skin smelled. He knew he was taking a risk in coming to see her. He knew she might prefer the memory of him to the man he had become. He rubbed his eyes.

After a few minutes the old shuddering clatter returned and then they were back on solid earth and Foole grimaced and massaged his sore thighs and got to his feet. Molly had got up some time before and not returned and Foole now sighed and buttoned his lounge coat and slid open the door of their compartment. He left Fludd snoring with his mouth open and his huge hands dangling between his knees.

The passageway was quiet, the twin lamps at either end were turned low and reflected in the warpled windows of the doors. Foole made his slow way to the rear with his hands outstretched as if leaning into a strong wind.

He struggled with both hands and opened the rear door.

The roar in the blackness was ferocious. He squinted against the cold and saw Molly huddled there at the railing, a tiny shapeless bundle. A solitary lantern burned above her, jittering with the shaking of the carriage trucks.

Couldn't sleep? he hollered to her over the noise of the tracks.

It's quieter out here, she shouted.

He nodded and stood close to her with his white hands gripping the frozen railing and they stayed like that for a while, leaning into each other. After a time Molly said something he did not catch and he leaned in closer.

I said, didn't you never feel no regret bout it Adam?

He looked down at her in surprise, the play of shadow about her face. About what? he hollered.

She shrugged.

I want you to listen to me, he shouted. He took her by the shoulders and turned her square to him and the wind whipped at her hair. The world will take from us what it wants. It doesn't mean we have to permit it. We are not here on anyone else's behalf.

She bit her lip.

Lives like ours are about what we manage to keep. Like you and Peter. That's something you've held on to. Charlotte is like that for me. His eyes were running from the cold. What did you do with that doll? he hollered. Did you lose it?

When she looked up at him the shadows were distorting her face. That doll, she shouted. That was all just pretend. It weren't life.

He felt a pain in his stomach as he looked at her. He set one hand on the railing and watched the freezing night unroll behind them. The lantern swaying and clattering above the door, the arc of the tracks in the gaslight in their infinite unravelling.

What if you could have it back, he shouted. Would you want it?

He reached into his coat and pulled the porcelain doll's head out into the cupola of light. He had not salvaged the muslin body and seeing her face now he regretted it.

Just don't let Japheth find it, he shouted. You'd never hear the end of it.

She took the doll's head from him in both of her hands. He could not see her face for the shadows and for the fall of hair obscuring it. It seemed to him then the darkness they moved through was not space only but time, too, that his century was already passing, and he thought of the girl as she would be when she was very old and he was long vanished from the earth and it seemed all at once terrible in its loneliness. The past is always just beginning. For us as for any, he thought. He set a cold hand on the girl's shoulder but he could not feel her through her thick coat and they stood like that as all around them the cold night deepened and scrolled past and away.

FIVE

William came up out of the mortuary feeling blown out, depressed. He could not say if Charlotte Reckitt had deserved her end and he told himself he did not care but it was not true. He thought of her ravaged scalp and the tufts of hair and blood on it and how her body had been cut up and the legs still, for god's sake, missing. Then he could not stop himself and thought of his daughters in Chicago, thought of Margaret. Swore under his breath and clapped his hands on his sleeves as if to dislodge the reek of the dead and stepped out into the fog.

Frith Street felt desolate in its brightness, the pale shapes swirling past, the cold mournful cries of costermongers in the mists. He could hear the lurch and creak of an omnibus over the cobblestones, the shout of a patterer trotting along behind it with his broadsides clutched in both arms, the soft tack-tack-tack of an undertaker's hammer several shops down. He pinched his eyes shut, lifted the brim of his silk hat, ran two fingers along his hot scalp. He could see the vague grey trees in Soho Square to the north. His shadowy self moving like water in the shop windows as he passed. At the entrance to an arcade he slipped among a crowd and made his way between the wooden pillars and mud-stained carts, past rickety tables with bolts of fabric laid out, past rows of folded spectacles, steaming pies, ball-peen hammers, inks, sheaves of paper, gloves and bonnets and stoles. He felt incandescent, and thin, as if not quite there. Men in stained cravats were calling out to him in the crush. Liverspotted hands in fingerless catch-alls clawed at his sleeves, grasped his wrists. He shook them off.

And then all at once he spun and jerked his right hand swiftly to his watch pocket and seized the small grubby wrist descending there.

She was a young pickpocket in a green bustle and a green bonnet and a strand of long brown hair had come unpinned at her throat. She looked tired and malnourished to his eye, her skin glassy, the blue veins visible in her forehead. He glanced out over the crowds but if any accomplice lurked there he did not see one. She clutched in her free hand a tiny kid glove of fine grey leather and her sunken eyes were frightened. He watched her writhe at the end of his grip like the eels he had seen hooked from buckets in the fish markets of New Orleans during the war and he glowered but did not have the heart to do more.

He let her go.

She stepped back without a word and rubbed her reddening wrist where his strong fingers had marked her and then she tugged back on the tight kidskin glove in a fury. When she looked at him her mouth was twisted to an ugly shape. Then she was gone in the crowd.

He stared at the space where she had stood and he thought of Charlotte Reckitt, startled by the sadness blooming inside him.

It was time he got out of London. He had come to this city trusting the Agency could run itself for two weeks but those two weeks had stretched to six and still he had come no closer to finding Shade. Sally Porter was right. Whatever Edward Shade had been to his father, he did not have to become that again.

But he made his way to the curb despite all of this and hailed a passing brougham through the fog and called ahead to the driver: Hampstead, man.

Knowing if Charlotte Reckitt had left any clue to the ghost of Edward Shade it would be there, in that tall gloomy terraced house where she had lived.

———

It was an ancient brougham with the box and bench uncovered and its strange outsized wheels hulking up on each corner. William huddled on the damp seat, staring at the driver's broad back, cursing his luck. The springs on the back wheels had known better days and on the uneven streets he ground his teeth and gripped the rail and felt his bones jar with the violence of it. The driver's hair was long and lay plastered in greasy strands over his collar. William looked away.

He changed his mind at New Oxford Street and had the brougham turn down past the Strand. At the Union Telegram Office near the Embankment he climbed out and paid the driver and went in rubbing the back of his neck stiffly. A warm dank fug of cigar smoke came over him. The Office resembled a small bank with its pillared entrance and its tall carved doors and the long counter along one wall just under the windows. William went to the standing desk and withdrew a slip of paper and a pencil from the mesh cubby and wrote out a message to his wife in Chicago. It said, simply: PUNCHED OUT. OFF THE CLOCK. HOME SOON.

He licked the tip of the pencil and counted off the letters in their small boxes and then set the pencil down and stood in line at the counter. There were silk ropes marking out the waiting area and the marble floor gleamed underfoot and the counter and railings and window trims were a deep polished oak as if reclaimed from a wrecked schooner. The telegraph clerk was a young man with a green eyeshade set high on his forehead and he reminded William of the dealers in the card dens he had haunted in the Panhandle some years ago though the man's fingernails were too clean and his skin too soft.

He wrote out his home address in Chicago and the clerk glanced at him and back at the name Pinkerton printed there and then back at him but said nothing. His business was his alone. He opened his billfold and withdrew a five-pound note.

When he came out the brougham stood at the curb yet and he paused and looked up the street in either direction but could see neither hansom nor carriage for the fog and he sighed and rubbed his neck and climbed creaking back onto the footboard.

Once again, guv? the driver grinned back at him. We was waitin for you. Just in case, like.

Wonderful, William muttered.

Hampstead?

William nodded and looked down at the cobblestones, at the brougham's big old iron-shod wheels standing at the ready. Driver, he called up.

The man half turned on his bench, blinking.

I'm in no rush, he said.

When they reached New Street in Hampstead he set one hand on his aching knee and got out of the brougham more stiffly than before. His shoe squelched into some deep pocket of muck and he shook it free. His topcoat and hat were cold with the damp from the fog and he paid the driver and went up the short steps and knocked on the door.

Charlotte Reckitt's terraced house was a steep dark residence of red brick and green railings with a patch of garden in the front withered and sad in the winter cold. He could see nothing behind the wrought iron in the upper windows but the sheerness of muslin, a ripple of sky over the uneven pane. The house felt desolate, empty. She had employed no help and had kept back from the windows during the day and William had from the very first found the place grim and cold, like a house whose owners had died. The steps now were smeared where the shoes of John Shore's constables had come and gone all morning.

He had expected no answer to his knocking and felt no guilt at having to break in. Whatever else this was, it was not an official investigation and his methods would not be scrutinized. He turned at the iron railing and glanced over the street and saw through the fog an old gentleman in top hat and grizzled whiskers clutching an umbrella and calling out for the brougham as it slowed. When it started again with a lurch the man's hand went to his top hat and William smiled.

The door swung open. A plainclothes police inspector in a grey frock coat peered out at him, his silver watch chain shining in the gloom. It took William a moment to recall the man's name.

Blackwell, he said.

The inspector nodded. Mr. Shore thought you might appreciate a hand, sir.

William removed his hat in irritation, held it roughly at the brim. Ran a hand through his hair and his hand came away black from the London smut. He had said nothing to Shore about his coming here. Is John here then? he said.

Begging your pardon, sir. The chief's occupied with the Fenians, sir.

The Fenians.

With the bomb, sir. In the Underground. Blackwell blinked. The one went off last Friday morning at Gower Street. You didn't hear, sir?

William ran a forefinger under the pouch of his eye, tiredly. He had heard nothing of it and did not know what to say. Was anyone hurt? he asked.

I believe so, sir.

He frowned and stepped inside and Blackwell shut the door. There were gold and silver garlands from the holiday just past still strung from the candle sconces on the walls and a scuffed brass trumpet standing on end in a window alcove amid fir needles. Then it's just you here? he asked.

Myself and the ghost, sir.

I don't suppose you found a bloodstained cleaver anywhere.

No sir.

An axe maybe.

Blackwell's eyes were heavy-lidded and bulged mildly and William regarded them. They gave the man an astonished expression as if he had just been swindled at cards. But then any swindler worth his weight must look just so, he knew. There's nothing here, sir, Blackwell repeated quietly. I'm just sort of watching the place. If you get my meaning.

William stood taking this in. He knew this meant Blackwell had been instructed to wait in case William showed up. Shore was a good man in his way but a jealous one and uneasy with the son of Allan Pinkerton in his city.

Anything of interest upstairs? he said.

There's just the one room that looks to have been lived in, sir. The chief supposed it belonged to Miss Reckitt. The parlour—

John's been here?

This morning, sir.

Appearing embarrassed as he said it.

William walked into the hall and set one hand on the balustrade and strained to see up the stairwell in the gloom. He half expected Charlotte Reckitt's shadowy figure there, glaring accusingly down. The chandelier in the entrance behind him had not been converted to gas and its arms loomed articulated and strange like some terrible spider. The wicks of the candles in the wall sconces had not been trimmed. His eyes followed the mouldings, the wainscoting carved in ancient Georgian fashion, all of it thickened under a layer of new dust. Plush white carpet had been tacked to the stairs and he could see the filth from the constables' boots where they had walked. He shook his head.

He started up the stairs, his bruised hand on the cool elm of the railing. The third step from the bottom groaned under his weight and he noted this in silence. On the second-floor landing a new clock built to look old had stopped at 11:37 and on either side a door opened into the back of the house. One stood open and his gaze took in the heavy furnishings of a study. He could see a lady's sewing room overlooking the street when he turned. Drawers upended, dresses and crinolines and hat boxes tangled in heaps, papers strewn across the carpets.

Did you find it like this? he called over his shoulder.

No sir. The detectives were rather thorough, sir.

He grunted. The floorboards creaked as he walked to the sewing room and stood with his hat in his hand and the damp

settling in his topcoat and he regarded the clutter. The door to
the bedroom at the front of the house stood half closed and this
he opened dully upon the gloom within and he frowned and
went to the far window and drew back the curtains. A cloud of
dust lifted and spun fractals in the cold light. It was a lady's
bedchamber and immaculate in its tidiness.

Blackwell had come up behind him and said, softly, Sir?

What's upstairs?

Two more bedchambers, sir. They're furnished but we don't
believe anyone is occupying them.

They're furnished.

Yes sir. The house must have been leased like that.

He went back downstairs and made his methodical way
through the scullery and larder and then through the kitchen,
opening drawers, unscrewing jars, tapping two fingers along the
walls for hidden compartments. The sink in the pantry was
made of wood and lined with lead and he ran a palm over its
joinings but felt nothing. He went outside, searched the water
closet. He did not know what he was looking for but could not
shake the suspicion that the woman must have left something
of interest behind. He poked his fingers through the cushions
and upholstery in the parlour and pushed aside the Christmas
ornaments and the painted eggs and wound the strands of gar-
land from the bookcases in order to riffle the pages of each
book. He made very little mess as he went and the inspector
followed behind him.

Why would a woman who lives alone go to such trouble
with the decorations? he asked.

I couldn't say, sir.

He made his way back upstairs to the study but turned up
no clue there either and at last he worked his way back to the
lady's bedchamber.

I guess John thinks it's ungentlemanly to search a lady's
room, he muttered.

Blackwell frowned. I believe he searched this room himself, sir.

William was hot now and he removed his topcoat and laid it on the bedclothes. Two candles stood in ornate silver sticks on the mantel. Under a chaise longue in the corner he could see shallow trays of clothes, untouched. At the dressing table he ran his finger and thumb along the antimacassar draped over the chair back but it felt clean and soft and told him little. He pulled the chair out, sat down. His reflection in the pier glass looked to his eye huge, pale, sinister. He pushed aside a silver hairbrush smudged with soot, a glove stretcher, a stack of unused envelopes. What would she need these for? he said.

To post her letters, sir.

He grunted. Who would she be writing to?

Blackwell made a noise and when William looked over the inspector was plucking something from the chiffonier and frowning.

What is it?

Your card, sir.

William frowned. He had left it on her doorstep on New Year's Eve to force her hand. He took it from Blackwell and pocketed it and the inspector watched him but said nothing and then he turned back and opened and shut the drawers of the dressing table without result. He went to the wall and got onto all fours and traced his hand along the perimeter of the baseboards and when he reached the ware table he shoved it rattling aside with one shoulder and a brass toilet can fell with a clang and he kept on. There's nothing here, he said. Nothing cut away at least.

No sir.

He sat back on his knees, pulled at his collar. This is ridiculous. Let me ask you something, Inspector. Did you find any signs of a struggle?

Blackwell cleared his throat. I understood she was tied up, sir.

Maybe.

Blackwell's eyes were fixed on him. You're not convinced, sir?

Convinced? he said. Why would she come back here? Who cut her into pieces? Who disposed of her? Why cut her hair, for god's sake?

Perhaps she thought she could get away. And was surprised at the last minute, sir.

They were both silent for a moment.

Perhaps not everything is connected, sir. Perhaps one of the details is confusing the matter.

Like what?

I couldn't say, sir. If she got out of the river alive she'd have need of a change of clothes. Perhaps she took the opportunity to change her appearance also. Cut her hair, for instance. Perhaps she was killed later in an ordinary manner. In a street robbery, for instance.

For god's sake. What rampsman cuts his marks up like that?

Blackwell frowned. Or what if it were a personal matter? A spurned lover? That would be consistent with the violence to her body.

But not her hair. I'm trying to put it together somehow. Charlotte Reckitt cut up and her hair cut off and her body left in sacks in two locations. The legs still unaccounted for. Someone was hunting her, someone I never caught sight of. She jumped from the bridge because she wanted it to look like she was dead.

So it was a deceit, sir.

But not for my benefit.

How can you be certain, sir?

It wouldn't make sense, he said, feeling his way towards it. He thought of his confrontation with her outside the theatre. Her small wrists crushed in his grip, the sliced whites of her eyes as she stared at him in alarm. I had nothing I could haul her in on and she knew that. She's an old hand at this, she knew the law, she knew I was out of my jurisdiction. She was trying to escape something else. Someone else.

Her killers.

Why run to Blackfriars? It's a long way and she ran directly for it. What was on the bridge? What was on the other side of it?

Perhaps it wasn't a thing, sir. Perhaps it was a person. An associate.

What if she was using herself as bait? What if she wasn't leading me towards the bridge, but away from something?

There's another possibility, sir.

William looked at the man.

That is, if it wasn't accidental, of course. We pull dozens of bodies from the river in any given week, sir. But assuming the lady was murdered—

You're thinking she was killed in error.

Yes sir. Perhaps the killer or killers did not mean for her to die. Something might have gone wrong. The disposal might have been an attempt to prolong the investigation.

I'd have thought if she was in that kind of trouble she'd have *wanted* to be arrested.

Blackwell nodded. Nothing is safer than a jail, sir.

My father used to say a wall is a wall from either side and who is to say which side is which.

Yes sir. Are we being kept in or kept out.

Exactly.

We were all sorry to hear about his passing, sir.

He looked at Blackwell a long moment and then left the room and made his way upstairs. Each of the two smaller bed-chambers was spare, immaculate, bedclothes tucked tightly in, porcelain bowls gleaming white under the beds. There was dust on the floor, wet boot prints traced in the dust. When he opened the armoire in the second room he found an array of expensive gentlemen's suits and jackets folded upon the shelves. A reek of mothballs from an open box. The clothing was crisp and had not been worn in some time and looked to William's eye ten years out of fashion.

Those will belong to her uncle, sir, Blackwell called from the doorway.

Martin Reckitt's in the Tench, William said. I expect he'll die in there.

In Millbank, sir, yes. But it's mostly a military prison now, sir. I understand there's talk of his being transferred south to the prison hulks when it closes next year.

William frowned in distraction. I didn't know it was closing.

A lack of funds, sir.

William crossed to the window and pressed a hand against the glass and the glass was cold. I'll want to talk to him, he said. He was a priest once, wasn't he?

So I'm told, sir.

But William's eyes were drifting now around the room and he did not say anything more and after a moment he walked slowly to one corner. A large birdcage was suspended there, covered by a white sheet, and he pulled the sheet gently back. The cage was empty. What happened to the larks? he asked.

Blackwell was stooped over a birchwood washstand and he paused now and straightened. Larks, sir?

William opened the little door and pinched a tiny grey feather from the tangle of grass. Why would anyone take her birds?

Perhaps they saw something they shouldn't of, sir.

The birds?

I don't know, sir. Blackwell paused. Either way, it shouldn't matter.

Why not?

They weren't canaries.

William stared at him. Are you making a joke, Inspector?

Shall I put out a description of the jailbirds, sir?

You can stop any time, Inspector.

It could be someone just took them on a lark, sir.

Blackwell. Stop.

Yes sir, he said. And turned back and pushed aside a brass pot in the cupboard to feel for hidden catches.

That night he tried to sleep but could not. The bed was warm from the swaddled hot brick laid in by the hotel maid and he got up resignedly into the freezing room. He wrapped himself in a blanket and retrieved Ben Porter's papers from the cigar drawer for something to do. He was thinking still of Charlotte Reckitt's body and waiting for his mind to clear. He sat in a wingback chair near the fireplace and rested his elbows on the bullets and then crossing his legs he sifted the papers in his lap. The lamps cast a weak sulphurous light a man with strong vision could just read by and he knew if he did not sleep soon he would be no good to anyone.

He rubbed his eyes.

Ben's reports went back some fourteen years. William read and reread what he could, feeling an irritation growing in him. He had believed Ben Porter to be an occasional informer and operative for his father in cases of criminals fleeing to England but this did not appear to be true. Porter had worked almost exclusively as a detective for his father for more than twenty years and during the last decade of his life worked solely on the peculiar obsession of Edward Shade.

According to the papers, Porter had begun haunting London's East End in 1869 when a description of an American thief had surfaced. He had taken work as a deal porter in a riverfront warehouse along the Surrey Docks in order to observe the area but had found no further leads. Then a rumour had emerged that an American by the name of Donald Rolson had taken rooms in Piccadilly and Porter had taken up work as a postal delivery clerk in order to acquaint himself with the neighbourhood. Rolson was rumoured to have set up a gambling den for gentlemen in the West End but Porter could not be certain and no sooner had such a rumour spread than the operation closed and vanished. What emerged gradually in Porter's reports and in William's father's replies was not a sense of the elusive Shade so much as a shadow, an echo of a man who may have never existed: six feet in height, with long arms, and a lean athletic build; or perhaps five and a half feet, with a portly build, and the short arms of a shopkeeper; a man with no facial hair and who kept his brown hair shorn close to the scalp; or perhaps a bald man, with carefully groomed whiskers; a man with catlike grey eyes and a quiet grimness about him; or perhaps a jovial and clumsy companion, who was drawn to the company of his betters; a man with no fear of God or law or country; or a man terrified of himself as well as all else. He might have been Edward Shade, or Donald Rolson, or William Peters Mackenzie. He might have been married, or not. One of the last letters from William's father suggested two Edward Shades might be working together and that Porter ought to keep an eye out for both of them.

William thought of his father with his powerful cooper's shoulders, his Scottish rages and righteous indignation, he remembered the sharp bite of the man's belt against the backs of his boyhood thighs. He looked again at the handwriting in the margins and at his father's wild surmising and he shook his head.

Ridiculous.

He pushed aside the papers in disgust.

SIX

8 2 Half Moon Street loomed up out of the fog.

Foole rolled a cold thumb over the head of his walking stick. He felt what he always felt, seeing it, seeing the small brass-plated sign he had screwed into the railing himself all those years ago: *Foole's Rare Goods Emporium. Imports & Exports. By Appointment Only.*

They had come by hired coach direct from the choking fumes of Gower Street station and he had got out exhausted. He stooped now in the walk with one hand on the railing and a yellow mist biting at his ankles, flowing past. He could see the front door standing open, Fludd fumbling in the gloom. A slow hammering of iron on iron started up from the roof across the street and though he turned and peered across he could not see the workmen. The windows in the terraced house opposite were dark and the drapes closed and the brown stucco depressing in the chill. He turned away.

There were smuts and blacks and flakes of soot adrift in the air around him like an evil snow. He could hear the clop and rattle of a hansom passing, disappearing down the cobblestones. A phantom, blurred in the mist, banged a trunk step by step up the whited stones towards him. That was Molly. Then Fludd brushed past, descended again into the fog where the coach was still unloading. All of it muffled, dreamlike, eerie.

The shabby main floor of the house was filled to overflowing with artifacts and objects shipped in from the corners of the empire. Ancient Asian vases, looking glasses from Australia, minerals and crystals from the mountains in East Africa, Indian headdresses, a chest of rusted sextants recovered from a wreck in a reef in the Caribbean. Foole loved the shadowy labyrinth of his Emporium. He had few customers. His prices were not listed.

Four years earlier he had leased this big house in its fashionable district just off Piccadilly and across from Green Park without having seen it and had paid the six months in advance through a land agent operating out of Chelsea. He had insisted on a residence expensively furnished, with tableware provided, with Turkish carpets and a lavatory pan on each floor and horsehair bedding covered in squares of holland under the feather mattresses. He had engaged a housekeeper and her daughter on the recommendation of an associate who had praised them for their discretion and had offered a generous salary. The previous occupants had broken their lease in a hurry when their second child was born dead and there was a sheen of illness to the house even now. Foole had made his way through the damp rooms following at his housekeeper's heels as she told him what she had gleaned of the place. She regarded that second child's stillbirth as a moral failure rather than a physical one and pursed her lips whenever the matter was broached.

Her name was Sykes and her wraithlike daughter's Hettie and she was a strong, wide-hipped hempen widow of forty. She would gnarl one hand into a fist whenever he called her to him and it was no delicate fist but strained white with knuckle and bone. He liked the hardness he saw in her, the austerity. Molly tolerated her as a cat would have done and that was good enough for Foole. Mrs. Sykes wore an apron stained with grease and blacking when she was not serving and a grim fringed bonnet that held her grey hair in place but there was in her eyes such an angry green intelligence that he wondered if she had talents yet untested.

Mr. Foole, sir, she said to him now. It's a fine big house to run, with only my Hettie and hardly a penny to the purse. How long do you mean to stay this time?

She was standing at the foot of the stairs wiping her hands on her apron among the foyer collection of Chinese vases on their shelves.

Foole smiled at her. It's good to see you too.

Fludd appeared in the doorway and stamped his boots and Foole put out a hand. Mrs. Sykes, this, he said, is my dear friend Mr. Fludd. He's returning to us after a long while abroad. I thought he could take the east room, across from Molly.

Ma'am, Fludd said shyly, doffing his hat.

Japheth Fludd. In the mighty flesh, is it? She gave the giant a strange sly look, as if assessing a shank of meat. O I heard stories about you, sir. I'll see to the room, Mr. Foole. But he'll be wantin to change those boots before he goes on up.

All three studied Fludd's boots a moment in silence.

It might have been the bad lighting or the recent exertions but it looked to Foole as if the big man's face under his beard had reddened. Foole cleared his throat. Japheth, you let Mrs. Sykes know what you need and she'll see that you get it. She's been a treasure to me these past years. He was looking at his old house-keeper fondly and wondering how much to tell her and then he could not help himself and he said, smiling, We may have another yet.

Would that be a lady, sir?

Why do you say that?

She winked, raised a finger to her lips. Now. Where's the wee one? Is she hungry?

Always, Foole laughed. I'd look for her in the larder.

Those first days back overwhelmed. There was much to be done in the airing of rooms and establishing of meetings and in the planning and weighing and diagramming of securities. Mrs. Sykes insisted on cataloguing each article or furnishing sold in his absence room by room in a ledger with Foole accompanying to sign off on each, if just to keep the staff honest-like, she explained, while she grumbled at the cost of outfitting a household with coal in the winter months. If you had of only returned to us in the summer, Mr. Foole, she'd scowl, I'd save you six shillings on the ton right easy. Them creditors of ours ain't like to stretch much further. He liked that use of *ours*, felt a gratitude well up in him to hear it. The basement buzzer rang constantly with rag-and-bone men, crockery girls, peddlers selling rabbits and pecks of peas and roots and herbs tied up by their ankles and dried. There were watercress girls in the mornings and butcher's apprentices in the afternoons and cockles-and-mussel men hollering in the streets outside before tea. Foole would work late into the night in a study behind the glass display cases with trunk lids standing open and the long mahogany desk shining in the gaslight and Hettie in her pallid thinness would come and go with a tray of dishes and vessels of hot water for washing. Foole would smile at her and gesture to the corner where Fludd was pencilling his accounts, where Molly was cleaning a satchel of picks and drivers, and he would watch the girl blush shyly to see them.

On the second morning, Foole came down to find Fludd with his shirt sleeves rolled back scrubbing the fender irons in the drawing room fireplace to a high shine. He clutched in one big hand a strip of dry leather and he paused and leaned back on his heels and ran the back of the hand across his face. Beside him sat a small twist jar of blacklead paste.

Good god, what is that smell? Foole said in a low voice. Has Mrs. Sykes put you to work already then?

She says you can't afford a proper lad. Fludd smiled wearily. Aw, I don't mind it. Easier work than breakin rocks.

Where is she?

Fludd shrugged.

In the basement kitchen he found his housekeeper with her skirts tied up between her legs hurtling pail after pail of cold water and carbolic across the linoleum. The silver tongue of the water hanging in the air a long instant as it fell. Then the crash and overspill and wash-back and sweep-through with the broom as she scowled and stomped up and down and guided the water

shirttails untucked, her hands on her hips and a sultry swagger to her backside.

She strutted on past, unseeing. The drawing room door opened, closed.

Mrs. Sykes cleared her throat.

Right queer one, that, she muttered, twisting and untwisting the washrag in her fists.

At noon on the third day a deliveryman rang the tradesman's bell at the basement door and was ushered by Mrs. Sykes in through the kitchen and up the back stairs to the Emporium. Molly took the small crate from him but she could not hold it and Fludd lurched forward and caught it and helped her set it down between the shelves. A scowl crossed her face and she did not thank him. All this Foole watched without moving from behind his desk. The warped floorboards creaking where Fludd walked.

There was a low fire burning but it gave off little heat. The crate held a sampling of small ammonite fossils still embedded in limestone blocks shipped privately from Geneva and under the straw packing in a false bottom were a variety of sapphire and ruby pendants taken from a Swiss jeweller. Molly turned each piece in the light of the window looking unimpressed then handed it along to Fludd who passed it to Foole. Molly said she hoped their partners on the Continent had a sharper eye than this. Foole was quiet for a moment and then he told her to have the pendants translated at a cut of seventy per cent by their regular tailor and to handle the transaction herself.

You mean to let the kid do it? Fludd said abruptly. Do she know the margins?

Foole blinked. The margins?

Molly laughed a sharp laugh and shook her head and wiped an exaggerated tear. Margins, she said. No one uses margins no more. We take a cut off the percentages in both directions, Jappy old boy. Margins, she grinned, shaking her head.

There have been some changes since you were last outside, Foole said. You'll catch on.

Aye.

Margins, Molly chuckled.

Molly? What's got into you?

The girl stopped smiling, looked at him. She put the last fossil back into the crate. Chewed at a nail, leaned over, spat some half moon into the fireplace. Nothin, she said.

Foole grunted, tugging at his whiskers. Japheth, he said. I'd like you to go over—

Nothin's got into me, Molly interrupted loudly. Except Charlotte bloody Reckitt an her weepy bloody letter. She pulled out a creased envelope and withdrew Charlotte's letter, glaring the while at Foole.

I won't ask where you got that, he said.

My dear Mr. Foole, she began in a quavering high voice. She squinched up one eye like a bat.

Molly.

I write you knowing how much time has passed between us—

He kicked back his chair and stood, his fingertips poised on the desk. That's enough, Molly.

—and just what your regard for me must have suffered these past ten years—

Aw, kid, Fludd said in his low rumble. That ain't right. And he stretched a long arm over her shoulder and slid the paper from her fingers. Where did you learn letters like that anyway? he asked. You read like a preacher.

She's a quick study, Foole said tightly.

Molly flushed. Did you visit her Mr. Utterson yet? You want to tell us the job?

Fludd turned from the girl, studied Foole. Utterson? The attorney?

Mm, Molly said.

You ain't still gettin reports from him now? Mr. Adam?

For god's sake, Foole said, is no part of my business mine alone?

Fludd paid this no mind and instead rubbed at his beard with an open hand and turned to Molly. Gabriel Utterson used to let Mr. Adam know what Charlotte were up to, he said. Was a time we used to see him regular-like. That were years ago now.

O-ho, Molly cried. She got angrily to her feet. A right regular romance, ain't it? How long was you plannin to keep this from me?

Fludd started to laugh. Kid sounds jealous.

I ain't jealous.

I'm to go see him this afternoon, Foole said. He held up a hand. Sit down, please. There's no secret to it. Charlotte left instructions with Gabriel about the job, I'm to go through the instructions and if I'm still interested I'm to call on her in Hampstead.

Molly sucked in her lips, her nostrils flaring. Ain't it lucky I got nothin planned for today.

I'm to go alone, Molly.

Why? She raised her voice. You afraid your plonk-eyed patty goin to be there?

Foole looked past her at his old friend, apologetic. The letter's clear on it, Japheth. I'm to go to his Gaunt Street address unaccompanied. I'll tell you this evening what I glean from him.

Aye you will. Fludd gestured at the letter on Foole's desk. But it don't feel right. Is that whole letter written like what Molly just was readin? As if there weren't nothin much between you an Charlotte needin to be aired?

O it gets worse, Molly called out. It gets near to disgusting.

The kid ain't often right, Fludd grimaced. But this might be one of them exceptions. Gabriel weren't never one of us, he weren't never to be trusted.

But he was never dangerous.

Bugger that. Fludd scooped at his beard. Don't you go alone, Mr. Adam.

He ain't goin to, Molly called.

Gabriel's queerer than he was, Foole frowned. He's cautious. That's what Charlotte's instructions mean. If I go in company he might refuse to meet. Even if the company is Molly. And if they wish me harm, Foole began, then trailed off.

He stared out the window. A cart clattered somewhere in the alley behind the garden wall and something passed like a darkness through the long grass there. At last he nodded. He could see the sense in Fludd's concern and although he did not say it he knew he himself did not wholly trust the letter either. Molly reached out and put a hand on his arm and Foole met her eye.

All right, he said, giving way. All right. He looked sternly at Molly. But you keep your thoughts to yourself and do exactly as I say. Understood?

Molly smiled a sly smile. O sure. Absolutely. Yes.

I mean it, Molly. To yourself.

She smiled and smiled. She had already scooped up a handful of straw packing from the crate and stuffed it now tidily back into place with a wink and she was humming to herself as she left the room. After she was gone Fludd got up and shut the door and he stood a moment listening and then he sat back down. I ain't goin to ask you where the profit is in all this, he said in a low voice.

Foole nodded. I appreciate that.

I know you and Charlotte have your history.

Well.

An I figure loyalty like that is a quality I ought to encourage in them what I work with. But I guess I hope there's some angle in it I don't see as yet. He glanced up. You ain't forgettin what her uncle were like?

Martin has nothing to do with this.

Martin Reckitt is a bad slice, he is. Even the Church didn't want him.

He was never a priest.

He were defrocked.

He wasn't. He was ordained but he never practised. He was never a priest, Japheth. He had a different calling.

Bugger that. You know what he done, Mr. Adam.

All he did was walk away from me.

An leave you to die.

Foole nodded and said nothing and then he said, He also nursed me back to life. He could have just taken what he wanted and gone. He didn't.

Aye an he could've cut your throat too. There ain't no shortage of ways to do a jack in. Just cause he took one way over another don't make it less of a betrayal.

It does to me, Foole said quietly. Besides, Charlotte is not her uncle.

You're wrong on that, Fludd said. He was looking at him strangely and then he cracked his big knuckles and folded his arms. There's somethin else, he said. I don't reckon there's any right way to say this. Last night I paid a old hello to our jill in Bermondsey. For old times' sake, like.

I know.

Fludd blinked. You keepin me tab open?

I wanted to make sure you kept out of trouble. How is she?

Fludd shook his shaggy head. She says if we waitin for Charlotte Reckitt we like to be waitin a long time. That business you mentioned from the letter, bout her bein hunted by a detective? It's bloody Pinkerton what's been huntin her.

Foole raised his face. Pinkerton?

Aye.

Pinkerton's dead, Japheth.

Not that one. The son. William.

Foole felt something in his stomach give way. He rubbed his face, stared out at the garden, the mists scrolling through the bamboo thicket, the bare apple tree against the stone wall. When he turned back Fludd was massaging one huge shoulder as if to ease some hurt from it.

Seems he were tracin some knuck Charlotte once worked with, Fludd said. Someone out of the swell mob. An somethin's afoot still, the beaks is all abuzz with it. Pinkerton's got a hand in it up to his bloody elbow.

A hand in what?

Fludd gave him a long level look. She ain't said the name. But we both know who.

Edward Shade.

Fludd nodded. Just like his da.

Foole got up and crossed back to the window and clasped his hands behind him and stood like that a moment as the fog curled past.

You want I should do somethin?

Foole was quiet. No, he said finally. Yes. Let's keep an eye on Mr. William Pinkerton. Have one of our snipes trail him and report back. Let me know if he crosses into Bermondsey again. Foole stared at the fog and brooded and stared. Do you believe in consequences, Japheth? he asked.

Never, the giant said. I live me life by it.

You frighten me sometimes.

Only sometimes?

Foole turned. Fludd was grinning at him in the gloom.

Late that afternoon he and Molly went to call on Utterson at his home. They made their way down to Piccadilly and hailed a hansom heading east and Foole directed the driver to take them to Gaunt Street in Bishopsgate. Molly gave him a look and they rode awhile in silence through the fogbound streets and then she turned to him and wiped a smut of soot from her face and asked him outright.

Bishopsgate? What kind of lawyer lives in bloody Bishopsgate?

He gave her a quiet secretive smile and reached across, picked at the lining of her breeches where a thread had come loose. You'll want Mrs. Sykes to give that a look, he said.

She scowled and folded her arms and glared out at the streets. They came to a halt outside a tall terraced house. It had long since fallen into ruin, the unpainted railings, the smeared brickwork, the ancient wooden door knocker all cracked and gone green with long use in the foul air. Foole knocked twice then stepped back and brushed at his sleeves.

He don't live here all on his own, now? Molly said, grimacing. Waste of bloody space.

It's his sister's house, he lives with her.

She laughed sharply.

Keep your tongue, Foole muttered. There's nothing amusing in it. She was a memsahib in the Raj before she came back to England and she's been in the flash longer than you've had teeth to pick at. Anything you say to her she will not forget.

O I can handle myself.

He gave Molly a long look. She'd as soon cut your throat as offer you a drink, he said. And that would be a kindness from her.

Just then the door groaned shivering back on its hinges, and he straightened. A huge Sikh in blue livery and a gold headdress and wearing slippers of an oriental cast nodded without speaking and Foole bowed gravely to him and introduced himself. The footman stepped aside, his white gloves extended palms up. Foole removed his top hat, his cane, his gloves, and then the footman stepped behind him and the floor creaked under his weight and Foole felt himself being delicately disarticulated from his frock coat.

Is Mr. Utterson at home? Foole asked.

The footman was gesturing to Molly and did not answer but when Foole glanced up he saw a woman had materialized out of the darkness of the hall.

Miss Utterson, he said, and bowed.

Keshub is a mute, Mr. Foole, she said. He cannot help you. *Fuelle*, it sounded like.

You are not alone, sir, she added.

Her voice, so like silk rustling. He had not heard it in years. She wore a thick mascara of ash and elderberry juice and had lined her eyes in kohl like some Eastern concubine and her long pale throat and sharp collarbone glowed whitely in the afternoon gloom. After a moment she stepped fluidly aside and half turned from him and he understood he was to follow. The footman preceded them down the long hallway, drew aside the drapery at a doorway, and the lady went past and through into the smoking room beyond. They had been lovers long years ago and friends after that and he thought her feline and beautiful still. The hard years had come out in her face near the eyes but the effect was to deepen and sadden a mystery latent in her and it made her the more desirable. She had travelled to the Raj in search of a husband in the spring of 1857 and returned fifteen years later alone and to Foole's knowledge was unmarried still. She had told Foole of that first journey across Egypt by land in terror of bandits and of sleeping outside on the deck of the P&O steamship under the Southern Cross. Flying fish in their shivering arcs like faeries of the sea. The wake of phosphorous in becalmed waters. India, she said, had assailed her eyes in a roar of reds and pinks and oranges, yellow saris cut with blue, the mingled spices of ginger, cloves, turmeric, the smoke of sandalwood and burning cow dung, the clang of bells and bullock carts squeaking in the streets. All this she had told him while running her cool hands over the skin of his back one afternoon years ago and he had listened with his eyes half closed and thought of his own Africa. She would be fifty-two now.

At the door he paused.

Long gaslit sconces burned low on the walls. His eyes passed over the indoor lily pond, its scarlet cushions arranged in a circle around the water, the soaring ceiling lost in shadow. On the walls were squares of a gold damask wallpaper, squares of a red and green trellis pattern of birds. A painted Japanese screen in one corner. A tall hookah in a black Japanese varnish in another, its pipes cabling snakelike at its base. Foole could hear the muffled sounds of the street through the white and blue drapery, drawn and glowing with the light of the outer world.

What is all this? Foole said with a smile. Molly had come through with him and stopped half concealed in the doorway curtain and he set a hand on the child's shoulder to keep her back.

You don't like it?

It's a wonder.

A faint curl of her lips. The eyelids closing a moment as her face registered the compliment. You'll have a drink, she murmured. It was not a question.

Her servant had receded into the darkness. She crossed to a sideboard and unstoppered a crystal decanter and poured out two cut-glass goblets of sherry and then looked across at Molly in the doorway as if considering. Then she moved away, sat down on a cushion with her legs folded to one side of her, smoothed her skirts around her.

It has been a long time, she said.

He smiled. Not so long.

You were away on pleasure?

Business.

Is there a difference? She crossed her long legs at the ankle with a slow catlike grace that he remembered from years past. My brother is not at home. Why don't you tell me the details and I shall convey them to him. What is to be discussed?

Charlotte Reckitt.

She waited.

She left instructions with Gabriel for me.

Charlotte Reckitt, she said, touching a jewelled finger to her lips. No. I don't believe I know her. Is she a whore's—

Rose, he interrupted. Molly snickered in the gloom behind them.

Mm?

Must we do this? When she said nothing he furrowed his brow and said, Charlotte's the best grifter still in the blush in London. Her uncle was taken to Millbank in seventy-four—

Ah, yes. The famous Martin Reckitt.

You remember Martin.

Of course. Gabriel is still representing him.

Foole paused, studied her cautiously. I had understood Gabriel was changing the kind of clients he took on.

He has kept a few of his more valued clients.

Foole leaned forward. Does Martin still have a hand in?

Martin Reckitt is a model inmate at Millbank, Mr. Foole. His good behaviour is a testament to his reformed ways. And nothing goes in or out of Millbank except through the proper channels.

Does he still have a hand in, Rose?

She folded her jewelled fingers, her eyes hidden in the low light. I do remember he had a niece, she said. Yes. Now I remember. Her lashes flicked languidly over Molly standing in her boy's suit beside the tapestry at the door. A beauty, she said softly, patting the cushion next to her in invitation.

The boy's all right where he is, he said.

The boy?

He could hear Molly breathing in the gloom but he did not turn to look at her and she did not step forward.

In the Raj, Rose murmured, we learned to be more flexible with our appetites. One must embrace the unexpected, no? But she was studying Molly with a cold flat stare as if weighing a shank of meat and Foole felt a sudden danger.

He cleared his throat. Rose.

Yes, she said at last, lowering her gaze. Go on.

Charlotte's been in touch. Gabriel has instructions for me, something to do with a project she's been organizing. I was to meet him here, today. Is he not here?

You were to come alone.

Foole frowned.

This is rather like in Madrid, I think.

It's nothing like Madrid.

You do have some difficulty in following directions, Mr. Foole. But she said it gently, and Foole sipped his sherry, smiled a sad smile.

That's not what I remember about Madrid, he said.

You still have a concern with her as well, I think. With this niece.

Foole felt his smile stiffen and he glanced away. I haven't spoken to Charlotte in years, he said quietly. But yes, there is that. Of course. There's always been that.

She leaned forward now and lowered her voice. My sweet sweet man, she murmured. I've been asking myself, what is this path my dear Mr. Foole walks? He doesn't write, he doesn't visit. What a surprise to find him in London again.

We've all kept ourselves busy, Rose. I think of you fondly.

She smiled a smoky smile.

And your brother, he is well, I hope.

My brother won't meet with you, she murmured. Since the Asperton affair, he prefers to keep his distance from the flash.

But Charlotte's letter was clear.

Your Charlotte has become a rather dangerous associate.

Foole wet his lips. What do you mean?

You would be wise to keep your distance, Mr. Foole.

You're talking about Pinkerton?

She held his eye. Mr. Pinkerton has been in London for weeks looking for your Miss Reckitt, yes. And not on Agency business, some personal matter. When we last saw her she said he had been asking about an old associate, someone his father had pursued. She did not say who. She was frightened. And then she disappeared.

Disappeared.

Last Thursday, yes. You must have heard of this. We understand the Yard is expecting her body to wash up downriver, but you and I both know what that is worth. Gabriel has made his own inquiries. The only thing he is certain of is that she did not leave town. At least not by the usual routes. Miss Utterson saw the effect her words were having and she fell silent and then after a moment she reached behind her and brought out a small scented envelope of rice paper. Miss Reckitt asked us to convey this to you.

The envelope was empty. There was an address for Hampstead written on the front.

This is hers? Foole asked in a rough voice.

Miss Utterson frowned in the half-light then let it fade in a long, slow, sphinx-like smoothing of her features. I would not recommend you go to her. I understand the police have occupied the residence.

So the job's off, he said slowly. And Gabriel's washed his hands of it. What does he believe, does he believe she's still in the city? What do you believe?

Miss Utterson regarded him. You remember, Mr. Foole, how it was between us? What happened in Spain? It seems what occurred was no accident. I have a gift.

Rose, he said impatiently. He shook his head, stopped. Remembering how it had been, the jobs they had worked together in the flash. She had dreamed during their last job in Madrid the precise events of the next day's heist, including the ambush by the police and the shooting of their cracksman. He had laughed it off the morning before the heist. That night, hiding in their hotel room, he had not been able to look at her.

She was quiet as if considering something. Then she met his gaze with her smoky eyes. The spirits manifest in me, she said.

The spirits.

The lost ones. Yes.

You're a medium.

I am a receptive. It is not the same.

He had heard rumours of Gabriel's interest in this realm but he had not expected this. He had seen advertisements for seances in the newspapers in the years following the Civil War but had never given it much credence. It seemed too close to a grift. He looked at her and then around him at the weird exotic furnishings and then he looked at her again. The shadows seemed to lengthen. He looked at his drink then set it with a click at his feet. He was thinking about Charlotte and Hampstead.

There is much confusion on the other side, she said. I hope it is not true. But the name Charlotte has been spoken.

For god's sake.

She tilted her face, long earrings clicking.

Rose, he said. His voice had an edge to it. If this is some kind of glim's pluck. He stared at her very hard. You know I don't take well to being rolled.

She set a cool hand on his arm. She said, In Calcutta our cook used to say, When a voice speaks that has been long silent it is natural to listen. That voice, it is speaking to you now.

I'm sure I don't know what you mean.

You do, she said. The spirits communicate through me, not to me. Gabriel holds the circle together and I am not told what is said until later. A receptive is asleep when it comes over her. So what I tell you about Miss Reckitt, it's the truth.

You're telling me the dead are talking about her.

Death is only a beginning, she said, meeting his gaze.

He glanced across at Molly where she stood listening. There was in her face a stubborn dislike that he knew masked fear. She was twisting one wrist tightly in a hand. You'll let Gabriel know that I stopped in, he said, getting to his feet. Thank you for the sherry.

As they were leaving, Miss Utterson reached down and gripped Molly's chin in one bejewelled claw and twisted her face up so that she might stare into it. Foole could see the fury in the child's eyes. I know what is in your heart, little one, she said to the child. I was damaged also as a girl. The world is not kind to the innocent.

Molly's eyes flickered.

Miss Utterson released her, smoothed her hair. The huge Sikh stood behind them, holding the door, eyes forward.

Mr. Foole, she said. You will come again I hope.

He pressed the inside of her wrist to his lips in reply.

Molly might have ceased to exist. But then the aging mem-sahib murmured, O do not give your heart to him, little one. She was holding her cool palm to Foole's cheek as she said this and she did not take her eyes from his.

Outside in the street he felt strange, broken with light, as if shining with some secret dread. It seemed all who passed in the busy crowds must turn from him and shade their eyes. Molly put a small hand on his wrist and said, O Adam, just because the beaks is lookin for her in the soup ain't the same as her bein in it. He did not know what to reply. It was a kindness for her to speak so and he found himself overwhelmed by the gesture. He left her at a cab stand in Bishopsgate with a full purse and he adjusted his gloves and stared into the fog and then set out for Finsbury Circus. It had begun to rain a faint brackish rain, more a mist than a rain, and Foole walked through it without regard as the water balled and spattered down the gabardine. At a flower seller's stall he purchased a clutch of blue irises, as if to disprove Rose Utterson's words, then changed his mind and started to throw them into the street and then changed his mind again.

The rain deepened. A hansom took him languidly through the wet and the chill and he watched the horse's wet haunches slide luminous in the sheeted water. He felt the shake of water from the reins passing through their guides, heard the crunch and splash of wheels on the stone streets. He checked and double-checked the address in Hampstead he had been given. Soon they had left the extinguishing city and were passing uphill through the half-built terraces and the low sky leaned down over the weeded lots and the muck and then they were turning up a lane of expensive new brick houses and the cab drew to a halt.

Foole studied the high terraced house. Then he got down. His heart was hammering inside him. He stood feeling the rain drip from the brim of his top hat and thought of how she would look as she opened the door, the smell of her hair in the wet.

The chill fist of petals shone in the light. The first hint something was not right occurred to him when he saw the whited doorstep, the scuffed boot prints there. When he knocked he listened but could hear no answer within. No lights were burning in the windows. He shifted the flowers from hand to hand. After a moment the door rattled and shuddered through its unlocking.

It opened.

A stranger in a grey frock coat stood before him, regarding the bouquet in the gloom, his protuberant eyes heavy-lidded and sad. The man was standing with the stiffness of a plain-clothes police inspector and then something sharpened in Foole, some pre-shaping of his loss, like the outline of covered furniture in a shuttered house.

Is Miss Reckitt not at home? he asked.

The inspector cleared his throat, peered past him at the hansom waiting in the street beyond, settled his gaze on the irises in Foole's fist. I regret to inform you, sir—, he began.

And like that a door slammed shut in Foole's heart.

All the Mornings
in the World

—————

1874

SOUTH AFRICA

They had met on the rooftop balcony of a sunlit hotel in Port Elizabeth and they had disliked each other at once. He thought her sly, watchful. She thought him cold. He took her hand in his and it felt hot, dry, scaled. She winced at his grip. She seemed to him tiny, pale, a theatrical creature insincere in her gestures and he seemed to her abrupt in the brutal manner of American men. A guest was tinking his timid way across the pianoforte in the bar inside and the sound drifted through the slatted windows to where the three of them sat as if it carried through water. He crossed his legs. She smoothed her dress. The third with them was the elder by twenty-eight years and he turned the ice in his glass and smiled, smiled, smiled under the latticed shade of the wickerwork.

There were whitecaps cresting and unfurling in the stark below, seabirds wheeling in the spray. Adam Foole would remember the sunlight on that afternoon, the white sand beach stretching away to the east like the curve of an eyelid.

She said her name was Charlotte. She had been an actress on the London stage.

He said he did not care for the theatre not as a boy not as a man.

Had he been wiser in matters of the flesh he might have seen the signs and feared the turn his life would take. But what was happening in him had not happened before and so he could not have known to call it by its name.

———

He was still young. He had come alone through the Cape posing as an ostrich-feather investor by the name of Bentley then journeyed east to Port Elizabeth where he checked into the finest hotel and waited for his accomplice to arrive. It was a seaport hotel frenzied with the wealth of the diamond trade, set down at the very bottom of the world, and out of this hot crowded stew he rode for days on end, returning from the interior with large purchases of feathers which he then crated and shipped to a rented storehouse in southeast London. That was the peak of the feather boom and no lady's hat was complete without its long curved ostrich sheen. He opened an office near the docks and hired a clerk and posted advertisements in the local papers seeking inland agents for his business. He was careful to protest loudly the expense of shipping in the lounge of the hotel, in the restaurants overlooking the offshore islands, in the post office itself. He stood several patrons their drinks and spoke of his business partner in friendly terms. He laughed, played whist, smoked late. Ate alone poring over his ledgers in the manner of any sober businessman and in short made himself liked.

Through all this it was the light that astonished him, the light he expected to remember. The hard flat bang of it like a sheet of tin as it shuddered and recoiled in the roadbeds. When he went out into it his eyes creased at the corners, glistened under the dust in his lashes.

He had believed his whole life that luck was just such a light and like any light must be accompanied by darkness and he had learned to seek out such darknesses wheresoever they lay. Though inclined to starched collars and tailored suits by nature he was no stranger to the grime of the road and knew the diamond fields in Kimberley had drawn the dregs of the world like soap scum sucked down a drain. Still he was surprised by the feel of that African boom town, how much it reminded him of the borderlands in the United States after the war. He stood on its depot platform watching the hopefuls arrive, their shoes and pans gleaming. He peered over the edge of the great open mine into the emptiness. He walked the main street in the dust and heat astonished by the crowds. There were rabbis with their long beards carrying pans and bedrolls on their backs and revolutionaries from Poland and Russians with shovels gripped wrongly in their soft white hands as if they were clutching leaflets or bombs. He saw ex-convicts from the Australias with tattoos on their knuckles and nary a tooth in their heads and he saw veterans of the Crimea with arms missing or loping along on crutches with a fold of trouser pinned up where a leg should have been. He saw bandits out of the eastern Baltics with colourful baggy clothes and pistols over their shoulders and he saw women in varied states of undress draped over the upper railings of rickety wooden saloons. Every man went armed even the street preachers staggering drunkenly on their crates and hollering at the crowds with their fists upturned. What he did not see was the law.

He waited. He listened. It seemed the diamonds were not transported on the new railway but rather trucked out from De Beers and from the other mines surrounding Kimberley in a convoy of armed coaches moving at speed through the low desert country. They crossed six rivers of variable size by cable ferry and by bridge and stopped only to water their horses. They rode at night with Boer rifles bristling from the windows and men crouched on the springbok perches on a precise timetable marked to coincide with the Port Elizabeth steamers' departures for England. The diamonds did not stop in any one spot for more than three minutes. At every waypoint a secondary guard recorded their passing and the hour and the minute and nodded to the driver as he clattered by.

Foole had arranged to meet his accomplice at their hotel in Port Elizabeth five weeks after his own arrival. Fludd had remained behind in London to handle the merchandise when it arrived not least because of his great size and formidable appearance. What was needed, Foole had explained, was a man who could dissolve into the illusion. They had heard Martin Reckitt was, by all accounts, that very man. An aging English thief with a reputation in the flash world for caution, sobriety, elegance in manner, he was gifted in the arts of manipulation.

He had quick fingers. He had studied in the priesthood but rather than mitigating his cruel nature his faith had twisted it, augmented it, until whatever viciousness he undertook was somehow made right in the eyes of his god. But although merciless and not to be trusted still Reckitt was a professional, with a reputation at stake, and he would not risk that reputation.

Foole was livid then to learn Reckitt had brought the girl.

It is not what you think, the older thief said, adjusting the cuffs of his linen jacket. They were sitting on cane chairs on the hotel balcony under a palm tree, out of the heat. She is my niece.

She's a liability.

She is an asset, sir. You will see.

Foole followed his gaze. Just inside, under the open windows, a young woman in a green bustle sat on a sofa, her languid hands outstretched to either side, a drink clutched in one and tipped dangerously askew. She lifted her pale face and looked directly at them.

No, Foole said. Absolutely not.

At twenty-six he was the younger by decades but there was already in him that heavy iron core that would in time frighten men thrice his age. Get rid of her, he said in his quiet way. Through the open latticework he could see the rooftop gardens in the evening light. A graceful curved path through the leaves. Ladies in white dresses under parasols, hats sculpted with flowers. He closed his eyes, pressed two fingers to his forehead. The air smelled of sap and roses.

My good Mr. Bentley, Reckitt was saying. You will find she has some rather unusual talents.

Foole opened his eyes. The young woman had risen and was gliding towards them and as she neared she smiled at her uncle. A wide mouth, big white horselike teeth. A mole at the centre of her brow fouling her expression. Green eyes too wide apart, a sunburnt nose too narrow.

He watched her fingers crawl nervously around the rim of her glass like the legs of small crabs and then he looked away.

Much later he would see in her a different creature, a creature of grace. Reckitt would be gone by then, that long dry month after the armed Boers had swarmed the port searching bags, pulling men from steamship cabins. Foole would lie back in the cool of his sheets and trace his palm in and out of the soft pale scoop of her hip. A pitcher of cold water sweating on the washstand across the room. Flies on the chipped blue enamel. The muslin sifting and billowing in the hot noon air. He would be aston-ished by the heat of what was in him, the pleasure he took from it, this thing he had not known before. He would run his hands the length of her thigh and marvel at the redness of his own scarred skin, the soft crease of her sex tucked away from him like a furrow in velvet. Her green eyes shut fast, as if she slept.

But she did not sleep. He would lie wordlessly beside her, knowing this, squinting out at the burning hour. The sky very blue, the ocean almost green where the sunlight shafted through it. The long beaches white with a purity that would seem to lift and fade even as he looked out at it, like a dream upon waking. In the heat shimmering up off the rooftops it would seem to Foole that everything, the horses in the dust with their tails switching, the omnibuses stopped and empty, the dusty board-walks under the porches, all of it trembled. He would lie with one hand on her skin and the other upturned and limp at his side and feel amazed, not quite himself, a ghost.

He could not get enough of her. It would astonish him, his desire, astonish and frighten him. He had not known such a thing was possible. Some days he would watch her undress, languid, mysterious, as if she were considering each gesture before the doing, one button unfastening, a pause, then a second button, each stay unhooked as slowly as if she moved in her sleep. Layer after layer, lace, crinoline, until the weird skeletal underbones of her dresses were exposed, each article laid out over each with such delicacy, such longing.

He was running his palm from her hip to her ribs and feel-ing her stir. Bending down, kissing her collarbone. Are you awake? he whispered.

Mm, she murmured. She pressed her lips to the pale hairs on his forearm. You taste like salt, she said. She sat up in the sheets and folded her naked back into his chest and he put his arms around her. They sat like that staring out the open window at the impossible blue harbour beyond and he felt a sudden fear, thinking of her uncle.

We should have had more sense, he said quietly. This is wrong.

You have your scruples, she said. I like that. A thief with scruples.

Her head on his chest, her hair soft and fallen across his upper arm like a shadow.

Everyone has scruples.

You believe that?

Just not always in the way people would like.

She shifted in his arms. The drapes stirred.

Not everyone, she said.

He could feel her small ribs swell and diminish as she breathed. In the heat where their skin touched he had begun to sweat.

She reached around and laid her hand on his chest. You still think you had some say in this, she murmured. You mustn't feel guilty. It was never up to you.

He smiled. With her hair loose and her makeup scrubbed away she looked very fresh, very young.

No? he said.

You have no idea, she smiled. She ran a finger lightly over his eyelid. You have the prettiest eyes, she said. Did you know that? Like the eyes of a girl.

He closed his eyes and laid his head back. Prettier, he said.

All that was yet to come, set out before them invisible and impossible and very real, like a hand opening over them as they slept. Reckitt eyed Foole from the great height of his age as if tolerating an unruly nephew and Foole frowned but said nothing. Years later he would marvel that the man could not have been much older than fifty who at the time seemed to him well into his seventh decade. The loose skin at his throat, the blue veins in his hands, the thorny eyebrows. The wet eyes that followed him across a room. Foole understood Reckitt was dangerous beyond the strict confines of his employment. As was his niece.

Charlotte he met again at dinner on the second evening. It was a circular table cut from a single piece of African blackwood with himself and the Reckitts and an elderly Frenchman in elegant dress filling it out. A quiet gentleman with thinning flaxen hair and a clean-shaven face like a Protestant minister sat to one side of Charlotte, blushing furiously.

Charlotte sat among them with her shoulders bare and she laughed and smiled and dazzled each man in his turn. All this Foole watched feeling something ugly and cold and lizard-like flash across his features. He laughed too loudly at her jokes. Nodded too emphatically at her stories.

She turned from him, of course. And what is it you do, sir? she asked the Frenchman to her right. Her blue silk dress flaring in the gaslight.

Ah, he said. I am the agent for a diamond buyer in Marseilles, mademoiselle.

Oh, wonderful, she smiled. How distinguished.

Mademoiselle is very kind.

She rested a hand, lightly, on the Frenchman's wrist. It must be rather exciting, I think?

It is an exciting country, my dear, Reckitt interjected.

The Frenchman smiled behind his waxed white moustache. His dinner jacket was a deep black, his collar a stiff and startling white. But it is very tiny in the scheme of the world, *non?* he said. He shifted in his chair and inclined his head as if to share some secret with Charlotte but he spoke to all the table. It is the question of, how do you say, quality? How do you access the stone? The stone is the stone, yes, but is also more. *C'est impossible.* He took her hand in his own and looked at it and he said through his dry lips, In Paris there is always the demand for beauty.

Foole rolled his eyes.

You must be careful not to lose your head, sir, Reckitt said. You French have a habit of it.

Monsieur?

Over beauty, of course.

Charlotte gave her uncle a look. How dangerous it must be, sir, negotiating such matters here. I cannot imagine it. Are there truly no policemen to protect you?

Foole darkened. It seemed so clumsy to him, such a dangerous turn. But the gentlemen at the table appeared not to have noticed.

Ah, mademoiselle, *les sauvages* have not the interest in the diamond. And the English know they must not harass the *compagnie*. We have the most reliable legal enforcement one could wish, *n'est-ce pas?* He winked. *L'argent, mademoiselle.* Money.

Oh, wonderful, Charlotte said, clapping her hands.

I do believe there has never been a theft of diamonds in South Africa, the quiet gentleman to her left said. Charlotte glanced at him and he reddened and studied his wineglass.

Is that the truth, sir? she asked.

Not if you ask a South African, Foole muttered.

A South African, Reckitt laughed. What an idea.

Is there such a thing, sir? Charlotte asked.

The Frenchman smiled. It is quite an untouched country, I assure you.

The roast on Foole's plate glistened grey in the low light and he poked at it in distaste.

You have the hands of a countess, the Frenchman was saying. *Très jolies. Non. Parfaites.*

Charlotte lowered her eyes. My uncle feared it would be most irregular for me to sit in the company of so many men—

Frowns, murmurs of protest.

—but I said to him, who could object to such gentlemen? Especially in such a wild place as *Africa*.

She lowered her voice at this last word as if uttering a particularly vile secret.

Oh is that where we are, Foole said sourly.

The Frenchman gestured to the waiter standing at the sideboard. *Pour mademoiselle*, he said with a flick of his fingers.

A dusky wrist disappearing into a white glove. A steady pour of burgundy in the hush, the clink of crystal on crystal.

Some would suggest this is no place for an unmarried lady, Charlotte said.

Ah but we are, how do you say, delighted by our fortune, the Frenchman said. He patted the tablecloth between them as if it were her knee.

You flatter me, sir.

Non. C'est vrai. He ran a long thumb over his waxed moustache then brought his fingers to his lips and smiled.

Foole looked down at his plate.

And you, sir, what is it you do yourself that has so seduced my uncle?

Foole looked up in surprise. Myself? he said. He could hear the annoyance in his voice. You have surely heard us speak of it, Miss Reckitt. We are establishing contacts for our import business in London. Ostrich feathers.

Ah oui, the Frenchman across from him smiled. There was much demand five years ago in Paris, monsieur. It is very profitable, *non*?

The English follow the French in all things, the quiet gentleman suggested politely.

Even as far as Waterloo, Reckitt murmured.

Ostriches, Charlotte said. I have heard they are terrible beasts.

Ostriches are birds, Foole said irritably, not beasts.

But very terrible. The Frenchman leaned in. Terrible claws, *oui*. You are not mistaken, mademoiselle.

I have yet to hear of an ostrich making a hat out of a person. Foole dabbed at his mouth with a napkin and set it crumpled next to his plate and met Charlotte's eye. But when ladies such as yourself demand hats worthy of their beauty, and here he paused and shrugged a little shrug. Well. We all must do our part. Even the ostriches.

Monsieur! the Frenchman said, colouring.

Foole waved a hand at the old man without looking. Charlotte was still watching him. Would you like to hear about the ostriches, Miss Reckitt? One must travel for weeks into the high country to find them. They're as tall as a dray horse, and thin, and when they run it's like they're trying to forget some terrible thing they've just heard. You can hear them from fifty yards away, they sound like wind in dry grass. It's said they mate for life because they cannot fly. Did you know they're the only creatures in the wild that are known to cry when they lose one of their young? The table had fallen quiet and he looked at each of the diners in their turn and he offered a dry smile. They have beautiful eyes, he added, sad eyes, and the longest of eyelashes. And when they're happy they dance a lovely, foolish dance in the dirt, kicking up clouds of dust. You can see it for miles. They have ferocious talons on their feet and they use these, yes, these terrible claws to scrape open tree bark, looking for grubs to eat. I've never seen one fight even in its own defence. What else can I tell you? He shrugged a little and looked at Charlotte with his strange bright eyes. When they're frightened they plunge their heads into the sand and stand with their backsides trembling. Oh, yes, it's quite comical to see. And then any hunter may simply walk up to them and lop off their heads with an axe.

Good god, sir, Reckitt exclaimed. You forget yourself.

Foole looked at him.

A dreadful thing to say, sir, Charlotte said quietly.

Indeed, the Frenchman insisted.

Charlotte's fist gripped its napkin tightly. I shall, she said, from this day onward, sir, never wear another ostrich feather. Tell me, why would you pursue such a cruel profession?

Foole watched her, impressed despite himself. She performed with such an easy grace for an audience that did not realize it was a part of the performance.

Ah, monsieur, the Frenchman was saying. Such manner of speech.

My young colleague exaggerates, Reckitt said to the table.

Foole stared at his lap and then he said, woodenly, Forgive me, Miss Reckitt. Gentlemen. I have been too long in the interior and I forget myself. He sighed and looked at her shocked countenance and understood that she was enjoying herself immensely. These long journeys into the country, he went on, they take such a toll. One forgets the delicacies of polite company.

Oh, Mr. Bentley, I have forgotten it already, she said prettily. Her long pale forehead seemed to catch in the low light and shine with a luminescence all its own.

Foole bowed gravely in acknowledgement.

It has been so delightful to have met you all, gentlemen, she said. How intrepid you all are. How resourceful. You have no idea what admiration I have for a man willing to pursue profit in such a dangerous, uncivilized place. She smiled at each in turn and each flushed with pleasure and then she folded her napkin, laid it carefully before her as if preparing to depart.

The table fell still.

I'm in buttons, the quiet gentleman to her left said suddenly.

The days passed. Foole saw her in the crowds of the shopping arcade, bent low over a display case of diamond necklaces. He saw her descending the hotel stairs, her face turned away, her throat exposed like the curve of a lily in a vase. He crossed the sweltering street near his office in the port and glancing to his left glimpsed a young woman in the haze flouncing from a cab and he looked again and saw it was not her. When he instructed Martin where to rendezvous with the horses on the third night he did not ask after the young Miss Reckitt. But on the rooftop gardens before dinner that evening he saw her seated alone with a glass of wine untouched before her and he went out to her without understanding why.

Mr. Bentley, she said, shading her eyes and peering up at him. What a pleasant surprise. Please sit, do. My uncle thinks you've been quite avoiding me.

I've been busy.

Busy avoiding me.

He shook his head. I assure you.

You did not care for my performance the other evening. She held up a gloved hand. No, please, don't deny it. It's all right. Martin tells me I must be more judicious.

Foole sat. Squinted across at her in the evening sunlight. Are you really his niece?

You doubt it.

He shrugged.

She reached forward and took up her glass and held it by the stem between two fingers and a thumb and she seemed to consider something and then she said, with a smile, Not by blood, if I understand your meaning. But yes, he is an uncle to me.

You mean he's like an uncle to you.

If that was what I meant, Mr. Bentley, that is what I would have said.

He looked at her a long moment. You're quite right. Of course. It is none of my business.

You think you are cross with me.

I'm not cross with you.

I know you aren't.

He frowned in irritation.

She wet her lips, her soft mouth parting just slightly. She set her glass back down on the tablecloth. Martin saved me from the streets when I was eleven years old, she said after a moment. She held Foole's eye. I was in the workhouse, she said. He came to the door, he was dressed very well, and he pointed at me and told the warden that I was his charge and he had come to take me away. I'd never seen him before in my life.

I don't understand.

I didn't either. I still don't. He doesn't speak of it and I don't ask. I thought for a time he must have known my mother but I don't know that I believe that now. She died when I was six from the cholera. When Charlotte looked at him her face was very clear, very pure, and Foole felt for the first time something like attraction give way in him. Martin took me in, she was saying, he taught me what I know. I owe him everything.

Foole raised an eyebrow.

You don't think he's that sort of man.

Foole shrugged.

There is nothing I would not do for him, Mr. Bentley. Nothing.

Foole nodded.

You're trying to decide how much of this to believe, she said.

He smiled despite himself. I wouldn't insult you by admitting as much. You are a mysterious woman, Miss Reckitt.

She smiled at him shy and sidelong. Are you admiring me, Mr. Bentley?

You'll know when I'm admiring you, he said.

She laughed. You make it sound like a threat, sir.

An elderly lady in lace drifted near, looking for a seat.

The difficulty, of course, lies in shaving off the overhead expenses, Foole said suddenly. Warehousing costs, shipping bills, import duties: one must understand the minutiae.

It is a problem of profits, yes.

The lady paused, smiled a faltering smile, drifted on her way.

And that is why I have come myself, you see, Foole added loudly, watching the lady pause at the next table. The French diamond agent was seated there and Foole watched him stand gallantly and pull out a chair that the lady might join him. He met Foole's eye and nodded and Foole nodded back.

Do you think he is really a diamond agent? Charlotte asked in a low voice.

I don't even think he's French, Foole smiled.

As the days passed Foole felt an excitement take shape in him. The plan was simple. They would ride out to a deserted stretch of road and string a rope across the way to throw the horses. The stagecoach would overturn, they would overpower the driver, disarm the Boer guard. All this he explained to Reckitt one afternoon in a saloon near the port. Trust me, he said, it's been done like this in the Midwest since the war. It won't fail.

We're not bandits, Reckitt said. That is not what we do.

Foole grinned. He instructed the older thief to meet him at a cliff just off the road outside of town on the night of the new moon and to dress for a hard ride. He insisted on revolvers and rifles but did not believe they would be needed. We're not in the business of killing, he said. It's just to keep their heads down. But when he rode up that night he found two men on horseback waiting for him in the blackness and he pulled up and unholstered his revolver and called across the rocky stillness and after a moment he heard Reckitt's hoarse voice.

Charlotte, Reckitt said. It appears Mr. Bentley has arrived.

Foole swore.

They rode out single file under stars that shone with the silver clarity of coal dust and Foole watched their spiralling axle and felt cold. They were three miners to any who might have seen them picking their slow way along the vacant road, their skeletal horses crunching through stones and dust, the air chilled on their knuckles where they nudged the reins. Bedrolls tight on the flanks, saddlebags full. The dull chink of pans and spades strapped behind the saddle. A blanket thrown over the shoulders of the second rider. At that hour the veld burned strange and blue like a stonescape ancient and glacial and unconsoling. Foole thought of the local Xhosa, their implacable eyes as they regarded him riding past at the high crossroads, he thought of the stories he had heard of their uprising and of the long smooth blades of their spears and he shivered. Go in fear of them, sir, a trader had warned him in the city. They's worse than beasts when they's hunting.

He pulled up at a low rise and set a hand on the hot neck of his horse and studied the country, its scrub and grassland stretching out below. At the far side of the valley a ridge of dolomite rose up and was lost against the sky. He could see the small orange flare of a cook fire burning at the side of the road some miles below.

Charlotte came up alongside him. They're so bright, she said.

He adjusted his hat, followed her gaze upward. Nodded. We'll have to be careful.

That's not what I meant.

He looked at her.

First diamonds of the night, she murmured.

Let us hope they are not the last, Reckitt said as he rode up. He had his left wrist folded up into his right armpit and he was grimacing.

Your wrist still troubling you?

No.

They sat there all three in the saddle, their horses snorting softly.

So where is this rift? Charlotte asked.

Foole gave Reckitt a look. Exactly which rift are we talking about? he asked.

The older man did not laugh.

They were riding for a narrow gully carved out of the limestone by some ancient glacial retreat and known locally as Chinaman's Gulch. The pass was bottlenecked at its exit and steep-walled for the duration and so named for the narrow mouth that could not fit a grain of rice turned sideways. Foole picked his slow way down a low escarpment then trailed out over the plain, cutting across the country and leaving the road behind. There would be a switchback some seven miles farther on and then a river and then the gulch itself and Foole did not want to come across any other travellers if it could be avoided.

The sky paled. In the hour before dawn they climbed down and rested their horses at a low stream in the veld. A man in a loincloth and carrying a spear materialized out of the shadows herding a cluster of sheep and in the early grey light he gave them a wide pass and kept his eyes averted. The thin ropy sinews of his chest, gleaming. His burnished fists. Foole crouched in the straw-like grass with Reckitt's rifle across one knee listening to the click of hooves in the rocky soil, the clunk of a beaten tin bell looped on a strap of leather around the shepherd's own neck. Then the man had passed on into the stony grassland and his disciples with him like a warning and all were lost to view.

At Chinaman's Gulch they dismounted and unhooked a coil of rope from the pommel of Foole's saddle and double-knotted it across the mouth of the gully at the rough height of a horse's throat. It hung taut and brutal as a cut of wire and near invisible in the crepuscular light. All this was performed in silence but for the crunch of their boots in the stony earth, their low breathing as they worked. Charlotte he sent fifty yards back into the scrub with the three horses and when Reckitt scowled in protest he only held up an angry hand and refused to discuss it. He would be damned if he would let the girl stay. On either side of the rocky opening were clusters of boulders from landslides of winters past and on the eastern slope a lone tree windswept and buckled into a weirdly human shape and there Foole dug himself in with his two pistols laid out before him on a flat white rock. Reckitt made his way some dozen paces farther on and crouched in the angle between two boulders where he would be able to see the stagecoach approach.

They waited. Foole could feel the cold sand under his knees. He sat with his hands pressed to the earth and his eyes closed. He could feel something else, a thrum in the earth, like a locomotive passing deep underneath. He wiped his hands on his trousers then cocked the pistols. His heart brutal in his chest. He was holding his breath and he exhaled now, slowly, carefully. Then he could hear it, the clatter of iron-shod wheels, the soft thunk of hooves in the sandy roadbed. He got to his feet, stood beside the tree.

And all at once it came into sight, the stagecoach, at a gallop, plunging through the gulch towards them, and it seemed to

Foole a long inhuman silence descended and held over him and Reckitt and that pass and then there was nothing, no stage-coach, no horses, only the faint calm dusky light in that long hour before dawn.

Then a screech, like hot iron doused in water.

A sudden thrashing in the grey air.

A screaming of horses.

He heard the rope crackle and zing free of its knot like a bullet by his ear and then the coach was smashing over onto its side in an explosion of dust and there were cries of agony in the confusion. All this Foole watched and heard with his kerchief drawn up over his mouth and nose and a pistol in each hand held at the ready and he stepped forward as if to wade out into that roiling frenzy like a man into deep surf and he raised one pistol and fired a high shot into the sky.

He could see three of the horses kicking in the dust, tangled in their traces. There was a man sprawled face down among them in the dirt where he had been thrown and he did not stir but Foole could not tell if this was the driver or the Boer guard. A second shot rang out and he thought for a moment Reckitt too was firing. But a third and a fourth shot punched through the branches of the tree in a splinter of bark and twigs and Foole turned his face and saw two men kneeling amid the wreckage with repeating Winchesters swivelling in the dawn light and then they began shooting in every direction with a wildness and ferocity that forced Foole to take shelter.

He was shooting with his head down and his eyes half shut when he heard, at last, Reckitt's rifle return fire. He crept to one side and peered across. He could see the older thief crouching in the dirt with his head held between his hands and his hat upturned beside him but the rifle was still firing and Foole did not understand.

Then he saw her. Standing coolly to one side of the boulders. The silhouette of Charlotte, firing and reloading and firing, as if it were a thing she been raised on and had always done.

———

They fled. Hats spinning off into the dust, clutching at their horses in terror. They slowed at last after some miles and rode on in wrathful silence under a red sky with Reckitt clutching a rag to his temple where a bullet had grazed him and sent him nose-first into the dirt. Two miles out they changed their attire and split up and rode in separately to Port Elizabeth. They would be several hours ahead of the stagecoach but feared being recognized in the aftermath. Foole dismounted at the hotel stables and folded a handkerchief across his neck and throat and then he stripped the horse and went on up to his room. A lamp was burning, the wooden shutters open in the heat. Charlotte was slumped at the writing desk, dust from the road streaking her chin.

Reckitt turned at the window, calmer. Sallow, the stubble along his jaw grimed, the dark eyes sunken. Foole could sense something had been decided in his absence and he felt himself withdrawing, his thoughts sharpening.

You'll want to conceal that, said Foole quietly, gesturing to the man's bloodied forehead.

Reckitt glanced at his niece, his expression tightening.

What.

My uncle feels this is not the job you described to him in London, Charlotte said in a low voice.

I was told you were methodical, Reckitt murmured. That you were a talent.

And I was told you would see a job through.

Meaning, sir?

Foole felt a stab of fury and swallowed it down. There was the sound of a door opening in the corridor and all three fell silent and then two men's voices approached their room and passed by and after a moment Foole added in a whisper, Meaning if you had held to your position and used your rifle as it is intended to be used we would not be in this position.

We do not use rifles, sir, Reckitt hissed. That is not our way. We are not rampsmen.

We use what the job calls for. I'd have thought you capable of understanding principles.

Principles.

Foole lowered his voice yet further. Had you done what you were supposed to have done, they would have stood down. The guards would have stood down. We would have what we came for. We wouldn't have failed.

Charlotte shifted in her seat, set a small hand on the rail of the chair. But there was a third guard, Mr. Foole. That is the salient point.

Reckitt blinked his slow cold eyes at her, said nothing.

A strand of hair had come loose over her face. She looked tired. Foole turned away. Think of the profits, Martin, he said. It's never been done before. We'll be the first.

Not under your guidance we won't.

Foole was still holding his saddlebags in the crook of one elbow and he bit at his free glove. I can understand her wanting out. But if you cut now—

We are neither of us cutting, Reckitt hissed. We are removing ourselves from a lunacy. It is not the same thing. You, sir, are most fortunate to still have your skin. Do you know what the Boers do to bandits?

We didn't have all the facts. That's all.

I nearly had my head shot away. You risked my niece—

You risked your niece, Foole snapped. I never wanted her along. If you cut now, sir, do not pretend it's because of her well-being. As he studied Reckitt in the lantern light he could see the cadaver beneath the man's skin and he did not like the feeling it gave him.

Reckitt's shadow twisted up the wall at a crazed angle. You would be wise to abandon this also, he said. You're no Dick Turpin.

Charlotte got to her feet in a rustle of taffeta. Foole understood the night was ending.

I'll have those diamonds, Martin.

Charlotte cleared her throat.

You will not, sir. Reckitt was regarding him sadly.

I'll stay, said Charlotte.

Foole paused, thinking he had misheard. He and Reckitt turned as one and stared at her. Her black hair cowled in shadow, her eyes liquid and dark. He started to swallow but his throat was dry and all at once he did not know what to say.

I will stay, she said again. Someone will have to. Or would you rather leave Mr. Foole to his own devices, uncle?

Some viciousness flickered across Reckitt's face, was gone.

Much later he would understand that it was not her fault. Still he should have recognized the con. The mark, the set-up, the art of the glide.

Which is what love turns out to be, when you get right down to it.

Reckitt abandoned them in the morning. Nothing could induce him to stay. The men were civil again though Foole for his part felt drained, exposed, despairing, and Reckitt appeared unmoved. Foole did not like Reckitt's arriving back into the London flash before him, leaving the man free to spin his account as he chose. He would write Fludd but the need for caution would preclude his giving any substantial details. All night he and Charlotte and Reckitt had weighed and considered options but had determined in the end to hold to the original design as planned. Foole would journey alone to Brindisi at a languid pace with the diamonds in his luggage and there find an accomplice waiting. Except this time he had insisted that accomplice be Charlotte not Martin.

In the railway station Reckitt stood with his small carry case between his ankles, his trunk already ticketed and stowed, a gentleman thief dapper once more in his frock coat and silk hat and brushing at his sleeves in distraction. His silver hair was shining.

The news will travel faster than us, Foole murmured. The moment you read of it—

I shall book Charlotte's passage to Brindisi. Yes.

Foole nodded.

The old thief took Charlotte's gloved hands in his own. If you change your mind, if something should go badly, he said, I shall wire you the funds for your return. Stay safe. He gave Foole a cold look. I entrust her to your care, sir. Do not fail me. The conductor was walking the platform, calling out to the ticket holders. Bursts of steam hissed from the boiler, passengers shouted. When he lifted his face Foole saw blackened steel girders, skylights stained from the smoke, an armed Boer staring down at him from a catwalk.

Go, she was saying.

Foole had already begun to think of another way. That morning he had watched the battered stagecoach come into the city after the steamer had sailed and seen the Boer guards climb down eyes scanning the crowds and watched as they took the shipment into the post office and locked it in the safe there until the next steamer could arrive. The evening papers were rife with rumour and conjecture. American bandits from the Midwest. Australian convicts. A sophisticated work of insider fraud. But Foole had seen the assistant postmaster with his stooped walk, the veined hands trembling with age, the visor askew over greasy hair as the diamonds were moved, and something had gone very quiet in his heart.

The days without Reckitt passed and passed. He saw Charlotte in the hotel lobby, saw her in the railway depot. He met her on the hotel balcony one afternoon and she took his arm and they made their way out into the white sunlight in light cotton clothes and went down to the harbour and entered a restaurant just the two of them as if they were man and wife. He looked at her and could not see the dusty rifleman standing in the low grey light reloading and aiming and firing with neither pause nor hurry. He was thinking of her theatrical work and it did not make sense.

You've done this sort of thing before, he said to her.

She smiled. Once or twice.

Who are you?

Miss Charlotte Reckitt. She extended her hand. Pleased to make your acquaintance, sir.

That wasn't my question.

You know how it is, she said with a smile. Why, outlawing is like drinking. She rattled the ice in her glass and gave him a sly look. After the first glass, there's no stopping.

As his plan coalesced in his mind he began to take measures. He wrote letters and travelled out of town and posted them back to himself via registered mail and as he picked them up from the postal station he smiled and chatted with the assistant postmaster. One afternoon he was writing when Charlotte approached him, lurked over his shoulder, studied the letter.

He set down his pen. You're hovering, he said.

She looked offended. I do not hover.

He said nothing.

Barrel has two r's, she said.

Her ankles he saw for the first time when she descended the stairs and came into the dining room that night. He had been drinking. He looked at the blue silk of her dress and her raven hair shining in tight curls and an unexpected joy filled him.

What's wrong? she asked.

The lightness he had felt earlier was in him again, a kind of elated recklessness. It was not the wine, or not only the wine.

He thought of her slender in the dawn with the rifle opening out before her and the clean balance of her, like a branch bowed out over a river. She did not eat very much. She had told her uncle she would help him as best she could and after she told Foole this there was silence as she looked at him and he did not understand what he was meant to say next. Later when she ascended the stairs he could not avoid seeing her skirts receding over the risers ahead of him like the wash of an outgoing tide. Inside her room he stood very still feeling her soft lips on his own and he did not know what to do with his tongue. She put her hot hands on his chest and pushed him slowly back onto the bed and in the darkness he saw her reach back and unpin her hair.

They met again in the morning. In the afternoon. It could not have been possible in any other city. Perhaps in Paris. She had moved into her uncle's room at the back of the upper storey and it felt eerie to be where Reckitt's belongings must have been. Foole would rise naked from the bed and cross to the window and rattle open the drawers of the bureau and she would watch him in silence. He wanted to give her something she had not known with any other man but he did not know what that would be. It took him a long time to understand that this longing was its own kind of gift. He took nothing from her that he could carry in his hands. He would stand over her in the soft afternoon light and pull the sheet from her damp legs and she would close her eyes and scissor her knees together and sigh.

He had not yet lost himself. In those first days he felt slaked and so drained he could not stand without a sudden weakness in his legs. A purity seemed to grow in him, a clarity of concentration. He spoke to her of the shipments from the mines, brooded and weighed and considered points of weakness. Watched the steamers in the harbour, the Boers with their rifles on the docks as the crates were loaded. She ran a hand along the sleeve of his jacket, plucked a loose thread from the cuff. He tried not to think of her uncle and what he would think to see them so. He knew there was a betrayal in this, an unprofessionalism which he would not have forgiven in an accomplice. Still it did not cease.

Through all this some part of him struggled towards a plan. Something simple and elegant in its simplicity. There were two Fooles, the man who lived his waking days, who ate and slept and made love, and the other, his shadow self, preoccupied and lean, unshaven and wild.

And that other was the truer.

And then at last a method started to make itself felt. He knew the Boer coaches arrived in the port almost to the minute with their diamonds set for embarkation to England. Those stagecoaches were heavily armed and rode the veld stopping only for fresh horses and would rein sharply up at the docks, bristling with rifles, a storm of dust in their wake. But after his failed heist he had learned the mine owners' contingency: if late to the port, the diamonds would be locked in the post office safe overnight. He had seen that safe and knew it could be cracked without difficulty. He knew also that the weakest locations on the Kimberley road were the unmanned ferry crossings and that a cut cable could delay a stagecoach by hours. But a cable could not be cut without alerting the Boers to the sabotage and in this way ensuring their heightened vigilance.

What we require, Charlotte murmured to him one night, is an act of God.

He smiled. Shall I call in a favour?

Mm.

And then we'll just pray that it knocks out a cable?

She rolled over and kissed his eyelids. Don't be ridiculous, she whispered. It doesn't need to knock out the ferry. We just need to make it look like it did.

So we wait for a storm.

We wait, yes. She pushed the bedsheet down off their thighs and straddled him and her face was ghostly above him in the shadow. She began to move her hips slowly. We wait, she murmured, and let the Boers forget about our failed enterprise at the Gulch.

We're weeks away from the rainy season, he said.

Mm. Weeks and weeks.

He gripped her wrists and drew her down towards him.

However will we fill the time? she said into his ear.

So it began. In the second week he went alone by passenger train to Cape Town and mailed two parcels marked Urgent back to his collections box in Port Elizabeth and the following week he stopped in at the post office just as it was closing and banged anxiously on the window. The assistant postmaster was an old whist player from out of the American Midwest to whom Foole had lost several hands some weeks before and they smiled at each other as the older man let him in. It was not a bank, there were no guards. The assistant postmaster's name was Holloway and he was stout and red-faced as a toad and Foole pitied him his part in this. But he slipped the man's keys from their nail behind the counter all the same when his back was turned and he pressed their effigies into the ball of wax he had brought with him in his coat pocket and then he slipped them back onto their hook before the man returned.

He had formed a negative mould of the post office keys and poured out the replicas later that night on a work table balanced above the hotel bathtub, using the fire stoked to heat the water, and a ladle supplied by Charlotte, and these false keys he kept in a small box in her steamer trunk. It amazed him that he trusted her so. He would walk through the arcades without her, peering into the shop windows with his hands clasped behind his back, and he would return to her carrying paper parcels tied with string and in them small figurines, china cups, a necklace of burnished ironwood beads. The port thrummed with its business. Each day hopefuls disembarked, each day the desperate and the lost ascended into the ships. None of them knew what he knew. There were languages on the streets, in the crowds, that he would never hear again and he stood on the footways watching the carriages clatter past and feeling himself in the grip of a glorious, secret fate.

Am I a fallen woman? she asked him one afternoon.

He ran his fingers through her hair, over the shell of an ear.

I keep expecting him to walk around a corner, she said. You know that look he gets? The one that means he knows exactly what you've been doing?

He's in London, Charlotte. He doesn't know.

She said nothing.

How could he know?

She looked at him a long moment. You're different from him, she murmured.

I'd hope so.

She smiled a wry little smile, the tips of her teeth visible, she looked away. I had no idea about you, none at all, she said.

You're like a stone when it's held under water. All the colours come out.

Later that night she said: There's something I need to ask you, something I need you to tell me.

Tentative fingers on his face, tracing his eyebrows, his lips.

If you lie to me I'll know, she whispered.

But whatever it was he was already drifting into sleep with the sweat silvering on his skin and he heard her speak as if from a long way off and then he was asleep. And in the morning he did not remember the question.

They moved to a smaller hotel. A blue corner building with its name whitewashed across the side wall of its second storey. Foole walked across the battered floorboards of the lobby feeling her gloved fingers on his wrist and his heart heavy inside him and at the reception desk he signed for them both. The register was old, the leather cracked. Sunlight fell slantwise through the greasy windows, illuminating the dust in the air. The loose stairs rattled as he and Charlotte ascended to the upper floor. Their room faced the street with a view of the post office and was hot from the morning sun and when Foole opened the window for air he heard the bed squeak under Charlotte's weight, like a farewell.

They were waiting for a storm but the weather held. In the meantime they were friendly to all, they were charming. They made themselves known. They took walks in the evenings along the harbourfront and leaned in close over shared dishes and bottles of wine. He had known women before but only ever as a transaction of currency and the desire he felt now was different from lust, a new thing. In the mornings she would lie face down on the bed with a pillow under her and the sheets kicked onto the floor and he would enter her very slowly, he would stir himself deeper. Some days she would sit in the washtub with her arms upraised as he ran a cool cloth over the soft black hairs in her armpits, as he squeezed the grey water over the nape of her neck, her shoulderblades, and she would look into his eyes with an intensity as private as grief. Her skin astonished him, its whiteness, as if it were lit from within. Nights she would straddle him with her hair still pinned off her neck and set her hands on her buttocks and arch her back and later he could taste himself on her lips. He was young, her body was the world. He wanted all of it.

She could be coarse, vitriolic, she could be mercurial and kind. She did not always want to be touched. One night she turned from him abruptly and pulled away.

He lifted himself onto one elbow. I thought you liked that.

You aren't even here, she said. She stood and began pulling on her clothes. You don't see anything when you look at me. You're thinking about the shipment.

I'm not.

You are.

I love you, he said. As soon as he said it he knew it was the truth.

She stood looking at him with an unreadable expression on her face and then all at once she seemed angry. He did not understand it. When she reached for her underclothes her hair covered her face like a sheet of rain.

Don't you dare pity me. You think you've corrupted me? You think you're the first?

Charlotte, he said, confused.

Don't you dare, she said again.

He watched her fumble angrily with her stays.

Where are you going? he said. Charlotte. Wait.

Get yourself a mirror, she said savagely, and try fucking that.

In the morning she was sitting at their usual table and he approached her cautiously but she just smiled as if nothing had happened and set her napkin down before her.

Look at that old lobster, she whispered, shifting her eyes to a table across the room.

He thought at first she was trying to tell him something about the night before. An aging couple at breakfast in the silence of a long and lonely marriage. The man with his red face and thick intimidating whiskers, like a colonial governor, an eyepiece pinched grimly into place. Beside him his wife in maroon crepe, her bloodless lips drawn tight, disapproval seamed into her brow. Hands lost in her lap as she ogled her menu. The man was reading the early edition of the local daily, the paper held stiffly up before him as he crackled the pages.

Charlotte grinned. That's not his wife. Her name is Mrs. Picquet and she runs the best brothel in Kimberley.

Not really, he said with a smile.

Oh, really. She's rather notorious, a very wicked woman. His name is Sweeney and he owns a ladies' boutique here in the city. *Très cher.*

How would you know this?

She winked.

I'm sure they're just conducting business, he said.

I'm sure they are, she smiled back. And where do you imagine her hands are right now?

That was how it was. Unexpected, unexplained, sudden and intense as a passing weather system and then without warning calm again. On that morning he had wanted to ask her where she had spent the night but he could not. He felt very young with her and there was no part of him, he realized, that understood anything between them.

They waited. The weeks passed and still no storm came. Huge carapaced insects like creatures out of some lost Jurassic age battered against the drapes, ticked against the lamps. In the mornings he would scoop them into his palm, brush them out the window. The theft of the diamonds began to lose all solidity, all reality, their days seemed to shimmer. Foole had not realized that happiness could be one thing, one thing only, repeated day after day, night after night, into an exhausted wholeness.

They walked the waterfront and rented cast-iron bicycles from a Hungarian at his stall and these they rode tottering and weaving past the omnibuses, laughing crazily at the horses in their traces, their bicycles' huge front wheels jolting over the uneven roads. They stood in line at the parks and bought French ices flavoured by papaya and threw away the little wooden spoons and instead licked the ices down to their fingers like children. Foole took her to the office he had rented and introduced her to the clerk who organized the feather shipments and while she wandered the small room running her gloved finger over desk and bookshelf and windowsill leaving curlicues in the dust Foole leaned over the accounts and tried not to look at her hips. In the third week he went back into the veld to collect feathers but he did not barter over their quality and the local tribes took his money and regarded him with pity. Are you sick? they asked him and he thought about it and decided he might be. He understood pleasant young Mr. Bentley did not exist and he mourned for him even as he tore that false life open, like a thick envelope, with everything spilling from inside it, everything being both happiness and time.

Then one morning he awoke and saw Charlotte at the window and beyond a roiling black sky. Wrapped in a sheet like a visage of her own death with her arms lost in the white folds and her white face very still, very beautiful, and only her eyes dark.

It's time, she said.

The storm lifted the roofs from the shanties east of the harbour. A hot wind came down punching loose the porcelain tiles from the central offices and the rain fell slantwise against the windows of the hotel. In the harbour the heavy steamers rolled, bumped in their berths. A rising wedge of water plunged through the middle of the city carrying over the roadbed broken ploughs, pieces of porches, the dipping corpses of dogs, and there were acacia branches adrift and spinning in the eddies. Sodden muck-like rags that once were shirts. Splintered crates. Wheels broken

by the current. By the second night the worst had blown past and
Foole and Charlotte rode quietly out of town following the
same route as before and when they passed through Chinaman's
Gulch rain-blasted now and scoured down to its limestone
striations he thought of Reckitt with them on that earlier ride
and it seemed to him a journey from another age, another life.

As the night eased into a red backlit dawn they found themselves astride their horses staring down at the outbuildings and
rickety fencelines of a waystation tavern. It looked deserted
though they knew it would not be and they skirted the property
though their horses were tired and they themselves hungry and
came back up to the road some two miles farther on. The long
yellow grass of the veld stretched out around them, a solitary
baobab rising to the east in the grey haze. They heard the river
at its height long before they saw it.

The cable crossing itself looked like it had not been tended
to in years, its laddered posts weather-stripped and leaning.
The cable swayed in the air where it spanned the river and he
could see the flat-bottomed ferry on the far side where it swung
and dipped and swung in the high water, the cable creaking
against its weight.

Are you sure they'll be able to get through? Charlotte asked
him. After this storm?

He got down from his horse and crunched slowly over the
stones to the timber that held the cable in place. His back was
sore. The air felt hot already. A silted quality to the light
made it seem as if they had ridden through a dreamlike blur
and he walked now around the posts and rested a hand on an
upright and stared down the length of the cable to the far
shore. The high water was fast and muddy and dragged at the
ferry. He looked again at the flywheel rusting there and he
returned to his horse and took from the saddlebags a very old,
very sharp knife.

Well, he said. I guess we'll find out.

And he set to.

It was a barbed knife he had been given in New Orleans by

a fisherman there meant for the gutting of fish and he liked it for the size of the blade, the crescent of its cut. He stood on a bite of the cable with one boot fast and he leaned his weight into it then sawed at the slack and slowly the cords frayed and ripped one by one. There was a groan, a sudden cracking as of green wood in a fire. He could feel the tug of the ferry in the high water as he worked and Charlotte was holding the horses steady and when he was through the cable jerked and snaked violently out of his hand and under his boot and into the water, singing as it went. His hand burned. He watched the ferry turn sluggishly into the river and spin downstream until some thirty yards away it ran aground on a sandbar. It bucked in the current and lifted and twisted but did not overturn.

Adam? she called to him. Is it finished?

He kicked away their boot prints in the dust. The earth was already dry as if it had not rained at all and he stumbled down the scree, squatted in the shallows with the river pouring cold over his ankles and he filled their waterskins and capped them and climbed wearily back up. Charlotte was leading their horses out and he rubbed at his face and looked at the waggon ruts and then at the sky.

Within the hour three stagecoaches came banging one by one through the low jacaranda, a cloud of white dust blooming big and bell-like behind them in the morning heat. A Boer sat perched high on the back of each, Winchester repeater upturned on one knee, swaying and jouncing to the ruts, while the drivers gripped the reins in both fists and leaned forward on their elbows. The horses were working hard through the haze of that cut and when they neared the ferry landing they slowed and the guards glanced nervously about. It was still early, the sun somewhere behind them. The first guard got down and kicked at the heavy cable in the dust and stared downriver to where the ferry had run aground. The door of the coach opened and a blond man came down, cracking his back. He walked the length of the traces, checked the stays in the freight webbing on top. At his side a Colt in its holster glinted. He stopped at the back wheel and stared out at the countryside with a hand on the bullets in his belt.

All this they watched over the grassy lip of a dune two hundred and fifty yards away. They had hobbled their horses a half mile back. They had taken off their hats and were shading their eyes and the flies were biting.

Seen enough? Foole said.

Charlotte twisted and slid on her backside down and the dune crested under her like a roll of surf. At the base of the slope she stood, brushed the white sand from her trousers. She was peering back up at Foole with a curious intensity.

Yes, she said. I think I have.

It was dusk when the stagecoaches clattered down past the port to the empty steamer berth and their drivers got down and beat the dust from their hats and the guards from the rear benches made their way into the shipping offices. Their vessel had sailed six hours earlier for England and they were no longer in any hurry. Crowds still pressed through the streets and Foole stood under a creaking barber's sign at the corner of an alley in a tall silk hat and he watched the guards make their tired way up the street to the post office. Then he turned and walked briskly back to his hotel.

They ate a quiet meal and Foole did not feel the delicious dread he usually felt when a theft began to succeed. He watched her small fingers on the knife as she cut delicately through the steak thinking that all this would soon be finished. He had understood from the first that this was a passing dream and like any dream it must be dispelled sometime but that time did not need to come so soon. She kept her face down, chewed sadly. Neither touched their wine.

They retired early to their room and doused the lights then paced in the darkness waiting for the hours to pass. They spoke of practical matters. How she would get out. Which steamship line to take to London. How much to tip the cab in Cape Town.

Anyone who leaves the country, he reminded her, will be under suspicion. When they ask you at the port, admit that you have heard of the theft. Be agreeable when they search your trunks.

I know how to handle it.

He nodded in the gloom.

You'll go overland?

Into the interior, yes. He scratched at his jaw, the bristles there like glass. I'm a feather merchant after all, he said. If I can slip over the border upcountry I can sail for Suez from the coast, continue to the Adriatic. Any luck and we'll find each other in Brindisi and take our time rounding Spain, let things cool off. I'll be travelling with a crate of feathers, of course.

She did not look pleased. How long do you mean to take?

He shrugged, his eyes small in the gloom. He wanted her to say something that she was not saying but he did not understand it. They had made no promises, he knew. Does it matter? he said.

I imagine not.

He looked at her and she met his eye and they stood like that in the silence. The hotel felt very still.

Give it three months, he said hesitantly. And then: You'll reach Brindisi before me. Be patient. Look for me at the Adelphi.

The Adelphi.

On the harbourfront. I'll be there.

She pressed a hand to his cheek in the gloom. She was holding something sleek and warm and when he took it from her he saw it was a small opal brooch. He stepped away from her and held it up to the window. The delicacy of its filigree, the fine lacelike twists of gold in their making.

It belonged to my mother, she said softly. Martin gave it to me when he brought me out of the workhouse. I asked him why he had it and he told me she'd left it with him once as a gesture of trust. He said it was a kind of promise he'd made to her.

Foole closed his hand.

Come here, he said.

Later that night he dressed and took the false keys and folded himself through the window while Charlotte held the sash for him. He crept along the roofline and dropped to a rain barrel in the alley keeping to shadow. He let himself into the post office and stood just within the door listening and then he locked the door behind him. Behind the counter he approached the safe for registered packages. Through the front window a faint greyness drifted in, a different shade of darkness. The safe was a modern cast-iron one built by a respected firm in Baltimore and Foole knew the make well. He had it open in under five minutes and then he sat a moment on his knees with his hands in his lap, peering in at the shelves there. He was thinking of Charlotte. He understood she had already said her farewell. How strange the morning would feel, with her gone and the sun rising as it would over any dawn, the red clouds smouldering out across the sky. There came a sound of footsteps and then a rattle as a hand tried the door and then boots receding along the boardwalk. The night watchman on his rounds. He did not wait long. He took out the three black felt bags and inspected each one and then for good measure removed the small amount of money and government bills from the filing shelf of the safe. Then he closed and spun the latch, locked the building behind him, and climbed lightly back across the roofline to the hotel.

In the morning her trunks were gone.

The swag lay tamped safely deep in his pillowcase and had not been tampered with. He lay a long time in that bed staring up at the ceiling mouldings. He kept expecting the door to open, her to lift the sheet and slip her cool legs into bed beside him. After a while he heard men shouting along the board-walks, the sound of running feet, then horses moving at speed up and down the roadbed. A police whistle sounded.

He rose and wrapped himself in the sheet and went to the window. The sky was washed pink, the cold rooftops of the city steaming in the early heat. The harbour waters were all shadow, and still, as if the night were coalesced there and sinking deeper. Men in red uniforms were gathered outside the post office and the assistant postmaster with his hair dishevelled was ducking through the door. He turned away.

In the sunlight on the bureau he found her opal brooch. He picked it up. It felt warm. He stood there in the rising of the sun at the bottom of the world and he held it in his fist as if it were her hand, and the heat of it her own.

The Woman
in the Thames:
Part Two

1885

LONDON

SEVEN

A dam Foole stood shivering on her doorstep in Hampstead, his fists full of irises wilting in the drizzle. He looked at the police inspector and he looked away. *You would be, sir, an associate of Miss Reckitt?* No he would not. He could hear the cabbie's mare shake her head at the curb and stamp a nailed hoof and he took off his top hat and felt the cold mist in his hair and he put it back on. He could not clear his head. *How long have you known the lady in question?* Knowing is such a complicated business. *As is the heart.* As is the heart. Foole stumbled back, glanced up, nodded politely. *I regret to inform you, sir, her body was recovered three days ago at.* Yes. *We're not at liberty to.* Yes.

He felt a hard anger like a knuckle in his ribs and understood he must hold on to whatever that was. He did not step into the house but turned, hearing his shoes scrape on the desolate stones, and at the curb he climbed unseeing into the cab.

She was no longer young, that was his first thought. Then: There has been a mistake. If I had returned a week sooner she might still be. He remembered the white curve of the African sun like an exquisite scythe on her arm in the furrowed bedsheets. The pale hairs on her leg, glistening with sweat. The languorous whup of the wooden fan turning its blades in the high ceiling and the slatted windows, the hot dust of the street.

The hansom jerked into motion. A shiver of reins in the cold, the mare skidding sharply, then going on.

———

He had not spoken with her in ten years, true. But he had watched her at a remove, had followed and been informed of her goings-on. For six years the attorney Utterson had written with news of her takings while Foole's purse permitted it and he had paid the man well for his words. Utterson was sly and troubling both but somehow too a kind of friend and despite Fludd's warnings Foole had found as the years went on that he came to almost trust the man. Through Utterson he had heard of Charlotte's affair with a banker in Lisbon and when it had soured he had gone to that city and in October of that year conducted a risky and ambitious heist of bonds meant to ruin the man's reputation. But instead of selling the bonds back at a profit he had surprised himself and Fludd both by burning them in a grate while the big man knocked over the furniture in frustration. It was always so, would always be. Through Utterson too he learned of her grift in San Francisco, in 1879, a haul of some fifty thousand dollars. That was when he had understood she was a talent to be reckoned with and when a few days later he learned she had married a man to pull it off he had gone into a week-long rage that even Fludd had not dared to interrupt. Through all of this he had watched and listened but never once approached her and he had found as the years passed that he did not want to do so. Still he would hear that she was in London and go through the streets with one eye open for her drifting figure. Had he thought of her less as the years passed? Each September on the anniversary of their Port Elizabeth heist he would purchase a clutch of irises and walk down to the Thames and stand alone, remembering. And then he would let the fistful fall and watch their stems separate and their petals drift and fill with water and sink.

Her earliest memory had been of water. That is what she told him. Of water warm and silvered in some sunlit green place, water pouring gentle from her mother's opened fingers.

He thought it strange that this should come to him now. Before her mother had died, before Charlotte had been sent down to the workhouse, she and her mother used to walk in Hyde Park in the summer during church hours and sit on the bank of the lake and watch the swans glide past. That is how she remembered it. She must have been four, five years old. The carved white marble of the swans and the luminous white shine of her mother's face in the sun. It was a momentary happiness she would carry with her for years and Foole had listened to her tell him this while a sadness ate and ate at his heart. They had been seated at an outdoor table licking flavoured ices in the shade of Port Elizabeth's railway station and he had asked her in a hesitant voice about her years in the Whitechapel workhouse.

She said all that was another lifetime. She said she had been six when her mother died and two weeks after her body was carted to the mortuary Charlotte found herself delivered perfunctorily to the workhouse gates by a ladies' aid society member. That lady wore soft white gloves, Charlotte told him, an expensive green hat, a pitying smile. They had stopped in at a bakery around the corner and Charlotte was still clutching the warm bread roll given her. Then a matron came out, a thickset woman with red freckled arms, and she pocketed the warm roll into her own skirts and steered Charlotte down a long hall and through an office and down a second hall. Charlotte without expression told Foole how she was stripped by the matron, doused by buckets of cold water, scrubbed raw with carbolic and a horse brush. That was the beginning of my second life, she said. She slept in a long room with toughened girls four to a bed and in the night under their creaking and coughing would come the scratch of the rats among their shoes and kicked-off blankets. Someone was always ill, she said. A fever would cut from one end of the ward to the other each winter and then begin its way back along the rows come spring. Days were filled picking out oakum with a spike while a matron read aloud from the Bible and meals were endured in silence and that was their true education. The girls were belted on the backs of their hands for infractions, locked in unlighted closets under the stairs. Some nights they were awakened and forced to walk single file with wicker baskets balanced on their heads and should any stumble all were beaten. In the yard during exercise they would stand some days with their foreheads pressed to the cold bars of the fence staring out at the world in its passing. We were all of us waiting, she said. For whatever came next.

Couldn't you have left? he had asked.

Many did.

But then your uncle came.

Then my uncle came, she nodded. Yes.

By late afternoon the light had snuffed slowly out as if a fist were closing over the sun and Foole felt himself borne aloft into a murky orange darkness. He recalled passing the toll booth, handing the three pennies around to the driver's hand with a dread growing in him. He recalled the lakes of muck in the streets, the deep slow pushing through of the wheels in the water, the cold rub of the leather seat under him. In Bond Street carriages banged up against each other and he saw an old woman struck into the mud as the fog came on.

It was not nightfall. He had forgotten about them, these London particulars. Fogs that came on without warning, thick as night, brown and choking.

Gaslights burned weakly in the shopfronts. Foole climbed down from the hansom on Piccadilly, stood shivering at the curb. He could not catch his breath. There were linkboys in the streets carrying torches to see their way and they moved like faint red horrors through the mists. He fumbled along the shopfronts, losing his footing on the tin cans of a milkwoman huddled out of the way. He could hear the grind and sizzle of a hot-potato stand nearby and smell the roasting chestnuts there but did not see it. When he held his gloved hand up before his face it looked ghostly in the haze.

He coughed and stumbled on.

How long did he wander. He felt something squelch underfoot and then a clattering roar whooshed past. Then brown fog.

Then he was leaning against a lamppost as a gas-lighter in a rubberized cloak banged his ladder against the crossbar. Get off with ye, he muttered. Then fog again. Some figure knocked him roughly down, ran past.

He was uncertain which street he had turned up. He paused, understanding he must find someplace to wait the fog out. At a broad stone stair he turned, and ascended, the granite balustrade brushing his gloved fingers.

He found himself blinking in the sudden warmth of an art gallery. Women in elegant frocks seated at the far wall drank from bone china and men in waterproofed coats leaned on their sticks at the tea counter and because he could not bear the lilt in their voices he turned and passed a watchman and went in among the paintings.

Later, much later, he would wonder at the unlikeliness of finding it. Such a painting, at such a time. He would wonder had he read about it in the *Times*, perhaps, on that journey to London. Or overheard some rumour in the streets. He had no recollection of paying the entrance fee though he must have done so. He remembered walking, yes, as if borne along by some current of light, he remembered the feeling of being not right in his skin. Everywhere were crowds murmuring amongst themselves, ladies in their kid gloves, gentlemen in their brushed top hats. He slipped into a secondary gallery and crossed the room and without pause, as if drawn to the thing, he went towards one wall where the crowds had gathered thickest. A window overlooked the street and the orange fog moved down below him and the lamplight in the room fell leeched and sickly across the waxed floorboards and it seemed to him that a hush had settled over everything. He was aware of the blood in his head. He stood jostled, and lonely, staring at the people around him, and then the crowds seemed to part before him and he stepped forward in his grief and he lifted his eyes and he saw the painting.

Charlotte.

He stepped forward, the blood thick in his ears. Of course it was not of her. He knew this. Seeing the crust of yellow paint where a brush or palette knife had streaked her throat. The wash of blurred soot where her hair was lost to the gloom. As he leaned forward he could see the red underpainting around her eyes, its eerie shadow like a world just beyond the visible. He had not lived his life by art. But he felt the gooseflesh rise on his neck, his arms. The woman in the painting stared out at him with Charlotte's face, Charlotte's eyes, in a haze as if through some atmospheric disturbance, her hair a bleed of colour, her face lowered. Her stare was lifted and sharp and held his in a harsh vortex of silence as if she were waiting for him to speak some answer of great moment. But it was an answer to a question left unspoken and to which he could say nothing, only nod miserably, and turn, it seemed always, away.

He had all those years ago in Brindisi failed her. That was the truth of it. He had left Port Elizabeth three weeks after the heist and journeyed north, overland, into Africa, the uncut diamonds hidden under a false panel in his trunk. He had filled that trunk with ostrich feathers and taken the slower eastern route, cautious, thinking of Charlotte as he went. She would be waiting for him in Brindisi before the month was out and it was her he moved towards. Then he got sick. At Maputo he understood he could not go on and he risked a berth in a Belgian trader sailing north along the coast past Zanzibar. In Djibouti he found passage to Italy. By the time he was offloading in Brindisi he was so weak he could hardly stand. He had been travelling almost seven weeks.

He had made his rendezvous on time but Charlotte was not at the Adelphi when he drifted, feverish, in. He feared something had happened to her. He made inquiries in his broken French but no one had seen her. Nor was there any packet of money waiting, a telegram, anything. Foole in his sickness understood Martin Reckitt had learned of their tryst and kept her from him, the diamonds, all of it. He was light-headed, starving. He had neither shaved nor washed in a long time.

The hotel bill rose. He sent a confused telegram to Fludd in London but wrote out the wrong address and it never arrived. The weeks passed. One day as he stumbled through the port on his way to the customs house he collapsed against a pillar and could not get up. In the sun the marble was hot on his neck, the sky very blue. There were dogs and donkeys and carts pushing through the crowds. It was then he felt a hand on his shoulder and through the haze of his fever he looked up and saw Martin Reckitt.

It was no dream. The old thief took him in his arms and supported him and led him to his hotel. Reckitt nursed Foole back to strength. On the second day Reckitt picked up the diamonds in their black felt bags from the customs house where Foole had stashed them. Still he stayed. Fed him, washed him. Sat with him in that miserable blank hotel room with his shirt off in the heat and squeezed a rag of water at Foole's lips when he could not drink. Murmuring the while about trust and betrayal and the seducing of his niece. He should have slit Foole's throat. He should have left Foole in an alley to rot. Reckitt had been a priest or almost a priest once and perhaps there was some last grudging mercy in him as he saved Foole's life. Foole would remember little of that time. He would remember asking after Charlotte. Was she ill also, was she in some trouble? Had the Boers interrogated her in Cape Town?

Reckitt had leaned over him in the wavering heat, his skin flushed. Charlotte's in England, Mr. Foole, she's well enough. Reckitt poured out a glass of water. I take it she never told you.

He struggled to rise. Told me what?

A viciousness in the old thief's eye. She's to be married. In the new year.

Foole fell back, tried to speak, slept again. In the morning when Foole opened his eyes Reckitt had taken the diamonds and settled the hotel bill and disappeared. There was no farewell. That day at noon the hotel staff turned Foole out into the street, still weak, not a shilling to his name. Reckitt was already sailing for England, already sailing towards his own fate, the

diamonds discovered in his luggage, the old thief apprehended
and condemned to twenty years in Millbank.

But on that first night after Reckitt's departure Foole had
sat shivering under the broken column marking the end of the
Via Appia, knowing none of that yet, confused, hurt. Peering
uphill at the lone café still open until the lights were snuffed and
then wandering down among the small fishing boats overturned
along the beach, the sand cold and hard-packed under his feet.
In the morning he had trudged up to the steamship offices and
watched the young clerk open for the day but something had
held him back, he did not go in. Instead he had gone in and out
of artisan shops while musicians piped faintly down through
the narrow crooked streets, eating the cold folded pastries the
old men threw out by the dozen at the end of each day, thinking,
crazily, that if he waited long enough Charlotte just might come
to him. It made no sense. But somewhere that mercurial creature he had fallen in love with was moving through the world,
in counterpoint to him, and he could not accept that the future
he had imagined, throughout his long dusty overland trek
through Africa, fevered, dreaming of their nights in Port
Elizabeth, was no longer possible.

His own earliest memory was not of water but fire. Perched in
an underground room on a cracked axlewood table, small legs
hanging over the edge into emptiness, shirt unbuttoned while
a huge fire whooshed and crackled behind him. The glow of the
flames gleaming in the polished wood. There was a man with
discs in front of his eyes and these discs burned with the flames
also. He knew his father stood somewhere in the shadow but
he would not approach though Foole cried. The man before
him was bald and his four front teeth were gold and a sheen of
sweat stood out on his flickering brow as he leaned in, pressed
his ear to the boy's chest, tapped two icy fingers on his back. In
his other hand a scalpel glinted and the man looked at Foole
and asked where it hurt. He would remember that fear, the

absolute certainty of it, like a thing he could hold on to and slip in a pocket. There was a dish with smears of rice paste half visible beside his thigh. The man said to him: I should just cut it out of you, neh? And be done with it, neh? He held the scalpel between his thumb and forefinger the way Foole had seen adults hold writing utensils and this somehow frightened him more. The man said: I can hear it in your chest, bolly. Right there. And he tapped Foole once over the heart. And all at once he could feel it too and though he did not know what it was he would imagine it there for years, alive, writhing in him, its little jaws working, eating his life from the inside out.

EIGHT

On the third afternoon when the fog had thinned but not
yet lifted William Pinkerton went back to Blackfriars.
He stood with a hand at the railing where Charlotte
Reckitt had fallen, he crouched low in the muck and studied the
bollards, he leaned out over the span in the high cold air seeking some evidence of her escape. A tangle of clothing, a scrab-
bling of mud on a stone. Anything.

He could feel the hems of his trousers clinging in a cold wet
crust to his ankles and he would stop now and then and shake
out a leg not caring how it must look. Then he would move a
few feet farther along the bridge, the grey street slime squelching under his boots. The river was high and the colour of burnt
cork and he watched the steamer ferries vanish through the
fog. A notion was forming in his mind that he could not shake.
He knew Charlotte Reckitt's body lay in pieces on Frith Street
and yet he knew too that a man saw only what he looked for
and he scowled and stared out at the drifting fog but could not
make sense of it. The hell with it, he told himself. The woman
was dead.

Curling his bruised hand into a fist as he did so.

What was it had happened? He stood in the chill, struggling to remember, passing a sore hand across his eyes in the
afternoon light. The night had been cold. He had felt the frost
on the bridge setts under his shoes, the slide and rasp of it. He
remembered there had been night watchmen blowing their

whistles somewhere behind him but he had not known if they were pursuing him, or Charlotte Reckitt, or some other. He remembered Charlotte across the footway, running for the railing, climbing high upon it and turning to glare back at him, breathless. The wind crackling her skirts whitely out from under her coat, the shape of her boots, a flash of stockinged ankles. Her hair in her eyes so that he could not make out her expression. He had lunged towards her and she had let go with her fingers and leaned back into the darkness with the shell of one ear visible and plunged straight-backed with arms outspread and then like that she was gone.

He awoke the next day before dawn with a fierce ache blooming behind his left eye like a sunrise of blood and the pain worsened in the bad air. He dressed with one hand on the towel rail to steady himself and went down for a breakfast of rashers and eggs and two cups of strong black tea without lifting his head to the day. Then paid and went out into the street and hailed a hansom for the wet docks at Wapping in the jostle and crush of the morning hire.

The day was a thin fog, a greying of the light as if tinted by a fine dusting of coal, and he turned up the collar of his topcoat. The hansom rattled on. Wapping was grim with its accidental courtyards and crooked alleyside shops. A stink of tan, tallow, gutted fish, rotting vegetable peelings oozed up from the open gutters. He saw windows packed with brass sextants and chronometers, sailors' compasses held open with their small paper tags dangling dustily in the cases. Sailmakers by the dozen with ropes and lines of tar coiled on tables and at each corner the slop sellers with their hammocks and oiled wetcoats and red or blue flannels knotted and swaying in the door frames. Waggons rolled past loaded with reeking mounds of pure. In the crowds newsboys were hollering out word of the Fenian bombing from the day before and he heard the driver in back clear his throat and spit and snort and vacate his nostrils.

Transport the lot of them, the driver hollered at him. Australia ain't too rough for their like.

William said nothing.

The driver said some word more that he did not catch then creaked back on his bench.

He rubbed two fingers at his temple to ease the ache. He saw girls in the streets bare-headed and leering never mind the hour and sailors in loose jackets and pantaloons. There were customs officers in brass buttons and blue coats and inked sailors with hoops in their ears and others with coloured wrappings on their heads. Wiry boys slipped barefoot between the carts despite the cold, lifting what little they could. When the hansom had come to a halt William got down and the driver gestured with his whip to the south, to the tall iron gates of the London docks standing wide there. He could see masts by the hundreds rising in the grey beyond like the stark spines of some ravaged forest.

One and six, the driver grunted.

William looked at him, his voice was soft. How much again?

The driver cleared his throat, squinted up at the sky as if anxious for rain. Call it a shilling, he said. Special, like, for you, sir.

William nodded. He gave the man one and two. For your trouble, he said.

More and more often now William stared into mirrors and his father stared back. Never mind his father had stood barely five foot eight in stocking feet and at forty weighed 165 pounds to William's 225, never mind his apelike arms that dangled near to his knees. For his father too could wrap himself round a barrel of molasses and lift it four feet onto a flatbed without strain. William remembered how the old man would oil his hair flat and how in July the heat would stand it out upon his skull in thick black curls. Scottish to a fault. He scorned anything not seen with his own eyes, not weighed in his own fist or poured through his fingers. He drank eight glasses of water a day and forced the same upon his family. Never touched a drop of liquor not even cold ale in high summer. Ate potatoes in their jackets with relish. For thirteen years he drove his children seventeen miles to church over dirt roads with his back rigid and his face unsmiling but one Sunday when the pastor spoke in defence of slavery he stood up and put on his hat and walked out and he did not ever go back. William feared him and loved him and loathed him every day of his life yet too not a day passed that he did not want to be him. His father was not a man of great physical beauty but the conviction in his fists could sway any man living. He had been a cooper when he came to America and then a lawman and when he set out as a private detective there was no such thing anywhere in the country and he became something else entire, a thing unstoppable and elemental and terrifying.

He woke throughout his life to a recurring illness which left a smell of burning in his nostrils. On such mornings he would squint out at the world under blood-coloured eyelids and speak to no one. The Scot in him distrusted doctors, the frontiersman in him blended his own medicinal drinks. Myrtleberry, celery, radishes, warmed milk. Other, fouler beverages. His beard he would trim with a pair of barber's shears kept handles-out in a Mason jar on a shelf near the rain barrel. Beside the barn a piece of mirror had been fastened with rope and nail and he would wash himself there in any weather for modesty. He slept when it grew dark and rose when it grew light and walked his daily constitutional come snow or shine. In the unheated house when the door banged shut William would kick off his sheets, shake his younger brother awake, and together they would start their chores. If there was a vanity in his father then it came from a love of what physical power could do. He had trained under a pugilist in the Glasgow slums and he took William on his eighth birthday to a warehouse on the Chicago docks to see Tom Heenan fight Johnny Roberts. Heenan was the taller but young still at that time and not yet a champion and when he struck Roberts down in four the riled crowd stormed the ring with knives and chains. William's father had held him against the far wall and insisted he watch the brawl. It's never what happens, lad, his father had murmured. Watch now. It's who it happens to. That's what matters.

His father spoke little about his own blood. He left it for his wife to sing Scottish ballads in the evenings with a misty eye. He did not believe in looking backward and took what he could from his life at hand and leaned knifelike into the future with it. But one afternoon when William was nine he spoke about his own father, dead in Glasgow. They were standing in the unscythed grass behind the woodshed. He said his father William's grandfather and all six of his own great-uncles had eyes the silver of cooling iron and that such eyes in the Scotland of his youth were believed the eyes of ancient Highland warriors. Eyes born with brutality in them. Or so legend claimed. Those men had been blacksmiths each and as if to prove the legend true each had killed a man in a bare-knuckle fight before his eighteenth year. The English had killed them all, one way or another.

William had brushed his own face in wonder. Do I have eyes like that too, Pa?

You, his father had grunted. You take after your mother.

As he approached the gates of the dock works he could hear it. A roaring muffled and thrumming up through the cobblestones like some vast machinery at work deep in the earth.

Then he came around a corner and saw them. Hundreds of men, blowing on their fingers, stamping their feet for the cold. Constables with truncheons and dock officers with their red hands bared kept back the crowds with a lazy swing of their arms and the labourers lingered in ragged shirts and coats, smoking, sullen, gaunt, unwashed and reeking, their fists plunged down the fronts of their trousers for warmth. It was only just half seven and all at once there was a ripple in the throng as faces were raised, listening, and then the great iron gates screeled open and there came a pouring of men through, shoulder to shoulder, the breath steaming off them like cattle driven to some enclosure beyond. He could hear the foremen on their platforms crying the names of men like a blessing and he could see the haggard and the lost of that city hollering and waving and showing the whites of their eyes in their desperation to be hired.

Somewhere in all that stood the Irishman Malone who had found Charlotte Reckitt's head.

William gripped his wallet in one fist, swore softly at the futility of ever finding the man. Then he went down into it.

A world all its own in its breaking. Slowly he went from basin to basin along the quays, the ships in their locks raised to differing heights. He could see the green copper sheathing of an American schooner with its weeds and barnacles looming high above him and creaking in the faint breeze and at its stern he saw a goat tethered and bleating and he could see beyond that the line of planks and gangways stretching from ship to ship along that basin. Other vessels drifted low under his eyeline and ladders leaned up against the edges of the stonework where dark-skinned sailors ascended in weary single file. He could see a heavy sack of meal misshapen and twisting sluggishly on its chains above a quay like a hanged man in his hood and he watched a thresher guide the burlap by its base as if to hold the ankles of the dead steady. He could smell the open crates of fish in their glister and the reek of bundled tobacco mingling with the cinnamon and rum. He passed a box of open horns and ivory with the flesh tufted and rotting at the bases and the stink of it made his eyes water. His soles stuck to and peeled from the slatted boards of the wharf and he realized it was old sugar spilled from the sheds nearby and he walked on, his steps blatting and slapping messily in the cold. Blinking and shivering and wondering if he was coming down with something.

He passed through the warehouses, the low sheds with their vast grinding wheels turning through their roofs like paddle steamers on the Mississippi, the brown water turning lazily under their laden barges, and he wended his way through the crates of cork, the bins of raw sulphur. The rattle of empty casks rolled along the cobbles, the clatter and hiss of chains slung up in a spray from the river, the brassy hammering of coopers at their barrels. He passed down into the storehouse vaults with their foul moulding dry rot and their spilled wine where orange lanterns smouldered on iron rings and then he ascended through the far tunnels and everywhere he walked men regarded him uneasily but did not slow at their labours and at each basin he stopped and asked but no man had word of the one he sought.

At last one foreman did not turn from his query but spat a slick of tobacco onto the wharf and stood waiting. William watched it bubble there like a dripping of grease. The ache in his skull beetled deeper. The man's crew was unloading a collier moored to a rickety dolphin a little ways out in the river and he watched the whippers in their black-stained greatcoats and fustians bend and hoist along the ladders.

Who? Malone? The foreman smeared a wrist across his forehead. There's a Molloy works for us sometime. Skinny little fellow, big hands, Irish. No lighterman though. He's a lumper in the right season.

Was he unloading a cargo of bulbs last Friday?

The foreman shrugged, rolled the wad of tobacco from cheek to cheek.

It's about the head.

What head?

Wasn't there a woman's head pulled out on Friday?

I reckon I'd remember it.

William frowned. You didn't find part of a dead woman here Friday?

Oh we got lots of stiffs round here. He grinned. But they all swear they're here to work.

William smiled.

Listen. I tell the lads to roll the bug-logs back out in the river. It's just too much bleedin fuss when you drag one up. You be at it all day.

Bug-logs?

The foreman squinched up one eye, spat again.

Are there any other docks would have been unloading cargoes of bulbs that day?

I don't keep the manifests do I.

Of course not. No.

Look at them buggers, he muttered. He nodded at a group of labourers leaning against a post where an unlit cauldron twisted and untwisted on its chains. Like they ain't even here. Ain't much to pick from in a morning. You just go down to the Bird & Whistle and hire the first damned butcher or old soldier from the Crimea you can find. Be lucky to catch a clerk or a old servant, any what wants the work. It don't take no skill but aught you can pick up a heavy and get from one side to the other. Pick it up now darlins, he hollered. Go on get your skirts dirty.

A ducking of heads, a sudden scrambling.

They ain't all worthless, he said. But nearly.

William nodded. She's adrift, he said, nodding at the collier.

Aye she's cranky. Like to get worse before she stiffens. The foreman did not offer his hand as he moved away but after a moment paused and called back over one shoulder. You could try out at St. Katharine, he said. They's just bloody crazy enough to be toolin a jill's head from the waters.

William tipped his hat but the man was already lost in the roar.

This is what he wanted to ask.

Where was it pulled out. How did it appear to the eye. Was it bundled and tied or no. How long had it sat unwrapped in the close air of the docks and who had touched it and who had not. Was there any other cloth swaddling it. Did anything fall from the package as it was lifted out. Where was the boathook that took it. Why haul it out at all and not pole it back into the river. What of the currents and where was the likely drift of it from.

How many other dead had been found that week. That month. That year. What of the woman's hair.

Yes. What of her hair.

Oh and who was the bastard pulled her and where did he live.

Scotland Yard's offices on the old palace grounds at 4 Whitehall Place had spread like a cancer until they had taken over the surrounding buildings and carriage houses, numbers 3 and 5, 21 and 22, and still there was not enough room. William's father had told him of a time when the old building had dwarfed its purposes but William could not imagine it. The public entrance was at the rear and he came in off the narrow cobbled street of Great Scotland Yard shrugging the cold from his neck At the Back Hall sergeant's desk he stopped, waited, announced himself. It was a tall angled drafting desk on a dais with a leather-bound records book laid out upon it and the hall sergeant perched behind it, high on his backless stool, a pencil in one hand and his other pressed flat on one knee. The man was a stout, rough-hewn veteran of the force, with a powerful neck and a grey walrus moustache that lent him an air of thuggish dignity. The second finger of his right hand looked to have been broken and reset badly many years ago. William asked for John Shore and the sergeant eyed him where he stood, grizzled and hatless, stinking yet of the dockyards, then leaned out and seized a runner by the scruff of his neck as he went past.

Take this here gent up to John Blunt's office, lad, he said. Mind ye be quick about it. We don't get so many American detectives we can afford to be rough with them.

William grimaced. His head was aching and he closed his eyes momentarily. I'm here to see Shore. Not Blunt.

Aye, the sergeant nodded irritably. I know the man ye want. Go on.

The runner ascended the stairs to the offices and William followed, surprised by the stiffness in his bad leg. Shore's office was a cramped low-ceilinged room cluttered with a black walnut bookshelf and twin bulleted armchairs and the chief inspector's desk filling the whole of the back quarter. A high window filtered in some light and he saw Inspector Blackwell there, next to the curtains, hair slicked, clothes smelling of peppermint.

Shore half stood in greeting.

A better morning, Mr. Blunt, William said.

Shore smiled wearily. It's a nickname.

A compliment I take it.

They always are. Shore sat back, round-shouldered and red-faced in his rumpled waistcoat. His shirt sleeves were rolled and he did not trouble to make himself presentable. He wore wire spectacles low on the bridge of his nose and he peered over the tops of them and then back down at his desk. There were boxes of files and reports strewn about the floor and William lifted a lidded box from one of the two leather chairs and set it at his feet and sat down uninvited. The chief inspector ran a harried knuckle under his chin.

These bloody Fenians. Tell me how blowing up the Underground helps to free the Irish from their English masters. Tell me what this poor flat had to do with it.

He crackled a report across the desk and William took it from him without seeing.

Shore unhooked the wire spectacles from his red ears. He was a haberdasher, for god's sake. On his way to work.

A haberdasher.

Some threat to the free Irish.

After a moment William said, My father fled Edinburgh to get away from you English. He used to say you can go in the harness or holding the reins and both are aimed in the same direction but which one would you rather.

Your father was a wise man.

William frowned slightly. Somehow Shore's saying it made him bristle. This Fenian business has been going on a while I take it, he said, changing the subject.

Aye. We're under an awful pressure. The Home Office wants this ended, Gladstone wants this ended. We'll tear them out by the root. He blinked and regarded William and frowned. What are you doing here?

I've been out at the docks. No Malone.

Shore sighed and leaned back in his seat and set a quiet hand on the papers before him. He looked at Blackwell and back at William. Dr. Breck should be here shortly, he said. He's been occupied with this mess at Gower Street. But you can ask him about your Charlotte Reckitt.

I will. The sacking her torso was found in might provide some direction.

The sacking. Aye.

Blackwell cleared his throat. He stood profiled at the window as if posing for a portrait. Maria Marten cut her hair when she went out to meet Corder, sir. To disguise herself.

Maria Marten? William said. Is this a recent case?

Shore grunted. Maria Marten was murdered by the Red Barn butcher. That was fifty years ago.

William shook his head. I guess we can rule him out then.

Shore had opened a box of loose tobacco as they spoke and begun to fill his pipe. William could see the red locomotive painted on the underlid and he watched as the chief turned the stem in his fingers and studied it as if thinking better of it then stuffed it back into his pocket with one hand and closed the lid of the box with the other. This was back in the days of Jack Ketch, he was saying. Before there even was a police to speak of. Corder was a wealthy farmer who had got Miss Marten in trouble. He lured her out to a barn one night and stabbed her twice and shot her through the eye for good measure and then buried her there, in a shallow grave. Went off into the provinces and wrote her parents for a year or so, pretending she had eloped with him. Story goes Marten's mother had a dream her daughter had been murdered and Marten's father went out to the barn and poked about in the dirt with a rake and pulled up something black and rotten and that was his daughter.

I guess Corder was hanged for it?

Shore opened his hands in a rueful gesture. Afterwards they cut him up in the lecturing halls and bits of him were sold all over the country. A leather seller in Oxford Street still has his scalp on display in a pickling jar.

I'd like to see that.

Aye. Remind you of back home I guess.

Well. We like to keep our pickled scalps in the parlour.

Shore laughed. What can you do, he said. It's the modern world.

There was an abrupt knock at the door.

Come, Shore barked.

A man came in. Leaning on a gold-tipped walking stick, his torso thin and hard like an old-fashioned scythe. He wore a sleek silk hat with a wide brim that darkened his spectacles into discs of shadow and wire and cast a strange crooked line to his nose. A purple cravat hung in a tangle off his collar where the tie pin had been stabbed at a crazy angle. William watched his head sway at the end of his neck, snakelike and grotesque.

Ah, Dr. Breck, Shore said. He rose in greeting from behind his desk. You will have heard of Mr. Pinkerton, out of Chicago. Mr. Pinkerton, our Dr. Breck. You know Mr. Blackwell.

William stood. The doctor's fingers were red and sore-looking as if accustomed to labouring without gloves on chemical tinctures, his nails edged in grime. His hand felt warm in William's own and it was withdrawn at once as if the touch of the living sickened him.

Doctor, William said. He hooked a thumb into his waistcoat. Mr. Shore tells me you have inspected the head?

Breck scowled at Shore. He means the one from the river?

Is there another? William asked.

More than you can imagine, sir, Breck said sourly, turning to him. He let go of his cane and removed his eyeglasses and withdrew a handkerchief from his vest pocket and proceeded to polish the lenses. It wasn't as cruel as it might have been, he said.

William thought about this a moment. She was dead before she was decapitated.

Correct.

Her arms were tied?

Who told you that, Mr. Pinkerton?

Mr. Pinkerton has several theories, Dr. Breck, Shore said. He came with me to view the head and torso.

He's only just putting it together now, sir, Blackwell said.

Breck scowled. In life the victim would have stood approximately five feet four inches tall, he said. She was black-haired. She had not eaten in several days. There is bruising to her arms as if she had been handled roughly. Tied up most likely. The stab wounds on the torso do not appear to have been executed in a passion. They are very deliberate, very shallow, and clean, as if the body did not twist at all as the blade was removed. The blade used was single-sided and curved slightly. The knife wounds are not deep enough to be the cause of death and the victim's lack of movement is consistent with the poison found in the body. She would not have been conscious at the time.

Shore grunted. Poison, you say?

Arsenic? William asked.

Always with you Americans it's arsenic, Breck muttered. No. Chloroform.

She was drugged then, Shore said slowly. Drugged, then tied up, stabbed, decapitated, and her body left in several places around the city. Is that what you're telling us, Doctor?

It's damned elaborate, William muttered.

Rather too elaborate.

The facts are what they are. I simply report them.

But how they're read and understood is a different matter, William said. So. She was drugged in order to subdue her, presumably. Why then tie her up?

They must have expected her to wake up.

Except she did not. She was stabbed while unconscious.

Too much chloroform, said Shore. Can that kill a person?

It would seem so.

Breck clutched the head of his walking stick with both hands.

Why so many stab wounds? Shore asked. If she was unconscious and not struggling?

How many stab wounds were there, Doctor?

Two to the upper left arm. Three to the torso. One near the heart. The angle of all of the wounds is from below. Which is commensurate with a taller assailant stabbing at her underhanded.

William considered this. What was she tied to? Not a chair. Could she have been tied upright, to a post? The angle you're describing would mean she would have had to be high enough in relation to her attacker—

A chair is unlikely, Breck interrupted. Unless it was on some sort of platform. Or unless the assailant was a rather small person. A woman, for instance.

Shore looked offended. A woman wouldn't do such a thing.

I'd still like to know, William said, why so many of these shallow cuts.

A weak assailant, Shore suggested. Or timid, maybe. Maybe it was their first time.

It was to wake her up, sir, Blackwell said quietly.

The men fell silent. William studied the young inspector, ran a hand over his jaw.

If she was drugged and tied up, sir. The shallow cuts would be to wake her up.

Interesting, said William. So they didn't want to kill her. Or not right away.

Perhaps they wanted information, sir, Blackwell went on. You said she had her share of bad dealings.

I said she was a part of the swell mob, William said. I don't know what kind of enemies she had.

Breck was already shifting his weight as if to leave.

A moment, Doctor, William said. Are you familiar with Bertillon's methods?

Breck regarded William with displeasure. I know Monsieur Bertillon, yes. And his theories. We communicated together on a case last spring.

If you would take the woman's measurements—

It is of course difficult without all of the pieces, Mr. Pinkerton. But I have already done so. As much as I can.

I'd like a copy of that sent to the Chicago office, William said. I'll have an operative go through our records. See if anything turns up with an alias attached.

It is the property of Scotland Yard. Not me.

Send your results to me, Dr. Breck, said Shore. I'll see that they get to Chicago, William. Now, Doctor. The bombing.

The doctor wrung his soft hands, unperturbed. If you bring me a body I will look at it. I can do nothing with a bucket of bits.

You have what we have, Shore said.

Breck wet his lips with the nub of a long pink tongue. He said, I can tell you that there was a bomb. Your unfortunate haberdasher was standing next to it. Or upon it. Or perhaps even carrying it. He would have been very close.

Shore regarded him with evident impatience. Wonderful.

Mr. Blackwell, Breck said. Would you be so good as to take me to the haberdasher's belongings?

One last thing, Doctor, William said. Charlotte Reckitt. Was she with child?

Breck paused, his long peeling fingers on the latch of the door. If she had been pregnant, Mr. Pinkerton, I should have mentioned it. Now if you gentlemen will excuse me—

The two men left and Shore stared at the door after it had shut for a long moment and then he said in a careful voice, What do you think of our good doctor?

William shook his head tiredly.

Shore stood and crossed to the sideboard and withdrew a small silver flask from the cabinet there and two glasses. Your father didn't much care for him either, he said. Breck's clever with a corpse though. He helped us in the Toms killing last year. A piece of wadding recovered from the body was found to match a broadside in the man's possession. How do you like your whiskey?

In a bottle.

Here's a glass. Shore sat back down with a groan. Our Mr. Blackwell's reliable, hm?

That's one word for it.

He was an amateur boxing champion last year.

Blackwell? I don't believe it.

Aye. You'd never know he was a reader of sensation novels.

Penny dreadfuls?

That Wilkie Collins and the like. Desk is full of them. I never could stomach a detective who was a reader.

William turned the glass in his hands, the smoky liquid darkening there.

Shore raised an eyebrow. What is it?

Charlotte Reckitt has an uncle in Millbank, William said, his smile fading. An ex-priest. I'll want to talk to him, I guess. Can you arrange it?

You want an interview with Martin Reckitt.

Before I leave, yes, William said. Just to be certain there's nothing I've overlooked. Maybe he knows something about Charlotte's business, who she worked with. I have a file to close. And then he caught himself, and glanced up. You know the man?

I know the man. Aye.

Well?

Well nothing. I can't see what Martin Reckitt could offer on this that wouldn't be a lie straight out. Bastard's been locked away for years.

William shifted his bulk in the chair, grinding an elbow into the armrest. His trousers were tight, pinching at his belly. You never mentioned him, he said, with a slow quizzical wrinkling of his forehead. Niece turns up in pieces all over the city and you never mention you knew her uncle?

Shore gave him an exasperated look. The man is in your files too. There's no conspiracy here. What could he possibly have to do with it? After a moment Shore picked up a small framed photograph and passed it across to William. It was a speckled picture of a little girl in a white dress standing next to a gravestone, her face serious and un-shy, some inscription on the base of the stone that William could not make out.

Fear not them which kill the body but are not able to kill the soul, Shore recited. *But rather fear him which is able to destroy both soul and body in hell.*

Cheerful, William said.

That's the grave of Fanny Adams. She was murdered twenty years ago up in Alton. Cut up into pieces in a field on a sunny day and the killer just walked away from it. She was ten years old.

Jesus, William muttered. What is wrong with this country?

It's a reminder, Shore said, ignoring the question. Instruments of vengeance, William. That is what we are.

William shifted the photograph from one knee to the other then set it on the desk in front of him. Blunt instruments, maybe, he said. Does he know about her death yet?

Who?

For god's sake. Charlotte Reckitt's uncle.

Shore's chair creaked and thumped as he tucked himself nearer his desk. You went out to New Street on Friday, he said. What did you find? When William said nothing he went on: Nothing. Because we'd already gone through it all. Because there was nothing there. What happened to Charlotte Reckitt is most likely some kind of revenge killing. Bad people betraying other bad people and suffering for it. Sometimes they do get what they deserve. You should go back to Chicago, William, go home. Shore's florid face turned in the weak light of the window, pausing as if to say something more. He grimaced. Then he said it. Staying here won't get you any closer to your Edward Shade.

William looked at him sharply. Edward Shade?

You thought I didn't know? You've been into every flash house in London asking questions. You don't make it much of a secret.

You've been following me.

Please. Nothing so dramatic.

William was leaning forward in his chair, turning the glass

in his hands. He said, quietly, Edward Shade's a ghost, John. He's not real.

Oh, Shade was real. He was real as a bullet. He died during your Civil War.

What are you talking about?

Your father never told you?

William could feel the blood rise in his cheeks. Told me what?

Shore's thick red fingers were still. Well, he said. I only know what your father told me. Shade was an agent for him in the war. A spy. He volunteered to go south to gather information and something happened, I don't know what, but he was caught. The Confederates tortured him. That was the last your father heard about him. I expect Shade died in a prison or was shot as a spy or suchlike. I understand some sort of evidence turned up, something rather compelling. Two graves, one marked with the name of a fellow spy. But then a year or so after the war was finished your father took to the notion that maybe Shade had survived. I don't know what changed his mind. I think he wanted Shade to still be alive, wanted to believe he just walked away from the war and disappeared. I guess he never forgave himself for failing the lad. He never told you about this?

William was shaking his head. There's a grave?

Aye. In Virginia.

Why would my father suddenly think he didn't die? It doesn't make sense.

I told him that myself.

William looked at Shore. There were documents, he said, in a file. In my father's home safe. Records of jobs Shade was involved in. All dated after the war.

Rumours of jobs you mean. And never any evidence of the man. Am I right?

He frowned.

Go ask old Benjamin Porter, if you doubt it, Shore said with a shrug. He and Sally were there when Shade crossed the lines. They were the ones he rode out with. They were the last ones to see him alive.

Sally Porter?

Aye. And Benjamin.

I was with Ben in Virginia, he said slowly. In sixty-two.

Shore regarded him strangely. Your father had those old Porters hunting Shade over here for years. I guess since they knew him by sight. I expect they're both still in the city somewhere.

William rubbed at his face with both hands. He was thinking of Sally Porter in her ruined hovel, how she had said nothing to him of this.

William? You all right?

After a moment he stood and buttoned his chesterfield and stared down at the chief inspector with a quiet grimness. Arrange an interview for me with Reckitt's uncle, John, he said. Let me finish this and get back to Chicago. I'm not here to get dragged into anything.

Shore's small eyes fixed on William's.

I'd say you're already in it, he said.

He came down out of Whitehall with his face grey and his bruised hand trembling. He had known his father as a violence and a scarring that burned coldly in his flesh. The old man's death had taken the shared part of them with it and left William alone in his regret. He could not explain to his wife that he did not now know what to do with his memory of the man. It had never been intimacy. His father had run a network of spies throughout the war and shared little of it with his sons. His father had discussed the particulars of Edward Shade with strangers at the Yard and never seen fit to confide in his own blood. William thought of Sally Porter in anger and then he did not. All he knew of his father's violent past, of his habits, his medical cocktails, of the stories behind each keepsake in the man's rolltop desk, the grapeshot that had been pulled from his father's saddle, the laces that had nearly garrotted him in Detroit, the dried daffodils and morningdew pressed in the pages of a Bible carried overseas from Edinburgh a lifetime gone. All of this and none had been the man in his breathing.

The death of his father meant William too had crossed a threshold. That was the fact of it. It had surprised him. Love was not the word for what he'd felt for his father. He knew some part of his own self lay diminished and mouldering in the wet earth back in Chicago. He pressed his hand against the cold cast iron of a street lamp outside Scotland Yard, he stared out at the fog.

NINE

Williaim Pinkerton. What was the famed detective's first son but a wisp, a rumour, a creature of nightmare walking the flash world, frightening all. Few had met him who did not count the days in chalk on prison walls, who did not nurse a broken bone. Foole was never among them. He had heard tell of terrible strength, true, of a man who did not sleep for days, who could survive without food or water in the stunted wastes of the western territories driving horse after horse bridle-first down to dust, who would drift along the water-rotted docks of New York with impunity. The man was thirty, no forty, no fifty, no the man did not age. It was said he could read a lie on a face like wind cutting across a lake. He could crush a pint glass with one squeeze and his weathered hands not bleed. In Chicago he frequented Madison's flash house those Fridays when he was in town and he would go down among the dippers and sharps there with a wary smile and stand unmolested at the bar and drink a cider very slowly, watching the flash world all the while watch him back. Some swore he could stare down a bull. Others swore his eyelids had been burned off as a boy and he did not blink as a consequence. In Virginia he was seen to leap from a moving train carriage onto a horse held up alongside and to then unsling a rifle and shoot a man down all before the other could draw. In the Black Hills he had beaten a sheriff into submission with his bare fists and broken every finger of both hands in the process and picked up his gun with the soft of his wrists when it was done. Foole had heard it said the only world he hated more than the criminal one was the world of the law and this was said with a knowing grin always. There were men who said his children were not his own. Others denied this and swore on their poke his brother's children were his also. All agreed the man was not like other men and lacked the common human appetites and whatever else he was a man without weakness, a man without pity. As the years passed Foole would listen while the myths grew and he would wonder and rub his eyes and try to imagine the true son of Allan Pinkerton in the flesh.

And this was the man who had hunted Charlotte to her end.

Fludd thought it the worst of luck. He came back from his inquiries sighing and shaking his shaggy head. Bloody hell, Mr. Adam, he muttered, seated at the plank table in the kitchen. I just got meself out of a stone jug, I ain't got no inclination of visitin its like again. Not for a while now. Don't make me get no closer.

Tell me about him, Foole said softly. Tell me what you've heard.

A long miserable look, ringed eyes peering under bedraggled brows. Mr. Adam—

Tell me, Foole said again.

As the mornings passed into afternoons, the afternoons into evenings, he would lean suddenly to one side with a hand splayed on the wall and eyes closed and see again that painting from the gallery. Or he would stare out at the drifting brown fog through the Emporium windows and recall in confusion the paint, the brushwork, the light in those eyes, and think again of Charlotte with a savagery that left him shaken. He woke and he slept and he ate with a woodenness that left Molly and Fludd anxious and made Mrs. Sykes crack a tea towel sharply out over her shoulder and purse her lips and leave whatever room he entered. He did not like the idea that William Pinkerton had been alone with

Charlotte when she died but Fludd's inquiries into the manner of her death came to nothing beyond a dark rumour of mutilation. It's Gabriel you want to be askin, the giant told him reluctantly on the second evening. No, he replied, I'll not, but knowing even as he protested that his old friend was right. When he left Half Moon Street at a troubled pace he could feel the big man's eyes boring into his back from an upper window and once he reached the cold of Piccadilly he hailed a hansom and rode distracted and alone the rest of the way to the Inns of Court.

Gabriel Utterson was a creature who had winched his survival to knowing both what others wanted to know and what they feared becoming known. Foole had considered him an accomplice once and then a friend during his long years of informing and then neither and then both again. He thought of the dozens of letters the man had written him about Charlotte and her affairs and he shook his head in disgust. As he crossed a frozen surf of mud in the street he tucked his chin in his collar seeking neither resemblance nor recognition in the faces of the law clerks he passed. At the end of a courtyard he found a thick oak door and he tried the latch and went up and at the third-floor landing he found Utterson's name set in a brass plate above a buzzer. He held his finger there a moment but did not press it and instead opened the door and went in.

It was the same high-ceilinged office, if shabbier than he remembered. Lit only by a single gas sconce behind a copying desk, tall doors opening out on the far side of the clerk's chair. But the man bent over a file there was no clerk and Foole regarded him in confusion a moment before clearing his throat.

What happened to your assistant? he said.

Utterson looked up in alarm. He had hard little eyes like the heads of nails, creased in the folds of his face, as if driven in. But there were purple rings now in the skin under them. He was softer than he had been a year ago, his flesh sagging in loops and flattened bags, like a water sack slackening and draining slowly. Foole took in the long austere hands, nails chewed to stumps, the cleft chin. A sprouting of wiry hairs from the cavities of his ears.

Mr. Adam Foole, Utterson said, setting down his pencil. Hello Gabriel.

Neither man smiled. The lawyer cast a disagreeable look at the door and said, I can see no purpose in a bell if a man is not inclined to ring it. Then he sat back, sighed. I've had to let three clerks go in six months, he said. Imagine it. Well.

He led Foole through to an adjoining office and shut the door behind them and pulled the curtains closed and then waved to a sofa against one wall. Foole walked over to it with his hat upturned in one hand and his gloves stuffed in the crown but he did not sit. In his other hand he gripped his walking stick in a grip too knuckled and fierce for a friendly visit. Utterson had rolled out a crank stool from behind his desk. Let me have a look at you, he said. How is business, no better? Did you return with your Mr. Fludd intact? Has his stay in America ruined him utterly?

Charlotte is dead, Foole said.

Utterson's colourless eyes diminished to slits.

Did you know it?

The lawyer wet his lips. I have heard talk, he said. Yes. He was silent a moment and then he rose and poured two glasses of brandy from a sideboard and Foole shifted his hat to the other hand and took his cautiously but he did not drink. How much do you know? Utterson asked.

Only that it's being investigated.

Investigated, Utterson said with a frown. A dirty yellow glow was filling the curtains from the courtyard below and Foole at last sat, watching it the while, waiting, and then Utterson said, Part of her was recovered out on Edgware Road, sir. Part of her was, he coughed sharply, pulled from the Thames.

Foole squeezed his eyes shut.

Her head, sir. A labourer on the docks recovered it, five days ago. Utterson leaned over his desk, the crank stool creaking in protest. I understand there are still pieces of her missing.

Pieces.

Her legs.

Foole was quiet, taking this in. I thought she drowned, he said at last. I was told she drowned. How is this possible?

It is London, sir. Anything is possible.

But if she jumped from Blackfriars—

Jumped, Utterson said sharply. He raised a hand to his chest, the slack of his throat spilling out over his collar. That seems hardly likely, does it not, given the condition of her body. Utterson lowered his voice. I do not like to say it, sir. But I have heard a rumour—

Who did she cross, Gabriel?

I cannot be certain, of course—

Who?

Pinkerton's son. William.

Foole blinked, frowned. He took a long slow sip of the brandy and stared at the floor and then he shook his head. William Pinkerton didn't carve Charlotte into pieces, he said.

No?

No.

As you say.

It's ridiculous. Why would he?

Utterson shrugged. But she was frightened of him, sir. She said his behaviour was becoming erratic, threatening. I believe she feared violence from him. She told me that he knew more about her than she could account for, old associates, details of past projects, something about her stay in Philadelphia last fall. Some of it went back years. She believed someone had been feeding it to him. Who could have done this to her, sir? I haven't any notion. If anyone has the idea of it, it is William Pinkerton. But then, Utterson added ruefully, we are neither of us so fool-ish as to inquire of him directly.

What did he want from her? Why is Pinkerton here?

Mr. Foole—

But he did not continue and Foole set his drink down and clasped his hands on his knees and sat with his back straight not understanding the man's reply. After a long silence he said, Charlotte gave you instructions for me.

They are of no consequence now.

What were you to have told me?

Utterson cleared his throat. He picked at some invisible thread on the underside of his sleeve and pursed his lips and belled his tongue in one cheek as if considering. She meant to break her uncle from Millbank, he murmured. That was the intent. I do not know the details. But when she was seeking advice on a crew I suggested you might be a useful addition. Naturally she thought you might not wish to be a part of it. Given your history together, and your history with Mr. Reckitt.

Naturally.

I assured her otherwise.

Foole nodded slowly.

The Tench is closing, Mr. Foole. It is emptying its cells. Mr. Reckitt is to be transported south to the prison hulks in March. My understanding is that some confederate on the inside had been working with Miss Reckitt to arrange a miscount during the transport. Utterson wet his lips. There would be no, ah, remuneration for such a project, of course. Not financially, that is. Which is one of the reasons she was anxious about finding a crew. I told her—

Rose couldn't have told me this yesterday? Foole said abruptly.

The lawyer was silent a moment. Then he glanced about him, shuffled the documents on his desk as if to some purpose. He said, These are not Rose's secrets to divulge, sir. Miss Reckitt left a message for you in my care. She instructed me to give you her address, of course. But she also wanted you to know that her uncle told her the truth of what happened in Brindisi. She said he feels remorse about it and wants to make amends. She herself was angry and then she was relieved. I believe, sir, she thought some future might be possible between you. Utterson looked as if he might say more and then he did not and then he must have changed his mind for he lifted his thorny eyebrows and said, gently, When did you see her last, Mr. Foole?

When did you?

The night she disappeared, sir. She was, as I say, frightened.

Foole ran his tongue along his teeth, remembering. I haven't seen her since the Royal Albert, he said. You were with me.

I remember.

She looked like she'd seen a ghost.

You didn't speak then, though.

No.

Charlotte was, ah, rather changed. In recent years, I mean. Perhaps she was no longer the person you remember. I imagine your feelings for her have not abated?

We're all of us changed, Gabriel.

But you would not be seated here, sir, if you had changed quite so much as that.

Foole said nothing.

When Mr. Reckitt was arrested, Charlotte became distant, colder. She disbanded her usual working associates and for a time I believed she had put the flash world behind her. I know she was living in Stratford, as a widow, for a while. And I know she eventually went abroad to the Continent, to Switzerland I believe. That was five years ago. When she reached out last August I could see how she had aged. I do not mean in her face, sir. I mean in her eyes. There was something about her that unsettled a person. As if she had been hollowed out and filled up instead with some uglier thing.

Foole did not know what to say. Her letter had betrayed none of that. He thought about how her uncle's arrest must have haunted her and then he looked up in surprise. Does he know? he said. Has Martin heard?

I imagine the Yard has been to see him. Or intends to. They will be making inquiries.

But you haven't seen him.

What occasion would I have? He is incarcerated, sir, with no hope of release.

Foole laid his walking stick across his knees. You should speak with him. Tell him yourself. He deserves to hear it from a friend.

Utterson's thin lips curled upward. A friend.

I am in earnest.

The two men's eyes met over the lawyer's big desk.

I find your interest in Mr. Reckitt's welfare surprising, sir. Utterson ran a hand along the rumpled curve of his waistcoat, considering the thing. Perhaps you should go to him yourself.

Foole watched the bad light glisten on the lawyer's face, his oily and pitted skin. He thought of Fludd's dislike of the man.

May I ask, sir, the nature of your concern?

You know the answer.

Ah, yes, he saved your life in Brindisi. You take that debt rather more seriously now than you once did. I recall a time when you felt he had ruined it. Utterson watched him with hard flat eyes. The minutes passed. You would do better to pay your respects to Miss Reckitt herself. Her remains are being held at Pitchcott's, I understand.

Foole looked up. Pitchcott's.

The mortuary. On Frith Street. I know a man there, I can arrange for a viewing if you'd like. Certainly the attendant has done favours for me in the past. Although I imagine it will be a rather explicit experience, perhaps, and not one for the faint—

Frith Street, Foole said, not quite taking it in.

She is in a better place, sir.

Did Rose's spirits tell you that? he said sharply. He had not intended to mention spiritualism and he was surprised at his own venom.

Utterson's green eyes burned as he looked up. He appeared to be searching for words. I was not a believer at first either, Mr. Foole. But it is not what you imagine. Death is not something to fear. His fingers flattened on the desk before him. There are some that pass over to the lowest sphere at once, he said. Others do not realize they have gone to spirit and it takes them some time to be at peace with it. But they are in no pain. It is as the Bible teaches, sir. There is nothing unchristian in it.

Foole got to his feet.

You will have heard our mother was removed to spirit two years ago, Utterson continued. It has been a comfort to us both, to hear that she is at peace. Grief touches all of us, sir. It is not a thing we were meant to struggle against.

Foole said nothing.

No, sir, Utterson went on. We must think of grief as a kindness. It is how we know we have loved.

A kindness, Foole thought in despair, knowing no such thing. She had been brought back pale and trembling into the world by an uncle she had not known and was given his name from the first. Come, child, he had called to her through the locked gate, a shimmering silhouette in the winter sun. Under his silk hat his face was double-wrapped in a scarf so that only the eyes were visible. She had stood trembling as he removed a glove and reached through the iron curlicues of that workhouse fence and set what seemed to her an enormous soft perfumed hand to her cheek. Then the matron had unlocked the gates with a clang and hauled the heavy black horse gate inward and cursed her for her laggardliness all the while. He had been so tall, so thin and elegant, so very old, she had whispered to Foole in the early morning light. He had been living at that time in a grand house south of Piccadilly and she had not dared speak the first two days of her stay for fear of the mistake that had been made. On the third day her uncle had called her to his study and told her a debt had been owed her mother and that he had not realized she had died or he would have paid it sooner. There was a sadness in him, a slowness in his eyes, as if all he looked at he would linger over lest it leave his sight forever. Was there love? There was love, yes. She learned her letters, her sums, she studied geography and history and classics under an Irish governess until she bore no resemblance to other girls her age. He dressed her well, he took her to the theatre, he took her to the parks and the exhibitions. Once a month he would descend into Whitechapel with her and they would walk through the grime and filth that she not forget the world that was real, and hidden, and hers by right. And on her sixteenth birthday he told her the truth of his vocation and the ambitions he held for her as a grifter and a thief. There is nothing possessed by any other that might not be yours, he told her. Take everything. From that night her true apprenticeship began. Despite appearances she was a creature of the uncivilized world and she owed no debt to any save her uncle and for him there was no law on earth she would not have broken.

I should have died in there, she said, biting at her lip. But for him, I should have died in that place.

You don't know that, Foole frowned.

He thought of it now and of her and felt many things but most of all he felt shame. He had been so young. They had been so young. A lifetime had seemed so long.

When he left Utterson's offices it was after midnight and he walked the empty side streets with his stick scraping the cobblestones and he saw no one. A darker night began to burn up out of the river and creep through the city and the coal fogs lifted, thinned to a watery grey, drifting web-like and eerie and serene. He had forgotten his hat and gloves on Utterson's sofa and walked now with his head bare and the cold running through his hair. A hurt was rising in him and he knew it had little to do with Gabriel or his sister but it was there all the same. When he reached the Strand he did not seek out a cab stand and instead cut north again and crossed a small unlit park and continued west. At a cobbled square he slowed and stopped and leaned casually against a stone balustrade and lifted his eyes. Across the street stood the Grand Metropolitan, brightly lit, palatial.

William Pinkerton would be asleep somewhere within. Foole set his hands flat on the cold pigeon-stained granite and studied the unlit windows, the marble columns vanishing up into the night. No part of him believed the man had thrown

Charlotte from the bridge. Pinkerton was not that man whatever he was, whatever his acquaintance with violence. All
around Foole stirred the sleeping figures of the ragged poor,
shifting, coughing, and for a long time he stood among them
like a visitant lost to shadow. After a time he heard a faint whistling, the scrape of shoes on the frosted cobblestones. Out of
the mists came three men, dissolute in evening clothes, silk hats
dangerously askew. Arm in arm with walking sticks folded up
under their elbows and a stink of gin in their clothes. One
would swing out his stick and strike the soles of the beggars in
their sleep as he went and the taller of the three tipped his hat
and winked at Foole as he passed.

Foole watched them go, his breath steaming. Then he
detached himself from the darkness and turned and walked
quietly away.

TEN

So Shade was real, had lived.

William stared trembling at the fog in Great Scotland Yard, thinking this. A fury was rising in him. If Sally Porter had known Shade in the war, had driven him in a creaking waggon through the backwoods of Virginia, then she had lied boldly and decisively. She had called Shade a figment, a madness. Perhaps, he thought, she wished only to save him from an inherited delusion. Perhaps she protected yet some secret his father had kept. William waited as the carts and omnibuses passed in the wet then crossed the road and continued on his way. No. His father had once believed Shade dead and whatever had changed his mind Sally was likely privy to. All at once William slowed and stopped and stood very still in his chesterfield with his fists bare and he stared at his shoes, remembering. In that first Christmas after the Confederate defeat his father had stood at the head of the table while the turkey cooled on their plates and he had raised his glass and drunk a toast. The great mahogany table gleaming, the dishes shining in the candlelight, his mother's round sad face upturned. It was the first time William saw his father drink wine. His father dabbing a napkin to his moustaches sombrely.

The toast had been to the fallen in the war. A long list. William had sat feeling his leg throb, watching his father. He had not known most of the names, recognized only a few. Mr. Lincoln, of course. Pryce Lewis. The spy Timothy Webster.

And the last in that litany, William recalled suddenly, watching a carriage creep through the fog, its side lanterns swaying, had been a boy named Edward.

He made his way along Haymarket in the rain to a scruffy Indian dining-house above a tailor's shop. He stood in the wet and peered up the stairwell at the crooked risers and old wormy wood handrail and then he wiped at his face and made his slow way up. It was a place he had found in his second week in London and he took a seat by the window and ordered a curry, a pint of bitter. On the table stood an ancient oil lamp that looked to have not been cleaned in decades. From somewhere came a clatter of dishes and when he lifted his face he saw the brass rail of the bar, shining, he saw a slice of afternoon light shivering in a drained glass smudged by greasy fingers. He looked away.

He was thinking of that autumn night in his twelfth year when he had first seen Sally Porter. The lantern casting its eerie crooked light across the kitchen, his mother unwinding slow roll by roll the stained cotton bandaging Sally's face. She had caught her face on a thorn of barbed wire twelve days out while fleeing a pack of dogs and opened the flesh in a ragged draw across her forehead and down her cheek. William remembered the low crooning of his mother as she worked in the gloom. He had been standing at the window with two fingers at the drapes to keep them shut. On a kitchen chair, the brown bandages in their coils like onionskin. The calmness in Sally's eyes. That steady gaze. While his father moved stealthily through the house collecting blankets for the others hiding in the barn.

He rubbed a wrist against his lips in distaste. So Sally had said nothing of the real Edward Shade, the man who had died in the war. If Shore were to be believed, then it was a thing she must have kept from him deliberately. He knew he owed him nothing and whatever debt she had owed his father she and Ben had paid back tenfold. Yet he had always believed both Porters friends to his father and he believed this still. He wondered what sort of anger must be in her and then he changed his mind and decided it was not anger. If Sally had told him his father had hunted a ghost, the reason for it would be rooted in kindness. *Or is that just what you want to believe?* he heard Margaret's sly voice in his head. In the street below he saw a man in a frock coat and bowler emerge out of the weak fog, walking fast in the drizzle. It was this which drew his attention. Walking fast, then halting, glancing about with a keen unsettled air, then walking on.

As he rounded the corner the man passed a slender woman with the fur collar of her cloak wrapped tight and William paused, leaned forward, rubbed the cuff of his jacket against the filthy pane. She was standing very still at the corner with her head down and her gloved fingers interlaced before her and the wide blue sculptural flora of her hat obscuring her face. Through the glass he watched her lift one pale hand to tuck a strand of dark hair under her hat and then she raised her face and stared directly at him in the window and even at that distance he knew her.

Son of a bitch, he whispered.

It was Charlotte Reckitt.

She held his gaze a long impossible moment. Then turned and slipped away around the corner and was gone. He could feel the blood loud in his ears and he blinked his eyes in confusion. He did not understand how it could be so and he frowned and absently rubbed his palm where the dirt of the city had seamed it black and then he turned his hand and saw the backside of it nigrescent with soot and he stopped. He thought about it. He had been sleeping badly. She might have been a ghost. But he got up from the table all the same and dumped a fistful of coppers down and banged his way back down the stairs and out into the cold.

She had been walking north up Haymarket and he went grimly in that direction but he did not see her where the thoroughfare met Jermyn Street. A costermonger arranging a bucket of wizened apples at his stall gaped when William materialized out of the fog.

He took the man's arm in a hard grip. A woman in a cloak, he said. Wearing a blue hat. Which way did she go?

The costermonger pulled back out of his grip, confused.

William had passed the mouth of an alley some twenty paces earlier and he turned, ran back. A beggar woman crouched just within in a squaddle of rags and William flashed tuppence to her between two knuckles.

A woman in a blue hat, he said, breathing hard.

She eyed the coin with a haunted gaze, nodded. Muck dripped from a water pipe to the left of her head.

Cor, she muttered. A jill what walks queer? Inky hair?

He gave her the coin and it vanished into her clawed fist, into her rags. She nodded a sharp chin down the alley where it disappeared around a crooked joining. Crowds of children huddled on the back stairs of the tenements barefoot and coughing.

Faces turned to watch him as he went. The alley twisted at the cutthroat's curve and doubled back and as he passed a gated courtyard on his left a rust-coloured mongrel hurled itself at the bars, barking. The alley opened out onto Panton Street and William stood a moment in the fog then saw a young crossing sweeper huddled in the cold with his straw broom tucked up under him. The child was shoeless and had wrapped old newspapers around his feet and tied them off with string at the ankles. He took the penny William offered and pointed across the street to a second alley.

Where does that come out? William asked.

Coventry Street, sir.

Where on Coventry?

The boy coughed a wet cough, his eyes glassy with the cold. Next the sweet shop, sir, he said.

William dug into his pocket and handed down a pound. The boy stared at it in astonishment.

He stepped out into the street and hailed a passing cab and told the driver to take him around the block to the sweet shop on Coventry Street.

That be Madame Froissard's what sells them chocolate ele-phants, sir?

I guess so.

Right you are, sir.

Be fast about it.

He understood two things from what had happened so far. The first was that the woman he was following knew the streets well and the shortcuts through. If it was not Charlotte Reckitt then it would be some other denizen of that world who did not fear the city's darker passages. No lady would seek them out even in daylight. The second was a suspicion that this woman, whoever she was, was leading him to some purpose.

The hansom doubled back to Froissard's purple and yellow awning and frosted window displays and William watched from across the street but he saw no sign of the woman. At the alley he got down and told the driver to wait.

Two news vendors were quarrelling on the footway and a small crowd had gathered. William drew an elderly man aside. He wore a battered top hat wrapped round with a strap of flypaper and dead flies attached and he was carrying a satchel of wares.

Catch em alive, sir, the man grinned. He was missing his four front teeth.

A woman in a blue hat, came out of the alley, William said. Black hair, cloak, fur collar.

The old man nodded his grey whiskers eastward down the street.

William muttered his thanks and crossed in the traffic and got back into the hansom and told the driver to go slowly. He knew she could not be far from him now. He told the driver the colour of her hat and what to look for and his eyes scanned the shopfronts as they passed.

Steppin out on ye, is she? the driver said.

Something like that.

Me missus ever step out on me, the driver grinned, I'd break her fingers. Ever last one.

At the corner of Leicester Square he got down again and approached an omnibus stop and asked a lady under an umbrella if she had seen the woman.

I'm afraid I only just missed the omni, she said. Perhaps your friend was on it?

He nodded. He thought a moment and then he ducked back into the hansom as the driver hoisted the reins over William's hat and he told the driver to catch the omnibus. They were off fast and pushing through the other carts and soon the high swaying housing of an omnibus came into view, the red and white painted advertisements for Tooley's Knife Polish on its sideboards, along the curving stairs to its roof. He could see, very clearly, the silhouette of the woman up top, in the garden seats.

Keep back, he called to the driver. But don't lose it.

The omnibus went along Long Acre until it reached Drury Lane. There it turned south and was lost to sight. When the hansom caught it the woman in the blue hat was just climbing down. Her boots slipped on the wet rungs and her skirts billowed out and she gained purchase and stepped up out of the street muck and scuffed her boots clear then adjusted her hat and set off east on Wych Street.

When he was certain of her direction William instructed the driver to go on past and then got out at the next corner and paid the driver more than he owed.

The driver grinned, tipped his cap. Give her a one for me, sir.

William slipped into the shallow entrance of a building and waited. He could feel the thrum of blood in his temples. A minute passed, then two. And then the woman was there, gliding round the corner of the building, and William stepped out before her.

Hello Charlotte, he said.

The woman stared up in alarm. I beg your pardon, she snapped.

It was not her.

The slack skin at her throat, the pitted cheeks. He shook his head, embarrassed.

Forgive me, he said, I was certain, you looked just like someone—

His voice trailed off. He could see she had been handsome
once. She had black intelligent eyes, long eyelashes. He felt
unsettled, the blood was still high in him, he could feel the earlier shock trembling through him still. London's fogs, its grey
river, the cold and scouring loneliness of its streets, all of this
was getting to him at last. He could feel something, a familiar
darkness, coming up in him.

The hell with it, he muttered.

There was a wrongness about his mistake and that wrongness
he knew was as real as a nickel. You could rub it between a finger
and thumb and make a wish on it.

He was thinking this standing in the cold while the traffic
flowed on over the tenebrous flagstones and the horses snorted
and flicked their tails and all at once he understood what it
was, what had been troubling him. Why he had pursued an
innocent woman through the tangle of London. Why he had
not been sleeping.

Charlotte Reckitt was not dead.

It made little sense. There was a craziness to it that echoed
his father's own obsession with Edward Shade but he could not
shake the conviction. He had trusted his instincts for years now
and because of that had survived great hardship but that was in
a different country, a different world. London's cutthroats and
fogs were making him jittery, making him doubt himself. He
still had not eaten. He walked now back through the fog to a
coffee house he had passed and took a table in the rear and sat
on one of the little wrought iron chairs built for French ladies
with his massive back to the wall and tried to think it through.
A chop was broiling and spitting on the gridiron behind the
counter. The light within was blue through the big glass windows and shadowed as the late afternoon shoppers shuffled past
but the air was warm and William could feel his cold toes begin

to throb as they thawed. If she was still alive there would be something, some clue.

He ate slowly, he wiped his moustache between bites. Perhaps there was some madness in the Pinkerton men. Some lunacy of detection, some impossible pursuit of the dead. Edward Shade, for his father. Charlotte Reckitt, for himself. He closed his eyes, rubbed at his temples, smiled bitterly. His father would have been about his age now when he first began hunting the man Shade.

As he was finishing, a huge shaggy man in a tight-fitting frock coat rose from across the room and approached his table through the cigar smoke.

You'd be Mr. Pinkerton I reckon? he said in a rough voice.

William tensed. Set down his utensils.

The giant blinked slowly and something shifted, flipped over in his eyes. Those eyes were vicious, the eyes of an ex-convict if ever such eyes existed. There were keloid scars stitched across the back of each wrist where they protruded from his sleeves and a lean savage scar at the base of his throat as if he had been garrotted once but lived to tell of it and the top of his left ear had been sliced clear away. He held a dented hat in one fist.

I seen you seated here, sir, an I said to meself, now maybe here's a gentleman willin to listen to a man's account.

Do I know you?

A law-abidin citizen like meself? the giant smiled, shaking his head. I don't see how.

William smiled faintly.

It ain't me what wants to talk, the giant said. It's me employer. Can I sit?

No.

But the giant had already pulled out the chair and sat, his thick thighs upraised, his enormous back bowed forward, his hands interlaced before him in a fair approximation of a peaceable man on a peaceable mission. His voice when he spoke was low and measured as if he were not used to holding his tongue around strangers. It ain't wise now, is it, sayin no without hearin none of the details, Mr. Pinkerton? he said.

William thought of his pursuit through the streets and the speed of it and the near impossibility of anyone tailing him. How did you find me? he asked.

Aw now, it were just chance, the giant shrugged. Just luck, like.

Luck, William said flatly. How long have you been following me?

The giant raised an eyebrow.

You're not English.

It don't matter what I am. Me employer has a regular interest in meetin with you. He has a proposal for you.

Why isn't he here himself?

He's grievin, he is. An he don't see as how he can trust you yet.

William studied the man's scarred visage and grunted. I'd say he probably can't. Grieving over what?

Charlotte Reckitt.

William leaned forward, interested. He adjusted the brim of his top hat as if he were outside in the weather and he pushed his plate clear and dropped a few coins onto the tablecloth. What's your name? he said.

Me employer's name is Foole, he said. You ain't like to know him neither.

That's not what I asked.

Me own name ain't important.

The giant was still seated with one enormous hand splayed on his thigh in easy reach of a weapon should any be concealed under a coat wing and William watched him. Then he got to his feet. Something in it did not feel right.

I'm not interested yet, he said. You can tell your Mr. Foole that.

Yet?

Yet. And he pushed his way past and through the panelled doors. The sudden rush of cold air came at him with a shock, the roar of the street.

The giant caught him at the cab stand outside.

Mr. Pinkerton.

William turned his face away, spat into a foam-flecked puddle in the street. In the early years he had been approached often by thieves and cutthroats proposing some business arrangement and he had not trusted them then and he did not trust this now. A gelding with grey socks lifted its head, rolled a big eye in their direction. A driver in patched woollens came out of the pub across the street and saw them and started across.

There's been talk, like. About that night on Blackfriars.

I'm sure there has been.

Talk, like maybe she didn't jump.

I don't give a damn what the flash world is saying, William said. He turned and climbed up into the hansom and shut the door sharply. Don't find me again.

But the giant leaned in, his head level with William's own. Where he gripped the door eight enormous fingers imprinted into the velvet lining. The cab creaked under his weight. You're paid up at the Grand Metropolitan until the end of the month, the giant said in a low voice. An it ain't the Agency payin the tab neither. You come here on your own time followin Charlotte Reckitt an wantin to know about Edward Shade. We got no wish to pry into your affairs, like—

The driver scrambled up into his perch behind, the hansom swayed. Guv? he called down.

—but you was called away by Mr. Shore the morning a jill's head were pulled out of the soup. An you seen it for yourself.

William watched the tight grey skin around the giant's eyes crease in the cold. The wiry black hairs of his beard, the grey interleaven there. He could see the brown teeth when the man grimaced.

Step away, he said. Driver, he called.

It be worth your while to listen.

Driver!

He can pay.

I'm not for hire. If your employer wants a detective, tell him to find an English one. He kicked at the door of the hansom, as if at a dog. Now get. Go on.

The giant flinched but did not move. Me Mr. Foole, he's got information about Charlotte Reckitt. Information what maybe you might find of interest, now.

Your Mr. Foole does.

Aye.

William had one hand on the upper strap of the cab. What information?

You can ask him that yourself.

What does he want in return?

Well he don't expect somethin for nothin, now. Will you meet with him?

William glanced off and then back up at the huge man. You tell your Mr. Foole when I want to talk to him I'll find him myself. He started to turn away and then he paused. Carts rattled past, crowds went on their way. Follow me again, he murmured, almost gently.

The giant released his grip on the door.

What he had meant by that last and what the giant had understood was: *You just tell me which fingers you want me to break first and I'll oblige.*

ELEVEN

Foole watched Fludd bang in through the kitchen door and swing a stiff knee out and straddle the chair next to Molly with his wet boots squeaking and when she shoved playfully at his shoulder he looked at her and she stopped.

Did it not go well? she asked.

O well enough, Fludd muttered. If you'd call climbin into a bearpit an pokin the beast in the balls without gettin ate well enough. He had both elbows folded miserably over the chair back and his chin rested upon it. Pinkerton don't take kindly to bein followed, Mr. Adam, he said. You know me thoughts. You take a cutter in your pocket if you still mean to talk to the bastard.

Molly snorted.

Foole fixed a sober eye on the giant, dripping, sullen. He'll meet with me then?

Fludd's nose was wet from the weather and he swiped at it, his knuckle folded into a handkerchief. Then from a plate on the table he took a biscuit in his teeth and two in each hand and he got to his feet. O he'll meet with you, Mr. Adam, he glowered. That ain't the problem.

After he was gone upstairs Molly gave Foole a grin. Poor old Jappy, she murmured. William Pinkerton don't scare me none.

Foole regarded her where she sat, her little fists balled, her legs under the table swinging.

He should, he said sharply.

———

He followed Fludd upstairs to the converted bathroom off the second-floor landing and found the man with his arms aspraddle deep in the cast-iron tub. The tiled floor was not cold but still steam was rising in sinister curls from the grey water around the giant's up-folded knees. Foole entered, picked a towel from a chair, sat. A low fire was burning in the grate. He watched Fludd pour from shoulder to chest to shoulder a carafe of hot water with his face turned away and Foole crossed his legs and he waited.

At last Fludd swore and glared in his direction. Go on then, he rumbled. Go on an say it. The meat of his arms shook, his beard trailed a dripping black knot of scum.

Tell me you don't think he would be effective, Foole said.

Pinkerton?

Of course Pinkerton.

The giant scowled, splashed. I'd like to grow me own pair of tits to play with too, he said, lifting his soft pink breasts in a weird gesture. Don't mean I should. Pinkerton's as like to roll you an you end up in a six-by-six as anythin else. He's dangerous, he is.

He certainly is.

Fludd looked at him suspiciously. Wiped water from his eyes with his fingers. Don't you go agreein with me now, he said. When he moved, a sheet of bathwater overpoured the tub, slicked out over the tiles. It's bloomin crazy, hirin a jack like that. I don't give a fig what kind of a detective he is. He'll check into anythin you sign before he starts to work for you.

I don't intend to hire him.

It's right bloody crazy as a bat in a barrel.

I don't intend to hire him, Foole said again, louder. He could smell the tarry stink of the man's bathwater, like a thing dredged up from the privy. But Pinkerton is tireless, he went on. You know his reputation. If he wants to find Charlotte's killer, he will.

Fludd was quiet, brooding.

He has all of the resources of the Yard open to him, Japheth. I don't see as how we can't manage it.

Manage it? Foole said sharply. We're not killers, Japheth.
We're not so inclined. I learned a long time ago that violence
is not my talent.

But it's Pinkerton's?

Foole studied his old friend. Yes, he said quietly. I believe
it is.

You sure that's all what this is about? Him bein effective?
Fludd stood and a greasy grey water poured steaming from him
and he rose huge and scoured and ferocious in the weak light.
A rug of black hair on his belly, whip scars cross-hatching his
thighs, an enormous red cock swaying between his legs. There
were rough prison-made tattoos Foole had not seen before tracing his shoulders and collarbone. The giant squelched from the
tub and took the towel Foole held out to him and began to rub
himself vigorously, his eyes fixed on Foole's the while.

I got me own talents, he growled.

I know you do.

You'll end up a victim of them Pinkertons yourself. There's
nothin you can tell him that he'll take as truth, we both of us
know it.

Well.

Tell me. What is it might induce Mr. William bloody
Pinkerton to work this angle for you? He don't want blunt, he
were clear on that.

Foole rubbed at his eyelids, frowning. I'll offer something
he wants more.

More than the truth? What would that be?

What do any of us want?

Fludd twisted his head, corked water from one ear with the
towel. O that's right easy, he grimaced. Whatever we can't have.

You ever hear tell of the Saracen? Fludd said later, calmer, seated
in front of a fire in the Emporium's backroom. The curtains
were drawn, the room dim.

Foole stirred his tea, considering. Lived down in Wapping?

Aye, in the tunnels, under the arches there. Six, seven years back. Big bugger, face all disfigured, like. You could see teeth through his cheek an nothin but holes where his nose ought to of been. Fludd ran a palm over his slicked hair, he cracked an eye, as if to gauge Foole's expression. Story goes, fought in the Crimea, come back with his face all tore up. Ladies was like to faint if they caught sight of him. He gone down to live under Roberts Street or thereabouts where he could disappear. Fludd gave him a dark look. He were a specialist, like. Worked the flash lay an got so he could pick an choose his kills. He wouldn't never look in your eyes, only sort of at the face around them. Like he were seein the meat an bone underneath. Pinkerton does it the same. You never met with him, the Saracen I mean?

Foole shook his head no, he dropped a rock of sugar into his cup. The tea glunked.

I never give him a thought, not in years. But just hear me out. This jack, this Saracen, it were sort of his calling card, cuttin off a head an floatin it.

There are a dozen reasons a head gets floated, Foole said.

Aye. Thing of it is, Charlotte Reckitt used to know the bastard.

Foole paused, the teacup at his lips.

I seen them together, down at Finchie's, years back. Word was, Saracen was a regular on Charlotte Reckitt's crews, she hired him for months at a time. When I get to thinkin what happened to her—

You think it was someone in the flash.

I don't doubt Charlotte Reckitt known the jack what killed her.

Foole frowned. The Saracen wasn't in the habit of leaving parts of his kills in sacks around the city. Unless I remember the stories wrong.

He didn't leave his kills nowhere. The bodies weren't never located. Fludd cleared his throat. When we was in New York, Molly told me a story old Mrs. Sharper an her sister used to tell to their dippers. To keep them in line, like. Story bout a regular customer even old Sharper's sister was frightened of. This was all years before Molly were born. Sharper called the customer the Grindbones, like in the children's rhyme. Him what cuts off the heads of the wee ones. Except this monster were real. Used to come round to Sharper's at night, lurk in the alley, watchin the windows. He only ever come for one girl, French Anne, an older girl. Molly says he were sweet on her like a cat with a cornered rat, an her right back at him. She took a knife to his good cheek one time she reckoned he were messin with another girl. Good as married, them two was.

You think she was talking about the Saracen.

It ain't just me thinkin it. Rumour is Charlotte Reckitt rolled the Saracen out of his share on a job one time, an the two of them parted ways in a ugly fashion. An it weren't no secret his fortunes took a downturn after that. When I were askin around I heard it from two different lads, this.

The flash world's talking about this?

Black luck travels fast, Mr. Adam. It's no wonder, when one of their own gets diced. Even a jill what retired from the flash years back. There's still those remember her name.

Foole gave him a long level look. The man would be what, sixty, sixty-five now? Is he even still alive?

The giant shrugged.

You're serious about this.

It don't strike me as unlikely, now.

Foole took a long slow sip of his tea. I'm listening, he said.

Fludd nodded soberly, he beetled his eyebrows low. A jack can keep a grudge a long time, Mr. Adam. I know it. An given what all the bugger suffered after your Charlotte boiled him, an his French Anne got the rot an were sent down from Sharper's? If I were the bastard, I'd date me misfortune to Charlotte Reckitt. An I'd be angry enough to want to rectify me troubles.

Foole ran a soft finger over the rim of his saucer. The house around them was hushed. That was a long time ago, he murmured. Why would he wait this long?

You ain't no stranger to long grudges yourself, Fludd said.

An here's me point. Maybe you don't need Pinkerton. If you was to locate a person knew the Saracen back then—

You mean the whore.

French Anne, aye. I were thinkin maybe if Molly were to ask around, like, maybe just inquire of old Mrs. Sharper an her sister. See if they known where the girl got to.

Foole stared at his friend. I can't ask Molly to do that, he said.

Aye, you can.

You don't understand. Matters didn't end well between those two.

Fludd shrugged his bulk. Suit yourself.

Foole stared into the grate where the coals pulsed and glowed with an unholy heat, turning the teacup in his hands. After a time he glanced down, the brown leaves drifting together, silting apart as in some weird latticing of fate. There was a little boy, Peter, he murmured. Four years old. He and Molly worked the crew together, he was like a brother to her. When she went back for him he was gone, the sisters had sent him down into the streets. Dead by then, I'd guess.

Footsteps approached in the corridor outside, passed, were gone.

She'd never go back. Not to Sharper's.

Aye she will, Fludd growled. If it's you doin the askin, she will.

In the evening he drifted upstairs to her bedroom, its door ajar. It was a narrow room wallpapered and dim with an in-cut gabled ceiling and under the slope she lay, blankets rucked up around the small of her back. A small green Arabian lamp was burning on her bedside table. Pressed flat before her was a rough paper excitement novel, the printing blurred and poor, the pages tissue-thin, and Foole watched her where she lay, this small creature with her broken past whom he loved, her cruel mouth that would pout or smile slyly, concealing the long teeth. She did not know herself yet, did not know the beauty that was coming. It would be a thing she would wake late to one morning

and never not know again. In the bedclothes next to her he saw
the chipped doll's head she had stolen from the girl on the
steamer, its glass eye staring at the ceiling, and he felt a pain in
his throat so fierce it seemed he could not breathe. When she
glanced up startled from her page he felt the living force of her
like a current that could pull a man under and close over his
head and leave no trace of him behind.

You just goin to lurk there like a bloody rampsman? she
said.

He had a hand on her door frame. He started to ask it and
then he could not. He said, instead, I'll be going out later.

She lifted herself onto one elbow. To Sharper's?

He stared at her.

A sly look, her eyes darkening. You like to catch flies, your
mouth hangin open like that.

I guess Japheth told you?

She grinned. He maybe said a little somethin bout it. It's
okay. It's a long time since I were frightened of them two, Adam.

Well.

An look at your luck, now. She gave him a pointed look. I
ain't busy this night neither.

He watched her there with the lamplight playing across her
eyelashes thinking the very opposite and feeling an old sadness
startle, bat-like and crooked, in his heart. I wasn't going to ask
it, he said.

I know you wasn't, she said.

They were the last of five half-blind sisters famously beautiful
once and none of whose husbands had survived their wedding
nights. The two youngest had been hanged as poisoners in
1862 and the second-born had been taken by the cholera before
that. Mrs. Sharper's fingers had been cut from her hand for
dipping in her own childhood and she had fashioned at considerable expense wooden replicas which she screwed into
the stumps and wore ungloved. All had emerged like a brood

of rats from the murk and filth of Wapping in the year of the Great Exhibition but remained denizens of that world with names still feared among the miserable and the destitute thirty years on. They had commanded a fleet of child dippers two dozen strong once but as their eyesight failed they had gradually conceded to fate and were now out of the trade. In her first year free Molly would wake crying and creep to Foole's bed in her pale nightgown and he would pull aside the covers and allow her in. She had been six years old then, dreaming she had forgotten the labyrinthine way back to their house. Do you want to go back to them? he would ask her, stroking her hair, confused. Do you miss them? And she would turn, mumbling, and sigh, already asleep, and have no memory of it in the morning.

Foole watched her now as they went, remembering. When their cab would go no farther Foole and Molly got out and made their way through dripping courts and under arches and down rickety stairs in the foul offing of the Thames. At last they stopped at a nondescript door, its white paint long since peeled into strips, and Foole stepped forward and knocked.

The door opened at once. An ancient sailor with powerful shoulders and tattooed knuckles leered out. A crutch was tucked up under one arm. His head was smooth as a shilling and shining in the faint light and where his left knee had once been his trouser leg was slack, pinned into place. When he caught sight of Molly something in his face opened, twisted up.

That ain't you now, birdie? he whispered. What you doin back?

We've come to talk to the sisters, Foole said. We'd like to speak with Mrs. Sharper.

Let us in, Curtains, said Molly.

After a moment the man grunted, limped aside. Shut the door behind them and locked it and squinted one last time out the peephole at the courtyard and then led them crookedly through. The house was dim, drafty, cold. There was a staircase leading up into darkness and a doorway just beyond that and from somewhere in the walls a high faint laughter came to them. At the drawing room the man Curtains called in loudly to announce them and then he took his leave. A single lamp with a rose shade was burning a sickly light and Foole waited for his eyes to adjust. He could smell sweat, an odour of pickled herring, cut daffodils from a vase on a pier table. Molly brushed against his side in the dimness and slowly his eyes distinguished the furnishings, the drapery, the pianoforte in its felted skirts. On an ottoman under a standing clock lounged a girl, soft, languid, not fifteen, staring at Foole with dull eyes. Then some huge thing thick and ancient stirred in the far shadows and then a cushion creaked in a different corner of the room and the girl turned her face dreamily between the two.

Leave us, a voice murmured.

The girl rose, her neckline dipping across her breasts, her gown faltering over one shoulder, her hair waterfalling across her face. The door shut behind her. A heavy silence descended.

Our guests must excuse us, sister, a second voice called softly. We can offer them nothing.

Slowly a seated figure materialized. Foole could see darkness pooling in cadaverous cheeks, clawlike fingers clutching the low armrests, chin upraised and listening. It turned its face sightlessly.

They are surprised, sister, it whispered. They see how we suffer.

They did not think the disease would have advanced so.

They did not think, sister.

Across the room then a second figure stirred so that the lamplight caught the horror of her blindness also. There were livid red scars at her eye sockets where the surgeons' knives had failed her. Skin white with powder, hair in an artful tangle. She wore an old-fashioned blouse with bone buttons and a high collar at the throat, a blanket across her legs. She was laying out a hand of solitaire on a table at her elbow, eerily running her fingertips lightly over each card as she turned it. Foole knew her at once.

You have brought your Mr. Foole to us, birdie, Mrs. Sharper murmured, her face turning from side to side. Twisting a card in her fingers. Or has he brought you? He cannot wish us to buy you back?

He don't, Molly whispered.

It was the first words she had spoken and now the sisters shivered and turned as one in her direction. Mrs. Sharper laid aside her cards.

O birdie, there you are, she said.

Foole felt his skin prickle. Molly had stiffened beside him and he put a hand on her hair and started to shake his head and then realized the pointlessness of it. We'd like to ask you about a customer, he said. A man who used to come here. He let his glance take in the shabby drawing room, its draped mantel, the blackened grate where no fire had burned in days. We're sorry to disturb you. We'll compensate you for your trouble, of course.

He wants to know about a customer, sister.

Who is he to ask, sister? We do not disclose details.

Not to him.

Only to relations, sister. Only to our own blood.

Molly gave Foole a veiled look. I weren't never your blood, she said. I were your property. You sold me.

Into a happier situation, child. You are happy now, yes? When Molly said nothing the old woman murmured, You see.

O how she wounds us, sister. Is that what she came for? To wound us?

Molly shrugged angrily out of Foole's hand. I come to ask after the Grindbones, she said. Not for nothin else.

Mrs. Sharper raised her ravaged face. The Grindbones, she murmured.

Molly picked up a small brass paperweight of the Crystal Palace, turned it absently in her fingers. He were acquainted with one of your dippers. We was told you might know where she gone to.

Put that down, Mrs. Sharper said coldly. Touch nothing.

We have had many dippers, child.

Her name were French Anne. You maybe remember her. You cut her face so she weren't able to work an you sent her down into the docks.

The thinner sister was tilting her face in the shadows as if to catch some scent. You talk to us about cutting, child? You who cut that poor boy?

What boy?

Peter.

I never cut Peter. I loved him.

And yet you left him. That was the cruellest cut of all. You went with your precious Mr. Foole and left him alone. Poor, thieving Peter. How he cried when you did not come back for him.

Peter weren't a thief, Molly said.

O but he was, child.

Incorrigible and corrupted, he was.

He weren't a thief. You sent him down into the streets even though you knew he weren't able to make his way. He weren't even six years old.

We asked him to return what he had stolen, the thinner sister murmured. He declined.

He left us to go with you, Mrs. Sharper said. He said he would find you, you would take care of him. What could we do?

He did not find you, child?

Molly was silent.

Come here, birdie. Mrs. Sharper held out her ruined hand. Let me see you. Even in the eerie light Foole could see the wooden fingers screwed into their stumps. She held forth that hand a long moment in silence as if to touch the ineffable and then she drew it back, and it disappeared into murk and gloom. Molly started to drift towards her.

Molly, Foole said sharply.

But she only gave him a vague distracted glance and continued on. He understood some private exchange was playing itself out, something rooted in hurt and fury and even, somehow, love. Molly kneeled down at the woman's feet and raised her face and Mrs. Sharper passed a hand slowly, methodically, across. The grey fingers crept like spiders over her eyelids.

How you have grown, birdie, she whispered. Such delicate features. You will be a beauty yet.

Molly opened her eyes. Her expression was unmoved.

Two long fingers under her chin, tilting her face upward. And what is it your Mr. Foole wants with Jonathan Cooper, child?

Foole held his breath. He had been staring at Molly, at something in her face which she could not strangle. Cooper, he said now, turning the name over in his mouth. Jonathan Cooper.

What have you told him, birdie? That Cooper had no face? Might your Mr. Foole want him for his particular talents, or has he offended in some fashion? Ah, yes, there it is. He has offended you. Her nostrils flared as she took a long slow deep breath and then her creeping hands fell still. It is true what you have heard, birdie, she continued. We had some sight yet when he used to come here, we remember him. We could see his teeth through a hole in his cheek. Grinning as if there were some joke in it all. But his eyes were awful, black all through, always weeping. O it was not tears. He was as big as a horse, but his back was twisted so that he could not stand straight. He came for Anne in the small hours of the night. He used to run a finger over her ear and whisper to her in his rough Italian.

Italian? said Foole.

Mrs. Sharper ignored him.

He never conducted any violence, sister, the thinner one called across. Not on yourself and not on any of our girls. But the two of them would quarrel so—

Such a fierce creature, Anne was. So jealous.

A jealous whore, sister.

Foole rubbed a damp palm on his trouser leg. His tongue felt thick, the bad air of the parlour oozed around him, made his thoughts sluggish. The stories they told you, he interrupted, speaking to Molly. About the Grindbones, what he would do to the littlest ones, what they protected you from. Ask them—

Ask us what.

Foole cleared his throat.

He doubts the truth of them, sister.

Their truth? Mrs. Sharper waved her ravaged hand at the darkness. The truth that is found in a story is a different kind of truth, but it is not less real for being so. We had always known the truth of Mr. Cooper's nature.

O we knew what he was, sister.

As did Anne.

As did Anne. That is why she left us, sister.

She never left you, Molly said. She was staring at the old woman with a fascination Foole did not like the look of. She never left. You sent her away.

We caught her stealing from us, birdie. We had no choice but to ask her to leave. We could not keep a thief.

Foole cut his tongue along his teeth as if to sharpen it. He withdrew two five-pound notes from his pocket and stepped forward and set them down in front of Mrs. Sharper on the card table. I should like very much to find French Anne, he said coldly. I should like to speak with her.

The banknotes disappeared into Mrs. Sharper's right fist and she clutched them to her chest and started to trace her thumb around their edges. There came a rustling as the banknotes vanished into her blouse.

The thinner sucked sharply at her teeth. Is it, sister?

It is.

Very well. You wish to find French Anne, Mr. Foole? Look for her under the lime.

The lime pits? he said. Is she dead then?

Mrs. Sharper glared a slow smouldering glare. French Anne is dead, yes, she said. But the woman who used to be her is not. She lives yet.

He stared at the old woman's clouded pupils and then she turned her face towards him and he felt the hairs prickle along his neck. She was looking at him. It was not possible and yet it was so.

She works the sewer mouths south of Blackfriars, Mrs. Sharper hissed. Lives as a mudlark in the cubbies. They call her Muck Annie now. She never comes up from the tunnels. Or so we are told.

The berserkers, sister.

Mrs. Sharper grunted and shifted her bulk. Foole could hear the click of her wooden fingers on the armrest. The tunnels are punishing, Mr. Foole, she murmured. No one survives them for long. They are the haunt of the berserkers now, even the police fear to go below. The berserkers will tear a man to pieces and leave him as feed for the rats merely for the pleasure of it.

Foole steadied the slender walking stick in his grip. How will I know her? he asked.

The scars.

Yes. Mrs. Sharper waved her ruined hand in the darkness before her face. Here, and here, she said. She drew her thumb in a long crescent from each corner of her mouth up her cheeks to her ears.

And the man Cooper? Is he with her?

Now the thinner shrugged slyly. It has been fifteen years, Mr. Foole. Our Grindbones was useful in frightening the little ones, nothing more. She turned her baleful face from side to side. In this life the lost stay lost, she said. And Mr. Cooper was always among the lost.

The dead do not come back, sister.

Is that not so, child?

Both lifting their faces as one and searching with their milky eyes in the gloom.

Child?

Birdie?

Is it not so?

Into the afternoon of the next day he slept. He dreamed an eyelash of light hovered beside his daybed and then it turned and lengthened and grew and when it bent over him he saw that it was a child. It bore wings of a burning light but its face was shadowed and he feared to look into it. *What is it?* he asked but the child only lifted one hand and pointed at his heart.

He awoke with his heart hammering. His shirt was damp on his chest and his left arm numb where he had rolled onto it and he got up still shaken. He splashed his face with cold water at the basin and dried himself and studied his eyes in the pier glass. He did not know them. Then he changed his collar and fetched his frock coat and went down the stairs to the Emporium. He found Fludd bowed over the rolltop desk beside the window working at some correspondence and he had the man go out into the weather and hail a hansom. He leaned into the fog as he descended the front steps to the street and as he stepped up into the cab it shuddered under his weight and he reached around and banged on the roof and called out his destination. They rode smoothly through the fog and it seemed to Foole as they went that the fog had no end.

At the door of the mortuary an assistant with a stutter met him and led him inside. His pinched mouth, black gums, the dirt in the wrinkles around his red eyes. They passed down a narrow corridor and through a heavy door into the underground itself without speaking and when the man leaned in close to hold the door open Foole could smell the gin in his apron. The assistant handed him a bull's-eye lantern with the shutter half closed and gestured him deeper.

Then the man vanished back the way they had come.

There were bodies laid out on metal tables along either wall and Foole went past them without a glance. Shapes rose up and disappeared in the shadows. He went quietly. It was not his first time among the dead.

At the far end against a brick wall weeping in the cold he found a row of cabinets. He set the lantern rattling upon a stained table and approached the tallest of the cabinets. He could hear the rasp of his shoes on the stone floor, the rustle of his coat.

The cabinet was not locked. The metal doors shivered and banged loudly as he unlatched them and the sound ricocheted off into the gloom. The upper shelf was filled with files loose in their boxes and the second and third shelves with jars of varying sizes their shadowed contents adrift within like deformed castings from Tussaud's waxworks and then on the lowest shelf he saw what he had come for.

It was a big tank, too heavy for him to move, filled with a coalescing darkness as if some horror floated just out of sight. He did not know at first what he was looking at. And then he saw it, pale, hooded, like a thing dredged from the ocean depths rubbery and reeking and unidentifiable, its wounds puckered and gilling in the formalin like tiny reefed mouths. A woman's torso, umbrageous and adrift.

He stood a long time there and at last reached down and lifted a smaller jar out and set it on the table beside the lantern. He unshuttered the lantern's eye and a cold light poured through its glass walls. He leaned in. A label had been affixed to one curve of the jar with several numbers and letters identifying the remains within. This meant nothing to him. As he turned the glass to see past the adhesive a kind of silt stirred in a slow cyclone in the foggy liquid lit as it was by that lantern and he understood that these were pieces of her that had come off in the formalin. And then slowly, languidly, the head drifted its face towards him.

He did not know her. She was slack, the cheeks belling upward in their floating, her eyes milky and smooth. The head was angled slightly backward from the weight of the brainpan as if to stare at the heavy threaded lid when it had closed and then one temple bumped the edge of the jar as it turned and he watched it, feeling nothing he could put a name to.

They had been two days out from Boston when New Year's Eve overtook the *Aurania* and he remembered standing in the icy night air of the saloon deck and staring through the blazing windows at the passengers laughing and drinking there. The piano hammering out some tune about a sailor and his paddle

all of it vaguely suggestive and ugly. The oblong cuts of light
sliding slantwise across the deck from the big windows. The
blur of evening suits and women in their silks and shawls and
elaborate twists of hair in the French fashion. He had thought
how they all must appear to any eye lurking out there in that
frigid black sea, last and only survivors of some catastrophe
perhaps, how they sailed onward singing and drinking in a light
of their own making while all around them darkness held them
and not a one looked out into it and saw it for what it was. He
remembered peering in through the fogged glass as if through
the wall of some aquarium and catching a glimpse of Molly
where she stood beside a brass globe of the earth with a stem of
crystal clutched in one hand and her face down-turned and how
the music had warpled and thickened in his ears when she lifted
her head. He had raised his hand but she did not respond and
then he had understood. She could see only her watery self
reflected in the glass. How small we are, how blind. How little
we see and how much we are seen.

The head drifted slowly past in its murky yellow keeping.

Charlotte, he whispered. Oh. Charlotte.

And closed his eyes.

TWELVE

William opened his eyes.

His head hurt. It was already noon. The bedding had come loose as he slept and had folded up around his skull like a shroud and he pulled it off and threw it aside in disgust. He could see the smudged soot where his hair had stained it in the night. He rose and dressed and stood by the window a long while, smoking, knowing he would have to return to Sally Porter's tenement though he did not want to go. The fog was thick in the street outside and the day grim and the gaslights had been turned on by the hotel maid before he awoke and then turned off again for the glass was still warm. His thoughts turned to the giant who had accosted him two days earlier and then to the man's growled hint about the ghosted Edward Shade and William frowned and clenched his teeth around the stem of his pipe.

At the narrow writing desk he sat and withdrew a sheet of hotel stationery and unstoppered a bottle of ink and wrote out the following:

Male mid-forties, accent of indeterminate origin. England? Australia? Brown eyes so dark as to look black, black hair black beard. 6'5" approx. 250 lbs approx. Claims employment through a Mr. Fool (any record in files of?), most likely an alias. V. threatening. Speaks rough. Identifying marks several: long scar at throat as if once garrotted. Top of left ear missing. Scars on backs of hands, knuckles: incl a circular burn on left wrist (hot poker? branding iron?). Scar above right eye shape of a star. Has air and look of a career criminal. Likely has served time. Cross-reference with Rogues' Gallery and misc. Identify. Send everything.

He blew on the paper to dry it and read it slowly back to himself and then folded it and sealed it and addressed the envelope to the Pinkerton offices in Chicago. He double-checked the hour and then withdrew a second blank sheet and dipped the pen into the ink and sat with the nib poised over the paper. Then he began a second, more halting letter. *My dear Margaret,* he wrote.

Yes the days here are cold it is the fog I do not care for. You would find it beautiful I think. It is like the paintings you admired so much when we were in New York last spring. Tell the girls the ponies in England are not so fine as what we have back in Chicago it is the bad air and no countryside that stunts them. It looks now like this business will be finished with shortly. All that remains is closing the file and you know how that can go well or ill there is no predicting. I saw Sally Porter last week she is quite ill. Benjamin Porter died before the new year. You will remember Benjamin from my father's stories they were fallen on hard times. I guess it is not easy. Write me when you can. I do not go to sleep without you and the girls beside me. Margaret if I

Here he stopped and wiped the nib dry with a cloth and studied the letter as it dried. It did not say what he wanted to say. It did not ever manage to. There were men with the gift for writing their mind but he would not ever be of their number. He stoppered the ink.

He was thinking of Isabelle his eldest and the long sickness she had suffered that autumn and how he and Margaret had feared for her. She would be eighteen this year. She had been sickly her entire life and the skeletal shift of her wrist bones through her skin left him fearful for her even now. He could remember the green smell of her sickroom and the condensation running down the panes of the glass in the morning light and how he would stand amid her kicked-off blankets and gaze down at her. How helpless he'd felt.

He wanted to write this but could not think how to start. After a moment he crossed out the last of the letter and wrote instead:

You were right. I should not have come.

Then he sat back and stared out the window then folded the letter in distaste and slid it into an envelope but did not seal it. He opened the lowest drawer of the desk. Dropped it in.

Within lay a stack of similar letters addressed and unsealed and all unmailed.

Margaret had come upstairs to his study one night last November after the girls were asleep. William had been seated with the lights off and one big hand open on his desk when she came in. The sycamore outside the window, its naked white branches upraised and the moon in cold profile burning beyond.

What do you aim to do? Margaret had asked him from the doorway.

She was carrying a candle in its saucer and its soft waxy light pulled him back to himself. She came in, set the candle on the edge of his desk among the opened files. Sifted languidly through the papers, the testimony of Charlotte Reckitt, the time sheets and official reports of his father's operatives. She picked up the rogues' gallery photograph.

Is this her? she asked softly.

He nodded. Charlotte Reckitt, he said. My father was certain she could lead him to Shade.

She's pretty.

He felt the blood rise to his cheeks. She's as crooked as my second finger, he said.

And she's in London.

Apparently.

They were silent then and William studied the slim outline of his wife. She was still a beautiful woman. There were owls that hunted from the fence posts of their yard but they were silent now and in the stillness William felt some part of him breaking. He had spoken of Charlotte Reckitt and his father's interest in Edward Shade and Margaret had listened in patience in the months since his father's death but he understood there were limits to compassion. He watched her turn in her night-dress and drift quietly back towards the hall taking the light with her. In the doorway she stopped.

You mean to go to her, Margaret murmured. It was not quite a question. When he said nothing she added, Because your father would have wanted it.

He shrugged uneasily in the candlelight. A sliver of shadow had cast itself knifelike under Margaret's nose and across her lips, giving her a ferocious aspect. He could not make out her eyes.

The hell with your father, she said from the doorway.

It was already late in the day and he knew that he would need to make his way to Snow Fields across the Thames to talk to Sally Porter. He wanted to tell her Shore's account of Edward Shade dying in the war and to hear her explain it. There was little enough sense in it he knew but he did not know what else to do with himself. He should not have slept as late as he had.

He locked his door carefully and made his way down the hall and punched the buzzer for the elevator. He carried his Colt Navy in the pocket of his overcoat. He liked very little about the modern world but he did like its firearms and its railroads and its elevators with their plush benches and fine mahogany detailing. As the cage rattled shut he nodded to the operator and set his hands into his pockets. The operator he noticed was a different young man, one he had not seen before. They did not speak.

In the lobby a familiar figure was lounging under the palm fronds.

Afternoon, Inspector, he said.

Blackwell turned with a start. Mr. Pinkerton, sir, he said. You're awake.

In body at least.

Blackwell nodded. He appeared agitated and shifted his hat from one hand to the other.

What is it? Has John arranged it already?

I beg your pardon, sir?

Don't beg, it's unbecoming. Has Mr. Shore instructed you to take me to Millbank?

Millbank, sir?

William studied him. Blackwell. Why are you here?

It's the legs, sir. They've found them in a sack near Southwark Park. In Bermondsey.

Both of them?

Even as he said it the question disturbed him and he ran a hand along his jaw.

Yes sir, Blackwell said. Both of them.

They went out through the glass doors into the grey after-noon. It felt quiet, dull, eerily empty for the hour and though it was Saturday William wondered suddenly where all of the traffic had got to. After a moment Blackwell returned in a hansom and offered his hand and William climbed grimly aboard.

They travelled across Westminster Bridge, through the toll booths, into the foul warren of Bermondsey. Soap scum frothing in the ditches. Crumbling wooden piles rising out of the green waters. The reeking tannery pits where men in rags stirred with long poles the drenched hides. The warehouses on their creaking wharves, the shabbily dressed children trotting alongside them.

William strangled a yawn, glanced at the man beside him. No jokes today, Blackwell?

No sir. Not today.

How about, Something's afoot?

Blackwell nodded unhappily. Very good, sir.

This will help us to get a leg up? Soon we'll have this in the bag?

Blackwell looked away.

The cruelty in his tone surprised him and he fell silent. The stink had soured in the days since he had last come through here and he watched the low slouching shopfronts and warehouses with a sadness. He thought of Sally Porter in her little room and felt all at once a pain in his abdomen and he winced and pressed a handkerchief to his mouth. He understood Sally had worked for his father almost her entire free life and that she would hold many of his father's secrets in trust and it was churlish of him to resent her for it. William told himself it was not her lack of forthrightness which bothered him so much as the concealing of it but this he knew was not true. The white lead paint on the sills of the buildings had blackened to a tar in the toxic air. There were ditches festering under the slat-board walks and slow mephitic bubbles oozing in the muck and he could see the frozen bodies of dogs twisted and strangled in the weeds. At times the fog would thin and he would glimpse ditches boiling red with the dyes and then the fog would close in again. He imagined Sally sitting very still in her shabby room listening to his footsteps recede down the hall and thinking of young Edward Shade in the war. A figment. A ghost. They turned up Jamaica Road and then up Drummond and they clattered past the huge chimneyed factory of Peek, Frean and Co., an awful sweetness pouring from its ovens into the streets.

The residents call it Biscuit Town, sir, Blackwell muttered.

The pain in his voice baffled William and he said nothing.

The hansom stopped outside an overgrown lot across from a factory with broken windows and a crumbling chimney and William at first thought the place deserted. Then he saw the pale faces in the upper windows gathered there and he studied their merciless curiosity with an interest of his own.

A constable was standing at the corner of the square with his truncheon loose in his fist though the onlookers kept warily off the street. Shopkeepers stood in their doorways with their aprons on and their shirt sleeves rolled each peering out from his respective darkness. The air was close, thick, reeking. The fog was dense. William could make out the skeletal figure of Breck crouching, straightening, moving about in the grey.

Well it's in the afternoon editions, Shore murmured as they approached. His eyes had a brittle shine to them. *Police Deny Knowledge of Head Found in Thames.*

Let me see.

Shore had been banging the rolled newspaper against his thigh with a soft dull thwap. You're in it too.

I hate these things. Too much appears in them that never appears out of them. But he took the paper and unrolled it and scanned the columns as the fog curled between their boots, seethed over the wet earth. SCOTLAND YARD IS ASSISTED IN THESE INVESTIGATIONS BY WILLIAM PINKERTON, CURRENT HEAD OF THE PINKERTON DEFECTIVE AGENCY, OF CHICAGO AND NEW YORK. He looked up. Defective?

Aye.

Don't you have copy editors over here?

Shore smiled a smile of small brown teeth.

Robert will be livid.

Your brother has a temper does he?

William trudged past the chief inspector to the sacking half hidden in the long weeds of the ditch. A temper, yes. It's what makes him such an excellent defective. Anyone touched this yet?

Aye. Dr. Breck, some of the lads when they first arrived.

William kneeled beside the sack and pulled off his gloves and lifted the opening cautiously wide. The legs had been stuffed feet first into the sack and he could see the pale split bone splintering out from the stumps. Something about it was more

terrible in its wrongness than what he had so far witnessed. He
had been to the slaughter yards in Chicago often in his work and
he thought now of the twisting shanks of meat rattling on their
chains in the cold storage and of the quiet chill he felt whenever
he went through. The echo of violence and pain almost like a
sound in those sober warehouses. He closed the bag. The sacking was dry and crusted with blood and it crumpled roughly
under his fingers.

Through the drifting fog he could see the figures of constables working their way over the rutted ground.

He thought of the open sky of the Midwest and the simple
bullet-riddled corpses of the bandits on display in their coffins
on the boardwalks there and of the good clean work of it all.

Well? Shore said. What about it?

William got to his feet, said nothing.

Aye, Shore grunted. Someone went to a regular lot of trouble to dump this.

What, in some weeds? In a ditch?

On the other bloody side of the city, Shore growled. Could
have saved himself the trouble and sunk the legs like he did the
head.

I take it no one saw anything.

Never do. Not in Bermondsey.

You've talked to the residents?

Aye.

William stood with his eyes fixed on the sacking and he
thought about it. How long has it been here?

Shore shook his head. Since morning, Dr. Breck tells me.
The blood's dried on the bag so the legs were stuffed in shortly
after they were cut from the body. But the sack's just cold and
only a little damp on the underside so it wasn't here in the night
when it rained.

And no one saw anything.

As I said. Poor woman.

A squelching of shoes through the soft muck. A sniff. Breck
loomed out of the mist, rubbing his fingers clean in a twist of

handkerchief as if he had just been sifting something foul. There are no footprints near the remains, he said curtly.

There are now, William muttered.

There are, however—and Breck half turned and gestured across a murky ditch thick with grey watercress—several indistinct marks leading back towards the park over there. Most likely from a pair of shoes wrapped in cloth to hide their prints.

What does that tell us? Shore asked.

That the dumping was done by a lone individual, William said quietly.

And that he or she had the foresight to conceal their footprints, Breck continued. Or that their shoes need to be protected from the mud.

She? William said.

Need to be protected? Shore said. Because they're of high quality, you mean?

Breck shrugged.

She? William said again.

Breck was leaning over his trunk and opening the lid and he did not look up as he spoke. Perhaps. It is possible the body was cut up because it was too heavy to dispose of all in a piece. And it is possible the footprints would have given us some important detail about our suspect. Such as a lady's footprints.

Possible, William said. But likely?

Possible, Breck said. He withdrew from his trunk a strange contraption. It appeared to be a bull's-eye lantern but had been outfitted with a complicated series of lenses and refractors and set upon a short handle and when Breck opened its shutter a powerful arc of light zeroed in on the sack. He had taken off his silk hat and he folded his coat over the open lid of the trunk and unhooked his spectacles and then he put on a leather mask with straps that crossed at the nape and buckled together so that a sequence of optical magnifiers on delicate rods could be swung out in front of the eyes. When he glanced up his eyes goggled gruesomely out. He gave a strange sort of leer.

Gentlemen, he said.

Oh for god's sake. Shore put a hand on his hat. You'll make us a sideshow, Dr. Breck.

You are already a sideshow, sir.

William watched him work with interest. The thin man kneeling in the muck. Guiding that dazzling beam of light with one hand inch by inch over the sacking, lifting its edges with a small steel instrument in the shape of a fork with the other. He pried open the mouth of the sack, sniffed at its underlining without disturbing the remains within. After a moment he cocked his head and said, Mr. Pinkerton. Do you know what a collodion slide is?

William frowned. He had no idea.

In the leather box in the trunk, Breck said. You will find a series of glass plates. Bring one to me.

It was a glass plate sticky with some adhesive substance and the doctor took it from him without a word and bent back to his work.

What have you found? Shore asked.

I cannot be certain.

Breck handed William the collodion slide and he held it carefully up and could make out two tiny white insects pressed between the glass.

This sack was not open like this earlier, sir. Has someone interfered with it? I instructed you to let no one near. Must I continually remind your constables what contamination means?

Shore said nothing. William said nothing.

After a moment Breck made a low throaty grunt and leaned in deeper. The hairs on the legs are dark, he said. But you will see, Mr. Shore, here at the very tips of the follicles they appear grey, do they not? Most interesting. Mr. Pinkerton, another slide.

William obliged. The doctor took a second scraping, a third.

After a moment Shore caught William's eye and they stepped back, away from the evidence. I wonder what hour the evening editions make the streets, he said.

William clapped his hands together for the cold. What are you thinking?

This was dropped here this morning. If news of the head was already out it's entirely likely the drop was deliberate.

What do you mean?

I mean maybe it wasn't about hiding anything.

William was silent.

We were supposed to find this bag today.

And it'll be in the papers tomorrow.

Shore nodded. But why in god's name would anyone do this? What's the point? To terrify people? To taunt us?

Maybe to send a message.

A message.

William shrugged. After a moment he said, You'll bury her now I guess.

That might be how you do things in Chicago.

Bury our dead?

Bury the evidence.

I guess so. I guess we're just crazy enough to do that.

She doesn't seem to have any relatives. Other than her uncle. No, we'll keep her out of the ground a while yet.

Until you've got a handle on this?

Or until someone comes forward with a claim to her. Shore ran the water from his forehead with a thumb. It was a wet fog and William could feel the damp seeping through his own coat. I keep meaning to ask, Shore said. The missus has been hoping to have you out at the house for an evening. Our cook makes a rather fine blood pudding.

Blood pudding.

Aye.

If I'm here long enough, he said, I just might brave it. In the fog the cold street looked ghostly. I've got a wife and daughters to get back to, John. And the Agency needs me.

That would be your defective agency?

William smiled.

Sounds like you have two wives, Shore said.

Margaret says it herself.

When Dr. Breck is finished I want you to get this cleared out, lads, Shore said suddenly to two constables at work search-ing the weeds. Be careful with it. Anything might be of use to us. He turned back to William. About Martin Reckitt, he said. Take Blackwell with you on Wednesday and see what you can get out of him. I've got you your hour.

William watched the men at their labours in the mist.

All right, he said.

He made his way back, at last, to Sally Porter's tenement behind Snow Fields.

He had been dreading doing so but wanted to hear her account for herself directly. If Shore's account of the Porters smuggling Shade through Virginia was true, then Sally had lied to him. Had sat shivering across from him in her darkness and lied. He could not think why she would keep such a detail from him except that his father too had done so. He thought again of that toast to the Union dead his father had raised in the year of the war's ending, that sad litany of names, of the boy Edward who completed the list. His father had once, it seemed, believed Edward Shade to have died. Whatever had caused him to doubt it remained a mystery. What was clear to William was that his father had believed it. And his father, whatever else, was never a fool.

The shop windows he passed were dusty in the chill and he could see the vague silhouettes of flypaper and thin strips of grey meat on hooks through the glass. Sally's lie to him, that Shade was never real, might, he thought suddenly, be connected to her knowing some truth about the matter. She might be able to tell him what it was that had so convinced his father of Edward Shade's survival. What secret was she keeping? He walked on over the clattering slat-board walks speaking to no one and ignoring the cries of the beggars from their ditch-side perches. He felt wearied by the discovery of the legs, saddened by the whole shabby business of it. He had thought to make his way to the pubs surrounding the London docks after but as the afternoon waned into evening he understood it would have to wait. After a time he took his bearings and turned left and slipped down a wretched alley and through a broken iron gate into the worm-rotted stairwell of Sally Porter's building. A dog was nosing some wadded rag in the shadow and when he came in it lifted its snout and growled. He stopped and regarded it. Then he turned away. The stairs shuddered under his heavy steps but at the third-floor landing he paused. Her door stood open.

He could see it from where he had stopped. He waited in that cold hallway and adjusted his hat and peered behind him, listening. There were raised voices coming from her room and he frowned and felt in the pocket of his topcoat for his Colt and then he made his slow approach.

It was a family.

Destitute and filthy and squabbling in the chaos.

He stood in the doorway a moment, confused. The old Porter desk had been upturned and pushed against one wall and the cracked elephant stood yet on the mantel above the old fireplace though someone had hung a rag from its trunk to dry.

The woman, girl, mother of that brood had let out a screech and was swatting at one child and then picking up a knife from the table when she saw him and then all fell silent.

Hello, he said, something sinking inside him.

She came at him with a directness and speed that alarmed him. He stepped back though he was thrice her size and well acquainted with knives. She stood in the doorway pushing at the head of a child in her skirts its face all filth and rage.

We ain't payin it twice, she snapped. We ain't payin you neither.

He held up his hands. Where's Sally? he said.

Her eyes narrowed. Ain't you for the rent?

I'm not for the rent.

A green blanket had been strung up on a rope cutting the bed from William's sight and a long low racked cough started from behind it and an elbow bloomed against the blanket and then a man's hoarse voice cried out.

Who is it, Maggs, he called. What do he want?

You got a tongue in your head, you ask him.

She had small sharp shoulders and hands the size of a child's and her reddish hair was filthy and shorn along her scalp where she must have cut it for the money. A flea-bitten child squalled at her thigh, tugged the hem of her dress. Its little knuckles blacked, its little face blacked.

What do he want? the man called again.

He don't want the rent, she hollered, then scowled up at William. Well? What is it?

I'm looking for someone, he said. He fished out a shilling. The woman who used to live here, he said, the old woman, the Negro. What do you know of her? Where did she go to?

Her hand absorbed the coin as if it were water and she tilted a sudden coy glance at him, slid one arm along the door jamb. He saw now she could not be older than sixteen.

You want to come in and talk bout it, mister? she asked. You just come right in, like.

I was here last week, he said. He stepped back and stared down the hallway and then looked at the girl. I talked to her last week. Right here.

Last week, was it.

She never said anything about leaving.

Goddamnit Maggs, the man called from within. Shut that damned door.

You wait, she barked over her shoulder. She peered back up at William with an expression of disgust. Last week's a lifetime ago, isn't it. All we was told was no one got theirselves murdered in here an the rooms was available right away. Never asked no other questions. She were a Negro?

He nodded.

A Negro woman?

He nodded.

Well she ain't hidin in the fireplace an we ain't cooked her an ate her. She shook her head as if giving up on him and started to shut the door.

He put out his hand, held the door fast. She didn't just vanish, he said.

The girl shrugged angrily.

People do, she said.

He came out of the tenement with his hackles prickling as if some shadow watched him through the haze but he could see no one. He took two steps backward into the muck of the street and squinted up at Snow Fields, its broken lightless panes, looking for Sally's window. His entire life he had lived with the knowledge that vanishings were real, that people disappeared. Why it should astonish him now he could not say. He trudged up Tooley Street and at Vine stopped and looked around him, uneasy, the air reeking with the sludge of the river, the buildings leaning crazily out of the fog. Wherever Sally had gone she had left her furniture behind and he did not know if this meant she was dead or had simply lighted out for other lodgings. The hell with it, he thought sharply. It had been years since he had seen her and whatever her love for his father she owed William nothing. There were figures drifting past now at the edges of the buildings but he could not make out their faces. He could not quit himself of a growing dread that some figure lurked there behind him with malice in its heart and he ducked into a small court and crossed it quickly, his soles slipping in the mud. At a gap in the far railing he squeezed through and went down towards Pickle Herring Street and the small iron-walled kiosk of the pedestrian tunnel squatting there like some armoured outpost set over the river. The bridges he knew would still be open to foot traffic but the Tower Subway would be quieter and if he had been followed he would lose his shadow here. He glanced behind him, dipped his head, paid his halfpenny, and went down.

It was a wooden spiral staircase that creaked under his steps and dislodged a fine sifting of dirt as he went. The brick walls were greasy with some filth, the gaslights in their blue globes sickly and dimming as he went deeper, as the air worsened. He came out into a vaulted chamber some fifty feet below the riverbank and stood staring at the round entrance of the iron tube as if staring at the threshold of some otherworld and then he peered back up the shaft of the stairwell to the small eye of light above him. In the tunnel were globe lights affixed naked to the riveted walls and visible from where he stood but even as he stepped through and began his slow walk under the river the air thickened into a grey haze.

The corridor stretched on, eerie in its solitude. Twin rails ran the length, laid once for a cable omnibus now long in ruin.

He could not shake the feeling that he was walking very gradually downhill, deeper into the earth, that the floor was lifting and falling under him like the deck of a vessel in a current. Through the tunnel's iron walls he could hear the heavy thrump of a paddle steamer in the river above. When he looked behind him he could not see where he had set out from and when he turned back he could not see where he was going and that passage in its grey hopelessness seemed to go on forever.

He heard them before he saw them. The crunch of their steps behind him, the huge rustle of their topcoats, a rasping cough. Hearing some purposeful thing in their approach and having known too many footpads to mistake it. He turned, fists bared, and waited. And then, through the haze: two monstrous figures, distorted and indistinct in the gloom, the sepulchral gas hissing behind them.

He did not move and the two figures behind him stopped and he could hear the blood loud in his ears, feel the weight of the river crushing down through the clay.

Show yourselves, he said.

His voice echoing off the length of the tunnel.

The two figures stood in their vague unsettling silence watching him from the haze. Then came a slight crunch of stones on the tiles underfoot and William felt the hairs rise on the back of his neck and he took a step back, knees bent, fists doubled.

Show yourselves, by god.

Mr. Pinkerton, a voice said.

William withdrew his Colt and very deliberately in the long silence of that tunnel he cocked the hammer.

There'll be no violence from us, the man said softly, stepping forward into the light. I assure you of that, sir.

The man who stood before him was small, narrow in the shoulders, thin-throated. His long whiskers were white, startling against his dark skin. He held an expensive silver-tipped walking stick in one hand and tucked a thumb into a satin waistcoat pocket with the other. The line of his mouth under the shadow looked worn, aggrieved, angry with some undefined hurt. William felt a kind of disquiet go through him. He did not put away his revolver.

My name is Adam Foole, the small man said. I believe my manservant spoke with you. If you'll forgive my seeking you out in this fashion—

What do you want?

The same as you, Mr. Pinkerton. To find the killer of Charlotte Reckitt.

William's eyes shifted to the other figure, massive, all stooped shoulder and thigh, his bowler hat crushed up against the ceiling. He knew that one at once. It was the ex-convict from the café. Tell your man to step forward, he said. Into the light. Where I can see him.

There's no need for that.

Step forward, he called.

The giant did not stir.

He intends you no harm, Mr. Pinkerton, the man murmured. His shadowed eyes, his face emotionless in the gloom, his small hands very still. He neither wept nor remonstrated and instead a current of tension tightened in him and William recognized it as an authentic grief. I understand you are a serious man, sir, an effective man. That is why I have come to you. To ask for your assistance.

I'm not for hire.

I do not wish to be a client, Mr. Pinkerton. I wish to enlist your help. Privately.

William's eyes shifted coldly between the two men. He had not yet uncocked his revolver.

It would be to your benefit also, sir.

What's your interest in Charlotte Reckitt?

I beg your pardon?

Your interest.

My interest is in her killer. The small man paused, raised his face. Charlotte mattered to me once, he said. Our lives diverged. I have always regretted the path hers took. She was not a bad person, Mr. Pinkerton, and never a cruel one. Whatever her affiliations.

William frowned. You and her, you were—

Intimate. Yes. I am not ashamed of it.

While he spoke William was listening for other sounds in the tunnel but he heard nothing. If there were others gathered in ambush they were not close. William could see the man's bright eyes glittering in the shadow of his silk hat.

There is a city under the city, Mr. Pinkerton. If you want answers, that is where you must go.

William shifted his weight, stepped closer.

Mr. Pinkerton, the giant said. That's near enough now.

The small man took no notice. There is a man, he said instead, named Jonathan Cooper. Called himself the Saracen. He was famous in certain circles for removing the heads of his victims and floating them down the Thames. You have heard of him perhaps? He worked with Charlotte and when they parted ways he disappeared. It was said she'd betrayed him, cheated him. The weak gaslight again caught the man Foole's face and his features were fierce, his violet eyes piercing. The mutilations to her torso, as if to make her suffer? The sawed-off head? This is Cooper's work, Mr. Pinkerton.

Anyone can cut off a head.

She knew him.

So you say.

Adam Foole smiled a tired smile. The only way to find this man, this Saracen, is to find the woman he was devoted to. A mudlark, goes by the name of Muck Annie. She lives in the sewers south of Blackfriars.

You want me to go into the sewers.

Into the tunnel arches, yes.

You know where to find her. You go.

And what would I do, should this mudlark lead me to the Saracen? Consider me, sir. He held out his arms, the walking stick dangling from a lilac glove. Whereas you, sir, you are the fearsome William Pinkerton. You can subdue a man and make him confess, no matter how fierce. No. If one wishes a task done well, one seeks out the talent.

Your man there looks like he could handle it.

But he is not the law, Mr. Pinkerton. Nor is he the greatest detective of our age.

William spat. I'm not the law either.

Well, the man said, clicking his tongue. Even better, perhaps.

It won't work, William murmured, drifting nearer. I know your sort. You and I would want different things out of this. His boots crunched in the slow gravel as he stepped off the rails.

All at once the giant slid languid and catlike from his position in the gloom and he loomed up behind Adam Foole and William saw the brass knuckles glinting there. That's near enough now, the giant growled. Step yourself back.

William looked at him.

Gentlemen, Foole said, half turning. That's enough. My man means no harm, Mr. Pinkerton. We simply wanted a private moment with you. Now tell me, please. What is it you imagine I want out of this?

Revenge, said William.

Not justice?

Not justice. And don't tell me they're the same thing.

O but sometimes they are, Mr. Pinkerton. As you know.

William felt a sudden quick anger. He did not ask which side of the law that placed the man on. It was a blurred line that made little sense in the distinguishing of right from wrong and in the end he believed it no way to measure a man's worth.

Just consider it. That is all I ask.

I'm not interested.

The man Foole frowned and belled out one whiskered cheek and then he nodded imperceptibly to himself. I made a promise to Miss Reckitt ten years ago, he said, a promise I wish to honour. I know you understand. I've been following your career with interest, you are not a man who betrays his word. We are not so different, you and I. He tapped his walking stick against the iron rails underfoot. There is a boy who works the lay in Waterloo Place. A gunsmith's apprentice, Albert. If you are willing to consider this, you can send to me through him. He will know how to contact me.

William glanced from the small man to his companion lurking in the haze. What makes you think I'd trust you?

Oh, trust, the small man said, scraping a half-circle on the tunnel floor with his walking stick. I wouldn't ask that of you. He met William's eye with a sudden hard expression that chilled William. She didn't deserve to die like that, Mr. Pinkerton. I know that you terrified her. But her death was not your fault.

William was quiet for a long moment. He did not see how the man could know that. He had shadowed Charlotte Reckitt for weeks and never seen this man cross her path.

I am prepared to offer something of value in return, of course, the man said. An account you might find of interest. I understand you've been into every flash house in the city asking after a man who doesn't exist. You've made no secret of it.

William could feel the thrum of the river through the iron walls and he ran a hand along the back of his neck. His hand was shaking. Edward Shade, he said.

Yes.

Shade's dead, he said sharply. He died in the war.

Who told you such a thing?

William paused, regarded the man.

Adam Foole raised his weary face, peered at him from the darkness. It wasn't the war that killed that boy, Mr. Pinkerton, he murmured. It was your father.

The
Ghost Special

1868

OHIO

The first time William Pinkerton heard the name Edward Shade he was twenty-two years old and drinking in the gaslit saloon of Cincinnati's Rand Hotel. He was standing with his father and George Bangs and all three had a boot heel hooked in the brass rail and their wide-brimmed hats set down before them on the bar. In time he would lose his father to that rumour as other boys lost their fathers to clouds of pox or sudden floods or to the flare of a spark in a curtain. His father with his grey beard and his thick ropy forearms and the skin of his hands so thorny and callused as to look diseased. His father with his burning grey eyes like a prophet out of some Old Testament squall. As a boy he had been his father's shadow and never once seen him proved wrong. He had learned from him in the fields outside Chicago how to tie a blanket to a saddle and in the sawmills how to lean his weight into a cut and in the rivers how to clean a trout with a flick of a blade. All this had been in him during the second year of the war when he had spied for his father in McClellan's lines and all this was in him still on that day, oiled and readied, like a bullet in the chamber of a rifle. It was the year of the Reno business. The war had been over three winters by then.

You don't like this, his father was saying to Bangs. His powerful neck turning.

I don't.

You don't like me going after John Reno?

I don't like your interest in a town like Seymour.

His father's eyes mostly smouldered with a peculiar light but now a darkness passed over them. He was not as big as either of his sons but he was hard as a plank of hickory and his fists were heavy as Scottish Bibles.

Seymour's a cancer, he said softly. Should have burned it to the ground years ago.

Maybe.

His father took a sip of cloudy water. The shot glass clicked down.

You won't find him there, Bangs said suddenly. Shade isn't the type to go west, Allan. If he even still exists. Or ever existed.

William ran a finger over the brass rim of his own shot glass, regarded the older men. I thought we were hunting John Reno, he said.

Bangs nodded at his father, as if weighting some invisible scale and eyeing the balance. Then he said to William, Your father has a notion there might be more in Seymour than just John Reno and his brothers. Edward Shade's been a puzzle since, what, sixty-six?

His father grunted.

Allan?

We'll take John Reno by surprise, his father said instead. Warrant or no warrant. Cut off the head of the snake. Then we'll find out what his brothers can do. Willie, he said.

Yes sir.

Go see to the horses.

William got up from the bar.

What you're suggesting is kidnapping, Bangs said abruptly. We have no jurisdiction in Indiana.

William met his father's eye.

That's right, his father said.

Bangs was shaking his head. The ends don't justify the means, Allan. They don't ever. You tell him, William, he won't listen to me.

William put on his hat.

Sometimes they do, Mr. Bangs, he said.

The Renos were a tough and brutal family of eight and John the second son. In the last year of the war he had galloped up out of the White River bottomlands with his brothers at his side, two miles northwest of Seymour, Indiana, a Colt strapped to each hip and the fingertips of his rawhide gloves scissored off. He was a powerful man with the straight shoulders and high cheek-bones of a Blackfoot brave and the long arms and big hands of his French forebears and he was black-haired and handsome as the devil himself. In the weeks following Appomattox he had bought up much of the nearby town of Rockford after several fires broke out and the rest he would take by fear and bribery until that town too belonged to him. In the fall of 1865 he took his brothers Simeon and William and Frank and stole and mur-dered his way through the county as if riding in a Confederate raid and in the spring of 1866 he stormed the Clinton County Treasury and blew out its walls with black powder. That was the year the Renos startled the nation by robbing the Adams Express Car of $15,000 while still at speed and this new thing, what could you call it, this train robbery, drew the interest of the Agency.

Then in early 1867 they stole $22,065 from the Davies County Treasury in Gallatin, Missouri, and the Pinkertons rolled up their sleeves and got to work.

Tell me about the man, his father said later that day. Bespectacled, light winking like twin coins in the lenses, his voice tired, his skin drained and grey in the afternoon gloom. Tell me about this Winscott.

William stood at the window watching the rain, his stained oilskin seamed tight at his shoulders, the warped floorboards creaking under his boots. A piano was playing somewhere in the hotel, a woman's low voice singing. A gust rolled across the glass, the thin walls groaned. He worried the papers in one hand and scanned the notes in the margins then flipped back to the first page. Dick Winscott, he said, thirty-six years old, black hair, a scar over his left eyelid. Runs the saloon in Seymour. He's been with the Agency since the end of the war, working out of the Denver office. Jim McParland vouches for him.

His father chewed a lip, his wiry grey beard working.

He's a big man, six foot two. Good with his fists. Complexion is real dark, dark like a Mex it says here. Has a tooth out in front. Carries a lot of hardware and is a good shot. Says he was with the artillery at Second Bull Run. Lucky enough or clever enough not to get himself killed. William glanced up. Either way it's a good thing for us. Active in Seymour since last spring when we sent him in. McParland did a job on his identity, there's a copy of a police record here, it says they even made up an old Wanted poster for him.

That's good.

William had seen the man in Denver two years before. Skulking in a stairwell, soiled outrider's hat shading his eyes, hot reek of the stables steaming up from his shirt. He could have been anyone in from the borderlands.

Concerns?

William ran a palm along his jaw. He had not shaved in several days nor washed and the dust of the roads itched under his collar. The Renos seem to trust him, he said. The trick will be to take John Reno without betraying Winscott as one of ours.

Why?

Jesus, Pa. I'm not green.

Watch your language. Why?

Because we still got a stable's worth of other Renos to pull in.

Good. What's the going concern here?

William glanced at the four pistols where they sat on the bed with the Enfield rifle laid out across them. To do it quick, he said. So as not to have to kill him.

And if he isn't alone?

William thought about this. He will be. Winscott says if he can just get him to the depot for the mail express we ought to be able to take him. And if we can get to him quick before he can draw we should have him trussed up before any of his brothers can even saddle a horse.

His father unhooked his spectacles, rubbed at his temple with two fingers. With its cropped grey hair and shorn beard his head looked hammered and square like a convict's. If he's alone I'll be damn impressed, he muttered.

Your head bothering you again?

Don't you start on that, his father said. I get it enough from your mother. William watched him with troubled eyes and his father glared. If he isn't alone we go ahead with it anyway, he went on. This is the one chance we've got to control the thing. What?

It's nothing.

His father put back on his spectacles, studied his son. Out with it.

You sure this is how you want to do this?

If a fight has to come let it come. And the sooner the better. You know my policy.

Show your fists.

Show your fists. Strike first and so hard they don't get back up. Fair is a fool's notion, Willie. His father crossed and uncrossed his legs. He seemed to have finished but then after a moment he muttered, God knows I have enough to do without getting complaints from you.

It wasn't a complaint.

I'll tell you another thing. After I am dead and the sod is growing over my grave then you'll know what it means to take over the management of everything.

All right.

But while I live I mean to be the Principal of this Agency. When I'm right I'm right and nothing will influence me other-wise. You tell that to Mr. Bangs.

What does he have to do with it?

Principal, he repeated. Until Death claims me as its own. Then you can pick over the carcass and much luck to the lot of you.

William blew out his cheeks.

His father took out a silver pocket watch, lifted it to one ear to check its gears. Where is he now, our Mr. Bangs?

William set down the papers in irritation and studied his father and started to say something then thought better of it and said nothing.

Is the special arranged? his father asked.

We've got our ops mustered down at the station. Five of them. They're brutes, he added with a shy grin. There's a head of steam up on the engine and we're just waiting on word. I believe Mr. Bangs is at the telegraph office. Just in case.

What have they been told?

Nothing yet.

His father grunted. Good.

William observed the descending darkness. He did not think word would come today. This Shade character, he said instead.

His father leaned forward, fumbled at his boots.

Pa? What happened in sixty-six?

He sat back and was still. What?

Edward Shade. Should I be worried?

No, he said.

All right.

I mean it.

All right.

His father was staring at him with hard bloodshot eyes and William saw in that visage something he did not like but that he knew was in him also. It had to do with fate and betrayal and some crueller thing that was a hole in the heart where remorse should have been.

After a moment his father steepled his scarred hands before him in his lap and scowled. You are twenty-two years old, he murmured. When I was your age I was stowed aboard a ship on the Clyde hiding from the redcoats and your mother was in steerage waiting for me. She would have followed me to hell if I had asked. You think you want to know about the world, boy. You don't.

William felt himself blush.

When you need to know the story of Edward Shade, his father said quietly, I'll tell it to you myself.

Many decades later at a police conference in Nebraska William would speak of those years with a kind of sadness for what had been lost. Don't mistake me, he would say, raising a glass to his lips. The outlaws and holdup men were killers and no good to anyone. Mostly boys too lazy to work and too full of bravado. In the southwest and middle borderlands especially most of them were daredevils home from the Civil War without much future to make up for the past. William would frown and study the cuffs of his dinner jacket as if lost to memory and then his eyes would clear and he would look at the young commissioner seated to his left and say, That war did nothing but corrupt the boys of a generation, sir. You can't cut a man in half day after day and come out of it normal. I knew men fit for nothing but the slaughter yards after it was over. He would cut a small bloody forkful of steak and chew it delicately and wipe at his moustache with a monogrammed napkin and then grimace. Well they were clever for all that, the outlaws in those years. No, dynamite wasn't in use until the eighteen-nineties. But Number Four black powder Coarse Grain could break up the doors of an express car and blow off your fingers to boot as well as any stick ever made. He would hear a weariness in his voice that he could not place and he would swallow it back down while the electric chandeliers burned on. It wasn't a federal crime in those years, he would add. Express cars were private property. A gang could cross state and county lines and vanish into amnesty. I guess that's how we got involved. How my father got involved.

He would listen politely to some query or other then and nod, a huge thick horror of a man with his grey eyes moist and

the crow's feet at their corners betraying long days in a saddle
under hard suns. His great hands liverspotted and trembling
which once had outdrawn outlaws. Well it wasn't quite like that,
he would reply. He would nod in silence and when the other had
finished he would say, But the express safes were supposed to be
burglar-proof. There was always a guard in the car with them
and even he didn't have the combination. They were locked in
New York or Chicago and not opened again until they got to
where they were going. Oh we weren't often at a loss. You could
learn a lot from the cut where a safe was dumped or a train
stopped. How many riders. Anything of interest about the
horses or the men. The first thing was always to ascertain if any
railroad employees had been seen in the area. No we had a network of sheriffs and peace officers and they were enterprising
enough. Our Agency never accepted the rewards you see only
our usual fee. I said rewards, sir. Don't get me started on rewards.

He would be thick in the waist by then, a heavy powerful
man with broad shoulders and a moustache stained to rust
from long tobacco. He would fold his napkin and set it on his
plate and blink his tired eyes. Well we were organized by that
time, he would go on. Though he was never garrulous and
would come to prefer solitude to company he could speak well
when he must. He would say, In the early years our contacts
would send descriptions of outlaws and their associates to our
offices in Denver and Chicago. Sometimes they'd even send a
photograph. That was how we recognized John Reno and his
brother Frank. Most of those boys loved to have their pictures
taken. They wanted to be known, you see. Yes we had all sorts,
saloon keepers, ranchers, railroad men, miners. You'd be surprised. Nothing was too trivial. My father used to say a ranch
hand's gossip was worth more to him than a dozen news reports.
Well. He was fascinated by rumours, I guess.

And he would go quiet then, and study the scrapings of his
plate, remembering.

————

The hotel was located six blocks from the rail yards and the two men father and son made their way out into the rain with their oilskin coats turned up and their heads low. Trudging through the mud of Central Avenue towards the river with a bowlegged gait each one and the grim unfussy approach of men well acquainted with violence. The rain came in at a low slant and the outlines of horses could be seen huddled to one side of the hitching posts. William regarded the thin orange glow from the hurricane lamps on the porch reflecting off their haunches and casting their crooked shadows out into the ruts and black pools of the street and he blinked the water from his eyes and went on. It was a cold ropy rain that chapped the knuckles and rawed the wrists and William regretted his gloves packed in his trunk at the hotel. The Enfield he had rolled in oilskin to keep the powder dry and carried it low at his side.

His father coughed and turned from the rain and spat then stepped up onto the clattering boardwalk and went into the depot. They wore two pistols apiece and they kept their heads both.

It was a small room with a low fire burning in a brazier at its centre and a wicket against one wall and beechwood benches set back to back running the length of it. It stood near empty but for the five operatives lounging with papers opened and pipestems bristling from their jaws and their hats wilting beside them or hooked over their knees. They were big men each one the better of William but when they saw his father they got anxiously to their feet.

All right lads, his father said, looking up at them. It's not time yet.

He swung off his hat and beat the rain from it and put it back on.

The rain was dripping from the hem of William's oilskin and he stood in a puddle on the floor wiping water from his face and stamping the muck from his boots. Anything might go wrong on the morrow and he knew any one of these men might not come out of it and he wondered again what sort it was elected such work for pay and what trust could mean to those who traded in flesh.

His father was going among the men. A nod, a clasp on the shoulder. The common touch. Has Mr. Bangs been in yet? he asked.

He were just here, Mr. Pinkerton, sir, one of the men said. A mouth wide as the base of a bottle, crooked yellow teeth like piano keys. His eyes were grim.

Where is he now? William asked.

The men looked at him then and he saw in their faces something thin, and hard, and severe.

Is he back at the post office? his father asked.

Yes sir, a second man replied.

Mr. Pinkerton? What is it we're here to do, sir? the first man asked.

The father peered across at the son.

Willie?

William met his father's eye. We'll tell you when it's time, he said curtly, and then he regarded the men. It's unlikely to be tonight. But be ready for it all the same.

A shuffling of boots. Much muttering and knuckles working in pockets.

William looked again at his father and set the rifle down on the bench then went back out.

He walked up Fourth and crossed Elm in the whirling rain then hopped back up out of the mud on the far side and stamped his boots and opened the door of the post office and stepped through. It was warm in there with the fire going and Bangs was seated on a bench under a poster advertising condensed milk and the miracle cures of Mr. Bilmacken's Goat Cheese and he looked up as William came in.

Nothing?

Bangs looped his spectacles back on, glanced at the clerk. Green eyeshade and gartered sleeves, a gnawed pencil tucked up behind one ear. Examining some paper laid out before him with a too-strained intent. Then Bangs stood and gestured

William out onto the porch and the bell rang and the door swung shut behind them.

Everyone still in place? Bangs said.

William nodded.

I think today's a bust, Bangs said. There's only the one express left and that's within the hour.

He was a small man, an ugly man. Walked with his left foot turned in and his left hand contorted into a claw and shoved into his coat pocket from an injury sustained before the war. As a boy William had feared him. He had small teeth not visible when he spoke so that only the tip of a pale tongue could be seen moving in the black and when he laughed his thin lips gaped open like the gills on a trout. Pocked cheeks from some childhood illness, hard green eyes behind crooked eyeglasses. He had been a journalist once and a guard at New York's Crystal Palace after that and he had balanced the Agency's books since its founding thirteen years earlier.

How's Margaret? he asked now, staring across at the lights of the depot.

Still beautiful, William said. Still fed up.

Bangs smiled. A woman like that likes to have her fellow close to home.

He likes to be there.

Well. Bangs nodded. This'll be done with soon enough.

It's the waiting I hate. The rain was easing now, the wind turning to the south. William folded both arms over the railing and clasped his frozen hands. The gaslights of the opera house were burning across the street, casting cones of light along the stone facade. He could hear the heavy waters of the Ohio churning far off in the darkness. He said, You think we can trust this Winscott?

I think so.

William thought about it and then he said, Tell me about Edward Shade.

You should ask your father about that.

I'm asking you.

The older man despite his ruined appearance was a hard and stubborn man. He seemed to be turning it over in his head and after a moment he shrugged as if he had decided something and then he said, What do you want to know?

What happened in sixty-six?

Bangs adjusted his spectacles with one finger. He said, An express train robbery in New York. The guard had fallen asleep and the thieves cut a hole into the door and clubbed him over the head while the train was moving at speed and then they jumped from the car and ran off. The guard was found unconscious with froth at his lips. There wasn't much to work from, the rough cuts around the door, some slivers of soap in the floorboards. But we had a feeling something was wrong. At one point the guard named a tunnel in the Bronx the train had just entered, right before the thieves struck. But if he was asleep in a windowless express car how could he have known that? He cracked. Confessed to being a confederate of the thieves and admitted rubbing soap on his lips to create the froth. The thieves were two men we hadn't known before, Crakes and Stone, and we traced them up to Toronto and arrested them and brought them south. We found a serrated knife in their room that matched the cuts around the express car door and had them sent down to the jail in White Plains, New York. The strange thing was that everyone we talked to insisted there had been a third man with them in Toronto, a man with a dark complexion and a scar on his face, a man named Edward.

William nodded.

It wasn't Edward Shade, Bangs said. There was no reason to think it.

But my father thought it.

You must have heard about this.

William was shaking his head. Did you track the man? This Edward?

Bangs smiled ruefully. Three weeks after the arrests someone dug a tunnel under the jail and Crakes and Stone escaped and we couldn't find them anywhere. Then a month later the

Boylston Bank in Boston was broken into using the same kind of tunnel, and over a million dollars' worth of securities was seized. It was Crakes and Stone again, of course. By this time your father was furious and sent two dozen operatives in to find them, but whoever was in charge, maybe it was this Edward figure, he was too clever for that. He approached Boylston's manager indirectly using a crooked attorney and offered to work back the securities to the bank for a fraction of their value. The bank agreed. I guess they thought it was cheaper than paying for our investigation. We couldn't do anything. We think there were four of them on that Boylston job—Crakes and Stone who were known to us, an English cracksman, and this mysterious Edward. All four of them sailed for Europe out of Canada and we could only watch them go.

What about the stolen amounts?

All of it worked back. Every dime.

William was puzzled. I don't understand, he said quietly. So what's all this about Shade?

Bangs was shaking his head and fumbling in his pocket for his pipe but when he pulled it out it was wet and he started to shake it dry and then gave up.

Mr. Bangs?

Look, kid, Bangs said. He's your father and I admire him more than any man living. But everyone gets it wrong once in a while. Here's what happened. A witness identified a third man running from the express train, said he was this tall and looked like so with a scar on his face like so. Dark skin, like a half Mexican. A similar man was seen in White Plains. No question. An informant in New York gives us the name Edward. And when we canvas the bank manager in Boston he claims a wealthy Mexican who was so tall with a scar on his cheek was seen opening a new account two weeks before the heist.

Okay.

Bangs gave him a look. Each of the witnesses said they saw the scar. Later every one of them retracted it. Both Crakes and Stone had thick beards, if that's what you're thinking. It wasn't either of them. Sometimes people think they see things and it turns out later to be, well, you know.

Wrong.

Yes.

My father doesn't want to talk about it.

He's embarrassed, I guess.

Was it very bad?

Bangs tilted his hat back from his forehead. There were jokes about it in the *Police Gazette* in New York, he said. At Christmas somebody mailed him a present of sticking plaster. For shaving cuts. It was kept out of the dailies thank god.

It could have been worse.

You think so.

You don't?

Bangs pushed himself upright from the railing, his bad arm hunched in the cold. He said, Worse doesn't come into it, kid. Not for your father. You know why we're here, don't you?

To take John Reno.

Bangs stared out at the rain. John Reno, he murmured. Sure.

They waited all through the evening and slept badly in their clothes with their boots and coats beside their beds and then waited all through the morning and afternoon of the following day. William could feel his father's impatience. The rain had blown past in the night and the city was crowded with clerks coming out of the counting houses and coaches mired in the muck and ladies holding their skirts in disgust.

He could not still himself and he paced under the big windows of the hotel lobby watching the doors for word and going to the station and coming back and in the afternoon as the daylight was again failing the telegram at last came through.

It's a go, he told his father with a rush.

His father merely grunted.

Dick Winscott would have John Reno on the Seymour platform awaiting the 4:10 postal express that day. William and his

father came at a run into the waiting room of the Cincinnati &
Indianapolis to find the big men watching the rail yards and
adjusting their hats and the depot clerk regarding them with a
disapproving air. Then the door clattered open behind them
and Bangs was shuffling in out of the cold with a scarf double-
wrapped around his neck and his eyes afire.

You ready? he said.

His father glanced at the men standing behind him and
William could feel his excitement. Is the car coupled? his father
said.

Bangs nodded. He took William's hand at the door and
wished him luck.

It's not us who needs it, William said. He winked. Don't
wait up.

And tipped his hat and went out.

Railroad men called it a ghost special. It crouched on the rails
in the cold snorting a great cloud of steam like some terror out
of an older age, a heavy eight-coupled tender locomotive accustomed to hauling freight, its boiler the size of a barn. There
were pigeons scattering up near the smoke box and landing and
picking at some spill of feed in the loading bays despite the
dark and the cold and William blew out his cheeks and felt the
first of his misgivings. Some of the men were already aboard
and others were hauling coils of rope from the sheds beside the
tracks. That engine had been built for power by the Grant
Locomotive Works and sold to the B&O in 1867 and William's
father had borrowed it for its speed. It gleamed black in the
gloom with its gold and red trim startling to William's eye and
a great clattering of pistons as the firebox was stoked and the
boiler cranked up to capacity. His father did not want John
Reno to know what was coming down the track and so the
tender had been coupled only to a single passenger car and the
fireman now leaned out of the cab and gave them a grim nod
and the men clambered aboard.

And then like that the brakes unclamped with a jolt and the wheels loosed and the twin pistons punched and spun. William took one last look at the station then trotted alongside and swung up and in.

It was an old velvet-lined carriage smelling of smoke and sweat with seats arranged along each wall in the manner of an omnibus and brass rails for their boots and webbing slung overhead for baggage and a weak gas lamp burning at each corner of the car. William stood with his father at the front while the men got seated and he was the last to sit and no man gave him more than a glance. His father did not sit but stood in the aisle with one hand out on either side of him gripping the posts for balance and regarding the men.

If you know me you know I'm not one for speechifying, his father was saying.

The big locomotive rattled up out of the hollow, the grey Ohio sliding past on one side.

Tonight we mean to go into Seymour Indiana and take John Reno out by force, his father said. This should go simple and without complications. You'll follow me when we come into the platform and stay close. Don't engage until we're in place and then don't hesitate. You know his reputation.

William felt the car shunt and shift on the tracks and they were moving now at speed through the extinguishing afternoon.

There'll be a man with him, a saloon keeper name of Winscott, his father said. We don't want him. He's not a killer by all reports but if he gets in the way.

He left the words hanging and the men nodded amongst themselves.

Reno's not too particular about killing so you'll want to be fast. He ran a hand across his mouth as if thinking about something and then he added, I've told the driver to go in hard and to get out at speed and he's given us three minutes on the outside before the postal express comes up on him. You know what that means, lads.

Two of the men were checking their revolvers. William

watched their deft hands at play. Click swivel turn click and the glint of metal winking there.

Is any of that not clear? his father was saying. Mr. Wyatt?

The man with the yellow teeth and wide mouth turned his face from the window and nodded. Sir.

I want you to keep an especial eye on his guns. He'll have two and a knife in his boot if our information is correct. Mr. Mueller?

A man bearded and broad-trunked and heavy-browed as a lumberjack with a great mane of reddish hair shuffled his boots and grunted. He sat with his hands on his knees and his big thighs splayed out over two seats and his gut sagging over his belt.

Mr. Mueller I want you to shackle the fellow. William will take his arms from the back and when he does so you get his wrists into the irons.

The big Hessian nodded.

His father reached into his waistcoat. Here is a photograph of John Reno taken last spring in Seymour.

The nearest man took it wordlessly and unfolded it then passed it on.

There's nothing about this man you should like or take kindly to, his father added. He's killed and stolen and done in just about every kind of honest citizen you can name and he's never thought twice about it. If you have a sister or a wife or a mother, this is the man she goes to sleep at night scared of.

William did not look at the photograph but handed it across to the man behind him.

His father took out his pocket watch, cradled it in his palm. You have thirty-four minutes lads, he said. Do what you need to do.

Twenty-nine minutes later his father picked up his hat by its peak from the seat beside him and set it low on his eyes and adjusted his revolvers then got swaying to his feet.

He ducked his head to watch the picketed fields roll past, the stands of oak in the middle distance grey and spindled and bare in the cold. William followed his father's gaze. The sun was low in the sky and had backlit the streaked clouds into a red inflamed welt of light.

Welcome to Seymour, his father shouted.

William could feel an electricity go through the carriage then and when his eyes shifted to the face reflected in the window he saw neither dread nor joy nor excitement but something else which he did not recognize and only many years later would understand was the look terror took on in the eyes of a twenty-two-year-old boy. He thought of his wife at home and of his new daughter in her crib and he realized there was no part of him that wanted to leave this earth. The riders at the depot in Seymour were killers and would shoot without hesitation and like his father he did not believe John Reno would be without associates on that platform. What troubled him was the not knowing. He would not know a member of Reno's gang to see him and could run right past a hand in a waistcoat or a knife in a fist none the wiser.

When he raised his eyes his father was looking at him.

Three minutes, his father hollered over the sound of the locomotive. Remember we get in and grab him and get out. If there's no need to make a fuss we don't make one.

William could feel himself nodding despite himself and he blinked hard and peered again at his fists. There was a loose thread on the cuff of his coat and he tugged at it and tried to think of nothing at all.

They came around a curve and slowed. The platform hove into view.

All right, his father was shouting. Mr. Wyatt, Mr. Mueller, William, you exit from the front with me. I want the rest of you out through the back. Keep your heads.

William felt a foreboding come over him. The platform was crowded with men and ladies in bonnets and bustles all of them awaiting the 4:10 postal express. He stared the length of the narrow platform but recognized no face. They came in past the water tower and a small wooden outbuilding once painted blue but weathered now and peeling in the cold and they were still at such speed William thought for a moment they would over-shoot the station until the carriage jolted sharply in a quick sequence of brakings and they came to a snorting halt in the centre of that crowd.

His father was glancing from the faces on the platform to the photograph in his hand to the faces again and then he shouted, There, in the blue duster. At the back of the platform.

William looked but could not see.

The men were already up and moving heavily their boots clattering in the aisle and the floor juddering under them. William swung down behind Mueller with Wyatt at his back and they cut single file through that crowd of onlookers, the more curious turning to regard them as they passed. The air smelled of rain and horses. He could not see where he was going and kept close to the Hessian and then the crowds parted and he saw the other men had formed a loose circle around two figures bent in conversation neither of whom had yet looked up. He saw his father step forward and speak some word and the bigger of the two men glanced up and went for his gun.

It was that fast. William lunged in from the back and grabbed Reno around the chest and one arm broke free but then he had him, he was pinioning his arms to his sides and Mueller was leaning into the fray twisting the outlaw's wrists and locking the iron handcuffs into place. The man was writhing and William tasted tar and spit and sweat in his neck and he had his face crushed up against the back of the man's head when Reno leaned forward then smashed his skull back into William's brow. He staggered dazed but he did not let go. Then Wyatt stepped in and struck Reno twice with his fists and reached down and slid the man's pistols from his belt with a soft liquid clatter and William's father was knocking Reno's hat from his head and shoving an empty flour sack down over the twisting fury.

The crowds had drawn back in confusion. Reno was shouting from within the sack and William scanned the faces for sign of any confederate but he could see only terror. Winscott was hollering bloody murder at them and grabbing for the arms of the nearest man and Wyatt stepped forward and set two strong hands on the middle of Winscott's chest and shoved him hard and he went backward into the crowd. All this William saw as he looked wildly about but he was already dragging the kicking man backward on his heels and Mueller was fighting to get a hold of one boot and then a second man had seized the other and they carried him like that through the recoiling crowds at a half run as if he were a sack of feed.

Goddamnit, his father was shouting. Get a move on, go—

William thought he saw a cattleman in the crowd pushing towards them and he did not see his father and then the cattleman went down and then they were hauling Reno still squirming up into the passenger car. When he turned he could see over Reno's thrashing legs his father behind them again. Winscott had pulled a knife and he watched his father turn and get in close to Winscott with one strong arm and with the other he hammered at him sharply on the skull with the butt of his revolver and the man's legs went out from under him like a calf on new ice and he collapsed with the blood already in his eyes.

Then his father was running for the buckboard and hauling himself up and waving to the conductor and they were away.

On board the men were whooping and slapping their hats against their legs and banging each other on the back and William turned from them to lean out the window and watch the platform shrink into distance. He could see no sign of pursuit.

His heart was still battering in his chest and he was breathing through his mouth as he made his way down the swaying carriage to the rear.

John Reno. In the flesh. Wrists in iron bracelets at his back. He had been tied and double-tied in a long winding zigzag of new white rope until he looked like a package of beef strung up for transport. His hat had been lost in the melee and his long black hair was greasy and standing in clumps on his scalp and his mouth and left eye were swollen. Mueller was holding him by the arms to keep him from sliding onto the floor.

William sat. Hooked a thumb in his waistcoat, nodded to Mueller. The Hessian grinned back. He could feel his own uneasiness as he studied the outlaw. The men were still laughing and hooting near the front of the carriage and passing a bottle amongst themselves and after a moment his father came down the aisle.

He held the creased photograph for the outlaw to see. Took off his coat and folded it over the seat behind him then sat down and William watched the big man's eyes shift to take in the two revolvers at his hips.

You don't know what you just done, the man said. This ain't even legal.

His father raised his eyebrows, smiled across at his son.

You look at me, Reno shouted suddenly.

His father looked.

The big outlaw had gone very surly, very dark. My name is John Reno and my brothers is Frank and Simeon and you give us two pistols apiece we ain't afraid of no man living.

Wonderful, his father said.

Reno turned his head and spat. His gums were bleeding.

William's father leaned in. Do you know who I am, John?

Reno grinned a bloody grin. You're a corpse with boots on.

Wyatt hollered from the front of the carriage. What size collar you wear, Johnny boy? There's a judge in Gallatin mighty curious.

Reno said nothing.

You may fear no man, his father said quietly. But you will fear me.

The carriage clattered and shivered, William swayed in his seat. Mueller's knuckles were white where they gripped Reno's arms.

You ain't the law, Reno said.

No.

His father was no longer smiling.

Reno turned his face, stared out at the passing fields. Beyond the windows the Midwest plains were vanishing and William could see the distant orange glimmer of a settlement.

The passenger car darkened further.

Now I'm going to describe a man to you, his father was saying softly. I'm going to describe a man and I want you to tell me if you ever heard of him.

In that first fall after Margaret's death he would sit alone in the evenings with a stack of his late father's books beside him and reread the popular tales of the Eye That Never Slept and in the reading he would once more hear, faint, under the crickets and the slicing wind in the long grass, the rasping half-articulated voice of his father. His own hands liverspotted and old. His father he knew had not written those books but there it was all the same. He would hear his father's shouted defence of his female operatives, see again the froth and spit as he stormed out of his office. Or his father's crumpling of receipt dockets and shouting down George Bangs's protestations. He thought of his father like a tide washing in and receding and leaving some polished strangeness behind in the sand, evidence of some other world. His father at his country house, striding out in all weathers on his twelve-mile walk or coming downstairs with his cheekbones red and steel-grey hair soaking the back of his collar from the cold bath he would take each morning. All that and the long brooding evening train journeys in which his father would turn to the glass and study his own watery reflection and speak to him over the clatter of the tracks about the nature of the hidden and of what might be seen by any who would choose to see it. William knew his father did not believe in the invisible world. But he would understand only very slowly in those years that his father was thinking of the phantom Edward Shade.

In none of those books was there any word of such a figure real or imagined. William had at one time believed this to be the shame of a man ridiculed but as he grew older he would come to think otherwise. He would come to believe his father wanted the story of Shade for himself, wanted to keep close and secret the delicious possibility of Shade's existence, even into his final years.

And as his father grew the more frail he would take to sitting in the garden among the flowers, his square head nodding, and William would sit with him in silence watching the bees work the roses. And it would seem to him sometimes that a third sat with them, some ghost his father's glance would shift to, shift from. In the end the old man in his confusion would look up at his son in astonishment, then lift a trembling hand and lay it upon his son's knee and murmur, his eyes wet: Oh I have been looking for you such a long time, sir.

And William would say nothing.

All that too would fade to sepia and fog. William's own eyesight would begin to weaken. In his dotage he would turn the pages of his father's books with his feet set square on the ground and his knees apart and he would look out at the fields and think of that day in Seymour when his father took John Reno and the western outlaws were born in blood and lead and he would shake his head for the madness of all that had happened once, all that was real.

Three days after delivering John Reno to the courthouse in Gallatin, Missouri, William opened the gate of his house in Chicago and waded the deep snow of the lane and stropped the ice from his boots on the porch steps with his suitcase standing between his legs and one hand on the frozen railing and looked up in time to see through the lighted windows of his living room his wife in her nightgown dancing with another man.

Standing in the cold, the air burning his lungs.

That man was her brother just in from California and he knew this and yet still the sight of it pained him. He swayed there in the snow-swept darkness for a long time, surprised by the hurt he felt. His face was wet, his hands were wet.

At last he watched her brother bow in an exaggerated fashion the orange light catching in his whiskers and his wife curtsied and then the man lit an oil lamp and went upstairs. William stood with his breath steaming out before him and frost crackling in his hair and he waited and when his wife had gone through into the back kitchen he picked up his suitcase and crunched down off the porch and around to the rear of the house and he went in.

She was twenty years old that winter and as beautiful a creature as any he had seen. She had strong white hands and a long throat and hair the colour of sunlight on a shallow stream bed in summer. Her voice was low for a woman and this was something he had always loved about her. They had been married one year and already he could not imagine any life other.

When he shut the door behind him she was staring at him in amazement with both hands gripping the back of a kitchen chair. She looked so young, so much a girl still.

Surprise, he said.

Good lord you give me a fright William, she breathed. She went to him and pulled his head down and kissed him and he pulled back and wiped the snow from his moustache and she kissed him again. Good lord, she said again. What are you doing here? I thought you said tomorrow. I would've had something laid out for you. I was just about to go up to bed. David just went up. She put a hand to her mouth. David's here, she said.

It's all right. I know.

We have stew, she was saying. Are you hungry? She paused then, she gave him a strange look. How long were you out there?

He shrugged.

Let me get a look at you, she said.

He stood obligingly.

You weren't shot.

No ma'am.

Well that was clever of you. You still have all your teeth.

Yes ma'am.

She was silent a long moment then and then she said, Oh, William. Oh you look so tired.

He did not know what to say to that.

Here, sit, she said. She took his hat from him and helped him from his oilskin then folded it dripping over one arm and went into the parlour. A puddle was forming under his boots and he scraped them on the roughage mat laid down just inside the door. I said sit, she called from the front hall.

He sat.

She came back in. Never mind about David, she was saying, David can wait. There's plenty of time for visiting. She set a saucepan on the stove and unpinned the cheesecloth from the top of the day-old stew and ladled some out and opened the stove door and stoked the coals and using the poker she shut the door with a clang.

How's the baby? he said, watching her.

She smiled without turning. When she's fed she's happy. She's missed you.

He nodded.

David's got plans for a boarding house in San Francisco. He's going to talk to you about it tomorrow. I think he's looking for investors.

Investors.

Just go easy on him, she said. I like to see him like this. He's hopeful.

He's something.

She poured him a glass of milk and set it before him at the table and laid out knife and fork and plate and then she gave him a long appraising look. So is it done then? she asked. Is it finished?

He shook his head.

You have to go back.

He opened his hands in a gesture he had learned from his father. There's still the others, he said. Frank's the real trouble. I expect he'll take over now his brother's been taken.

Will they try to get him back?

If they don't I'll look a fool.

No you won't.

I will. I told my father to expect it. William glanced at her. He set out his big hands on the table and closed his eyes. It's not the Renos I'm worried about, he said tiredly. The whole country out there is angry. There'll be a vigilante mob five hundred strong if the governor's not careful.

Your father'd like that.

William opened his eyes. She came over to him and nudged the table clear of his chair with her hip so that she could sit in his lap and then she sat and folded her arms around his neck. She wrinkled her nose.

I haven't washed, he said.

He put his hands on her waist as if to lift her but he did not yet.

And what does Mr. William Pinkerton think of it? she said.

Of what?

Of vigilante justice. Do you agree with your father?

He frowned and peered at her but said nothing. When he saw she was in earnest he said, My father was born in a place where justice had nothing to do with the law.

You think it's different here?

I think it could be.

She kissed him softly. Good answer, she said.

He kept his eyes on her as she got up and smoothed her skirts.

Hiya, he said. Come back here, you.

She slapped at him with the dishcloth. Watch those hands. I'm married you know.

You got a sister?

I thought you were hungry.

I thought so too.

Well, she said. Aren't you going to ask what I think?

About what?

She gave him a look.

Okay, he said. What do you think Mrs. Pinkerton of a mob breaking into a courthouse and dragging a man out by his boots and stringing him up without a trial?

I'm glad you asked, she said. I don't think I like it. No sir.

His gaze drifted over to the stove where the pot of stew was simmering but she was not finished. Her voice went serious. She said, Sometimes when you're asleep and having a bad dream you make this little whimpering sound. Like a pigeon.

A pigeon?

She puckered her lips and cooed, cooed.

I never.

You do. You do so. I have to reach over and shake you by the shoulder. You don't wake up but you roll over. I guess the dream changes. At least you stop whimpering.

I don't whimper, he said. She seemed so very beautiful, smiling at him in her heavy winter gown, her hair down her back in that long thick Celtic braid.

I think that's what this country is like right now, she was saying. It doesn't want to know about justice. It's there, it's just not a part of the dream. But it could be. We're asleep and when the whimpering gets too loud something will come along and shake us out of it, into a different dream.

William rubbed at his face. Or maybe we'll wake up.

No one wakes up. Not really. You still want that stew?

He grunted.

You aren't hungry?

He smiled. My jaw's getting tired.

She put a hand on the back of his neck and it felt warm and clean and right to him. He put his own rough hand up and they stayed like that a moment as the snow whirled down in the silent blackness beyond the windows and the oil lamps dimmed.

You look tired, he said after a while.

I feel tired.

He twisted in his chair, put his arms around her. I don't mind tired in a girl. Just so long as she's got green eyes. You got green eyes?

You know what colour they are.

He pressed his face into her neck, smelled her hair. He was still a young man. His entire life lay before him. The house creaked in the darkness.

That's all right, he murmured. They don't need to be green.

Inventing
the Devil

1885

LONDON

THIRTEEN

William woke with his fingers creeping through the cold scoop of his bedsheets, missing his wife. All night and into the morning the man from the tunnel had come to him, a crescent of light etching a cheekbone, a splinter of whiskers, that sorrowful liquid darkness in his eye. Foole. Adam Foole. He opened his eyes, breathing, remembering the grief that man had kept under control on behalf of a woman he had loved. He thought of Margaret in their blankets on winter mornings, fitting her bed slippers to her feet, while the mattress shuddered gently under. She hated how her body had thickened after the children but he did not mind it and he loved the soft heat of it still.

A weak daylight was leaking through the curtains and he kicked clear of his blankets, crossed the freezing floor, poured cold water from the carafe at the basin and wrung out the flannel and began to wash. Shade was likely dead howsoever his death had found him. Shore believed it, the man Foole claimed it, different though each account did prove. Margaret would ask him what was in his heart. He had learned over a lifetime to trust her counsel and his own thoughts did refract and clear in the hearing of it. He thought of Adam Foole's quiet sure grief as he levelled his accusation against William's father. The hell with it. What was in his heart? His heart told him the Saracen was real, though there was no reason to believe it and though the mudlark Muck Annie was most likely decomposing in some churchyard lime pit.

Could his father have killed Edward Shade? He knew what Margaret would say: I loved your father too, Willie. But that man was capable of anything.

He had been fifteen years old when he fell in love with the eldest Ashling sister, blond, vain, flighty. For months he could not see beyond her dazzle to any girl else. Dreamily he would skip his classes at Notre Dame, buy her chocolates, roses. That sister's name was Alice and she would swoon in his arms and brush her lips against his jaw like a heroine in an English novel and he felt his own new raw strength course through his arms as she did so. Alice Ashling would go riding with two of her schoolgirl friends in the public parks in the afternoons and William would stand with a hand on the trunk of a sycamore watching her canter and turn and canter past again. Staring at him boldly, smiling the while, her girlfriends all a-giggle and calling her away.

That was in October of 1861. In November she danced all evening with an older boy of nineteen, already an officer in the Northern Cavalry, while William lurked at the edge of the waxed floor and crushed the flower in his lapel. She had arrived at the ball on his arm but she would be leaving on another's. William was desperate, devastated. Visions of his own enlistment in D.C. where his father was gathering intelligence, visions of some heroic act under fire in a cornfield of Virginia. All of it nonsense. When he rubbed at his wet eyes and turned away there was a younger girl standing beside him, white dress, flowers wreathing her hair.

He almost knew her. The night deepened, the dance floor tilted and drained away. Together they watched Alice curl into the officer's arms.

That's the wrong sister for you, Pinkerton, the girl said.

And then he knew her. Margaret Ashling, fourteen years old, quiet and lovely, smiling a sardonic smile at him from under her lashes. She held out a tiny hand for him to take. To his surprise he took it.

How lucky you are, sir, that I happen to be an excellent dancer, she said, guiding him towards the bandshell while the violins swelled around them. You just follow my lead.

Margaret loved to tell that story. Whenever friends asked how he had found her she would give William a cool smile and say, Oh, *he* didn't find *me*—

At which he would shake his head, reach for her hand, and laugh. How did I find her? he would grin. I found her difficult, and stubborn, and headstrong—

At the hotel desk in the green light under the low-hanging fronds he rapped a knuckle on the counter and waited but when the clerk checked there had not yet been any telegram from Chicago. He frowned. He was more interested than ever to hear if his description of Adam Foole's manservant matched any in the Agency files and if there were any record of his employer Foole. He thought of that man's slight frame, his shadowed skin, the eyes like amethysts pressed in wax. As the doorman held open the great glass door and the cold roar of the street sucked at him he buttoned his chesterfield and hunched his shoulders and strode through. Even after twenty years of detective work he found himself confused by his own nature and the havoc it could wreak. He would confess freely his fascination with the criminal world, his fondness for rogues of all stripes, his equally determined desire to mete out justice in a fist or at the end of a rope. Margaret thought his fearlessness, his introspection, his restlessness all emergent from the same dark and molten core: a love for a father whom he did not think loved him rightly back. It's a hard thing, learning to love the man you are, she would tell him, running her fingers through his hair of a night. Goodness isn't dependent on anyone's approval, Willie.

William jogged across the street, pushed through into the warm restaurant with its Restoration-era mouldings and steamed windows. A wood fire was burning in a great hearth at either end of the dining room, bracketing the empty tables. What he wanted was to talk to Margaret about the man Foole. What he wanted to chart was the cast of her silence. He was seated at the far end of the room with his back to the fire and his deep-set eyes watching the door through force of habit when the waiter came, fussed, went. Adam Foole's mention of his father and Shade would not let him alone. He thought it likely he was being manipulated and yet the man claimed an intimacy with Charlotte Reckitt and she of anyone might have known how Shade died. William frowned. He was a man who trusted his gut over his head and had learned to do so by measuring the quarts of his own blood spilled. There were facts and then there were facts, he knew. If you draw a spade, his father liked to say, don't try to play clubs.

He unfolded his napkin across his lap and studied the table-cloth and asked himself, as he had asked his entire life, what his father would do.

The sky was white, a white sun burning a sightless funnel through the haze. He caught John Shore in the narrow lane of Great Scotland Yard, just leaving. A cold wind crackled around them, riffled the loose papers stuffed under Shore's elbow. The chief inspector shook his harried head, glanced anxiously in the direction he had been proceeding.

Jonathan Cooper? he muttered. Aye, I remember him. Whole generation of us came up in the Yard hearing stories about Cooper. The Saracen, he was called. What's your interest in it?

William shrugged. It's probably nothing.

I'm late as it is. Walk with me. Shore started off at a clip and William jogged to catch him. Maybe ten, fifteen years back, he said, heads started turning up in the Thames. Nineteen of them in the end, one shy of a nice round number. The chief shrugged, his face red, breathing hard as he went. A lot of murders go unreported around here, a lot go unsolved, a lot are never writ-ten up. At least they used not to be. The curious thing about these heads is that the bodies were never found. And the heads all had the same kind of cut, some rough ragged chop. I'm told it was a very distinct cut.

Like the Reckitt woman's?

Shore slowed. Is that what this is about?

A market cart clattered past, trailing cuttings of cabbage. Two small urchins with rags tied to their feet with twine were following, darting between the legs of the horses, snatching up the leavings in the cold.

So he was real, William said. Cooper existed.

Cooper didn't do in Charlotte Reckitt, William. The man's been disappeared for ten years at least. He's in his grave by now.

Is that fact?

Shore waved at a passing hansom but it did not stop. I never saw a body, if that's what you mean. But I'd stake my reputation on it. A man like that doesn't just stop killing. What are you up to, William?

William did not answer. He said, instead, What can you tell me about him?

Not much. He was a big bugger. He served in the Crimea with a raiding force of bashi-bazouks. They'd burn the Russian villages and cut off the heads of the Christians. Women, children, all of them. The heads were thrown into the Danube. Floated the whole bloody way down to Varna where the English and French were camped and our lads started picking them out of the reeds with boathooks. But by the time the raiding party got back to Varna the cholera had struck and the French camp had set up pickets to keep the English sick out. I guess it was a mess. I guess the army wanted to keep the whole matter quiet. Cooper wasn't court-martialled but he fell sick on the boats when the army sailed for Alma. He must have recovered in time to go into the fight or maybe the army just thought it was an easy way to solve the problem of what to do with him. A musket ball tore up his face in the first assault. Entered through his left cheek and came out at the right corner of his mouth and took twenty-three of his teeth and a good part of his tongue with it. That was in a vineyard before they'd even reached the river.

He'd climbed a tree to get a bead on the enemy. It's said he was left hanging there for hours by his feet before he managed to get down and go looking for a staff surgeon. Somehow he didn't die. Shore gave him a long, tired, appraising look. You really want to know about this?

A hansom cab stopped at the curb and Shore clambered up. Leave it alone, William, he called over his shoulder. That's my advice to you.

William held up a hand and took a step back. The driver leaned forward with his loop of reins and then on a whim William stepped swiftly up and set a hand on the door and leaned in. One last thing. Ever hear of a man named Adam Foole?

Adam Foole?

Clear, the driver called angrily. Clear off now.

Foole, yes, William said.

Shore grunted. Never heard of him. What's he?

William started to answer and then looked off down the street and let go the hansom and stepped back. No one, he said.

In the afternoon he returned to the Grand Metropolitan. The polished marble columns, the hush, foreknuckles rapping twice on a mahogany counter while across the gleaming floor a gentleman under a palm lifted his face from a newspaper, startled spectacles glinting. The desk clerk was deferential, tugging at his cuffs. Ah, still no telegram from Chicago, Mr. Pinkerton, sir, no. William cracked the vertebrae in his neck wondering if the delay meant much or little. Upstairs in his rooms he scraped his shoes tiredly and did not take off his chesterfield but collected the files on Shade and Charlotte Reckitt and carried them down to the smoking lounge on the second floor. High windows, long Persian carpets, long bulleted sofas empty at that hour but for two gentlemen in a blue cloud of smoke well out of earshot. William seated himself before the fire, the day's whiteness blooming through the curtains. He was looking for any word or description that might match Adam Foole in either file or verify the man's accusation but after an hour he still had nothing. Was Foole speaking as an accomplice of Shade? He thought it unlikely. Charlotte Reckitt, he knew, was the probable source of the man's story. And yet Foole's calling Shade a boy had the ring of truth to it. *It wasn't the war that killed that boy.* William unfolded his legs and plicked at the knees of his trousers and fanned the files out before him. He picked up the rogues' gallery photograph of Charlotte Reckitt. Youthful, cold, brutal. Hooded eyes unkind, a wide mouth, raven hair pulled flat for the camera. He shut the file.

Whatever else, he had not lied about the Saracen. William knew that did not make the man or his other claims trustworthy. But it was something. As for Cooper—the Saracen—if there was any truth to him at all then he was worth attending to. That would require blueprints to the sewer tunnels downriver from Blackfriars and William wondered briefly at which city offices he ought to make his inquiries. He knew Breck would be prying apart the microscopic secrets of Charlotte Reckitt's flesh even now and turning up some hint, perhaps, as to the Saracen's whereabouts. William started to loosen his collar and then he caught himself and stared at the carpet, smiling angrily. The Saracen's whereabouts, he thought. So you believe it after all.

Just then the gentlemen's laughter drifted across, bright, watery, false. William grimaced. He realized what it was about the man Foole: ten years gone and their marriage never realized and what would he, William, do, were Margaret to be killed? Would his heart too chart such disaster, such ruin? The dignified grief in the man astonished him. He told himself he would risk the same given such calamity but he could not be sure. All this he saw without seeing and he thought of his ancient father in the reading room of the new city library in Chicago, turning the pages of some report that did not require his attention, the stiff watermarked papers rustling, a vision two years past and that man never again to be seen on this earth. William belled his tongue against his cheek, closed his eyes. A man knows nothing of himself, he thought, until he is tested.

And then?

He opened his eyes. And then god help him, whatsoever he choose to do.

Long nights, wearying nights. On Tuesday William rose tiredly and washed and dressed and ate and at ten o'clock made his way by hansom to the Metropolitan Board of Works. The mist was brown, murky, room after room of smouldering fog closing up around him.

London, he thought in disgust, wiping his handkerchief along his throat.

The traffic was thick, the going slow. He got down at Trafalgar Square and walked the Mall in haste until he reached Spring Gardens. He entered the Works building already irritated and tired. At the reception office he gave his card and asked to see the official responsible for sewer oversight and explained in a low flat voice that it was a police matter. The clerk regarded him skeptically but directed him along the hall to the next department and there he again gave his card and explained his purpose and there he was told, again unimpressed, to seat him-self and wait.

An old woman was asleep on the chair facing him, black hairs asprout her upper lip, her low snoring somehow consoling. He closed his own eyes. There was something in that old woman, some resigned fortitude, that made William think of his mother. An hour passed, clerks came and went. As the second hour closed he rose again and again inquired and was again told, coldly, that he would be attended to in time. He wondered if he should have enlisted Shore's help. At noon the old lady snorted awake and slid out from under her feet a small hamper that contained a roll of bread, a twist of sausage. She ate with her eyes downcast, her dry thin lips chewing rapidly like a rabbit. Then she leaned back, folded her arms, shut her eyes again.

At last a rumpled clerk came out, blinking. William glimpsed behind him rows of copying clerks, waistcoated, in gartered sleeves, their diligent heads bowed. The man was clutching the door handle in an oddly effeminate manner, wrist turned back, William's card held out before him in his other hand as if it were an unwashed thing.

Mr. Pinkerton? he called. Peering about as if William were not the only man there.

William got to his feet, his muscles stiff. Here, he said. He stepped forward, looming, he lowered his voice. I've come about plans for the sewer tunnels—

I know what you are here for, sir. The Bazalgette plans, yes?

William did not know what a Bazalgette might be.

It is a police matter, you say?

William nodded. There was in the clerk's fussiness something he instantly disliked. Chief Inspector Shore sent me, he lied.

The clerk studied his size, his callused hands, his long dark moustaches. His fingernail flicked William's visiting card, flick, flick. But you are not with the Yard yourself?

Obviously not, William said, impatience creeping into his voice.

The man raised his eyebrows.

I'm an American detective, William added, forcing himself calm. Our agencies are working a case together. He felt a growing irritation with the small man, his self-importance. For god's sake, man, I've been waiting here hours. Is all this necessary? You can show me a copy of the plans or you can show me to your superior. Either will do.

There was a smugness to the clerk as he apologized. But surely Mr. Shore knows that the MBW does not keep its plans at Spring Gardens, Mr. Pinkerton, he said. I can't imagine what he was thinking, sending you here.

What are you saying?

You'll want the Public Record Office. On Chancery Lane, sir. The public consulting room there, for research matters. The clerk gave him a veiled shake of the head that made William want to punch him. You'll bring your credentials, of course, sir.

Perhaps a letter of introduction from Mr. Shore would be of assistance.

The hell with the letter, William told himself. The hell with the damned English bureaucracy. An hour later he was entering the Public Record Office off Chancery Lane still in a black mood, the winter afternoon already extinguishing behind him. An old man in woollens with the fingers cut out and blowing on his hands for the cold squinted up at him, his pale eyes unfocused.

Can't never get warm in here, he whispered, not never, sir, no.

William feared him mad but then the man cleared his throat and said, in a high-pitched voice, Yes, yes, and what is it you come for then?

Records of public works? William said cautiously. Sewer plans, actually.

The old man nodded and led him down a long gaslit hall to an empty room filled with tables, haphazard chairs, muttering the while. You a writer too then? he asked.

A what?

That Mr. Dickens come here regular, once. I remember him well, I do. We used to talk about songbirds. We both liked them birds of a season. Fascinating man, that Mr. Dickens. Don't much care for his writing though.

William shook his head, removed his hat, set it down on a table. Is there someone I can see about plans for the sewer lines? he asked. It's a police matter.

Ah, them sewer lines always is, the old man said mysteriously.

But he disappeared with William's card back into the hall and shortly afterwards a plump hairless man in a green waistcoat came through, cod-like eyes abulge. William started to explain himself again but the man waved William's visiting card in his direction and held up a hand to stop him.

I know who you are, Mr. Pinkerton, sir, he said. What is it I can do for you?

William liked him at once. The plans he brought out from a locked records room were rolled and tied off with twine and the man set them down on a tilted drafting table and clipped them into place and smoothed them down with soft fingertips. He said, It's not the main line but the street lines you'll be wanting, sir. These are the drafted plans drawn up by Mr. Bazalgette, sir, as he had hoped to build the lines. But the construction often had to make do, sir. What's here and what's down there, he said, jabbing a squat thumb at the floor, are not really the same thing at all. Oh it's no one's fault, sir. There were chambers and rooms and old sewer tunnels already in place in some instances. They just used what they could find, shored it up. Following the spirit of the plans the while. You said it was for police use?

That's right.

This here, and the clerk riffled through the papers until he had found the sheet he sought, this is the branch line that runs down towards the Thames below Blackfriars Bridge. You can see the outflow chambers, sir. This one, and this one. I know for a fact that this tunnel was never built. It should show two parallel tunnels, quarter-sized, that snake along from here, to here.

You know for a fact? You've been down in the tunnels?

Two years ago. He half opened his mouth, sawed his tongue along a row of crooked teeth. I was in Works before transferring here, we were conducting a safety survey. Terrible places, those tunnels. I don't know how men do it, go down there regular, like.

I've heard stories.

Ah, yes. You mean the berserkers.

The what?

The clerk gave him a quick searching glance. The berserkers, sir. It's said they live in the tunnels, never come up into the light. Keep rivers of rats with them and swarm a man who ventures into their territory. The rat catchers and sewer workers tell dreadful stories about them. I never saw sight of them myself, sir. The mudlarks, now they're another story. We saw three, four, five of them, scuttling away when our lanterns caught their nests. Mighty shy, that sort, collecting the trash from the sewer mouths. No sir, the real danger down there is getting lost. It's easy to get turned around, and the sound of the tunnels can make it rather disorienting. We used chalk lines to mark our way when we went. The clerk was quiet a moment, remembering. Then he said, Well, the risk of getting lost and the treacherous footing too. Those are the dangers, sir. You walk the masonry of those dykes at your peril. A slip into those waters and you'd be dragged under and drowned for certain good, sir. You're not needing to go down there, I trust?

The building around them was quiet. A sound of dripping water somewhere. The afternoon dialed darkly down.

William studied the man, frowned. You've been a help, he said.

At his hotel that evening he stripped to the waist and scrubbed himself at the standing basin and thought about what the clerk had said. He had taken a copy of the tunnel plans with him but he understood it was likely inaccurate. He thought about his father and about the Saracen. In the morning he would go to Millbank to meet with Charlotte Reckitt's uncle. He stared at himself in the clouded glass, the sacks under his eyes, the two days' stubble showing through. A smear of ash at his hairline where his hat had been, his greasy hair crushed flat.

And Adam Foole? he brooded. Who was he? What was he after?

William tightened his grip on the basin. His murderer's eyes glared out, black, unblinking.

Go find out, they told him.

FOURTEEN

He was born on a kitchen floor surrounded by keening women in a big house in Calcutta in 1848.

His name was not Adam then, it was not Foole. Through an open door a late sun was sinking into haze and in this way he was born to the coming dark. Wrenched free from his mother's dying, wrapped in a sheet, passed hand over hand to a wet nurse looming at the lintel while slicks of blood cooled on the tile floor surrounding. That was his world and patrimony. And yet for the bastard-born he was raised nonetheless with love, in the long shadow of a Bengali girl who had hired herself out for tinny, raised by an English merchant-man father who captained a fleet of six vessels and owned a profitable shipping company and adored his half-breed son. That father would drift wraithlike as a curl of smoke on the fringes of Foole's memory and though he had no voice and did not speak there would be no figure else of greater importance. Of his mother he would recall nothing neither face nor smell though he would pull at the edges of his mouth with his long thin fingers years later and stare at his reflection and try to see the stranger in the glass. There had been two before him both girls and one an albino and both had drowned in the year of his birth. He wondered at these ghosts as he would at the faces in railway stations, at all those who would stare through him thinking they had seen an apparition themselves.

For he must have heard stories, he must have been told. How else to account for that memory of two girls in white holding hands at his bedside while he hid his eyes and trembled. There had been such resentment in their faces. When they vanished they left behind fading wet footprints and a terror that ate away his childhood. He thought of his first years in Calcutta now as a kind of aborted life, as if he were spying through the broken slats of a fence into a courtyard where a child who looked like he looked, who laughed as he laughed, who played alone with a hoop and rod did not hear his calls and did not look his way. White Town was but a blur in his mind. Heat in an alley behind a bakery kiln, the kick and sprawl of broken crates where old loaves were dumped to waste. He remembered the monstrous bulk of black cattle snorting in the heat near a river. Boot prints filling silently with water. The cry of peddlers. The calluses of his father's hand at his neck as they trudged uphill through a warm rain.

His father, yes, that. Captain Edward Benlowes was a tall Yorkshireman with shoulders like planks and a wiry beard that stood out from his chin like some benevolent Assyrian king's. A sheen of oil would glisten on his forehead when he came slowly up the old street each evening, shuffling past the sandesh bakery and the colonial offices, doffing his hat, rubbing at his hair in the dusty light. Foole remembered that, or believed he did. There had been such power in his father's wrists, such pragmatism. Captain Benlowes had contracted his first vessel with the East India Company in 1841 and throughout that seething decade had shipped opium along the coast between warehouses and depots never once failing to deliver his cargo on time. Somewhere Foole held a memory of being hoisted like a travelling satchel over his father's shoulder in the humid evening air while insects batted against a screened porch and an old woman stood nearby, arms folded, smiling. Was it a true memory? He wanted to think it so.

But all that he knew he knew only through the telling. That was the truth of it. A shy child, a watchful boy. He had walked late but never fallen. He had spoken late but in full sentences. Somewhere a photographic plate existed taken by a bellows camera when he was two years old and in the cloudy image he stares unsmiling, uncurious, black-haired and pale-eyed, a fat flushed English boy from the colonies hot in his little white suit.

All of that was his first life. He remembered so little of it, flashes, broken fragments, the faint scent of spice or the smothering heat of the summer evenings. He was four years old when his father determined to take him on a business voyage to Baltimore and though no stranger to his father's ships in the port still he had not sailed before. Was it not strange in such an age to take a shipowner's child along like so much ballast? All his life he would wonder what had possessed his father: had a nurse been dismissed, was Foole to learn the trade that would one day be his own, had his father woken from some troubling dream warning what was to come?

They set sail at dawn under a red sky with the quiet sailors padding barefoot along the spars and hauling at ropes in silhouette in a choreography of rigging and silence. The boy perched on an overturned crate at the railing watching the brown land fade into haze and feeling the lift and roll of the waves take over. His father's schooner tacked away from the coming weather into green seas, past the calm red outline of desert hills, south and east and south again into open water where the sparkle and flare of shoaling fish startled the boy he was. Days passed, weeks passed, under a gauzy webbing of stars and noon skies white as salt. His father led him through the stations of the ship with a patient eye for all he saw while the midshipmen grunted at their work and avoided his gaze until one evening on deck without his father a pod of dolphins was sighted to starboard and he begged the second mate to see. Whatever happened the man held him there by his scruff leaning him farther and farther out until he swung half suspended over the cresting waves and the salt spray flecked his lips, his jaw, and he started to fear. He squirmed in that grip while the mate crooned, Aye I could let ye go, lad, ye'd be eaten by fish and no part of ye'd ever be found, and when he started to cry with the wind punching at his face the mate only scowled and shook the boy until his little teeth chattered. Bollocks, he hissed. Don't ye go weepy on me, ye ain't worth the weight of ye.

His father heard of it. He said nothing but still his father somehow heard. He could remember being locked in his father's quarters while the ship lay becalmed and hearing above deck the roar of his father's voice, the rumble of some heavy thing dragged sternward. He tried not to listen, watched a fly crawl across muslin curtains, blink into motion. The mate kept his distance from then and when they put ashore in Cape Town he trudged down the gangway with his satchel strung over one shoulder and not a look back to crew or captain and Foole never saw the man again.

All that was soon forgotten. After weeks at sea he jogged unsteadily alongside his father feeling the weirdness of packed earth underfoot. They slept side by side in a rented room in clean sheets and when he closed his eyes he could still feel the roll of the ship and when he awoke his father had returned from a street market with fresh fruit and warm white bread. In the mornings his father met with shipmasters in warehouse offices while he waited bored, his feet drumming the floor, and in the afternoons they wandered the Company Gardens flapping their arms at the birds and whooping and smiling at the shy black nannies as they passed. There were prams with enormous wooden wheels standing in the paths and ladies in white seated on benches and under the azure sky the trees were very green, the earth very red.

The accident when it came was nothing, ridiculous, it could have been avoided. They had set sail from Cape Town into a wilder ocean and the first storm had struck on their second day out and it did not let up for weeks. He was sick, seasoned sailors were sick. His father stood at the rail soaked and battered and leaning into the wind with a fury that contained both joy and desire while below decks Foole swung in a hammock, greening, and the pitch of vomit slid from wall to wall underfoot. The ship would rise and rise and crest and then plunge violently back down the steep black water shuddering and creaking the while until the boy feared the timbers must split and the sea pour in. At some point his father came below, sea water streaming from his beard, his right hand cradling his left in a wrapped cloth where a splinter had gone through. It was nothing, a broken bite of wood, a loosed rope in the strong wind. But the fever came over him gradually, the arm weakened gradually, the wound went bad and the gangrene set in. As the Americas neared his father went among the crew less and less often and the stink when he did so was black.

It was the first mate who piloted the schooner past the shipyards and up to the Baltimore waterfront and the same man who carried his father to a lodging house above the harbour. He'll be at peace here, the mate said, and cleared his throat, and added, I'm sorry for ye, lad. He clicked a small bag of English coins down on a writing desk, and shut the door firmly when he left.

His father was lucid, his father raved. He slept often and like the dead. His arm had swollen to the thickness of a melon and was green-black and he screamed at the touch of it. Foole was too frightened to leave his side and ate only what the maid brought him out of pity. After two days the desk clerk came and stood over his father frowning and a short while later a surgeon came and withdrew from a small satchel several ferocious-looking instruments and folded his frock coat over a chair and rolled his sleeves past the elbow. Get the boy out, he said sharply. That was all he said. Foole was taken next door to a restaurant kitchen and seated among the steam and bustle of the Negro dishwashers and there he ate thick slices of bread and strawberry jam and though the sweetness of it turned his stomach he could not stop eating. When he was at last brought back to the lodging house his father's arm was gone and the doctor was leaning over a basin scrubbing the red foam from his knuckles and he could see blood freckling the man's sleeves. Through the open window a fishmonger was calling out his catch. The curtains shifted. On the bed in a square of sunlight the man his father lay, mouth open, his thick beard inexplicably cut short, dead the half-hour at least.

How much of that was true?

All of it, he would say. None of it.

He stepped gingerly through the iron flood doors on the north side of the Thames just before midnight, and started up the stairs, Fludd trailing some ten feet behind. They had waited in the haze with their backs to the wall like cutthroats to give Pinkerton time to exit and after twenty minutes set out in the same direction. The giant had said nothing the long walk north along the tunnel and that silence Foole knew was its own rebuke. He could feel still the soft thrum of the river through the rock overhead, the slick of the tunnel walls shining weird in the gas. There had been a brutality and economy in the American's gestures, the way he had held the revolver at his trouser leg, thumb cocking the hammer, silk hat darkening his face as he watched them go. The father in the man, yes, that. But also a weariness, a sadness at the eyes the father had not suffered.

Around and around, up and up Foole trudged, his hand on the iron railing, his heart drained and sick of it all. Charlotte in the sunlight walking through warm sand. Her face, her hair adrift in the green mortuary light. That snowy morning in New York when he had opened her letter. He ducked his head at the top of the tunnel stairs, slipped out into the night. After a moment he heard Fludd grunt, squeeze his bulk through the narrow door.

The outline of the Tower rose before them.

What is it? Foole said at last. He could not keep the irritation from his voice.

The giant's shoes crunching heavily. Foole could see the huge outsized hands, the brass knuckles glinting.

Say it, Japheth.

Say what.

You think me reckless.

Aye, I do. Bastard's like to start his peeping now until he learns the truth. A man don't dance with the devil, Mr. Adam.

The devil, Foole muttered, turning away.

The river was dark. A family of nine lay huddled asleep on a stone bench cut into the wall, heads lolling, mouths agape. Foole walked over and slipped a guinea into the folds of cloth in the mother's lap. Then they turned north and walked in silence and came out of the shadowy mouth of an alley onto Gracechurch Street like visitants emerging from a dream and they mingled there with the night crowds flowing along the footway.

Fludd was rubbing slivers of frost from his beard. He said, Before sundown tomorrow Pinkerton's goin to know who we is an who we ain't an like as not what we ate for breakfast. He ain't a man we employ for this sort of a task. Not jakes like us, we don't.

Foole slowed before a dressmaker's leaded window, studied their warping reflections in the glass. Crowds swirled past, rivers of light, rivers of pitch.

And just who are we, Japheth? he murmured.

But Fludd was regarding him with an expression of almost grief and did not reply.

His father had lain six days buried in that cemetery in Baltimore when on the seventh day the man in white appeared. A man with long sharp vulpine teeth, plucked eyebrows, tiny spectacles squinching his eyes to slits. The boy he was sat huddled on a bench in the gravel yard of a Catholic orphanage, watching the man glide towards him, a withered nun in her winged cowl dipping at his side. He felt the hairs on his arms prickle. He was four years old and alone in the world and still he could feel the wrongness in the man. His father had been laid in a pauper's grave loose-boxed under a shovelful of lime and Foole had stood at the gravedigger's knee while a ladies' aid member set her gloved hand to her hat and struggled to find her tears. That gravedigger with his African skin and trousers tied with rope and his heavy stooped shoulders proclaimed a prayer none of which the child understood beyond its final cruel Amen. All his life to come Baltimore would be that: a city of open graves and hot wind and skies rolling blackly overhead.

The man in white did not announce himself. He took the child in hand and led him past the staring orphans in their grey wool shirts and had him repack his father's satchel and took him from that place without a kind word or smile. There was a letter with some signature and seal at its bottom which the man showed and the holy sisters nodded gravely at it and regarded Foole from the depths of their eyes. He did as he was told, he did not cry. But he missed his father and it was a physical pain, a hurt in the hollow of his breast. He missed the sea in his father's skin, his ropy forearms as he swung the child whooping skyward. And he missed Calcutta, too, already fading from his memory, the big house in White Town near the bakery, the heat and clatter and noise of the Bengali processions along the riverbanks under a setting sun. In comparison this forlorn land, this America, seemed cold and vast and brutal, a land where the loved could be swallowed by the earth and lost forever.

The man in white took him in a hired coach to a bustling hall and lifted him up a steep set of stairs and down a corridor lined with windows and into a small plush private room. There was a window, and Foole remembered the seat underneath it, soft, maroon, and the man's quiet meticulous gestures. That man wore a long cream coat whose tails he folded up over his thighs as he sat down and a tall white top hat and his head, when he removed his hat, was hairless. Foole remembered the creased skin at the back of the man's skull, the way his ears pressed flat against his head like white knots of bone, the eerie stillness in his face when he turned around.

His name was Fisk, the man said, speaking at last. He peered at the boy from over the rims of his spectacles. He worked for a woman who had once known Foole's father, he said, a woman whom his father had written from his sickbed, begging that she care for the boy. Should his employer so agree, the boy would be raised in a city called Boston, far to the north. Even as they spoke his father's schooner was being negotiated down to cover the debts incurred by its incomplete voyage and the big house and the shipping business back in Calcutta would be similarly disposed of. He, not a legal heir, could lay no claim to the properties. All this Fisk said with a quiet contempt and then he unhooked his spectacles and rubbed at his eyes and added in his crackling voice, It is a pity about your colouring, boy. If you are lucky you will be mistaken for Spanish. Foole sat, absorbing all this. And then came a sudden swift jolt, and the child put out his arms for balance and stared in horror as the small room began, incomprehensibly, to move.

It was his first journey by rail. As the train gathered speed he sat with his nose against the glass, the fields and forest scrolling past and the train rattling up through the boy's bones and settling, a low throb, into the nerves at the base of his skull. The dining carriage was wondrous, the sleeping compartments cold, the scent of oil and polish in the wooden floors unlike anything he had known. The journey passed, the days passed. Boston when they arrived was cooler, calmer than Baltimore, the wide boulevards strangely clean, and Fisk hailed a coach under a red evening sky and took Foole across the city and past the Commons and into its outlying estates. As they rode Fisk sat facing the boy, his hands crossed on the handle of his cane, his head drooping and jerking awake. But his eyes all the while remained fixed on the boy in his dread.

Fisk's employer, Foole's benefactress, awaited them in the vast marble foyer of her mansion. Foole had seen big houses before but nothing so grand, so forbidding, so cold and clean and silent. The gates stood open, the long drive was lined with sycamores, hedges, vast lawns. Then the house was looming up before him, a great stone fortress, and he had stared at the windows in their shimmering rows feeling whelmed with fear. Fisk had alighted at once, cleared his throat in impatience, and tapped the child on the backside with his cane as he clambered down. He leaned his face close and whispered, Best begin your begging, boy, then brushed past and ascended the entry stairs and pulled sharply on the reception bell.

She was dressed in a grey silk and wore her black hair up so that the streak of white at her temple startled. She clasped her long pale fingers at her belly and lowered her chin and studied the child where he stood still clutching his father's old sailor's satchel, shivering, small, and her gaze was steady, curious, intent. He wanted to hide his face but did not dare.

This is the boy? she murmured. Her voice was low, surprisingly gentle. Is he hungry? Have you eaten, child? Stand straight, do not be afraid. Ah, yes, you have your father's eyes.

She had been standing on the first riser of a wide curving marble staircase and he had not seen this until she stepped down and walked towards him. She was smaller than he'd thought.

O you sweet poor creature, she said. She knelt, lifted his chin in her fingers. Her eyes were two different colours, one grey, one the green of a sunlit sea. What shall we call you? Certainly something English, something to help you get along in the world. Edward, I think. After your father.

Foole trembled. The great house around them creaked.

After a moment when it was clear he would say nothing she rose and brushed at her gown and turned and regarded Fisk lurking in the shadows. Mr. Fisk will show you to your arrangements. Tomorrow we shall have a look at the nursery and see that it is made suitable. For tonight, the library will suffice. Mr. Fisk?

The man in white bowed gravely.

See that young Master Edward is settled. Take him down to the kitchens for his supper.

Fisk nodded. As you wish, Mrs. Shade, he said.

And he took up the child's battered satchel and crossed the marble floor and guided him down a dark passage into the shadowy rooms of his second life.

FIFTEEN

A fine mist was drifting sidelong out across the river. A frenzy of rooks burst black and savage in the air over the south bank and William stopped with a hand shielding his eyes, taking in the metallic sinew of the Thames, the cries of rivermen adrift over the waters. The rooks rose and wheeled as one in the cold light and there was a wrongness to it, like a warning.

Mr. Pinkerton, Blackwell called. It is near eleven, sir.

He grimaced. He had insisted on their walking to Millbank, despite the cold, wanting to turn over in his head some of his confusion. He did not know if Martin Reckitt would have heard of the man Foole. An uncle could hardly be expected to recall his ward's dalliances in detail, especially from long ago. As he had drifted into sleep the night before he had decided not to follow the lead on Jonathan Cooper, the Saracen, bristling at Adam Foole's insinuations. Then of his dreams he recalled only fragments, the tissue-thin drafting plans for the sewers unrolled on a stone table, a clerk shouting at him that Muck Annie's hole had not been built to specifications. He awoke exhausted, troubled, and knew by the hollows under his eyes that he had decided nothing.

At a pie stand just past the rotted timbers of Lambeth Bridge William stopped and Blackwell paused then came back towards him and he bought the inspector a mince pie and they walked on. The pie vendor banging the lid of his cart behind them in the cold, grinning toothlessly into his fists. William pulled off his gloves, held the pastry steaming in its brown paper between two fingers. The heat of it scorched the roof of his mouth.

I remember when it froze five years ago, sir, Blackwell said, blowing on his pastry. You could walk right across it, bank to bank. There were barmaids out on the ice with brandies for sale. A queer feeling that was, standing on something that shouldn't hold your weight.

It took William a moment to understand his meaning. He let his eyes drift out over the river, shimmering in its steel.

They have a history, sir, Blackwell said. The chief and Mr. Reckitt, I mean.

William felt the hairs on the back of his neck prickle. He folded the remains of the pie very slowly in its greasy wrapper. What history? he asked.

I don't mean to speak of it, sir. It's not my place.

William put out a hand and held the man's arm. What history?

Blackwell cleared his throat. Well the chief has a, well, a weakness for the chippies, sir. You might have noticed it. Oh he's a fine husband, I don't doubt, but he has a weakness.

This sounds like gossip, Blackwell.

Not gossip, sir.

He gave the inspector a hard look.

It's not gossip, sir, he said again. Mr. Reckitt's crew were passing bad notes on the Continent and the chief went to Paris and arrested one of the screevers himself. I suppose Mr. Reckitt had an eye out for revenge. The chief was a regular at Nellie Coffey's house in the Borough. She and the chief used to meet at the Rising Sun on Fleet Street and exchange, ah, information. She was the widow of Big Jack Casey, you might have heard of him? Had the one leg? Well Mr. Reckitt arranged to have a gentleman step in at an unsuitable moment and notify a night watchman of a theft on the premises. Being a gentleman of some standing, this would have involved the detaining of all of the guests for questioning. And Mr. Shore would have been, ah, interrupted, sir.

You mean in the act.

Blackwell flushed. Yes sir. In the act. Fortunately we learned of Mr. Reckitt's intentions on the evening in question and avoided the scandal. The gentleman-associate came to us and confessed. Cold feet and such, sir, I expect. Rumour of it passed up the line all the same though and Mr. Shore was overlooked for promotion the following year.

When was all this?

Seventy-three, I think it was, sir. Mr. Reckitt was taken the next year. Arrested at customs with a bag of uncut diamonds traced back to a heist in South Africa.

William stopped walking. Why are you telling me this, Inspector?

Blackwell turned to face him, his blue eyes flat, his cheeks raw in the chill. Because no one else was telling you, sir, he said.

William's father too had loved a woman not his wife. William had known this even as a boy though he did not know the nature of that love, even now, and would sometimes tell himself it was a chaste love, a love of friendship and not of passion. His father called her Kitty but to the world her name was Kate Warne and she came to the Pinkerton offices in 1856 with no experience, a slender widow of twenty-six, brown-haired, with bold cheekbones and a gift for accents and the intelligent eyes of a schoolteacher. She had taken from her handbag an advertisement for the position of detective and his father had scowled, refusing her an interview. Detective work was not for women. But later that morning he had, inexplicably, relented, and by ten o'clock he had put her on the payroll as a full detective. William remembered the stubborn way his father's neck would thicken and bull into his chest whenever his mother mentioned Kitty's name. He trusted her as he trusted few others, he would tell her. A married man shouldn't trust her kind, she would reply, leaving his father apoplectic and stuttering. Her kind uncovered the plot to kill the president-elect, he would shout, even if Lincoln's people didn't want to pay the expense of it. Oh I've heard about her expenses, his mother would shout back. And don't you talk to me about being reasonable or the Drysdale case or how she traced that $130,000 again, hush now, stop, the boys are listening. But his father did not stop. When Kate fell ill with pneumonia William's father sat vigil at her bedside and when she died he did not come home for three days straight. That was in January of 1868. She would have been younger than William was now, he realized. His father had her buried in the Pinkerton plot, next to where he himself would lie. His mother never would discuss it and her humiliation, like so much about her, could be savage in its silence.

William himself had never been unfaithful. He would drink late in outpost saloons under fiery candle wheels, make his way upstairs to whatever creaking bed alone. On railway carriages he would eat in silence, his dark eyes unfriendly. He was indifferent to a well-turned ankle, to the flare of a pale throat in an elevator cage late at night. Yes he knew how women looked at him. He just did not care. There were men with appetites in his line of work as in any but he could not be counted among their number and the truth was he loved his wife and desired no other.

William watched Blackwell cross the white gravel of Millbank's outer yard and call through to the gatehouse. The prison was silent, the street around them empty and desolate. Blackwell called and called and he shook the cold bars of the gate.

After a moment a hooded figure crunched around the corner of the gatehouse and peered at them through the bars and then worked a clasp. The gate swung inward with a slow heavy screech. Blackwell gave William a look and they stepped single file through onto the dead black earth of Millbank and the porter—a small man, cowled in his cloak—cast a quick sharp glare at them as if at a shank of meat at market found wanting and then he stumped back inside.

William had been through many prisons in his life and seen terrible things. He had seen the small brick jail in Denver where men had been hauled kicking into the rafters on coils of rope and the ancient Tombs where Manhattan's indigent were dumped to die. He had been beneath the stones of Kingston Pen and seen men's limbs lost to frostbite and he had prowled the haunted underground cells of Newgate with neither escort nor guide. But not Millbank, never yet Millbank.

Of course he had heard of it. What lawman had not. It stood near empty now, though it had once held thousands of men in a solitude and silence that broke the spirits of prisoners and wardens both. Its stone walls were the grey-yellow of the high California canyons and rose around them sullen and cracked in the sulphurous light and as he walked William could not shake the feeling of being watched. The small openings high in the walls would not be within reach of their occupants but in the central tower rising up before them the windows burned with a greenish light. A stink of vinegar filled the air as if some wrong thing had burned there. William held his handkerchief close.

They followed the porter in. A low coal fire was burning in the grate.

Gentlemen, the porter said. He had taken down his hood and stood side-whiskered and ancient with his backside to the fire, his stubby hands held out behind him for the heat. I'll ask ye to sign the ledger on the perch. And to relinquish any firearms ye be carryin on your person.

This last was said with a direct look at William and William glanced at Blackwell then back at the porter but did not move.

The chief told him you were an American, sir, Blackwell said.

Meanin no offence by it, of course, the porter added.

William cradled his Colt in one hand, passed it upside down to the porter. Is that it?

The ledger, the porter said.

William dipped the pen, wrote his name in his big crooked hand.

It was a .36-calibre Colt Navy and in Chicago he kept it the way some other men kept secrets: it was the first thing you saw. You saw a gun and there was a man with it like he was on retainer and first the gun said hello and then the man nodded and said hello too.

He sucked at his teeth.

Nodded at the porter and they went on in.

The porter guided them to the inner gate where a warden took their charge and they followed along a windowless stone hallway and through an iron door without speaking and as they went the darkness at first distinguished them and then made them as one. The immense weight of stone around them pressed deep. The halls were unlighted and the floors covered in gravel from the yards and at each heavy safety door the warden would pause and turn sideways in the gaslight and pull slowly through the ring of keys tied to his belt as if he had not covered that distance in many years and did not himself trust his way.

At last the corridor widened and they came to the cells. The doors stood open and the cells bare and William saw neither the incarcerated nor any guard. As they went Blackwell talked to him in a low voice about the military use of the prison and its now-empty cells and the reasons for its dismantling and when he asked what would happen to Martin Reckitt Blackwell only shrugged and said the chief had recommended the decommissioned naval hulks south of Portsmouth.

The warden led them along the angled corridor towards a narrow iron staircase. The cells stood all to the right and facing them were small deep-set windows spilling an eerie grey daylight down the walls. At the top of the stairs he made his way down to a turning in the corridor where a single cell stood barred fast and where seated upon a hard bench picking at a strand of oakum sat an old man with shorn hair in brown prison-issue clothes.

The old man stood slowly. He set the frayed rope aside in a tangle.

Martin Reckitt? William said.

The prisoner regarded him for a long quiet moment and then he nodded slowly. Mr. William Pinkerton, he said.

He was informed of our visit, sir, Blackwell explained in a low voice. But not its purpose.

Martin Reckitt was thin as a rail, his skin greasy as if some deep illness were seeping up from his core. A bruise on one cheek had browned like bad fruit. His eyes were small and bloodshot in a face the more deeply etched for the bad light in that cell. But his ancient fingers were thorny with calluses and still strong and when he moved there was a lean muscular stiffness in his shoulders and neck as if he had slept a long time on a hard surface and it had not broken him.

And what are you in for, sir? he was saying. His smile did not reach his eyes.

William inclined his head. He waited while the cell was unlocked and then went in and sat at the end of the bench and withdrew a notebook from his pocket.

Mr. Pinkerton means to ask you some questions, Blackwell said sternly. He stood just inside the cell. You'd be wise to listen and answer honestly. No nonsense from you now.

Martin Reckitt studied the young inspector with a baleful smile and then he looked at William. I'm innocent, he said.

William shook his head. A case of mistaken identity, was it.

It always is, Mr. Pinkerton. In all but the eyes of the Lord.

William gave him a quick puzzled smile. Except I'm not here to talk about you, he said. I want to talk about Charlotte.

Charlotte.

Your niece. Yes.

Martin Reckitt shifted on the prison cot, he turned his face aside. When he glanced back his expression was careful, composed. I haven't seen Charlotte in years, he said flatly. The last I heard, she was lawful and not causing any trouble. You should leave her be.

Blackwell scratched at the back of one hand, bored. He said, Charlotte signed herself in as a visitor two months ago. We know how often she came to see you, Mr. Reckitt.

William waved the inspector quiet. Tell me about her and Edward Shade, he said.

He was watching the old thief's face as he said it but the man did not flinch and his calmness betrayed nothing, neither recognition nor confusion. She worked with Shade before he died, did she not? he pressed.

I've been inside ten years, Mr. Pinkerton. I know nothing of such matters. I'm old and tired and would like to die outside, that's all.

That's not likely to happen, Mr. Reckitt, Blackwell said.

Reckitt looked across at the inspector standing by the cell door in his black morning coat and said, I'm surprised to see you with a chaperone, Mr. Pinkerton. The great American detective.

William turned to Blackwell. Give us a minute.

Blackwell frowned. My instructions are clear, sir.

William waited.

Blackwell hesitated, glanced from William to Reckitt and then back. Just a minute then, sir. I'll be just along the hall.

He called for the warden and the hunched figure came slowly back along the corridor and unlocked the cell then locked it again and William sat in the silence listening as the clinking of the keys and the scrape of the two men's footfalls passed away. Then he turned to the aging thief.

Edward Shade, Mr. Reckitt. What did you know of him?

Reckitt blinked wetly. Shade. Shade?

William still had not opened his notebook. He said, I'm not interested in your niece, Mr. Reckitt. Unless I have to be. I'm interested in the man Shade and what happened to him.

Did your father send you? Reckitt gave him a sly look. He used to be rather interested in the whereabouts of Mr. Shade, if I recall. It was the first question he'd ask any of us, back then. I expect he is still—?

William cleared his throat. My father died last year, he said.

Ah. Such a loss. Sometimes I think there is a wall separating all of us from the world, Mr. Pinkerton, he said gravely. Free and not free alike. Sometimes I think that wall separates us from ourselves. If you'd like to know about Charlotte's acquaintances, you should ask her yourself.

William nodded in distraction, his thoughts adrift. He nodded and he nodded and in the silence he started to inform Reckitt about his niece's death but then he did not. Instead he said, surprising himself, You and John Shore—

Reckitt smiled a thin smile. Oh. I've known Inspector Shore a long time.

Chief Inspector.

Reckitt looked surprised. Chief? Well. Time shall creep in its petty paces, he said softly. We are here until we are not.

Not you. You're here until you're transferred.

I was referring to the condition we call life, Mr. Pinkerton, he said in a withering tone. The transfer means little to me. Reckitt rubbed at his wrists as if to ease an ache in them. It is a strange feeling, outliving one's prison, he said, a rather strange feeling. I have found my days at Millbank not so trying. They have given me leisure to reacquaint myself with the word of the Lord. Do you know, sir, had I a second life I should have devoted it to the Church?

You tried that. They wouldn't have you.

Reckitt regarded him a long cold moment. No, sir, it was I who wouldn't have them, he said slowly. He blinked his moist eyes.

You tell it however you like. About your niece and Shade—

Reckitt gave a slight bony half shrug, almost theatrical. He said, In the seminary, Mr. Pinkerton, I was one of the more studious candidates. I had my faith, of course. But what interested me was how translation had changed the Bible itself. The Good Book was not written in English, sir. It was not even written in Latin. Some of it is from the Greek, some the Hebrew. And yet we are told the word of God is absolute. Does that sound sensible to you?

William said nothing.

Reckitt clicked his tongue. Nor to me, he said, nor to me. Language is created by men.

Mr. Reckitt.

Consider the devil, Mr. Pinkerton. The Satan. Only as an example, nothing more. In Hebrew, *satan* is not a name, only a word, meaning adversary. The figure of the Satan, when he appears in the oldest stories, is a servant of the Lord, sent by God to tempt the people of the earth by testing their faith. His task is to report back to God about who passes, and who fails, such tests. We invented the devil, sir, sometime in the Middle Ages. Nothing is absolute. Everything in the human world is translated by time. Even evil. Once I understood this, I was no longer fit to serve the Church.

William wanted to ask the old thief about the man Adam Foole, Charlotte's old lover. It seemed possible that the old man might recall some detail about him. But something held him back, some hesitation, he could not say just what it was. The old man was not forthcoming about anything and perhaps it was simply this. Perhaps it was something more. They could hear Blackwell pacing in the corridor, the click of his heels on the flooring.

Mr. Reckitt, William said. How did your niece first encounter Shade? Who introduced them?

Do you believe in love, Mr. Pinkerton?

William looked at him, exasperated.

Love is the great divide, Reckitt said. It is what we cross and how we cross out of ourselves. You must know I did not ever marry, sir. But I have loved. And I do love, I love my niece. I know the truth of it is love, because the word is inadequate to its meaning. The Bible tells us only a man incapable of love is a truly dangerous man.

What does this have to do with Shade?

John Shore, sir, is a man incapable of love.

For god's sake.

We were children together, in the same neighbourhood. He was a troubled boy, a bully. I was older than him, and bookish, and even still I was afraid to pass him in the street. He went into the police force because he understood it was a way of holding power.

William sighed, impatient.

It was as if Reckitt could sense the shift in him for he fell silent and then he was regarding William with a strange intensity. Why are you here, Mr. Pinkerton? he said cautiously. Why are you here, speaking with me now? What is it has happened?

William closed his notebook. Your niece is dead, Mr. Reckitt. She was found twelve days ago.

Slowly Reckitt's thorny eyebrows knitted together. He said nothing.

She was murdered. I'm sorry about it.

The ancient thief turned his face aside and they sat a long moment in silence. Then William got to his feet, he ran a hand through his hair, he set about buttoning his chesterfield.

Charlotte's dead? Reckitt said slowly.

William nodded.

Charlotte?

Her head was recovered from the river, William said. Her torso was found at a building site on Edgware Road in a sack. Her legs were discovered on Saturday, in Bermondsey. This man, this Edward Shade. His old associates are the only lead we have.

He watched the old man absorb the lie. At the cell door he turned. If you remember anything about Shade, you know how to reach me.

I never knew an Edward Shade, Reckitt whispered. He did not raise his eyes.

Anything at all, William said.

Can I see her? Mr. Pinkerton?

William banged on the bars. Blackwell, he called. He turned back. Who else worked with Charlotte in those years, Martin? Who else might have known Shade?

When Reckitt raised his face his eyes were black with fury. Some brutal thing passed between them, some understanding about human suffering and the ways it might be increased. He swallowed.

The man you want to talk to, he said, is Adam Foole.

SIXTEEN

Frightened? Foole said. Edward Shade's been dead twenty years, Japheth.

So show me a body, Fludd muttered. He gestured with his spoon and an orange light flared in its curve. Fact is, Mr. Adam, you crossed a line with those Pinkertons. Worst what you can do, to a certain kind of jack. I told you for years it weren't over. Past has a way of dippin a man's pockets when he don't keep an eye out.

This from you.

Aye, Fludd said with a heavy look. This from me. It ain't up to us to decide what dead is.

Foole thought of Charlotte in the stillness of the mortuary and then of the American enshrouded in the tunnel darkness and he shook his head. Pinkerton's of use to me, he said with a soft vehemence. If the Saracen can be found, Pinkerton will find him.

He's like to find more than just the Saracen.

He's not dangerous to us, Japheth. A rough laughter drifted up through the carpet from the flash house below, faded away. Foole shifted the claret aside, interlaced his fingers on the table. Pinkerton imagines he's hunting Shade for his father, he said slowly. But he's not. He's doing it for himself. That's what makes him dangerous. Do you know what I think, Japheth? I think his father told him nothing about what happened.

You mean between you an his da.

Foole nodded.

That ain't a reassurance, Fludd grimaced.

They had come down King's Cross in the hour after dusk, the two of them, crossing with care the three slimed steps, the broken knife-edged planking that led here to Bottle's flash house. Fludd had hauled at the bulleted door with both hands, set his weight and leaned out, and then Foole had felt the sudden blast of heat from within. Dense smoke, the reek of unwashed flesh: Foole had held his pocket closed and his hat to his head as he trailed Fludd in and down. They had brushed by ramps-men with tankards asway, maltoolers with their fly forks fumbling the skirts of bonnet girls, they had glimpsed a child with a malformed spine grinding an organ on a low stage in a corner but they had not slowed. A knuckler had pushed past with a glass of max, his bad eye tamped like a white marble in mud. Then at a heavy oak door at the far end of the bar Fludd had banged thrice in quick succession and after a moment a small slot in its face had opened and the white rove of an eyeball pressed itself against the visible light.

Bottle, Fludd called, ducking his face to be seen. It's Japheth.

The slot shut again. There was a rasp of bolts and then the door swung wide to reveal a man in evening dress grave and solitary as an undertaker. Foole glimpsed thinning hair, a liverspotted scalp. How old they had all grown.

Why Mr. Fludd, the man said in a thick Scottish accent. You have come back to us. And Mr. Foole, sir. Table for two?

Three, said Foole. Molly's to join.

Aye, an bring her a bucket when she do, Fludd grinned. Kid can drink like a fish.

Bottle had led them upstairs, along a narrow corridor, their footfalls drumming over the hollow floor. In a panelled room at the front of the premises, on a small table, they found two thick tallow candles burning down, as if the men's presence had been long foreseen. A bottle of claret wrapped in a white cloth had been left uncorked and breathing. Foole ordered a coconut soup followed by a salmon curry and Fludd the artichoke ragout and then Bottle withdrew, returned moments later with the dishes, withdrew again.

Foole leaned close. I thought he'd be taller, he said with a quiet intensity, as soon as they were alone again. Pinkerton's son, I mean.

O he were tall enough, like. An light on his feet for his size, what makes for the trouble.

He's not much like his father. Less fire and brimstone. His father was wrathful but he doesn't have that in him. Foole said this and then looked up as if surprised by his own words.

Fludd nodded. You thought he'd be different.

I thought there'd be—

A resemblance.

He regarded Fludd's face in the candlelight but could see no ridicule in it. Yes, he said softly. A resemblance.

They ain't your blood, Mr. Adam.

It was said in kindness but he felt all at once foolish, tired. He had lived always with a tight control over events and it seemed to him now that matters were descending, that he was losing himself in the face of some grand design not of his own making.

Fludd snapped open a napkin and reached for the claret and poured out two glasses. To Pinkertons, he said. To them what's here, an them what's gone. The glass vanished in his huge hand, his fingernails black-rimmed and bitten.

Foole drank.

But Fludd had suspended his own glass at his lips and he growled now over the rim, his gaze steady, Still I'd go three rounds with the bastard without gloves, I would. Though I'd rather come on up behind him with a cosh in me fist an him asleep. Then he grunted and took a deep drink, set the glass down, wiped the claret from his beard. Law don't never make for a clean tool, Mr. Adam. An Pinkerton's a law unto hisself.

Foole frowned. You make it sound Biblical, Japheth.

Blame it on me upbringing, Fludd said, then fell to brooding. He shifted a meaty fist on the table. You'll be wantin to tell the kid about it, he said. I know you won't be eager to. You just need to decide how much to tell, when she gets here.

Foole studied his cracked hands.

You can't protect her from it, Mr. Adam. I just come out of a stone jug. Dancin with a Pinkerton's like to land all of us back inside. Molly won't be treated no softer on account of her age.

There was a distant crash from the bar below and then a muffled cheer but in the soft dimness of their little room Foole took no notice and after a moment he said in a tone all at once cold and brutal as a steel cable: Edward Shade never existed, Japheth, not legally. There are no papers in his name, no photographs, no outstanding writs or warrants. Nothing. No one else knows the truth of it, except you. I was careful.

You never told Charlotte?

I never told anyone. Least of all the Reckitts.

The giant's face contorted in the candlelight.

No one can trace a ghost, Japheth. Not even William Pinkerton.

Except you ain't a ghost, Mr. Adam, Fludd murmured, and his low voice was like sheet metal shaken in darkness. You ain't a ghost yet.

Edward, Mrs. Shade would whisper at night, and the child would look up from his wooden toys startled. The speaking of his father's name felt so strange to him, preposterous. Some afternoons Fisk would come upon him in the half-light of the stables and hiss: You should not be in here, Master Edward, and he would flee in a clatter of harness leather and iron, as if from the name itself. At supper, when his governess asked him sternly, And what do you say, Edward? he would set his spoon respectfully astride his soup bowl and murmur some assent that seemed to come from a different throat, a different child. And yet that name now belonged to him, and what might have been a kindness, a way of keeping a loved one alive and near, became in time its own erasure. Slowly he answered to that name as if it were his own. Slowly Edward Benlowes faded, his rasping voice forgotten.

What did the child feel in Shade House, what did he think of its occupants? Was it fear? Mrs. Shade herself should have terrified. She was skeletal, a grave woman with death in her eyes, with skin so pale it glowed at times almost blue. But a sadness filled her, inhabited her movements. Widowed at thirty-one, young yet for the fortune she possessed, she never spoke of the husband dead three years that winter, his surveyor's coach overturned into the raging Ohio. His body never was found. She often was tired, true, and in the evenings would clutch a hand to her throat to catch her breath, the tendons in her neck standing sharply out. She climbed stairs slowly, spoke in halting phrases. On summer mornings she would rise from her untouched breakfast and drift onto the garden terrace among the dahlias and the roses bearing an expression of stricken regret. Foole would watch her, anxious, fearful.

Mrs. Shade was a freethinker, an atheist, an abolitionist. There was a greatness in her, in an age when women were refused greatness. When the child asked Fisk one day why the estate's small chapel was boarded up, the man shrugged a sour shrug and said, Because she wants it that way. Her faith lay elsewhere. In the autumn she insisted the child begin his lessons though just five years old. He was to study four hours each morning and she brought a governess up from New York for the task. Mrs. Shade insisted he eat lemons, oranges, grapefruit during his lessons. A scientist in New York had discovered citrus opened new channels in the brain, she explained, and then with a sly smile added: It makes one think, does it not? Foole was dressed in little tailored suits each day and kept obedient but Mrs. Shade was fiercely opposed to any physical punishment. She told him once, A man is judged for his beliefs, Edward. You must never believe in anything that you have not first thought through. He learned through Fisk and the cook that her mother's parents had fled the Revolution in France, only to have to flee Bonaparte again, and then again, as the smaller countries of Europe were eaten up by the French Empire. My parents believed in nothing, she herself said one evening. Nothing but human dignity, Edward, that and the importance of good walking shoes.

In the afternoons he was given his run of the estate. He would scale drainpipes, prowl the slate roofs, hunting the half-wild cats with hands spread and a ragged fishing net slouching between. Or he would peel off his clothes and swim naked in the man-made lake among the lily pads and weeds. He would play with an older boy, James, son of the coachman who had drowned in the Ohio, who lived with the cook in a cottage off-grounds. That boy was pliant, and gentle, and twice Foole's size. Together they would dig elaborate traps in the lawn for pirates and thieves, they would hide on his governess until dusk had fallen. They were more than friends, as boyhood allows, inventing a private language of bird calls and grunts, cutting each other's hands with a flint arrowhead, swearing fealty each to each in the infinite undying twilight that is a childhood.

All that he would remember as if it were a fairy story of impossible dimensions. And like all such stories there came a blight to this one also: a sharp pained cough, his benefactress doubling over in her chair, blood in a handkerchief folded and double-folded and secreted away. No she would not discuss it. But in the fall she disappeared for six weeks, travelling out west, to the high dry sierras there, leaving the child behind on the estate in its sudden gloomy vastness. The man in white, Fisk, went with her. Foole remembered his stern upright figure glaring straight ahead as the coach started slowly down the drive. She returned from that trip with blood in her cheeks, her eyes ablaze, and for a time she came alive. And then slowly, surely, she began again to wilt.

So the months passed, receded. Calcutta, his father, all that he once had been, receded. The frail silhouette of Mrs. Shade, coughing, took their place.

It was on the last night of his first year at Shade House when he awoke in his blankets, startled, heart hammering. The two girls in white were standing at his bedside. He had not seen them since Calcutta. Moonlight fell aslant the floor in a silver oblong and in that shining he could see his breath and he started to shake. The girls' eyes were filled with hatred.

Papa? he whispered. Have you seen him? Is Papa there too?

But they said nothing, only stared in their loathing, and then in the stillness they were gone, devoured by the dark.

He was five years old.

In the flash house Foole was rubbing at his eyes with the heel of his hand when Molly came in. He could see by her face that something was wrong. She had been quieter since their visit to Mrs. Sharper and her sister, a soft core of sadness in her, but it was not that. Fludd, the wings of his waistcoat spread and a dainty pink finger picking at his teeth, caught Foole's expression and turned also.

I never seen him until he were right behind me, Adam, Molly said. I swear. Like a bloody shadow, he is.

The man who squeezed in behind her wore an elegant black coat with tails and a green satin waistcoat and his oiled brown hair was pressed and combed back from his ears. His cheeks were pitted and shiny in the light. He sat in the empty chair and set his hat aggressively upon the table. When he crossed his legs Foole noted his spats and the false ruby in his cane. There would be a blade hidden there he knew. The man was a fence by trade and long a part of the swell mob and rumoured to have accepted human cargo in lieu of outstanding debts. Foole had borrowed twenty thousand pounds from the monster two years earlier and not yet paid back a penny. His name was Appleby Barr.

Barr regarded Fludd where he sat glowering and then he turned sidelong to face Foole. I had heard you were in London again, he said quietly. I did not believe it. I expect you will have a payment for me?

Foole furrowed his brow, he cleared his throat as if to speak but he did not speak.

That is not the answer I was hoping for, Mr. Foole.

I have a few projects in the planning. You'll have your money.

I certainly shall.

Foole smiled tightly. Then what is the concern here, Mr. Barr?

It is a question of when, sir. What manner of project?

Profitable ones.

Barr licked at his lower lip. A thick blunt tongue, white as a grub. I shall need more than that, Mr. Foole, if you wish to appease my associates. What sort of return are you expecting?

You'll have your money, Mr. Barr, Foole said again.

Molly chewed at her nails, leaned over, spat into the carpet.

Fludd's low voice rumbled from the shadows. That ain't the way to ask for it now, is it, he said, his huge strangler hands open on the table.

Barr looked unimpressed. Mr. Fludd, I presume?

Mr. Fludd, Foole said, gesturing wearily. Mr. Barr. Mr. Barr is a business associate of ours.

An investor, Barr corrected. Who has yet to see a return on his investment.

Some prospects is just a losin proposition, Fludd grunted. Sometimes you just cut your losses, like.

Mr. Barr's prospects do not lose, Foole said. Do they, sir?

They do not.

Fludd turned his shaggy face towards Foole, raised his eyebrows.

You'll have your return, Mr. Barr, Foole said quickly. He wanted to avoid further provocation. I assure you of that. But I do need a little more time.

You are out of time, sir.

Another few weeks. My reputation as an earner is worth that much, surely.

It used to be so.

A jack can't pay what he can't pay, Molly muttered.

Barr sat with his oily face calm and he ran a finger over his hair, smoothing it. He said, Ah, child, but there are many ways to make up what is owed. Are there not, Mr. Foole?

Foole frowned.

Next time, sir, it will not be me coming to visit, Barr said with a shrug. He pinched up the fabric at his knees.

An it ain't like to be Mr. Foole they find waitin, Fludd growled.

Barr nodded coolly, a flicker of a smile at his lips. Mr. Foole, Mr. Fludd, he said, rising from his chair. He set his hat delicately on his head, screwed it into place. At the door he paused. Might I recommend the '72 Chateau? An excellent companion to the salmon.

And then the door closed, and Foole sighed, rubbing his temples with two fingers.

Just how much you in the bag for? Fludd said, as soon as the man was gone.

O we're all ears, Adam, Molly said. She sat in the chair Barr had been using and wriggled on her haunches. It's all bloody warm now. Like sittin down in his lap, it is.

Cork it, kid, Fludd said. You're the one what brought the bugger.

Molly was making a show of standing, draping her coat over Barr's seat.

It's only business, Japheth, Foole said. It'll be settled soon enough. Mr. Barr is a useful man to know. Maybe the cleanest fence in the flash. I'd regret offending him unduly.

Then you best pay him.

We'll need the funds first. Foole tried to smile but did not quite manage it. We've been shifting stock through Mr. Barr since eighty-two. He's floated us a few times when he needn't have. He has his own pressures, I'm sure. This visit wasn't much more than a gentle nudge. Foole could hear the roar of the flash house below. I think Mr. Barr looks on us with a rather friendly eye, he said.

Fludd grunted. Eyes glistening in the candle fire like the heads of twin nails.

Molly looked up, met Foole's gaze, and there was in her face some troubled thing. She dragged a shoe over the carpet, back and forth.

What is it, Molly?

She shook her head. Nothin. I were just thinkin. You should find that mudlark.

Fludd raised his face in surprise, studied Foole.

Seeing the girl's expression cloud over Foole thought of her that night after Sharper's, in the carriage as they rode slowly back towards Half Moon Street. How she had laid her head on his shoulder, the light warmth of her curled there, her soft breathing. For days now he had glimpsed her standing at the Emporium windows lost in thought and had understood, grievously, what had been stirred up in her from that visit. Foole had lost his own share of loved ones. But for Molly there was only the lost child Peter, eaten by the outer darkness of London.

Mrs. Sharper said Annie's down in the cubbies, Molly muttered. If you think the Grindbones likely done in your Charlotte, it don't seem right not to go on after him. You don't want the not knowing, Adam. You want to feel like you done all you could.

Foole nodded.

I don't know as how you get down there and back out in one piece. But a dipper used to work the lay with me maybe knows somethin. Used to hole up down under Blackfriars in the winters. I can ask him, if you like.

Foole felt Fludd's eyes on him. He said, softly, We already have a man in mind.

He ain't agreed to it as yet, Fludd said.

Molly paused, studied them with her small eyes. Who is it?

Pinkerton.

Pinkerton?

Aye. Pinkerton.

You met with William Pinkerton, she said slowly.

Foole nodded.

He had thought she would be angry but instead she only nodded and folded and unfolded her hands, solemn and thoughtful. We operated a long time without never attracting undue attention, Adam, she murmured. You always said it were the best way to keep in the clear. Not bein noticed, like. She looked up, frowning. An now you bring in William Pinkerton? You can't mean to trust the bastard.

Trust has nothing to do with it.

But you'd send him down into the cubbies. On flash business.

You want to go instead?

I ain't scared to. She scratched angrily at her ear. We can always find some jack to go, Adam. But using Pinkerton in the risk? A faint down-turn at the edges of her lips as she considered. What don't I see? Is there some roll to it? Jappy?

It weren't me decision.

Foole rapped a patient knuckle on the arm of his chair. It's been decided. Rightly or wrongly. It's a calculated risk.

Calculated me arse. Molly leaned across, picked a chunk of salmon from Foole's plate with her fingers. It's our bloody necks in the noose too, that bastard ever gets a wind up. Them Pinkertons keep a record of every jake in the flash an they share it out to the four and ten, Adam.

I don't believe we're in any danger.

You don't believe it? Molly muttered. You send Pinkerton in, there's no knowing what will happen. Or even if he's to come out of it in one piece. Those berserkers, they cut their own tongues out, to stay quiet. A mollswop I known, she told me them berserkers keep hordes of rats. Herd them like sheep. She lowered her voice. I heard they eat people who get lost in there.

Fludd loosened his collar. Maybe they'll eat Pinkerton an be done with it, he said.

He was nine years old and standing at the great library windows watching the rain blow in sheets against the glass when he heard the maid in the hall cry out. The cry was terrible, forlorn. In the marble foyer he found the house servants gathered, hushed, none at work. She's dead, the cook told him, her voice breaking. She was clutching a letter. Poor Mrs. Shade is died, Master Edward, bless her soul. Foole started to cry. The last time he had seen her she had kneeled before him in the gravel drive of Shade House and kissed him farewell and her lips had felt cold on his forehead. Then she had smoothed her skirts, adjusted an elaborate floral hat brim over her eyes. She was to travel to a hot springs in Colorado for the waters.

A strange lightness came over him in the days following. He drifted on the edges of rooms, uncertain, he was noticed less and less and fed only intermittently. His governess packed her bag the second day and was gone. The cook did not attend to her duties after the fourth day. He and the boy James sat with their legs dangling through the railing posts on the second-floor landing and watched the adults wander through the house, removing statuary, silverware, valuable books. On the sixth day Fisk found him and told him no provision had been made for him in the will. The estate is to be divided among Mrs. Shade's relatives, he said curtly. They will sail out here from Ireland in the new year. In the meantime I am to close up the house and begin a stock-taking.

Where will I go, sir? Foole had asked.

You, Master Edward, Fisk had said, shall be reacquainted with the real world, I should think.

He and the boy James were sent south by rail to Washington, D.C. They arrived cold and frightened and slept two days in the railroad depot with their little suitcases at their feet, watching the travellers striding past, dragging upturned crates across the floor in the hours between trains to pick through the garbage bins for food. On the third afternoon a fruit seller took them to a police station for the constables to deal with. He could remember a sergeant walking through the cold dusk and them climbing endless stairs in an apartment house where carts rat-tled past every half-hour and where they were fed plate after plate of scrambled eggs and great, thick, hot slabs of ham. He remembered the shine of grease on James's lips.

He had thought they might live there. But in the morning the sergeant returned them to the station as if they had done something wrong and later that afternoon a nun arrived and took his friend away holding the wrong suitcase in her enormous hand and two hours later a very old priest in a black suit came for him. They had been separated as a matter of principle and they would not ever see each other again. Foole wore his friend's baggy clothes for six months with the sleeves rolled back and the waistlines ballooning under his fist before he at last gave up hope and when he could no longer remember his friend's face he traded the clothes for a box of marbles and the suitcase itself with *James Gray* in copperplate for a pair of good leather shoes.

He slept in that orphanage for three years, slept whether awake or no. The long chilly wards with their tiers of beds, the gangs of boys brutal in the dining hall, the quick illicit nature of their deceptions. He learned not to remember Mrs. Shade, Shade House, the kindnesses of a life now lost. There was anger in him, at first, that she too had died and abandoned him, but slowly that anger drained and left only emptiness. All was grey in his new home, the walls, jerseys, the skin on the backs of the nuns' hands. The boys had been put to work stitching or repairing clothes and the older ones would work in the wood shop in the basement and all were beaten with hollow canes as a matter of course. At night they would move from bed to bed while the ward master snored in his enclave and they would trade their goods and whisper rumours of an easier world beyond the orphanage walls. A world of pickpockets and fine suits and easy women. Foole there learned that size did not equal power and strength was sometimes weakness. He learned the trick to not getting caught lay in being among the unsuspected. He learned compassion by its lack, he learned blood by its plenty.

Then one April morning in his eleventh year he stuffed his belongings into a pillowcase and walked out of the front gate of that orphanage with a boy named Cullen at his side. That boy took their few coins and all of their food and disappeared on the second night and Foole never saw him again. He slept under bridges, he stole from street sellers. He begged and dealed and sold to pawnshops. He learned in time to steal pedigreed dogs from the finer houses and then return them for their rewards. He was twice beaten and once near raped and those men he fled from with his shirttails flapping and shortly thereafter he made his slow way by road north to New York City.

He was small for his age but quick and savage with the razored instincts of a survivor and it was not long before he found himself adopted into a gang of pickpockets and thieves. He learned the art of the lift and they worked in teams of three under a master thief and they kept only a small portion of their takings. His violet eyes were startling but he had heavy shaggy eyebrows that gave him a glower beyond his years and his looks attracted notice in the daylight. He learned to prowl the night streets outside the theatres and to slip between the carriages of the wealthy and he would dream as he did so of one day walking among them undisguised. That was a world of grand dinners and fiery candelabra glimpsed through closing doors and of fine white horses that would knock a street lad into the mud without slowing and he loathed it and longed for it and lived in the shadow of it learning his trade the while.

He was thirteen years old when the war broke out. There was a wildness in the streets, a reckless electricity in the crowds. In September of that year he lined up with several hundred others at the enlistment tents for the New York Light Artillery, hoping to acquire the signing bounty of one thousand dollars. He had smudged his face and roughened his clothes in an attempt to look older but the tired men around him in line jostled him and laughed at the disguise. It was raining and the water tipped from the brim of his hat as he looked away.

When Foole reached the front of the line the enlistment sergeant was seated at a table under an awning, shuffling papers. The grass had been trampled to mud. Name, the sergeant barked. Then he glanced up, paused. How old are you, son?

Eighteen, sir.

The sergeant frowned past Foole in his ragged coat at the lines of men in the rain. Someone snickered. You want to fight for your country, son? the sergeant asked.

Foole thought of Mrs. Shade, buried somewhere in the western deserts, he thought of his father dying in a lodging house in Baltimore. Death was life. He said, in his roughest voice: I want to kill the bastard enemy, sir.

The sergeant eyed him grimly up, scratched at his chin. That's what I like to hear, he grunted. Welcome to the United States Army, son.

SEVENTEEN

William left Blackwell at the gates of Millbank and drifted down to the Embankment. He glared out at the river seeing nothing in the orange light and shaking his head as he did so. Reckitt had named Adam Foole. Had *named* him. Whatever else, then, Foole was telling the truth about having once been a part of the Reckitts' world. It did not mean that Foole's account of the killing of Shade was true. Nor did it mean Foole's clue about the mudlark was to be trusted. He frowned out at the river. But Shore had heard of the Saracen, that killer was real. William thought of the sewer lines and the berserkers prowling them and the likelihood of finding a solitary mudlark long ago eaten by the city's darkness and of finding her alive. There was just enough truth in the man Foole's accounts to make something possible. Just enough truth, he scowled, to make a dangerous lie.

He started to walk towards Whitehall, hesitated, his breath clouding the cold air. The brown waters of the Thames muscling past, the city rooftops millionfold in the haze beyond. His mind kept returning to that one undeniable fact: the old thief had named Adam Foole.

Go on then, he muttered. What are you waiting for? Go seek out your mudlark.

He smiled all at once at his heart's delusions. But?

But take the man Foole when you do.

———

Margaret Ashling would be a mystery to him his entire life. He thought their happiness unlikely, chanced, as all happiness must seem in retrospect. After twenty years he still held her chair out for her at dinner with a wonder tilting inside him that she had chosen him, had married him. He would watch her from bed as she sat at the vanity and combed her long hair, seventy strokes each night, and he would not speak only listen to her breathe knowing that nothing in his life would be as beautiful or as complicated as the silences between them. It astonished him how young they had once been. He had loved her name from the first, the aristocratic lace of its syllables, the knots it made of his tongue. Margaret, he had murmured, staring in his pyjamas into the looking glass at Notre Dame, then blushing and rinsing his mouth at the unmanliness of it and hoping the other boys had not heard. But he could not help himself. Margaret Ashling. A name he could lean into, a name to keep pace by. She was two years his junior and small but there was something in her that made him feel foolish, brash, like a dulled knife, and he mooned over her during his classes and while playing rugby and cricket in the autumn evenings. He never did learn to predict her reactions. She would prove calm and then furious, patient and then stubborn, she would break upon him like a wave and leave him staggering and then just as quickly stop and apologize and the rage in her would snuff itself out.

I feel I hardly know you, he whispered to her in the third month of their courtship, standing at the edge of a frozen pond while their friends skated past. He brushed her wrist with his glove. Her cheeks were red in the cold.

Because you don't, she said, and bit her lip. Not yet.

Scotland Yard felt big and empty at midday although there lingered a waft of night dirt in the halls from the full pails. He passed no one on the stairs and when he reached Shore's office the chief inspector was not in. William tried the door and was surprised when it opened.

A weak daylight was coming in through the coal-grimed windows and he let his eyes adjust before closing the door behind him. It was then he felt a movement at the edge of his vision, a sort of slow unfolding in the dimness, and when he glanced across he saw the long thin figure of Dr. Breck behind Shore's desk. He was in the process of closing a drawer.

I guess John doesn't mind you sitting there, William said.

Breck shrugged curtly. I wondered if he would send for you.

But he had not been sent for. Neither Shore nor Blackwell had informed him of a meeting. True, he was not present on official duty, and perhaps, if he were Shore, he would not bring a man like himself into an investigation either. He thought this and then he scowled at the idiocy of it. No, he would use a man of ability, rules be damned. He thought of Martin Reckitt's account of Shore as a bullying child and what Blackwell had told him about his personal antipathy towards Reckitt and then he grimaced at the murkiness of it all. But in their world everyone was tainted, eventually.

He glowered, looked up. You have some results?

Breck ran his hand along the leather armrest of the chair, a smooth eerie gesture. Did you know, Mr. Pinkerton, there are doors in the Queen's Treasury covered in human skin? A colleague of mine at the Royal College of Surgeons was showing them to me. Most interesting. Made from the skin of William the Sacrist.

William removed his gloves and set them in his upturned hat. A saint?

A thief. Notorious, in the thirteenth century. He stole the royal Treasury and hid it in a bog before vanishing away.

Not quite vanishing. William sat, the leather crinkling under his weight.

A sound of muffled voices from the hallway, approaching the office. The door opened and Shore came through, Blackwell in tow. William twisted in his seat but seeing the chief inspector's eyes something caught in William, some flare of caution.

Shore grunted. I won't ask what you're doing here.

I came to see you.

He gave a sharp resigned shrug of his shoulders, not waiting for a reply, and his black mood seemed to ease. Well you might as well stay and hear Dr. Breck out. He crossed to the light stand. The office filled with a soft yellow glow. How did it go at Millbank? Did good Mr. Reckitt give up anything of use? Nothing? Not even to the great American defective?

Breck gave a strange high-pitched chuckle.

William shifted in his chair so he could see the two men better. Millbank was, he cleared his throat, interesting. Reckitt hadn't heard about his niece.

How did he take it?

How do you think?

Shore struggled irritably out of his coat, sat at his desk. Cat's out of the bag now, I reckon.

Should I not have said?

Shore unfastened his cuffs and shoved his sleeves up his forearms as if he were about to reach into a washbasin. Doesn't matter, he said, but there was in his gesture a kind of furtiveness. William watched him wondering if Blackwell's insinuations, and Martin Reckitt's allusions, had muddied his own sense of the man.

And what about you, Doctor? Shore said. What did you bring me? Something useful, I trust.

Breck wiped at his lips with a handkerchief. Forensically speaking—

In plain English, please.

Breck looked from Shore to William a moment and there was in it a kind of complicity. He said, The hair from the legs is dark at the roots. He took up a slide and held it to the light and then passed it across to Shore. At its ends you will see the colouring to be much paler. Nearly grey in its discoloration, even. Upon examination my assistant detected minuscule traces of sand, sawdust, and coal—

Shore set the slide down with a soft click on the table. Coal, he murmured.

Anthracite, to be exact. The sand is more interesting. We found no trace of it in the sacking. It consists of silicate, ferruginous silicate, and quartz. When we split the sawdust with a microtome it turned out to consist of pine and oak.

You can tell all of this? William said, amazed.

Breck unhooked his spectacles and held them down before his face as if to peer at the lenses before continuing. The stains on the inside of the sacking that held the legs are also from anthracite, intermingled with traces of mildew, he said. All of this could indicate a location, from which the sacking originated. The sand might offer a possibility as to where the legs were kept prior to being wrapped up.

I'd like to take this fellow back with me to Chicago, William said with a slow smile. He looked from Shore to Blackwell with his eyebrows raised and then back at Shore.

I think Mrs. Breck might object to that, sir, Blackwell said.

Shore grinned. She might not.

There's a Mrs. Breck? William said.

The doctor rose and limped across to the coat rack and took from the pocket of his topcoat a second collodion slide. He said, The three small insects found on the inner fold of the sacking from Southwark Park are *anophthalmi*. A species of blind beetle. They are quite colourless, quite devoid of pigment.

Are they from the park?

No.

Blind, murmured Blackwell. So they come from under the earth, sir?

From the dark, to be exact. Taken together with the other fragments it would not seem unlikely that the body was kept for a time in a cellar. I might suggest a vault—

Except for the sawdust, William said.

Correct.

It would seem our killer has gone to ground, Blackwell said.

Shore gave him an exasperated look.

Is there anything more? William said. Anything from the torso to help?

Indeed. The skin was covered with *Saccharomyces cerevisiae*. A bacterium. Used in the fermenting of alcohol.

Shore was rubbing at his face, the cords in his thick fore-arms cabling under the skin. The sawdust—

Suggests this cellar must also hold firewood. Or perhaps even be used for sawing it.

It's a pub, Blackwell said suddenly.

Aye.

This will be a popular assignment, William said with a wry smile. He crossed to the far wall and studied the big city map. He drew a line from Edgware Road down to Southwark Park and stood staring at the Thames in between. What about the locations of the drops, he said. The torso was found on Edgware Road. That was in the early hours of the morning. The labourers wouldn't have been on site until when, six o'clock?

Four-thirty, sir, said Blackwell.

William nodded. That leaves very little time. Whoever did this acted fast. That means they were decisive, did not hesitate. The torso was probably deposited first.

The head was collected at the docks.

Which means it was dropped upriver from there. It was collected by a lighter man at work. How long would it take such an item to drift downstream from the bridges?

It was caught in a mooring cable, sir, said Blackwell. It could have been there for days.

But Charlotte Reckitt only disappeared the night before. How is that possible?

Maybe it isn't Charlotte Reckitt.

Facts, Shore said. Let us work with the facts, gentlemen.

What about the state of decay? William asked. Can we tell anything about how long the head was in the water?

Breck clasped his hands behind his back.

The three men waited.

The doctor said nothing.

Shore cleared his throat. Doctor?

Breck gave him a slow look with his watery blue gaze. Less than three days, he said reluctantly. Perhaps not even one.

William turned back to the line on the map. The Thames I can understand, he said. From any bridge the head could be dropped rather easily. But the torso would be heavy and bulky. The legs too. Why would the killer distribute them so far apart? He would have had to carry at least one of the packages some distance from the scene of the killing. Perhaps both. Why go to such trouble? And if he were going to such trouble, why not dump both at the same time, in the same location?

Edgware Road is a short walk from the end of the Number 11 omnibus route, sir, Blackwell said.

You're not suggesting the bastard carried the torso on an omnibus, Inspector?

At that hour? Would a hansom not make more sense? William said.

It would certainly draw less attention, Shore said.

But?

The chief inspector frowned. But that would mean two things. The driver, first. Somewhere there is a witness to this parcel being picked up—

William interrupted. Not only picked up.

What do you mean?

Not only picked up, he said again. What would have struck the driver as odd would have been the dropping off. A big package like that, at a strange hour of the night, in the middle of a deserted construction site?

What if it wasn't obvious? The package might look like construction supplies.

In the middle of the night?

Aye, said Shore. And our killer would have risked being seen.

Blackwell cleared his throat. What if it was a private carriage, sir?

Shore looked disgusted. A gentleman of standing would never be involved in something like this. I've been an inspector fifteen years. I've never seen such a thing.

William shrugged. Where I come from, it's the more likely. We're not in America.

So you keep reminding me.

Shore was shaking his head. What about Southwark Park? Is there any link between there and the building site?

The omnibus route, sir. The Number 11 changes to the Number 3 during the week. The Number 3 runs into Southwark, sir.

William regarded Blackwell feeling something almost like admiration. How do you know so much about this, Blackwell?

My brother, sir. He was a cad in an omni over Blackfriars.

Are we talking about the same omnibus for each route?

Blackwell shook his head. Hard to say, sir. On a private route the driver can change over at his leisure.

Pubs, William said abruptly. If they're fermenting in their cellars wouldn't they have access to a horse and waggon?

Aye.

So we might have just a delivery waggon being used here then.

Shore stood and crossed to the window and there folded his ruddy arms. We keep it simple, he said. We know we want a pub with a cellar. It should be somewhere near the Thames. And we suspect we want a pub with a delivery waggon. The cellar should hold coal and firewood.

What about the omni routes?

Leave those for now. Start by asking at Edgware and Southwark if any carriages or waggons were noticed in the area around the suspected hours. We're talking about some rather large and heavy items. It shouldn't be hard to find a witness noticing something. Dr. Breck, can you have a sketch drawn up of the woman as she must have been in life?

I can arrange that.

Shore nodded. Inspector, you take the drawing from pub to pub and make inquiries. Do not reveal that she is dead. Say something else—say we are looking for her on behalf of, I don't know, a relative. Perhaps an unexpected inheritance. See if anyone recognizes her.

Yes sir.

There's a limited number of places in London that will fit with the good doctor's findings. We just need to be thorough.

Blackwell cleared his throat. We might put out a reward, sir, he said. In the interests of being thorough, sir.

You disapprove, Mr. Pinkerton? Breck asked, his eyes alight.

William grunted. He had been frowning at Blackwell in distaste. Our agency never posts them, he said slowly. Our operatives never accept them.

Shore bared the pink of gums in a grin, and there was in it, William thought, something unsavoury. Aye. Your father used to refuse them as a policy.

And I can tell you why, William said. We had a case in Chicago a few years back, before the telegraph had made much impact. The lakes had just been opened. The city was something of a boom town in those days. My father had given me this case to work. It was the murder of a local bar owner's wife, found bludgeoned to death outside the locked doors of his residence. They were wealthy, prominent. Some thought it was a political killing. He had evidently been involved in passing an ordinance that affected the hiring of non-local labour, something to do with immigrants and lower wages. Of course the police couldn't find any motive. I was brought into the investigation late, the evidence was poor, the witnesses already worked over. I didn't know what else to do. The bar owner insisted on posting a reward. One hundred dollars. The police matched it. I allowed it. I went to the newspapers with the offer.

And?

And the killer himself came forward. Turned himself in. He was a vagrant, he'd been out of work for some time, had a wife with a child on the way. But he claimed the reward, and we could see no legal reason not to give it to him. He gave it to his wife to provide for the child.

The law allowed for it?

The law allowed for it. I asked him after his sentencing—he was to be hanged before the week was out—why he'd killed the woman. He told me he'd trusted a reward would be posted, if the murder were careful enough. He told me he knew he could not provide for the child. He asked me how much a life was worth, and what was a father's life worth if he could not keep his baby alive.

The men were silent. The light shifted in the window.

I believe, Shore murmured, we are in no danger of that here.

If you post a reward, John, we both know the public will flood you with tips. Even if you only look into the useful ones, you'll be busy for weeks following up.

We might find something of use, sir, Blackwell said to Shore.

You'll find something of use by good detective work and careful thinking and a compliant public. Not by wasting your time on gossip and hearsay. William looked at Shore. Let me ask you this. What would Charlotte Reckitt be doing in a pub cellar with her hair cut short? Drugged and tied up?

You make it sound like she was there by choice, Shore said. Charlotte Reckitt had plenty of bad credit with plenty of flash folk. Not to mention her uncle. We'll check the flash houses first.

William clicked his pocket watch open, clicked it shut.

You should get yourself some rest, William. You don't look well.

William rubbed at his eyes with the heels of his hands.

I know what I look like, he said.

It was in 1862 in a ramshackle military hospital outside Antietam that William woke feverish and in pain and saw Margaret at his bedside and understood their life to come. They would be wed after the war and he would not leave her again for the rest of his days. But nor would he live them alongside her. Theirs would be a marriage of leave-takings and returnings, a marriage forged in railroad stations and dusty travelling satchels and late envelopes and unwritten recriminations. He could not be other than he was. He understood his entire life he would seek out death and sidle up next to it and set a powerful hand on its shoulder

and pin its arm into the small of its back and he would do this
in the Ozarks, in the Black Hills of Dakota, in the warehouses
of the New York waterfront, any place he was called on to act,
on trains moving at speed through mountain passes and at
poker tables on paddlewheelers in the Mississippi and galloping
bareback down dirt roads outside New Orleans. He awoke in
that military hospital with his left knee swaddled and the pain
rising in waves through his body so that he would tense and
flinch and ease and tense again for hours on end while the boys
around him cried or moaned or lay staring at stumps where two
days earlier arms had been and he watched Margaret wend her
way down past the other cots and come to him wearing a stained
white dress and he felt the luckiest of all those lucky enough to
be alive. She had journeyed all night on special trains under a
warrant issued by his father and had come to him at that hospital to bring him back from the war. She had just turned fifteen
years old and was taller than when he had seen her last and her
eyes were no longer the eyes of a girl. Seeing her he understood
death would not take him. He already belonged to her.

He was sixteen years old then and not yet shaving but when
he reached for her hand his own hand shook like the hand of
an old man.

He slept out the afternoon deep into evening. Outside the hotel
the sprung hansom bowed and rocked as he climbed in, as the
wheels jounced into motion. The sheen of sweat on the mare's
hindquarters smouldered in the cold air. At the bottom of
Regent Street he stepped down and put on his hat and stared
out at the deserted gloom of Waterloo Place. The driver gave
him a questioning look but said nothing and then snapped the
reins and went on.

William crossed the vacant square with his gloved hands
loose at his sides, his shoes loud on the cobblestones. Made his
way past a statue of a robed figure, laurels in its fists like snakes.
At its base six gas lamps burned weakly like globes of fruit on

twisted iron stems and a man in rags stood in their light, his bare hands on the wheel of an overturned barrow, his bewhiskered face upturned in rapture.

He found the shop without trouble. It was set back from the square, a dark cobbled lane, bollards blocking the entrance. Gold lettering curlicued onto the glass: *Gleeson's Gunsmithing–Locksmithing–Bladesharping–&tc.* A weak light burned within.

He entered decisively and walked past implements and keys, tiny blades shivering on hooks as he went. A smell of oiled metal, wood shavings. In a corona of light behind the counter a figure dipped and straightened over a sharpening box, feet paddling the grinder. It was a boy, fifteen, sixteen. He withdrew a long cleaver from its slot and set it carefully aside and wiped his knuckles on his apron and approached.

Narrow vicious eyes, pimples in a burst of grease on his forehead. He caught William's eye and stopped short, out of reach, his left hand in shadow.

We're closed, mister, he said. You'd be best back in the morning. Mr. Gleeson's not in the shop at this hour.

Albert, he said. He could feel the size of himself there, the shadow he must be.

The apprentice peered at him, hesitant. Do I know you?

William lowered his chin so his hat brim would catch the lantern glow and bury his eyes in darkness. He said softly, the menace in it unmistakable: You are acquainted with Mr. Foole, Albert?

The apprentice cast an uneasy glance into the gloom.

I have a message. I'll be passing through Waterloo Place tomorrow night. Ten o'clock. I want him to meet me there. Tell him I'll do as he asks, but not alone. See that Mr. Foole gets it.

The apprentice ran a black knuckle under his lip, as if gathering courage. And who do I say it's from, sir?

But William had already turned and started back up the aisle, wrestling his gloves on as he went, and he did not bother to reply.

EIGHTEEN

Foole went, as instructed.

A splatter of gaslight on the cobblestones. Shadows clinging to the brick and mortar walls in the gloom. Foole could see nothing in Waterloo Place, no figure, only darkness and the statue like a twist of knuckled stone above its gas lamps. He did not call out. He walked slowly into the open, the chalky scrape of his stick loud on the cobbles, his scarf wrapped tight at his throat. He checked his pocket watch: five minutes to ten. Then came a low huffing of breath at his back, and he turned sharply, and there the man was.

He had been watching, of course. Thickset, vengeful, he loomed up before Foole in the faint light, the vapoured heat of him rising yellow and eerie from his shoulders and coat. The curve of his top hat's shadow concealed his eyes. Then he stepped closer and lifted his face and Foole watched the man's deep-set eyes scan the square.

I've come quite alone, sir, Foole murmured. I assure you.

Pinkerton seemed to glower down with a swift and mercurial fury and then this too was gone. He said nothing until he had searched him. Ran his hands along Foole's arms, under his armpits, he kneeled and felt firmly the length of his trouser legs. He got to his feet and unbuttoned Foole's topcoat and ran a hand smoothly over the inner lining and he withdrew from a waistcoat pocket a pocket watch and then replaced it without giving it a glance. He plucked the silk hat from Foole's head and the cold air squeezed suddenly at his pate and Pinkerton reached into the hat and ran his fingers over the brim slowly and methodically and then he handed it back and nodded.

I was surprised by your message, Foole said quietly. But pleased that you would take up my offer.

Don't be pleased yet. Pinkerton inspected the walking stick.

I carry no weapons, sir. I have always felt it takes a kind of courage to refuse a fight.

Pinkerton grimaced. There was a menace in the man he had not felt upon that first meeting. I never met a man who ran from a fight out of courage, he said. You're an American?

Foole buttoned up his overcoat. He took the walking stick back and weighed it in his hands then looked up at the bigger man. I was raised there.

Raised where?

Ah. Not in Chicago, sir. Foole smiled a cautious smile to see the stillness creep across the man's features. Come now, he said. You're a public figure. You must expect me to know some few things about you.

While I know nothing of you.

That, Foole said, I find difficult to believe.

Pinkerton lifted his face and Foole stood in silence and after a moment he heard the quiet slow footsteps of a constable walking his beat. When he was gone Pinkerton said, You aren't American by birth.

Foole said nothing. He was reminding himself with impatience that this man could prove both his accomplice and his undoing. Dangerous, fiery, ill-tempered, violent.

And you do not come from wealth, Pinkerton continued. He had removed his gloves to search Foole and had held them in his teeth as he did so and now he pulled them back tightly over his wrists and flexed his fingers as he spoke. He said, You're too careful in your dress and your manners. You're too aware.

Ah.

There's no shame in being a self-made man.

Foole had so often stated the same that he wondered a moment just how thorough the detective's research might have been. He said, Once, when I was a boy in the schoolhouse, I traded my only two pennies for a single brand-new penny. When I brought it home my father beat me for my stupidity. Foole tugged at his whiskers. Everyone's attracted to the shinier thing. Especially if they don't know its real worth. When I grew older I determined to make of myself a brighter and more attractive spectacle. Foole glanced at the sky as if to determine the hour. It was black and starless. He said, He was a cobbler. Respectable, until debts got the better of him and drink did the rest. He studied Pinkerton to gauge the effect of his lie. What's any father like, really? You love them and you resist them and you want something from them that in the end they fail to give. Foole started to turn away but then paused. He met the detective's eye. I was sorry to hear about yours, he said.

There was a tension in the detective's shoulders, a ferocity in his stillness.

He said nothing.

In the Civil War Foole had stood once beside Allan Pinkerton in a crowded army mess tent while a hot rain gattled the tarps and chewed up the mud outside and he had slid one shifty eye to gauge the man drenched and snorting beside him. He was not tall but there was a solidity to him that reminded Foole of the men who had once been engaged to saw down and drag clear a stand of timber from the Shade estates. His wrists were strong, hairy. He flared his nostrils and spat and ran an open hand over his beard to crush the rain from it. His blues were steaming and hung heavily on him, like a horse blanket. Drowns everything but the damned blackflies, he grinned at the cook ladling out their mess, and his voice sounded like the soft burred voice of a shopkeeper. Friendly, brisk, freighted in its friendliness with its own wants. All this Foole had observed with the quick eye of a boy from the streets but when Allan Pinkerton turned his broad face and stared down at Foole the man's eyes terrified him, deep, lightless, the eyes of a dead man who did not yet know he was dead.

What he saw now when he looked at the son was a distortion of that father, a marred reflection, a twisting and warping of a great man gone wrong.

The detective led him north out of the square up Regent Street then turned east on Coventry keeping to the crowds until they had reached the green of Leicester Square. Two rent boys strolled arm in arm towards them in magenta neckties and green and cream overcoats but upon seeing Pinkerton's face the young men ceased their whistling and veered to the left and kept on. There were other men lounging under the solitary gas lamps waiting for some encounter and the detective led him past to a small round building at the limits of a far hedge. It was fitted with a low child-sized door and he glanced around him then withdrew a bent wire and picked the lock. A rancid air rushed past. He was standing just behind the detective's shoulder and he could feel the man's physical power but he did not flinch. Inside he glimpsed stairs, descending into shadow.

We're not entering by the river?

Pinkerton was silent a long moment and then he said, Charlotte didn't die in the river.

On a hook to the left of the door Pinkerton found a lantern and on a plaster shelf above it the sparking flint and these he took down. They were covered in a grime of dust. He turned his back and unhooked the glass door to check the tallow candle within. Then he crouched and held the bell of the flint-work over the wick and scraped twice and watched the wick catch and waver and lean violently to one side and then burn tall.

You have a map, I presume? Foole said. You must have instructions?

Pinkerton gave him a long slow searching look, the lantern casting his features in eerie relief. I met with an old friend of yours the other day, he said. Martin Reckitt.

Foole paused. About Charlotte?

Among other matters. He said you and I had much to talk about.

Foole could feel a hardness in his throat. Mr. Reckitt was always a capable man, he said with forced calm. Perhaps not the most reliable. I have found it best to take his accounts on caution.

Yes.

We were never friends.

The detective inclined his head. Associates, then.

Foole wondered just what Martin Reckitt might have said to the man. He did not believe Reckitt knew his most damaging secrets but then the aging thief was nothing if not resourceful. He said, You have two fists, Mr. Pinkerton, like any peeler. But connecting them is a skull with a brain in it. That is more rare. I'd suggest you exercise that intelligence carefully when dealing with a man like Martin Reckitt. The Yard never managed to.

You don't have much faith in the Yard.

I prefer American defectives.

Pinkerton lifted the lantern and the light caught the craggy planes of his face distorted and grey-skinned and stern. Beneath his dour moustache he was smiling.

My brother insists there's no such thing as bad press.

Only bad printing.

Pinkerton grunted, his smile fading. Come, he said. He doffed his hat to clear the lintel and stepped with a shiver through. Let us go find your mudlark, Mr. Foole.

The stairs were dry. He paused on the third step and took the lantern from Pinkerton that he might shoulder the door more firmly shut and it screeled to with a clatter that echoed deep below them. Then the American took the lantern back and continued on past. They wound their way down into darkness. A weak corona of light cast over the stone walls, the spidering cracks lit in the ancient bricks, their wet footprints trailing behind them like some doomed path the sightless might once have walked. The air tasted of dust and iron.

The stairs ended in a worm-eaten wood door and Foole reached out and tried the handle and his hand came away wet. The door did not give. Pinkerton pressed past. Set his shoulder to. The door punched wide with a loud shriek and he staggered through.

It was a long arched corridor and Pinkerton paused only a moment then turned right and walked quickly over the ill-fitted stones. Water in the cracks, water shimmering like mercury at the edges of the light-fall. There were streaks of black moss growing on the walls where moisture trickled. At every twenty yards or so an alcove opened to their right and each alcove was barred by an iron gate and he could see Pinkerton eyeing each but neither man spoke and they went on. The corridor curved, branched, curved again and Pinkerton kept to the left until it began very gradually to slope downward. At last they came to a three-way fork and the American paused and walked back some ten feet until he reached the nearest alcove and when he set his hand on the gate there it opened with a rattle and he hoisted the lantern and peered in. Foole followed. Within he could see another set of stairs.

We're not there yet, Pinkerton murmured.

They went in. Foole could hear the slow roar of running water as they descended. The smell thickened, the air went tarry and rank. This second stairwell was steep, and slick, and Foole set a hand on the slimed wall as he went holding his walking stick in his fist for balance. He knew men had been lost in the lines, knew to avoid the smaller branches where the air was bad and chokedamp could strike. The night before, the gunsmith's apprentice had stood in the Emporium office anxiously turning his hat in his bitten fingers as he delivered the detective's message. Fludd had listened glowering. He had stormed out in disgust and then come right back in and the two of them had talked through it. Foole said he would be careful. Fludd warned him the tide would rise five hours after midnight and careful was not enough and that he would need to be above it by then. Foole said

Pinkerton could have no reason to let him come to harm. Fludd said Pinkerton was a bastard and a man of violence and harm was like breathing to him. An if you get yourself lost, his friend growled, don't stop to think about it. Follow the waters out. Down there rats been known to eat a man to the bone an him still alive. An rats ain't the worst of what's down there.

All this Foole was thinking as he followed the huge shadowy figure of the detective. They came out, at last, upon the wide parapet of the London sewers.

Pinkerton lifted the lantern high. Coins of light on the dark waters before them. A vast arched ceiling vanishing into blackness. In one hand he had withdrawn a map and unfolded it deftly with his thumb and two fingers and he held it up in the light. He looked left, looked right, studied the map again.

Foole watched him. Lost already?

Pinkerton smiled grimly. Not just yet, he said.

They tied handkerchiefs at their noses and mouths like bandits and went on in silence under a penumbra of light and as they walked Foole felt a kind of dread coming up in him. He strained over the rush of the waters to hear any cry or rustle of men with murder in their hearts. He knew if the berserkers came upon them it would be sudden and swift and brutal.

The parapet was wide enough to walk abreast and Foole moved with hands at his sides and his walking stick gripped fast and he could hear the big American breathing fiercely through his nostrils alongside him.

After a distance Pinkerton slowed, held a hand out to stop. He shuttered the lantern to a slit and they stood, listening. The low rumble of the waters. Foole's blood loud in his ears. He could hear nothing else.

What is it? he whispered, his handkerchief shirring.

Pinkerton unshuttered the lantern, their shadows sliding up the curved wall.

But then it came again: a weird distant hooting, like the call of a night creature. The cry filled the tunnel elongating and distorting as it sounded and Foole shivered to hear it. He could not tell from which direction it came, ahead or behind.

What the hell is it? Pinkerton whispered through his handkerchief.

Foole listened. It did not sound human.

Pinkerton walked to the wall, made a deliberate mark in chalk. Let's keep moving, he said.

It was a wide tunnel high and well ventilated and the waters moved at a steady drift, muscling past, scraping the filth and detritus of a world city against its bed. The corpses of dogs, cats, rats washed down from the slaughterhouses, even the coiled tumbling entrails of horses turning end over end in its current. The cavern veered left and then left again and then a smaller branch sewer opened on the far side but Pinkerton kept on. The chamber widened until it seemed a kind of reservoir of muck and the stink deepened into something older, thicker, a stench they had to wade through as they went. Punctured here and there high up in the walls were the narrow clotted outfalls of old sewer lines, a steady trickle of crud leaking from their openings into the reservoir. When Pinkerton lifted the lantern Foole could see suspended from the ceiling long spindled stalactites of putrid matter hanging over the waters and he glanced at Pinkerton and the skin around the man's eyes was drawn and pinched in the strange light but he kept slowly on.

After a time there was a sound from the far side of the chamber and then a light appeared, a luminescence hovering, moving bumpily forward in the darkness. Pinkerton stiffened, shuttering his lantern too late. Foole heard the click of his revolver.

A second light appeared, more distant, a third. And then Foole saw the dim outline of a man take form. He had tied to his front a small bull's-eye lantern and the half-shuttered light crossed and crossed again in the gloom as he went, wraithlike, about his business. The man was back-bent and his arms were long and he did not look their way though Foole knew they must be visible. Instead he passed silently on in a long greasy velveteen coat, pockets weighed heavily down, a sack clinking over his shoulder. Then a second man appeared wearing a canvas apron stained with what looked like blood and this man carried a long staff with some sort of flattened blade at its end like a monstrous hoe and he walked with his bald head bare and his grey skin gleaming in the weak light. There were three of them in all moving single file in some strange procession and as the third passed he raised a forlorn hand as if in warning or entreaty and his face was cadaverous and terrible. Then he too was lost to view in a gloom beyond which it was not possible to go and the two of them stood again alone.

Tunnel men, Foole breathed in relief. Salvagers.

Pinkerton looked at him gravely.

They went on. After a short length they heard a steady scraping and then saw tied to the parapet on the far side a skeletal hull rising and falling in the waters. It was an old peter boat fitted out for dredging at one time but now pitched and paired for nothing beyond shore work. It had no stern, no aft, but a sharp cutwater at either end, the bow scarred from grapples hooked there years past. It rode shallow in the current. All this they saw at a glance and Foole knew it would belong to the salvagers they had just seen.

Pinkerton studied it uneasily from the edge of the walkway, the foul waters between. His handkerchief sucking in around his mouth at each breath, sucking then billowing back out.

Careful, Foole murmured. That's more than deep enough to drown in.

Pinkerton regarded him with unreadable eyes then consulted the map and made his mark in chalk. It was then they heard that eerie cry come again, closer this time, distinctly anguished. Foole stared in alarm at the big American and neither spoke as the cry swelled past them and dissipated. Then came a second cry, a response.

This sounded higher, nearer, and Foole could make out the long slow bending of the vowels as it replied.

Did it just say *clear*? Pinkerton hissed.

No, Foole whispered. It said *here*.

The cry came again, louder. Pinkerton raised his face to the darkness behind them and then Foole too heard it: footsteps, clattering towards them. It sounded like a great horde of men running.

Foole twisted in alarm. This way, he said.

But Pinkerton was already running. Foole could hear the low hooting cry pass them and the clatter and chink of what sounded like chains and he too was running fast, his walking stick low at his side, Pinkerton just ahead with the lantern swaying wildly and casting the tunnel and the rushing waters into bizarre spirals of shadow, spirals of light. His hat flew from his head, spun out across the gap and landed upright and adrift in the black currents and was gone. He did not slow.

That chamber came to an end at three wide sewers, each line opening at an angle, and Pinkerton paused, breathing heavily. He set down the lantern and unfolded his map. Foole could hear the clatter of feet behind them.

Pick one, he snapped.

Pinkerton squinted at the map.

An ancient brick walkway had been erected across to the centre line, overspilling now with sewage. It reached a span of nine feet at least, the wash of foul matter making the crossing treacherous. Foole stared, gauging it. Then he picked up the lantern and looked at Pinkerton and turned and ran nimbly across. The going was slick and dangerous and when he was in the clear he turned and set the lantern down at his feet and held out a hand to Pinkerton.

The detective glanced uneasily behind him. Foole saw he had his revolver low at his thigh.

Don't think about it. Just come.

Foole could see for a moment his companion plunging into the murk and being dragged under and then he put it from his mind. It was not what he wanted. The detective had pulled the handkerchief down from his face and was glaring at the narrow brick walkway.

Goddamnit, he muttered.

Then he turned and strode back into the darkness and disappeared. Foole called out to him in a loud whisper but there was no answer.

He heard quick footsteps and all at once the detective emerged from the shadows hurtling towards him at speed and then he was leaping with his arms outstretched and legs wide. He seemed to hang an impossible long moment in the air before his right foot came down, hard, on the edge of the old brick crossing, and the bricks crumbled and gave way. Then Pinkerton was rolling like a fallen horse into Foole and the two men crashed against the wall at their backs. There was an eerie sucking sound from beside them and then a strong current of filth poured through the breach in the bricks into the tunnel below. Foole could hear men shouting behind them. And then he was scrambling to his knees and Pinkerton was shuttering the lantern and they both were crawling blind around the corner into the line and they lay with legs outstretched trying not to breathe and listening as the figures rushed past.

Tunnels and turnings, lightlessness. When the walls had again fallen silent Pinkerton got to his feet, shook out his pant leg. The smell was terrible. Then he unshuttered the lantern and Foole stood and they went on. Some of the lines were dry, wide, others deep and ancient. In great submerged caverns they crept high on the walls across narrow catwalks of rotting wood, the lantern guttering between them. Pinkerton would pause and study the map and then go again on.

They found themselves in an older sewer line and it narrowed as they went until they were stooped and walking slowly. The ancient bricks had rotted over the decades and given way and there were huge glistening lumps of matter deposited in the breaches. Vegetable peelings, the drainings from stables and streets, rotten mortar, wood softened and trailing rags of muck, even the outlines of kettles and pans and stoneware jugs all the one colour and glued together. At one turning Pinkerton lifted the lantern and a huge black rat crossed the spill of light and moved up the tunnel. Then a second appeared and a third and all at once there was a sound of rushing air and the far wall became a roiling mass of rats pouring past, a river of darkness, and they stood unbreathing as the rats flooded past and were gone. Pinkerton ran a grimy hand across his forehead, streaking it.

Wait, Foole said, panting. The air was bad, his breathing shallow. Stop. Wait.

We're nearly there.

A sound of dripping water, faint, came and went with Foole's breathing. His heart was labouring. He set his hands on his knees and doubled over, the handkerchief at his lips.

We should keep going, the big detective said. We should finish this and be gone.

Foole straightened, studied the man.

What is it.

Nothing.

Pinkerton nodded, walked a few feet farther. The corona of light receding on the walls and the low ceiling overhead.

I keep asking myself why, Foole called softly to the detective's back. Why did she jump? What was she so frightened of?

Pinkerton was standing peering up the tunnel and he turned now, and lifted the lantern, and regarded Foole with his black eyes glinting. It wasn't the jump that killed Charlotte Reckitt, he said. I don't know what this Saracen of yours is capable of. But whatever she met with that night was a damn sight worse than a broken neck.

Foole blinked sharply.

Forgive me, said Pinkerton.

A moment passed. Another. And then as if by unspoken assent Foole rose and they went wordlessly on. The air worsened. Foole was thinking of Charlotte in the freezing Thames and the water closing over her face and her hair adrift and then he bit hard down on his lip, he cleared his head. He watched the flame in the lantern shrink but it did not go out. At each turn Pinkerton stopped and double-checked the map and marked an arrow in chalk on the wall. They passed under what must have been the public privies, the wood floor rotting above them, and turned left down a narrow passage splashing through a puddle of clean water and came at last to a set of glistening stairs leading upward. Foole could just make out a faint glow of light ahead.

This is the place, Pinkerton whispered. Come.

It was a long wide dry chamber with alcoves in the facing walls enshrouded by darkness and a few solitary stubs of candles burning down at the feet of huddled occupants. A puddle oozed near the door and Foole saw the shrivelled hams of a man squatting over it and he looked away. There was a cough from someplace deep within and then a second answering cough and then the silence of many figures observing. Pinkerton walked slowly the length of the arches holding the lantern aloft at the beggars and mudlarks hunched in their robes, wattled arms clutching their rags to ward off the light.

In the far corner Foole found the woman Mrs. Sharper had described. An ancient crone swaddled in rags, her huge grey feet bare and outsized with the crusted mud of the river. Livid scars stretched from the corners of her mouth up her cheeks, like some grinning cruelty made flesh. Her throat corded with the strain of twisting her face from the light. It was a stone alcove shallow and level with the floor and at one time must have opened onto a drainage line but had since been bricked over and sealed and she had laid out her scavenged goods and filthy straw to make her bed. Her gums moved, chewing at a long strand of grey hair. Her hands were liverspotted and trembling.

Foole crouched. Pinkerton set the lantern down beside him on the slick stone.

Are you the one they call Muck Annie? Foole asked.

She spat out the knot of hair, scowled up.

Muck Annie, he said again. Is that you?

Her face dipped and greasy tendrils of hair obscured her eyes, her nose. Sharp broken teeth, brown in the weak light, great gaps between. Her mouth was open slightly. Her lips were wet.

We're looking for someone, Foole said. A man that used to sleep here.

What's he? she demanded suspiciously. She was glaring at Pinkerton. Her voice creaking as if from long disuse.

We can pay you, said Foole.

At this she grinned a weird lascivious grin and the scars twisted and she glanced furtively from side to side and then picked at the front of her dress and leaned forward. She extended a wizened claw. Go on, you, she said. Give it here then.

Foole heard something stir in the blackness beyond. He glanced at Pinkerton but the big man did not seem alarmed. He was studying Muck Annie with a dead expression.

We're looking for a man you once knew, he said. Jonathan Cooper.

She did not react. The rustling of her rags was like a thing uncoiling from a nest.

He glanced at Pinkerton then back at the woman. Jonathan Cooper, he said again. Do you know him or not?

She licked at her lips. Aye, she said. I knows him. He what took me leavings off to the Lascar an never come back. I got something of his own here, I do.

The Lascar, Pinkerton murmured. What's the Lascar?

You mean the opium dealer? Foole said. In Wapping?

But she had twisted in her rags to fumble about behind her and then she turned back with a battered tin kettle with the top missing and held it on its wire stem towards them. Go on, she said. Pity a poor maid. Go on, sirs.

How do we find Jonathan Cooper, Annie? Foole said.

She gave them a sly look. You never do.

Is he dead?

She shook her head.

Foole withdrew a shilling from his pocket and held it gleaming before her and all at once she froze, as if transfixed by the coin. Annie, he said.

You never finds him, she whispered fiercely. He finds you.

NINETEEN

William awoke in a fever with his hair hot and plastered to his neck and the sheets sticking to his spine and he shuddered and slept again and when he awoke next the windows were dark and he had kicked clear of his blankets. He stumbled to the dresser and poured a glass of water from a pitcher there and the silver arc of it was like mercury in the faint light and left him light-headed and cold. He fumbled his way back to bed, slept, woke, slept again. Shivering through it as if sick with some bacillus of grief bred of the ditches and the drains.

A spill of lantern shine on slimed walls. The half-crazed leer of Muck Annie. Then came a grey light filtering in through the windows and he opened his eyes and sat up in a tangle of blankets feeling weak with his head aching but with his thoughts, thank god, clearing. He did not know what day it was. He rose and staggered towards his wardrobe and began, shakily, to dress.

No he could not eat. Only twist his spoon in the light of the sitting room windows and watch a blade of light flicker across the ceiling and down the wall's mouldings. He set it with a click down on his plate and ran a handkerchief over the back of his neck and it came away damp. He felt the floor tilt. Stood again and waited with both hands grasping the edge of the table. When he went at last out he was careful to lock his door and pocket the key and he walked deliberately out of the elevator and through the lobby greeting no one.

At Scotland Yard neither Blackwell nor Shore was in. The desk sergeant scanned his ledger with his crooked knuckles then gave William a street address in Drury Lane for the inspector. Cor, that can't be right, the sergeant muttered. He flipped back two pages and was quiet then looked up with a shrug of his battered old shoulders. He said that he was certain the chief would be at his club. Did William know the way and all right. Then he frowned at William's pallor and said, You might want to sit a minute, sir. If you don't mind my saying.

He minded. There were smudged lanterns screwed to the outer walls of the hansom he flagged down and they rattled as the cab swayed and started off. The driver's whip came lazily down from above and the beast took no notice but went on at her same steady weary pace and William sat back huddled in the nook feeling the cold wind on his face and he squinched his eyes shut.

The driver shook him angrily awake.

Right, now. Out.

He did not protest. His heart was beating fast and he climbed down from the hansom and peered up at the grim facade of Shore's club and heard through the blood in his temples a low whistle and when he turned he saw the driver leaning down to him, holding out a cupped hand. The man wore knitted gloves with the fingers cut away and his nails were black with dirt.

He found Shore seated in a high-ceilinged dining room among mostly empty tables, his back to the window. He was eating with two forks and William glanced at the bloody cut swimming in its juices and felt his stomach churn.

Mr. Blunt, he said. Desk sergeant said I'd find you here.

What, eating? Shore grunted, he patted his pale green waistcoat. Should I be offended? Chewing and chewing as he spoke, his cheeks packed. He reached for his wine and took a drink and swallowed and then said, Didn't I instruct you to get some rest?

This is me resting.

I almost believe it. Shore was pulling apart the soft meat on his plate. Sit. We've started teams of two covering pubs in the city, he said, showing the good doctor's drawing of the woman. It could take a while. I've put Mr. Blackwell in charge. If I've learned nothing else in twenty years, I've learned patience. What. What's that look?

What look?

Like you're eyeing up the tastiest bits to bite into.

Of that?

Of me.

William's head was thick still and it seemed his skull trailed slowly behind him. He took out his pipe and a pinch of tobacco and stuffed its bowl with trembling hands. There's no look, John, he said. I'm just tired. Is there anything I can do?

You're the great detective. You tell me.

William looked at him.

What.

Is there a problem between us, John?

Shore sighed. Ah, it's not you. Jesus. I've my bloody hands full. This Fenian mess. A review scheduled next month. A half-dozen crimes with no suspects and a half-dozen suspects with no crimes. Mr. Blackwell's canvassing his streets without a partner and all I can do is pray he doesn't slip up. What I want is this to-do with Charlotte Reckitt wrapped up and I can't say I care too much how it ends. So long as it ends.

But you want evidence.

Well. Evidence is always preferable. Shore regarded him now with a clear expressionless gaze. You look terrible, William. You should get yourself back to your rooms, lie down.

William's shirt felt damp, it was sticking to his ribs. He wiped at his face. I went into the sewer lines, he said, in a low voice. Into the overflow lines south of Blackfriars. On a tip. I went looking for Jonathan Cooper.

Shore took a long slow sip of his wine. I thought you might do something foolish.

I didn't find him.

You're lucky you came back out.

William dabbed at his hot temples. I came back out with a name, he said. The Lascar. An opium dealer. Does that mean anything to you?

Not in relation to Charlotte Reckitt.

William waited.

Shore worked at his teeth with his tongue. At last he said, Lascar Sal is who you mean. Operates down out of Wapping. Wretched area, that. Bloody Chinese box of a place to find, I'm told. He cast a quick glance at the hushed tables nearby and muttered, We let the house operate because it keeps the worst off the streets. It's an arrangement. Not perfect, I know, but. He paused, studied William. I don't know what you're up to, William, but I find it hard to accept as Agency business.

Well.

When did we meet? Seventy-two? When I first sat down with your father I realized the Yard wasn't even modern in its methods. You know I worked with him for years. There was never this sort of nonsense.

What sort would that be?

Skulking about the sewers. Running grifters off bridges into the Thames.

William smiled tightly. My father had his ways too.

I have some idea what Agency business looks like, William. It doesn't look like this. It's mostly background checks and paperwork. This Charlotte Reckitt business you've been on about, there's no client involved, is there? Since when did the Agency start hunting the flash on its own?

William met the man's stare.

You just be careful, Shore said grimly. I'm telling you that now. I've had some comments from the higher-ups wondering about you being here. You know I'm glad to do what I can for you and I'll leave you to your inquiries. But keep it legal. Or if not legal, at least out of the papers.

William rubbed at his forehead. I'll do my best.

Shore started to eat again. Scrape and click of cutlery. How did it go with Martin Reckitt? he asked casually. A sly glance up as he asked it.

William shrugged. I gather there's no love lost between the two of you.

Mr. Blackwell informed me that he was not present for much of the interview.

That was my fault. Reckitt wouldn't talk with him there.

Well? Anything of interest?

The blood was pressing at the back of William's eyes. He blinked hard. He said the two of you grew up together. He said you'd taken an interest in him.

Shore paused in his chewing, studied William tiredly, swallowed. Thing about a gifted liar is, there's always just enough truth to make the lies dangerous. Some of Reckitt's stories are genuine red-letter jobs.

I know it.

Martin Reckitt's a liar who nearly cost me my job. That's the only truth.

William looked at Shore wondering where that truth left off and the lie began. He knew there would be more to it and he thought of Blackwell's account of Shore's chippies but he did not care to embarrass the man. The daylight shifted across the ceiling.

Shore was saying something about Blackwell. He's in the pubs up around Edgware Road today, he was muttering. He thought it might be prudent to investigate the locals. Observed that the sack might have been carried on foot from a nearby location. Makes some sense. Of course I don't imagine it would be easy to locate him. But if you're looking for something to do, you can keep him on the narrow for me.

William blinked, confused. Is Blackwell a drinker?

Mr. Blackwell? I should think not.

Then I don't understand.

He has his limits.

You don't trust him to handle this.

How many of your operatives do you trust?

All of them, William said. None of them. Why put him in charge then?

Mr. Blackwell's been useful in the past. Shore pulled the napkin from his lap and dabbed at his mouth with impatience then folded it twice into a clean triangle and set it on his plate and got to his feet. At the cloakroom he took his coat from the attendant and shoved his arms through but did not put on his hat and he regarded William where he swayed. Did you ever get in touch with old Ben Porter? he asked. Did you ever ask him about Edward Shade?

William gave him a quick sharp look. He thought there must be something taunting in the man's question but when he looked at Shore the chief's face was quiet, his expression earnest. William shook his head.

Benjamin Porter died last year, John, he said. Sally's gone too.

Shore paused. What, dead? He banged his bowler softly against his belly as if to punch it taller and then he set it low on his head. I'll be damned.

Well.

We didn't work together much. But I always did like him.

William did not know what to say to that. The attendant behind the polished counter of the cloakroom was studying with great intensity the ruff of a fur coat. The panelled oak walls seemed to pulse and draw back and lean inward. Then the attendant stepped forward and opened the door smoothly and the air from the street felt startling in its clarity, like blown ice. William turned up the collar of his chesterfield.

There was a new brougham set low on its iron wheels at the edge of the pavement and William glimpsed a young woman with blond hair watching Shore. The chief inspector nodded to her, then turned back, a reassuring hand on William's arm. I've an appointment I must take, he said. Go find Blackwell, get this all finished soon. The sooner you get out of my city the better. You have a way of making a man look bad.

I doubt that.

You know my wife thinks you're a handsome devil. Said so at breakfast this morning.

Well.

I tried to tell her what you were like but she wouldn't hear it. I guess she's got her tastes. He winked. But I've got my eye on you, he said. He stepped away. Edgware Road, he called.

William raised a hand and smiled with the fever that was in him and his smile felt gluey and hot and too bright in the grey chill of the streets. He watched Shore glance furtively about and then clamber up into the creaking brougham and then a small gloved hand drew the curtains shut. The carriage swayed on its springs, the driver snapped the reins, the roar of the street took over.

There were parts of him now as he felt himself growing older that would plunge vertically, like a mine shaft dug out of his life, into old fears and unresolved moments. Quarrels he had held with Margaret in their early years together. The silence in the house at the birth of their first daughter, Isabelle, the impossible quiet as the walls creaked around him and Margaret's screams fell abruptly away and how he had stood with one hand on the fireplace mantel and stared at his father across the room as the two of them waited. And then the thin thread of a newborn's cry, and the sudden fire blazing inside him. He did not know how much of this remembering was to do with the death of his father. He thought of Isabelle, of the croup that had come so much to her in her first winters. The savage coughing like a dog's bark, the heat of her skin, how he would walk with her the length of the house for hours at night and how Margaret would look at him in the morning, her eyes red-rimmed and hazy. He remembered the dropper of ipecac and the languid shift of his daughter's arms heavy at her sides, and the calomel powders in their small blue jars. How they had filled nightly the gutta percha bag his father had brought back from England with scalding water and how they had laid this down in their daughter's crib in a desperate attempt to keep her temperature steady while the snows came smoothly and whitely down over their world, tacking against the glass and melting and streaking the darkness beyond. He had never known such fear.

And he remembered his own early years with his father, how his father would open an enormous Bible someplace thick in the Old Testament and the boy that he was would struggle to read the verses aloud. His father would sit forbiddingly beside him at the kitchen table with his knuckles in his beard like some ancient desert patriarch while Robert cried in his crib. Holding a gnarled rootlike finger under each word and William would sound them slowly through. Balanced crazily on the adult chair, his feet kicking in the air under the table. His father would explain nothing of the verses to him and he learned not to ask. When he shut his eyes at night he feared the Godhead would pour out from the dresser, an eerie mist enshrouding both father and son and no part of it loving only terrifying and wrathful.

It was a warren of narrow lanes east of Edgware Road, ill lit, filthy, its ash-brown bricks as old and air-pocked as any in London. He found Blackwell gingerly picking his way out of a tight alley on the edge of Portman Square and he watched the inspector pause and withdraw a folded sheet of newspaper from his sleeve and lean down with one hand on the wall and wipe at his shoes. Then wipe at his fingers one by one. Then drop the crumpled newsprint to the ground.

He had come upon him almost at once and he could not believe the chance of it. He knew this corner of London had pubs the way Manhattan had jewellery rigs and that he should have been hunting the man all day.

Your Mr. Shore sent me, he said, coming up alongside him. His head throbbing. I think he wants to keep me occupied. Any luck?

Blackwell was clutching a broadsheet and William took it from him and unrolled it and it was the drawing Breck had made. The face resembled Charlotte Reckitt around the eyes, perhaps, in the severe set of the jaw. The inspector was looking at William with something like concern. You should be abed, sir, he said. You look like death.

I'll sleep when I'm dead, William grunted.

As they cut across Seymour Street and stood under the eaves of a papery shop Blackwell told him which thoroughfares he had so far searched, which pubs he had entered, and there were bruises under the man's eyes. He had been on his feet since four o'clock that morning and had learned, he said, nothing at all. At the corner of the next block he showed a lad behind the spigots the drawing of Charlotte Reckitt but the lad was either foreign or simple and only gurgled some indecipherable reply. A woman with a washrag over her shoulder peered at the picture and shrugged. There were a few sullen men drinking under the windows in the smeared light but none had seen the woman either.

They entered a small pub in the confines of Great Cumberland Street and asked if there was a cellar on the premises and the barman there laughed a toothless laugh and said, Aye, and a carriage house with oats and hay for when the duke comes a-callin. The barman was sixty years old if a day and one sleeve was pinned to his shoulder and William studied his bleary eyes and said nothing. Blackwell showed the drawing.

They turned east on Berkeley Street and north on Montagu Street and passed two pubs on either side of a haberdashery but Blackwell explained neither would have a cellar. At the end of that block they entered a corner pub and stepped down into a smoky darkness and stood at the bar a long while before anyone came out to meet them. The girl who emerged from the back had a smudge of grime on her cheek and mouth and she could not have been more than ten. William wondered what else they served beyond ale and food but he did not ask. Blackwell showed the drawing and she tucked a greasy strand of hair behind her ear, bit her lip, shrugged. She told them she weren't like to answer nothing except to paying customers. William bought a pint and she drew it off with a practised flick of the wrist and carried it in her small hands and he saw when she set it on the counter that she had to lift herself up onto the balls of her feet to do so. Blackwell showed her the drawing again. Never seen her? No never.

So it went.

On Gloucester Place they walked up two flights of stairs and entered a rickety pub grey and shabby in the light of its big windows and they asked two girls in gaudy shawls who were eating beef stew with their fingers but neither had seen the girl.

On Upper Dorset Street they found a proprietor who thought he recognized the woman in the drawing. He asked them what they wanted her for and Blackwell said it had to do with an inheritance, a distant relative who had passed. The man had thick hairy forearms like a sailor and dense white eyebrows but was otherwise bald as a saddle. He thought he had seen her in a brothel off Drury Lane and though Blackwell took note of this William knew it would come to nothing.

They crossed back down through Byranston Square and walked west on Upper George Street and had no better luck. The weak daylight drained off. Their shadows melted in the dusk. By then it had been failing for an hour and then it had been two hours and then the streets had filled with men coming off shift then emptied again and by that time the pubs were lit and roaring.

After a while William swore and stopped and looked grimly at Blackwell.

Well, he said. I guess Charlotte Reckitt is keeping her secrets still.

Blackwell nodded. Whatever happened on that night, sir—

William stared down at him.

That is, whatever state of mind she was in, when last you saw her—

For god's sake. She jumped from Blackfriars Bridge, Inspector. What state do you imagine she was in?

Blackwell flushed. Distraught, sir?

He turned away, discouraged. He had been watching the inspector all afternoon and thinking of Shore's lack of faith in the man and he wondered now through the haze of his thoughts what sort of enmity lay between them. He put a shaking hand to his chest like a man twice his age and felt his heart thrumping rapid and shallow like the heart of a caged rodent. The day was done. Done and they had nothing for it but a heat behind each heel that would blister up as soon as they took off their shoes. Charlotte Reckitt had vanished into the depths of the city and been carved up without a trace. But there's always a trace, he told himself. Almost always. You just want a bit of luck in the finding of it.

His knee ached. He left Blackwell going through his little black notebook and went limping down to the corner to find a cab.

But Charlotte Reckitt had not been distraught. Breathless, yes, from the run, but calm and assured under the gas lamps of the span, the crescent of her hair fuzzed in its glow. It was as if she had intended he run her down. As if she had desired it.

He thought of Adam Foole's grief and felt a splinter worry away in his skull. He had known by nightfall that something must soon break. She had descended from her doorstep in Hampstead, looking left and then right, then walked south the half mile in the twilight to hail a passing hansom. William had watched her go with his hands plunged into his chesterfield and his hat drawn low over his eyes. It had taken him some minutes to find a cab of his own and he followed her to a theatre in St. Martin's Lane. The carriages and hansoms were jammed and moving slowly and he paid and got down and walked ahead. He watched from under a closed shopfront facing the theatre as the gaslights blazed and blazed, as the audience arrived in their finery and drifted laughing up the wide steps. A beggar shuffled near, crooning, shuffled away. The carved doors had been propped wide with chains hooked to their frames. He watched the arrivals in their hooped gowns and sleek silk hats mill and laugh and make their way inside. At last Charlotte Reckitt had appeared in the window of her cab and he waited for her to step down and when she had gone in he started across. In the lobby he waited with some muttered excuse to the ushers as the doors closed and the house lights dimmed and he could hear through the walls a muffled viola begin in a mournful key.

She had come out before the first intermission. She did not see him. She collected her beaver fur from the cloakroom and moved swiftly towards the front doors and it was then he had stepped out, taken her elbow in a fierce grip, and said: But Miss LeRoche, the performance is only just beginning.

She had recoiled. Glared at him and started angrily to protest.

Hush, he said.

An usher lounging behind the ticket counter with a pipe in his mouth had quickly stuffed it into one pocket, straightened his cap, regarded them with a ferret-eyed suspicion as William steered past.

You are mistaken, she was whispering to him. You have the wrong person.

And all at once he had grown tired of it. Miss Reckitt, he had said. Twisting her to face him at the top of the steps outside. I'm not interested in whatever you might have done. That's not what I'm here for.

She had said nothing for a long moment, studying him with her dark eyes. The night air was cold. There were hansoms lined up at the cab stand down the street, the horses dipping into feed bags, the drivers with their legs crossed on their high seats, whips low.

I'm interested in you, he added.

In me, Mr. Pinkerton? Or in Edward Shade?

He let her go, all at once uneasy.

Come, sir, don't look so surprised. You have made no secret of it. She drew on her long gloves, held her coat out to William.

After a moment he took it from her, held it up, and she slipped her arms in and turned around. Do you think to frighten me? she had said, suddenly coy. By stalking me at my home, by following me on my outings? You should know me better.

The usher was walking slowly across the lobby carpet towards them.

He said: What I know is a man like me isn't good for business. I know the sooner we talk, the sooner I leave you alone.

The stippled light over her face, the tiny white hairs along her upper lip.

This game we are playing, she had said softly. It has been amusing, sir. I shall enjoy playing it a while longer. And she stepped gently forward against him. Her coat was open and he felt the heat of her breasts against his side and then she slipped her wrists into his enormous hands and William watched in confusion as her face twisted into an expression of absolute terror.

Help! she screamed. Help! Assault!

William shoved her backward, cursing. But already the usher was running towards them and a second man from the street had turned in shock and started up the steps of the theatre and William felt his muscles tense and he set his feet wide and his fists low.

Here, you now, the usher was calling.

He glanced helplessly as Charlotte Reckitt fluttered down the steps her skirts billowing. Then the two men were upon him and he held the one at arm's length as the other knocked his hat from his head and seized the collar of his coat. William hurled the usher backward and wrestled the second man against the iron railing and he struck him hard in the mouth and the man slid sideways and fell to his knees. And then William was taking the steps two at a time and running into the fog after Charlotte.

She had turned onto the Strand filled as it was with traffic and he did not see her and then he saw her in a hansom some fifty feet away. He seized the first cab he saw and climbed aboard and followed her through the press of carts and carriages and when she jumped down at Ludgate Circus he jumped down also and followed her down Bridge Street. She moved quickly despite her gown and he was breathing hard when he reached Blackfriars Bridge but she was only twenty feet from him by then and he could see, yes, that he would catch her on the span and there would be nowhere for her to go.

TWENTY

In the second week of October 1861 Edward Shade was officially mustered into the Flushing Battery of the 34th New York Light Artillery. He was handed a slip of government paper with the advance on his bounty amounting to forty dollars inscribed in purple ink and he glanced up as the man next to him with a scarred face and unshaven throat carefully folded his own bounty into his shirt front and then he, three months shy of his fourteenth birthday, did the same. He had no belongings but an old bent hat two sizes too large and a pair of good leather shoes and he found himself in a long wooden bunkhouse filled with the indigent and idealistic both, every man but he untying bundled sleep sacks and spare boots and long underwear. None of those goods would reach the battlefront when it came. All this was at a training camp on Long Island, the rain plunging through the winter dark until the fields fairly drummed with it and the men waded through the cold clear waters muttering about having enlisted in the navy.

Flushing Battery's captain was a fussy German by the name of Roemer who struggled to pronounce his *w*'s and whose voice, excited, would scramble to a shrill pitch. Roemer's eyes were very blue and his ruffed hair very red and his left eye slid inward giving him a sinister visage. He had learned his shoemaker's trade in Stuttgart before emigrating in 1839 and he had still the sharp waxed beard and mocking eyebrows of his trade. He was much hated. Roemer rewarded tidiness, promptness, boots kept in polish despite any weather, and punished severely any minor infraction. Private Shade, tidy, prompt, polished, found himself praised and soon promoted, never mind that as battery corporal he stood three-quarters the height of the next-youngest recruit.

Roemer did not care. He wanted glory and death. He drilled them in the rain with a tireless ferocity, their field guns wedged on tremendous wheels, positioned, aimed, unlocked and dragged again through deep mud, the gun crews mucking their loads of hollow shells across the fields and back until it was too dark to see and the languishing men had lost their boots in the mud and Roemer himself had vanished into a thin orange outline of lantern shine and blown rain. Edward slept a godforsaken sleep each night and woke early and stirred his bunk crews to attention in the gloom knowing Roemer would soon stomp through. Roemer in full regimentals, Roemer impatient to spread his misery.

All the same it was gentler than orphaned street life. The world of his father's cutters, the world of Shade House and its vast elegant rooms, all of that had been obliterated long ago by the scrabble and grime and soft core of hunger that had been life in the gutters. When an ex-printer with black-rimmed nails and thick forearms pushed him aside for the second time and scooped up his food Edward met the man's eye and then walked out of the mess tent. That night when the bastard went to the privies Edward followed carrying an iron pipe as long as his arm. He called to the man by name to turn him and then struck him sharply across one ear and when his hands went up Edward struck him twice in the groin with the pipe and the man's bowels erupted. He crushed a rib on either side of the man's barrel chest and when he was finished he threw the iron pipe into the open trench of the latrine. Come after me again and I'll kill you, he said flatly. The man never did.

At the end of October Roemer promoted him to sergeant in charge of his own cannon with a crew of five and on the thirteenth of November Flushing Battery was ordered south to Camp Barry in Washington. One week later in a freezing rain the entire battery, pale, dispirited, were shipped by cattle car to reinforce General Milroy at Camp Cheat Mountain in West Virginia. By the first of December they were peering grimly across the Staunton Turnpike at the white drifts of smoke from the Confederate camp on the facing mountain. Roemer brooded, paced, brooded, staring out into the dusk and the sheer drop with madness in his eye. The days passed. Occasionally they would fix their range and fire shot and shell for hours on end and the older Confederate guns would reply but there was in such probings a tired, depressed air.

Then on the thirteenth of December came the bloody storming of Allegheny Mountain. Edward was struck in the knee and again in the thigh while loading a cannon in the freezing wind and carried away from the guns screaming. He had not ever known such pain. As no arteries had been hit he lay shivering in hospital at Green Spring Run near Cheat Mountain for several days with little attention. They had cut two balls from his leg and a third had passed clean through. Nineteen others from his regiment had been wounded that day and three horses killed and the confusion and stink of flesh was overwhelming. On the second morning in the field tent a nurse leaned over the next cot and spoke to the dying boy writhing there calling him Sergeant Shade and Edward had raised his own weak head at that, meaning to speak up. But something held his tongue. The boy's lower jaw had been shot away and his face and chest heavily bandaged and no one could have known him by sight. Someone had confused the paperwork at the cots. A priest came that afternoon and sat on an overturned crate with his Bible open on one knee and addressed the boy as Sergeant Shade out of New York and Edward lay listening to the prayer with his eyes on the ceiling where the shadows crawled like flies and shortly thereafter the false Shade died.

All that night he lay awake, thinking. In the morning a new snow had fallen and covered the yard and the crates and the flatbed waggons in silence. The sentry was asleep. He lifted his head and stared out through the open tent flap at an impossible whiteness and he climbed out of his cot and buttoned his coat

with shaking fingers and vanished back into the civilian world
a ghost.

Foole studied his face in the pier glass. Cracks at the corners of
his eyes, the skin sallow and bruised. His aged eyebrows, his
nose raw in the cold, the heavy grooves lining his mouth. Somehow the light in his eyes had failed him. He stood in his baggy
nightshirt feeling a cold seep through his stockings and thinking of Pinkerton, the mudlark, the tunnels. They had emerged
exhausted and shivering into Leicester Square and parted ways
with a silent handshake. They would meet again in two nights'
time at a public house on the edge of Shadwell and proceed in
search of the Lascar's opium den and there had been in the big
man as he walked away some slow assured sadness that Foole
had noticed and weighed.

He drifted across the room to the small writing desk under
the window and sat, the folds of his nightshirt blooming around
him. The curtains stood cracked and he could see the grey
winter sunlight in the windows of the terraced house opposite.
A widow lived there, he knew, a lonely woman who used to find
any excuse to exit her house whenever Foole exited his. The
follies of the grieving. Before going into the sewers Pinkerton
had interviewed Martin Reckitt and discussed him, Foole. He
did not believe it any real risk. No one but Fludd knew the truth
of Edward Shade. He tried to imagine Reckitt sitting across
from a man like William Pinkerton and betraying the confidences of the flash world and he could not do it. But then the
Reckitt he had known hadn't yet been ten years in the Tench.

What he wanted was some clarity. After a moment he withdrew a sheet of writing paper from a cubby and dipped a pen
into a jar of ink and began to forge a letter of introduction from
Mr. Gabriel Utterson, solicitor, to the wardens of Millbank
Penitentiary.

Sometimes the only way to get, he thought, is by going.

———

In the mid-morning chill he walked through the crowds of the Mall with the falsified letter in a satchel and cut through St. James's Park and made his way down to the brown flats of the river, the low wall of the Embankment blue in the frost. He went alone and told no one of his going. When he looked out he could see the Albert Embankment across the river and the silhouettes of lampposts with arms upraised like crucified thieves. He crossed the frosted setts at an awkward slide.

After Brindisi he had sworn off revenge but some part of him still burned at a low boil and something else, some reluctant thing in his heart, made him understand visiting Reckitt now was the closest he would come to seeing Charlotte again in the quick. Was it a farewell he sought, was it some kind of leavetaking? A settling of accounts? For ten years he had kept himself from the Reckitts, their old haunts, their old accomplices, struggling to forget South Africa. The old thief would think his coming now a weakness, he knew. As perhaps it was.

At Millbank he presented his falsified letter with its seal to the gatekeeper and stood with his hands clasped in the small of his back waiting while the massive gates were lifted from their anchors and drawn back. I never seen you here afore, the gatekeeper muttered, opening the visitors' book in the gatehouse. Foole blew on his cold fingers. He was dressed like a junior solicitor and carried a card to that effect and he frowned importantly.

The visitors' hall was in a central wing on the lower tier. A long narrow room with spider-cracked walls and plaster peeling overhead and a row of dusty tables under windows. Foole shivered as he waited. Through the far door he saw a guard escort a grey withered man in brown prison-issue clothes. His wrists and ankles were shackled and he walked with a pained shuffling gait and it took Foole a moment to recognize his old accomplice. His chains were unlocked and drawn clanking through an iron anchor set into the wall beneath the table and then relocked and then the guard walked bored back to the far door. Reckitt glanced balefully behind him, as if longing to be returned to his cell.

Millbank had roughened him. He looked so much thinner, almost transparent, like a sheet of tissue paper held to a flame. Foole tried to see in the creature seated before him the confidence man of Port Elizabeth, that old elegance, but he could not do so. His fingers swollen, the nails cracked. A blue web of veins visible in his cheeks, his forehead. When he closed his eyelids he looked almost another man, leaning his face back into the shaft of sunlight coming in through the high window.

So Adam Foole has come to Millbank, Reckitt said, his voice creaking. He opened his eyes and met Foole's stare and his own eyes were clear, pale, calm. It is true then, he said. About Charlotte.

Foole cleared his throat.

You would not be here if it weren't, Reckitt said. His eyes hardened. I have been reminding myself that we are all here by the grace of the Lord. That His purpose is kindness.

Kindness, Foole muttered. He felt already unbalanced. He remembered uneasily this man's talent for seizing and twisting a conversation.

What I did not expect, Reckitt said, is how difficult the fact of it would be to accept. I understand it is true. Charlotte is dead. But I do not believe it. I do not believe it because what happens in the outside does not happen in here.

Foole was silent. The grey light fell in squares across the far wall.

We are born dying, Reckitt murmured. Tell me, who would design it so? Why would the good Lord give us a body which must suffer? Reckitt paused. Unless He is not the good Lord after all. Unless goodness is not His concern.

If I wanted to talk faith I'd go to a priest. A real one.

There are no real priests. Reckitt studied his ravaged hands. You think I sound mad. I do not care. A man can stare at a thing for years and not see it for what it is.

Foole shook his head. I came to tell you I mean to find him, he said. Charlotte's killer. I mean to make him suffer.

That is not why you came. What are you doing back in London?

Charlotte wrote me.

Charlotte.

Foole nodded, watching the thief's sudden stillness. What she was working on, he said. She wanted to bring me into it.

Reckitt lowered his face and now Foole saw undisguised that plunging darkness he had once feared, years ago, a vortex inside the man's heart vicious and without end.

You are a liar, Adam Foole, Reckitt said softly.

An ugly satisfaction rose in Foole, rose and was gone, leaving only a heaviness in its place. He was surprised by his own meanness despite their common grief and all at once he wanted to get the meeting over with. William Pinkerton came to see you, he said.

Reckitt tilted his head to one side, as if he had not heard.

William Pinkerton came to see you and you spoke with him.

I imagined shame would have kept you from coming here, Reckitt murmured. Do you know how the Church defines shame?

What did you tell Pinkerton, Martin? What did he ask?

Reckitt removed his hands from the table and settled them in his lap, the chains clinking. He studied Foole. The nature of the devil, he said quietly. That is what we discussed. Evil.

Evil.

Among other matters, yes.

I was one of those other matters.

Reckitt gave him a long hooded look. I see I am not the only one Mr. Pinkerton has visited, he said. Do you know what the devil is, Adam? He is our own deceit. Our own deceit made flesh. We make him by being what we are.

Pinkerton is not the devil, Martin.

Not Pinkerton.

Foole wondered if some mania had devoured the man after his long years alone in Millbank. You saved my life once, he murmured. Then you took what was mine by rights and left me in Brindisi to die. If you had—

I did not save your life, Adam.

Foole blinked.

I did not save your life. I spared it. Reckitt's reptilian eyes held his own in a hard bright stare. I have often asked myself, would I know the truth if I met it? If I stood before it, would the truth know me? The ancient thief leaned in closer, he lowered his voice. Charlotte never came to you in Brindisi, as she was supposed to, Adam. Why? All those years ago, when she came back from Port Elizabeth, when I came to you in Brindisi. I spared your life why?

Something went through Foole then, some presentiment of dread, a lightness in his skull. He could hear a machinery working deep in the blood box of his ears. Why? he said.

The old man gave him a disgusted look. Because she was with child.

With child.

Reckitt raised his fists over his head and shook his chains for the guard. The clatter was harsh in the quiet room. Foole watched the figure detach from the wall, drift lazily towards them.

You're lying.

Reckitt shrugged.

Charlotte never had a child. You're lying.

All right.

Prove it. Where's this child now?

The old thief looked at Foole and Foole saw then all of the loneliness and brutality that was in himself also. The guard shambled nearer.

Reckitt leaned in close. Foole could smell the sour-milk smell of his skin.

It died, he said.

In better years the crates that arrived at the Emporium arrived sometimes weather-worn, the grey wood shrunken from salt water, jungle rainfall, the sudden cold of the English weather, and Foole would brace a knee against the first plank and with a crowbar begin to twist and pry back the warped nails in their beds. He had such a feeling inside his chest as he came out of the penitentiary. The sky was brown, the light in the faces he passed white and eerie. At a busy corner he waited for an omnibus and when it reined to a stop it was already packed. He clung to the roof seats as the nails in his heart creaked and bent slowly back.

He did not believe Reckitt's lie, he was not so foolish as that. He got off the omnibus in a black mood, vicious with himself for having met with the man. Already the day had deepened though it was only just noon, the cold crackling its way across the slate roofs of the city. He was walking fast to keep his body distracted. Past a papery shop, writing implements and leather notebooks fanned out in its windows, past a tailor's, a dry goods emporium, and on. He could not say what he had expected from Millbank but if he was honest with himself it was something to do with forgiveness and grief.

His throat began to ache. The warped nails prying loose. He slowed to a walk and then he stopped, a still figure in the centre of the footpath, while the city flowed on around him and under him and past.

Mr. Foole? a voice said at his elbow.

He glanced up and saw a florid face, a throat wrapped and double-wrapped in a scarf. It was Gabriel Utterson.

The unlikeliness of it left him staring in confusion and he raised his eyes and saw across the street the arched entrance to Utterson's court offices and he saw the solicitor's leather satchel tucked up under an elbow as if he was on pressing business and Foole did not understand how he had walked so far.

Gabriel, he said thickly.

I'm just stepping out, sir. Is it pressing? Then Utterson paused, peered into his face with a cold assessing eye. You *are* looking for me, sir?

He was startled to feel the man's grip at his elbow, to feel himself guided to one side. No matter, the solicitor murmured. I am pleased to have found you. I had intended to seek you out.

Foole buttoned the uppermost eyelet of his coat and turned up his collar. He wanted only to be alone.

I've been thinking of what we discussed, the solicitor said. Rose has been much distressed. About Charlotte, I mean. He shifted his bulk, grasped Foole's arm again. Rose believes she has found a contact for you. But it is complicated, there are conditions to be met.

Foole did not immediately reply. Seeing in his mind's eye a blood-soaked bed, stained sheets bundled by candlelight, hearing the long low keening wail.

I've offended you, Utterson said. It was kindly meant, sir.

You haven't. Foole held up a tired hand. You haven't, Gabriel.

The solicitor's left eye twitched under its lid. Rose says there has been talk, on the other side. She is willing to try to reach your Charlotte. The circle can be closed Tuesday next, sir, if the signs remain favourable. But success is not certain. I am told the attempt would be much magnified if you were to bring with you a particular companion.

How particular?

Not your Mr. Fludd. He would tear the room apart looking for conspirators. No, Rose has someone else in mind. A great advantage to reaching Charlotte would be if someone who was with her near her end were to sit with us. One of the last to see her alive. Something flickered in Utterson's eyes, a quick sleek menace, and was gone.

Foole did not at first take the man's meaning and then he did. Pinkerton?

Indeed.

That's madness, Gabriel. That's inviting the devil to dine.

Utterson folded his chin into the scarf at his throat. We would need to be cautious, yes.

The man will start a file on all of us.

I rather expect he has already started on you.

Foole paused, his breath clouding in the cold. I won't ask Pinkerton, Gabriel.

Are you so protective of him?

I won't see the man provoked. Nor should you.

Utterson's eyes were sharp. I hear stories, Mr. Foole. Stories I can scarcely credit. Midnight excursions among the mudlarks of Blackfriars, for instance. I was sure they were mistaken, that you would not keep such company as William Pinkerton.

Company you would share.

To facilitate the seance, sir. Only that.

The two men stood under the cold archway while crowds of law clerks crushed past and the horse-drawn omnibuses rattled by in the loud street. Foole thought of Charlotte sitting convalescent at an afternoon window watching sunlight play across a turned-over garden and he imagined a silence inside her. He refused to concede his private business to a man such as this.

Adam, Utterson was murmuring, you know my sister's integrity. She makes no assurance of contact. It is not a deceit. Sometimes the worlds come together as we would wish, sometimes they do not. Rose can only promise she is willing to try.

High overhead the stone buildings loomed, canescent and sinister.

If one opens their ears, it is a beautiful message, sir, Utterson was murmuring. Beautiful. And yet so few wish to hear it. How stubborn we are. How easily frightened.

Foole could glimpse a melancholy in his voice like light through the cracks in a floor though it was a light he could not stand on and a floor that would hold no weight. Grief was selfish, grief was angry. He would damn any who would take it from him. He knew this the way he knew he was right-handed and that a scar cut like a question mark deep into his cheek under his whiskers. Grief was a part of him, a part of how he had lived, what he had been made from.

I'll sit with her, he said. But I make no promises about Pinkerton.

———

He was a dead man when he left the field hospital outside Cheat Mountain and already buried in a soldier's grave when he fled north, into Ohio. The war had drained the country even then and he walked in ruined shoes through deep snow feeling the wind biting at his neck and seeing no sign of life. Waggons standing unhitched in the road. Farmhouses with doors standing open and snowdrifts blown inside. Christmas morning found him asleep in a barn rolled in straw and the animals long since gone. When the year turned a week later he was huddled under a railroad bridge in west Pennsylvania with two other deserters none trusting the others while a low fire burned in a rusted barrel. He was by that time wearing women's gloves with the fingers cut out and a farmhand's woollens and boots that reached halfway to his thighs. The men huddled with him looked old and savage but they gave him his space and he wondered for the first time how he himself must look. When he broke the ice to clean his face the next morning he saw hollow eyes, a gaunt stare, the haunted face of a grown man. All night trains rattled past overhead, snow sifting through the ties all around them in the darkness dreamlike and sad.

By the tenth of January he had caught a boxcar in the freezing wind and ridden across the state to New York, starving, feeling a lightness burn up out of his legs and hands. He did not know what he was. He was not exactly a deserter but nor was he a free man. He would think sometimes of his old captain, wondering if he had found the death he had sought. Foole tried his hand at pickpocketing in the railroad stations but he was too weak and miserable-looking and could not get near his marks. He knew legally that Sergeant Shade had died and so at last he gave up and enlisted again under a new name in a regiment out of Rikers Island. Once more he pocketed the forty-dollar advance on his bounty and shortly afterwards he leaned his rifle against a rough barricade in the frozen mud pits around the unfinished Capitol and fled from his picket into the night.

A door had opened, he had glimpsed a new kind of war. In February he made his way north to Boston, he enlisted under a third name in exchange for a further forty dollars. This bounty he accepted like a boy just in from farm country, like a boy dazzled by the sight of it. He had burned through that first bounty in dice games with the other recruits but now he had it in mind to set something aside for a venture after the war. He jumped again and re-enlisted back in New York the following week feeling a kind of eerie shadow at his back and here his luck failed him at last. The parade ground was clear of snow but hard-packed and cracking from the frost when he heard a familiar voice call out, Sergeant? and when he glanced lazily back he found himself staring up into the crossed blue eye of Captain Roemer.

Sergeant Shade, Roemer said. He was leaning on a crutch, his left trouser leg folded back and pinned at the knee. His sharp teeth smiled in disbelief.

You're mistaken, sir, Foole said. And walked calmly away.

But that night two soldiers came for him in his bunk and hauled him half dressed into the cold and beat him severely. He was handcuffed, interrogated, beaten again.

It was the end of March by then. He was held in a stockade in that northern military camp for several weeks with two other deserters and there was a desperation and a fear etched in each face for they knew what lay ahead. Roemer had come limping into the stockade one day with a quiet triumph and explained to the guard that the three prisoners were to be shipped south to the Army of the Potomac as deserters and cowards. There would be no court martial. In the Capitol they would be held until the army mobilized and sailed for the James River. When the battles began the deserters would be shackled in irons and shoved stumbling into the front lines without weapons and forced at gunpoint to run at the Confederate positions.

Be ground up like meat, them three, one of the guards, a Texan, grinned.

But I expect the boy won't be much troubled by it, Roemer said, eyeing Foole shivering through the bars.

Why's that?

Because he's already dead, Roemer said. Isn't that right, Sergeant? Aren't you already dead?

Leering and dragging the swaddled elbow of his crutch across the bars as he spoke.

TWENTY-ONE

The scarred, vicious face of Muck Annie haunted William in the days following. He had left Foole at the sewer entrance two nights earlier on the understanding that they would meet again, this night, at a public house on the edge of Shadwell. He had stooped in under the crooked timber door frame and peered about at the dejected in their cups feeling a sudden uneasiness and then turned and gone back out. But ten minutes later Foole had approached, whistling softly under his breath, and together they started down into the crowded East End. The streets were lit only by old-fashioned lanterns creaking from hooks that had been nailed into the lintels of public houses in the murderous days of George III and there were no lights else but for the flare and sheen reflecting off the puddles and rivers of muck in the streets.

St. George's Street. Whatever else it was not England. Bearded Jews with their ringlets and prayer shawls wading powerfully through the crowds like some ancient warning from the East, their shoulders wide-set, their necks bullish. Walking five abreast and wringing empty sacks in their fists. Peddlers with stacks of stained silk hats tottering on their lice-ridden heads, tiny pickpockets running barefoot through the sludge. Once the crowds parted like a sea and out of the throng William saw emerge a very short Turk in a tall white headdress and in his fist was a rope and at the end of that rope a brindled cow. Drunk Swedes with faces painted like acrobats shouted out some mournful song over the heads of the crowd. Laughing at their own misery as if it were some joke. Pigs ran loose underfoot. At the corner of Cannon Street Road William met the dark Asiatic stare of a woman selling Bibles from an overturned crate and he looked quickly past her. Just beyond, like a pale horror rising from the blackness, the limestone tower of St. George-in-the-East. Foole mingled, Foole did not slow. The air was cold. They passed two ladies in fur collars leading a monkey on a leash north towards Shadwell station and William looked at it and understood it would be dead within the week. They walked downwind from Jamrach's Menagerie, the reek of offal and shit and animal fear shouldering past them, they passed the walled rose garden of the old Wesleyan graves. At a pie stand he saw a thin man wrapped in rags exhibiting a bucket of turtles to a gaggle of urchins. Cloth caps folded into little fists, eyes agog. The man swung the turtles in an elegant dance and he saw the man's milky stare and he knew that the wretch was blind.

Then they were turning north into Victoria Street and all around them came the spice from cooking fires and he saw in the crowds the grim faces of Chinese and Indians and Malays. He could smell hashish and opium, cinnamon and oranges. He felt dizzy with the noise. Squalid figures squatted over cook fires in alleys stirring pots with weird sticks wrapped in beads and feathers and half-breed children half stunned from the cold whistled to them from dilapidated courts. Ahead in the darkness William could see the taller darkness of the viaduct. They passed four gin saloons each identical to each where a piano clattered off-key on the boards within and the stamping and roars of men reached them from out of the smoke. The dazzling brightness of a Ragged School, beggar children lounging on its stairs and picking tobacco from their lips and passing a bottle of some black liquor. Foole led him past Quashie's where a tattooed barker called to passersby some display of wonder and talent within and William stared at a monochrome poster of a man in a mask cutting the throat of a girl.

They were seeking a shabby yard known as New Court and at an arched passageway Foole pulled him aside out of the crowds. It was quieter there. The passage opened into shadow beside the Royal Sovereign public house but they did not go down it. After a moment a Malay sailor stumbled through the front door of the pub and leaned up against one wall in the weak light of the windows with a hand for balance and started to piss. The two men watched in silence. He was wearing a Confederate uniform.

William grunted. Now where do you think he got that from?

Then the sailor was staggering away from the wall like a man from a losing hand of cards and pulling at his fly with both fists and then without so much as a glance he went back in.

The moral few, Foole murmured.

The moral few. William laughed a caustic laugh. Four men equal a lion.

How many times did you hear that in a day?

William regarded Foole in the dimness, trying to make sense of the man. Where did you fight at? he asked at last.

I didn't. Foole shrugged an apologetic half shrug. I never saw action. I was stationed with the Fifth in Washington as a quarter-master's apprentice in the railway drops. We kept you boys fed.

We weren't fed. We could have eaten our shoes.

Foole nodded. Well. We tried to.

William levelled his gaze and stared down Foole, a man slight, elegant, dapper in his cutaway and starched collar. He did not believe a word the man was saying.

I, like you, found the war a more complicated thing than most wish it to be, Foole said quietly. It's hard to have faith in our fellows when you see what they're capable of.

Yes.

I would not relive those days for anything. I still dream of them.

Their breath like smoke in the cold. Frost crept in slow webs over the cobblestones. Beyond was a shabby square of a dozen or so lodging houses and William could see the stiff grey lines of washing not taken in, a cart upturned on its handles with one wheel pried away. Seated on a sunken stair was a cripple in an old sailor's coat, his crutch crosswise in his lap, head nodding. After a moment a group of four well-dressed gentlemen emerged from the shadows smiling dreamily each to each and they did not even glance at Foole or William as they slid past. One of them was brushing his fingertips back and forth over the deckled pages of a city guidebook and William could almost see the black poppy boiling the man's blood.

Sightseers, Foole murmured contemptuously. But I expect she's in.

The Lascar's a woman?

Used to be, at least. She's old Latou's widow. Lascar Sal. You've heard of Latou.

He had not.

Welcome to Shadwell, Foole said. He tapped his walking stick on the bricks of the arch. Sal's is the only den left now. He fixed William with his glowing catlike stare. They say Charles Dickens used to come here.

Just then a tinker burst staggering backward from the door of the Royal Sovereign his arms wheeling for balance. The man started to laugh in the cut of light cast from the open door and then he wiped at his face and muttered something in German and went back inside. William watched this in distaste. He said he thought it strange a place like Sal's could exist when the substance could be purchased at any chemist's. It's everywhere, he said. They feed it to teething babies, for god's sake, you can buy it over the counter. Why come here?

Ah, but this is pure, Foole murmured. From Canton itself. There's an art to the mixing I'm told.

An art.

It's like cooking.

William shook his head in disgust. There's no art to feeding a starving man, he said.

Foole lifted a patched curtain with care and held it for William to pass. In the doorway slouched two men, hands deep in pockets, coats rucked up over their wrists, and they were smiling absently out into the night. They had the leeched grey throats of men staring down the grave.

The interior was small, perhaps eight feet by eight, the water-stained ceiling low. William stooped, took off his hat. The Lascar's room was sparse, dim, lit only by a solitary lantern in the far corner half concealed by a divan where a bundle of wet rags had been thrown and left to dry. He could see a small framed watercolour of what must once have been St. George-in-the-East, hanging now askew on its nail, and there was a low shelf just off the floor near the divan. Five leather-bound books, with gold Chinese script upon their spines. A polished box of dominoes with dragons carved into its sides, the lid left up. A scale for weighing opium. A three-legged chair propped against a wall.

Where is she? William said.

There was a doorway at the far end of the room and Foole was staring into its gloom as if to discern some shape in the beyond. Then William felt a slow thrum rising from the dirt floor and the watercolour began to rattle and the walls were shuddering and then the full fury of the East London line thundered under their feet and past. He glanced at Foole. And it was then he saw, under the rags on the broken divan, the tiny translucent body of Lascar Sal.

He had seen many dead in his life but the hearts of those dead had stopped and Lascar Sal's beat on. She was skeletal, shrivelled, she seemed scarcely able to lift a wrist to wave the two men forward. There was a waxiness to her skin and her eyes had shrunk to slits, the lashes ringed in a crust of tears. She was breathing fast laboured breaths and her ribs rose and fell like the shallow ribs of a hurt animal. All this William saw and did not see. She lay with her birdlike ankles crossed and a heat rising from her skin the two men could have warmed their knuckles by and her long white throat with its ropy swallowing as she smoked her pipe over her lamp.

Sal? Foole murmured.

Her eyes unfocused, her face turning. Dearies, she said. A whisper like dried leather. You'll pay up according, dearies, won't you? You'll pay up according?

Foole held out a hand as if to assure her but he did not touch her and it hovered over her still form for a long suspended breath. We're looking for someone, he said. We'll pay for that.

You'll smoke a pipe won't you, like a good soul, dearies? You'll pity poor Sal?

William could almost not hear, so soft was it.

We're looking for a man named Cooper, Foole said. Goes by the name of the Saracen.

Her eyes closed and her eyes opened. Her lips moved soundlessly.

Foole withdrew a shilling from his pocket and held it before her in the low light and William felt something at his back and turned. The two addicts at the doorway were staring at the coin in Foole's fingers.

No ships, no ships, she whispered.

Foole set the coin with a quiet click down before her and the Lascar's sinewy white hand very slowly drifted to the coin, slid it scraping across the floor and under the blanket.

They waited.

She did not stir. Foole glowered at the two men in the doorway and then he tucked the hem of his coat around his legs and took up his walking stick and shuffled past William into the room beyond.

It was smaller than the first, darker, hushed but for the quiet bubbling of the pipes. Against one wall a tattered bed slouched on ancient iron bedposts, two figures sprawling out upon it smoking. Three others lay huddled in blankets against a wall and not one stirred as the two men picked their slow way over them, peering into the faces of the dreaming dead.

All were men, all were old. Sallow figures sunken in bliss and lost to the world. The skin of each burned with an awful luminosity as if lit by a lantern from within and when William rolled one onto his side to see his face the man felt papery and light as a wasp's nest.

Foole passed on into the third room, and he followed. A narrow closet, unlit but for the weak light at their backs. He stood pressed close to the small thief neither man speaking and it was then they saw, laid out on his ancient back with his bony hands folded at his chest and his huge eyes shut in their sockets, what was left of the fearsome Saracen.

There could be no uncertainty. He was huge, even wasted as he was. An old man, his cheek dried and pulling away from the old wound there so that the red slash of his mouth could be seen in all its horror. Weird scars curled down across his face and over the ruin of his nose and the skin there had discoloured to the stained brown of old tea and the scallop of one mangled ear gleamed in the light. He was very near death, William knew.

It's not him, said Foole.

It's him.

Foole looked like he was going to speak but then he did not. William tried to put a hand on his shoulder but he stepped away like a man avoiding a draft. He was still staring down at the figure in its rags.

There's nothing for us here, Mr. Foole, William murmured. And then: Adam.

Foole looked up. His eyes were creased and sad. He didn't kill her, he said.

No.

Look at him.

William studied the dying man in the bad light. I see him, he said.

They made their way back out into the night and the air felt cold and clean on William's face. He was tired. He glanced sidelong at Foole, knowing it was time the man held up his share of the bargain and told him what he knew about Edward Shade. They did not retrace their steps but went north towards Shadwell station and Foole took them through a warren of unlit courts and alleys. William struggled to keep his footing, to keep pace. He could feel eyes watching from the pitch but shook this feeling off. His Colt was in his coat pocket, the weight of it against his ribs as he went. There were lanterns in some few of the yards they passed, a smell of livestock.

Hold up, William hissed. Mr. Foole?

His fingers moved across the fungal slick of the bricks and over the sharp lead gutter of a rain spout or what he trusted must be a rain spout and then he kicked some clattering twist of metal and stumbled and his foot rolled over a soft cold thing like a dead cat and caught the ground again and he righted himself and kept going. Foole was ahead of him now.

There was a light. All at once he found himself face to face with a figure in a battered top hat and a patched cloak and the man was leering a toothless leer. He held in one hand an ancient bull's-eye lantern, its leather strap crossed and double-crossed over his sleeve like the lashing of a harness. His grizzled jaw, his cheeks pitted from some long-survived smallpox, his one eye turned lifelessly out.

Pity a poor lad, mister, the man whispered.

William shook him off.

Give us a copper for the old missus. Just a copper, like.

The man was tugging with strength at William's sleeve though William was a good head taller. Get off, he snapped. Go. But as he began to shoulder past he felt something like the brush of a crow's wing at the back of his neck and he raised his fingers to the spot and they came away wet. It was blood.

A sudden shadow, a shock of pale hair in the lantern light. He could not say how many there were. Only that he fell into the cold muck with his arms cradling his head as the kicks came sharp and furious at his back and ribs and elbows and hands. There was blood in his eyes. He thought he saw a massive shadow block out the light in that alley and then there were men lifting into the air like sacks of wheat thrown from a waggon and that giant silhouette was wading like a reaper through the fury but then William shut his eyes in pain and when he opened them it was only Adam Foole, torn and bloodied and quick, his walking stick carving through the four men surrounding him, striking first one and then another with a violent grace and at each gentle touch from his stick a froth of blood would explode in the weak light and the men would clutch their faces and crumple.

It could have lasted moments, it could have lasted hours. He could hear Foole breathing in the darkness. The man did not stoop over him, he did not offer his hand. But only stood swaying upon his walking stick and staring wild-eyed around him as if they might return at any moment. William rolled slowly onto his elbows and sat up and he saw two urchins crouched in the light of an overturned lantern and when they locked eyes the small boys vanished.

Son of a bitch, he said. His ribs ached but he did not think he had broken any bones. There was a wetness at the back of his collar and down his back and he knew the blood there would ruin his shirt. He pressed a handkerchief to the cut.

Foole said nothing.

You came back. William fixed on the thief through one swelling eye.

He watched Foole shrug.

Why?

A long quiet look. Then the man said, softly, I always keep my word, Mr. Pinkerton. I always pay my debts.

But there was a sadness and a disappointment in his voice and William studied him thinking of the Saracen and feeling overwhelmed. He asked no more. He had lost his hat and the shoulder of his chesterfield was ripped at the seam. His face in the morning would be mottled and lumpen and yellow. He imagined what Shore would say and he winced.

Foole was coughing with one hand against a brick wall and the other clutching his ribs and his feet were straddling some foul muck of the street and then he straightened and looked at William. Four men equal a lion, he said.

Some lion, William said.

Limping they found a wretched pub next to a butcher's stall with sawdust on its floors and a lantern burning at either end and there was murder in William's face as they stumbled in. No patron looked twice to see their state. They dragged a table nearer the fire and gestured for a bottle of gin.

Foole's hand shook as he poured. The cold bottle with its paper label in the firelight, the gin glowing like silver nitrate.

Foole raised his glass. To Jonathan Cooper.

To Cooper, William muttered. May he never awake.

They drank. Poured a second and drank again.

Foole held the gin in his mouth and then swallowed. It's the not knowing, he said after a moment. He looked up, vulnerable, as if something had been peeled away. I'd heard rumours about the Saracen. I thought, I don't know, perhaps there might be some truth in them.

William dabbed gingerly at his neck. What will you do now?

I should ask Charlotte that.

Ask Charlotte—?

It's nothing. A joke.

He sipped at his gin and felt a warmth prickle in his throat and then he blinked heavily and knew he would soon be drunk if he did not slow.

Foole was staring at his hands as if deciding something and then he looked up, his eerie bright eyes shining. Do you believe the dead can be reached? he asked.

The dead? No.

But you do believe in an afterlife.

William opened his hand and stared at the cross-hatching there in the firelight and then he said, Mr. Foole, I believe the dead live on inside us. In our memories. That is the only after-life I believe in.

I was contacted by an old friend yesterday. A spiritualist.

William said nothing.

You do not approve.

I'd never have taken you for a believer.

A believer? Foole said with a bitter laugh. He wet his lips. When I was four years old I was visited by two small girls. They would stand at my bedside in silence. They were my sisters. Foole paused a moment, then said, My sisters drowned the year I was born, Mr. Pinkerton. Yesterday, when my friend asked me to a seance, he asked me to bring a companion. To make up the numbers for the gathering. I told him it could not be done.

William regarded this man in his grief and felt something, a sudden anger, on his behalf. It's natural to want to believe, he said sharply. But don't let your loss belong to someone else.

Foole's face darkened.

Did you ever read of the Reno business, back in sixty-eight? William said. It was in all the papers. When Foole nodded he went on, Well, the next year, after the brothers had all been killed or strung up by the mobs, a rumour started to go around. Their gains from the various holdups were never recovered and it was said all of it had been buried somewhere near Seymour, Illinois. Scores of treasure hunters turned to mediums to find it from the dead men. William eyed the smaller man sitting bruised in the shadows and he felt for his split lip with the tip of his tongue. Our general superintendent in New York at the time was contacted by the vice-president of the Adams Express Company. One of our important clients. He'd had an intuition, this man said, that he ought to contact a certain medium about his company's stolen money. He wanted Mr. Bangs—that was our superintendent—to go with him.

I've heard such stories.

Yes. Well the medium could tell him nothing, of course. When asked where the Express Company's money was at, a spirit, Sim—one of the dead outlaws, presumably—had only excuses, vague allusions, all unverifiable. He named an accomplice, Sheeley. There never was a Sheeley with the Renos.

Mr. Gaither—that was our client's name—admitted later to us that he didn't even believe in spiritualism.

But he went all the same.

Exactly. Just on the possibility of it.

He knew it was all lies and deceits and yet he went all the same. Foole lowered his voice. It's a question of hope, of course. Having that possibility, no matter how unlikely. Living with it.

There's hope, and then there's gullibility, Mr. Foole. I'd be sorry to see you taken advantage of.

Foole smiled a quick barbed smile. It is such a relief to hear you say it.

Say what?

My friend asked me to speak with you. You were the last to see her alive, the last to touch her. He believes your presence might make contact possible.

My presence?

At the seance.

William stared into his gin. I wasn't the last. You know that.

I would be in your debt, sir.

You already are.

Foole raised his eyebrows, his expression faltering.

Edward Shade.

Ah. Foole picked up his glass, set it back down. His face was flushed.

What is it?

I fear I have misled you, he said. What I told you in the tunnel—

William was quiet while the firelight played over the table, the glasses, his bruised knuckles. That would be a shame, he said.

I did not lie to you, Foole murmured, leaning forward. But I know you are a man of facts, not conjecture—

I'll take the conjecture.

Some of this is nearer to rumour.

William said nothing, waited.

I cannot promise it is entirely true, Foole said. That's all I mean. Edward was small, even for his age. And he was always hungry. He would eat anything, just eat and eat, as if he could never get full. Foole regarded William with a cautious gaze as if weighing his next words. Then he said, Edward loved your father.

You knew Shade?

A long time ago. He used to say your father was a great man.

This was after the war.

Yes. After the war. Impatience had crept into the man's voice. Edward and I met in New Orleans in eighteen sixty-five. That was a terrible year. The war had stripped the city. I daresay they deserved it. But grift became a way of surviving. Either you were quick or you were dead. Edward was very young still but he knew how to work a street. I had established an import business there the month the war ended and I hired Edward to help me with incoming cargo on the docks.

He worked for you.

Only briefly. He could not keep out of trouble. I let him go when the customs officials started harassing me. It seems Edward couldn't leave the army's supply depots alone. My business had been flagged, as it were. Very troublesome, that. Years later I saw him near the warehouses in Detroit. I was just passing through. He invited me to an evening at a rat baiting and it was there I met Charlotte.

He wanted to ask which side of the barrier she'd been on but he did not.

I courted her, Foole said. I didn't know then just how involved she was with the criminal element. I loved her from the first. Foole said this and then lowered his face, as if embarrassed.

Tell me about Shade.

Foole cleared his throat. I met Charlotte again ten years ago here in London. It was she who told me what had happened to young Edward. She said your father had been hunting him for years, that they had worked together in the Secret Service during the war. Edward had done something terrible, had run from his post, or leaked secrets, or some such. Your father hunted him relentlessly. In eighteen seventy-three the boy grew tired of running. He went to your father's mansion in Chicago, to your mansion. He broke in. Waited in the dark with a revolver for your father. A struggle ensued, Edward was shot. Your father dispatched the body.

William stared at the small man in the firelight, the mottled bruising along one side of his face. In eighteen seventy-three, he said.

Foole nodded.

In eighteen seventy-three Edward Shade tried to kill my father. In his own home.

Yes.

He was in my father's house. With a loaded gun.

Foole furrowed his brow. I could be mistaken. Perhaps I am.

William left the unlikeliness alone for a moment and tried to think his way through the account but it did not make sense. It would have been self-defence, he said abruptly. An armed intruder in his house? Why would my father not alert the police? Why would he not tell me?

Foole turned his sad bright eyes on William, shrugged.

How would your Charlotte Reckitt know this? William muttered. Who would she have heard it from? War offences were forgiven in sixty-six. My father couldn't have prosecuted Shade even if he wanted to.

Forgiven? Foole turned the word in his mouth, as if testing the possibility of it. But who did the forgiving? Not your father, I would wager. Not the men who suffered in the field.

Why would my father keep hunting a man he knew was dead?

Perhaps to hide the murder? Foole shook his head. I really couldn't say. Tell me something. What was your true interest in Charlotte?

I never had any, William said, distracted. I was only ever interested in Shade.

Foole was quiet a long moment. What would you have done, had you found him?

William's fingers were still crouched on the rim of his glass. He felt the blood slow in his throat. He looked up. I guess that's the question, he said tightly.

TWENTY-TWO

E dward Shade made his first escape before the barge had left the Hudson.

It was March 3, 1862. In the pre-dawn darkness the foam in the ship's wake seemed to him to glow with an other-worldly light and when he turned his face to the wind a long crack of red light could be seen seeping up out of the east. But the deck he lay crouched on, handcuffed and huddled in a threadworn blanket, was still black, the boards slick and freezing. Others sat shackled half asleep nearby and a guard stood in the lee of the wheelhouse with his hands tucked under his armpits for warmth, shoulder turned to the wind. He could hear the low thrump of the engines, the water slapping past. He rose in silence, just levered his elbows onto the railing, hoisted his hips up, and let himself over. He felt nothing. Then his back struck the icy waters and he went under. A sailor leaning out over the stern witnessed his plunge and cried the alarm and fired a warning shot that went wide and after a long slow turning of the barge and the criss-crossing of lamplights across the waves a lifebuoy was hurled at his head and he slapped his way to it and struggled to hold on. He was hauled up half drowned, given a dram of rum, left shivering in his frost-stiffened clothes while a puddle seeped under him on the deck. By the time the sun had risen he was coughing and could not get warm.

His second escape came one week later while trudging through the churned mud of Camp Barry in the gloom of the

Capitol's half-built dome. In the wind its scaffolding would lean and rattle like a broken door and though he was still weak from his sickness the sound of it made him bitterly resentful. They were returning from digging a line of fortifications at gunpoint and were shackled at the ankles each to each and he being the smallest and frailest walked the rear. He had lifted a key from a guard as he drifted into line and now as they turned a corner he bent down at a half walk and unlocked his chain and it slithered heavily clear and he started to run. He made it as far as the rail yard pilings before a shot rang out over his head and he stopped, hands raised high, his eyes fixed on the boxcars in the distance.

He was stripped and beaten badly for that. Four grown men in outsized boots, kicking and stomping, his spindly child's limbs snapping out and then curling back in again. They left him crying in the straw, laced with blood, bruised, too broken to tremble. He was but one of eighteen in that stockade and the least vicious of all but after his second escape he became known as a wily and dangerous convict. He did not care. He would be damned if he would permit the Union to tear him to pieces. Daily he ate, he dug, he hauled, he slept, daily he brooded over his escape. Weeks passed, the Peninsular Campaign drew nearer, the wheat fields where he and his fellows would be shackled and driven into a grinding hail of shrapnel and bullets. He slept badly. On moonless nights his death came to him silent and shrouded and studied him through the bars.

He watched the others with hard eyes, he kept his distance. They had come to believe him a bad omen, a boy marked by evil, and though he did not understand this he was grateful for it. Some of those men were deserters, some thieves, one barrel-chested sergeant had strangled a corporal in a card game, all of them were sly desperate men. He stole another man's spoon one night and after the man had been beaten for it and the stockade overturned in the search he began to sharpen it, very quietly, muffled by straw. After the second week he became aware of a figure lurking, slyly, at the edge of his vision, and he understood his third escape would be his last. That figure was a tall thin man with a broken nose and a shaggy white beard stained to copper from tobacco and his eyes were creased to slits and Edward could not be sure when the man was peering his way.

Edward was careful, Edward was patient. He studied the guards' turnovers, he listened through the walls for the crunch of their boots in the gravel as they took the shorter route behind the stockade, he took note of the different mechanism locking the outer door from the inner. He knew the number of paces to the high corner of the camp fenceline and he knew too where a washing line of old clothes could be found the second street over. He knew the operations were under way for a major offensive and that they would be shackled and shipped out soon. He waited for the next new moon and kept his head clear.

In the third week the old man who had been watching him sidled close. Edward had taken a fistful of rotten rice from the floor and crawled back to his corner. The old man's two bottom teeth had been knocked loose and in the gap his tongue looked grotesquely pink.

I've been watching you, he whispered. His voice creaking.

Edward sat unmoving, hair long in his eyes.

I said I've been watching you.

I heard you.

The man wheezed, it might have been a laugh. His knees were folded up near his shoulders, twisted, crablike. I always knew the world would catch up with you.

Edward paused in his chewing, rice clinging to his knuckles. He studied the man's face.

Do you not know me, boy?

I know you, Mr. Fisk, he said.

And then Mrs. Shade's trusted servant, broken now, withered, six weeks out from his own death on a grassy hillside in Virginia, leaned in close and muttered: They know what you are planning, boy. They *know*.

———

He had been dreaming about the Saracen. He heard his door creak in the morning cold and he rolled stiffly onto one elbow and cracked an eyelid and watched Fludd hesitate with his hand on the latch of the door. Mr. Adam? the giant murmured. You awake?

No.

The giant wiped his hands front and back on his shirt front and stepped through into the gloom and crossed the room with very small slow steps. Give us a look at them ribs, he said. When he sat on the edge of the mattress the bed buckled under his weight and Foole slid against the big man's sloping thighs. He scowled, shut his eye. He could hear through the opened door Molly two floors above hollering down some curse about hot water and towels. After a moment Mrs. Sykes's voice rose from the depths of the Emporium muffled and fierce as if from the bowels of a ship but he could not make out her reply. There was a thump above his head and then a second thump and the door juddered on its hinges and then there was silence.

O they been at it all morning, Fludd said. I just come in here to hide.

Foole groaned.

Fludd was quiet in the grey light. After a time he rose from where he sat on the corner of the bed and he drew back the curtains on a grim drizzling morning. The pane was streaked and filthy.

Foole said, That was you in the alley. Last night, dealing down those footpads. That was you.

So me fists tell me, Fludd said. Curling his blotched hands spider-like open and shut in the grimy light of the window. He didn't see nothing, your Mr. Pinkerton?

Foole coughed and as he did so he felt the bruises along his left ribs come alive.

Fludd frowned. You always was contrary, Mr. Adam. You sure he ain't playin you?

Foole rose clumsily and swung his bare legs out dangling over the bed and then he got to his feet with a grimace. The

floorboards were freezing. He stood with one hand on the brass
bedpost and stooped and cleared his sinuses and raked his fingers through his hair and they came away black. The night
before was coming back to him, slowly.

You followed me, Japheth, he said. He met the giant's eye.

Aye.

You likely saved my life.

Fludd grinned a sudden shaggy grin though the lines of
worry did not leave his eyes. Well, he said. I weren't goin to let
me boss and saviour get his throat cut now, were I?

Foole stood there with his nightshirt flapping at his knees,
legs trembling in the cold. He stared at his white toes gripping
the floor.

You follow me again, he said, I'll cut your throat myself.

He felt the blood rising in his skull. It was a hot dark wrath and
it did not subside all morning. At the open door to his study he
found Hettie stooped at an overturned basket of laundry and
he swore to see it and in the Emporium office he dismissed
Molly for the ragged state of her clothes and in the dining room
he sent his breakfast back uneaten. Later he stood glaring out
at the mid-morning street traffic through the display windows
amid shelves of coral from the South Seas and Hettie came in
to feed the fire and saw him and withdrew in terror. He felt
ashamed but whatever was in him would not leave him. After a
time he sat at the small cut-away and shifted a fossil and wrote
out a curt note to Gabriel Utterson confirming the seance and
then without further thought he sealed the note and gave it to
Fludd for delivery.

He did not trust that Pinkerton believed his account of the
killing of Edward Shade. That was a part of it. But some other
thing would not let him alone. What he had felt, staring down
at the Saracen the night before, was the horror of his own
future. He had understood that this was the fate of any man
strong enough to live out his youth, in his world, in their world.

He was surprised that he had asked Pinkerton to the seance. What was it Mrs. Sharper had said to Molly that night? The dead do not come back. He was not certain they ever left.

The heart is a locked room, he thought. To you as to any.

But first there was something he needed to do.

After dark had fallen that night he went back through the filth of Wapping. Kicking his way through the trash and rats in the wet. This time he did not knock. He stood listening at Mrs. Sharper's door and when he did not hear any stirring within he slipped a slender file into the frame's gap and worked a bent pick into the keyhole and after a moment the door clicked and creaked inward. He held the handle, listening. Then he slipped through.

Sharper's house was silent. He stood in the dim as his eyes adjusted and then he removed his shoes and set them outside on the step and closed the door. He padded soundlessly in his stocking feet to the room under the stairs. He could hear a raw unhealthy snoring from within and when he opened the door he saw the one-legged doorman, Curtains, asleep on a cot. A tattooed forearm dangling, mouth agape. Foole took the man's crutch from where it leaned against the foot of the bed frame, slipped back out.

At the drawing room door he paused, glimpsing the light underneath. He cracked the door an inch. The rose lampshade in the middle of the room was still bright. Foole could see the pianoforte, the draped tables, the utter black of the cold fireplace. But there was no one within, and he set the doorman's wooden crutch just inside the room, and closed the door.

He went upstairs, testing each riser to avoid creaks, and on the upper landing he went from door to door. Linen closet, water closet, a study, an unused bedchamber filled with old junk. At last he found the sister asleep in a tiny bedroom, the window blocked out so that the room felt suffused with the horror of her blindness. Foole carefully shut the door. He lifted a tall standing lamp from a pier table and laid it crosswise in front of the sister's door in hazard.

At the last door he paused, listening, and heard the slow muffled sounds of a figure beyond. He knew this must be Mrs. Sharper. He opened the landing window, balancing in the sudden cold of the sill. Then crossed in his stocking feet along the roof tiles to the next window. The sash stood open. He let himself soundlessly in.

He saw her at once, readying for bed. She wore a flannel nightgown streaked with brown at the back and had already unscrewed the wooden fingers and Foole could see the knuckled stumps where she had been carved up. He was thinking of Molly, the sad still centre of her.

Mrs. Sharper froze. Who's that? she hissed. Who's there? She turned her eyes sightlessly in the gloom, her face upraised, as if scenting the air.

Foole stood beside the windowsill, watching.

I will know you, Mrs. Sharper said softly. You will rue this trespass.

A long moment passed in the darkness.

Her spine was curled, her neck and wrists bone-thin. She looked, Foole thought, frail and mean. Do you come to harm an old woman? she hissed, swift, vicious. An old blind woman? Or do you come to rob me? I warn you, there is a man in the house below.

Mr. Curtains cannot help you, Foole said.

Who speaks? A long, slow, calculating pause. You. Mr. Foole. You should be more careful.

Adam Foole, she said, her face twisting. It has been a long time since a man climbed through my bedroom window.

Molly's boy, Peter. Tell me what happened to him.

Mrs. Sharper raised her face and a dry smile crossed her lips. The boy? I do not understand, Mr. Foole. What is he to you?

Foole withdrew a safety match from his pocket and scraped it alight on the windowsill and then he crossed the room with the flame bending back towards him and he crushed it against the blind woman's hand. She shrieked, snapped back in terror, clutching the skin to her mouth.

He shook the match into smoke. Tell me about the boy, he said again, his voice calm.

We sent him away, she said. For thieving. I know nothing more than that.

Foole withdrew a second match, struck it alight. A scrape, a hiss of phosphor. The blind woman backed away, bumped up against the dresser. That is not the truth, said Foole. What happened?

He stole nothing, she stuttered, he didn't steal from us. Wait.

You sent him away for nothing?

We never sent him away.

Foole stepped closer.

We never sent him away, she repeated. He died. He was killed. He was struck down by a carriage in the street and we buried him in St. Aldwyn's. He's dead.

Foole held the smouldering match to her face. He's dead?

Dead. Yes.

He was very close to the old woman and the smoke would be in her nostrils, the heat near her eye, but she did not flinch. Why did you lie? he said.

In the matchlight her face was etched with a vicious loathing, her milky eyes scooped, unblinking. Why? she murmured. The poor girl. You took her from the boy and he was buried three days later. When she came back to us, we knew what it was she sought.

She's blamed herself all these years.

Herself and us.

Yes.

But herself less than had we told her the true. That the boy died going out into the streets to the corner where the two of them used to dip. Mrs. Sharper glowered with her wispy hair wild and her dry mouth atremble. We loved that girl, Mr. Foole, she said, as she loved us. You will not understand it because you do not know what it was between us. We let you have her, yes. We allowed it. Because we wished a different life for her.

Foole remembered their vicious covetousness from that time. You forget how it was, he said. Don't make yourselves out to be saints. You were well paid for her.

And what if we were?

Foole extinguished the match, stepped back out of her reach. That isn't love. It's profit.

Mrs. Sharper's face was cast into crags of shadow. We must invent our monsters, Mr. Foole, in order to cast ourselves against them. Call us what you will. But the truth? You are no different than we.

Foole could feel the confusion in his face. He thought of Molly at six years old, sliding like smoke through the streets, the steady sober concentrated grief that was in her when he first hired her.

You are not her only protector, Mrs. Sharper whispered.

He had held the girl as she screamed and cried and struggled against him locked in a dream, her tiny body so soft, so thin. He studied Mrs. Sharper's face as if to seek some semblance there of the conflicted heart but saw only cruelty and the gnarled impress of age. He started to speak and then he did not and after a moment he backed through the darkness to the door, his stockings silent on the floorboards.

She swung her arms in a slow arc, sensing his withdrawal. It was a kindness, she hissed into the shadows. Do you hear? A kindness.

Foole slipped his shoes on in the cold outside, his stockings wet, his toes numb. He knew Molly would be asleep when he got back. He would go to her in the morning perhaps, sit at the edge of her mattress, and as she raised her face and stared sleepily at him he would tell her he had been to see the sisters a last time. He would tell her he had learned the truth about her Peter and that she deserved to know the facts of it. He would say

Sharper had lied. That Peter had found a protector, a ship's carpenter, and had travelled to the Continent, and that somewhere in a small mountain village in Austria he was alive and well and learning an honest trade. She would lie in silence listening and he would press his hand into the bedsheets and tell her that there were many kinds of not knowing and that certainty and conviction were not the same thing. He would tell her he had lived alongside Charlotte's absence a decade now at least and had felt her proximity all that time. And when he got up to go the impress of his hand in the white sheets would remain, fingers splayed, palm open, like a hand extended in offering.

Edward would think to himself, years after the war, that there are confluences in a life, moments of deep exchange between strangers, when the strands of two different fates draw together and the cutting of one necessitates the cutting of another. Such a confluence had come upon him there in Camp Barry, in 1862, though he did not know it then.

It was the night before the new moon. Three men in frock coats and top hats came brutally in swinging their lanterns over the faces of the prisoners and he knew at once that it was himself they sought, that he had been betrayed. The man Fisk clawed through the straw and withdrew the bent spoon honed now to a blade and a stout bald sergeant seized Edward by the hair and hauled him sacklike through the gate, outside into the cold. He struggled, kicking, terrified. He understood there would be no trial and he would that night be tied to a stake in the frozen mud, blindfolded, and shot for treason. As he twisted in their grip he glanced back and saw Fisk under the high barred window, a silver outline, eyes hidden in shadow.

What came to him then, unbidden, was a memory of Mrs. Shade gliding in a mauve dress among the roses at Shade House. He remembered the pale languid turning of her parasol, its Japanese design, the sound of bees in the sunshine. He had been, he understood, happy, and had not known such happiness again. He crushed his eyes shut. Her voice was low, kind. Her fingers were long and thin, the joints swollen. He could not recall her face.

The men dragged him to a harnessed waggon with a lantern dipping on a cane stalk above the driver and they hurled him onto the flatbed and then all three climbed up with him and the waggon jolted and set off at a fast clip. The men wore their hats low at their eyes and Edward could see nothing in their faces and he did not understand where he was being taken. The men swayed and rocked and he drew his knees up to his chest and eyed the passing streets. They rode out towards the gloom of the city and slowed at the camp guardhouse but did not stop and then they were turning along rutted streets and passing abandoned brick houses. No one spoke.

At a nondescript house with a single lantern burning weakly above the front door they got down and he was taken roughly upstairs to a small sitting room and shoved into an upholstered chair facing an empty desk. It had been a long time since he had sat on something so soft and his skin recoiled at the brush of it. Only one of the men stayed with him. That man's face was scarred and hard-looking. Edward glanced at the door, glanced at the curtains billowing before an open window. He wondered at the height of the drop, wondered if he could reach the sill without being tackled or shot.

The door at the far end of the room opened, a bearded man came through. Black-haired like the devil, thick and burly, solid through the chest like a cannon, with eyes small and deep-set with malice. He sat at the desk and took a cigar out of a box in front of him and leaned back and glowered. Edward felt a low thrum go through him, a sudden presentiment of danger.

This is the lad they call Shade? the man said in a deep Scottish burr. He chewed at the end of his cigar. I understand you've been something of a nuisance in the stockade. Escaping and such.

Edward said nothing. He was neither chained nor handcuffed and he sat with his feet carefully spread and his weight balanced and he felt the coiled tension in his body. He was care-ful not to look at the open window.

You're thinking you can still run, the man said. His eyes flicked up, fixed on Edward's. You can't.

Edward flushed.

I understand you've made escape something of a career, the man continued in his gravelly murmur. How many times have you jumped for the bounty? Three?

Four, sir, the man in the top hat who had escorted him in said.

He has no next of kin?

Not according to his records, sir.

The bearded man leaned forward, interlacing his thick fin-gers before him. He had the cigar between his teeth, still unlit, and he said very quietly, My name is Major Allen, son. Do you know what it is I do?

Edward regarded the Major cautiously.

I offer people with unusual abilities a chance to redeem themselves. I offer them a choice.

What kind of a choice? Edward said cautiously.

Ah. Major Allen held his cigar out at arm's length, turned it end over end in his fingers, smiled grimly. A choice between living and dying. Tell me. Do you want to live?

Did he want to live? Years later he would struggle to under-stand why he had answered as he had, why he had let himself be spared. The debt would in time come to feel Biblical, fated. He had been saved over others by a man who did not officially exist, a thief-taker, the dreaded Eye, a man who wrapped him-self in darkness and walked among the enlisted men a ghost, a rumour, feared and faceless and unseen. In time Edward would come to love the shifting nature of the man the way he loved the skin of a river. In time his love would twist and expand into the angry complicated love of a son for a father he had not ever known.

I want to live, Edward said softly.

The Major watched him, wreathed in shadow. Nodded.

He was the civilian head of the Army of the Potomac's Secret Service, Edward would later learn, a man of unchecked power. His real name was, yes, of course, Pinkerton.

Allan Pinkerton.

TWENTY-THREE

It was the last Tuesday in January, 1885, and William Pinkerton stood in the middle of Gaunt Street listening to the drift of footsteps in the darkness. The cabman had found the address with difficulty and he stared now up at the silent house, its weak gas lamps burning a smoky and sinister light. It had been three days since he had accompanied Foole down into Shadwell, three days since Foole had poured out the last of the gin in that tavern and torn the label from the bottle and scrawled out the address to the seance in pencil on its reverse. William had protested but the small man had pressed it into his palm beseeching. The falseness in Foole's account of the killing of Edward Shade had angered him, true. His father had ever been a man of violence. But he had hunted Shade long after that confrontation could have taken place and if nothing else this alone proved the lie. William had not come this night because the man Foole had begged him. He had come because something remained unfinished between them. He had come because the man was other than he seemed.

A weak fog crawled over the setts in the street. No one had entered or exited the house since the hansom had dropped him. At last he started across, his ribs still sore, the sticking plaster at the back of his neck scratching. He knew a man usually suspected his own failings in the men he met. His brother Robert trusted no one on the wrong side of the law and thought the difference between right and wrong a clear one. But William knew the law had as much to do with power as rightness. It was built by men for its own purpose, like a steam locomotive, and what was done with it was the work of men who had places to get to and schedules to keep. He thought of Foole. Of course there was a wrong side to the law.

He sometimes wondered if there was a right one.

If Shade had indeed survived the war then his father might have found any kind of moment to take justice into his own hands. He knew this. He did not think his father capable of murder but killing was another matter. William's own war had lasted a meagre six months but had scoured clear any uncomplicated idea of goodness and mercy carried over from his childhood. At sixteen he witnessed the worst the world could do to a person and the sight of that had stayed in him always. It must have been the same for his father. In the early months of the war before the Peninsular Campaign his father would write him letters from Washington. Curt missives sent to his dormitory in Notre Dame with instructions rather than advice. He would sign them under his pseudonym, Major Allen, S.S. of the Potomac. He would explain that the secret to warfare was discipline, that fighting armies rarely engaged but at the moment of contact one side invariably broke and ran. Hold your position, son, and a man will be all right, in life as in war. Most bodies pulled off the battlefield are shot through the back.

Then in the grim spring of 1862 the character of the war made itself known. William had enlisted by then, was there alongside his father. After Malvern Hill his father never again made such claims. That was a season of evil unbounded. He thought of the balloonist Ignatius Spaar, his scarred visage, the anxious twitch of his eyebrow like a wink that made him seem always to be teasing. The look of the man as he ran low into the trees towards the Confederate sharpshooters. That. And that preacher in the burned hamlet in northern Virginia, a rag on a stick, beseeching the retreating soldiers to lay down their arms.

Waving his arms and hollering from the peaked roof of his church. What was it he had cried?

Repent, boys, repent. For the wrathful Lord sees all.

He remembered the sound of the rifle. That preacher when he fell fell in a slow silence and landed in the muck with the slap of a wet sack of earth. Eyes rolled up to the sky, arms wide, a burnt hole in his cheek like a kiss.

Whoever in that long line of soldiers had shot the man did not stop. William himself had trudged past, staring, too tired to care, and he remembered how no other had fallen out of line to bother with the burying.

He rang the bell.

A tall bearded Sikh with long indigo eyelashes and a red turban opened the door and let William inside. The house was hushed, cold. He could smell marigolds in the gloom. The Sikh turned wordlessly and moved away with a silent tread in his slippers and after a moment William followed. His own footfalls echoing on the inscribed wood floor. It seemed a third walked with them there and he shivered to feel it.

No he did not believe the dead did speak. He thought spiritualism a refuge for scoundrels and grift. He had known many professional liars in his time and all had insisted a man must first deceive himself before he can be deceived. The mark, they would grin, must be the most convincing liar of all.

The Sikh led him past a lighted room with a fish pond and through a beaded curtain and down a second hallway into a parlour. The gas lamps on the walls cast an eerie light and the air was heavy with incense. William noticed this first. Then the gold and red wall hangings with their prints of elephants and tigers. It was a small room made smaller by the plush dark armchairs and the tall row of draped windows. There was a chill in the air. He saw others had already gathered but he did not see Adam Foole.

At the far side of the room two folding doors of lacquered wood stood wide. A slender woman with long bare arms and heavy bracelets swayed beside them and William knew her at once for the medium. She wore a white fabric wrapped around her in some complicated oriental style and she looked in the dim light very still and very beautiful like a naiad carved from marble. He watched her turn slowly between the two men with whom she spoke and her eyes he saw were outlined in black pencil and her lips were very red and he felt something quicken inside him. Just behind her in the open doorway stood a plump man, straining at his waistcoat, smoking soberly. Every so often this man would touch her arm and murmur into her ear and she would nod without looking his way.

William felt a presence at his elbow and turned. A lady in a green shawl, a scarlet bustle, mother-of-pearl buttons. She had a thin catlike jaw and prominent teeth and her hazel eyes were large and set wide in her face. Grief had drawn its deep lines like a thumb through soft wax. She greeted William with a quiet smile and held out a gloved hand and he looked at it and then he shook it. She told him she had come to communicate with her daughter. She smiled as she said this. Her daughter had sickened four years ago at the age of eleven and had passed over within a fortnight. She followed his gaze across to an ancient man in a tall worn silk hat seated alone in a corner and she told him that gentleman's name was Gables. His son was lost in the Crimea, poor man, she said. Oh but he's been to so many of these sittings. Miss Utterson gets excellent results.

William furrowed his brow. He had shifted his stance so that he could see the door over the lady's head but Adam Foole did not appear.

You must be a pugilist, sir? she said.

I beg your pardon?

She touched a finger to her face. Your bruises.

William smiled vaguely. No, he said. An accident.

An accident, yes, she was nodding. Yes. She stared up at him and there was burning in her face a kind of beatitude that left William moved. She looked tired and happy. We must be careful, she said, in this world at least. Our flesh is so fragile, though our spirits endure. Of course Miss Utterson does not always reach through. But that is how one knows it is real, you see. It is rather crowded on the other side. There is so much noise.

Noise?

Interference. She paused. Are you not a believer, sir?

Well.

It is quite all right. I shall tell you what to do. She patted his arm quickly and she smiled and smiled. You must reveal nothing to her, she whispered, you must give her no details. Then you will see. She will know things she cannot possibly know. And then you will believe.

He could still see no sign of Foole. He watched the medium glide from guest to guest and then turn with a sinuous grace towards them and drift across the soft blue carpet with her eyes fixed on the lady in the green shawl.

Miss Utterson, the lady said warmly. How do you feel tonight? Shall we have success?

The medium grasped the lady's outstretched hands and peered into her eyes as if seeking some answer but she did not reply. Then she turned and lifted her face and regarded William where he loomed and she said, in a throaty murmur, You must be Mr. Pinkerton.

She spread then clasped her jewelled hands and her bracelets rattled and William inclined his head. He was going to ask her if her spirits had told her that but he sucked at his teeth and did not say it.

You have been to India, he said instead.

She smiled. The webbed lines under her eyes, the loose skin in the hollow of her throat. Combed blond hairs invisible above her lips. She was older than he had thought.

Oh, India, said the lady in the green shawl. I've always wanted to experience India.

We are more than just experience, the medium said quietly. Her painted eyes were fixed with a luminous intensity on William. But we are also what we were. I spent many years in the Raj, it is true. It was difficult to leave it in the end.

It looks like you brought it back with you.

The Raj is always with you, once you have become a part of it.

Extraordinary, the lady in the green shawl murmured. Most extraordinary.

She took no notice of the lady but began to speak to William of the strangeness of that continent. Of the fields of rice in the winds blooming golden and tidal like corn. Of the crowds in their colours and the tall narrow houses painted blue and yellow and red and of the long surf rolling in at Madras. She said back then travellers were strangled in their sleep and the Bengalis worshipped a goddess with a tongue of blood and a necklace of human skulls and yet she herself had feared only the holy men wandering the cities with their roving eyes and tangled hair halfway down their shoulders and the knuckled bones in their backs articulated and sharp. It was not a country, she said, but a world. Not a world, she said, but a passing through time. One grew old there. She said on her first afternoon on the river she had seen the body of an old woman in the mudbank being eaten by pariah dogs.

Of course death is only a gateway, she said. Our bodies hold us like locks.

Like locks, murmured the lady.

Locks, said William.

She nodded. We cannot transcend without first breaking them open.

Exactly, murmured the lady.

William frowned. By transcend you mean die.

She shook her head. Nothing dies. It is only born into the next life.

William studied her hard eyes and wondered what she had seen in this life that would lead her to such a pass. He did not yet know if she deceived or was herself deceived.

She leaned closer. He could smell her skin. She wore no scent, no perfume. You think you do not believe, sir, she said. But nobody comes here who does not seek someone. You must not be frightened.

Frightened of what?

Of what happens this evening.

William smiled a cold smile. And what is it you seek?

She did not take his meaning or else chose to ignore it. She said, calmly, My mother, sir. But she has already found me.

William said nothing. He watched the soft man from the doorway come up behind her and nod in greeting and without turning to acknowledge him the medium said, This is my brother, sir. Mr. Utterson, Mr. Pinkerton. Mr. Pinkerton is the guest of Mr. Foole this evening.

Utterson nodded. His eyelids were sleepy but the eyes behind them were as hard as any William had seen and stared out of the slack grey skin of his face with an unfriendly sharpness. The man leaned in close to his sister and said in a surprisingly soft voice, They are ready, my dear.

William looked from one to the other. Mr. Foole has not yet arrived, he said.

The medium smiled her strange smile.

And just then the tall Sikh drew the beaded curtain aside and Foole stepped into the parlour. His face, discoloured by a heavy bruise on one cheek. A scab of dried blood crossing the bridge of his nose. His forehead was knotted by worry, his silk hat unbrushed and dull. He looked drained, and desperate, and anxious. William's eyes met his, held.

But already the medium was allowing her brother to take her elbow and lead her through the folding doors and then the gaslights dimmed as if being choked slowly into darkness.

He had witnessed too much suffering and horror as a young man at Antietam to think spiritualism's embrace of death anything but madness. The grave was the grave, the dead the dead. The worms fed and were fattened. Had it not ever been so? Because he had been fast and strong for his size he was named runner on a crew of eight for a Parrott cannon that day and he had begged his father to let him serve. Nights still came to him

now when he would awaken in a panic, twenty years on, a man
who occupied his time with violence and blood by choice but
for whom the nightmare of that morning still thundered in
his skull and made him sick. It was September of 1862, his
seventeenth year. The night before the battle he had felt a roiling in his gut that the men of his battery called death belly.
By common assent it meant he would not walk away unscathed.
That crew's last runner had been ripped in two at the waist
by a splintering wheel as it fragmented off a cannon ten yards
away and it had taken the pickers three days to bag the lad and
haul his pieces by horse to the overfull graves. The gunner on
William's crew was a boy of twenty and seemed impossibly old
at that time, in that place. He showed William how to soak
knots of rag in cold water and stuff them into his ears and said
the noise when the firing began would be a physical thing, he
would feel it rustling the sleeves of his coat. He showed William
how to mark out a line in the dirt and grass from the limber to
the cannon and explained that when the battle was under way
the smoke from the cannons would roll in great sheets over
them and he would see nothing but blur and fog and flares of
light in the exploding chaos. All this proved true. They were
positioned on high ground and fixed their mark on the cornfield where the Texans would come rushing through and when
the battle was joined the world dissolved into flame and smoke
and a shuddering earth that was nearly impossible for William
to keep his balance upon. His task was to carry the ten-pound
shells one at a time from the limber along the line to the gun
crew and he would stagger with the shell held low in both hands
and his elbows locked, his eyes trained on the marks in the dirt
showing him the way. He could see only a murky fog, hear only
the roaring. Thirty minutes into the battle a Confederate battery had fixed their position and the hill burst around them and
exploded into flame, whistling twists of iron scantling, spikes
of wood, rock, dirt. There was a high whine, like a mosquito at
his ear. And then William felt himself lift into the air and hang
there for an impossible length of time and then a gentle pain

enfolded itself around him and massaged his knee between its thumbs and then it started to crush him with a fury and it tightened and tightened yet further and when there was only the pain and the long darkness of what came next he closed his eyes and descended.

The air in the seance room was heavy with the scent of marigolds. William stood to one side of the folding doors and held his handkerchief to his mouth and breathed. He had heard stories of spirit cabinets, of floating objects, of ghostly figures manifesting in the corners of seance halls. Here afforded no such possibilities, cramped as it was. A bare round table without cloth of any kind filled the space and the chairs surrounding were squeezed close with their laddered backs scraping the walls. Thick purple drapes hung from iron rods at the ceiling and a solitary lantern was burning on the table. Beside this, a small wooden box with its lid flipped back. Inside: a small brass bell.

He waited for Foole and put out a hand and Foole glanced up. I started to think you might not show, he said.

Foole smiled a tight smile. Mr. Pinkerton. You came.

William touched the skin under his own eye. How's your face?

Embarrassing.

They took their seats as did all the others and only the widower Gables stood with one hand resting heavily on two seatbacks as if uncertain which to take. The medium pressed her jewelled hands flat on the table and raised her head.

We are only nine, Gabriel, she said.

Her brother glanced at the gathered sitters. Who's missing?

She dipped her head and the gold hoops at her ears caught the light.

Never mind it. I shall make the tenth.

You cannot, she said. She gave him a quick sharp look. You must be the guide.

His eyes took in the sitters one by one and then William watched his slow eyelids lower like the eyelids of a caiman and he said, Tonight I shall be both. It will be fine.

He pulled the extra chair away from the table and took it through the doors and returned after a moment and folded the doors shut behind him. They sat in silence as he took his seat, fastened the lid of the bell box shut, replaced it in the centre of the table. He reached his left palm towards Mr. Gables, the ancient widower shrunken and trembling, and took the man's fingers in his own. You must not, ladies and gentlemen, under any circumstances, break the circle. Do not let go of the hands of your neighbours. It would be most dangerous.

Dangerous, William said with a quiet smile.

Dangerous, sir, yes. We are bridging worlds in ways we do not entirely understand.

They all sat in the light of that dim lantern with the curtains close at their backs and the bell set out before them and their arms were stretched wide across the distances. William glanced at Foole but the small man was studying the medium with a quiet seriousness and would not meet his eye. Something did not feel right.

The medium had already closed her eyes and was breathing long slow steady breaths.

Her brother said, I must ask you to concentrate now. All of you. I want you to focus your energy on the one you wish to contact this evening. Think of that person. Remember their smell, how they looked to you, the sound of their laugh. Many of you will have brought an item that once belonged to them. You do not need to share it. Only think of it while we wait.

A minute passed, two minutes. He heard a soft murmuring from across the table and realized the medium was speaking to herself. It sounded like Latin.

William watched Foole's eyes move between the medium and her brother.

Ten minutes passed. Fifteen. A quiet settled upon the narrow room, a warmth began to fill it. William could feel his eyes closing, he began to drift in an almost sleep. And then all at once the bell in its wooden box clattered harshly and his eyes opened in alarm. His blood loud in his ears. Everyone sat unmoving, hands grasped in the faint light. The bell sat yet in its box in the centre of the table.

There has been contact, the brother said calmly. Have any sitters present felt anything?

No one spoke. The darkness of the drapery surrounding was absolute, it might have been folded from pitch. William breathed quiet shallow breaths, listened to a creak in the ceiling overhead, the slow shirr of the drapery. He glanced at Foole's face, the thin gash of his mouth in the gloom. The smell of marigolds was overwhelming. For a long while the medium sat murmuring her prayer. Then the clapper in the box rang again, stark, violent, brash. William felt Foole startle beside him. The sound fell away.

There has been contact, the man repeated. Have any sitters present felt anything?

Now a lady's voice said, I do, I feel something, yes. It was the lady in the green shawl. Her eyelids were crushed shut.

The man was studying her dispassionately. What do you feel?

Hands. I can feel hands. On my neck. She gave a brief shiver as she spoke but did not open her eyes.

Do you feel anything else?

Oh they're cold.

Rose? the man said gently. Is there a message for this lady? Is there some word?

The medium sat with her face uplifted and her eyes closed and the light cast a strange cage of interlaced shadows over her lips and cheekbones. Her mouth was parted slightly and her tongue pressed against her lower teeth as if she might speak. A long silence followed and then at last she spoke. Her voice was soft, hardly more than a breath.

The spirit says, You have come a long distance to be here, she said. The spirit says, You must travel a long distance back. There is a woman who brings a message from the shining world.

A young woman, with red hair. Her hands are white. She is reaching towards you.

William felt an uneasiness rising in him.

The medium's brother inclined his head towards the lady with the green shawl. Mrs. Caldwell? Do you know this spirit?

She wet her lips. My mother, she said softly. She died October last.

It is not your mother, the medium murmured. She is here also. It is not her.

My aunt?

I am hearing a name. It begins with an H. Hester? Does Hester mean anything to you?

No, she said.

The H is important. Can you think of anyone whose name begins with an H?

My aunt Hettie.

It is not her. Anyone whose name has an H in it?

The lady was turning her face side to side in the weak light and William watched the purple curtain behind her ripple and elongate and ripple. Could it be Martha? My sister? We lived in Hull when we were girls—

The medium was silent and then she gave a sigh as if some breath not her own were leaving her body and she opened her eyes and said, smiling, Martha says hello, Susan.

Martha? Is it her? Truly?

She asks what you would like to know.

Oh, god. Oh, god.

There was a long silence then in that blackness and William felt the dampness of Foole's hand in his own, the strength in the sinews there as he gripped and gripped. William's feet were flat on the floorboards and he could feel a low drumming as if someone was tapping their heels in a quick fearful tap.

She says to tell you, Lizzie is happy, the medium said. Her suffering has ended. She says Lizzie's hair has grown back. Her eyes can see again.

Oh, Lizzie, the lady murmured. Lizzie, Lizzie, my little bird.

And she started to cry, soundlessly, her sharp narrow shoulders racked by it.

Do not break the circle, the brother warned. Hold fast. Hold fast.

They were silent then a long time and the medium began to murmur her prayer over and over. Perhaps twenty minutes passed, perhaps more. The lady in the green shawl had ceased crying and sat luminous and filled with grief like a vessel that had found its purpose and William studied the lines in her face and thought of the grifters he had known capable of manipulating such suffering. When he glanced at Foole he saw a man transfixed by longing and regret and he wondered suddenly if Foole too found this crooked and dishonest. The bell in its wooden box rang again.

There has been contact. Have any sitters present felt anything?

No one spoke.

Rose? her brother said. Rose, is there a presence?

She rolled her head slowly forward as if following some scent with her eyes shut and her arms outstretched and then she shook her head. It is gone, she said.

Ten minutes passed. They waited again.

The bell clacked loudly.

There has been contact. Have any sitters present felt anything?

Foole cleared his throat.

Mr. Foole, sir? Did you feel something?

No, he said. I thought I did. It was nothing.

Nothing?

No.

I have a presence, the medium said abruptly. A presence is coming through.

Whom does it seek? her brother asked.

She sat very still as if listening at an open window to music playing somewhere. She said, hesitantly, A man comes to us tonight, a man in pain.

What is his name?

William could feel Foole gripping his hand hard.

She was silent.

Whom does the presence seek? her brother asked again.

The spirit says, Do not mourn. You are loved even still. Yes?

The spirit would like to tell you that there is nothing to for-give. What was left unfinished on this side will be finished on the next. The spirit says, The war. I see the war, and a betrayal.

Did he die in a war?

A name. Ignatius.

William felt the hairs on the back of his neck prickle.

Ignatius, the brother said. Is it the spirit of Ignatius who comes to us?

She grimaced, as if in pain. All at once she turned her sight-less face and something had shifted in her and when she spoke now her voice had roughened to the husk and gravel of a man's voice, a faint Virginian bend in the vowels. What is this place? it said.

Do not be frightened, her brother murmured. His eyes looked carved from darkness. You are between worlds. You are here with a message for this world. What would you have us hear?

You sound so far away. I lost so many things, I lost—

What would you have us hear?

It was silent.

How is it in that world? the brother asked.

It shook its head. I was in a river, it said. A black river. Then I was on the shore.

How is it in that world?

It sat slumped with its sightless gaze fixed outward and said nothing for a long moment. Then murmured, as if by rote, Other than the world as it was.

Yes. Good. And what did you take with you to that shore?

My skull opened like a flower, it said. The night smelled of dust, someone was crying. O someone was crying—

And what did you take with you to that shore?

I took a darkness with me to that shore.

And in the darkness?

In the darkness another darkness.

The man's eyes were fixed on his sister and there were twin pricks of light deep in the sockets there and William stared at them feeling a kind of horror.

And were you young in this world?

I felt old. My legs wouldn't hold me.

You were. You were young, as are we all. And were you forgiven?

It had lowered its face and with its arms outstretched it looked to William like a figure crucified and sorrowing. At last it murmured: She is here, Edward.

Foole gave a low groan, his eyes staring.

Who is with us now? the brother pressed. What is her name?

She is here, it said again, face lowered and lost to sight. She is at peace. She says do you remember the flavoured ices in Port Elizabeth, long ago. She says it is that warm and peaceful here. She knows what is in your heart. She wants you to know she does not blame—

All at once William felt his right wrist twist, his grip give way. Foole was staggering upright, his chair falling away in a clatter, his face very white. And then the medium was staring with her eyes glassy and dazed and her brother was shouting and Foole had pushed past all of them and the circle, whatever it was, whatever it had been, was broken.

Later that night he saw. He sat in his underclothes at his hotel window and through the leaded glass saw. Night, coalescing in the cobblestones below. A lamplighter in a cloak appeared like a messenger out of the shadows and he watched the hooded figure lift a long hooked stick from one shoulder to reach the street lamp above. Everything felt so far away. The ordinary world in all its wonder and strangeness. He heard again the medium's dreadful voice as she spoke the name Ignatius. He thought of the balloonist Ignatius Spaar, whom he had fought with at Malvern Hill, thought of the man's soft Virginian accent, the crackle in his voice. Spaar had died in that battle. I see a war, the medium had murmured, I see betrayal. Down in the street the lamplighter unhooked the wrought iron casing, the small pane of glass creaking open. Something inside William was clicking through its chambers, at the edge of violence, like a revolver seeking its bullet. The lamplighter turned a cog with the sharp point of his hook until a hiss of gas from the fishtail jet leaked out. It was not the war that killed that boy, Foole had told him in the tunnel. The man you want to talk to, Martin Reckitt had said, is Adam Foole. The figure swung down the staff, reached hand over hand for the end, adjusted the wick, hefted all of it smoothly back up to pass through the gas. The man, the boy. Adam Foole, Edward Shade. A bloom of flame, a spill of light across cobblestones.

She is here, Edward, the spirit had said.

William crushed his eyes shut. Something stilled inside him. He was thinking of the seance, the clatter of the overturned chair, the alarmed shine in Foole's eye, and all at once he opened his eyes.

His hands were shaking.

For he knew who Adam Foole was.

The Balloonist

────────

1862

VIRGINIA

Thirty-two years later in the shadow of a new kind of war William Pinkerton would sit across from a lady columnist from a New York daily and try to describe the horror that had been Malvern Hill. The great ocean-going turbines shuddering up through the floor, the sound of violins drifting past the portholes. This would be in the first-class viewing lounge of an Atlantic passenger liner, William smothering the palsy in his hands, returning from a police conference in Glasgow. Somewhere in the Europe behind them aeroplanes were dropping bombs on boys cowering in trenches and he could only shake his head helplessly at that, and frown, and in his frown was the bitter squint of a man who could no longer see as he was accustomed to seeing.

It would mean so much to hear the truth of it, Mr. Pinkerton, she was saying. Especially now.

He ran a weary claw over the blanket in his lap. The truth of Malvern Hill.

Oh, yes. My readers would be so fascinated.

He peered out of the porthole at the passing grey of the ocean, of the sky. Somewhere out there German warships slid like smoke over the waters.

Your father was the head of the Union army's Secret Service at that time. Did you join him out of a sense of patriotic duty? Or was it because you'd heard he had fallen ill?

William crushed his eyes shut. He had been sixteen then, he had been immortal.

Oh, don't look so abashed, she laughed. You were very young, Mr. Pinkerton. I understand he was sick with malaria at the time. You were still a boy but you stayed by his side. You must have been awfully brave.

I didn't know what brave was, William said. If I'd had any idea I'd never have gone to the war. He looked at her with a watery gaze, his eyes searching her face. He said, Pull your chair closer, young lady. My ears don't work so well as they once did.

Her smile. Like lightning in a cornfield. Something about her made him think of his wife.

I was asking you, sir, if you were afraid. Your father was very ill.

William grunted. In Virginia everyone was ill. The mosquitoes were feasting on all those poor New England boys. I dropped out of Notre Dame to go down there, that was in April of eighteeen sixty-two. Just in time for the march on Richmond. I don't know what my father thought of it. He knew McClellan from before the war, when the general was with the Illinois Central. They were close. He resigned when the general lost his command. William looked at the columnist and smiled. You know Lincoln was the legal consultant for the railroad at the time? Small world.

She raised her eyebrows, said nothing.

I don't know what I was thinking, he went on. I stayed because I guess my father figured it was safer for me to serve under him, where he could keep an eye on me. Rather than charging through the fields with the infantry. He was probably right. He never expected he'd get sick. He wasn't sick when I first got down there. William paused and blinked and stared at his hands. Do you really want to know all this?

She smiled her dazzling smile. My readers will be fascinated.

You said that already.

Mr. Pinkerton, she said, and he could smell the perfume rising from her. Whatever else, he thought, Margaret never wore perfume like that. She said, My readers are the proud mothers and sisters and wives of our boys in France. What they'll want to hear is the story of a patriot who served his country and returned home a hero.

He could feel the thrum of the big engines kicking down as the vessel began to shift its course and he remembered the weird dappled light in the wet trees outside Gaines's Mill all those years ago. The beauty of the blue fields at dusk. The eerie crawling figures of the dying in the dawn mists after battle. The spray of men ripped to pieces and the sounds of horses screaming, the clatter and boom of the artillery.

What they'll want to hear, he said, is the story of a boy who returned home. That's all.

She leaned forward and set a cool hand on his wrist. He dabbed at his mouth with a handkerchief. Her hair was cut in a bob and black and her skin very pale, her lips very red. In an earlier decade he might have found her a wonder. Now seeing her he felt only tired, and alone, and he was not surprised by the lack of fire in him, and this lack of surprise is how he knew he was old.

She said, Is it true, Mr. Pinkerton, that you went down to see your father because he had stopped writing letters to your mother?

Where did you hear that?

Oh, we journalists have our ways. She winked. Your mother was worried because she could not reach him and sent you down to make sure he was okay. You found him already weak.

William was quiet.

And you stayed with him in the battlefields. Despite the danger. You carried him on your back during the retreat. It is a beautiful story, Mr. Pinkerton. Especially during wartime. So many of my readers have husbands and fathers serving in France. It will be such a comfort to them, to be reminded that love can be stronger than war.

It isn't.

Her smile faltered.

It isn't stronger. And I didn't carry him on my back. I've heard that story. It isn't true. It didn't happen like that.

How did it happen?

The only thing my father ever let carry him was a sorrel that he loved more than his own two boys. And when that was shot out from under him he got up and walked home from the war and he never looked back at it.

I know this is a difficult topic.

It's not difficult. Ask me something else.

She cleared her throat.

Ask me something else.

You left your fiancée in Boston to go to your father.

Margaret. Yes.

But she waited for you.

He shook his head. She was one of the Ashling daughters, he said. There were three of them, famous beauties. I knew I was going to marry her from the moment I saw her, at the winter dance in Boston. She was with me in the field hospital at Antietam after I was injured. I woke up and she was there. My father was already back in Chicago by then.

It's such a beautiful story, Mr. Pinkerton.

It felt odd, speaking about this to a stranger after so many years. He still kept his wife's framed photograph on his bedside table each night. Still spoke to her under his breath in the mornings. He frowned suddenly. You wanted to ask me about the war, he said.

That's what I'm doing, sir.

No it isn't.

She gave him a long appraising look and then closed her little notebook and curled her fingers over the top of it and smiled gently. Can I get you something to drink, Mr. Pinkerton?

No.

Soda water? Some tea?

Ask me something else, he said.

———

When his father collapsed in the storehouse headquarters at Gaines's Mill it was two days before the Confederate offensive at Malvern Hill, and already dusk, and the slaughter had slowed to a groan. The door to the storehouse had been torn off and taken someplace away and the flies were thick in the doorway. Though the great batteries had fallen silent in the trees the hollering of boys clutching rifles and of men screaming in fear was still clattering and echoing in the fields. There was a gutter of the lantern and William had looked up to see his father step back from the map and stand very still and then all at once he fell. William lunged forward. Caught him under the arms and staggered under the man's bulk and then fell with him, ungainly and awkward as a calf. His father had been in a fever for days and not sleeping, skin blistering with sweat, shirt sleeves drenched in the heat, a greyness in his face. He had conceded nothing to it.

A runner was sent. The litter bearers took their time but came at last and rolled him moaning into the sling and William walked alongside them in the mud off the boardwalks with a hand slick on his father's boiling skin. Loaded waggons were being dragged across the camp and there were men with their haversacks rolled standing in groups near the southerly road. Someone was shouting. Someone was always shouting.

In the hospital tent they set his father shuddering down among the rows of the dying and his eyes rolled whitely back in his skull. William had never seen his father sick and the sight of it made him afraid. That tent was a large tent, along the walls hung lanterns creaking on their iron rings. The sick and the mutilated were dumped on rough beds of piled corn shucks, the smell was staggering. He saw boys with their bowels shot out doubled over and seething with the pain and they made no sound. Others blinded with stained bandages wrapped over their faces, others with arms in slings, with wrists dangling wrong. He saw orderlies digging with calipers for bullets or grapeshot in the legs of half-naked men, their colleagues holding them down as they writhed. The ground was wet with muck and William's boots slucked quietly where he stood and he realized in disgust that it was blood that had soaked the earth and when he looked behind him he saw a slow foaming gutter of blood running through the mouth of the tent. He was all of sixteen years old.

Pa, he said. I'll go fetch a doctor. You just stay here.

A hot thorny hand grabbing at his wrist. Willie?

I'm here Pa. It's me.

Willie what is it Willie what.

But then his father closed his eyes and began to shake violently and his teeth were clenched.

He went out. There were wounded in the aisles trying to walk through their pain and William pressed gingerly past them and lifted the flap of the tent. There was an ancient sentry posted at the door in the twilight, he held out a grimy hand. In his eye something unhinged and terrible.

I'm looking for a doctor, sir, William said. There's a man needs quinine in there.

Don't everyone. The sentry's weathered face stared him down. As if gauging the boy's age in a baffled stupor. A jerk of his bearded jaw. Go on through there, son.

The slick mud of the boardwalk. A small tent standing open just beyond.

It was the field surgery. When William stepped in through the open flap he was struck at once by the stink. The ripe wet smell of shit and burned flesh. No one took any notice of him. A trestle table had been rigged up using an old door and two sawhorses and there was a man writhing upon it. His wrists were gripped hard, his head was held in place, there was an orderly with his bare arms wrapped around the man's leg at the knee as if he were a colt to be branded. A doctor in his shirt sleeves was bent over the wounded with his back to William and his arms were working furiously. Blood pouring down the table into the mud. A steady wet rasping. The muffled groans of the sufferer. When the doctor turned his face William saw he had his teeth clenched down around a lit cigar and sweat dripping from his nose and all at once William understood he was sawing off the man's leg.

He did not speak. Left the tent in a daze. His hands clutching at his thighs, doubled up and retching. The air was hot, the flies thick. He staggered through them. He could hear horses nearby, the creak of waggons loading. He stared out at the fires in the field beyond. There was a small pile of grey firewood in the long grass behind the tent and as he turned to go he caught the glint of eyes staring back at him. A dog, standing very quiet, very still. Then an orderly came out of the darkness with something in his arms and he dumped it onto the pile and gave William a strange look as he went back inside and William saw it was a man's leg, and that the sticks were not sticks, but feet and arms and hands.

When he got back his father had twisted onto one side and his legs were hot to the touch and spraddled the bedding like a bad saddle and William did not know what to do but wrestle him back into place. He felt sick and frightened and young. There was a man wearing a stained apron over a vest and shirt sleeves walking down the far aisle with two orderlies at his side and William waved to him in a panic and he came angrily over. Thick-necked, thick-wristed, like a pugilist at a country fair. Sleeves tied off into knots and blood in his knuckles. He was a doctor.

He's sick, sir, said William. Despite his youth he was tall and the doctor had to raise his eyes to meet his own. It's the fever, sir. The malaria.

What's a goddamn civilian doing in my tent? the doctor said.

He's sick with the fever, sir, said an orderly. He's not a civilian. This is Major Allen.

I'm not talking about the patient.

William flushed.

The second orderly had already turned away and William saw this with a rising sense of terror. The doctor was wiping his hands up and down his apron, back to front, like a butcher. His pale whiskers bristling, bruises under his eyes.

Please, sir. He's on General McClellan's staff, sir. He's the head of the Secret Service.

He's a spy?

William felt the heat rise to his cheeks. He's *the* spy, sir, he said angrily. If you want to call it that. Don't let him die, sir. Please.

The doctor turned his face aside and spat into the mud and wiped his mouth with an open hand and stared hard at William. He said nothing. Then he reached for his notepad and scrawled out a ticket for quinine and stuffed it with distaste into William's hand as if it were a soiled handkerchief and turned and without so much as a glance at William's father walked away.

It had been that way for weeks. After a month of hot rain and foul vapours the mosquitoes had bred in the millions. Malaria had boiled up out of the swamps and into the bloodstreams of the Federal army and for weeks already men had been shivering in the ranks, collapsing in the pickets. Some too weak to sight their rifles, some too weak to lift a hand. Even when the Confederates rushed in waves of grey from the treeline, screaming. Even when the bayonets slid between their ribcages. There were men in the field tents who had been carved to pieces by enemy fire and men who had been gutted by disease and the wounded would die bravely, the sick would suffer in cowardice. That was how it was. Ask any surgeon. No soldier worth his brass fell out for shitting his pants. The quartermasters ran out of quinine by the third week of June and after that the doctors left the shivering masses to their fevers.

William ransacked his father's pockets and turned out a riveted leather billfold and this he tucked down the front of his tunic. He took his father's Colt and checked its chamber then slipped it into the pocket of his coat and he squeezed his father's shoulder.

In the lantern light his father's chin was a crescent of

darkness. His flushed throat trembling, as if palsied. A boy across the tent started to scream.

He went out.

The Confederates had not overrun them but William could see the chaos of the camp and the exhaustion of the men as they kicked down their tents, slung up their packs in the firelight. There were soldiers standing in a daze around small fires and the air was already cooling though the ground felt hot still and the heat poured up off it like something pestilential and evil. William went quickly, standing aside in the mud when tired men crowded past on the boardwalks, and at last he shrugged up his shoulders and just waded through the muck. There were others hurrying through it also. He could not see what it was he sloshed through though he had some idea having watched the soldiers void themselves in it and the cooks dump their scraps and the sutlers kick aside their opened cans like razored shells into the stew of it.

The quartermasters had already started to crate up their stores and they took what they could but the packing seemed crazed and fearful and made no sense. There were shelves of tinned beans and boxes of cigars left unsealed but a crate of soap had been nailed and cross-nailed shut. Some stared at William and some shook their heads and some did not bother to reply. The sutlers were rougher. Laughing and pushing each other drunkenly aside. One lashed out with a boot but lost his footing as he did so and William turned away.

As he was leaving a boy his own age took him by the sleeve and drew him aside out of the light and said, I know where you can get quinine.

William looked at him. There was a hunger to the boy, a viciousness, that made him uneasy. He wore a filthy Union infantry shirt.

Goin to cost you though.

How much?

A pale tip of a tongue. Crooked brown teeth. He cocked his head and said, Five dollars.

The boy's small eyes were wet in the darkness.

Show me, William said.

The boy set off through the grass behind the tents and he did not look back to see that William followed. There were fires in the night, wearied soldiers sitting around them. As they walked William slid his fingers down his shirt and took out five bills from his father's wallet and slipped them into his trouser pocket. The boy led him to a small fire where a man sat turning strips of bacon over in a pan with a knife and he raised his eyes and watched them approach but he did not stop at his labours.

Orville, the boy said. This here's lookin for the quinine.

The man frowned. A long line of stubble along his jaw. Thick black moustaches and heavy eyebrows and greasy grey hair clotted down his back. He punched out his cap and set it on his head and grunted. He don't look sick.

It's not for me, William said foolishly.

It's six dollars, the man said.

He said five.

Seven.

William looked at the boy and the boy spat and shrugged and no one said anything.

All at once the man smiled. All right, all right, all right, all right, he said. Let's just take it easy now. You hungry?

He held out a leaf of rasher on his knife but William did not move to take it and instead put his hand in his pocket.

Says he's got money, Orville, the boy said. He sidled over and sat on a log near the fire and reached into a satchel and withdrew a tall green bottle. It was whiskey.

I said quinine, William said.

There's quinine in it, the boy said.

You put that away, the man said. And you. You seat yourself down.

He bit the bacon from the blade and chewed it slowly. The boy was dragging a stick through the dirt with the bottle clamped between his knees and William frowned and turned his face into the darkness. He could hear enlisted men stamping through the muck, muttering.

The man grunted. Interesting uniform you got on there.

William glanced uneasily around.

Where you say you were fightin today? the man said.

William blinked. He took his hand from his pocket and in it was his father's Colt and his hand was very steady.

I'll take the bottle, he said. Five dollars. If it's really quinine.

The man rested the blade of his knife on his thigh and he stared up at the Colt. He smiled a disappointed smile. It's quinine, he said.

The boy did not smile. His two hands still clutching the bottle by the neck.

William held out the five dollars to the boy and the man nodded and the boy took it and William took the bottle. It was not heavy. He took two deliberate steps backward away from the fire without turning around and the boy watched with glittering eyes. Then he turned and went.

At the hospital they had taken his father from the tent and dumped him outside in the cold among those suffering dysentery and other hopeless cases and it took William several minutes to find him. He was on the far side of those dying boys and he kneeled beside him and put a hand on his wrist and his father opened his burning eyes.

Willie, he whispered. Your mother was here.

He did not know if there was quinine in that whiskey but he uncorked the bottle and cradled his father's skull in his hand and drew the bottle to his lips. A flare of light from a passing torch burned through the buckled green glass, passed and was gone.

Go on, drink, he whispered. Good. Like that.

His father drank off a third of the whiskey then started to cough and twisted onto his side and coughed and coughed. William tucked the bottle in his shirt, the glass cool against his skin. Then his father lay back on the rugged husks and William watched him and after a while he lay down next to him, feeling the heat pour from his father's flesh, and he pulled the coat up over them, and closed his eyes, and together they slept.

The next morning dawned muggy and hot. There was mist in the long yellow grass. Bodies lay around them tangled on the corn husks and all looked grey and still and he could see in the nearest the white staring eyes of the dead. He lifted his face and looked at his father and then tucked his coat more tightly against his father's sleeping form and rubbed at his neck and he rose.

The sentries were gone. The low mist crept over the ground and there were no fires burning in the camp. The mud underfoot had thickened. Tangles of rope, broken crates, clothing and dry goods strewn over the field. During the night most of the tents had been struck, Porter's V Corps had moved out with the waggons, there were only the dying and the stragglers left. He reached for the whiskey in his shirt but it was gone.

He did not know what to do. He went out in search of something to eat but could find only a box of salt crackers and these he tore into with his teeth bared and the crumbs exploding. A weak sunlight was coming in through the grey trees. On a low rise he found the sutlers' tents slumped and pulled off their stakes and their goods turned out in the mud. On his way back he lifted the flap of the hospital tent and saw the beds evacuated. He did not go into the surgery.

There was a man standing over his father when he returned and he felt something cold go through him. The man's back was to him and he was rubbing one hand slowly on his pant leg and the sound of it seemed all at once eerie and awful and menacing.

William came up on the other side of his sleeping father. The Colt still in his pocket.

What do you want, he said.

The man was wearing a forage cap with a small brass balloon insignia on it. He lifted his face.

He had no eyebrows, no eyelashes. His eyes were very blue. He had been burned once and the skin had scarred over and the man's cheeks and mouth and nose looked soft and pitted and shiny like poured wax.

William took the Colt from his pocket. What happened to you?

The man grunted. Slept through the muster, he said. Look at these poor bastards.

William watched him.

The man looked up and saw the Colt. Jesus, lad. I got left behind. It happens.

William said nothing.

I ain't a deserter.

I meant what happened to your face.

The man's eyes fixed on William and then his mouth twisted into a smile. A hydrogen balloon ignited it, he said. I was an aeronaut before all this. A balloonist. The man gestured at William's father with a gnarled hand. I reckon you're going to want some help with him. What is it? Malaria?

I think so.

The burned man nodded. I'd say so.

If I can just get him to headquarters.

The burned man stepped closer in the warming mud and leaned over his father and stared at his face and after a moment said softly, I'll be damned. When he looked up the expression in his eyes had darkened. You know who this is?

Major Allen. Of McClellan's staff. William lowered the Colt. You know him?

I'm an aeronaut, kid. We're in intelligence ourselves.

William took a step forward. Will you help me with him? he said in a low urgent voice.

The man peered around as if thinking better of it. At last he nodded. I guess we're going the same way, he said.

They took little. Someone had been through William's things in the night but he still had his bedroll and a pair of dry socks and a waterskin and he took these along with whatever food he could scrounge up. All this he slung over one shoulder and with his father slumping wearily between them the three began the slow walk southward to the James River. The road was rutted and the mud two feet deep in places and everywhere they saw evidence of the Union army's retreat. Rifles discarded in the mud. Sacks of food. Thick officers' coats with fur collars and the arms stitched in relief. They touched none of it.

There was no sign of Confederate scouts though they knew the rebels would be coming. They talked little. William's father drifted and muttered and shook his head and coughed. His skin was hot and bloodless. By mid-morning they had come upon the army's rearguard and began to pass the soldiers on the side of the road, some turned out with boots pulled off and rubbing at their feet, others sitting with their rifles between their knees and faces bent earthward. All were weighed down with ransacked stores from the fleeing sutlers, cigars stuffed in their mouths, pockets packed down with bars of soap, crates of cigars on their shoulders, some crazed few were rolling enormous slow barrels of whiskey over the ruts in the road. There was a terrible carnival aspect to it all. One soldier lay spread-eagled in the road, drunk. Another shifted boxes of foot powder from a broken tin trunk into a wheelbarrow.

They walked shuffling past. A burned man, a sick man, a boy. No one challenged them.

They slept in a clearing with their backs to the trees, listening for the sound of an army on the road. The cold grass sticking to their legs. That night the temperature dropped and they folded hands into their armpits for warmth. They did not risk a fire and in the morning when they rose William's father was worse.

He's going to die, the burned man said.

No he won't.

You've got to get him to a doctor. He won't make it out of here.

He's my father.

The burned man squinted up at the grey sky. I know it, he said. The day grew hot again. There were waggons on the road when they set out and the drivers told them to head for Savage's Station. All were heavily laden, none could spare a space for William's father. William cursed them and they kicked out their boots but it was half-hearted and pointless and no one drew a gun. The great wheels banging and creaking over the ruts. The starved horses with their drooping heads, their breath pluming out before them. It started to rain a warm mist-like rain and William wiped his hair back from his face and they went on.

They reached Savage's Station along the railroad by noon. Rows of high grey tents in the rain. A confusion of men. A fenced perimeter stood in place around the hospital and they passed pockets of infantry huddled in the trees and then they were in the chaos of the evacuating camp. The hospital was a clapboard shack with wounded figures huddled outside it and there was a big tent with the flaps tied back and a dark smell in the beyond. A big waggon train stood sealed and under guard without the horses to haul it away. They pushed through the crowds and at the entrance to the hospital William set his father down on a broken ladder that served as a bench and the burned man stared fiercely out at the figures in the rain.

You'll have to manage him now, he said. I need to find Colonel Lowe. Runs the Balloon Corps. I need to report in.

William looked at him and he shrugged.

What, the burned man said. You thought I was army? Aviators are civilians, kid. The uniform doesn't mean anything. He twisted his ravaged face, nodded at William's father. Get him to the infirmary, he said, and turned to go.

William looked around at the whirl of men and the grey blanketed wounded in the muck and something in it all made him uneasy. Wait, he called.

The burned man turned.

I don't think we should stop.

He needs medical attention, kid.

Not here.

He needs quinine. Look at him.

William got to his feet.

The burned man had taken two steps out of the yard and paused and now he came back. I know who your father is, he said quietly. I mean before the war. I know what he used to do. I know about the Agency.

William had been assured only two men in the ranks knew his father's real identity: Benjamin Porter, and General McClellan himself. If you know who he is, he said cautiously, then help me get him out of here. The Confederates are coming, this place will be overrun.

It won't be.

Please.

I'm not getting myself killed over this, kid.

So come with us.

The burned man took off his cap and raised his face and closed his eyes and the rain was coming down over him and into his open mouth. Your father, he said, was investigating graft in Philadelphia when my brother was working for the post office. Started working in the office with him, got friendly. Turned on him. My brother got seven years.

William stood quiet in the rain.

He's still in jail.

He was guilty.

Maybe.

William met the burned man's gaze. He was guilty and got put away, he said coldly. I wish I could say I was sorry for him. Maybe he's lucky. If he's in jail then he's not down here.

The burned man scowled, nodded. Well he was a bastard.

William looked at his father.

Not him. My brother. You really are his kid? Pinkerton's?

He nodded. William.

The burned man studied him. Ignatius Spaar, he said.

I can't carry him myself, Mr. Spaar.

Spaar scowled at the Federal soldiers leaving through the gates with their packs clanking and rifles slung. My brother always was a bastard, he muttered. He always was that.

———

Against his better instincts he waited but he did not approach Sumner's staff and the hour came and went while Spaar hunted for some word of his fellow aeronauts. William sat with his father, he stood with his father, he dragged his father through the mud to the southerly road. Then out of the shifting crowd a figure stepped forward and set a hand on William's arm and when he turned he found himself staring into the wide power-ful face of a black man, the rain running from his chin. He reached up and wiped a hat shapeless as a feed bag from his head and his nostrils flared.

Look like you ready to drop, the man said in a soft rich voice. A flash of gold teeth.

Mr. Porter? William said, confused.

Aw, now. Take it easy. He reached down and hefted William's father with one massive arm and crossed to a narrow shelter beside the fence and propped the feverish man against a barrel and murmured, Now what you so poorly with, Major? and lifted his face and felt for his heartbeat.

It's the fever, William said. We're trying to get him some-where safe.

Shoot. That ain't here.

I know it.

Sally's back at Harrison's Landing. She goin to know what to do.

Benjamin Porter and his wife had been working with William's father in service to the Union since the outbreak of the war, running spies across the lines under the guise of slaves. They had been friends of the Pinkertons since fleeing the South three years before when they had hidden under the floorboards of the Pinkerton kitchen. William trusted the man the way he trusted his own brother. He could not stop himself now from reaching up and holding the man's arm and he felt a sudden upwelling of relief but then they heard the sound of firing from behind them and men were running.

Spaar materialized out of the chaos and looked at Ben with a curious expression. A grizzled old sergeant was with him.

Mr. Spaar, Ben said. You a long way from the balloonists.

Spaar tilted his cap back from his eyes, the rain swishing from the leather brim. I'm looking for them now, he said. Are they all up at Harrison's Landing already?

The sergeant who had returned with him ran a hand over his face to wipe away the rain. You all should get out now if you're going, he said. Magruder's units are coming out of the west. Jackson's in the north. It'll get hot here.

Get out to where? William asked.

Malvern Hill. The companies are regrouping. They'll make a stand there.

Ben shifted William's father on his shoulder. This here is Major Allen. Of McClellan's staff. Ain't there some waggon he can ride out on?

The sergeant squinted. If there was a waggon I'd be on it myself, boy. You get him over to headquarters at Malvern House.

Malvern House.

Yes.

Spaar grimaced. How do we get there?

A Spencer repeater started shooting from the lines its quick sharp crack and then several others started up and the sergeant was already turning away. Follow the goddamn army, he called. You'll know it's ours by the backs of their damn trousers.

And trudged through the thick mud with his shoulders hunched and his long hair matted down his back and his Colt slapping at his leg.

It was late afternoon when they set out and still raining in a long slow languid rain and the water was warm on their necks and soon they were soaked through. Discarded packs and greatcoats and rifles littered the ditches but they did not stop to pick through them. The soldiers escorting them had been drinking and would stumble to their knees and shoot at every shadow in the fog. No one helped them carry his father and the mud on the road was deep, the going slow. Behind them the big guns started to sound but they walked on without a

word and by dusk the guns had fallen silent and they understood Savage's Station had been overrun.

A lifetime later William would watch the columnist slide one
long thigh up over the other, adjust the hem of her dress in the
quiet of that cabin. The ocean light fading, the brass portholes
burning bright and cold high up in the walls. He reached for the
pitcher of water, an orchid of light.

Mr. Pinkerton? She tapped her pencil against her lips,
flipped back through her notebook. Tell me about the balloon
battle, she said. Tell me about Malvern Hill.

Malvern Hill.

She gave him a soft, sympathetic look. If you can, Mr.
Pinkerton. I know it was a long time ago.

Fifty years.

Yes.

A steward in his pressed whites came to the door, glanced
in, went on his way. William studied the columnist there in the
silvering light, deciding something. Margaret's ghostly double.
A faint scent of salt air and whitewash reached him, the tang
of oil rubbed into the millwork. What did he remember? Fifty
years ago someone, somewhere, had been singing a low hymn.
There had been crying in the twilight. Hogs feeding on the
dead all night as the wounded wept and called for water. Then
the skies opening in the early dawn, the rain coming down,
him wading hip-deep through the grass and his trousers cold
and soaking.

There had been boys, huddled at the mouths of tents.

Terrible eyes.

He told her, It wouldn't stop raining. Wheat was in the
shock, oats ready for harvest, corn waist-high. We'd been retreating back up the peninsula all week. They call it the Seven Days
Battles now but that isn't accurate. At the time it just felt like we
were running. We called it the Infernal Week. We didn't know
where anyone was. It seemed half the time we were just afraid

of falling behind the Confederate lines. We kept hearing they
were coming up and coming up but we didn't see much of them.
But we'd pass wounded on the side of the road, boys with their
feet shot off, men with their arms in slings. So we knew someone somewhere was fighting. Malvern Hill was the last of it.
After that the Confederates fell back.

You were assigned to the Balloon Corps?

William frowned. No. Well, during the battle, yes. I'd
been a despatch rider all week but because of my light weight
I ended up in the balloon. We went up to try to get a sense of
what was going on. We had a direct line by telegraph with the
General's headquarters and we sent them our observations but
they didn't help much. I think we helped the howitzers locate
their targets some. The heavy Parrott guns looked all wrong
to us. But our batteries had the high ground, wide sweeping
fields of fire. It was nearly a perfect day of killing. He went
quiet for a moment, then said, The Hill was bisected by a long
Quaker road. There were two streams down below where the
forest broke and these funnelled the Confederate forces into
a narrow assault. It was only just a mile wide or so. It made for
a slaughter.

She shivered. I think I'd be terrified to go up in a balloon.

Scared the tar out of me too.

What happened to your balloon when it broke loose?

When it what?

Broke loose. Didn't your balloon break loose? Wasn't there
a free flight over the Confederate positions during the battle?

No.

There wasn't a free flight?

No.

She studied him but did not say anything for a moment.
Glanced at her notebook, pale brow furrowing. It must have
been a very confusing time, she said.

Not that confusing.

I hope the war in France isn't as terrible. For our boys over
there, I mean.

William smoothed the blanket on his knee, his big hands gnarled but still strong. He said, The war for the Union cast a long shadow. I'd guess maybe every war does. But used to be you'd meet a man who'd fought in it and there was an understanding between you.

Mm.

I don't know. I think when a man comes back from a war the rest of his life is already written. Whatever happens. It's all a long descent from that place. Most of us are glad to be leaving it. Some of us don't ever really get to. It doesn't much matter. You live with it.

He saw in his mind's eye two boots standing upright in a thick stew of mud. The leg bones sticking from the tops where the body had been sheared away. He heard again the heavy slucking noise as the corpses were rolled from the muck.

There were things that happened in that time, he said slowly. Things that never made sense then and never made sense afterwards. My father never got over some of it. Maybe he never cared to. I know I never did care to dwell on it.

My grandfather disappeared at Shiloh, she said after a moment. There's a grave for him back in Kansas but no one's in it. My grandmother never gave up hope that he would come back someday. Just walk up to the door and knock on it. When the railroad came to buy out her house she refused. She didn't want to leave, in case he couldn't find her.

There was always talk of deserters, William said. It happened.

She smiled. The O'Malleys down the street from us knew a family whose husband returned from the war six years after the surrender. They had all of them given him up for dead. I think my grandmother thought about that often.

Well.

She died at Shiloh too, my father used to say.

A lot of boys died and weren't ever found. Sometimes there just wasn't—

She leaned forward. Yes?

It's nothing.

Please, she said. Go on.

He paused and then he said, Sometimes there just wasn't enough left of a person to collect up and bury. On the peninsula the torpedoes were the worst of it. The Confederates used to bury cannon shells using a friction timer under the roads. You'd step on them and be ripped in half.

Awful.

But it was the exploding shot that would obliterate a man. There'd be nothing left of him. Just a cloud of blood. He paused, looked at her. I'm sorry, he said. You spend a lifetime not talking about it and then start in on a young lady like yourself.

Don't be, she said. I've heard worse. Is that what happened to Mr. Spaar?

Who?

Ignatius Spaar.

William smiled vaguely, waited.

The balloonist. You were with him during the campaign? His body was never found.

A shake of his grizzled head. I'm sorry, he said. I never heard of the man.

She peered down at her notes in confusion. You flew with him, sir. You stated as much in an interview with the New York *Sun* in eighteen seventy-three. You said—

I know the article. It was a fabrication.

A fabrication?

The man who wrote it was fired.

The columnist adjusted her hair behind one ear. You know the article but you've never heard of the man?

His face hardened. He said, I'd say somebody somewhere got the facts wrong, and the confusion got written down instead of the truth.

I don't understand, Mr. Pinkerton. Are you saying he didn't exist?

William cleared his throat, he glanced impatiently at his pocket watch.

Mr. Pinkerton?

I'm saying the man is a ghost, Miss. You can write that down in your little book.

Of course his father did not die. They stumbled up Malvern Hill in the settling twilight and filed past the Union pickets quiet and grim and no one stopped them. It was the last day of June eighteen hundred and sixty-two. They moved past the cannons upturned on their wheels and glaring sphinx-like through the gloom as if to challenge any who would pass and they wended their slow way through the campfires burning low and miserable in the damp. Malvern House was dark with only a few candles burning in the windows and as they approached a sentry waved them back and warned them off and they found their way to a nearby tent and laid William's father out for the night. Spaar had already slipped away in search of his aeronauts. In the morning William and Ben rose and took William's father up to the porch of Malvern House and William stood with his hand on his bare head feeling the heat beginning to rise out of the ground and he watched his father shiver in his blanket there with his eyes yet closed. Ben's great bulk creaking there in the chair. There were ninety thousand Federals in that camp and by noon of that day all were in the lines. William knew Lee would be coming up fast and that an assault must soon begin and he felt sick at the sight of his father and went out to find Ignatius Spaar in the hope he might be of some use.

Spaar found him. William, he called. How's the Major?

William tipped his cap, squinted. You find your balloons yet?

The aeronaut looked dishevelled, tired, a sheen on his waxen skin where the sweat stood out. His blue cap was stained with a pale dust. He looked like a snake oil salesman down on his luck and fierce. Don't you worry, lad, he said. He'll recover. I reckon we're in a strong position here. The rebels won't get close to him.

William nodded.

Spaar was leading him down towards a copse of trees where an older man stood examining the sky and this man palmed his kepi from his head and rubbed it at the nape of his neck and watched them approach. A small man, lean as a rope and looking just as strong, long Gaulish moustaches sweeping down from his chin, his skin baked to leather as if he'd been nailed for weeks to a fence in the sun. William liked the look of him at once.

Good lord, the man muttered. This bloody heat.

I was told the corps's disbanded, Spaar said as he approached. We out of iron shavings?

Shoot. Folk do like to talk.

It ain't true?

William's shirt was plastered to his back and he could feel the sweat trickling down his ribs.

Not hardly. *Intrepid*'s near to ready. How's Thaddeus?

Still sick.

The fever?

Spaar ran a hand over his mouth, nodded. No telegraph yet, I see.

The older man shrugged. Whole crew got eaten up by the reserves. We had to abandon the poles back at Gaines's Mill along with a load of shavings. That's what your folk are talking about, I'd wager. But we've got plenty of iron back at Harrison's Landing.

Spaar turned to William. This is Clovis Lowe, he said. Keeps folks in line around here.

Some, Clovis grunted. You're the new floater?

The what?

I haven't told him yet, said Spaar.

Ah.

What did he call me?

You think he's ready? Clovis asked.

William stared suspiciously at the two of them. Ready for what?

He followed Spaar's gaze across the field towards a rocky stream, a war balloon filling under the trees there, and even as he watched a wind caught the balloon and it twisted and rocked dangerously and there were men shouting and running and then it righted itself like a buoy in a current and its envelope continued to expand.

The hell with that, he said. I'm not going up in that.

Spaar looked at him and grinned a ruined grin.

It had been christened *Intrepid* and stood as tall as a five-storey building with a gas envelope of thirty-two thousand cubic feet. Its wicker basket had been reinforced to the weight of five grown men and could carry a telegraph operator two miles into the air. The Confederates feared it more than a Federal battery and had launched sniper assaults by night and sabotage attempts by day in their efforts to burn the thing to scrap. Still it hovered like a dark globe of silence above the battlefields in its infernal machinations and the soldiers would lift their eyes skyward and see it in all its wrongness and feel the hand of dread come upon them as if it were an omen and not built by the hands of men. William had felt it himself on days while the batteries boomed into smoke and men lay dying in the corn and he stood now close to it in wonder and watched Spaar set a hand upon its webbing.

The net lifted and lifted, trailing over the ground like a thing alive, a jellyfish of gas. William watched it sway at its tether. He glanced uneasily at the corps men working the tubes, holding the cables fast, smoothing out the canvas underlay as the balloon filled and filled. Six men with heavy brooms were sweeping the site clear of debris. Two enormous wooden gas generators on wheels with nozzles and thick tubes attached sprawled across the grass to a small central box attended by a Negro in shirt sleeves and from there the gas poured along a third tube into the envelope itself.

Spaar drew him forward, past the hulking sentinels set at watch with rifles at the ready. They walked down through the long grass to the balloon.

I can't go up in that, Mr. Spaar.

Spaar laughed. The basket was four feet in length and two in width and had been painted in brilliant red and white stripes. White stars lined the rim. He let his fingers crawl across its edge.

I mean it, sir. I'm no good with heights.

Spaar held his hand on the basket. The rivers of scars across the knuckles, the weird waxen colouring of the skin. I know what you're afraid of, he said. You think it'll be like standing at the edge of a bridge or a cliff. It's nothing like that. You'll see.

There was a strange odour to the envelope, a brownish whiff of gas in the air. Sweat ran down William's ribs.

I can't do this, sir, he said.

You can. You're half as heavy as anyone here. I need someone light. I need to get altitude fast.

William was shaking his head.

Listen, lad. The reason you get shaky at the edge of a high place is because your centre of gravity is below you. You lean out and you feel like it's pulling you down. An aerostat is nothing like that. Someone called something to him from near the generators and Spaar looked back at the balloon and nodded and then he stepped back and studied William. In an aerostat, he said, your centre of gravity is above you. When you lean out, the pull on you is to swing you back under the envelope. Your body understands instinctively. I never heard of a man getting sick from the height.

All I'm saying is these men better not stand under the basket.

Well. They got hats on.

And he grinned.

The man Clovis came over with one hand in his greasy hair and he nodded at the two men. There's no part of me that likes this, Ignatius.

I know.

Thaddeus will spit in his coffee when he hears you're going up.

I'll talk to him.

Especially on the one cable.

So get me another.

Clovis grimaced.

Spaar shrugged. You tell your boy I've gone up on less. We'll use the flags to signal. Keep a runner close. They'll start the attack soon.

Clovis nodded. He reached into his pocket and took out a revolver and handed it to Spaar. You won't need this, he said.

But it's nice to have.

Yes.

There were men holding the guy lines of the balloon steady and Spaar climbed up onto the crates and started to hoist himself into the basket when he paused and looked down at Clovis. You see any of that back pay yet? he asked.

Clovis smiled.

You see the paymaster, you tell him I'm looking for him, Spaar called over one shoulder.

And swung up and in.

Clovis took William's elbow, helped him up. Then he stepped back and shouted instructions to the groundsmen.

William felt his guts shift. It was like stepping into a boat, the soft wicker floor belling down under his weight and slewing sideways and him gripping white-knuckled the edge of the basket. It was not more than two feet deep.

Spaar had one hand on the ballast bags and was double-checking the knots and he looked at William crouched in the bottom of the basket, both hands out for balance. Listen, kid, he said. When we start to go up the Confederates will start in with their shooting. Don't mind it. Once we clear five hundred feet they'll stop.

William swallowed. Five hundred feet?

But we'll make that height in minutes. Don't worry.

Wonderful.

Hold on now.

William was already holding on. What will they be shooting at us with? he asked.

Spaar grinned. Everything they got.

Jesus.

Never mind it.

But they can't hit us?

Well, Spaar said. They haven't managed it yet.

The aerostat was enormous and bull-necked and strained against its ropes and William felt a sudden lurch as the basket shuddered under him and began to drift upward. After only a few feet it caught and held again and Spaar was leaning over the edge checking the balance of the basket and then he called down his okay to the groundsmen below and they loosed the ropes and all at once the balloon began to rise for real. He could hear the screel of the windlasses letting out and then that had faded and Spaar was standing with one hand on his black hat and the other at his hip and his feet planted wide like a sailor at the stern in a rolling wake.

You can stand up, kid, Spaar called.

William was staring at the gaps in the wickerwork of the basket. His fingers poked through and gripped the pliable walls and the walls rippled under his grip.

You sure this is safe? he said.

Spaar grinned. He took hold of either side of the basket and jumped heavily against its floor and the basket lurched and swung and William cried out.

Oh it's safe, Spaar laughed.

There was no other sound. They had ascended no more than fifty feet when William got to his knees and was astonished to find his dread gone. The air was cooler, less humid. The balloon crackled and snapped like a flag in a wind and William closed his eyes, felt the slow rocking of the basket. They rose higher. When he looked down he could see the languid circling of the vultures riding the currents, the ripple of heat coming up off the earth in an eerie distortion of the light. He had seen nothing like it in his life. Overhead all was endless grey in a haze of high cloud and he stared at the shifting wisps like tendrils of fog and felt himself grow light-headed. It came over him without warning and in a rush and then there was a hand on his shoulder and he stumbled and it was Spaar, drawing him back in.

His heart was hammering.

Looking up's the danger, Spaar said softly. Look at me. William. I said look at me. That's how you lose your balance up here. You keep your eye on the ground.

William thought of his father shivering on the porch of Malvern House. He bit into the side of his mouth and tasted blood. He could see the brickwork of that building on the hill, the maw of its chimney.

When do the guns start? he asked.

Spaar looked around. They should have started, he said. He shrugged. I guess they can't shoot at us without giving up their positions. I guess we got lucky today.

The afternoon came on hot. They rose higher. The balloon turned on its solitary cable like a hat in a slow-moving river and William watched the hill below in perfect clarity. The pale lines of the earthworks, the cannons hub to hub in a long snaking mile along the crest. The soldiers in blue huddled in their lines. And the long slope of the hill with the white road descending down the centre. He could see the twin streams on either side through the trees and the wide field and the shimmering of the forest as if its leaves were made of iron and he knew with certainty that the enemy was massing within. The balloon twisted, the netting on the silk slapped and crackled in the high air. He held on.

Everything was very still.

And then it started.

William felt a distant shudder and boom of artillery. He followed Spaar's gaze north to a cloud of smoke rising from a knoll in the distance and then the earth at the base of the hill heaved and shattered into a cloud of dirt and then again and then the big Federal guns on their rise started in reply. He could see blue soldiers running into position along the crest of the hill and the light caught and flared in their bayonets.

Spaar took his eye from the spyglass and studied William with a sober look. It's beginning, he said. Then he went back to his observations.

William said nothing. The Confederate batteries sounded unsteadily for a while and then fell silent and William knew they had been destroyed. Then a second battery opened its uneven barrage and the Federal guns shifted their aim and after a time these too fell silent.

What are they doing? Spaar muttered.

Even to William it seemed awkward, uncoordinated. And then he heard the faint screaming of men in a fury and he peered over the rotating basket in time to see a wall of grey break at a run from the trees and pour forward towards the hill. There were hundreds, there were thousands of men pouring like a pestilence across that field. The Federals let them come on and held their fire and they came on to the very edge of the field and then the Federal cannons opened fire and obliterated the first wave. The Confederates wavered, men in grey still running and then only a pink cloud and the men gone and others ran through where they had been as the dirt twisted around them and it felt to William at that height horrifying and Biblical and savage to behold.

My god, Spaar muttered. The basket still spun on its axis and he reached across and fumbled with the cable. He had the signal flags in his hands but had not raised them yet.

William watched the Confederates come on. A second wave punched out through the trees and the cannons tore into them too but they kept on and he watched them hurl themselves uphill past their writhing brethren almost to the breach and then the Federal infantry opened fire and the rebels collapsed back into their clothes in the tall and mutilated grass.

All at once *Intrepid*'s basket wobbled violently and William pitched forward and grabbed at a rope and glared at Spaar.

What was that? he said. Mr. Spaar?

Spaar did not answer. He was leaning dangerously out and staring downward and then he crowded over William and watched the ground from the other side.

They had stopped spinning. The balloon felt suddenly calm.

And then William understood. They had come untethered. They were in free flight over the battle.

Mr. Spaar?

Spaar was gripping the edge of the basket.

Mr. Spaar? He took hold of the man's sleeve. Put us down. Get us down now.

Spaar shook him loose. I can put us down. I just can't say where that will be.

You can't steer this thing?

No one steers an aerostat, kid. Except the wind.

The wind.

Spaar paused and looked at him. This isn't my first flight, kid.

William stared wildly down, watching Malvern Hill recede. They had begun to drift over the Confederate lines.

William, Spaar said. Listen to me. The currents move us in their own directions. We just go up or down until we find the wind we want, and we ride that. We're perfectly safe up here. When we're ready to descend we'll go down fast. It'll be fine.

Some bitter thing was rising in his throat and he swallowed it painfully down. He could see the dust and clouds of smoke far below them, the men dying in their thousands. They sailed over a clearing and he could see masses of Confederate cavalry standing at the ready and the slung grey peaks of tents in the trees. The sky overhead was vast and silent and clear like still water. Below them a vulture wobbled, dark and evil, an auspice.

He stared at the aeronaut. What do you mean by fast? How fast?

They came down a half mile behind the Confederate lines. The aeronaut had reached up and seized a thick cord and torn the rip-panel open and the balloon had lurched and started at once to plunge earthward. William felt his stomach give out.

The netting on the envelope was crackling and snapping above them. It seemed to William the floor of the basket was pushing up against him and he could not keep himself steady.

Get down, kid, Spaar shouted at him. Hold on now.

He was holding on. He was in the bottom of the basket and gripping its sides fiercely and then something went past him at a high whine like a hornet and then a second arced past and then he understood they were being shot at. He could not see the shooters.

He raised his face. They were plunging at an angle and still high above the earth and he saw the battlefield to the south and when he looked up he saw the envelope widening and filling like a kind of parachute. There were men shouting and pointing and he saw a regiment of Confederate infantry raise their rifles as one and begin firing but he heard nothing and felt nothing and then they were skimming over the treetops. Something caught in the wicker of the basket and they spun sharply. Branches snapped, slicing the basket like knives.

He awoke on the ground. Sprawled out and not himself. Both wrists aching. Spaar was kneeling over him with a revolver in his hand and the man's face was bleeding and for a moment William did not understand how he had got there.

Well that wasn't so bad, was it? Spaar murmured.

William tried to speak but something was in his mouth and he got to his knees and vomited.

The basket had been torn into pieces and was hanging weirdly from its ropes in the branches of an oak and the silk envelope had snagged and tangled in the high leaves. There was a line of debris on the earth surrounding them, shattered branches, torn leaves. William got to his feet and swayed and his arms windmilled and he sat abruptly and stayed down, the trembling in his legs subsiding. He felt all at once afraid.

The rebels will be coming, Spaar said. And if they find the aerostat they'll find us. Spaar pocketed his revolver and ran his sleeve over the cut on his burned face but it did not slow the bleeding. He was looking at William's hands. Are they broken?

William turned his wrists painfully.

Can you move your fingers?

He moved his fingers a little.

All right. Come on then.

It was hot and still in the trees. The basket sawed quietly on its straps. He could hear distant rifle fire, the faint shouting of men. He thought of swimming with his brother Robert in the mountain rivers when they were little and how they would holler at each other submerged.

William, Spaar hissed at him.

He opened his eyes. Spaar had taken his revolver from his pocket and was staring through the trees to the east and standing very still. They remained that way for a long moment, straining to hear. No one came.

We need to hurry, Spaar said. He had started to climb the tree and then he was cutting through the ropes with a small sharp blade and William limped over to help. As the pieces came free and fell with a clatter into the grass he dragged them clear and laid them flat as he could manage. He collected the bracken from the ground and laid it over the garish red and white wicker and he tore up fistfuls of grass to do likewise. Spaar was cursing and the tree was shaking and the netting would not come free. William glanced fearfully around at the trees but he did not see anyone. Then Spaar swung down and walked around the tree unlooping a rope in its tangles and William came forward and the two of them billowed and dragged and hauled on the silk as if they were snapping laundry from a line. And the thing came free.

Spaar was breathing hard. How are your wrists?

They were less sore but his ribs had started to ache and were growing worse but he only shrugged and began rolling the envelope up and stamping it down. They buried it between the roots

of the tree and covered it in torn grass and when William looked
up he could see torn pieces of coloured silk and webbing in the
leaves overhead.

It'll do, Spaar said.

He handed the revolver across to William and then reached
into his pocket and pulled out a case of matches and he pointed
at the tree. You get up there and you wait. Don't let that aerostat
get into Confederate hands. You get down and you burn it if
you must. Understand?

What are you going to do?

Spaar wiped again at the cut on his face. I'll try to get back
to our lines.

William said nothing. Then he held the revolver out. You
take it.

No.

I mean it.

Kid, I never shot a gun in my life. Listen. I'll be back with
some help. You just stay put and keep real quiet. You can do this.

Spaar put a hand on William's shoulder. Then he turned
and walked off into the trees towards the sound of the fighting
and soon the dappled sunlight and the shifting trunks of light
and shadow had absorbed him.

It was already late in the afternoon. William climbed painfully into the lower branches of the big oak and sat with his
knees propped up and the revolver in his lap and he watched
the forest around him. He heard boots passing nearby but no
one came in sight and later he heard the sound of a repeating
rifle shooting into the leaves farther off but nothing returned its
fire. The war felt very far away, the woods felt silent. He saw a
buck come into the clearing below and stand with its antlers
raised and ears swivelling and then it turned and slid noiselessly
into the underbrush. The sunlight shifted like drops of liquid
over the grass. William closed his eyes. He told himself he must
not sleep. He slept.

Hello floater, a voice said softly.

He opened his eyes. The blood loud in his temples. It was

dusk and he cocked the revolver and stared below him. There were men in the clearing, six of them, they wore Federal uniforms and the man at the front was squinting, shielding his brow. It was Clovis Lowe.

You didn't think I'd leave you to a Richmond tobacco prison, he called up.

William's legs were stiff, his ribs hurt. All at once he started to shake and he could not stop. He climbed painfully down.

Where's *Intrepid*?

William gestured to the brush. The black leaves like twists of iron on their cold branches. The pieces of the basket under the bracken and grass. Then the faces of the soldiers were dissolving in the gloom as they dragged the aerostat clear. He saw a waggon and spectral horse standing some feet away and he said, Mr. Spaar didn't come?

Clovis had lit a cigar and was smoking quietly and the light was craggy and grooved on his face and flared at each breath and now he paused. He's not here?

Sir?

Spaar's not with you?

He was going for help. He didn't find you?

We clocked you as you went down, lad, Clovis said. We been on the hunt all afternoon.

William could hear the rasp of the silk envelope dragging through the grass, the sharp breathing of the men at their labours in the shadows of that place. No one spoke. All was hushed. The trees surrounding were smoke from some horror that would not dispel and all he saw seemed to wither in that strange darkness and waste away to dust, as all things must in time, to waste away and be washed from this earth.

William was looking at the columnist feeling an unaccountable sadness and he moistened his lips and coughed into his handkerchief and looked away. How many of us were there?

If you can recall.

I can recall. You don't forget a thing like that. You try not to. Working with my father in the Secret Service were a few of his earliest operatives. Timothy Webster, he was good. He was in charge of the field agents. They captured him as a spy in Richmond in eighteen sixty-two and hanged him as a spy. John Scully and Pryce Lewis were arrested as well. Lewis was an Englishman and fearless. They'd been sent south to try to get Webster back up north. William fell quiet and his thorny eyebrows drew together and then he looked up and said, My father loved all three of those men. There was some talk about Lewis and Scully betraying each other in prison but he never believed it. Who else. Sam Bridgeman was a fine detective but a drunk. He came to the Secret Service from the New York police and knew the business. John Babcock could hit a hawk in flight at two miles. Seth Paine got so reckless as the war went on that my father thought he wanted to get caught. I remember him rolling up his sleeves and showing me his arms, they were covered in scars of his own making. Cigar burns, knife cuts. I think he liked it. Ben Porter and his wife, they were escaped slaves, excellent operatives. The female agents as well. Kate Warne and Hattie Lawson. My father always believed in those two. He and Katie were close for years.

She was writing fast as he spoke and then she looked up and said, What about Mr. Thiel?

Gustav. Yes. He worked for my father too. That's where he learned the trade.

He later became a rival.

William shrugged.

Do you remember any of the balloonists, Mr. Pinkerton?

The aeronauts. Yes. There was Thaddeus Lowe, I never had much to do with him. He fell sick with malaria during the Seven Days but I'd seen him in camp before that talking with my father. Always wore black, a long black moustache, hollow eyes. Looked like a carnival magician. I think I was a little bit afraid of him. His father, Clovis, was like a twisted nail. William smiled. Like he got pulled out of something wrong and never put right. I liked him. There were others. Jim Allen, he had been ballooning since the fifties. I think he hated Lowe and Lowe hated him. They were all like that, big egos, like actors. There was a Negro I liked very much, Cleveland Coombs. He was a part of the ground crew. I don't know what happened to him after the war.

She was watching him closely. He passed a finger and thumb over his eyelids flickering soft as a moth. What you remember is not how it was, he said. I know that much. I close my eyes and I see it and I know it wasn't like that.

There was a sadness in her, too. He wondered just what sort of person she was, what sort she would grow to be. He would not live to see it.

He said, I wish I could have been more help to you.

No, honestly. This has been very helpful.

But you can't write it.

I beg your pardon?

Not like it needs to be written. You can't tell it direct.

She inclined her head. I'm not sure my editors want the unadorned truth.

Or your readers.

Or my readers.

He was gripping the edges of his armrests and he could feel the trembling in his liverspotted hands. He had grown so old. The war that was raging in France was not his war, the world it would build would not be his world. There was no one left from his world. His brother Robert, his wife, John Shore. His father. All of them gone. He looked up at her and said, Well. I'll say good night to you now.

She glanced at him in surprise. Oh, yes. I mean, of course. It's late for an old man.

I shouldn't have kept you.

He stood, he dumped the ship's blanket on the seat of his chair. Waved a gruff hand at her. Never mind it. Be sure to mention the Agency. Say something nice about it.

She smiled but remained sitting.

Was there anything else? he asked.

She was studying him with her clear eyes and her legs were crossed prettily before her and she looked youthful and alive and her black hair fell in a slash across her face. A shadow crept over the floor like a living thing. She said to him, There's just one more thing I wanted to ask you.

What is it.

It's not about the war. Not exactly.

What is it.

It's about someone your father used to know.

He stared at her impatiently.

There is a boy, Mr. Pinkerton, mentioned in several accounts. A Mr. Edward Shade—

*Men Who
Do Not Exist*

1885

LONDON

TWENTY-FOUR

All the while deceived, William thought.

Shaking as he thought it. He had been all the while deceived. He had trudged the darkest alleys of Billingsgate, clasped the man's hand in friendship, toasted with blood on his knuckles to fathers lost, all the while deceived. Late that night after the seance he had stood at his washbasin, brooding, raking his fingers over his face, amazed, wrathful. Going over it all in his mind to see if it made sense. It did not make sense. And yet he was sure. How Foole must have been laughing. In the morning he walked the great high streets and remembered against his own desire Foole's quiet smile. He had liked the man. That seemed almost the worst of it. In the afternoon he rode through Hyde Park under an icy blue sky where the gas balloons ascended and descended on their tethers and the ladies gripped the railings in exhilaration, their white coats winking open on the frozen lawns, and he thought of Foole standing over the Saracen, close to weeping. There were leafless trees branched and cold like capillaries in the lungs of the dead and William saw this from the open seat of a rented carriage with a blanket over his knees and a scarf at his throat and he understood he had been waiting for something that had at last arrived.

Shade.

He was careful. Over the following days he met his few underworld contacts in dingy courts, he lurked in the file closet at Scotland Yard with his coat off and shirt sleeves rolled.

Adam Foole did not exist, had no record, no listed address. He found nothing on the gunsmith's apprentice Albert either. An old file on Rose Utterson's illegal activities in the Raj had been marked in pencil in the margins from some background check years ago. He traced the brother Gabriel through court records, the public registers. One name among the solicitor's clients caught his eye, gave him pause. He did not know if either sibling was a part of Foole's flash life or whether they knew the truth about him but the one seemed likely and the other increasingly possible.

At his hotel he rang the bell at the front desk then stilled it and waited. The concierge was a man his own age with a neck too thin for his uniform's collar. A telegram from Chicago had been misfiled days ago and he now sat himself in the lobby under one of the palms with the roar of the street coming through the opening and closing doors and the cold air in bursts and he opened and read it at once. It began: *Mr Pinkerton, sir; man described is Japheth Fludd. V dangerous. 1879: assault of off-duty constable, sentenced 5 yrs, Sing Sing. Served full term. Approach with caution. No record of priors. No known aliases. No known accomplices. Employer Fool not known to us (alias?).*

Hours passed, days passed. A tension began to thrum in him, like a rope drawn tight. He ate enormous dishes of roast beef, fried bacon, curried potatoes. He circled the idea of Foole with a languid predatory intent. A red sun sank into the rooftops, the city burned on in the dying light. The man Shade was out there somewhere. He thought of his father, he thought of his wife. What would Margaret say?

She would tell him: Go on get the bastard and be done with it.

It was Sunday and he was on his way to Scotland Yard when by chance he saw the Utterson woman again. He stood clutching a paper cone of roasted chestnuts in one hand and did not at first know her and then all at once he did and he crushed the paper without realizing it and changed direction and began to walk behind her. He did not care if she saw him and he walked with his eyes glowering and a cane in his fist like a cudgel.

It was the first of February, and cold. There was about her now none of the Raj, none of the exotic or otherwordly. Dressed in a mauve dress long out of fashion but elegant still with its declining bustle and long thick skirts. A white hat with thick pelican feathers and purple flowers arranged at one side, a white winter shawl wrapped at her shoulders. Pale kidskin gloves clutching a parcel. This she shifted into one elbow as she gestured to an omnibus heading east and took up her skirts and stepped out into the street and climbed inside.

He followed.

Catching the ladder as the vehicle lurched into motion and hoisting himself up onto the freezing roof and sitting astride the bench there. A conductor swaddled in scarf and woollens folded one elbow up onto the roof and William paid him and the man vanished back into the cabin below. The sky was grey, the air bitter on his face. The omni creaked, rolled on towards Bishopsgate. He huddled into himself, fumbled for the chestnuts.

She climbed down just as the omni turned south and William clambered down after her, his knuckles frozen, his ears chapped. She turned up Gaunt Street threading her slow way home and it was a different borough by daylight, the drab slouching of the shopfronts and the chimneys black in the cold.

He caught her at the railing of her front steps.

Miss Utterson, he called.

He said it only the once. She looked older without the kohl at her eyes, her cheeks raw from the chill. Seeing him something passed across her face and was gone, a kind of impatience, and she glanced up at her house.

Mr. Pinkerton, she said. How very unexpected.

A coal waggon passed noisily in the street and a maid with a shawl at her shoulders came down from the next house and ran a few steps after it and then gave up.

If I could have a word, William said.

She shook her head and studied the brown paper parcel in her hands as if considering and then she said, I'm rather busy, Mr. Pinkerton. Is it something I could answer briefly?

William smiled a sharp tight smile.

I see, she said. Her face had hardened.

Perhaps we could speak inside, he said.

Perhaps not. What do you imagine you know, sir?

I imagine nothing.

She began to turn away.

What I know is that Utterson is no longer your legal name. He watched her face as he said it but she betrayed nothing. He said, I know two members of your household staff were arrested for theft in Bombay in eighteen seventy-one. I know the charges disappeared or were made to disappear. That same year your husband relinquished his post in the government and went away and you returned to London alone.

A sad affair, she said. I fail to see its interest—

I know, William continued, that your brother represents clients of wealth and dubious character. And that among them is a Martin Reckitt, who has retained your brother at a handsome salary for ten years. I know that his business is not only legal.

She regarded him with expressionless eyes.

Miss Utterson?

Her gloved fingers left four dark prints on the frosty railing, like the marks of a ghost.

You have my attention, sir, she said.

I arrived in the year of the Mutiny, she said.

Sitting with her legs tucked up under her on the low cushions, turning a tiny silver spoon in her tea.

That was a terrible time. Fear is a terrible thing, Mr. Pinkerton.

It was a strange room, a room built for heat and pleasure. The drapes pulled back, alabaster moulding on the ceiling. Panels of gold wallpaper afire in the daylight, red fish huge and unmoving in the water at his feet like smooth glittering stones of ammolite.

It started in the North, she said. I was supposed to have been there. I was meant for Delhi. But when I arrived the most horrific stories were just beginning to reach the South. Englishwomen wandering in the roads without clothes, nothing to eat, drinking water from the ditches. Men cut into pieces in the streets. Babies speared and thrown into the rivers.

Studying him with eyes black and flat and reflective, obsidian stones, utterly smooth and without depth. The shadows at the edges of the room liquid and slow. He felt his blood thicken, a languid heat rising in him like sleep.

We heard the most incredible stories. One about a young memsahib, a Miss Wheeler, who was taken from the slaughter at Cawnpore. They had been under siege in the barracks for months. Children were shot going to the well in the yard. Women were dying from disease. At last the survivors were offered safe passage down the Ganges but when they launched the boats the Indians opened fire. Murdered all the men except a single boat, which escaped. The Indians came down to the river and waded in and bayoneted the babies and burned the school-girls alive and took the women onto the riverbank to divide amongst themselves.

William set his tea down on a low table beside his cushion.

I appall you, she said.

No.

No? You are no stranger to atrocities, of course. She nodded. This woman, this Miss Wheeler. She was the daughter of the general defending the barracks and she watched her father be killed. She was taken by a local sepoy, a powerful man. It was said that in the night she rose and took up the sepoy's sword and sawed off his head and then went from room to room in his house cutting off the heads of his sleeping wife and children and then she went out into the yard and hurled herself down a well. You cannot imagine, sir, the pride we felt hearing that. I think about it now and I feel ashamed, quite ashamed. The Indians

were inhuman, absolutely savage. But so were we. Fanning ourselves on our porches while the soldiers stood guard around us.

She took a sip of the tea cooling it with her tongue and
turned the cup in her long pale fingers as if it had no handle.
She said, A few years ago an Italian priest who had been in the
Raj came here to call. He was returning from his time there and
soon to set out for Ireland, of all places. I cannot fathom how
they do things in Rome. He told me he had been at the deathbed
of a woman in Cawnpore who spoke flawless English and that
she confessed she was, in fact, the notorious Miss Wheeler. It
seems she had lived all those years in perfect happiness with her
sepoy. The sepoy was still alive, so were his wife and children.
In fact he had wept at Miss Wheeler's death and paid for an
elaborate funeral. I thought he had made some mistake, that
priest. But he had not made a mistake. None of what we had
known then was true, you see.

William felt his eyes grow dark. I have something to ask
you, he said. It's not about the dead.

Everything is about the dead.

He was looking at her with a fixed intensity, his big scarred
hands loose in his lap. He said, softly, How did you learn what
he is? Did he confess it to you?

Who? Confess what?

The truth of your Mr. Foole, Miss Utterson. His past.

A doubt flickered at her lips. This is why you have come?
She sipped at her tea. Adam Foole is a man of honour, Mr.
Pinkerton. His secrets are his own. I would not wish to disturb
them. And I should not betray them if I knew them.

You've already done that. I want to know why.

She narrowed her eyes. You are referring to the sitting?
Something the guide said? That was not me, Mr. Pinkerton. A
spirit spoke through me. You witnessed it yourself.

I witnessed nothing.

She passed a long jewelled finger over her eyes. Adam was
kind to me once, a long time ago, in Madrid. I sat for him because
I wished to repay his kindness. I wished to ease his grief.

By deceiving him.

By bringing him peace. Not all deceptions are false, Mr. Pinkerton. Sometimes it is through untruth that we stand in the light of a greater truth.

A greater truth, William muttered. When did he first tell you about Shade?

Shade?

Edward Shade, yes.

Who is he?

William studied her. Perhaps you don't understand the seriousness of my interest in your Mr. Foole, Miss Utterson.

She inclined her head. But I do understand your interest in our gathering last Tuesday. You wish to make sense of it, do you not? You wish to know why Adam left the circle in such distress.

I know why he left.

I beg your pardon.

William glared, suddenly impatient. My friends at Scotland Yard do not approve of fraudulent actions conducted in the name of religion, Miss Utterson. It would be a shame if they were to become interested in your activities.

I think it time you took your leave, Mr. Pinkerton.

He did not move. I can think of several Agency operatives with experience in exposing carnival frauds, he said. The newspapers find it always a compelling story.

She studied him a long dignified moment and her face seemed very old to him then, as if she were staring down a century of grievances. She said, gravely, It is not a fraud, sir. You would be acting wrongly in persecuting us. We harm no one.

He set his hands open on his knees. How is it done? How do you manage it?

I don't know what you mean.

The deceit.

She regarded him with a wounded expression. There is no deceit. Not as you mean it. I am in a kind of sleep when it occurs. A waking sleep. I do not remember much of what is conveyed. She ran a pale fingertip lightly over the rim of her saucer, frowning. Sometimes, it is true, we must induce a state of wonder in our sitters. Sometimes there is resistance. The circle must be receptive, you see, if the worlds are to align.

Show me, he said.

I cannot sit for you. Not at present.

Show me, he said again, and there was a violence in his tone that had not been there before.

She began to shake her head but she stopped and looked at him. Show you what?

The trick. How you do it.

She held his eye. A long moment passed. Then she rose and led him along the hall and through the parlour and into the seance room. It felt smaller, shabbier in the day. The bare table, the bell box, the chairs tidily tucked up under. The ceiling was low, stained by water. It might have been a storage closet once, it might have been a pantry.

The summoning is not a trick, she said. That is real.

The bell in the box, he said with a gesture. Is there a string? Is that how you ring it?

She hesitated as if arguing something with herself and then she sat down and slowly unlaced her boot. She showed him her toes in their stocking and then she sat rigidly in her chair and raised her leg without altering her body's position and she held her foot under the middle of the table.

There is a magnet in the box, she said. I wear a second magnet on my toe. It sets off a contraption that rings the bell.

That's why the table is so small. So you can reach the bell.

Yes.

That's why you work in this room. Only a small table can fit.

Yes.

William prowled slowly around the table studying the woman seated there. He said, almost tenderly, Is there no truth at all in what you do?

She looked up at him. All of this is just the theatre, Mr. Pinkerton. We do not believe what we believe for rational reasons. But the spirits are real. The other world is real.

Who would accept that? Seeing this?

Sometimes the spectacle is necessary. Sometimes we must be kept in awe in order to find our faith. Is the Christian church any different? Turning wine into blood?

William set his big fists on the table. Explain Ignatius to me, he said slowly. Why did you choose that name?

I chose nothing, Mr. Pinkerton, she said, her voice taking on an edge of impatience. He came unbidden. Sometimes a guide can frighten a sitter. Ignatius, I understand, frightened Adam. I do not know why.

William thought of his own Ignatius, the balloonist Spaar, also a Virginian. He thought of the coincidence in it all. But he knew spiritualists and frauds turned such coincidences to their favour and he did not speak of it. You said Port Elizabeth, he said instead. What happened in Port Elizabeth? What were you referring to?

Not me, Mr. Pinkerton. Ignatius.

Who was the *she*?

There was something in Rose Utterson's face, a flare of pleasure, when she said, Ah. But you know the answer to that already.

Charlotte Reckitt.

She nodded. Port Elizabeth is where he met her.

In South Africa? William took a step towards her. Why was he there? What year was that?

She turned her face away. I've said enough, she said. Ask Adam if you wish to know more. His heart is his own.

This last was said with a wounded dignity and William understood all at once the conflicted nature of her feelings. She was in love with Foole. And yet for all that he did not think she knew the truth of the man. But that would mean some other had indeed manifested in her that night and this he could not accept either.

He watched her but she did not flinch. At last he said, quietly, Adam Foole's real name is Edward Shade, Miss Utterson.

That is nothing to me.

It's your Mr. Foole's deepest secret.

Hardly.

But she had spoken this last too quickly, too dismissively. William cracked his knuckles under his thumbs one by one and studied the medium's still face. My father hunted Shade his entire life, he said. He never found him. He's the reason I'm in London.

Your father is?

Shade is.

Something stirred in her then. A slow reptilian look from under the woman's eyelids. You expend your efforts on the wrong pursuits, Mr. Pinkerton. They will not bring you happiness.

Is that your professional opinion?

The presence with us that night, the guide spirit. Ignatius. He knew you also. She raised her eyebrows. He sensed a loved one near him, Mr. Pinkerton.

William shook his head, he studied her with his cold eyes. Be careful, Miss Utterson.

Death is hardest for those it leaves behind. Have you lost someone of late?

You know I have.

Ah. Your father.

It would have been in the papers.

She regarded him with sudden pity. Longing is the source of our unhappiness. But it does not need to be. Why not leave this pursuit of Edward Shade, let yourself believe? Your father, sir, is at peace.

My father. William put on his hat, turned to go, turned back. My father's not at peace, he said angrily. Not yet. But he will be soon. And you can tell your Mr. Foole that for me.

TWENTY-FIVE

Foole drifted, half drained, through the days following the seance. He stood in his sleeping robe staring at the winter traffic turning off Piccadilly, he walked his halls in velvet bed slippers, he spoke little, he waited. Yes that was the sense of it, waiting.

As if something were coming.

Slowly his thoughts coalesced. He dreamed the same dream three nights running, a dream of doors opening upon a solitary figure in a dripping chesterfield, hands clasped at his back. That figure was William Pinkerton. Edward, Pinkerton said. She is here. He would wake startled, glaring at the shapes in his room, recognizing nothing. After the seance he had stormed out into the darkness of Bishopsgate with his frock coat open to the weather and his knotted fingers working at the air. Striding past several cab stands unseeing before at last pausing, retracing his steps, hailing his passage home. Oblivious of the cutthroats in doorways, the drunks wheeling through the unlit streets. Rose's voice had thickened into the voice of Ignatius Spaar. That was the fact of it. Spaar: aeronaut, spy, victim of Allan Pinkerton's wartime ambitions, a name mouldering now somewhere in the marshy earth of northern Virginia. Darkly in Foole's mind the possibilities turned. Rose Utterson and her brother lived capable of any deceit, he knew, even of those they shared affection for, and both were formidable seekers of other men's secrets. If the Uttersons had learned of his past and set out to ruin him in front of Pinkerton they could not have managed it more effectively. But Foole himself had stared down ghosts in his childhood and he believed in the singular viciousness of the dead. The living, ruthless though they be, were always tempered by self-interest. Rose dared not risk him without risking her brother, herself. Not so the dead.

He brooded. On the third morning Fludd heard him out, all menace. So Pinkerton knows, the giant said at last, combing his fingers through his beard. He knows, an it were them Uttersons what told it?

Well. Or Spaar's ghost.

Bollocks to that. Fludd rubbed at his wrists in the darkness, as if to ease an ache. You know what needs doin.

Foole met his eye. Not that.

Can't keep smoke in a bottle forever, Mr. Adam. It's like to get out, one way or another.

But Foole turned back to watch the orange fog seethe in the street below, saying nothing more. He would not condone murder, would sooner flee the city than take that course. He was remembering again how the circle had hushed, Pinkerton creaking in his seat to stare, his grip slackening in uncertainty in Foole's own. She is here, Edward, the spirit had murmured. Foole had staggered to his feet in horror, speechless, uprighting all. The stupidity of it appalled him now. No, the detective would not need long to disentangle the truth.

And then? Foole clutched the blanket tighter at his chest, glared. The fog crept past.

And then the bastard would come for him.

He had been fourteen years old, condemned for treason, dressed in rags and shoeless and stinking, the first time a Pinkerton had come for him. He had not known it then, of course. He stumbled out of his meeting with Major Allen of the Secret Service of the Potomac with his wrists unshackled and his legs free, thinking he had just met an old soldier, nothing more. He kept peering about as if some mistake had been made but if so the mistake was his. In a filthy cell back at Camp Barry a pallet of straw held his shape where he had lain now for weeks awaiting his death and he did not believe such a death had been averted. He was taken downstairs in that house by the burned man in his frock coat and seated in front of a fire and there he waited alone. He looked at the windows, looked at the door. He did not know if it was some trick to test him, if he was being watched. Ten minutes passed. An enormous black man with monstrous hands and a neck thick as a dray horse's came in, went out, came back. Edward watched him fearfully. The man was coatless, a pistol holstered backward at each hip like a gunslinger. He wore a yellow vest with a gold watch chain pinned to the lapel and a heavy gold ring on his left hand and when he spoke Edward glimpsed two gold front teeth.

Mr. Edward Shade, he said, pausing on each syllable, his voice a bass rumble. I guess you best come with me. But he stood sizing Edward up, not moving. Ain't much to you, is there. I suppose that be you own sweet luck, boy.

Edward did not understand his meaning. He got to his feet then followed the monster outside into darkness and they crossed the muddy street without speaking. His bare soles ached in the cold, he felt light-headed, he trembled in hunger. The man led him down a side alley and through an unlocked gate and knocked twice at the door of a lightless building and the door opened.

Go on, in you get. Ain't no changin you mind now.

It was a two-roomed safe house for Secret Service operatives and almost totally empty. The scarred man Edward had seen at his meeting with Major Allen was in the first room, fixing bedding to a small folding cot in one corner, and he rose and regarded the boy with his ravaged face.

It all right, Mr. Spaar, the black man murmured. Go on with you.

The burned man, Spaar, opened his mouth in a stiff expression. Just you don't better kill him tonight, Ben, he said. Not like the last one.

Ben grinned. Oh I don't reckon that be necessary. Ain't that right, Mr. Shade?

Spaar made a strange sound, low in his throat, a laugh. Don't look so frightened, kid. The Major's the one you should be afraid of, not Mr. Porter here.

Ain't that the truth.

Edward thought of the Major, his scorched eyes, leaning back in shadow.

You cross the Major, Spaar said, tugging at the brim of his hat and pausing at the door, then you'll know what fear is. He wrapped a scarf over his mouth and nose until only his eyes showed, he drew on a tight pair of gloves. Then he opened the door and went out into the cold.

The man Ben had settled himself on a ladderback chair against the wall. Go on, he said, best get youself to sleep. You life about to get complicated, boy.

You just plan on sitting there all night?

I do.

Edward did not undress but crawled under the covers of the cot and felt it shudder under his weight, the sudden slouching give of it disorienting. He closed his eyes, his head swam. Does the army even know where I am? he said. With an enormous struggle, he cracked an eye. Is this even legal?

Aw, now. Country's at war, boy.

The country can go to hell, he mumbled.

Ben smiled, his gold teeth gleaming in the low light. You still ain't gettin it. You don't belong to the United States Army no more. You belong to Major Allen now. And the Major ain't no part of nothin. From this night on, if you goin to die, boy, you be dyin for him.

Edward closed his eyes, he opened his eyes, the darkness had deepened. He shifted onto his side, folded his hands between his warm knees. Ben was still awake, still watching.

How much is he paying you? Edward asked sleepily.

Benjamin Porter sat hulking in the corner beside the door, fists folded on his knees, face lost in shadow. Payin me?

I owe the man my life, he said quietly. It ain't a damn question of nickels.

All week Foole did nothing. Grief was at work within him and for almost the first time in his adult life he did not know his next move. Charlotte's death was no less fixed and yet he had no further leads on her killer. The Saracen worked to kill only himself, no other. Charlotte's uncle withered in a barren cell at Millbank, betraying no one, dying day by day among the rats and beetles. Pinkerton, clever, brutal, would care nothing now for her murder. None of them had any hand in her destruction. Before sleep Foole would smudge the pier glass with his fingers, mar his own reflection. Each night looking a little older, more haggard, than the last. At noon on Thursday he sat alone at his lunch and took out Charlotte's letter and ran a whorled thumb over the signature, going through all the ways he had failed her. On Friday he held that letter over a lit candle and turned it this way and that as the flame ate towards his fingers. Blaming her. All things must end, he told himself, not quite believing it. On Saturday he stalked the rooms of his house and stood in the kitchen listening to the rain on the window, alone. There was a clatter and then Mrs. Sykes materialized in the scullery door, a bucket of soapy water at her feet, her cautious grey eyes filled with pity. And he understood: Charlotte was gone. Nothing would bring her back.

Mrs. Sykes shooed him down, set a kettle on the stove for tea. Revenge never set a scale to balance, Mr. Foole, she said. Man like you ought to know that by now.

He thought of Allan Pinkerton, the old detective's relentlessness. He looked away.

I lost my mister to the loop a lifetime ago, now. Not a day goes by I don't think of it. Mrs. Sykes pressed two scalded hands to the nape of her neck, tired. But I didn't never stop my own livin on account of it. It weren't for me to do. If you take my meaning.

Foole squinted at her as if through a blurred glass.

I had my Hettie, sir.

Yes, he said slowly. Well.

There's those what need you right here, she said. An it ain't too late to save them.

You mean Molly.

I mean Molly, aye. She pressed her chin down into the soft of her throat. And I mean your own self too.

It might have been Mrs. Sykes's words, or the passing of the days, or some third thing. But he awoke the next morning with a clear head and a coldness taking shape inside him. His grief and shame were still there but had dulled. He sat with Molly and Fludd in the Emporium, a low coal fire burning in the grate, trying to talk it through. Molly still knew nothing of his life as Edward Shade and Foole looking past her glimpsed Fludd's murderous expression and turned away. The giant had wanted it told, he knew, from the moment they left Pinkerton in that tunnel under the Thames. Had thought it unfair for the girl not to know, to be a part of their crew, at risk, in peril, but oblivious to it. It ain't any way to manage a crew, Mr. Adam, Fludd had said. Now Molly scratched at the scabbed back of one hand, stared at the fire. Foole started to tell what Fludd had already heard, the account of the seance, its implications. But when it came time to explain the story of Edward Shade he glanced at Fludd and paused and then he left it out, surprised at his own hesitation.

Molly listened to the rest, disbelieving, swearing a blue streak under her breath. Leaning against a shelf with her arms folded. Pinkerton? Jesus.

I could gill him, Fludd suggested quietly. He turned a knife in the firelight. Could slick his ribs, be done with it.

Molly snorted. Right, an get every bloody beak in the city up for blood. Pinkerton's not just any blueleg. A touch like that like to get us more trouble than ever.

The giant shook his shaggy head. We disappear then.

Need blunt to disappear, Jappy.

So we pull a job. Are we bloody flash touches, us three, or not?

An what job would that be?

Any job.

Just scoop up a bucket of blunt an be gone, is that it? Takes months to set up a grift. You been in the jug so long you forgotten how it goes. She paused, her cheek lined in the silver light of the window. What's he up into, anyway? How do Pinkerton even know we're flash?

Balls of brass, kid. Mr. Adam? It's your carriage, we're just ridin it.

Foole, brooding, said nothing.

Mr. Adam.

Slowly Foole lifted his eyes, he met Fludd's gaze. The fire smouldered in the grate. After a moment he nodded imperceptibly. Tell her the rest, he said.

Mr. Adam's got a history with the Pinkertons, Fludd said abruptly.

Aye, we all do. Then Molly bit at her lip, glared. What history?

With the old man himself. Allan.

Molly was silent.

Allan Pinkerton were a major in the United States Army, during their war, Fludd said. Mr. Adam served under him before deserting. Just a kid. Not much older than you. The giant scooped at his beard, glanced at Foole, at Molly. What do the name Edward Shade mean to you, kid?

She shrugged, suspicious. Why? What's he?

You never heard him talked about? In the flash houses like?

Bloody hell. Just tell it already.

Edward Shade, Fludd said, is the greatest thief in the smoke. Never been caught, never been touched. Half in the flash don't even think he's real, other half never even heard of him. There's those in the Yard what think he's a folk tale. But the Pinkertons believe. Shade's the jake William Pinkerton come to London to find, on account of his father. Old Allan hunted Shade for twenty years. It were a kind of obsession for him, like. Made him half crazy, by some accounts. Blamed Shade for any theft he couldn't solve, an even some he could. An now his son is at to seein it through. Fludd leaned forward, the chair creaking. Pinkerton had it that Charlotte Reckitt known Shade once. He were here to ring her, nothin else.

Molly nodded slowly. Then this Shade's to blame for what happened to her.

Somethin like that, aye.

So we knick him then. An clear ourselves with Pinkerton in the bargain. He'd give us a pass if we sewed up this Shade, I reckon. She looked up. How do we find him?

Findin him ain't the problem. Fludd paused, frowned. You an me is both lookin at him, kid.

Molly blinked, glanced uncertainly across at Foole in the firelight.

Fludd rose to his feet. Meet the mysterious Edward Shade, kid. In the mighty flesh.

Molly stared past the giant, her face clouding, then suddenly fierce. Edward Shade? That's your name, Adam, for real?

Lower your voice, kid.

You always said the past never mattered, she said, ignoring the giant. You always said it were today what makes us us. You an your bloody stories. She whirled on Fludd. Pinkerton had a blood feud with him an you never thought to tell me? Edward bloody Shade my arse.

You can see now why we got to get out of London, Fludd said quietly.

She rubbed at her face, set a hand shakily on a chair. Only place to hide from the Pinkertons, she said, is the grave.

Now Foole looked up from the fire, his eyes sharpening.

Not even there, he said.

At the sound of his voice her expression again hardened. He could see her shock, the baffled hurt of it, but he offered no apology. His past, for god's sake, was his own.

You're both right, he said softly. We need blunt to clear our debts, get out of the city. He interlaced his fingers and he looked at his companions with a black expression. And I know what we can steal to make that happen.

Edward had awakened on that first morning as an operative of the Secret Service of the Potomac with his head aching and a smell of fresh coffee in the air. Sunlight had tangled itself in the curtains. He was alone. Someone had left a tray on the man Ben's empty chair and when he lifted the silver lid he saw buttered toast, scrambled eggs, three thick slices of ham. He ate, he wiped his hands on his shirt, he sat on the cot thinking. At last he rose and opened the door and stepped out into the alley.

A black woman was taking down some washing from a line and she paused over her basket and regarded him and he looked past her for any sign of Major Allen's men. But then the woman snorted and addressed him by name and he looked at her again, astonished, and she laughed.

Shoot, she said. You never reckoned the Major was just goin to leave you lonesome, now?

She set two fingers to her mouth and whistled and a moment later the huge black operative, Ben, came out of a door down the alley, wiping his mouth on his sleeve, his pistols and belt slung over one shoulder. Ben looked bigger, more scarred, in the daylight, his nose flattened to a crooked angle as if it had been badly set years ago, his huge hands callused and rough.

You eaten then? he said in his deep voice.

But did not wait for an answer and only leaned down and kissed the black woman on her forehead, and then shoved past Edward towards the street with a grunt that he should follow.

And so began Edward's training. He did not see Major Allen. As the days passed he learned the slow dangerous art of being a spy. Ben instructed him first on how to conduct a rough shadow, how to follow a mark and be seen so that the mark could know he was being tailed. The trick, Ben said, was to remain aloof, not to lose the mark but not to approach so near that you could be confronted. When Edward asked what to do if he was challenged, the man shrugged. Make the bastard nervous, he growled. With the scarred man Spaar, Edward learned to eavesdrop on conversations in cafés, in restaurants, in train stations. With Ben's wife Sally he worried away at different accents, catching a Virginia lilt almost at once. On his fifth day Spaar seated him before a mirror with two dozen electric bulbs blazing around it and pulled out a carpet bag filled with sticks of chalk and paint trays and dyes and described the art of makeup and disguise. Edward learned to rely not on the altered appearance but on the physical gesture that would distract a person's attention. He learned to walk quickly while appearing casual, to move slowly while appearing to hurry. He learned that nothing is as it seems, and that to trust one's senses is to trust a treacherous thing. Every night Ben sat broodingly at the door to bar his way, hinting at Major Allen's furies, his rage, his impatience, his intolerance of failure or weakness of any kind. In the second week Ben worked on Edward in a makeshift pugilist's ring in a depot warehouse near the rail yards. He knocked Edward down, knocked him down again. When the boy cried out Ben cracked his knuckles in disgust.

You think the Major goin to show you mercy?

Edward was on his knees, the breath knocked out of him.

Get up. I seen the Major take out a man's fingernails with a hot poker. You get on up now. You don't want to make the wrong impression, boy, when he test you tomorrow.

Edward raised his bruised face. Tomorrow?

Ben grimaced. I said get youself up, boy. We losin daylight here.

Foole's idea was simple: steal a painting.

But not just any painting, he said, watching his companions in the firelight. It's called *The Emma*. And it's set to command thirty thousand pounds at auction.

Fludd gave a low whistle. Thirty thousand pounds, he muttered.

We could work it back for a third of its value and be gone without any warrant ever being issued.

Molly, sullen, frowned. You want us to chalk out a bloody painting? A painting, *Edward*?

Foole studied her until she blushed and looked away. He held up a hand, folding down his fingers one by one. An art heist could be set up and executed quickly. And it had never before been done, to his knowledge. The reason was obvious: a work of art of any value would be impossible to fence, being too identifiable. But this would make the target an easy one in that the security would be minimal. And they could negotiate the painting back to its owner at a fraction of its value, say, ten thousand pounds, in exchange for the dropping of any charges. This particular painting, this *Emma*, had made the front page of the *Times* at least once a week for months now, and its noto-riety would ensure its value. They would employ their solicitor, Gabriel Utterson, to attend the exchange in their stead and negotiate on their behalf, as legal representative.

Utterson, Fludd scowled. You mean to trust him again? After everything?

We've worked together fourteen years. Foole withdrew from inside his frock coat a folded sheet of newsprint and smoothed it out and passed it across to the giant. It was an article on the painting. I don't muddy the waters, Japheth, when it comes to business, he said. It's not a matter of trust. It's a matter of profits. And Gabriel understands profit.

Molly glared darkly at a spot in the carpet, hardly listening.

Fludd shrugged. Right. Supposin we agree. Supposin we reckon this a live possibility, now. What do it require?

Just us. No outsiders. But I haven't cleared it all in my head. We'll need to know the building. Hours, routines. We'll need an approach and an exit. We'll need to know the gallerist and his resources. His name is George Farquhar, he's a wealthy man already by all accounts. Famous in all the right circles. We'll want details, specifics. How he spends his leisure time. His wife's relations, if he's married. Where he lives.

Timeline? Fludd prompted.

Foole rubbed at his whiskers. Ten days. Maybe two weeks. Not a day longer.

Two weeks? Can't be done, Mr. Adam.

Foole looked at Molly in the gloom, he shook his head.

It has to be, he said.

Monday afternoon arrived cold but dry, the London zoological gardens deserted. Foole had sent a runner to Utterson's offices that morning and received an immediate reply. The solicitor would see him at the gardens at two o'clock. He had descended into Piccadilly for a cab with his hat and walking stick under one arm and Molly trailing sourly behind. Twisting a stubborn shoulder, solitary, quieter than usual. They walked now through the cold gardens, the two of them, a father and his daughter out for a winter stroll. A lonely keeper drifted along the paths disappearing and emerging around the shrubbery. Molly ran her fingers through the low-hanging trees leaving a trail of broken twigs. Foole said nothing. He peered up at the grey sky, glanced at the girl, shivered. The iron stakes lining the pens stood grim and dark as if stained by shadow, the cages desolate and unswept.

But there was still in the air that earthy fug of animal fear as they passed the hippopotamus pool, emptied now of its water, the walls of its tank splotched and peeling.

I ain't stupid, she said suddenly. Don't look at me like that. You never asked me along to work Utterson into the blind, *Edward*.

Stop that, Foole said.

Stop what.

Foole put out a hand, slowed her. I'm not Edward Shade, he said, his voice gentling. It's true I was, once. But that person died in the war.

That's a load of bollocking fancy talk an you know it.

He shook his head. It was a different life, he said. Like what you lived with Mrs. Sharper and her sister. Their birdie. You don't talk about her. Who you were to them.

But it ain't a bloody secret from you neither.

Foole frowned. To their left the monkey house loomed shuttered and dead. At the elephant park he stopped and leaned his elbows over the railing and looked at the ruins beyond and there was a slick of ice visible in the drained pond.

Mrs. Sharper, she cut me plenty, Molly said. But you was different, Adam. You didn't never lie to me. Not from the very first. I never asked you to tell me about your life before, it weren't mine to ask after. But— She fell quiet.

What?

She looked at him. Jappy knows you in ways I don't. It's embarrassing.

Japheth and I go back twenty years. That's a long time.

She plugged up her bottom lip, grimaced. I weren't never birdie, she muttered.

You were to little Peter.

She shook her small head, her hair in her eyes. Peter, she said. I remember how it was. How you were.

Don't you bring Peter into this.

You're right. I'm sorry.

She looked at him. I reckon the war were awful.

I could live fifty lifetimes and never get far enough from it.

He raised his eyes and saw a figure at the far side, watching them. The man wore a silk hat and a fur-lined coat buttoned high and he knew from the shape of him it was Gabriel Utterson.

Molly, he said.

But she was already looking across. You should have told me, she said quietly. That's the point.

They crunched their slow way around the enclosure, over the frozen grass.

Your office would have been warmer, Foole called.

Utterson clapped his gloves, his breath smouldering in the cold. We have a problem, sir, he announced. William Pinkerton came to the house yesterday. A quick displeased sideways glance, his gloves all at once still. I did not speak to him myself, I was occupied at the office. But Rose insists he was rather aggressive. I understand he suggested some impossible relation between you and a certain elusive thief.

He heard Molly suck in her breath and he looked angrily away. We work our own jobs, Gabriel, you know that. We bring no one in. Who does he mean?

Of course your business is your own, sir—

What thief?

—but I cannot be under scrutiny. I will not permit it.

What thief, Gabriel?

Utterson looked at him, his hard green eyes shining. William Pinkerton believes you are, you once were, the notorious Edward Shade.

Foole started to laugh, stopped. You are joking?

The solicitor's expression was blank, unreadable.

Foole blinked, glared in bafflement at the elephant enclosure beyond. What would give him such a notion? That damned seance?

Or the manner of your departure perhaps, Utterson said coldly. I did warn you. Sometimes Rose is successful. Sometimes, unfortunately, a sitter will—

What. Leave in disgust?

Break the circle. Utterson held out his open gloves, fingers splayed. Rose did not mean to have upset you.

But she didn't. It was Ignatius speaking, was it not?

Utterson's thin lips were white and crackling in the cold and Foole watched his tongue creep along their edges. We do not select the guide, sir, he said softly. We are conduits only.

Foole frowned, weighing the truth of his words. The solicitor was all falseness and cruelty but Foole could see no advantage in his betrayal. He felt Molly, tense, beside him. He knew she carried a stiletto in her boot, knew too that he himself could strike Utterson to the pavement with the knuckle of his walking stick before she could even draw. At last he nodded. You and I go back too many years, Gabriel, to play each other false. It would be too easy for either of us to ruin the other.

The threat hung in the silence between them.

You asked to meet, Utterson said at last, his distaste sinking back into the folds of his flesh, his face taking on a flushed stillness once more. What is the business?

Foole took from his pocket a small gilded notebook and flicked through the pages, stopped. There is a man of considerable social standing. He will lose an item of great value to himself soon. Whoever recovers it will need someone to negotiate its return. For a fee, of course.

Ah. Utterson's eyes were narrow, lightless. The poor gentleman. I'm pleased to hear it will have a happy ending. But I haven't accepted such work in over a year, I regret to say.

It would be for the usual percentage.

Utterson's voice was very low. I'm not in the game anymore. I'm sorry.

Foole stepped forward. I need to get out of London, Gabriel. Because of Pinkerton.

If what you tell me is true.

Utterson paused, considering. And it would be in my interest for you to absent yourself, he said slowly. It would keep Mr. Pinkerton from my affairs. But you have debts, sir, and Mr. Barr has proven most patient already. Will the job prove so profitable? His shaggy eyebrows lowered as he caught Foole's expression. Come now, I have heard of your investment loans, do not look so surprised. You must learn to live within your means, sir.

Foole frowned. This job should fix that.

It will need to reach completion rather soon, I expect.

Within the fortnight.

Utterson gave him a quick sharp look. Haste, sir, is never an ally.

Not haste, Gabriel. A window of opportunity.

Ah.

If you agree, I'll be in touch with further instructions as I know them. Standard hook and line. After the job's been executed I'll require you to reach out to the gentleman yourself, suggest a neutral location to meet. One of us will direct him to you on the day of the exchange, same as always. I expect he won't press charges.

Not if he wishes to negotiate, sir. It is illegal to buy back stolen property from declared thieves. You're certain he will co-operate?

Well. Foole peered up at the white sky. It's always easier when they do.

Just then a keeper came whistling out of the trees rolling a barrow in his arms, the wheel squeaking weirdly. He glanced bored across at them as he went then disappeared towards the monkey house. Utterson took the notebook with George Farquhar's name and street address and pocketed it and nodded to them both and then he walked swiftly back down one of the deserted paths and was lost to view.

Foole watched him go. I guess that's a yes, he said, turning to Molly. Your impression?

She glared after him. I prefer the sister.

Me too.

But I don't reckon he set you up. Not with Pinkerton, at least.

Foole nodded, brooding. That's my sense of it too, he said at last.

William Pinkerton, Molly muttered. William goddamned Pinkerton.

She stared out at the grey light in the gardens, the trees wrapped in their heavy wadding to keep out the cold like men turning into their collars. Foole set a hand on her shoulder. He felt her trembling under him like water in a ditch when a carriage rattles past and supposed it must be the cold and he thought again how young she was. Feeling a sudden impossible sadness for the world as it was.

TWENTY-SIX

William Pinkerton had been alone with his rifle in a burning canyon in New Mexico when his father fell. That was in June. He did not hear of it until eight days had passed and he had returned to Santa Fe with a man roped and trussed to his own saddle. He threw his satchel over one shoulder and did not wash the desert from his face or hands but rode at once for the railroad station and climbed aboard the first express heading east. All that long journey he stared at the passing fields feeling nothing at all and that nothing he knew would be in him for always.

The old man had fallen on the sidewalk outside his house and bit through his tongue and septicemia set in. He was dying. When William walked into the front hall out of the evening sun he was wearing a clean shirt and his face was washed but there was a ring of dirt around his collar and wrists and he was carrying his satchel still. He took off his hat in the stillness and stared at the polished furniture in shadow as if he had not seen it before.

Hello? he called.

He feared for a long moment that his father had already died. He walked the length of the hall listening to his own footsteps and opened the door to the morning room and crossed to the back porch and stood looking out. His mother was sitting stiffly on the swinging seat there. But when he let the screen door bang behind him she looked up, her face drawn, and he knew it was not yet so.

Oh, William, she said.

He stood over her and enfolded her in his arms and he held her like that and when he let her go the chains on the swing creaked. She wore a sun-faded green dress and had pinned her grey hair and she looked to William very old. He saw her glance at the house and then back at him and then she said, Did you just get in? You look hungry. Let me fix you a bite of something.

He shook his head. He was still holding his hat and he put it down and sat in a wicker chair opposite. How is he?

A shrug of her shoulder. He comes and goes. Robert's here.

From New York?

She nodded.

I came as soon as I heard, William said. I haven't even been home yet. Where are Margaret and the girls?

They were here this morning. She smiled. They've been wonderful.

William nodded.

I'd like to see him, he said.

His father was resting in the second-floor guest bedroom because of the light and when William went in he saw at once that the old man was near death. His throat was thin and corded and his chest sunken and the skin everywhere looked yellow in the evening glow. William would not have known him. He could speak only through one corner of his mouth and the words came distorted and strange. As if he were speaking through a mouthful of cotton.

Willie, his father said.

He came to the edge of the bed. How are you feeling, Pa?

A grimace. Eyes closing.

I heard you had a fall, William said.

He saw a thin tear crush out from the corner of one lid and trail down his father's temple into his thinning hair. He had never seen his father weep. He filled with pity and with something close to shame and he looked away. There was a chair beside the bed and he pulled it out and sat down. Huge and clumsy in it. He did not know what to do with his hands.

Then his father opened his eyes and stared at him and his eyes were very pale and very clear. Willie, he whispered.

I'm here.

I don't want to die. Don't let them bury me.

You're not going to die.

His father lay still and prostrate in the bed and a white sheet was across his legs like a funeral shroud and he worked his mouth and he started to tremble. William was looking at him in his frailty and terror and he wet his lips and swallowed but he did not know what to say. He was his father's son and too much so. The door stood closed behind them as if to keep the softness of the world out. It was a small room and it caught the red sunlight aslant in its windows. The big willow was green on the lawn and he could hear the gardener cutting back the rose bushes under the window. After a time the old man closed his eyes and slept and William sat on in the silence, his big hand on the old man's wrist, the bones there light as paper.

It was raining. He got down from the omni and splashed his way through the setts and crossed into Great Scotland Yard, the water seeping through the collar of his coat. Inside the doors of Back Hall he shook out his hat, brushed the beads of water from his arms. The floor was puddled, slick. He made his way downstairs to the freezing records closet. In his pocket he carried the folded telegram from his offices in Chicago. Because Shade had left no trace, no record, no paperwork, William had no legal cause to pursue the man, nothing that would stand in court and not be dismissed as intimidation or harassment. What he needed was a methodical approach. His first task then must be to create a trace of the man. Then he could identify Shade the next time he transgressed.

For twenty years Shade had haunted the streets, a subterranean figure, not even a suspect in his own crimes. Some grief had divided Shade from William's father in the war, some betrayal lost now to the grave, if Shore's account could be trusted. Nearly lost, he corrected himself. There was still one at least who knew the truth of it. If only William could find him, make him confess. For he knew little more now, a month later, than he had known when Foole first approached him in that tunnel under the Thames. His father had wanted Shade held to account, true. But he did not know if his father's rage was cause enough for him, if it had ever been. There was in him, he knew, some part of his father that he would have better been without. He paused at the records door gripping the handle, scowling at his wet shoes, while two constables stumped past. Helmeted, eyeing him suspiciously. The hell with it, he thought.

He'd see Shade in shackles yet.

The records closet was a long narrow windowless room underground. Just within the door stood a cabinet with brooms and mops and a bucket and beside this a small desk and a broken chair which William suspected was used mostly by the groundsman on his night shifts. There were candles in their sconces set at the front and back of the room but they gave very little light. The rest of the room was filled with shelves piled high with papers and boxes and cabinets, all labelled in a faded brown spidery script nearly illegible now and ordered to some system long since abandoned. William had gone in that first day baffled and belligerent until a passing constable had shown him to the small cabinet with the files he was looking for and he returned there now in his search for Fludd. He was crouched on the floor when the door opened and the candles guttered sideways. He glanced up. It was Blackwell.

Mr. Pinkerton, sir, the inspector called in. I was told I might find you here. Have you a moment, sir? He shut the door, lowered his voice. It's about the Reckitt murder.

William stared. He had not given the case much thought since the seance.

Blackwell shuffled forward, brushing against the loose papers.

In his frock coat and silk hat he seemed to cramp the narrow space. You were called in to identify her, sir, were you not?

Why are you whispering?

Whispering, sir?

Speak up, man. Yes, I saw her.

Blackwell cleared his throat. And were you certain about it, sir? The identification?

What is this about, Blackwell?

The inspector frowned, uneasy. Is it possible, sir, that a mistake was made? Is it possible the dead girl is not Charlotte Reckitt?

William thought of the woman he had mistaken for Charlotte in the street several weeks past, his frantic pursuit of her through the alleys, all at once interested despite himself.

It's just that I might have found a lead, sir. From the drawing, sir.

Go on.

A publican's wife. She disappeared shortly before the body was found. Two separate men identified the drawing as bearing a resemblance. And the pub in question fits Dr. Breck's criteria, sir.

What does the husband say?

I haven't approached him yet, sir.

William smoothed his moustache. You know it's likely nothing.

Yes sir.

It's probably a mistake. You know that.

I do, sir.

Does John know?

The chief? Blackwell blinked. I haven't written to Brighton, sir, if that's your meaning.

Brighton?

The chief's in Brighton, sir. Did you not know?

What's he doing in Brighton? Holidaying?

In February, sir? Blackwell smiled stiffly as if William had made some witticism. I should think not, sir. He raised a hand to his collar but his elbow caught on a leaning stack of reports and he bent swiftly, caught and righted them. Mr. Shore isn't due back until day after next. But I wouldn't wish to waste his time, sir, if it is indeed a mistake. I have a tenement I'd like to make some inquiries at first, which she's said to have frequented. Blackwell eyed the leaning stack of reports warily then raised his face. What is it you're looking for here, sir? Might I be of assistance?

William waved a hand as if it were nothing. Did you want me to talk to him?

Mr. Shore?

The husband.

Ah. Blackwell nodded in relief. Well, sir. I should hate to go alone.

William gave the inspector a firm look. You just let me know when, he said. And then he started to turn back to his task. But Blackwell did not move and only stood peering at William in his damp clothes and William blew out his cheeks. Was there something else?

The body, sir. To be clear: you were certain when you identified it?

I thought I was. John recognized her too. And there was a neighbour brought down from Hampstead who confirmed her as well, if I remember it right. William's legs were cramping and he got now to his feet, sore, feeling his age. If it's not Charlotte Reckitt in those jars—

Sir?

—then where the hell is she?

Blackwell nodded. I was thinking, sir, rather: whose body is it, then?

William fumbled for his pipe. Well, he said. That too.

Robert was folded in his shirt sleeves over the railing when William came down to the porch from the sickroom. As his brother straightened and turned, his straw hat snared in the low-hanging oak twigs and he plicked it thornily free. The screened door banged shut. Summer hummed in the green. A dappled light was filtering through the leaves across his face and William saw how his brother had aged. He had shaved his moustache since the winter and his great round cheeks looked tired and when he smiled his lips were thinner, his jowls slacker. William had still not washed the travel dirt from his neck or wrists but Robert came across and hugged him with a great fierce embrace all the same. He could smell the expensive per-fumed aftershave at his brother's throat and feel his brother's shoulder blades oaring under the tailored cotton of his shirt and when he stepped back he saw a grey streak of dirt imprinted on his brother's stomach. His waist had thickened.

When did you get in? Robert said. His voice was low, sombre, as if at a sickbed.

William shrugged. Are you here alone?

For now. I need to go back to New York tonight but I'll be back Monday. I didn't want to bring the children yet. I didn't know what sort of condition he'd be in.

William nodded, squinted. The air was hot, still, rising up out of the ground. New York, he said after a moment.

Robert belled his tongue against the wall of his mouth in a gesture William recognized from their father. That mess in Hoboken with the postal employee. Our operative thinks he's found a way through it. I take it New Mexico was a success.

I didn't have to kill the fellow, if that's what you mean.

Robert smiled. That's what I meant.

The porch boards creaked under their weight. William was still gripping his brother's wrist, staring with the sober affection of an older brother who did not see as much of the younger as he would have wished. Even as a boy Robert had displayed an inky smartness William had lacked. He would as soon read as ride, would help his older brother with his schoolwork. He had graduated from Notre Dame's business college then slipped to the New York office with George Bangs and started plotting to open further branches, to widen the watchman patrol in its lucrative ordinariness. William, held up in Chicago under their father's brooding eye, famous for his drinking, gambling, camaraderie with thieves into the late hours at Mike McDonald's saloon, understood none of that. In contrast his brother was calm, cool, all profit and calculation. It had ever been so. As a boy in the summers William would wander down through the rapids in the small river below their house seeking some crooked boulder to perch upon in his hunt for the biggest trout. Robert, quiet, stolid, would in the meantime dip current-side to a proven eddy and haul out a half-dozen smaller trout. But his brother also was a man of great physical courage and together they had ridden several times the outlaw trail with loaded rifles and there was no man William would rather have at his back.

Robert was fumbling now at his pockets, as if looking for something. You'll keep him alive until I can get back? he said.

William grunted. I'll just tell him we found a lead on Edward Shade.

Edward Shade. Good lord.

There was a sound behind them. Their mother had drifted to the screened door and stood blurred in the cool of the kitchen, hands shielding her eyes. You boys hungry?

We're fine, Ma, William said.

Bobby?

Robert glanced back at her then reached up and disentangled his hat from the oak leaves. Some of that cold chicken sounds good, he called, raising his eyebrows at William as he spoke. His eyes were anxious but he smiled a low smile and shook his head and added in a conspiratorial whisper: Hell, Willie. Edward Shade? He gave a quiet laugh. You know talk like that could lead to a full recovery.

He was thinking of that afternoon as he returned through the rain to his hotel. Thinking of his brother, of the summer's red sunlight flush on his wrists, of how much he wished their father had lived to see him close in on Edward Shade. A dip in the footway outside his hotel had turned into a black puddle and a crossing sweep stood next to it, brushing the water away as

William approached and splashed through and went inside. It had been a strange finding of Shade and even now he lacked any evidence beyond his own conviction. But that conviction was like steel. Never mind Charlotte Reckitt. He did not know if Blackwell would prove correct in his investigations but in the end it did not matter. She would turn up one way or another. They always did. In the hushed lobby the concierge saw him and waved him over. A package was waiting. It was heavy and he felt the weighted slide of articles within and he stared at it a long moment before deciphering the scrawl.

It was from Sally Porter.

He made his way back up to his room and shut and locked the door and left the key in the lock and then he began to strip himself from his clothes. The maid had been in and a washtub stood half filled with water that had cooled but there was a ceramic jug of hot water stoppered up beside it on a stand and a stack of folded towels and a bar of Pears soap. He stood holding his trousers in one hand bare-legged but still in his stocking feet and he stared at the water. Then he went back into the front hall and took the package from the pier table and went into the sitting room and sat half naked with his white knees shining in the gloom.

He cut the string carefully with a knife and poured the contents onto the writing desk and withdrew the letter. The familiar slanting hand, the cramped spidery scrawl of the housekeeper Sally once had been. He sifted through the objects, a steel belt buckle, the snub-nosed twists of two bullets, a creased and folded Civil War photograph from Cumberland, 1862. William saw his father at the centre, he saw Benjamin Porter as a young man at its edge. It was an image of the agents of the Secret Service of the Potomac. He opened the letter grimly.

Dear Billy;

I am writing this to you now Because I believe you should know the truth of Edward Shade no matter how strange the fashion of it seem As it mattered to your father it is not

*Surprising it should matter to you. He would not have
wanted it that way but we do not always see eye to eye with
our kin & I know that now my Mr Porter is gone bless his
Soul. But I shall be straightforward with you as God is my
witness and hold to my own Conscience if not to his. You do
not get to choose the pattern if you do not make the quilt.*

*Yes I knew Edward Shade. He was an Agent for your
father in the Secret Service during the war which I suspect
you know & not what you came to me for But I will tell you
what I know & I hope it will help you to put some of this
behind you. Lord knows your father did not ever manage it
& my Mr Porter was loyal to him to the last.*

*You will see his Reproduction in the photograph I
include it here for You to Know him. It is not a good like-
ness I am sorry to say.*

He held up the photograph and stared from face to face. In
the front row, at one edge, a young man crouched, a boy yet, his
face blurred and eaten by time. He could make no detail from it.

*Edward being small & quick etc & having no other
object in view But his activities for your father was an ideal
operative he was a strong boy of fourteen when I knew him.
I should not call him a boy. He was smart & likeable both
& he had a gift for accents. Your father I think liked to
think of him as a kind of adopted son or that is how it
seemed to me Took him under his wing tried to teach him his
Letters etc. My Mr. Porter liked to say your father saw
Something Of Himself in the boy. They both had tempers I
can assure you that. But he always was proud of you &
Robert this had nothing to do with that.*

*It was in the second year of the War just before the
Peninsula campaign & the Union poor were then dying by
the Hundreth under the guns of the Enemy No you had not
come up from Notre Dame yet I do not believe. The sight of
it was v. dispiriting etc. Your father approached us &*

relayed that the General (that is McClellan who as you
know your father Loved more than any other man) was in
want of reliable Information behind the Confederate lines.
As we were a small group that he trusted & as Edward was
one of us When he volunteered I was present & I heard it
myself what some folk said later about coercion is a lie. No I
did not like it at the time as Edward seemed v. young to me
But it was not my place to say. 12th April being a new moon
on that night my Mr Porter & me guided Edward down
through a dry creek past the sentries & Mr Porter gave him
the horse & carriage we were riding on & sent him on his
Way we returned on our own two feet through enemy country
two Negroes in the Confederate south on our way to Fort
Monroe & that was a walk I do not care to remember.

Five weeks after he crossed over the reports ceased. As
that was the onset of a cold spring & as we heard nothing
more Your father may he Rest In Peace grew v. agitated &
anxious & sick etc. On 1st July he sent a Virginian operative
south to inquire after Edward I did not know the man well
But what I knew I did not like. Ignatius Spaar was his name
I believe you knew him some He was not a regular operative
& he never told a story about himself that was not flattering.
Well it is perhaps not kind of me to write that. That summer
the Army of the Potomac was pushed off the Peninsula & it
was a bad season to be issuing an operative we all of us considered it ill-timed even your father. When that Virginian
too disappeared after reaching Richmond I don't believe your
father was under any Illusions he had received not more
than two reports before the operation went cold. In August
Washington informed him both men Shade & that Virginian
Spaar had been arrested by the Confederate Secret Service
& were being held in a military prison.

He wet his lips. Spaar and Shade? He thought of the spirit
Ignatius whispering to Foole at the seance and he thought of
Spaar during that terrible retreat in the Peninsular Campaign.

Straggling through thigh-thickened mud, the rain lashing their hands and throats. Spaar had vanished into the treeline at Malvern Hill and William had always believed the man captured and killed by Confederate forces. Sally's account did not make sense. Unless Spaar had deliberately cut their balloon loose, had brought them down behind Confederate lines on purpose in order to get nearer Richmond. He furrowed his brow. Richmond. Where Shade was.

Billy I do not like to write about that time it is painful even now to think what that poor boy suffered. Maybe your father felt so too & that is why he did not speak of it to you. I always did Respect & Love your father he was a man of Principle & Feeling but when he heard about Edward he did not come out of his tent for several days. Were you on the front lines then? If so then you will recall how much thinner he had become & weaker etc & how there was in him a new & destructive choler I have seen it since but not v. often. Your father wanted to send a small raiding party consisting of his own operatives behind the lines to rescue his agents But the General was opposed to it & Washington refused to negotiate the exchange.

I have always believed it was this even more than the General's renunciation of his command which embittered your father to the War. No man escaped unscathed it is True & True too the conflict was already felt by him to a personal degree as I know you were brought in to run the lines. But Edward when he volunteered had asked only one assurance in exchange for his service & that was to be returned whether alive or dead to the north If dead to be buried there If alive well it does not matter does it. Your father made him that vow I watched them shake hands there was a lantern burning in the tent it was v. solemn & moving a sight etc.

When in the event that hostilities ceased at last your father's v. first action was to journey south through the

devastation into Richmond & there begin investigating the
circumstances of Edward's disappearance. My Mr Porter &
me did not travel with him at that time instead we remained
in Baltimore as there was much to be done in regard to a
ring of stock thefts. But your father wrote almost daily. He
had little hope of locating Edward alive after so long a
period He knew after all We all did How pestilential the
conditions in those prisons. After several weeks he found a
marked grave in the Confederate Army Cemetery in
Richmond. It contained the remains of the Virginian operative, Ignatius Spaar. The inscription told of his Great
Sacrifice for the Confederacy.

Your father dug up the Body and Removed the bullets I
send to you now they were in the Virginian's Remains it is
clear he was Shot & Executed as a Spy. No we could not
then and I still cannot now make Sense of the inscription
Perhaps it was a cruel kind of joke. That happened in the
War you will remember. Death became so common.

Now Billy you asked about Edward Shade. I did not
answer you not truthfully. Edward survived the war. In sixty-
six your father come home one night and ate with your
mama in the kitchen like they did always do. When he gone
on up to his study he found a boy was waiting there to shoot
him dead & that boy was Edward Shade. I should not call
him a boy he was a man by then. I do not know just what
transpired between the two of them that night but there was a
struggle, your father he fought Edward down & he took his
revolver. Edward got out through the window. Six times your
father shot into the night & six times he missed. Your father
bless his soul was many things but he was never a poor shot.

If all that is not enough to make a man like your father
crazy then I do not know what would do it. He did not ever
much talk about that night with Edward in his house holding a loaded gun on him.

As your father knew that if Edward did not die in that
prison it could only be by turning on the Virginian he had

sent down & Betraying him to the Confederates it is not surprising your father felt Betrayed himself. I do not know what else Edward could have confessed to as I do not know which secrets he carried in him but certainly he knew enough to make his life worth the Preserving.

Edward disappeared. No we did not ever hear from him again. There was that nonsense later about the break-ins, the senator's residence, the stolen items posted in packages to your father but I do not believe that was the doing of poor Edward.

Your father thought to the End of his Life that Edward would turn up again. That is what he was looking for. I do not know if it was Vengeance or Love in your father all those years perhaps both. My Mr Porter & me we have been on the private payroll of your father some thirteen years to the day with one overriding purpose & one only We were to collect & report back on Edward Shade & to apprehend him if possible. To this end we have lived in San Francisco New Orleans Paris & London that last being six years now. Those reports being uncertain at best nevertheless Allan did not ever stop his belief in Edward's existence.

What do I believe? I believe Edward is dead. I expect he is lying in an unmarked grave somewhere out west or maybe in South America. I believe your father felt grief & guilt & anger & that anger kept him from Seeing the Truth of It. I believe you Billy would be wise to let the matter lie & go back to Chicago.

What I have written here is the Truth God bless.

When you read this I will be gone from London I shall look up my Sister in California if she is still Alive & God willing.

I remain, your loving, etc.

He set down the letter and rubbed at his face. The sharp stubble burning his palms, his thoughts slow. She had said nothing to him that morning of his visit, only to confide such details now. What had altered in her? If what she wrote was true, then the man Foole had not lied to him, not entirely, when he told of his father holding a gun on Shade at his house. William got to his feet and crossed the room and crossed back. Ignatius Spaar had spied for his father and laboured as an aeronaut in deep cover and his father had never once told him. He had for many years after the war lived with a crippling guilt about Spaar's disappearance. His father had known the truth of it and never said. He felt a sudden unexpected fury. And Shade? Shade had betrayed them all.

He ran his fingers lightly over the papers. He tried to imagine Sally Porter labouring over the letter, writing him the truth as she knew it, pouring sand on the wet ink and lifting the pages and reading them over with care. He thought of the regret she must have felt at deceiving him that morning. The bath in his bedchamber was cooling. Go on find your sister, Sally, he thought. Find your blood and make your peace. Outside the rain was rattling the windows. He heard the maid knock with two soft knuckles at the locked door and then call in to him but he did not answer and after a time she went away.

TWENTY-SEVEN

In the morning a black regret overtook Foole. He paced the cluttered aisles in the Emporium considering Farquhar, the painting, Pinkerton, while the old floorboards groaned underfoot. His knuckles were cold but he did not request a fire. Fludd had warned him against approaching the detective but he had not listened and nothing had come of it but complication and misfortune. So. And Molly had stared at him reproachfully when she learned what he had kept from her. But it was not his past or not only that. He was never one to wallow in his own mistakes but still he did not like making them and he felt now only shame and disgust at having done so. He tugged at his whiskers, he glowered. If you do not like your situation, he told himself angrily, then change it. A weird bright rain had started to fall when he went into the foyer and found Fludd huge and shadowy and disapproving in the white backlit glow of the windows.

I want you with us at the gallery, Foole said and his voice was curt. Change your coat.

Fludd set his hat on his head. Aye.

Molly, he shouted.

But when he turned around she was breathing hard at the foot of the stairs and her foot was resting on a crate of Namibian war rattles and she was looking at him in alarm. He corrected her ribbons and adjusted the lace in her cap and he gave her pink dress a hard appraising glance. She had done her hair in

ringlets despite the shortness of it and the effect was strange
though suitably innocent for his purpose. Fludd came back
downstairs dressed in a faded black morning suit with scuffs on
the elbows and the trousers high on his ankles as if he had
bought it from a dead man and he had coloured his beard and
stained the moons of his fingernails like a labourer not used to
daylight on a weekday. Foole grunted his approval then took the
bowler from the big man's hands and gave him a battered silk
hat. He withdrew from his billfold several pounds and passed
them across to Fludd and then he leaned out into the hall and
called for Mrs. Sykes.

She came in wiping the backs of her hands on an apron and
untying its strings and folding it over one arm. Her hair wild, a
streak of flour on her chin.

Mrs. Sykes, he said. How would you like to take the morning off?

She looked at him as if he had just poured salt in the marma-
lade. What, and double the work for tomorrow? I'd guess not.

Foole frowned. I'd like you to go with Mr. Fludd to an exhibition of paintings. Would you be willing?

Now Mr. Foole, she said tightly. There's a goose in the pantry
if it don't get dressed it goin to be getting back up onto its two
feet an walkin out of here on its own. Leave you lot eatin lentils
and potatoes and not a thing else.

Foole raised an eyebrow.

Mrs. Sykes, Fludd said, and cleared his throat. You got to
think of it as a holiday like.

A holiday? she said.

Aye, Molly laughed. All Soul's Day, what with him on your
arm.

Mr. Fludd will be your companion, Mrs. Sykes, Foole said.
It would be a great favour to me. Unless you feel the two of you
might need a chaperone?

She flushed and turned her face away. But when Foole saw
the wounded look on the giant's face something inside him
turned to ash.

Forgive me, he said, his voice gentler. I shouldn't tease.
Japheth, you go on and bring Mrs. Sykes when she's ready. We'll
proceed apace.

What about Hettie? Molly asked. She don't get a holiday too?

You ain't in the house, Fludd muttered. That's the holiday
for her.

Edward was taken to the Major's office in the third week of
April 1862. The bearded Scot stood at a window in his vest,
distracted, his back to the room and his hands folded behind
him and the fingers flexing silently. He did not turn. His shirt
sleeves had been folded back and rolled to the elbow. Edward
studied his broad back nervously, his shaggy black hair. Outside
it had started to rain.

I understand you might have the makings of an operative
after all, the Major said at last, returning to his desk. His voice
was low, subdued, his eyes looked tired. I have an assignment
for you. I'm told you can read?

Edward was passed a slip of paper. On it was an address, a
handwritten description of a woman. Tall, aristocratic, widowed. Tight auburn curls, eyebrows a little too thick, a mole to
the left of her nose. Speaks with a Texas lilt. The paper did not
identify her beyond this nor was Edward told her name. He was
to find her and shadow her during the day but under no circumstances was he to approach her. He did not know if it was
a test or a genuine operation but he was surprised at the seriousness he felt in his labours. As he trailed her carriage across
the capital and memorized the addresses she visited he let himself imagine the Major's interest in her was not professional.
Certainly she was a beauty. There was a lithe grace to her both
predatory and haunting and he watched her auburn hair dip
across her face as she bent to smooth her skirts. It had rained
all the week previous and the roads were mudded and the widow's carriage rattled high over the ruts. Edward, quick on his
feet, kept the carriage in sight with little difficulty. The widow

visited several elegant homes in the west quarter and on the third day lunched with a member of the general staff. Edward understood this by studying the officer's uniform although he did not know the man. Daily he watched, brooded, slipped along the streets, and as he did so he felt for the first time his new power, the delicious power of secrecy, of trailing a victim unseen and unknown and holding her fate in his hands.

But nothing happened. For four days he followed her, memorized her movements, recorded her moods. He witnessed nothing incriminating. He feared his observations had failed.

But the Major did not appear disappointed. On the contrary. We'll catch that spider yet, he grunted. He did not smile but his hard eyes crinkled at the corners.

You did a fine job of it, lad, he said. And picked a piece of tobacco from his lips.

Edward could not recall the last time a kindness was spoken to him with such ordinary ease and he stared at his shoes, uncommonly touched, a lump in his throat.

Foole would have liked to have walked. Instead Fludd strode down through the rain to a cab stand at the gates of Green Park and brought a hansom back up to Half Moon Street. When the driver climbed down he punched open an umbrella patched with grey squares of oilcloth and this he held blooming above Molly's head as she came down from the house. Then he hurried back to Foole but Foole waved him irritably off with his walking stick. His hands were red in the cold and he looked up at the house as if to go back in for his gloves but he decided against it. The hansom was new and well-sprung with a blue wool blanket laid out upon their knees and they rode through the cold in a smooth and almost dreamy comfort. The rain had tamped down some of the city's stink or perhaps Foole was growing used to the smells. He could not be certain which. Molly smiled her sweet smile, pointed to sights as they passed, played her role of innocence like a star turn upon the boards.

As they clattered east down Piccadilly they passed the walls of the park and the ancient brick edifice of Devonshire House with its iron railings gleaming in the bright rainfall and at Old Bond Street Foole banged on the roof of the hansom with his walking stick that the driver should turn north. They drew to a stop outside the entrance to the Burlington Arcade. Across the street stood Farquhar & Son's Fine Arts Galleria.

The gallery had not been built to be ugly. Foole's glance from the halted cab was casual and haughty as if merely double-checking the address. But in its stonework he saw balance and rigour despite the gaudy columns added to its entrance, already pitted and soot-stained, wrong in a false Italian style and garish like brass earrings on a young beauty. The stone blocks of its facade were large, the masonry deep, on the wide sills stood low sharp iron railings like an invitation to a burglary. He smiled cheerfully and Molly smiled back. The windows were lit and shining through the rain and he could see even at that distance the bovine shapes of ladies ascending the steps and moving through the rooms two by two like visitants to some foundered ark.

An art heist.

It had never been done before so far as Foole was aware. There was, as Fludd had sworn, little sense in it. Foole suspected this would be both the challenge and the grace. He would need to approach it as he would approach any bank job or vault job but he would need as well to be mindful of the differences.

Inside was the tall cold room with the wrought iron chairs and tables and ladies taking their tea and Foole smiled and led Molly past. At the entrance to the first gallery was a table with small brochures like programmes to an opera and he took one with a dignified bow, Molly on his arm. There were crowds even at that hour and he was pleased to see this. At a small exhibit of watercolours of the Thames he stopped and read a few lines and studied the guard seated on his stool near the entrance and then he moved with Molly forward to the second long gallery and paused and read further. The brochure said nothing about any works in the gallery except the one astonishing painting all had come to see.

As they drifted with the crowds Foole studied the floor. The gallery consisted of two long horseshoe-shaped rooms, connected at each end. In the centre at the rear a wide staircase with satin ropes for handrails ascended to the second floor and opened onto a hallway from which several small alcoves extended. At the front of the second floor, in the largest space, hung the most famous painting in England. Foole's painting. His Charlotte.

They let the crowds carry them up. It was, it seemed, the work of one Joseph Wright of Derby. Wright had titled the painting *Iphigenia in the Mirror*. He had come to London to have his subject sit for him and had worked on the painting on commission but he had never been paid and the painting had been thought lost for ninety years. It had been found hanging in the cottage of a retired schoolmistress outside Derby who claimed her father had accepted it in lieu of payment of a debt. The intrepid Mr. Farquhar had known the work at once. He had offered the schoolmistress ten pounds but she had insisted on twelve or no sale. All of this was written up in the brochure provided as well as the expected price at auction. It was believed the work would fetch upward of thirty thousand pounds. Foole smiled to himself and passed the brochure to Molly and folded his hands behind his back and shifted in the crowd to get closer.

There was a gentleman in a green frock coat standing at the door taking one and six from each viewer as they passed and providing them with a ticket stub for re-entry. There was something condescending and reserved about the man despite his elegance and Foole liked the look of him and suspected he must be Farquhar himself. The fellow would do nicely, Foole thought. Very nicely.

He paid and went in.

And there it was. Though titled *Iphigenia* by Wright the newspapers had taken to calling it simply *The Emma*. For the woman whose face Foole had known so powerfully was a young

Emma Hart, later Lady Hamilton, lover of Lord Nelson and the most notorious seductress of her day. Wright had only painted her the once. She had been born into a life of drudgery but by the age of sixteen was dancing naked on tables for the private stag parties of her betters. She had slid from bed to bed trailing silk sheets behind her and found herself eventually wed and living in Naples to a dying man twice her age. There she had displayed herself to Goethe and to visiting monarchs and had studied the classical ruins around her for their elegance and fascination. Buried inside her was a fascination of her own that she longed to reach.

Wright's vision of Emma had been an unhappy one. A study of frail lights burning against an overwhelming darkness. She sat central to the canvas surrounded by gloom but for a single candle burning low on the table to her left and she stared with a livid and scorched expression directly out from the canvas. Her eyes were the eyes of Charlotte. Her dread and furious sorrow was Charlotte's. He knew that farewell, knew what she was leaving. In the background all was shadow but as he stared Foole began to distinguish a second figure, only just visible. It hulked there unaccounted for and ominous and Foole knew it at once. He wet his lips and leaned upon his walking stick and the room seemed to go quiet around him and he might have been alone with the painting for all that he was aware of the crowd around him. He stared. That figure, he knew, was her future self coming towards her. It was her death.

Mr. Foole? a voice said at his elbow.

He turned in surprise. He did not at first know the man.

What an unexpected pleasure, sir, the man was saying. And how are you enjoying London? How is your lovely daughter?

It was the phrenologist from the *Aurania*. The man who had ruined him at whist and taken his silver pocket watch as payment. Foole smiled an elegant smile, slid into his role. She is excellent, sir. We both find London most stimulating.

I'm pleased to hear it. I trust you are staying away from the cards?

Foole had taken the man's elbow and drawn him to one side of the crowd and he frowned at this jibe but did not respond to it. He had caught a glimpse of Fludd's massive figure drifting through the crowds, Mrs. Sykes on his arm, her cheeks chafed with cold. He lowered his gaze, cleared his throat. What brings you to London, sir? he asked.

The phrenologist tugged at the cuffs of his grey coat, raised both eyebrows in answer. Why this painting, of course, he said. All of England has an interest in it. I wanted to see it for myself before it was lost to the auction.

Perhaps you will be lucky, Foole said. Perhaps its new owner will appreciate a game of whist.

The phrenologist smiled. Ah. Very good.

It is an extraordinary beauty, is it not?

Indeed, sir, the man nodded. But just then a colour rose to his cheeks and he lifted his chin as if swallowing back some sourness and Foole followed his gaze. It was Fludd, drifting towards the painting. When the phrenologist glanced back down at Foole his white lips had thinned and his eyelids were heavy and there was in his face some slow horrified dawning.

Foole withdrew from his vest pocket the silver pocket watch with the unblinking eye inlaid upon it and he clicked the lid smoothly open with his thumb and he cradled the watch in his left palm. Well it is 11:52, sir, he said pleasantly. Midday does approach.

And he looked up, and he met the man's startled eye with a cold and murderous gaze.

Edward was issued a small gambler's pistol with an enamelled grip which he tucked into the fold of his stocking. He would stump up the Major's stairs at five o'clock in the morning and scrape his boots and enter to find the Scot already seated at his desk, coffee steaming before him. Edward's task was to scratch out the man's dictation by the light of a weak sconce lamp and to lose nothing in the speed. The Major kept him close. In the afternoons he sat in drafty waiting rooms, hat on his knee, while a cold rain drummed the windows. At night he lugged a satchel filled with papers across the mudded street to the safe house and made a fair copy of the day's correspondence. Some nights he found a clothed stranger asleep in his cot, sullen-looking, bearded, dirty. In the morning that man would be gone leaving only the folded blanket and a stink of tobacco as proof that any had been there at all.

A kindness began to creep in. One Tuesday the Major took him by carriage into the city. At a tailor shop he stood shivering in stained underclothes while a Frenchman fussed around him with swatches of fabric and scissors. Across the street a haberdasher wrapped a cold measuring tape around his skull, disapproving. Later a barber waved a straight razor in a mirror, smiling at the Major, pretending to shave the boy's smooth cheeks. Perched on an army waggon under an overcast sky the Major told Edward how he had come over from Edinburgh in his youth. His ship had been wrecked off Nova Scotia and he and his wife came ashore on a beach somewhere off Sable Island, half drowned. This was in the cold under a web of stars and they were taken in by a fisherman there for the week until word could get out and a ship could come for them. He and his wife were the only survivors. Edward listened to this thinking of Mrs. Shade's descriptions of his true father, trying to recall through a haze some memory of the Atlantic, of ships, of salt water and wood.

On the last night of April before Edward was dismissed the Major reached into his desk drawer and withdrew an important-looking envelope. There was a government seal upon it.

This, lad, he said gruffly, is a pardon for the man who sold you out. Fisk. You know the man I mean? The Major rose and walked to the stove in the far corner and banged open its grilled door. A pulsing red heat from the coals within. He stuffed the envelope in using a poker and then he shut the door with a clang and blew on his fingers.

His brutal eyes lifted, met Edward's. The bastard'll burn too, he said softly. Just that easy.

The next day at Camp Barry he stood beside the Major in the General's quarters listening to a proposal to move against the Confederate capital of Richmond. He was wearing his new suit, a grey silk hat, a pink pinstriped vest. Afterwards the Major waded the deep mud of the mustering yard and they entered the stockade and Edward stood in the hushed gloom staring at the condemned men there feeling nothing. The air reeked. He did not say a word. He could see the tangled white beard of Fisk where he lay in the straw, frail and sick, a bony wrist covering his eyes.

That afternoon in a hired carriage as they rattled back through the streets the Major reached out and gripped the boy's forearm. His fingers felt hot. Where do you hail from, lad?

Edward looked away. No place, sir. My people all are dead.

The Major grunted and withdrew his hand, a cigar smouldering between his teeth. When this is all over, you'll come to work for me in Chicago, he said quietly. He raised an eyebrow, studied the boy's reaction in the settling darkness. You know who I am, what it is I do?

Edward stared. Yes sir, Mr. Pinkerton, he whispered. Thank you, sir.

The Major turned his face to the window. You're wrong about your family, lad, he muttered. There's the family you're born to, and the family you make. It's the latter kind that lasts.

Foole stayed at the Farquhar gallery late. He sent Molly home by hansom with a fatherly pat on her arm and dignified instructions to the driver and he watched her sweet crestfallen happiness and wished it could have been real, that this could have been her childhood in truth. When she had gone he sat in a café at the entrance to Burlington Arcade and watched the constable walk his beat and the gallery's watchman trade off his shift and the crowds ebb and flow.

When he returned to 82 Half Moon Street it was late and he fumbled on the unlit step like a burglar then withdrew his key but when he went to unlock the door he found it already unlocked. He went in feeling uneasy. The house was cold. He stood just within the door then closed it behind him and stood longer, listening to the floors creak above him. On the pier table he saw the gloves he had forgotten. Then a muffled clatter came from below and he crossed to the stairs and peered down. He could see the dull orange glow of a light from the kitchen there and without taking off his hat or setting down his walking stick he moved stealthily down and stooped and entered the kitchen.

The counters, wiped and tidy. Pots hanging from their hooks in the candle fire, the linoleum gleaming as if just waxed. A metallic stink of poison in the air. At the cutting table with her back to him and her face turned away stooped a wide-hipped figure, feet planted powerfully apart, elbows sharpened and moving.

Mrs. Sykes, Foole said.

She looked around at him in alarm. Mr. Foole, she said. Why you scared the daylights out of me, you did. I were just, but then she faltered and trailed off and glanced behind her at the candles burning down in the pantry where her bed had been laid out. He could see the straw ticking and the fusty brown blanket and a basin of water under the nearest shelf of dry goods. There was a nightgown folded upon it. The door to the scullery was closed and he heard muffled snoring from beyond and he knew Hettie would be asleep in her own darkness there.

Forgive me, sir, Mrs. Sykes said. But you shouldn't be down here. It ain't right.

And you shouldn't be working this late. He waved a tired hand, stepped forward and removed his hat and sat down at the table across from her. Neither of us cares about what's proper. You must know that. Did you enjoy the paintings?

I don't mean proper, sir. I mean it ain't right.

He gave her a long searching look. Something shifted in her, and she put down the silver and the polishing rag and regarded him. Are you all right, sir? she asked.

It's nothing. I'm tired.

She screwed the lid back onto the bromide. Might you eat a wee bite, sir?

The way she asked it made him think of Mrs. Shade a lifetime ago and he sat with his head sunk into his chest and his palm flat on the table and then he nodded. Did you know, Mrs. Sykes, that I was caught in the American war?

Aye, sir. Mr. Fludd might have said so.

Foole paused, studied her. Did he tell you the circumstances?

Ah, no sir. He said it was no business of his to tell. Only that the two of you met in the war. She gave him a look. Should he not have said?

Probably not, he said, but he smiled to soften it. I wasn't even fifteen. I enlisted for the pay. Imagine. I had no idea what it would be like, the killing. He looked up at her. I shouldn't be here by rights.

Go far enough back in any life, sir, an the same's true of all of us.

I guess so.

She smiled.

There was a major I served under. A good man. Tough, stubborn. But he knew what he knew and there was no telling him different. He was a cooper in Scotland in his youth and he ran from the English all the way to America. He wasn't so big but he had thick cooper's arms and when he shook your hand it felt like a vise. He taught me the one lesson I've never forgotten: revenge, justice, they're just two sides of the one coin. Whichever side you stare at doesn't matter. When you spend it, it's worth the same. I loved that man. I loved him like a father. Foole raised his face. He tried to have me killed.

Mrs. Sykes put down the rag on the table and stared. He done what?

He sent a man to kill me.

She gave him a long appraising look. It don't do to dwell too much on what's gone, Mr. Foole, she sighed. It ain't easy, I know it. I tell Hettie the past is writ. But tomorrow ain't never existed before. Not in the whole history of the world.

As she spoke he watched her eyes shift towards the door behind him and he wondered at it. He heard a heavy footfall in the hall above and knew it and he listened to Fludd pause and pace and pause and then go noisily back up the stairs and he was surprised to hear the giant still awake. He wondered if his friend was wanting him for something. But then he saw Mrs. Sykes blush and dip her head to hide it and all at once he understood why she was awake at that hour.

He flushed suddenly. Forgive me, he said to her. I'm keeping you.

Nonsense, she said.

I am, he said. Tomorrow will come early enough.

All right, she said.

I'll be going up now.

All right.

He took the candle and went up. He saw no sign of Fludd as he returned to his room nor as he shut the door nor blew out the candle. He stood a long time in the darkness watching the grey ribbon of smoke from the candle fade. Somewhere above him a door opened and shut and then a heavy tread descended the stairs and passed his room and descended again and then the house was silent.

Fludd and Mrs. Sykes? He took off his coat and trousers and necktie and went to his window, he stared out at the gaslit street. It felt unexpected, what was in him, like an immense and secret happiness.

Could the world be other than it was? He passed a hand over his eyes. Just so.

The world could be other than it was.

TWENTY-EIGHT

His unkillable father. Knifed fourteen times, shot four, badly beaten twice, struck once in the throat with such force that he was hospitalized for a week. He had suffered a stroke in 1871 that should have crippled him for the rest of his days but had through force of will dragged his dead leg behind him on daily walks and slowly regained a semblance of speech. In his late years he would change his shirt in his afternoon office while William sat in an armchair and went over the morning's meetings, watching the old man undress. There was the ugly body, the ropy sinews and slack skin under the arms, the flattened breasts shuddering as he bent at the waist, the folds of flesh bunching there. But the eyes were hard, small, dark, and the set of his mouth was impatient with intelligence. As he had aged he had lost his physical sensitivity and by the end he did not shake a hand but gripped it, he did not close a door but slammed it. All was strength and the exhibition of strength as if he could defeat his own decline through stubbornness alone.

On William's first night back from Santa Fe he sat in his pyjamas at the foot of his own bed, his white feet planted on the carpet, while Margaret brushed and brushed her hair at the mirror. He was thinking about his father's unkillable nature. An attempt had been made on his father's life in Windsor, Canada, over fifteen years ago. That was in 1868, the year of the Reno business. His father had gone north in pursuit of the last of that gang and a salesman walking behind him on the ramp as he disembarked from the ferry withdrew a revolver from his samples case and held it to the back of his father's head and pulled the trigger.

He did what? Margaret lowered her hairbrush, studied him in the mirror with shining eyes. You never told me about this.

I didn't want you to worry.

Was the gun not loaded?

William grunted, shifted his bulk. The bedsprings shivered, creaking. It should have killed him, he said. I guess Pa felt the man there at the last minute and turned around and somehow got his thumb jammed in the hammer of the revolver. Broke his thumb doing it.

Your father, Margaret said.

William studied her straight back, her white neck, her long hair drawn down over one shoulder. He nodded. He knocked the fellow down. The man later told the police he'd been hired by us for the publicity, that it was all a stunt. That night he escaped or they let him go. Our operatives caught up to him of course, we took him down to the docks and questioned him ourselves. Turned out he'd been hired by Sam Felker.

Sam Felker?

William nodded vaguely. Some four-flushing penny detective trying to make a go of his own business in Detroit at the time. I guess he'd been thinking to get Pa out of the way. He laid his head back on the pillow. He was remembering the gleam in his father's eyes, the triumph as he studied the assassin's swollen face in the half-light of that grimy room. The sound of the man's bones cracking. Freighters bellowing and men hollering on the docks outside the warehouse, the three operatives motionless in shadow, their fists double-wrapped like pugilists.

What happened to Felker?

William raised his head. Margaret was still watching him in the mirror. Felker? Nothing. I think he went broke a few years later.

She doused the lamp and slipped into the bed beside him. I never imagined I was marrying into a family of lunatics.

He smiled into her hair in the darkness. Ma's not crazy.

Your mother's the worst of the lot. But she said it gently with a smile in her voice and then she slid a soft leg over his thighs and straddled him. She held a finger to his lips. We have to be quiet, she whispered. The girls will hear.

A low cloud lay over the city. He had worn his oilskin and was walking fast his shoulders hunched and walking stick raised but the rain held off. In the streets he slipped between carts and waggons, squelched through the mud, shouldered past beggars and clerks and shoppers all massed on the footways and seemingly pushing against him. His stomach was tight. As he went he thought how easy it would be to lose Shade. His visit to Rose Utterson might have already tipped his hand and the man could be preparing his departure even now, could be already gone. Edward Shade had not eluded his father for twenty years by being careless. In the crooked lane some of the peeling red and black posters had been ripped down by the rain during the night and lay crushed in the muck of the setts. William kicked aside a broken milk tin, its bottom blown out, and watched it rattle sharply off a bollard. He saw no one. After the roar of the streets the lane felt eerie, still, a place out of time. The stained brick walls, the mist drifting through, the quiet dripping of water into the gutters. At the small gunsmithing shop with *Gleeson's* in gold script on the windows he paused, glanced behind him, scraped his shoes, and then went in.

A man looked up as he entered. He had blooming whiskers badly kept and a leather apron tied off over a green frock coat and in his hand he gripped a small sharp hammer. The shop was dim, dusty, cold.

William walked straight for him, his eyes level. You're Gleeson?

Hadley Gleeson, sir. At your service. Wiping his hand in his apron, holding it out. And what are you in need of today, sir?

Where's the boy?

The gunsmith cocked an ear as if he had misheard. Albert don't get in till ten o'clock, sir, he said slowly. If it's about a piece, I'd say I know the trade a fair bit better than the boy do.

I'll wait.

It's not about that Showalter girl now, is it?

William paused.

He swears it weren't him. Now I'm inclined to believe a girl in distress but Albert, well, he may be rough but he ain't so rough as that.

William gave him a look. It's not about the girl, he said.

Although there was an alley-side loading bay into the cellar there was no back entrance. William took in the shop, smaller, shabbier in the daylight, and drifted to one corner, the gunsmith watching him the while. When the boy came in William had been lurking to one side of the door and he waited until the door had shut and then he stepped forward. Gleeson called to the boy at the same moment.

Albert, he said, this gentleman here has some business with you. Make it quick now. I've a week's worth of work for you and half a day to get it done.

Albert had already turned in alarm, his greasy pinched face squinching down. His hair was thinning and long over the ears and William found it difficult to imagine the boy getting any girl in trouble. He put a big hand on Albert's sleeve and drew him, struggling, to one side of the door.

You remember me? he said softly.

Albert glared fearful from under his eyebrows. The gunsmith Gleeson was watching from behind his counter, a hunting rifle in one hand, a small gun key in the other.

I have a message for Mr. Foole. William withdrew from the lining of his oilskin a five-pound note and he crushed it into Albert's palm.

A quick sly nervous glance across the shop. I'll see he gets it, I will.

William nodded. You tell Mr. Foole there has been a

development in the Blackfriars Bridge matter. Tell him Charlotte might not have gone for a swim after all.

He squinted up, as if looking for some advantage. Charlotte? Just tell him. William turned to go. And Albert?

The boy studied him, sullen, pale. Aye?

You stay away from that girl.

All morning he waited, drifting from shop to shop, smoking in the shuttered doorways. It did not rain. A man is nothing without patience, his father used to say. Patience and a loaded gun. When Albert went out at noon William followed as far as the Fisherman's Hook pub two streets over and he watched through the streaked windows as the boy ate alone and sucked the sauce from his fingers. At two o'clock the gunsmith Gleeson went out with a heavy satchel clanking over one shoulder and shortly after that the boy took down the sign and closed up shop and proceeded at a brisk pace in the direction of Piccadilly. William slid like a shadow along the wall, following.

Albert turned from the tumult of Piccadilly into Half Moon Street and trudged up the steps of a tall terraced house there and he buzzed the tradesmen's bell and then turned and slid around the side of the house. It was number 82. A low wrought iron railing with a swing gate propped open ran alongside the pavement, and the steps, William noticed, were a cut white stone which the gunsmith's apprentice had sullied with his boots. William stood in his oilskin under a gaslight across the street and watched the side yard where the boy had disappeared. He could see no movement and at last he risked cutting across to the far side and walking slowly past the house. He caught a glimpse of the gunsmith's apprentice talking to a young boy. He walked on twenty paces then took off his coat and folded it over his arm and cut back to the far side of the street and retraced his steps.

It was then he saw Albert, walking quickly back in the direction of Waterloo Place.

William took off his hat and ran a hand through his hair there in the street and stared after the apprentice and then he turned and peered up at the house. It must be Foole's, surely. But he did not go up. He took careful note of the address and set his hat on his head and slipped his arms through his oilskin. Just then the front door opened and the boy emerged.

You, boy, he called roughly. He jogged across the street, caught the boy at the gate. But when the child turned he saw in surprise it was a girl, ten, maybe eleven years old. She stared up at him with a snub nose, freckled, her red lips down-turned in a pout. Her dark eyes were hard, too knowing. He instinctively lowered his voice. Do you work here? Who's your master?

The girl scowled. My what?

He was in no temper. He thought of Foole coming down the street and he grabbed the girl by the upper arm, he pulled her onto the footway. Who lives here?

She glared sullenly up at him. An what's that to you? Let go my arm.

I'm looking for an acquaintance, lives near here. A man named Foole.

An acquaintance, is it. Do tell.

He stared off in the direction the apprentice had gone. What did you and the gunsmith's boy talk about? he asked, all at once uncertain. He was starting to think he had made a mistake.

The girl blinked.

Albert. The apprentice.

She glanced angrily away.

And then William understood. He had the wrong house. For god's sake, he muttered. Your name isn't Showalter by chance?

Just then there came a sharp cry from the house and he turned and saw a stout housekeeper shaking out a rag, glaring down at him from the step. What's this then? Fondlin the wee ones when you don't reckon anyone like to catch ye, is it?

William gave her a startled look, loosened his grip on the girl.

She slid nimbly out of his reach. Bloody damned American bastard, she swore.

And then she was gone at a run down into the bustle and crowds of Piccadilly and lost to view. He turned, one hand on the cold gate, his eyes fixed on the housekeeper. You, he said.

Me nothin. I've a mind to call for the constable.

I'm looking for someone, William called up. He opened the creaking gate. Wait.

I don't give a black rat what you be lookin for. Off with ye now.

Wait. A Mr. Foole? Adam Foole.

Go on. Get. She stumped back into the house, slammed the door.

William climbed the steps and paused listening and then he knocked sharply. She did not answer. He lifted his eyes and glimpsed two gentlemen, canes looped over their wrists, standing on the footway watching. He grimaced. He would need to return to the gunsmith's apprentice and find a more direct line of questioning, he knew. He started to go, then paused, his eye catching on something to one side of the door: a small brass plaque, screwed into the railing. *Foole's Rare Goods Emporium. Imports & Exports. By Appointment Only.*

Son of a bitch, he muttered.

There had been another side to his father. All was not brimstone and fire, or not only. He was also a man whose greatest pleasure lay in making something from nothing, in the building of spaces, architectures, lives. He had stumbled back out of frailty and retirement when the fires swept through Chicago fourteen years earlier, devastating the old Agency offices. William had watched him pick his way through the charred rubble, leaning heavily on his arm, already describing the massive building he would erect in its place. And for ten years the old man had designed and planted larches on his sprawling ranch property in Illinois, the farmhouse and pavilions filling with art and books and murals

of General McClellan from the war. William stood in the shadowed foyer of what would soon be his mother's house in
Chicago, listening to the old clock punch through its minutes,
feeling the living presence of his parents on the floor above. His
mother would be snoring, his father down the hall in the morning room half awake and in pain. William put on his hat, sighed.
The summer lane was abloom with darkness beyond, fragrant,
and dense, and heavy.

He stood listening like that, remembering. Knowing his
father would soon be gone from the earth, that he would not
again hear that voice, see that face. Let him stay like this, he
thought, though the man suffered and faded daily. He closed his
eyes. Let him stay like this, Lord, he whispered. Let him suffer
just a little while longer.

TWENTY-NINE

In those first long months after the war Edward would remember his time at Fort Monroe with the Union army and how his own happiness had eaten away at him. How he had stared at his face in the small shaving glass tied to a post in the tent by one of the older conscripts, seeking out some resemblance to the Major. The cut of a tooth. Flare of a nostril. If he saw in Allan Pinkerton the slope of his own shoulder he could be excused perhaps on account of his past. All this he would think of in years to come with a kind of heartbreak and bellicosity. He took to standing the way the Major stood with his arms crossed and wrists tucked under and his chin sucked down to his chest and he would screw his eyes into slits and bite down on a stick as if it were a cigar. He too would argue or sullenly disdain the Washington cabal. He too admired General McClellan in his stern elegance. He too regarded the ragged Negro runners emerging from the wilderness with the pity and compassion of a man who had for twenty years fought for their freedoms. All this and the almost undetectable burr that would come into his voice as he grew agitated as if he too had put a childhood in the Gorbals behind him. He was not yet what he was, what he might be.

Then came the news from Richmond of the arrest of the Major's spies and Edward's life took its last impossible turn.

He had been a different creature then. The war raging and his several lives already ended and a man whom others feared offering him kindness. Foole sat in the drawing room, thinking this, the big bay windows looking east into the fire of the rising sun. He watched the slow creep of light across the carpet like a luminescence alive and with purpose. Up over the piano, down the potted palm standing in its curve. Setting the twin wooden pails from Antwerp alight, the brass candlesticks from Ghent. He watched this and thought: That is how the past creeps.

Something had passed between him and the detective that no other had a share in. He thought of the shadows in Rose Utterson's voice that night as the possession took hold of her and how in that moment he had recoiled like a man burned. Pinkerton had gone back to question her. And now, it seemed, he had come by the Emporium. Foole sat with his fingers interlaced before him, only his eyes moving, sucking at his anger like a sore tooth. Molly had told him about it the evening before, describing the man in his dark moustaches and the strength in his grip. She had rolled up her sleeve, bared the bruises from his fingers. I weren't afraid of him, she said, too boldly. I reckon he were afraid of me.

Now the light was crawling over the table's long curve, over the ladderback chairs. Fludd and Molly sat with heads bowed. They were going through the morning papers seeking word of the painting and the coming auction. The more publicity now, the greater the impact of the theft later, he knew. He stared tiredly at Fludd and Molly where they sat, the big circular table gleaming under the gaselier, watched them slit their uncut pages steadily in the stillness. Folding the penknife and passing it across and unfolding it again. So far only a small article on the third page of the *Gazette* had mentioned the painting and the auction and Foole had read it with misgiving. The article seemed uninterested, cursory. Everywhere instead was talk of empire and savagery and the wounded honour of the British lion. Last night news had reached London of General Gordon's death at Khartoum and the morning pages were filled with it.

Bloody hell. Fludd was running his big hand over his beard in puzzlement. Mr. Adam, he said, where's this Khartoum at then? It ain't in Africa is it?

Molly glanced up from her newspaper. Where's what?

Khartoum. The Khartoum.

Foole lifted one sore shoulder and rubbed at his eyes. You're meant to be looking for articles on the *Emma*.

Molly took the newspaper from Fludd's grasp and studied it. Oh, the Khar*toum*. In Mexico. Where that General Gordon got hisself killed.

Fludd frowned. Mexico?

You ever been there?

Fludd shook his head.

Right, she nodded. Mexico. Whole city's carved out of the rocks what they live under, like. All built out of tunnels and such. That's where it gets its name from. Khar-tomb.

Fludd stabbed a thick finger at the paper. That says there an expeditionary force were sent from Cairo to relieve him. Got there two days too late.

Molly scanned the article, nodded thoughtfully. Oh they mean Cairo, Mexico, she said. It's a city near the ocean. It were called that on account of its pyramids.

Pyramids me arse. Where do it say pyramids?

They got pyramids in Mexico. Not like in Egypt but they got pyramids.

Mr. Adam? You hearin this?

Foole grunted. They have pyramids in Mexico, Japheth. Mexican pyramids. Where they do not have pyramids is in Mr. Farquhar's gallery. Keep looking.

Just then Fludd stood, his face reddening, his big shoulders bunching to avoid the gaselier. Mrs. Sykes stood in the door. Aye, that General Gordon, she said. Ask me, any jack what's foolish enough to just sit and wait while a horde of savages walks right on up to his door and rings the buzzer don't deserve much else. Imagine.

Fludd cleared his throat and said, shyly, You don't consider it were maybe just a wee bit noble? Fightin them savages?

She snorted. Noble now, is it?

Fludd's face fell.

There's some as wouldn't know noble if it climbed up into their lap. As she spoke she stared at the floor and she could not bring herself to give the giant a direct glance. She wrung her hands out in her apron, glanced up at Foole. You wanted to see me, sir? Will you be wantin some tea and biscuit?

Foole shifted in his chair. Molly said a man came by the house yesterday?

He did, sir. And mighty pleased with his own self, he was. Manhandling the lass like that. I didn't care for the look of him.

What did he want?

Mrs. Sykes blinked. Why, you, sir. He was to askin after you.

Molly chewed at her lip. Albie from Gleeson's come by first, sayin he had a message for you. I reckon he were followed.

Foole felt something shift inside him, some deep misgiving. What was the message?

Molly shrugged. Never said. I expect it weren't nothin. An attempt to get Albie to lead him here.

Mrs. Sykes was wiping her hands on her spotted apron, the old yellow stains of some mess not quite bleached out there. She cleared her throat. Will there be anything else, sir? Tea and biscuit?

Biscuit, aye, Fludd said loudly. Be lovely.

Mrs. Sykes paid him no mind.

Tea would be fine, yes, Foole said.

And for Miss Molly? she said.

Molly grinned at her.

As she turned to go Mrs. Sykes gave a quick pointed look at Fludd where he stood stiff and formal with his arms at his sides and then she went back out.

I do adore a nice bit of biscuit, Molly said. She stretched her arms in a theatrical gesture and smiled and rubbed at her belly. O my. Yes.

Fludd glowered.

Yes yes O yes, she said. She licked at her lips.

What was all that about? Foole asked. You two having a fight?

Fludd grunted and crackled the pages of the paper before him and seemed not to understand. Nothin in the *Telegraph* bout the painting, he said.

Foole leaned forward in his chair. We'll negotiate it back with Mr. Farquhar directly, he said. That should keep the police out of the matter. We'll sail for New York out of Liverpool immediately. That will mean limited tickets. We may not all be travelling together.

Just as well, muttered Fludd.

An then where, Adam?

I was thinking San Francisco, Foole said with a smile. To begin.

Just then Mrs. Sykes came at an angle through the door with her strong arms outstretched and the wide silver tray low before her. She set the biscuits down in front of Molly and poured a cup of tea for the child and a second one for Foole and all the while Fludd sat with his big hands before him on the table and said not a word and he watched her every move.

She did not look at him. Mr. Foole, sir, she said, with a dip of her head. Miss Molly.

But her bonnet had been straightened, Foole saw, her stray hair tucked up under. She was wearing a fresh white apron that seemed to glow where it traced the bloom of her hips.

In the first two years of the war the Major ran a network of spies throughout the American South, recording troop numbers, morale, condition of railroads, cost of food staples. He used runaway slaves, deserters, civilians seeking to cross the lines, prisoners of war. For the most precise and delicate tasks he used a cadre of volunteer operatives, sent into the Confederate cities with falsified papers and credible stories. The greatest of these last was the Englishman Timothy Webster, tall, thin, clean-shaven, with long aristocratic fingers and fine leather breeches and a case of cigars for each officer he met. Webster travelled in a private coach under the guise of an English lord touring the battlefields and he soon fell into the confidences of the Confederate elite. He worked Richmond and sent reports back every fortnight. Then in January 1862 word came north that Webster was seriously ill and the reports ceased and in March the Major sent two operatives, John Scully and Pryce Lewis, south to bring the man back. Lewis, a fiery riverboat gambler before the war, had interrogated a Confederate sympathizer in Washington in 1861 and this very sympathizer, a young woman, recognized him on his second afternoon in Richmond. Before nightfall he and Scully found themselves arrested at gunpoint. The Confederate spymaster, a man named Cashmeyer, beat them both senseless and left them in separate cells. Cashmeyer, the Major swore when he heard. The bastard's a devil.

Mr. Lewis and Mr. Scully wouldn't never betray Tim, Ben said. He be all right.

Edward, standing at the door of the tent, said nothing.

In the following days the Major, doubtful, paced and swore and barked out letters to his superiors in Washington. He feared Webster feverish and frail would soon be arrested. But Washington refused to negotiate and Mr. Lincoln did not reply directly and the Secretary insisted that the Union did not employ spies and so could not vouch for the release of any such prisoners. Then in the middle of April Timothy Webster was carried out of his hotel on a cot, too weak to walk, and taken to the Richmond prison.

They mean to hang him, the Major said hoarsely to Edward and Spaar.

Spaar rapped a knuckle twice on the desk. You mean to exchange him. They don't hang our people. They don't hang ours and we don't hang theirs.

The Major's mouth was tight, his lips bloodless.

And the others, sir? Edward asked. Lewis and Scully?

They'll rot in prison. I know what those places are like. They'll be dead by Christmas from a plague. The Major dropped his cigar into the mud in disgust and walked away.

Something turned in him, flared, caught the light along its own fineness like a razor.

Pinkerton did not return to the Emporium. As the days passed Foole's uneasiness began to fade back into noise and in its place he started to work out the theft with his old obsessive drive. He and Molly and Fludd watched Bond Street and recorded the hours of the night watchman on his rounds. Fludd took down a detailed description of the locks on the doors of the gallery and Molly learned what she could of the night watchman. He was an old sailor with thick wrists and a slight limp and he lived alone across the city. Fludd raised his eyes at that but Foole made a dismissive gesture with his fingers. He wanted no violence and he wanted no witnesses. Every second evening all that week they walked from Half Moon Street to the gallery without hurrying and they timed the distance and wrote down any interruptions or obstacles as they found them. One afternoon they climbed to the rooftop of the bazaar across the street and stood at the stone balustrade with an unrolled copy of the floor plans of the gallery and peered across at its windows and tried to find some way to enter. They knew the doors required two keys for each lock and they knew the galleries themselves were locked after closing. They did not know if the upper windows could be opened. On the sills were iron railings with spikes to discourage the pigeons and the sills themselves were very narrow. It seemed, Foole thought, possible. Fludd returned from a pawnshop in Whitechapel with three shabby old paintings and Foole laid them out in his study on the floor. One by one he cut them carefully from their frames with different-sized blades. They did not go into the gallery again.

It was on Thursday in the dark hours of the morning that Foole descended to the kitchen and worked the knife sharpener with his foot and held a small narrow jemmy against the stone and shaved it to a fine point. The jemmy was threaded at one end and he unscrewed the end of his walking stick and fit the piece into the hollow there and then re-screwed everything into place. He had brought his black frock coat with him and he laid it open on the carving table and over the inner stitching he ran his fingers until he found the loop of fabric and this he pulled. Two knots of strong cording fell out. He rolled open the heavy oilcloth bundle and its contents clattered softly as he did so and then he stood studying the picks and skeleton keys and tiny blades gleaming there. He removed only three and these he attached at either end to the knots so that they did not rattle and then he closed the oilcloth and tied it fast and lifted up the frock coat and dusted it and set it to hang on a peg of the door. He took down a large bottle of paste from an upper shelf and poured several heavy dollops into an emptied jar and screwed the lid into place. On the floor was a simple wooden doorstop and he stood looking at it a moment and on a whim he bent down and took that also. He took a stick of chalk cool and silky in his fingers and broke it in two. Slipped each half into a separate pocket. Then he stood listening. Rubbing the dust from the pads of his fingers with his handkerchief as he did so as if he could erase all trace of himself.

They had decided on Saturday night for the theft. It would be Valentine's Day, the night of Farquhar's dinner party, and Foole had one last errand still to complete. He needed to get close to Farquhar, he needed a copy of the man's keys.

Saturday, he thought.

All was silent. He cradled the candle, he went back up.

When he found the Major chewing at an unlit cigar on the river landing at dusk he was astonished to see his cheeks wet and when Allan Pinkerton only shook his head and handed him the newspaper article he too feared he might weep. Timothy Webster had been hanged on a grassy field outside Richmond. The crowds had gathered by the thousands and stood crookedly on the beds of waggons and propped telescopes on the open doors of carriages as Webster walked the steps of the scaffold. He died well by all accounts and when the noose had been fastened to his neck he had been heard to say, Make it tight. None of that had mattered. The drop had been sharp and the rope slipped and Webster had landed in a crumpled heap under the scaffold wheezing in pain. They had dragged him back onto the platform, the crowd hollering all the while. When they drew the noose again tight he had cried out in protest but then the drop fell open and his neck snapped like a chicken bone and he kicked and shat himself and swung slowly and was still. All this Edward saw in his mind's eye and he put his hand on the Major's sleeve and felt something like compassion. The Major did not shake him off.

That was the twenty-eighth of April, 1862. The Army of the Potomac had been ferried south and established its perimeter on the banks of the James in the days preceding and was preparing its slow advance on Richmond. It was the very day Edward first heard about the Major's son. Standing at the troughs with Spaar, his balloonist's cap tucked up under one arm, the slow pines swaying on a rise beyond the river. The Major's eldest was to come down for the siege of Richmond, like an underclassman on his holiday.

It's not like that, Spaar said. Major's more proud of that boy than anything. Do him a world of good, having him down here.

What's he like?

Willie? Spaar grinned. Like chewing a mouthful of nails, I'd guess. A bit like you, kid.

Edward kicked his way back down to the river but did not see the Major and that night he lay awake with his hands cradling his head and he stared through the tent flap at the stars. The spies Lewis and Scully were suffering in a prison somewhere in the rat's nest of Richmond. He thought of the stockade at Camp Barry, its blood-soaked straw where he had stared down his own execution. The Major's grief over Timothy

Webster's hanging had been genuine, shocking. And then he
could not help himself and he tried to imagine what the boy
Willie must be like. An underclassman with a straw boater
and silk waistcoat and soft clean fingers. Dazzling teeth. A
rose in his lapel.

Edward's tent was downwind of the latrines, the stink and
flies were savage. He raised his eyes, arguing something with
himself. The stars in their gauzy silver spirals, the snoring and
coughing of men all around. This was the filth of his world. In
the morning he rose early and went down to the river and dipped
his hair and washed out his mouth. Then he trudged back up
past the sentries and at the Major's tent he went in unannounced
and when the Major lifted his tired eyes from the map of
Richmond laid out before him Edward crushed his hat in his
hands and said, angrily: I'll go. I'll break Lewis and Scully out.

The Major regarded him. You won't, he said. If the grey-
coats catch you there'll be no trial, lad. They'll string you up
like a horse thief, leave you to rot on the rope.

Yessir.

The Major grunted, screwed up one sleep-bruised eye.

Good lad, he said.

THIRTY

William sucked at his cheeks and bit into the angry flesh and crossed Piccadilly at a jog. He found Shore lurking under the arch at Hyde Park Corner with the buttons of his coat loose and his silk hat tipped back on his head and he took the man roughly by the elbow and pulled him aside.

You told me Edward Shade died in the war, he said.

Shore looked up at him startled. William, he said.

He didn't. He's here. In London.

Shore shook him off. Glowered and brushed at his sleeves. What is it with you Pinkertons? he muttered. You're all mad.

The cold park was busy, a bright sun flaring against the old Iron Duke with his finger upraised on his frozen charger. In the beyond a dark blue sky stretched deep and clear and roofless in the cold.

He calls himself Adam Foole, William said. But it's Shade.

There were ladies rustling past in fur collars and with opened parasols turning on their stalks, as if it were spring already and not just some reprieve from the greyness, there were gentlemen with small white dogs on leashes, breath pluming out before them.

Adam Foole, Shore said. I know that name. How do I know that name?

I asked you about him.

Shore grunted. Aye. You were looking into that bastard Cooper.

The chief inspector was studying William as he would a feral creature trapped in a coal scuttle. He looked disbelieving and then indignant and underneath it William could see a third thing, a kind of pity. He nodded towards the gate and started to walk.

Tell me, he said.

So William told. It was not his habit to bring men into his confidence and he spoke haltingly, cautiously, even now. Everywhere were the crowds. Men in heavy coats walking horses, ladies in top hats riding sidesaddle. Nannies with prams jouncing and creaking. William recounted the gradual drift of his activities, the encounter in the tunnel, his expedition through the sewers and into Shadwell. Shore knew something already of his meeting with Reckitt in Millbank but he recounted it in greater detail. He told of the seance and the man Foole's horror when the spirit called to him by name. He told of Sally Porter's letter. As he talked they passed ragged figures curled against the trees, feet tucked up under, and hot-cider sellers and carts steaming with beef pies and potatoes roasting in their skins. Shore listened. The grass in Hyde Park was dead, scruffed at the bases of the wooden posts.

There's something between Shade and Charlotte Reckitt and Reckitt's uncle, William said. Some history there. I haven't got it all sorted yet. Charlotte and Shade were lovers.

And that's why she jumped that night. On Blackfriars.

Maybe.

Shore grunted. There's always some damned history. Hell of a couple months you've had.

You've been busy yourself.

Aye. Fenians and muggings and this bloody business coming up in the papers. Did I tell you about the department review? Fat lot of nonsense. My father used to carve a pig into trotters of a morning and wipe down his apron by noon. Old bastard never knew how lucky he was.

Then on to the next pig, though.

Shore smiled bitterly. Aye. There was always a next pig to

stick. He shook his head. So. You sail over to confront Reckitt because there's a chance she's an old acquaintance of Shade. She dies, the business looks to be left unfinished. But you meet a man later with a lead on the Reckitt woman's murder and he turns out to be, according to a ghost—tell me I've got it wrong—none other than Edward Shade himself.

William took a long ragged breath. I know how it sounds.

You have no evidence. Nothing. Only a damned spirit conjuring and your own conjecture.

It's him, John.

Listen, William. Your conjecture is worth a hell of a lot more than any other man's, at least to me. You must know that. But speaking as a chief inspector and not as your friend, I'd be negligent if I didn't tell you this sounds damned thin.

I know it.

You tell this to anyone else you'd be laughed back to Chicago. Shore started to walk again, slowly. I'd half expected to get back from Brighton and find you sailed for New York. I'd thought you might have let it go. Got back to your own life.

You never did.

Shore glanced at him and then away as if not quite satisfied and at last he said, I'm damned sorry about your father, William. You know I am.

He could feel the chief inspector's small eyes on him. He wondered briefly if the man had known already about his investigations into Foole but dismissed it. He thought of Foole in that tunnel under the Thames and the regret in his face and he thought of the man's strange violet eyes at the seance. There was the weight of his small hard body as they collapsed in the sewers and the ferocity in his visage as he stood wavering over William in that alley wiping blood from the head of his walking stick. He thought of all this and he thought of the articulated precision in the man's voice when he spoke as if placing each word one by one down.

So what is it you want? Shore said. If you're not mad as a hatter, that is.

William gave him a long slow dark look. I want Edward Shade. I want him to answer for what he's done.

And just what exactly is that? Do you have a single particular offence that you can charge the man with? Anything? Shore hooked his stubby fingers over his lapel and the hand hung there, a red crablike thing in the cold. I'll be frank, William. I'm not convinced you've found the man, and I'm not convinced the man's a criminal. If you want my assistance, you need to convince me. Find me a reason. Find me evidence of a crime. Until then anything you do to this Mr. Foole is done to an innocent citizen. You understand what I'm saying.

William ran an angry hand over his moustaches.

You met with Shade in the Thames tunnel, you say? How did you find him? Your father was looking for years. Ben Porter was looking.

William hesitated. I didn't.

You didn't.

I didn't find him, John. He found me. William rubbed at his wrists in the cold. His bad knee was aching. I know what you're thinking. But I think maybe he's been trying to tell me something.

Like what?

He turned his palms up. I don't know.

There came a low thump from somewhere ahead of them and then a ricochet rolled back towards them from the trees and William knew it for what it was. The sound of a gunpowder trace going off. He could see the silhouettes of skaters gliding along the ice of the Serpentine unconcerned and he raised an eyebrow and Shore shrugged. He said the explosion would be from some lunatic blowing a hole in the ice so he could bathe. William thought he must be joking but as they passed over the stone bridge he could see at the north end of the waterway a mound of block ice tumbled there, a slash of dark water opened and gleaming in the rough green surface.

He felt unexpectedly deflated, lessened by the admissions. Saying it all aloud had made it sound half crazed and he knew

Shore's doubts were sensible. Tell me about the Reckitt case, he said, shifting the focus of their talk. Any progress?

Charlotte bloody Reckitt, Shore growled. I'd have pitched her head back in the drink with my own bare hands if I'd thought it would drag out like this.

Blackwell's no closer then?

He barked a laugh. Mr. Blackwell has his notions. Thinks the evidence suggests a crime of passion. Thinks he has the pub and even the man responsible, seeing as the man's wife matches Charlotte Reckitt's description and has been missing a month. He believes there's a cellar on the premises that might contain Dr. Breck's sawdust and insects. Shore squinched up an eye. I told him if he thinks he can close the case quickly I don't care if it's the bloody footman to the Queen.

A crime of passion, William said. Nothing to do with Charlotte Reckitt?

Aye. The publican's dear wife is in France, he's told, visiting relatives. Might not ever return, he's told. Some kind of a row between them, she's up and off to her mother without a word to anyone, hardly a stitch of her clothing packed and taken.

How sure is he?

Not very. Not yet.

If that wasn't Charlotte Reckitt fished up out of the river—

I wouldn't put too much stock in Mr. Blackwell's notions just yet, Shore said. I've been a police detective twenty-seven years, William. The simplest explanation is always the right one.

Except when it's not.

Shore gave him a queer sidelong look and William raised his eyebrows and then the two men smiled.

William did not mention his conversation with the inspector in the records closet. On a low knoll ahead a hot-air balloon drifted at its tethers in the dead grass. Men in heavy coats and scarves leaned into the anchor ropes to hold the basket in place and the balloon was painted red and white with an advertisement for Pears soap curving across its face. Two ladies in winter shawls clambered aboard and the aeronaut loosened a bag of sand and the basket rocked and began to drift upward. The ladies shrieked and laughed and clutched at their hats with gloved hands. The crowd broke into muffled applause. The balloon lifted higher and higher, its long slouching tethers sloping down from that other world of buckling winds, of drenching light.

It was then William saw the man. He wore a tall silk hat that gave him extra height and his enormous flesh seemed squeezed into his morning coat so that the buttons strained across his chest. His black beard was trimmed, his chin shaved clean in an empire style. He kept his head up, he walked casually. William knew him at once.

Adam Foole's manservant.

He said nothing to Shore but started after the giant and Shore quickened his pace to keep up. The chief inspector was talking about the Great Exhibition that had been held in Hyde Park when he was a boy, the Crystal Palace with its walls of steel and glass, the great trees it had been built around.

Foole's manservant stopped at a bench and checked a large pocket watch in his vest and after a moment two men came along the promenade and shook hands with him and they began to walk. One of them wore the dress regimentals of a British officer. Men doffed their hats as he passed. William interrupted Shore, gestured.

Who's that?

Shore followed his eyes. Ah. Colonel Vail.

Vail who was in Afghanistan?

The very one. Our hero of Kandahar. You've heard of him?

We have newspapers in Chicago, John.

I keep forgetting you Yankees can read, Shore smiled. The colonel's leaving for the Congo next month. I almost pity the poor man. Look at him. A feather in the hat of your every bloody ladyship in London. You can't go out to a dinner without him being seated beside your host. I reckon he's had to let out his uniform more than the once this winter.

Shore glanced again across. Now that other's a big bastard. Him I don't know. But on the left is George Farquhar, the gallery owner. Sir Farquhar someday, I'd wager. He's a friend of Lord Dugan's. His wife was rather a famous actress some years ago, there were rumours she was the mistress of the Duke of York. Has a notorious collection of diamond jewellery, rivals Lady Margaret's, it's said. Mr. Farquhar's been drumming up publicity for a painting they say will fetch a record price at the auctions.

The auctions.

Christie's. You never read about this? People lining up out the door to see it? It's been front page of the *Times* for a month.

William shrugged.

I thought you Yankees could read.

I don't read the gossip.

Shore smiled. Gossip is news too, my friend. They say this painting could command thirty thousand pounds. It's a painting of Emma Hamilton. Rather saucy, I understand.

Thirty thousand pounds for a painting?

Aye.

I don't believe it.

Rumour has it your Mr. Amherst is interested. The financier.

William saw Foole's manservant nod gravely and turn and make his way through the crowds and then the two men continued in the opposite direction. He felt something, a lightness, as if he had just glimpsed some stitching in the fabric of it all. Some hidden fold that held the thing together. You don't just get lucky, he thought. You don't.

It was just after midnight when he awoke. He could hear the dog barking from the wire enclosure next to the pumphouse and then it went quiet and then he heard the slow drag of boots climbing the porch steps and a pause and then a soft knocking. Margaret was asleep beside him and he rose from the bed and wrapped himself in his night robe and walked barefoot through the house and down the wide stairs and drew back the bolt and opened the door. It was Robert, half dressed, his hat pulled low over his grey face.

He's gone, Willie, he said. He passed just after midnight. Never woke up.

William nodded. He stood there nodding in the darkness with his hair standing out upon his head and the sash of his robe hanging unevenly and then he looked up and he said, Do you want to come in? And then he said, He's gone. Jesus.

I should go, Robert said. Ma's back at the house. And the kids are awake.

But he did not go.

Come in, William said. Come in. You want a pot of coffee?

He turned and walked past the stairs and into the kitchen leaving the door standing open behind him and after a moment he heard Robert step inside and shut the door and follow him through. He thought of Margaret upstairs.

Margaret's asleep, he said. Should I wake her?

Even as he spoke it he knew he would let her sleep. There was nothing to be done at that hour. Robert had stopped at the threshold to the kitchen and taken off his hat. William lit an oil lamp, set it on the planked table, and the scrubbed room bloomed into light. The two brothers blinked and blinked.

William felt nothing. That was the shock. He had imagined this moment for days now but had not thought it would feel so strange, so disconnected, as if it were only a rehearsal for the loss that was still to come. He banged a pot down on the stove and struck a match and poured out a half pitcher of water and then he sat heavily, his big hands open on the table before him.

Robert said, It's better for him. It's better this way.

Yes.

He didn't want to keep suffering.

William studied his brother, the clear brown eyes swollen with exhaustion. He did not tell him how their father did not want to die. He did not say it. He said, instead, I guess so.

I wanted to let you know, Robert said. I wanted to come tell you.

I appreciate it.

I guess there'll be plenty to do. Arrangements and all. Ma says she doesn't want a big funeral. I don't see how we can get around it.

William looked at his brother. How is she?

Robert rubbed at his unshaven face. Aw, you know. She's stronger than any of us.

William nodded. How are you?

It's strange.

It is. It's good you were with him. At the end. You were always his favourite.

Robert made a quiet noise in his throat.

What?

Jesus, Willie. His brother pushed back from the table, hands white-knuckled on the edge of his chair. He stared at his boots and after a time he said, I should go, I should be getting back.

But he did not go.

William could hear the floorboards creaking overhead. He thought Margaret might come down but she did not and they sat on together in that late kitchen, their blurred reflections warpling in the windows. Neither brother spoke. The water started to boil. William got up, pulled the pot from the stove. The water was crackling and belling up into vapour and he watched it feeling nothing at all and then it was still, a clear, lightless, rapidly cooling thing, holding the shape of that which held it, and William stared at it a long time wanting to plunge his hands into it but he did not and his brother did not speak and slowly around them the huge night deepened into morning.

When he called in at Scotland Yard three days later it was Monday again and the sun gone and a fog curled over the Thames. He removed his leather gloves finger by finger and signed in with the sergeant at the desk. It was a man he had not seen before. Then he pushed his way through the crowded halls and up the stairs and found Shore gruffly directing two labourers outside his office. There was a stink of fish oil in the corridor and he wrinkled his nose at it. A massive frame of glass stood angled between the men and they were walking it carefully through into Shore's office and they leaned it up against the back wall with a grunt and it only just fit.

Right, lads, Shore said, though the men were old enough to be his brothers.

What's this?

Shore grunted. A gift from the Kaiser's police. Have a look.

William stepped closer. It looked to be sixty or so photographs of different women seated in the same studio. Young women, old women, some blond, some dark, dressed in rags or finery and smiling or glowering. It might have been a rogues' gallery. William frowned and let his gaze drift from one to the next. Something was strange about it and then he knew what it was. They each had the same eyes.

Not just their eyes, Shore corrected. It's all the same woman. Just done up differently.

William looked again and then he could see it.

Makes you think, Shore said. We all of us have more than the one face but used to be I thought that was just an expression. Look at her. I think of her whenever I find myself staring at a photograph of anyone. You see what you look for. We think it's a kind of evidence.

Isn't it?

Shore shrugged and sat behind his desk and pushed a stack of papers to one side.

I guess you didn't send for me just to show me this.

No.

William took off his hat and ran his hand through his hair. Well?

A man matching the description of your Mr. Foole was seen entering Millbank two weeks back, Shore said. Signed in as a law clerk to one Gabriel John Utterson, barrister. Under the name of Mr. Guest. He was visiting our dear Mr. Reckitt.

William rubbed at his eyes. Do I look a little less crazy now?

Shore grunted. Needless to say Mr. Utterson denies know-ing the man in question and claims his clerk Guest—who does exist—was with him in chambers all that day.

Rose Utterson was the medium at the seance.

She's the one called him Edward?

William nodded. Her brother was there too. I met him. He knew Foole by sight.

Aye. I expect your Mr. Foole will turn out to be a client.

So we bring them all in. Catch them in the lie.

No point. Utterson will just change his story. Or someone somewhere will get paid off and the whole thing will leave you looking foolish. No. But, and here Shore paused and stared blearily at William. I've found another connection. I know where to find your Mr. Foole next.

And where is that?

At a charity dinner this Saturday, a Valentine's dinner. For the Knights of the Guild, in honour of our Colonel Vail, before he sets off for the Congo. The host of the evening is none other than Mr. George Farquhar.

William moistened his lips. The men from the park, he said.

Aye. Now, this Adam Foole, Shore said. I had him looked into. Seems a rather respectable gentleman. Has taken a house off Piccadilly, on Half Moon Street. Some kind of import busi-ness, an Emporium for select clients, quiet, keeps to himself. No complaints from neighbours. No trace of him in our files. You still believe this is Shade?

It's him.

Shore sucked at his cheeks, considering. I can imagine what a man like Edward Shade would want with the Colonel.

William could imagine it also. There would be wealth attached to the Colonel, prestige, extended absences from England. He sat with his knuckles steepled before him and his big feet planted on the carpet and he stared out the dirty glass thinking about Foole and the charity evening and the possibili-ties there. How did you hear of this dinner? he said at last.

We're the CID, William. We keep an ear to the ground.

When you're sleeping maybe. How?

Shore smiled. Wife's on the committee. I saw a copy of the guest list. He's to come alone.

William got to his feet, started to pace. I want to be at that reception, John.

I thought you might.

I want to see Foole myself. If he has some sort of grift on Vail I want to see him working it. He nodded as if considering something and then he met Shore's eye and he said, You should be there too.

The wife'll make bloody certain of it. These evenings are planned months in advance, they're damned exclusive. I don't know if I can get you in.

Find a way.

And tell them what?

Tell them I'm principal of the Pinkerton Detective Agency. Tell them I'm a handsome example of American manhood.

So you'll be in disguise.

What about the entertainments after dinner? You could offer my services. William cracked his knuckles one by one, feeling his way towards an idea. Do you know, I think we can use this nicely. I think we can start a record of Adam Foole.

How?

You remember that dinner with the Sûreté officials last fall?

In Paris. Aye. Shore drummed his fingers on his desk. What are you thinking? An exhibition of Bertillon techniques?

Why not?

I can think of a reason or two.

But William was not listening. We'll make it an exhibition of fingerprinting as well, he said grimly. We'll draw Adam Foole from the audience as a volunteer.

For god's sake.

He's a ghost, John. I've double-checked the Agency's records and there's nothing anywhere on this man. He doesn't exist, not officially. I want his measurements. I want to be able to identify him when the day comes.

When the day comes. Shore sat very still with his chin lowered and his throat in rolls around it and then he looked up and his expression was weary and a little sad. I'll see what I can do, he said. Are you all right?

I'm fine.

You don't look fine. Shore unlocked his desk and pulled out two glasses and unstoppered a bottle of whiskey from a shelf behind him and he poured two knuckles into each glass. The dark liquid smouldering and folding in over itself burning clear in the winter light.

To luck, said Shore.

William held his glass to the light. I never found luck in a bottle yet, he said.

Aye, Shore grinned. But that there's in a glass.

THIRTY-ONE

Foole saw Pinkerton first.

Looming just inside the door of the Farquhars' palace, his broad back pressed up against a marble bust, nodding with great seriousness to a knot of whiskered gentlemen. Among them the stout figure of Chief Inspector John Shore, ugly wide face flushed. He watched Pinkerton turn to shake the hand of a man at his elbow and saw with surprise it was Farquhar himself. Foole had not seen Pinkerton since the seance and he felt a sudden plummeting dread in his stomach. The big detective did not see him.

Foole stepped fluidly back across the lintel and let himself be jostled up against the iron railing by the other arrivals, women in their sable cloaks and fox furs and their companions turning sideways to fit through the door. He considered abandoning his purpose, finding some other way. There were carriages and hansoms stopped along the cobbled street, their orange lanterns burning through the fog. Foole peered out with the easy distracted frown of a man of means and tried to think. He did not believe in coincidences. And yet there were advantages, he reminded himself, to knowing where the two men would be this night of all nights. He felt the sweep of cold air on his face, and steeled himself. After a moment he turned and pressed back in. Let Pinkerton stare. He had come to take a man's measure and leave with the means to his house and he would not be diverted.

Still he was careful. He moved slowly along the line of arrivals and shuffled up next to Mrs. Farquhar and greeted her with a smile and went through. He had thought to arrive late, never mind the hour. It was a Saturday evening in London in the dead of winter and behind him the fog was already choking. He glanced cautiously around for Pinkerton but could no longer see him though he felt or feared he felt some eye upon him. He had come dressed the part. Fitted in an expensive evening jacket tailored for him only two days previous, his high collar crisp and startling against his throat, his walking stick and top hat and white gloves. He had come to be seen.

Farquhar's was an imposing mansion, cavernous, marble pillars flanking the entrance hall. Pink ribbons and white streamers tied off in bows lined the railings and sills of the hall. It was chilly and Foole shrugged out of his coat and took off his gloves and hat and glanced quickly across at the coat check where the gentlemen guests were crowded and he slipped instead along the far wall and down a corridor until he reached a small cloakroom. And there he found a coat stand thick with the Farquhars' own coats. He glanced around and then shifted his hat and coat to one hand and began riffling rapidly through the pockets of the coats but he did not find Farquhar's keys.

Might I be of assistance, sir? A butler with the pallor of a corpse stood watching.

Foole turned, smiled. Forgive me, he said, surely this isn't the coat check?

No sir. The butler shook his head gravely. Shall I escort you to your party, sir?

Foole nodded in relief. Thank you, he said. I'm afraid I'd only get lost again.

He mingled, he chatted, he laughed and charmed. He was a small man but handsome and he knew this and used it to effect. Ladies admired the delicacy of his wrists, gentlemen were drawn to his laugh. He moved through the crowd watching for Pinkerton but each time the detective drew near he smiled and turned away.

At last he reached Farquhar and the gallerist's wife and smiled and introduced himself again. At her throat a lattice-work of diamonds gauzy and shimmering and impossibly lovely. Her hand when he leaned down to brush his lips across it felt cold, a diamond on each finger. Farquhar's eyes were small and creased and sat in their folds of skin like buttons and Foole felt a shiver pass through him to see it. The man was not tall. His wife towered above them both, her throat old and sagging. She might have been twice Farquhar's age. What scandal had been strangled there, Foole wondered.

Yes, Mr. Foole, of course, Farquhar was saying with a smile. His voice was crinkled, friendly. It is such a pleasure, sir, to have your acquaintance.

Likewise, sir.

You are a collector, I understand.

Foole inclined his head.

Mrs. Farquhar's long pale fingers lingered a moment on his arm. And is there a particular area you are interested in, Mr. Foole?

Until now, American painters, early century. But I mean to fill my house here in Piccadilly with British works.

You have seen *The Emma*, sir?

A little flush for my means, I fear. But yes, I have seen it.

A fine sport, all the same, Farquhar beamed.

And you are located where, sir?

Half Moon Street.

Why, Mr. Foole, Mrs. Farquhar said with a shy smile. We are almost neighbours.

We shall have to arrange an appointment, sir, smiled Farquhar. Perhaps this coming week. But tonight, sir, I insist you enjoy your-self and concentrate on nothing but the excellent company.

Mrs. Farquhar smiled and smiled. George has several accomplished watercolourists in our collection here, she said. I would be pleased to show you.

I have heard as much, laughed Foole. But I couldn't possibly steal you from your admirers.

They stood the three of them in a narrow eddy out of the crush of the crowds and Mrs. Farquhar fanned herself politely as they spoke. Foole clapped the gallerist on the shoulder as they discussed the details and Farquhar himself never felt a thing. Foole's hand deftly picked the man's pockets, hunting his keys. He found nothing but a handkerchief and a penknife and an emerald ring sized for a lady's finger.

As he slipped back into the crowd he glimpsed the American detective. Pinkerton leaned against the balustrade on the second step of the stairwell, looming over the crowd, vengeful and dark. He was watching Foole with great interest. The guests in their finery drifted between them with drinks in hand.

Just then a tall matron in a blue gown reached out and took his arm and when he turned she smiled a gruesome smile and introduced herself and her companion. They were just arrived from Boston, she said, and had been told he was a countryman.

Delighted, Foole said with a bow.

When he raised his eyes the detective had disappeared.

The bell rang, they went in to dinner. It was a large dining room ablaze with gas like the great room in some modern guildhall, its vaulted ceilings painted luridly with cupids leaning over in perspective and dropping golden apples down upon the viewer, its carved mahogany beams gleaming like great black planks torn from some Spanish galleon. All was opulence and sheen. The long tables were laid out along three walls with the Farquhars and Colonel Vail seated at the centre. Pinkerton had been seated directly opposite Vail, next to Shore and Shore's wife, and Foole to his surprise was at the main table also. An enormous sculpture of a swan carved from ice was slowly dissolving on a wheeled cart between the tables. The assembled forks and knives and spoons gleamed in their ranks like instruments at a surgery and Foole saw his own face distorted and swimming in the bowl of his soup spoon. The room was hot and despite the thick curtains along the walls the dozens of voices thundered

up echoing off the ceiling and Foole found it difficult to hear.
Wine stewards stood at the ready and servers moved silent as
wraiths from guest to guest ladling out soup from great copper
tureens and Foole studied the face of each server as if seeking
some resemblance. They were the invisible and the absent and
this, he knew, gave them power.

He had been seated next to an old man with a powerful neck
and a long scar running the length of his cheek and his white hair
combed over a bald patch at his crown. He was a clergyman.

Church of England, the man said.

A pleasure, sir, Foole replied gravely.

When the clergyman gripped Foole's arm his hand was
enormous, and scarred, and just visible were the faded blue
lines of a tattoo. I were a sailor near twenty years, before I could
rightly purchase my living, he said. It were a rough life. The seas
belong to God. They don't leave a man in peace.

Indeed, Foole said. And how do you know the Farquhars?

The clergyman grunted. The who?

Foole cleared his throat.

Ah, just a little joke, lad. Mr. Farquhar contributes chari-
table works to the parish. We go back a way. You're from the
colonies?

Foole grinned a puzzled grin. I'm over from New York. If
that's what you mean.

Welcome to London, lad. This your first visit?

No.

Ah now.

I keep a residence here, Foole added after a moment. I come
more often, since my wife passed.

The clergyman shook his powerful head, his eyebrows con-
tracting as if a drawstring around his skull had been pulled
tight. She is in a better place, sir.

Yes.

Foole glanced uneasily past his companion to Pinkerton,
across the way. The big detective frowned at Shore and then
stared balefully down into his soup in a savage absorption.

Foole nodded at the clergyman without listening. He could hear Mrs. Farquhar talking about the fall of Khartoum.

A man next to Farquhar leaned in and said, loudly, Do tell us about *The Emma*, sir.

Farquhar smiled, a cat with a canary. I purchased it for twelve pounds, sir.

A hard bargain.

Indeed, indeed.

The clergyman laughed a sudden soft snorting laugh and there was a gentle derision in it and Foole realized he liked the man immensely.

Someone should tell the poor fellow, God doesn't bargain.

Someone ought to indeed, said Foole.

Mighty pleased with themselves, aren't they? The clergyman leaned over his soup bowl and took a delicate sip from the side of his spoon and Foole wondered anew at the strange manners of the man, his roughness, his refinements. I wonder if it will ever change for us. I look at my brother's two sons, sir, and I think about it. There's a writer we have out in Hertfordshire who writes about that sort of thing. He thinks there will be flying carriages.

Foole turned some pale disfigured thing over in the broth with his spoon, watched it sink again from view. He smiled. Flying carriages? Pulled by what? Birds?

The clergyman smiled too. They'll fly on their own power. Like a locomotive.

Impossible.

I should imagine so. Though the good Lord has given us a most astonishing world already.

Mr. Farquhar leaned across and said loudly, And what do you think, Mr. Pickins?

The clergyman looked up in surprise. About what?

About what, he asks. About General Gordon.

You do know they arrived only two days after the city fell, Mrs. Farquhar interrupted.

It isn't a city, my dear.

Of course it is. What is it then?

Khartoum? Something like a walled village, I should expect. Colonel Vail, you were in the Sudan, were you not?

The Colonel was shaking his head. I was in Egypt, sir. But my understanding is that Khartoum is indeed a city. A walled city, that is. A village could hardly withstand a siege for so long.

Foole felt Pinkerton's eyes on him and glanced across but the detective was not looking at him. Mrs. Farquhar took a long slow sip of the wine. Foole watched the diamonds at her throat flare in the gaslight. She said, The newspapers were all full of him a year ago. Do you remember that, darling? They said he was the only man suitable for the task. The *Pall Mall* made him out to be quite the dashing figure.

Yes, Farquhar smiled. Chinese Gordon. Sounds rather fierce, what?

I remember it because we had just met the General, in Palestine. When was that, darling, wasn't that just one year before the whole business started?

Farquhar pursed his lips. Two years before, wasn't it?

No, one year. It was one year before. Your mother was just passed. She turned her attention back to the table and swept it with her chin raised, her long throat exposed. We had no idea he was so important, you see, when we met him. He was a most peculiar man. I suppose all great men are, is that true, do you think? She smiled. General Gordon told us he was conducting research into the geographies of the Bible. He told us one night that he believed he had located the mountain where the Ark ran aground after the Flood. He said he was interested in where the Garden of Eden might have been.

How wonderful. How strange.

Isn't it, though.

What was he like?

Mrs. Farquhar smiled and folded her chin into one cupped hand, her long thin fingers curling up the side of her face. Sunburnt, she said wistfully. He walked with a kind of stumbling motion, then would glide a ways, then stumble again, as if he were always deep in thought. I suppose he was.

They say he has a very quiet voice. They say it's amazing he can make the savages hear him.

Yes. She nodded. Very quiet.

He was a gentleman, her husband added. Impeccable manners.

Ah.

Did you ever meet him, sir, on your adventures?

The Colonel inclined his head. Regrettably, no, he said. Though I have known several of his friends and companions. I should have liked to have asked him one or two things.

What would you have asked him, sir?

The Colonel smiled.

He would have asked how he managed to subdue those blasted Taipings without so much as an English musket.

It has always surprised me, the Colonel said softly, how matters of the greatest importance can appear so slight from England, and how the most trivial matters can appear of consequence. The Colonel cleared his throat and his gaze fixed on Pinkerton. The table had fallen silent. Here, I would imagine, is a man who would understand the difference.

Pinkerton's eyes were hooded but Foole saw him glance flickeringly in his direction.

Colonel Vail, said Pinkerton, and nodded his head slightly. You honour me.

Indeed, you are both men of action, said Shore with a mild smile. If only the good General had the two of you with him in the Sudan.

There were murmurs of assent and concern around the table. Shaking of heads. Frowns.

I understand a subscription is being raised, a lady said across from Foole. For a charity. In his memory.

How interesting, said Foole.

I heard that Her Majesty wrote a letter to his sister.

How interesting, said Foole again.

Oh, that is such a beautiful gesture. Such a beautiful gesture.

Well, said Farquhar with a shake of his head. I understand Mr. Gladstone was seen at the theatre on the very evening word was received about Khartoum. Rather embarrassing for him, I should think.

Mr. Gladstone is not easily embarrassed, the Colonel said.

It is a wonder he sleeps at all, Mrs. Farquhar said loudly. Leaving the poor man to his ruin, out there. The expeditionary force should have been sent months ago.

Foole shifted his eyes and met Pinkerton's gaze. The two men studied each other and the room seemed to Foole to recede at its edges. Pinkerton's eyes burned like twin black coals, lightless and charred. Foole lifted his glass.

Pinkerton looked away.

He waited until the detective was absorbed in conversation with a soft flushed woman to his left and then dabbed at his lips with his napkin and excused himself to the clergyman and slipped out to find the water closet. The grand hall beyond was emptied of its guests and there were servants in satin waistcoats setting out rows of chairs. Two workmen in leather aprons were assembling a low rough stage in one corner of the hall.

He ascended the wide stairs and stood on the landing out of the lights and watched the servants pass through the hall from the kitchens below carrying their platters of food and he waited until he was certain the upper floor was quiet. Then he made his way along the carpeted corridor, studying the paintings in the low light, trying the doors of the rooms as he passed. The first two were not locked and opened onto a dressing room and a small bedchamber belonging to a woman and Foole disregarded each but the third door was locked fast and he slipped a slender wire into the aperture and cracked the mechanism easily and went through.

Farquhar's study. He did not open the curtains, he did not turn on any light but stood letting his eyes adjust. He could make out leaning tubes of rolled canvases, framed paintings turned to the wall, the big desk. Foole had done his research into the gallerist and knew Farquhar made his profits by touring through the small villages buying up paintings from the unsuspecting local poor. He would find in a season a lost Turner or a Gainsborough and use these profits to float his more ambitious purchases. Not theft, but not honest. He knew also that wealth was beside the point as Farquhar had married the daughter of a lord. There was a high bookshelf crammed with reference volumes and a cabinet with papers in disarray. The carpet was white and thick and very soft under his feet and he was careful to leave no impress of his footsteps where he walked. He paused when he heard someone approaching from the hall but whoever it was walked on past.

He took from his coat the sealed envelope for Farquhar and propped it conspicuously upright against the desk lamp. From an interior pocket he withdrew a soft lump of wax and kneaded it with his hands to warm it until it was suitably pliable and this he split into several smaller lumps and folded them carefully into his handkerchief. He opened the drawers of the desk one after another but he did not find the man's keys. In a locked drawer at the bottom of the desk he found a loaded revolver and he held this in his hand a moment feeling the cold weight of the thing and then set it back and locked the drawer. He lifted the papers on the desk and shifted the dossiers but the keys were not there. He checked the cabinet, he ran his fingers lightly along the bookshelves. Then he saw the man's chesterfield hanging from a hook on the back of the door. He crossed the room quickly. Reached in.

And pulled from the folds of the pocket a ring of heavy iron keys.

Three minutes later he was slipping sideways from the gallerist's study and shutting the door with both hands behind him lest it make some sound and creeping noiselessly towards the stairs. Folded into the handkerchief in his pocket lay the soft wax impresses of each of the man's keys. The hallway was empty, the stairs bright after the gloom of the study. He could hear the muffled sound of the party far below, the low tidal rumble of conversation.

All this time, said a voice near him, you were lying.

Foole froze.

Pinkerton stood in the shadow of the landing, watching him. He came forward with his arms folded at his chest and his dark face melancholy and wrathful. Hello, Edward, he said.

Foole held his hands loose and easy at his sides. And for the first time in twenty years he nodded to that name. I did not think to see you here, he said.

Pinkerton smiled a bitter smile. I'm sure that's the truth.

The truth is not as complicated as you imagine it.

I imagine it to be very simple, Mr. Shade.

Foole observed the man's suppressed fury and thought of the party below and how alone he was with this man. Then he nodded. If you'll excuse me, William. I'm expected back.

He started towards the railing.

What I don't understand, Pinkerton called to him, is the why. Why risk it? Why come to me, of all people? A man like you must have dozens of contacts. Any of them could've traced her killer. He stood very still. Did you want to be caught?

Foole paused, turned. You flatter yourself. You've caught nothing.

No? Your man Fludd was released from prison in December. Your Mr. Utterson is the representing attorney for Martin Reckitt. You went to see Mr. Reckitt at Millbank in disguise.

What of it?

You're flash. Through and through.

Whatever you think you know, Foole said, you're mistaken. A name is of no importance.

A man can change, is that it?

Martin Reckitt's a friend.

Curious friendship.

Foole smiled a cold smile. Aren't they all?

Pinkerton took a step forward. I've informed Mr. Shore about you. I'll let the flash world know my interest in you. The

Yard will call for you on every damned investigation from here to Edinburgh. In America my Agency has already flagged you and your man Fludd. I'll ruin you.

Foole shook his head. I live an honest life.

Something hardened in Pinkerton's face. His eyes shifted, took in the door to the study. You have an interesting sense of direction. Are those Mr. Farquhar's private rooms?

Foole wet his lips.

Pinkerton stepped closer. What would happen if I were to turn out your pockets? What would I find?

Foole could feel the wax impressions of the keys, huge, heavy, dragging at his side. You came to my house, he said abruptly, changing the subject. You harassed and threatened my serving girl. The child has been terrified. You should be ashamed.

Pinkerton met his eye, his gaze fierce. I know about the war, he said. I know what you did for my father. What you did to him.

Foole stared. I never did anything to your father.

Pinkerton loomed within reach and Foole was aware of the enormous bulk of the man, the thickness of his chest, the sour wine on his breath. Downstairs a click and scrape of cutlery on china, the muffled thrum of all those voices speaking at once. He made to push past but Pinkerton grabbed at his arm and his grip was iron-like and brutal.

You gave up my father's operative to the Confederates, he whispered angrily. A man died because of you. A man my father trusted.

I never betrayed anyone.

You as good as killed him.

Foole shook himself free. As good as? he hissed, suddenly angry. There was the roar of the dinner party as a door opened downstairs and then closed and Foole could hear the slow click of heels in the stairwell. Didn't you ever wonder why your father told you nothing about it? He looked at Pinkerton and a long-dampened hatred began to rise. He said, very softly: Spaar

came after me, he betrayed me. I had no choice. He was shaking
and he started to go and then he turned back. I shot the bastard
twice to make sure, he said.

And then he pushed past and went back down.

THIRTY-TWO

A fter dinner in the whorl of chair legs scraping back and napkins collapsing William lost sight of Foole and of the Colonel and when he turned in his seat his big thighs straining he could see nothing but movement and drift. He kept turning over in his mind the thief's words from upstairs. Earlier he had watched Foole stand and walk to the Colonel's seat and speak some emphatic message and Vail had glanced uneasily around then shaken the small thief's hand in reply. William could not think what Foole might be up to but he did not like any of it. He glimpsed Mrs. Shore gliding towards him and he turned at once and crossed the hall and ascended the stairs without looking back and in the shadows of the small landing he found, smoking a cigar and staring out of the darkness at the guests below, the Colonel himself. Coat standing open, face drawn. He was quite alone.

Forgive me, William said. I didn't mean to intrude.

Vail's eyes glinted obsidian in the half-light.

You are William Pinkerton, are you not? the Colonel said after a moment. You look as uncomfortable as I feel, sir.

I wish I felt as comfortable as you look.

Vail turned and peered back down at the guests. He reached into his pocket and withdrew a second cigar but William waved his hand no. There was a low green divan on the landing but neither man sat.

Look at them, he said. I was recalled here to be at the very centre of the empire, Mr. Pinkerton. And do you know what I have found?

No, sir.

I have found there is no centre. They are the centre. He gestured with his cigar. Them.

I've always supposed the British Empire wasn't really a place, William said.

Then you are a wiser man than I.

William cleared his throat. He glanced quickly along the room but saw no sign of Foole.

London is not really a place either, Vail said. I shall be relieved to be gone from it. I think Gordon was relieved as well. He looked at William sharply. I did know the man, he said. General Gordon. It is not such a large empire that one can avoid such meetings.

You said you never met him.

The Colonel shrugged. It was a damned foolish spot of nonsense, sending him down to the Sudan. It was bound to end in disaster. I wonder sometimes who makes these decisions. Do they even trouble to think about it?

It was not William's empire nor was it of interest and Gordon to him remained only a man taken apart in warfare and he had seen his share of that kind of suffering. He knew what the flesh was worth.

The Colonel shifted a stiff shoulder in his dress regimentals. He said after a moment, The man made it perfectly clear how he would conduct the campaign even a year ago. He said he was in favour of vigorous military action. Vigorous. That was the word. Retreat was never on his mind. Maybe he'll be proved right, a man can never tell. He said there would be no way to protect Egypt against this Mahdi if Khartoum fell. You can't fortify the south of that country, it can't be done. He said, and I remember it well, You might as well fortify against a fever. He believed if the Mahdi took back all of the Sudan his followers would spread throughout the region. But he was like that. He was a born fighter. He never was a statesman.

Sometimes a man can surprise you, William said. Sometimes he can be two people.

The Colonel grunted. Gordon? There was never a man more completely himself. Stand him at the head of an army and he could march it anywhere. But task him with the delicate problems of statesmanship and he'd look at you in confusion. The Colonel shook his head. He was very Old Testament in that way. Never mind the paradoxes of the Gospels. For Gordon it was always wrath and fate and might. All that slavery business last March is where he went wrong.

We've had our own problems with that.

Vail nodded. Your father was an abolitionist, I understand.

William was surprised the Colonel had heard of it.

I'll miss him, said Vail, and for a long confusing moment William thought he was referring to his father. But then the Colonel added, He thought the Sudan could be civilized. He thought the slavery question could be strangled in its sleep. He was a strong, amazing, foolish man.

William felt a growing discomfort. He glanced at the room below but could see neither Foole nor Shore among the guests. The servants were rearranging chairs in their rows and shifting the settees and plush sofas into position for the evening's entertainments.

You have just come from Afghanistan, Colonel?

Indeed. With the Amir there. And it was bloody cold, I can tell you that. I'll be glad to get down to the Congo in the spring. At least until the flies start biting.

A lady in green silk shrieked with laughter. A glass shattered.

You'll be needed down there for your demonstration, Vail said.

I guess so.

They stood awhile then in the darkness and a figure came halfway up the stairs and stopped with a hand on the balustrade as if trying to determine who they were before turning and going back down.

I was in Alexandria six years ago, the Colonel said. They wanted me for the Sudan post but I was already promised for an expedition in the Cape of Good Hope, I had to decline. I take some comfort in the fact that fifteen years from now all of us will likely be in our graves and none of this will matter at all. It will not matter that Gordon has arrived there first.

Fifteen years? William said with a slight smile.

Too brief?

Too long.

The Colonel smiled. They were quiet for a moment and then Vail said, We have only one task on this earth, sir. And that is to live a just life.

Who can say what that is?

Indeed. It's different for each of us. But always it is the surrendering of one's fate to God's will. I think of dinners such as this with a kind of horror. I understand the honour but it makes so little sense. Why do they not throw dinners for those who need the food? The Colonel tilted his face, the greying hairs at his temple in their tufts. He looked again out at the ladies in their taffeta mingling below, the gentlemen wheeling and drifting past. The gaslights in their sconces glittered up off the marble floor like port lights reflected in a harbour. All of this is meaningless, this—he stretched his hand the length of his body in a strangely effeminate gesture—is all just transitory and passing. Our bodies will age and die but we shall not. They call it courage, what men like us have. It is not. It is simply a different perspective.

William said nothing. The sound of a viola tuning up could be heard drifting up from the low platform in the corner of the great room. The Colonel turned then and gripped his shoulder, a sharp strong bruising grip.

There, said Vail. That's flesh. That's what I hate.

William gave him a hard surprised look. You did not seem to hate it so at dinner.

That man you saw tonight, at dinner. That is the man I wish to be rid of.

They were silent then and William felt a strong affinity for the man, an affection, rising. He saw in him something of his brother Robert, something of his father. The goodness sometimes found in physical strength. The directness of it.

I wanted to ask you, sir, he said.

Vail's pale eyes studied him.

That gentleman you were speaking to earlier, at dinner. Mr. Foole. What did he say to you?

The Colonel frowned. I beg your pardon, he said. I don't know any Mr. Foole.

Adam Foole. You do. I saw you together.

Vail shook his head.

A small man, William prompted. Silver hair. Very startling eyes, almost purple.

Ah, Vail smiled. Yes. He didn't give his name.

What did he want?

Oh, nothing from me, Vail said with a puzzled laugh. He was asking after Mr. Farquhar.

The entertainments began. A soprano just arrived from Finland rose wraithlike and pale and stood like a white flame in that vast room. She sang unaccompanied and William who had been lurking at the far side of the hall seeking some glimpse of Foole found himself instead arrested by her. He could not discern any language in what she sang but there was Margaret combing her long hair before bed and he went to her and held the brush and their eyes met in the mirror and then he was back in London, listening, his eyes were wet.

Then the girl finished and the room stood as one and applauded. He moved grimly and quickly along the rows. He found Shore and his wife seated near the front on a green velvet settee and the chief inspector shifted his bulk and the springs creaked under him and then his wife leaned across the man's lap to tap William on the thigh with her closed fan and give him a watery smile.

Where's Foole? he whispered to Shore.

But he was thinking of Farquhar and of what the Colonel had said. He knew the gallerist a wealthy man and much in the news of late with his valuable painting *The Emma*. He thought of Foole's presence in the upper study and of the huge manservant meeting with Farquhar in the park and he understood this evening must be, for Foole, part of some design. Nothing else made any sense. He tried to put all of it together but he could not. Not yet, he told himself.

He felt an elbow in his ribs.

At least try to look interested, Shore hissed.

A man limped slowly down the rows to stand before the guests, his gait stiff as if from some old wound in the hip. He wore thick drooping moustaches and a purple waistcoat like a gypsy bandit from some hill country and he stood with his long white fingers twitching and introduced himself. He had come with a rare and wondrous device he called a zoltascope which presented the most marvellous of images. Paintings in light, he exclaimed. Images of a world which is not. As he spoke two assistants in white suits erected a tall white sheet at the front of the room and drew it taut and stepped back to one side.

It is not a trick, he said, it is not witchcraft. Though there are those who have condemned it as such. It is an example of the wonders of science. What you shall see, ladies and gentlemen, you shall not believe.

William leaned over to Shore and murmured, Foole's been working. I followed him up to Farquhar's study during dinner. I don't know what he was up to.

Shore twisted his chin slightly and nodded behind him. He's watching you now.

Where?

Back of the room. Had an eye on you since you sat down. What did you say to him?

The gypsy was calling for the lights to be dimmed and his

assistants were going from sconce to sconce in the great room and the gaslights one by one were sinking into blackness.

I've seen that look before, Shore whispered. There's murder in it.

A beam of light appeared. Smoke folded eerily through it. The white sheet burned there in the darkness like a beacon. William had seen such a device twice before and both times it had struck him as a faintly sulphuric and unnatural display. The first time had been at a conference on charlatans in San Antonio and the magician displaying the machinery had explained that they had once been used to conjure devils and to display the faces of the dead.

The room held its breath. Through the drifting smoke appeared an eerily lit village, a river threading slowly between its winter streets. There was a bridge, a church steeple, a woman peering into a shop window. A house at the edge of the village with one light on.

And then it began to snow.

He heard a gasp and Mrs. Shore shrugged up her shoulders and glanced above as if to check for snow there. Shore's thick hand fumbled out, grasped hers.

It was a thick snow, a soft snow, it came down fast but did not thicken on the ground. A line of geese appeared and flew slowly past the church tower. A horse and cart appeared and crossed over the bridge and left the village. All of this in absolute silence. A shepherd appeared in the foreground and drove a flock of sheep across a hill and out of sight and then the image of the village went dark.

He could hear the guests around him murmuring uneasily and then before them glowed the image of a man, bearded, wearing a red cap and with a thick grey beard. He looked vicious, a kind of mountain bandolero. And all at once his eyes shifted, rolled back in his head, rolled forward until he was staring with fierce contempt at the room. His eyes rolled again.

Nobody moved. All held their breath. William could feel the alarm and tension in the bodies around him, the tautness of the legs, the fright corded in the throats of the ladies.

William shifted in his seat. The impresario was bent double beside the zoltascope with his wrist working, shifting the glass plates up and down. The images began to vanish and reappear more rapidly. In that beam of light a thin sheen of sweat was visible on his lip. He withdrew the last plate and reached carefully into a box at his feet and took out another. This one had a corkscrew lever.

Ladies and gentlemen, the man announced with a flourish. There are those in the scientific community who call what I am about to show you a chromatrope. We do not usually expose it to the general public due to the dangers involved. I warn you: do not look directly into the centre, it can have a rather disturbing effect upon the more sensitive viewers. Last year a gentleman in Leipzig was hospitalized for several weeks after suffering an attack of nerves.

Then came a beam of white light, smoke. A geometrical pattern appeared before them. It was luminous and brilliant and coloured like a stained glass window, and slowly, very slowly, it began to rotate. It turned faster and then the image was blurring into a stream of colour and light and William felt a brightness at the back of his skull and he closed his eyes.

Then the lights came back up. Men began to laugh, ladies applauded softly in their gloves.

Shore pinched his eyes shut, he blinked, he shifted in his seat.

Right, he said. He set his jaw. Let's get this done.

William rose with the applause and walked to the front of the room tugging at his shirt cuffs. Pale faces dialing towards him, ladies with their fans shushing the air. Shore had slipped away and he came back in wheeling a serving cart on small wheels and the squeak of it was unsettling in the stillness. Set out upon that tray were the instruments of their trade. Pads of ink and paper, calipers, yardsticks, a photographic cabinet still closed. William cleared his throat. He did not look in Foole's direction.

He raised one arm.

Many of you will know my excellent colleague, Mr. John Shore, chief inspector of Scotland Yard, he smiled. He added wryly, Don't let the title fool you, he is a very able detective.

A quiet surprised laugh from the audience. Shore shaking his head.

Ladies and gentlemen. He clasped his hands white-knuckled in the small of his back. For over thirty years, he began, my Agency has been engaged in investigating many of the more dramatic robberies in the continental United States. My father, the late Allan Pinkerton, my brother Robert, and I myself, often have had cause to personally take part in running down the thieves. One of the problems we face in modern crime detection is what to do after a crime has been committed. How are we to identify the perpetrator? Even more, how do we do it as the days and weeks go by, and the trail grows colder? You will wonder, perhaps, how it is we can catch a man after so much time has passed. You will wonder, perhaps, how it is that the National Detective Agency has never yet failed to arrest a railroad holdup man. Witness testimonies are often contradictory. How then can we be certain we have the right man?

In the stillness he could sense the intensity of the ladies' eyes on him.

It is called by some the Bertillon method, he said. It was discovered by a Frenchman of that name. You see, although as we age we change in appearance, nevertheless there are elements that do not change. Aspects of our physiognomy that stay the same despite the years. Namely, certain measurements of our faces and our hands in relation to the rest of our bodies. The distance of our eyes, for instance, from each other, as well as from our ears and our noses. The length and shape of our jawline. The length of our forearms against our palms, our fingers, our thighs. All of this when recorded carefully and noted against a criminal's outward appearance—the colour of his eyes, his hair, his skin complexion, scars, and so on—all of this gives us the man despite his superficial changes. Who can hide himself from himself?

The room was silent.

Mr. Shore?

Nobody, said Shore.

Nobody. Exactly. And tonight we shall see how it is done. First we shall need a volunteer. Are there any criminals in attendance?

A general soft laugh rippled through the room.

I would ask my colleague, but I'm afraid we might find a match in our files.

Shore's big flushed grin. More laughter.

William scanned the guests. Several ladies had lifted their hands but he let his eyes rove past them. You, sir, he said. You look rather suspicious. William extended his long thick finger at Foole where he lingered near the curtains at the back wall. Foole shook his elegant head, held up a hand with a casual smile.

Come now, sir, William said loudly. There's no harm in it, I assure you.

No, no, Foole was mouthing with a smile on his lips. A young woman beside him set a hand on his forearm and smiled. A gentleman shifted to make room. Others were turning to look.

Shore was already moving through the crowd towards Foole.

No, thank you, Foole called out to Shore. I have seen the thing done before, sir.

A round of applause for our courageous volunteer, William shouted.

Ladies applauded. Men chuckled, called out to Foole in encouragement.

William could see the small thief's fury beneath the smile.

But then Shore had him gripped under one arm and was leading him down through the guests towards the front of the ballroom and William had stepped to the cabinet and started to clean the measuring calipers with a soft grey cloth.

Ladies and gentlemen, William said, setting aside the cloth. Our brave volunteer. He made a show of studying Foole's proportions. Ah, excellent, he said, and winked at the audience. I make it a point to never ask a volunteer bigger than myself.

More laughter.

And what is your name, sir?

Don't do this, Foole said under his breath. Still smiling.

Mr. Adam Foole, ladies and gentlemen, William announced with a flourish.

The room erupted in applause.

Stand here, sir, just right here. Excellent. There are many ways, he said, seizing Foole's wrists in a ferocious grip and twisting his arm to its point of weakness. Yes, many ways to measure a man. We shall show you all of them.

General applause. Foole smiling through his teeth.

Ah, now, said William, you must allow us to get a clear imprint of your fingertips. The patterns on a man's fingertips are unique to him and do not change all his life. This is important, as we leave invisible prints of our fingers on everything we touch.

He could see ladies rubbing the tips of their gloves together as he spoke, gentlemen studying their own hands in interest.

Foole's eyes were fixed on his, steady, level, vicious.

We begin, he said, by dabbing a man's fingers one at a time in ink, and then impressing them onto a formal paper. As he spoke he stabbed Foole's fingers onto the dark pad, then quickly rolled the man's fingertips onto the paper.

Ah, yes, excellent, my good sir, William smiled. He held up the paper for the audience to admire. And now for the other hand, he said.

Foole smiled. Perhaps, sir, a second volunteer could illustrate the difference between fingerprintings? he said loudly.

William gripped his left wrist and drew him unwilling back to the table.

Perhaps, William smiled.

And rolled the thief's fingers into the ink, onto the paper.

When he had finished the room erupted once again into applause.

Ah, but we're not done yet, he smiled. He led Foole to a chair and sat him down and with a calipered instrument began to measure the distance between the man's eyes, ears, the length of his nose, the distance of his jaw from his brow. He measured the length of Foole's arms and of his torso and he had Foole stand and roll up his sleeves and he smiled to see a small white scar on his left forearm.

Normally we would inspect a man and record any unique details, he said. Scars, moles, tattoos, and so on. Given the delicacy of our volunteer, we shall refrain from such behaviour this evening. But we certainly must do our best to record this gentleman's eye colour, hair colour, height, and so on.

During all this Shore's pen scratched dryly across the formal documentation for the files. William had Foole sit and stand and extend his arms until his frock coat bent out around his waist and then sit again in the little wooden chair with his knees pressed firmly together and at last Shore unbundled a camera on a tripod using both arms and squinted through the aperture then moved the apparatus some five feet farther into the room and then leaned again into the billowing black cloth. William said, with a smile, Last but certainly not least, we always take a photograph of our criminal. In this way we can help witnesses identify possible suspects. Now, sir, I must insist you do not move. Or we shall have to take the photograph again, and show these fine ladies how we restrain uncooperative suspects.

Foole lifted his chin. Sat very still. He stared grimly at the camera and there was in his eyes a ferocity William had not seen before. The etched grooves deep in his forehead. The raked white whiskers along his cheekbones, his stern moustaches.

A soft crump as the bulb flared and then it was done.

William smiled. Now sir, he said loudly to Foole, you will not want to commit any crimes on your way home tonight. Or we shall certainly identify you at once.

The audience laughed appreciably, Shore laughed, William laughed.

And Foole as he got to his feet was laughing too. Laughing and laughing, his thin lips pulled back, his sharp yellow teeth glinting, his eerie catlike eyes on William the while.

———

An hour later in the murky gaslight William was descending
the steps of Farquhar's palatial home feeling a weariness pour
through his limbs. The house was ablaze behind him, the evening still going on. He clutched under one arm a clerk's leather
satchel and inside this the Bertillon measurements of Edward
Shade. Photographic plates, fingerprints, a copy of the man's
signature in alias. Something his father had failed in, his entire
life. The night was very cold and there was in him a violence
which he was coming to understand, gradually, as he aged,
would be the condition he was to live in always. He was his
father's son. He saw again the misery in Foole's eye as he glared
at the camera. On the corner a cabman's mare was wheezing,
tired head drooping, the ridge of her spine and the drag of her
reins. All the horses in London were sick. William called to
the driver, climbed up. The hansom set off clattering down the
cobblestones. William closed his eyes. He should have been
pleased. Instead he felt his failure, thinking of Foole outside
Farquhar's study, their aborted conversation. What he should
have done, he realized, was keep the man talking, hear the man
out. There was a truth in any man's lies. Even Edward Shade's.

No it was not finished. William swore. He would need to go
back to Half Moon Street.

THIRTY-THREE

T he night deepened.

They were three and they moved through the fog-bound streets silent and blurred. A short slight gentle-man and his hulking manservant, a servant boy drifting some steps behind them. Each walked sharply in the stillness dressed in an elegant black evening coat and a silk hat though the small man with the pale whiskers was clearly the man in charge. He was not old but his face was grooved and lined with care. His eyes, yes, his eyes were old.

They passed the gates of Green Park and then the silent edifice of Devonshire House and they did not see any other soul as they went nor did they speak nor cough nor breathe. They paused as if to converse under a gas lamp on a corner each man peering in a different direction. Then the boy stepped back into a doorway and was devoured by shadow but for the white slash of knuckles and the glint of an eye and the two men turned north along Old Bond Street, walking with a studied ease. The small man was smoking a cheroot. As they came alongside the Burlington Arcade the small gentleman paused and studied his reflection in the windows of a tall stone art gallery and adjusted his cuffs and dropped the cheroot and ground it under the toe of his shoe.

He removed his gloves, dipped a hand into each pocket. Sifted the chalk in his fingers.

The bearded giant glanced along the street both north and

south but saw no movement and then with a nod from the smaller man he withdrew a painter's tube from under his coat and handed it across. He crouched and interlaced his fingers into a step and the small man bit the walking stick between his teeth and looped the tube over his shoulder and stepped up into the waiting hands.

In a single fluid gesture the giant lifted the small man high over his shoulders and the small man coiled and leaped into the air and he caught the stone sill of the second-storey window. He swung a long slow moment. Already below him the giant was melting back into the shadows. He folded his legs and swung to the left and hooked an elbow and a forearm onto the sill and hoisted himself up.

It was a shallow sill just wide enough for him to crouch sideways on one knee and the first thing he did was to pull back on his gloves. He then quickly unscrewed the tip of his cane and withdrew the short iron jemmy there and leaned into the casement and cracked the lock in a smooth sharp powerful movement. The broken lock clattered to the floor within and he sat listening and then he tucked the walking stick under one arm and drew the window noiselessly upward. And he was in.

It was an unfurnished room, he knew it well. There was no light but for the weak gaslight coming up from the street but even still he could see on the far wall the tall portrait of Emma Hamilton gazing sorrowfully out at him. He stood for what seemed a long time staring at her in reverie though it could not have been more than several minutes. Then he got to work.

He walked to the door and stood listening for the guard on his rounds but at first he could hear no sound at all and then a long slow shirring like waves on a beach at night came to him and he smiled. The guard was asleep.

He took off his frock coat and laid it open on the floor. Its arms loose and sprawled, like some collapsed victim. From the coat lining he withdrew the wooden doorstop and wedged it under the door. He crossed to the wall and hoisted the velvet rope aside and with great care he lifted the painting from its hook and set it face up on the floor. The gilt frame was heavy and worth several hundred pounds itself. He removed from his coat pocket the small jar of paste and a sharp folding knife and he opened the blade. The canvas was strong and thickly woven and he sawed slowly and he did not hurry. He was careful to cut behind the edge of the frame and not to damage the visible image in any fashion. When he had finished he turned the painting upside down and unscrewed the jar of paste and dabbed the end of the velvet rope into the paste. He moistened the back of the canvas to make it more supple. Every few minutes he would pause and lift his face to listen.

He rolled the painting with its image turned outward to keep the paint pliable and to prevent its cracking. Slid the canvas into the hard tube, screwed a cap onto its end, left the frame lying shabby and ravished on the floor of the gallery.

He did not hesitate. He put back on his coat and collected the doorstop and his walking stick and he paused at the sill to be certain he had left nothing behind. Then he folded his legs out the window, drew the casement shut, bit down on his walking stick and rubbed his forearm over the edge of the sill until his chalky fingerprints had been wiped clear. Then he swung himself down with a casual grace until he was again hanging from the windowsill by his fingertips and let go and dropped the fifteen feet to the ground.

The giant reappeared. Smoothed the back of the man's coat, adjusted the collar. At the corner the boy stepped out of the shadows and joined them. No one spoke. They walked unhurriedly back along Piccadilly, paused at the corner of Half Moon Street just long enough for the small man to light a second cheroot and glance about for witnesses, and then all three slipped away among the houses there and were gone.

Seventeen minutes had passed.

Any man lurking on that street would have seen a light go on in the second-floor window of number 82. And then the heavy drapes pulling shut, and the house again going dark.

THIRTY-FOUR

Years later when he would think of the funeral and all that attended it a fog would descend, brown and slow, blurring the edges of his grief. Somewhere in that haze were the facts of it. His father fallen hard and having bit through his tongue and the gangrene setting in. The septicemia that killed him. That. But when William later recalled those weeks in July of 1884 there was always that other thing, a haze of sorrow, obscuring all. Had it seemed so in the moment? He could not recall. Moments are like that, Margaret liked to say. Moments are seeming or they are nothing.

On the second morning after his father's death he had stood before the pier glass in the hall while Margaret adjusted his collar and set her cool hand at his heart and he had looked down at her. Her eyes like sunlight on green river stones, her eyes like the quiet after long applause. He asked her if it wasn't too early to go across. She told him he was a good man. He asked if the coffee in the carafe was still warm and she told him she would see.

Fireworks had lit up the sky for two nights running. It was the Independence celebrations. They had sat on the verandah of his mother's house in silence while the girls slept within and had watched the spill of broken light and felt the tracers on their eyelids in the warm air. After each explosion his brother Robert had cleared his throat and coughed until William could not stand it and he had got to his feet and bid them all good night. His mother had risen from the old swinging bench and come to him and held him and he had felt embarrassed by the heat of it all.

A small funeral, she said to them in the morning kitchen, och, that would be best. Immediate family only, he agreed. Robert brooded, Robert disapproved. He thought a show of public mourning more suitable. You'll not, their mother insisted. I'll not see that for the poor man ever. The block of butter melting languidly in its dish. A fly battering itself against a pane. Robert meeting William's eye over her head and holding it while the clock on the landing sounded the hour.

By then the obituaries had already begun in the national dailies and the international papers as well and their mother clipped each one with her ancient heavy sewing shears and pasted them into a memory book with thick leather covers and wide pages and a ghoulish lock of their father's hair. William could not bring himself to go to it though Margaret sat with her for hours leafing through it. The obituaries were posted over from the New York office and Robert thought to instruct them to cease but William told him to leave it alone.

Robert scowled. It's unhealthy, Willie.

It's what she has left, he said.

All that week William slept little. In the mornings he ate an early breakfast of steak and eggs and left the house with his collar unironed and vest unbuttoned. In his father's sunlit bedchamber he would go idly through the clothes with Robert, dabbing a wet cloth to his lips, the muslin curtains glowing. They had done so as boys too when their father was away on business and William thought of this with a sudden upwelling of sorrow. A Bible sat on the nightstand, a paper folded to mark its place. The paper was blank. His father and his faith. Wherever he might be now. In the mid-morning their mother would come with cups of tea and kiss them on the tops of their heads and go.

What he was thinking, sifting through his father's suits, was the power and vitriol that flesh had once held. He could count on the fingers of a single hand the times his father had confided in him, had looked at him with pride, had sought his judgment or advice. The old man had been impossible, unpredictable. William would smooth his fingers over the fabric of a lapel, lift his father's sleeve. The worn cloth light as a wasp's nest, Robert coughing someplace near.

He had always been the favoured son. That from Robert, not in resentment.

His first operation without oversight, the Farrington business, had ended in brutality, a kind of failure, and he had feared his father's wrath. He could still recall the taste of metal in his mouth, the dread as he had descended the arrivals platform in Chicago. But instead of disappointment he had met with the fierce satisfied grip of his father's hand on his sleeve, a long shrewd grin of approval. There were newsmen crowded at the station exit calling for comment and his father had taken William's suitcase from him, and nodded, and let him walk through first.

The Farrington brothers were sullen black-bearded behemoths with fists the size of a man's skull. Each had stood near seven feet tall and the smaller of the two had wrists so thick William had had to rig the cuffs to fix him. That was Hillary. Levi could crack a squirrel at fifty yards if the light was right. They had worked a Southern Express Company safe out of twenty thousand dollars at Union City with three other men and holed up in a rickety general store in the swamps near Lester's Landing, Kentucky. It had been a botched hunt from the first and when he at last stormed their hideout he took a bullet to the gut in thanks. He'd gone in at dusk through the swamps with a former Memphis policeman whose fingertips had been buffed to softness and were quick on the hammer and with two cane-fed whites who poled the skiff in a mistrustful silence. There were birds screeching in the twilight, the dirty river pushing sluggishly past the woodyard and landing.

That general store was a rough log cabin built on stilts with a door at either end and a single window covered by bearskin. Through it an eerie orange light from an oil lamp was visible. He remembered the silence of that place, how he had walked in through the front door while the ex-cop had circled around back and how he had found five men and a woman sitting in the room playing cards and how he had asked casually for directions to the Tiptonville Road. Levi had risen huge and shaggy like a cave bear and he shot first and hit William and then he turned, shot low through the closed back door, hit the ex-cop crouched there. Then he kicked through that door in a splinter of wood and nails and knocked the wounded man aside and vanished into the swamps. William had set to, swinging his fists and his revolver and lumber and furniture until no man stood against him. He had been bleeding badly but the bullet had only just taken the skin with it. The button of the ex-cop's heavy Kentucky denim had turned aside the other shot and passed it under the skin to the man's back. Afterwards William had forced the woman to hold the candle while he cut out the slug with a corn knife.

Then word came in that the other brother, Hillary, had been seen near Verona, Missouri. They found him holed up in a settler's cabin on the edge of the Indian Territory. The man was in place with rifles and ammunition and was slowly picking off the posse William had gathered. He pulled his deputies back, and thought about it, and went among the posse until he found the cabin's owner and he bought the place outright for two hundred dollars. He outfitted a waggon with hay and rolled it against the cabin wall and was prepared to set it alight when the big man came out with his hands empty.

Why hello Hillary, William had called out with a grin.

Two days later he had engaged a stateroom on the steamer *Illinois* bound for Columbus, Kentucky, Hillary Farrington huge and hairy and quiet where he crouched on the cot. He was too tall to lie down and so sat up into the night and after a long while William had offered him a drink in the saloon. What was it in him that pitied a man as terrible and vicious as that? What had gone wrong in him, his father used to ask. The night air had been warm. The big man had raised his cuffed hands over William's head as they got up on deck with an easy gentleness as if to embrace him and then he crushed him against the rail and reached for the Colt at William's hip and neither man had said a word. They had wrestled in silence. Just grunts, muffled gasping over the quiet slap of river against the hull. When the Colt went off the sound seemed desperate and sudden and real.

Something changed in their struggle then. The bullet had grazed William's scalp and there was blood running into his eyes. Hillary had him by the throat when William twisted the man sideways and up over the rail and then Hillary was gone into the darkness of the paddlewheel.

There was the sound of it. There would always be the sound of it. The crunch and whump and weird watery slapping of a heavy body diced and shunted and sprayed outward in a dark cloud under the river. William had slid down onto the deck with his back pressed against the posts of the railing and shook and shook.

If any part of the man was ever dredged up he never heard it. Two weeks later his brother Robert beat Levi to a pulp in the main street of Farmington with the butt of a revolver and the matter was closed.

The morning of the funeral dawned grey, muggy, a weird light shining behind the clouds and casting no shadow. They had hired two long black carriages and rode to the church in a grim silence and William wondered at the nothingness he felt. The pale faces surrounding. His daughters quiet at his side. The church itself was cold and grim and the pews felt wrong to him, hard and uncomfortable, he shifted his weight but could find no trick to it. When he rose to speak his voice sounded thin to his own ears, strained, as if he had not slept and did not believe his own words. The old Chicago attorney Luther Mills declared his father a reformer, a great man fighting the evils of the modern world. He and his brother and George Bangs and three others carried the coffin out to the hearse. It was not heavy. They might have been carrying furniture. The horses stamped in harness. Low white fences, porches, oaks, then the wrought iron gates of Graceland Cemetery. The black-ribboned wreaths and heavy white flowers lining the gateposts, dragging against their own weight as in a slow current of sorrow. The small knot of newspapermen standing respectfully aside.

What did he recall of that morning? Margaret's gloved hand on his wrist. He could hear his frail mother weeping and he peered around him but could not comprehend what he saw. Figures in black, grey faces. The pastor had fallen silent with the book closed upon one finger and he extended a sorrowful hand that all there might bow their heads all but one and that one glared about him with a hollowness where once had been some gentler thing. Somewhere across that green field of the dead a bell was tolling. There were stones and monuments gleaming whitely under the strange light, the rain-blown sky steeped in it. Nearby lay Kate Warne decomposing in her burial clothes and the remains of Ignatius Spaar attendants both and buried with their liege and William thought of this and then he tried not to. He felt light-headed, sick. He stepped forward with his brother and together they took up the shovels and turned them. A scrape of iron, a sift and slide of dry soil and small stones. Robert's eyes were wet. He could hear Margaret crying softly near him.

He stood like that at the edge of the earth, staring down into darkness, the cold sky whorling over his head, and he felt the worst of it enter him like a sickness and settle there in his blood.

The worst of it. Yes that.

What he felt was not grief, or not grief only. Not grief only but also the black amoral joy of a man adrift. He had nowhere he needed to be.

What he felt, staring down at his father's rosewood coffin, was relief.

THIRTY-FIVE

When the knocking came it came urgent, maddened, and they froze each across from each in Foole's study and locked eyes thinking the same thing. The hour had passed midnight and not stopped. Foole could feel the blood loud in his ears. He did not think the Yard could have traced them so quickly. Then he knew in a sudden swift panic who must be outside.

Pinkerton.

He had not yet told the others of his humiliation at the dinner party. Fludd withdrew from a hidden sheath behind the bookcase a long curved blade, an evil thing Foole hated the sight of. He gestured at Molly and she started to roll the painting carefully back up in its scroll.

He did not kill the lamps. In the hall where no lights burned he drew aside a corner of the curtain but he could not see the step nor the big American with his dead eyes and strangler's hands. He thought of what Pinkerton had done to those ramps-men with their coshes in the alley behind the Lascar's and he set his jaw and hurried. He could hear the knock sounding again and there was something else, a kind of scraping he could not identify. He wondered if the detective was picking the front lock. Fludd went to the stairs moving with a murderous silence and Foole in his study peeled off his frock coat and his shirt as Molly held out his robe wordlessly. He clawed his hands through his hair to muss it. When he descended he found Fludd already looming silent in shadow. Foole did not look at the knife in his fist. He could see through the stained glass of the door the blurred outline of an arm, a shoulder, but no distinguishing mark to them and he felt all at once the hairs on the back of his neck stand on end. The knocking sounded a third time, angry, commanding.

Yes, yes, coming, Foole called out irritatedly. He had a hand on the bolt to draw it back when he saw too late that he still wore his shoes, crusted with the filth of the streets. He knew Pinkerton would see it at once but there was nothing to be done. He opened the door.

A cold blackness. A rush of freezing air on his face.

There, on the step, with one fist upraised and darkness tangling her hair, stood Charlotte Reckitt. He stared at her in confusion.

Charlotte? he whispered.

Hello Adam, she said, and her voice was what he remembered, water in sunlight.

American Detective

———

1862

VIRGINIA

He was no one's son.

He was small with black whiskers still coming in and burning violet eyes and a soft accent that might have been Virginian and there seemed great beauty in him, like a buried suffering. In that second week of May 1862 he was still a boy and the seething streets of Richmond still mysterious. He wore Confederate grey as if it belonged on him, a man among men, nodding his slow nod to all. His uncle had been with Jackson in the Shenandoah, he said. No they were not licked yet, he said. He was down from Baltimore the only son of a captured courier there and he had carried his father's mails across the lines and no sir he did not think he would go north again. He could be found staring across the grey river in the morning light running his fingers over the malformed lump of his left shoulder as if to massage a limb that was no longer. There was smoke rising above the Chickahominy. He smoked and shared his tobacco with any who asked. Officers with sabres at their sides, stiff white gloves shining. Barefoot boys younger than himself running messages from the Twenty-Third Virginia at Camp Lee. In the afternoons the Capitol gleamed its marble truth over a martial city and the clatter of regimental drums could be heard from the old fairgrounds and all day the guns on their great wheels would bog down in the streets and the powerful horses would heave against their weight in the muck and old men would come out of the shopfronts wiping their hands on their aprons to watch. He walked among them, one of them, fierce.

But he was not that one. In truth he had been sent from the North to move among them like a viper through tall grass and he felt the poison of it as if he were sick with it himself. The man who had sent him was a burly Scot with hard hands and a barrel chest and caustic blue eyes and who answered to the Union rank of Major. The boy's task was clear. Break two Union spies from prison before they perished by bullet or by rope or by plague.

He was alone in that enemy capital, without ally or recourse. And should he fail or be caught he would meet his death blind-folded and roped to a stake under a hail of executioners' fire and be kicked into a shallow grave outside the walls of Richmond. No man would know to mourn his loss.

No man but one.

One week earlier while a dying sun reddened below the treeline Edward had stood in a clearing, south of the Union pickets, watching as the Porters finished their preparations. The jour-ney would take most of the night. The Major stood with a hand on the boy's shoulder as if to claim him for his own, his hat pulled low to conceal his face. Ben trudged the perimeter of the waggon and squatted to check its axles then rose and tightened the straps on the withered mule. Sally called to her husband some instruction and then gathered her skirts and clambered into the flatbed and kicked through the straw for buried sup-plies. When both were satisfied they straightened and regarded the boy. No one spoke. Edward held a tied bedroll under one arm and he had wrapped a small ivory-handled pistolet in an oilskin and stuffed it into the bedding and he carried nothing else. He gave the Major a look and the older man nodded and stepped back. Sally was crouched in the straw, a shawl at her shoulders. Edward and Ben climbed up onto the bench seat, crushed together. In the gathering dusk the flies were biting.

Edward swiped at his throat. When he glanced back the Major was already gone.

Darkness came on. They rode east and then south and then east again in the night forest. A single lantern burned weakly on a rod over the mule's crooked back casting all into eerie relief. Ben had removed his earrings and gold chain and without a weapon at his side he looked somehow more sinister, more dangerous. He led them down ancient grassy tracks through the forest and twice he lost his way and retraced his steps and they went on. They passed a solitary house standing dark in a clearing but no one came out to greet them and they rolled creaking past and did not stop. At the marshy shores of the James, Edward got down and took up his bedroll and his small hat and he nodded to the Porters and they nodded gravely in return.

Godspeed, Sally murmured.

Ben shifted on the bench, clicked the reins. You be safe now, he grunted.

Edward walked the remaining distance alone. The moon was out and once onto the riverbank the light was enough to go by. He was careful to wade through mud and wipe his shirt cuffs and backside with dirt and bark. He slept that night in a stone farmhouse under the baleful glower of two widowed sisters. They were gold-skinned with long Iberian faces and sad eyes and dressed alike in grey homespun dresses and might have been twins to Edward's eye. Rebel sympathizers both and key links in a Confederate fifth column. Before dawn a boy his own age in ragged trousers stood whistling at the gate with a lobster cage slung over one shoulder and the sisters woke him and gave him a packet of cold chicken and corn cakes and led him across the yard in their nightdresses like homesteaders fleeing a fire.

Edward had felt nothing at first, neither fear nor dread nor gratitude. The boy rowed him across the smoky waters to the Confederate shore and shipped his oars at the far bank and folded his fingers to his mouth and called a bird cry into the ominous woods for the pickets to know. Edward huddled in the stern watching the water run down the oar shafts in the half-light, listening to the waves slap at the hull. When he stepped from the slow roll of the rowboat into the shallows to splash ashore a soldier materialized out of the trees with his Enfield lowered and his eyes lost in shadow. The Confederates had commandeered a thatched cottage two miles away and a peat fire was burning in its hearth when they arrived and Edward held his hands to the smoulder of it, nervous. He fumbled his pass from the cuff of one soaked boot with stiff fingers. The infantry captain interviewing him sat on a three-legged stool before the fire huddled in a blanket and he seemed very tired. Edward watched the day come on through the dirty windows and when asked he unstitched the packet of letters from the lining of his coat and passed them across.

The captain told Edward passes were being revoked. Spies had been at work, he explained. There was a Union force preparing to march on Richmond.

Edward nodded, said nothing.

The captain said he had not seen his wife and daughters in over a year and he did not believe he would see them again. He said his smallest had been born blind. There were tiny etched lines at the corners of the man's eyes and his lashes were so pale as to look dusted in the early light.

Well, son, he said. Tell Mr. Davis if you see him there are brave men here who just want to fight and be done with it.

Somewhere bacon was sizzling in a pan, a man was coughing. Somewhere a door had been left ajar.

Everything lay still before him, a lifetime yet unlived. He walked in the middle of the road and was picked up by a passing waggon carrying bolts of silk to Richmond and when he reached the city he again showed his pass and was escorted under armed guard to a nondescript stone building behind a hedge. He was instructed to report to the intelligence-gatherer Cashmeyer on the second floor. He swallowed uneasily, stared at his scuffed boots, then went up. In an airy antechamber he was told to wait

and sat under a tall portrait of Jefferson Davis drumming his
fingers on his knees and through the windows he could hear
birds singing. The gentleness of the light, the elegance of the
marble pillars beyond the doors were at odds with the cruelty
of its purpose. For the Major had warned him about this place.
No traveller entered Richmond without first registering with
Cashmeyer's people. He was the rebels' Pinkerton, a captain in
the Confederate secret service and an investigator out of the
provost marshal's office serving under General Winder and one
of the men responsible for the arrest of Lewis and Scully and
the hanging of Timothy Webster. He had fingers, Southerners
said, like a spider.

A soldier came out, studied him, unimpressed. Come, he
said. Let's go.

Edward rose. Rumpled yet in his travelling clothes, mud
crusted on his boots.

Cashmeyer got up from behind his desk and shook Edward's
hand and gestured to a sofa under a window. He offered tea,
biscuits. The man had very small ears turned outward from his
head, he was wide-shouldered, his blond hair thinning. His eyes
were so dark as to look black in the sunlight.

Your uncle was in the Shenandoah? Cashmeyer said.

Yessir.

I know your father. I was sorry to hear of his arrest.

Spies, sir, Edward said, letting a venom creep into his voice.
Someone spoke out of turn, I reckon. Sold him out.

Any idea who?

Edward shook his head angrily. I'd cut his throat if I knew
it, sir.

Cashmeyer sucked his lips into a frown, studied the boy.
Then he rose and crossed to the window and peered through
the slats with his face hidden. He never mentioned he had a boy.
You have some colour to you, son.

Edward cleared his throat. My mother was Spanish.

Spanish?

Yessir.

The Spaniards are the niggers of Europe, Cashmeyer said softly. It is a sad fact but true. That is what comes of a history of being conquered. He stared out of the window at the streets of Richmond, lost in thought. A lad has two bloodlines in him. Which will be the stronger? Does he have a say in it, or is he already what he will be?

Edward said nothing.

Cashmeyer grunted, half turned, hands still clasped at his back. Some would say that is what this war is about. A man's right to choose his own self. Is the North to rule without our consent? Or do we have a right to our own destiny?

Yessir.

Cashmeyer turned back to the window. But they would be wrong, he murmured. That is not what this war is about.

A moment passed. Edward stood with his hands damp at his sides, waiting. The captain said nothing more and at last Edward said: Sir?

Cashmeyer turned, as if surprised the boy was still there. Welcome to the free Confederacy, son, he said. There'll be a room for you at the Spotswood. We'll find a use for your talents yet.

He took a room on the third floor of the Spotswood Hotel as instructed and rose early the next morning and walked uphill to the Capitol through the rain. The days began their slow passing. A Negro chambermaid near his age made eyes at him each morning but he ignored her. He recorded what he could in a small notebook at night by candlelight though he sent no reports out. The breastworks were of split pine logs with a 64-pounder and a traverse of 180 degrees, he wrote. There were seventeen batteries surrounding the capital, he wrote. The defending soldiers were equipped with Enfields from England smuggled in via Bermuda. He observed that sickness had thinned the ranks of the infantry but that the cavalry remained strong and he noticed that hay of any quality was scarce, the prices wild and fluctual. He estimated some 75,000 fighting men stood to arms in Richmond. He hid the notebook and the small ivory-handled pistolet between his mattress and the headboard. He did not approach the prisons.

Edward walked now among the Confederate officers in the rain and he saw the same faces as in the North, the same fever, same youth, same blood. In his second week in Richmond he made his way out to the old fairgrounds at Camp Lee and stared at the scaffold that stood yet where Timothy Webster had been hanged. The grass was still trampled down to mud from the crowds that day and he stood on a low rise alone against the cloudy light and stared across at the devastation of it. Webster had died well, had warned the soldiers to make the noose tight. Edward never met the man but wished he had. The two spies remaining, John Scully and Pryce Lewis, had been arrested seven weeks earlier while trying to locate Webster and when Webster went to the scaffold and they did not rumours started up. It was said Lewis had betrayed him to his death. It was said Scully had revealed the Major's networks in the South. But the two men remained in prison and the Major did not believe the talk and Edward, if nothing else, trusted the Major.

In the last days of May after McClellan had taken Mechanicsville and the Union guns rolled to within five miles of the city he became aware of a man following him. The man wore a long unkempt beard and stained grey trousers like a labourer down on his luck but his eyes were clear and very blue. Everywhere a quiet hardness lay across the city and its inhabitants waded through the muddy streets with their hats low and their eyes fierce in the knowledge of what was coming. Edward would leave his hotel in the morning and see the man lounging in a doorway across the street, thumbs hooked in his pockets, his watch chain glinting in the sunlight. An able-bodied man in the heart of the Confederacy doing nothing. Conspicuously.

He learned from a shoeshine boy that the man was an agent of Cashmeyer's and something cold and evil turned over inside him to hear it. He had by that time worked out several plans to free Lewis and Scully but each time as the hour drew near some unexpected interference arose. He had learned that the two men were being held in Castle Godwin, a fierce scorched-brick building set back from Carey Street with grim slitted windows in its rear and a rotted fence running the perimeter. He had taken to walking past it on his morning rounds but he ceased doing so in his uneasiness. At first he had thought to work his way into the prison as a visitor but when that seemed to draw too much attention he had abandoned it and began to collect sticks of dynamite for an assault when the Union army began its shelling. As the shells struck he would shatter one wall of the prison from earth to sky and walk through that breach and carry Lewis and Scully to freedom. Then McClellan hesitated at the Chickahominy and did not advance and then Edward grew anxious and started to look for another way. He cultivated a friendship with one of the younger wardens thinking to find some weakness there but that man was redeployed into Lee's army and killed at Glendale and Edward did not think it wise to approach another. What he needed, in fact, was some accomplice. Some second man.

Then in the second week Cashmeyer's agent was replaced by a different man, much older, and in the third week Lee began his counterattack and the Infernal Week boiled over in all its fury and the Union forces were pushed back past Malvern Hill and Edward found himself again alone.

He was ogling the windows of a harness-maker's display on Carey Street in early July when he saw in the rippled glass two dark figures pass at his shoulder. He stood very still, his own reflection blurred and pale. Then he turned and followed.

This was after the Union retreat, after the slaughter of Malvern Hill. He was trapped in Richmond by then. He followed the men towards the centre of the city and walked slow and kept his distance. The smaller of the two, a man with a bony neck and a delicate white suit, spoke furtively and rapidly.

The taller only listened. Then the taller nodded farewell and slipped alone past the lintel of a storefront and inside. Edward crossed the street at a jog, followed him in. It was a butcher's shop and the man he sought stood at the counter with his back to Edward and he was holding out a hand for a wrapped paper package. The man chuckled and tipped his hat to the butcher and brushed past Edward's shoulder and a moment later the shop door banged open and then he was gone without so much as a glance Edward's way.

His beard had come in since Edward had seen him last, yes, his accent was thicker here in the heart of the Confederacy. But the scars were the same.

Ignatius Spaar.

At breakfast the next morning Edward found the two men in silent concentration over plates of sausages and eggs and he sat at their table in his grey cotton suit and took off his hat and held out a hand. Both men lifted their faces: surprised, interested, calculating. Spaar took Edward's right hand in an awkward left-handed grip, grunted in greeting. His companion set down his knife and fork, smiled. He was an attorney-at-law out of Texas named Marvell.

I've seen you about, son, Spaar said pleasantly, still chewing. You're that courier came down out of Baltimore. Folks say you crossed the lines alone.

Yessir. Edward dipped his head. My mama always said I was lucky as a duck in a puddle.

I couldn't speak to luck, young man, the attorney said. But you're certainly brave.

Thank you, sir.

His father was arrested, Mr. Marvell. In Baltimore.

Marvell crushed his eyes shut in sympathy. I am sorry to hear that. I am.

You're not from Richmond either of you, then?

Marvell chuckled. I don't know as anyone is, really.

Edward lifted an eyebrow, smiled vaguely.

I'm just to passing through myself, Spaar said. I come up here to the capital on wheat business. Trying to establish some sort of norm to keep the prices steady. Won't do if our boys all starve to death before they have a chance to knock on Mr. Lincoln's door. He smiled around the room in the clean July sunlight and then he fixed his pale eyes on Edward and he held his gaze. Smiling with all his long teeth, his burned skin webbed with scars.

Edward looked away. And what's your business in the capital, Mr. Marvell?

Ah, his is an interesting affair, Spaar said.

Marvell wiped at his mouth, set his crumpled napkin in a ball on his plate. I'll tell you, son. You've heard of those spies captured here in Richmond, last April?

I heard a little, sir.

Marvell shrugged. Well. I've come to offer my services to the Confederacy. To defend those two men in their case.

Edward smiled a confused smile. Defend them?

Marvell nodded.

I don't understand. You mean you want to help them?

The attorney laughed. I don't wish to help them, no. There's no helping those men. I wish to help the Confederacy. They shall need to go to trial. And when they do, the law requires they be provided with counsel. You might say I have come to expedite the process.

To expedite it.

It's all somewhat strange, son, Spaar interjected. But it wouldn't do for the Confederacy to appear to be flouting its own laws. We have allies we need to court, see. Britain, France, and such. It makes it far harder for Mr. Davis to draw in their support if we appear to be less than lawful. Is that about the matter of it, Mr. Marvell?

Marvell smiled. And to think I feared I had bored you, sir, with all my talk yesterday.

Edward had always liked Spaar in spite of himself. There

was in him something brutal and merciless but too the man could be easy and fine and strong. Someone had told Edward once that Spaar never won a game of cards against a private and never lost a game to an officer.

They rose now from their breakfast with Edward wiping at his mouth and they went out into the white sunlight of that July street, the smell of the heat coming off the walls of the buildings and the dust under the hooves of the passing horses. Their shadows long and crooked before them. Marvell took his leave: a nod and two fingers to his brim, an excuse. Edward and Spaar walked on slowly, talking the while. When clear of any's earshot Edward dropped the accent and said, Affable fellow, interesting line of work. How did you meet?

Would you believe by chance?

Edward cast a sharp sidelong look. I don't believe I would.

The man ran a finger along his ravaged lip where the sweat was already beading. They had been walking west through the city and they made their way out towards Camp Lee where Webster had been hanged those two months gone. The scaffold long since dismantled. The grass scavenged and yellow.

What are you doing here, Mr. Spaar?

Spaar kicked a heel through the ruff and gave Edward a long cool look.

The Major sent me, he said at last. I came to find you.

To find me.

Spaar nodded.

Is there a message?

Yes there's a message.

Edward waited but Spaar said nothing, only picked at his teeth with a long blade of grass and stared thoughtfully down at the camp, the soldiers drilling there, the guns and horses gleaming in the sunlight.

What's the message?

Spaar's hairline glistened in the heat. I've been sent to bring you back, Edward, he said. I've been sent to get you out.

———

That very night Spaar strode into Edward's hotel and tucked his walking stick under one sleeve and argued loudly with the clerk for a reservation that ought to have been in place but was to his great astonishment not registered and Edward happened by and interjected politely that if there were some error he would be pleased to share his own room. The clerk stared at him in relief. Oh but there were two beds one on either side of a street-facing window and he did not mind, no, anything to help a fellow patriot, gentlemen.

Spaar's orders had been clear. He was to locate Edward and smuggle him north again under the cover of a private loss. He had left a loaded cart and horse at a farmstead three miles west of the city and he would take Edward through the trees to that isolated spot at the earliest moment. When Edward asked how he had crossed the lines during the fighting at Malvern Hill Spaar got a strange look and the cords stood out in his neck and he said, tiredly, The Major wants you back in one piece, Edward. We need to go.

Edward gave him a cautious look. Something did not seem right though he could not explain it. I can't, he said, not yet. Not until I've done what I came here to do.

Spaar raised an eyebrow. Meaning what?

You don't know?

Spaar shrugged. I don't know what you were sent here to do, son. My instructions don't take it into account.

Edward frowned and rose and crossed to the door and listened.

No one's listening, Edward. We're quite secure. What's your purpose here?

But Edward crossed the room again and sat next to Spaar and cupped a hand at the man's ear and whispered, I could use your help. I'm here to break Lewis and Scully from Godwin.

Spaar pulled back, squinted at Edward. The hell you are, he said. Alone? Who have you contacted? How do you aim to proceed?

Edward met the scarred man's eye and smiled. About that, he whispered. Your Mr. Marvell might prove of use.

A day passed, a second, the two men turning over in their heads possible approaches. He told Spaar about Cashmeyer and General Winder's undercover agents. Marvell had come to offer his services to the Confederacy and as such would have access to the two prisoners. Access, Edward brooded, that he himself had failed to secure. If Marvell could be drawn to their purpose then a plan might be executed. Spaar disagreed. His methods were the more brutal.

On the third night Spaar slipped out into the darkness alone and returned an hour later with blood flecking his wrists and trousers, his blue eyes haunted.

Edward locked the door behind him. What did you do? he hissed.

What needed to be done, he said. Mr. Marvell will not trouble us now.

The next morning Spaar walked to Winder's headquarters to report his presence in Richmond and to offer his services as counsel. He returned with a slow wide grin and tipped Edward's hat playfully back on his head and said, They've heard of me. Mr. Marvell, who successfully found against cattle thieves in Texas. They found my offer rather compelling.

Edward grinned.

But there was a strange look on Spaar's face sometimes when he thought Edward was not watching him. In the afternoons Spaar would vanish into the cold halls of Castle Godwin to meet with Lewis and Scully and weigh their health and condition against what would be required of them and Edward would begin to prepare their escape. He had Spaar press an imprint of the warden's keys and then had a duplicate copy made and he took to walking through the hotel stable yard with an apple for the old sorrel in its stall there. He bought items of spare clothing from several different shops over the course of a week and he was careful to wear some of them when he went out. He bought two pairs of boots. Spaar took an interest in

Edward's earlier failed attempts and grilled him on the names of his accomplices. He said it was to prevent such mistakes being repeated. Edward did not entirely believe him. Spaar smuggled the duplicate keys to Lewis. He told Edward that the two men were kept from each other and that they were thin and depressed and there was an anger in Scully that was not in Lewis. He said Lewis would run his fingers over the edges of the bricks in the wall of his cell with a kind of obsessive calm and he feared the two men were weakening. One morning as Edward was inspecting the wheels of the small straw-filled cart in the yard the hotel clerk came out with a message for him and he realized he would need to be more careful. He had already visited John P. Jones seeking a pass north and had suffered the clerk's ferret-like stare and sour questions but now upon his return he was given his requested papers without a second glance. That too should have given him pause.

On the evening of the twelfth he and Spaar walked again back out to Camp Lee as if to take the air and there Edward drew in the dust with a stick a rough map of the city and he went over the following night's plan and then he wiped the map clear with the toe of his boot and gave Spaar the stick and had Spaar explain it all to him word for word.

You've got the one chance at this, kid, Spaar told him. You come north with me, whatever happens.

Evening faded. Cicadas sang, the linden trees were eaten by shadow. Then the stars wheeled up over the horizon and the skyline was sucked down and the man-made lights of the world came on one by one until the face of the earth and the face of the waters burned alike with pinpricks of light.

Edward nodded.

Tell it to me one more time, he said.

Finally a night would come years after the war when he would sleep a long dreamless sleep. When he would not wake with one hand lurching for a pistol and his eyes roving through the darkness. There would be great fields of the ploughed dead by then and half a nation still smouldering in ruins and he would stand at the cold hotel window of a city across the ocean and stare out at the bird-stained horsemen in their stone shakos and marvel at the ancient cruelty.

The war would end. The dead would not. That was the dawn of industrial war and Edward would understand only slowly that killing on such a scale could be a kind of commerce. When he knew that, he knew some faith in his fellow man had been compromised and he could not come back from it. He would wonder about the boy James Gray from Mrs. Shade's estate, whom he had not thought of in years. That boy had been two years his elder and ripe for enlistment and he would wonder if his bones lay now in some field of the Ohio rolled in a man's coat two sizes too big or scattered in pieces under the muck of some earthworks long overrun and gone to grass. He had seen too many dead to think otherwise. But perhaps the boy had gone west. Or died in the poorhouse before the war began.

On the night of the new moon he and Spaar walked out of their hotel together in the quarter-hour after ten o'clock. They carried nothing but their jackets and they did not slow as they passed through the lobby. They wore their derby hats low. Outside Edward slipped down an alley and entered the rear stables through an unlocked gate in the fence and Spaar took his hand and wished him safe passage. They would rendezvous at the bridge road leading south of the city. As he stepped away he glanced back. Spaar was watching him with a look of murder in his eye.

Inside the gate he took the sorrel from her stall and walked her to the cart in its corner of the yard and he hitched her into harness and walked her by the bit from the yard talking to her the while in a low voice. In the alley he stood with one hand on her nose and leaned towards her and murmured and when she was calm he climbed onto the cart and set off.

The streets were very dark, the city unlit. He made his way through the narrow lanes among the houses avoiding the main

streets as he could. He carried passes for himself and Lewis
and Scully and in the bed of the cart were two rolled bundles
of clothes for the spies and a pair of old boots for each. In a
quiet side street under a row of linden trees he heard a voice
call out to him to hold up and he turned in alarm and saw a
cavalry captain approaching him on foot. He thought it
strange the man was not on horseback but he did not ask. The
captain asked for his pass and Edward handed him the paperwork nervously.

Where you headed at this hour, son? The captain looked to
Edward like the scion of some plantation bloodline playing at
war. He ran a gloved finger over his nose, he frowned. There's
a curfew in effect, son.

Yessir.

The captain walked around to the bed of the cart, peered
into the straw there as if hesitant to touch it. After a moment
he took off his white glove finger by finger then turned over the
straw and withdrew the bundle of clothes. He held up one of
the boots. What's this?

Edward shrugged. I'm to shovel the latrines at Camp Lee,
sir. It's a change of clothes for the ride back. You can smell them
from here, I reckon.

The captain stared. Chewed at his lip, flicked again through
the papers.

Edward could smell the fresh soap on the captain's skin
and he saw the man was wearing his dress tunic and had
shaved that evening. After a moment the captain grunted and
then he handed back the papers and said, All right, son. Go
ahead.

Edward was sweating heavily along his spine as he clicked
the reins and went on. He slowed at each crossing and sat listening and then continued on his way. He had been careful to
grease the axle of the cart and it rolled with great smoothness
through the quiet city. He had given himself twenty minutes to
reach the prison and he would slow and open his pocket watch
to gauge the time and then go on. He knew Lewis would be

working his way free even now and that he would need to make his way soundlessly down two floors to reach Scully before both of them could get out to the yard. That way would take them through two doors and along a corridor frequented by the night warden and once in the yard the two men would need to move some of the trash against the far corner and clamber over the wall into the alley below. All of this would take by Spaar's reckoning some fourteen minutes.

He paused, clutching the reins, he rode on.

When he reached the prison he slowed and got down and walked the sorrel into the alley and he stared at the shadows for some sign. He clicked his tongue twice and listened but he heard nothing. The brick wall of the prison was very tall and lost in shadow and the prison beyond it was a huge blackness against the night sky. He left the sorrel standing with her head down and walked into the gloom with his arms outstretched and calling softly, Hello? Hello?

There was no one. The alley was deserted.

He tilted his pocket watch into the weak light from the sky. The half-hour came and passed. Then it was eleven o'clock. Eleven-thirty. Still there was no movement. The sorrel nickered and he stood with one hand on her neck in the darkness. She was long-legged and high-backed and built for running not pulling loads of any weight but a war was on and horses scarce. His thought had been to sacrifice the cart to the weeds once clear of the city. To split up and for two to ride at speed and two to walk overland.

His eyes were sore and he rubbed them with his thumbs. At the mouth of the alley something clattered like a bucket knocking over and he glared fearfully down into the shadows. His mouth was dry. He understood something had gone wrong.

At last he could wait no longer. He glanced around a last time then snicked the reins. The cart moved down the dirt alley, the wood creaked quietly, the sorrel's hooves almost silent in the dust. It was thirty minutes past midnight. He turned his back on the prison, he rode on.

The narrow lanes were deserted, the leafy trees still, the houses dead.

They had not come.

He rode the cart back through the lightless streets listening to the harness jingle. He could not think what had gone wrong but as there had been no ambush he knew it could not be a betrayal. His first thought had been that Scully or Lewis had been transferred abruptly. His second thought was they had been killed. But for all he knew they might have simply been too weak to escape or been caught in the act or even just lost their nerve.

Spaar was waiting in the darkness at the bridge road and Edward felt a dread settle in him at the sight like a warning of things to come. He slowed but did not stop and Spaar swung up beside him on the bench. He could see in the man's face that he understood something had gone wrong. He did not ask.

Spaar got down one block from the hotel and went on ahead. Edward backed the cart into its place in the silent yard and unhitched the sorrel and removed her harness and walked her into the stable. He was afraid now that someone might hear but no lights came on in the windows and if any in that hotel saw they did not approach. When he went up the room was dark but he could see Spaar in his hat and coat seated at the edge of his bed and Edward took the certificates of passage from his pocket and slid them under his mattress. He felt angry and foolish and very frightened. All around them the hotel was still. A faint light was coming in from the street below.

Well, kid? Spaar said at last.

He shook his head, the gesture meaningless in the gloom. He said, angrily: I waited in that alley for two hours.

After a moment Spaar said: We go in the morning. You agreed.

Now that it had been said aloud it seemed to Edward a terrible thing.

You gave Lewis the keys?

Spaar sighed.

You put them in his hand?

Lewis and Scully are friends of mine. I don't like leaving them either.

Edward bit at his lip. I want to find out what happened. I want to know if there's another chance.

He heard Spaar shift on his mattress, kick off a boot, then another. His voice when he spoke was measured, wary. That's not what we agreed. I'd guess Lewis thought it would have been suicide.

He felt he had failed them and failed the Major back at his camp and he was afraid he might start to cry. After a long moment he said quietly: For who?

Spaar said nothing.

Edward lay back in the darkness still clothed and feeling a heaviness in his chest and hating himself for it. He thought Spaar unusually pressed to get him to leave Richmond and he did not quite understand why. He shifted onto his side, rucked the pillow up under his ear. You know I never killed no one yet, Mr. Spaar, he said. I guess fate's been saving it up.

Spaar was slow to answer. At last he murmured, It's not worth the saving. Weren't you at Cheat Mountain?

Yessir.

And you still think you've never killed anyone?

Cheat Mountain. Edward ran his tongue over his cracked lips. You didn't know what you were shooting. You couldn't see anything for the smoke. It's not the same.

Killing's killing. In the final reckoning, not seeing it won't work in your favour.

The final reckoning.

Yes.

You mean like Judgment Day.

You don't believe there's going to be one?

Edward rolled his small shoulder in the gloom, the stiffness in it. I think it's already come, he said.

They were quiet a long time then and Edward folded his arms up under his pillow and he stared at the ceiling and he said, You sleeping yet?

No.

I keep thinking about Mr. Webster. How he wasn't afraid.

What makes you think that? They listened to the sound of footsteps in the street below pass and fade away into the night. Being afraid's nothing, Edward. It means nothing.

I know it.

We'll be north of the lines this time tomorrow. Get some sleep.

He closed his eyes and listened to Spaar breathing and he realized he did not trust the man. He opened his eyes. What'll the Major say when he sees us?

The Major gave me clear instructions, said Spaar and the reply seemed strange to Edward even then. Go to sleep, Edward.

He did not think he could sleep but somehow he slept. The night deepened. Sometime before dawn a man crossed the room his bare feet making no sound and a goose pillow clutched in his fists. Leaning over Edward long and willowy and grey as a ghost and then placing the pillow firmly but gently over his face and leaning his weight into it even as Edward began to thrash and struggle up out of sleep.

Then Edward's eyes were open, he was writhing and kicking out. He felt something on his chest, the weight of a man's knee pinioning his arms in place, he could smell the soap on a man's hands and he twisted to one side and loosed one arm and tore at the pillow. A flat emotionless face. A webbing of scars. Eyes calm, resigned.

Then Spaar leaned back into the pillow, crushing the life from him.

Years later he would stand with a dying friend on a concrete breakwater at the mouth of the James and stare out at the whitecaps in the slate ocean as a ferry approached and he would try to account for those days. Seabirds wheeling and crying in the high air. Dazzling in their whiteness. And him leaning with his thumbs hooked in his trouser pockets and the lower buttons of his frock coat unfastened and the wind whipping his white hair to spume. He was old by then though not in years and stiff with a kind of fascinated sorrow for what he had outlived. The slow unfolding of that night. How he managed to withdraw his pistolet from its hiding place behind the headboard and club Spaar on the temple with the stock. His sudden gasping for air. He had rolled off the bed tangled in the sheets. He remembered the fear, he said. It was like a taste he could not wash from his mouth. The hotel room, he said, was silver and very still in the moonlight like a room underwater. Then he was standing. Spaar had been coming at him with a knife when he raised the gun and fired and when Spaar collapsed he walked terrified over and stood above him and levelled the pistolet at the dead man's face and pulled the trigger a second time.

There was the heavy tread of men on the stairs and then a long silence and then his door exploded, the frame splintering and swinging at a crazy angle in to knock the plaster from the wall. A half-dozen Confederate soldiers were shouting at him. In his fear they looked enormous, hulking. The landing beyond was lit by candles and in the eerie light he could see Cashmeyer smoking quietly and other residents standing in their open doors staring wide-eyed in and then he was being struck to the ground by a sergeant and his hands twisted behind his back and his wrists and ankles shackled. His nightshirt was rucked up over his waist. He could not understand how they had arrived so quickly.

He raised his head. A sticky black pool of blood was seeping across the floorboards, staining the bedclothes in its ink. He saw the clawed hands of Spaar, twisted in death.

A stew of teeth and brain and bone where the face had been.

There was blood on his face but it was not his own.

He was dragged like a bag of feed into the street and thrown into the bed of a waggon and his skull cracked against the boards and he felt his eyes run. Someone slapped the horse in its traces and then they were moving slowly through the darkness and he could smell the rank vinegar smell of pigs in the wood underneath him but when he raised his head he saw two soldiers squatting on the wooden rails with their rifles standing in their fists and their eyes hard on him. He was thinking of Spaar, he was thinking of Allan Pinkerton. He could make no sense of what had just happened. His eyes were wet from the stink in the wood and he turned his face away.

They took him to Castle Godwin, its scorched bricks, its terrible slave pens, and he understood as he was punched and kicked from the waggon that they would kill him. But they only held him unsteadily while Cashmeyer unfastened his ankles and frogmarched him across the mud of the yard. There were torches burning in sconces. He could see General Winder standing in a long oiled coat like a whaling captain just come ashore and his white hair was uncombed but he clenched his sharp jaw in disgust and went in before Edward reached him. Inside men were moaning in their cells. There were stone stairs. Wet straw on the floor under barred windows. Doors unlocking, locking.

Am I being charged? he mumbled. He crushed his eyes shut, opened them, he was coming slowly back to himself. Captain, he said. It was self-defence, sir. The man attacked me.

Cashmeyer stood him swaying against a brick wall as a soldier unlocked his cell and Edward could see figures moving in the darkness beyond like tall grass in a night wind except there was no wind.

Cashmeyer's eyes were lost to shadow. He wants to know the charge, he said.

One of the soldiers grinned at him.

Edward bared his teeth in fear. You can't arrest a man for defending himself.

You're not under arrest, Cashmeyer said.

Edward stared at him.

You're not under arrest, he said again. You're not even here, boy.

And then someone had taken his arm and shoved him forward and they were locking the cell again and he kneeled there in the faint light with his wrists still shackled. His jailers paid him no mind. He gritted his bloodied teeth thinking of Lewis and Scully somewhere in that prison and that he was closer to them now than he had ever been. He stared with glassy eyes through the bars of his cell, listened to the men around him cough and scratch at their flea bites. Feeling weak and whip thin, a smell of sickness already in his skin. Turning it all over in his heart.

In the morning they came for him and took him to a stained room with a drain in its floor like an abattoir and there they beat him until nightfall. They cut up his face.

They did not ask him anything.

All week they came for him.

Please, he would say. Please.

Shut his mouth. Shut your goddamn mouth, boy.

Please. Please.

And then the ropes at his wrists would tighten, the crank would click through its gears hauling him again upward to the ceiling, his shoulders cracking under the strain. Somewhere a man was screaming like a child.

One night the cell door opened and Mr. Marvell came in and crouched near him and said, You are in a mighty spot of trouble, son. I don't know as there is anything to be done for you. I'm sorry.

Edward closed his eyes, stoppered his ears. When he awoke the man was gone and Edward stared at the stone floor where he had been and he could not say if it had been a nightmare or no.

———

Was it madness in his thinking, or a new clarity? Through all
of this he struggled to make sense of Spaar, of the scarred
man's cold rage. He remembered a conversation between them,
crouched in the grass above Camp Lee, the cicadas in song. A
warm orange backlit glow seeping down under the rim of the
horizon. He had told Spaar he would not go without Lewis
and Scully.

Spaar had sighed, withdrawn a long slow knife from a sheath
under his coat. He stood a moment turning it in the light and
then said, softly, I can't leave you here, Edward.

Edward remembered staring at the weapon, smiling. What
will you do? Murder me?

Spaar's smile had faded, pity in his eyes. It was the pity
Edward thought about now, curled shuddering on a pallet of
rotting straw at the bottom of a bleak stone cell. That, and the
dead man's muttered reply: Aw, kid. Just how much do you
think a life is worth? No one sends a man into Richmond that
they can't stand to lose.

A delicate white spider was crouched two inches from his
face. It started to move, slowly, away. And at last he understood. He shivered, moaned. He had become a liability. Ignatius
Spaar was a man of vicious talents and the Major had sent him
to Richmond for a reason and that reason was not to get
Edward out.

Spaar had been sent to kill him.

He got sick. Two men held his wrist to the arm of a chair and a
third put a bayonet blade through his left hand. The week
passed, then a second. One afternoon they came for him and
he lay feverish and moaning in the filthy straw and they turned
him over with their boots and then they went away. A man
came to look at him, he pried back his lips, peered into his
throat. Unwrapped the bandages from his left hand to look for
gangrene. Later a lady stood at the cell bars holding a cloth to
her nose and asking him some muffled questions but he could

not understand her. Someone had given him a pair of shoes and
then in the night some other had taken them from him. He lost
count of the days. Some part of him understood that he had
vanished and would not be heard from again.

Then one morning he was taken from the prison in fixed
cuffs manufactured in Chicago before the war and he was loaded
into a coach under armed guard. His shirt hung slack and
befouled from his shoulder blades like a wet towel from a
branch. He stared into a pool of brackish water in the yard and
saw his hair standing on end and the huge whites of his eyes and
the outsized yellow bandages on his hand. His neck looked too
thin for his collar. There were two soldiers lashing heavy
wooden crates onto the rear of the carriage but he was shoved
inside without explanation and sat on the rear bench with a
guard staring in at him through the open door. The guard was
very young, younger even than Edward, he was bored, he was
cold. Edward felt the carriage sway as each crate was loaded. He
did not care about any of it. He shook his head and the blood
moved inside his skull like water in a half-empty jug. He asked
weakly where they were taking him.

The young soldier grinned. To hell, he said.

Please, Edward begged. Are we going north? Is it an exchange?

But the guard only pulled at his peeling upper lip, leaned
against the carriage door, shrugged.

There were two horses which meant they were to travel at
speed. But when the coach turned south outside Richmond and
then west Edward felt his hopes fade. The sun slid across the
sky, eased into the west ahead of them. They rode roughly
onward into the setting sun over the washed-out roads and the
red light drenched the carriage and lit their faces a violent red
and he closed his eyes to see it.

On the second day he thought they must be riding for Texas.
That evening they stopped at dusk at a roadside inn at the edge
of a high field and he could see the still shapes of cows grazing
there and he looked at the sky and wondered if he would soon
be dead. They would leave his body to be pulled apart by dogs

in some distant pasture. The stars were already out and wheeled right down to the horizon. The two soldiers sat inside for a long time leaving Edward handcuffed to the carriage in his thin clothes and listening to what sounded like artillery in the distance. He did not try to escape. When they returned they brought some meat and bread wrapped in an oilcloth for him but he could not eat it and his guard shrugged and set it aside.

Don't eat then, his guard said. But there was something new in it, pity maybe.

They rode into the night. A lantern had been lit on either side of the driver and cast a weak swaying light over their faces and Edward felt the eerie strangeness of that journey in his bones. It was river country, it was hill country, they crossed several bridges and went on in silence and there was an uneasiness in the young guard that made Edward wonder through his fever if they were nearing Union lines. He felt the coach dip, he felt it rise. He heard the clatter of hooves on hammered planks and then the slow rolling thunder of the coach wheels as they reached a larger bridge. He could hear the river under them. And all at once there was an enormous cracking sound and he felt a sudden jolt and he was thrown forward onto the floor. The guard across from him had braced himself with one hand on the roof and a boot kicked forward against the door and he was staring in sudden alarm out the window even as Edward felt the coach begin to slide.

Captain Redd, the guard was hollering. Captain!

Edward swore.

The horses were screaming. And all at once the roof was rising to meet him and he felt the soldier's elbow sharp in his spine and there was a long weightless moment and then one wall smashed with a bracing violence into the river. Something struck his face. Water poured through both windows in a black foam and engulfed them and he felt himself knocked power-fully backward and under and then he could not breathe.

He spun, he kicked out hard. His hands were still cuffed before him and he pushed himself upward and gasped in a small crevice of air and he felt the water rising fast. The bandages on his left hand felt huge, heavy. He could see the soldier in the far corner gasping also and he felt the boy's legs kick out and strike his ribs and he grunted and went under again. Then he had taken hold of the boy's shoulder and was pushing him under and lifting himself into the air and he could feel the boy thrashing under him there. He had twisted his body up to fill the narrow slash of air and the young soldier struggled but could not get up. Then the soldier went still. Started to drift.

The water was dark and very cold. The confusion of it was what he would remember. The feeling of weightlessness and the strange impossible uncertainty as to which direction was up. The weight of his boots and clothes was dragging him down and he kicked and writhed and struggled through the small window. His boot caught on the door and then somehow it gave way and he was out and kicking for the surface of the river. He surfaced in an explosion of breath with his hands over his head and his face streaming. There was blood in his eyes, in his mouth.

He saw no sign of the older captain. He rowed his elbows oar-like through the mud of the shore and hunched his hips and slithered and dragged and sawed himself gasping up onto the riverbank. Rolled onto his back his chest heaving and his boots still in the current.

He could not have said how long he lay in that place. His wrists bound before him, his head thrown back, his white throat naked and soft. He was sick and he slept shivering and he dreamed the cottonwoods uprooted themselves and came down the riverbank and dipped their branches in his mouth and drank from him. He could hear the river on the stones and when he lifted his face he saw the wreckage of the carriage its wheels standing splintered in the foam, its doors staved in, and he saw the huge soaked mounds of the horses half submerged in the current and the waters pulling at their manes. Where should have stood a bridge stood now only pilings and sky. The sun slid behind the trees. The forest darkened and grew cold. He slept.

He opened a feverish eye. Something was moving through the mud in the gloom.

He closed his eye.

At some point the river paled to a molten silver, dawn came on. Edward was shaking and very sick and when he raised his head he saw a bearded man in a patched coat come down to the river on the far bank and stare across at the wreckage of the Confederate coach and he made no sound when he vanished back into the trees.

When he next lifted his head the man was nudging him in the ribs with the toe of one boot. Edward grunted in pain. The man left him and sat and pulled off his boots and trousers and he folded his ragged coat and shirt over a branch and he waded out into the river looking pink as a plucked chicken with a line of grime at his throat and wrists. He returned dragging from the river a low raft piled with rope and Confederate boxes and four boots and the two Enfield rifles all salvaged from the swamped coach and then the man was bending over him, turning out his pockets, and Edward was too weak to protest. He was a very big man bearded and thin like a starved ox. His collarbone stood stark and his shoulders sharp and his every rib was articulated in the sunlight. There was a savagery in his crooked nose and fierce thin lips and Edward thought for a long and terrible moment that he had been found by one of the Comanche but then the man kneeled and scooped Edward into his arms and he carried him through the cottonwoods and along a ravine and up into the hills.

The man's hands were gentle, his skin dry as snakeskin. He laid Edward frail and trembling upon a blanket, he offered him water. He took out a pouch from under his coat and poured several long iron keys onto the ground and selected one and unlocked Edward's cuffs. These he pocketed carefully. He stripped Edward from his coat and trousers and he rolled him into the dry blanket and carried him nearer the fire. He said nothing. A day passed. Perhaps two.

It was at dusk that Edward awoke at last and he found himself in a high encampment propped against the wall of a stockade and the man who had saved him was watching him from near the fire. They were alone. He seemed to be a tinker and his cart stood nearby with a canvas shell stretched across it and his varied tools laid out for the working of leather and metals and a starved horse stood some ways off regarding them with a single terrified eye.

Ye ain't dead then, the tinker said.

His voice was hoarse from long disuse and he spoke with a strange bent accent like an Englishman but not like an Englishman. Whatever he was he was no Southerner.

Edward's tongue felt huge, dry as a sponge in his mouth. He swallowed painfully.

You got a name? the tinker said.

When Edward still said nothing the tinker busied himself at the fire scraping a pan over the stones and something sizzled. Edward shut his eyes. Opened his eyes. The streaks on the man's sleeves where he had cleaned his knife. The twin Enfields stacked against a log.

Shaking his huge shaggy head. He squinted one eye as if to take the boy's measure and there was something new in it, a kind of menace. I recognize that look, he said.

Edward raised his slow head.

Like a cat starin down a hole. Just what sort of man are you?

Edward's teeth were clenched, he was shaking with the fever. Firelight shone slick on the stones. Just what sort, he said, are you? Steeling himself for a fight.

The huge tinker studied him then all at once he grinned. He had a tooth out in front.

Edward balled up his fists.

But the giant only held out a hand, huge and black as if seamed with coal. Easy now. If I were goin to kill you, you'd be dead already, he chuckled. Me name's Fludd.

Fludd.

Aye. And behold, I, even I, do bring a flood of waters upon the earth, to destroy all flesh, wherein is the breath of life, from under heaven. The tinker's eyes were very dark and strange as he spoke. After a moment he added, softly, An every thing that is in the earth shall die.

Edward glanced around at the encroaching darkness. How long you been alone up here? he asked.

The man Fludd grinned and grinned.

Long enough to find God, he said. An long enough to lose Him.

It's not courage if you're not afraid, the Major would say. Cigar smoke like a strange incense in the fabric of his tent. His shirt sleeves rolled back, beard wild, the big pre-war map of the valley laid flat on the table before them. A man who doesn't know fear is a man I don't trust, he would say. But it's what you do with the fear that matters.

Or he would set his big hand on the boy's hat and crush it down over his eyes as the cavalry rode out in clouds of red dust and say, A man can be read just like a book. You can flip through him and find the page you want.

Edward, who had watched Allan Pinkerton and loved him. Who had studied the way the older man's eyes in a crowded room were always moving into the corners, towards the swell of curtains or the opening of doors. Studied his ropy forearms and the bullish sinews in his neck and the way he would chomp down on a cigar through his bristling beard as if he would bite any hand that came near him. The Major was gruff and strict and quick to shout but he did not shout at Edward even the once and there was ever a gentleness in his eye when he looked at the boy. He said he himself lived without fear and that this was only possible because he was so often afraid. At sunset on that fateful night he had stood with Edward while the Porters crouched in the muck inspecting axle and harness and he had told Edward he wished he could go with him.

He said: I will find a way to bring you back.

One gnarled hand gripping the boy's shoulder. The crease as his blue eyes hardened.

You won't have to, said the boy. I'll bring them back, sir. Both of them.

Look at you, the man said. You could be my own son, lad.

*The Eye That
Never Sleeps*

1885

LONDON

THIRTY-SIX

No one noticed it was gone, sir. Not all weekend. Blackwell's scuffed bowler was drawn firmly down to his eye line, his shoulders swaying with the growler. Not until Mr. Farquhar found the letter, that is, he added.

Their driver rattled over some sort of obstruction and turned a sharp corner and Shore put out a strong red-knuckled hand and gripped the door. What letter? he said.

The letter in Mr. Farquhar's study, sir. It contains rather explicit instructions.

The growler struck another loose stone and Shore glowered. Instructions?

Blackwell sat with his fists clutched between his knees and his shoulders swaying side to side. The pale cloth of his trousers was streaked with soot from his fingers. He nodded uneasily and he said, Yes, sir. Instructions, sir.

What kind of instructions?

As to how the painting will be negotiated back, William interrupted impatiently. He blew out his cheeks and put a violent hand to the seat beside him as the growler swung around again and he turned to Blackwell and said, Do you have this letter now? Who's been in contact with it?

The inspector fumbled with his pockets and unbuttoned his greatcoat and reached into its lining and withdrew the crumpled envelope. Shore moved to take it but William reached past with his calfskin gloves still on and very carefully he pried the envelope open and poured the letter out onto the seat beside him. He was careful to touch only two of its corners as he unfolded it. The stationery was an expensive card stock with a London watermark and the writing was in the tall elegant hand of a man with skill and a desire to show it.

Who's handled this? he said. I mean besides Farquhar and yourself?

Blackwell shook his head. I should think Mr. Farquhar's wife, perhaps. Perhaps the constable who interviewed them.

A sudden latticing of shadow and light as they passed under a railway arch and on. William peered down to the bottom of the page and turned it carefully and held it to the light and then he looked up.

Well? said Shore. What does it say?

William looked at Blackwell a long moment. It says *The Emma* has been temporarily removed from the gallery, for the purposes of safekeeping. It says there have been rumours of criminal intent towards it, and in the interests of preserving a work of national interest, the interested parties have taken it upon themselves to protect it, et cetera. He cleared his throat, scanned ahead. The painting can be negotiated back for a fee covering the costs incurred. A representative will make contact with Mr. Farquhar—here William squinted, held the letter high in the light of the carriage window—in the next few days, et cetera. No charges are to be laid, as no criminal offence is intended. Police are not to be involved. It mentions you directly.

It mentions me? Shore scowled. Give it over.

You're not wearing gloves.

To hell with gloves. Give it to me.

But William frowned and waited and after a long angry moment Shore drew on his heavy gloves. William handed the letter across.

Shore was shaking his head. *Please advise Mr. John Shore of Scotland Yard that his presence is not encouraged.* Is this a joke?

The growler lifted onto two wheels then rattled banging back down as it swung around a corner and William was thrown heavily against Blackwell. Where did you say this was found? he said, picking the inspector's bowler from the floor.

In Mr. Farquhar's study, sir.

At his residence.

They could hear the driver cursing his horses.

Indeed, sir. Blackwell was regarding William with interest. It seems it was propped against a lamp on his desk, sir. Where Mr. Farquhar keeps his private papers. One supposes it was left there on purpose, so that it wouldn't be overlooked.

It was found this morning?

Yes sir.

Nothing else missing? Shore glared. The keys to the gallery? Papers? Mrs. Farquhar's diamonds, for god's sake?

No sir, nothing. Not according to Mr. Farquhar.

William reached across and carefully took the letter from Shore and slid it into his inner pocket. The thief didn't take the keys because he didn't need to, he said calmly. This is no amateur.

He bloody well is. Overlooks her diamonds but takes a painting? You can't fence a picture like *The Emma*.

He doesn't need to fence it.

If George Farquhar refuses to negotiate, the thief has nothing. A painting he can't unload.

William grimaced. But he won't refuse. It's still more profitable for Farquhar to pay out than to lose the painting entirely.

Just then the carriage struck another bulge in the stones of the roadway and set their teeth ajar and Shore cursed and reached through his window and rapped on the roof. The carriage drew tight in to the street's edge. The chief inspector swung open the door and climbed swearing down.

We'll walk the rest of the way, he snapped at the driver. It's not a bloody derby, man.

William had come to the gallery at Shore's invitation. Good Mr. Farquhar has suffered a misfortune, the chief inspector had said, and William thought at once of Foole prowling the upper rooms of Farquhar's mansion. Edward Shade's fingerprints lay carefully labelled and packaged on the writing desk at his hotel and there would soon be an Agency file on Shade and then a rogues' gallery entry and then the man, Shade, Foole, some other, would be caught the next time he committed a crime. His father had hunted the thief for years and never come so close. Close, he thought, surprised by the unhappiness in the thought. Having traced and recorded the man ought to be enough.

It was not. He thought of Charlotte Reckitt, pickled in that mortuary cabinet, he thought of Blackwell's doubts as to her identity. He thought of powerful Ben Porter, collapsed in a rat-infested tenement, his ancient widow somewhere now on her way to California. He thought of his own father, mouldering in the black earth in Chicago. All of their parts in it were finished.

There was a watery yellow fog in the air, burning his vision, and William rubbed the heels of his palms at his eyes as he walked. The cold of the morning crept in under his collar. It was an old macadamized street with the stones pulled sharply up over the years and with stone bollards set every few paces along the shopfronts to keep the carriages from molesting the passersby. Their footfalls were loud in the fog and William could hear Blackwell sniffling as they walked and in irritation he reached into his waistcoat for a handkerchief and handed it across. A dray clattered past in the fog ghostlike, blurred. They turned a corner and came out at Bond Street and there were silhouettes moving in the mists and Shore jogged across the Sunday traffic and William followed with his silk hat low on his head and Blackwell was behind them in the mist like a wraith.

As they approached, a long thin figure detached itself and drifted towards them.

Look what's crept out of its lair, Shore muttered. And then, louder: It seems you have beaten us to the quarry, sir.

There was a tightness around Breck's grey eyes and he

glanced at Blackwell in distaste before saying, sourly, I have warned you, Mr. Shore, if you do not instruct your constables not to interfere with a crime scene I shall be of no use to you.

Shore rubbed his gloves together. Aye, so you have. Mr. Blackwell, please see if anyone is still here. The night watchman, perhaps.

No use at all, Breck repeated. I mean that. I have other matters to attend to at the hospital, they are no less pressing.

Dr. Breck, William interrupted. What have you found?

Other than that the London constabulary force is made up in equal measure of cattle and of feed?

William smiled. Other than that, yes.

Breck turned his back and kneeled at the edge of the street running his fingers through the mud in its grooves and he said, You, at least, Mr. Pinkerton, will appreciate what I have found. He stood and turned twice on the spot and stared with pouched eyes at the ground and William saw the knees of his trousers were black with muck. The doctor turned and held up a vial of reddish liquid. Do you know what this contains?

Blackwell had just emerged from the gallery and was approaching through the fog as Breck spoke and he said, Does it contain the solution, sir?

Breck gave him a sharp mistrustful look. The solution?

To the problem, sir.

Ah. Breck scowled. Amusing.

Blackwell smiled politely and rubbed at his cold nose and said, Mr. Shore, sir. The night watchman is still inside. Seems he heard nothing. Noticed nothing amiss until this morning when Mr. Farquhar arrived having found the letter. It was then they went upstairs to the gallery and discovered the theft together. He says he has no idea when it happened, or how.

That is because he was asleep, Breck said.

You'll want to talk to him, William said to Shore.

Breck glanced coolly across. You'll be assisting in this investigation, Mr. Pinkerton?

Never mind him, Shore said. What did you find?

Breck ran a filthy hand along his neck. Ah. The man you are looking for is slight of build. He is small, but athletic. He did not come in a cab or in a carriage. He climbed to the gallery alone using the outside of the building but he had an accomplice waiting here below. He is well-dressed, a gentleman, and he was recently in America. He has been in the gallery several times over the past few weeks and is a professional criminal recently in trouble with the law. Not here, but overseas. Most likely in the United States.

William listened to all this feeling the gears clicking in his mind and he paused and he studied the thin doctor and then he said, quietly, How can you know all that?

You see what you expect to see, the doctor said impassively. I expect nothing. He gestured at the street. The only recent wheel grooves standing at the curb are from a single wide-gauge wheel, which suggests a private carriage. Hansoms are narrow gauge. As it last rained early Saturday evening but only lightly, and as there is only the one impress in the mud, it is reasonable to assume this carriage belongs to Mr. Farquhar, whom I know arrived at the gallery this morning. Therefore the thief arrived here on foot. There is a smudge of white chalk on the underside of the window ledge which I am certain will also be found on the upper side. This will be from the thief's fingers. It is smudged because he has tried to conceal his fingerprints. This means his fingerprints are likely to give him away, and that he knows this, which in turn suggests he is both familiar with the technique of fingerprinting, and fearful that his prints will be recognized. This is a recent technique, only coming into use in the last few years, and only so far in Argentina, France, and the United States. Therefore he has been handled by the authorities in one of these countries at some point recently. He will have been well-dressed so as to draw little attention to himself as he walked through this area late at night, and either he or his acquaintance must have been recently in America as he was smoking this cheroot, which is an American brand, and somewhat expensive.

Breck was gesturing with the toe of his scuffed shoe to the ground-down heel of a small cigarillo.

None of that would stand as evidence, William said.

It does not matter. It is correct.

Justice isn't a matter of correctness, Doctor.

No?

It's a matter of proof.

Breck gave him a strange dark smile. Justice, he said softly, as if tasting the word.

The gas in the sconces was standing at a high flame, casting a corona of light up the walls. A man's footfalls echoed through the galleries ahead then faded and as they went upstairs Shore said, It's the same damn thing with that scarecrow always.

Breck?

Blackwell.

William pulled off his wet gloves. I didn't know he was a problem.

Shore barked a laugh. Not a problem. Seems his theory on that girl's head we fished from the Thames might pay out after all. A publican, missing wife. He's done his digging. Fine detective work. I told you all this last week.

Yes. The Charlotte Reckitt case.

Shore shrugged. We're calling it the Thames case now.

You have doubts too?

Not doubts. An open mind. Shore put a hand on William's arm, slowed. I have a favour to ask. Mr. Blackwell means to confront the man, this publican, tomorrow.

And you don't think he can handle it.

Whoever did this to that woman is not a fellow to take lightly. I'd hate to have a second head in the river.

William thought of the severed head in its jar and the savage wounds on the torso and he nodded. Okay.

Shore studied William as if reconsidering his request and then he grunted and turned away. This painting, he said, this *Emma*. It seems some industrialist in America has had an eye on it. The papers have been claiming he's one of two probable high-bidders, against some French aristocrat. You don't suppose one of them is involved?

It's more likely Farquhar himself.

You're not serious.

William looked at the chief inspector's appalled face and smiled. No, he said. I guess not. But I do know this. When the press gets wind of this it's sure to increase the notoriety of that painting. And the more famous, the more valuable. Farquhar sells paintings for more than you'll see in a lifetime. He knows how the market works. You'll want to talk to him.

Shore led him into a high-ceilinged gallery with plaster mouldings running the span and naked wood boards which rattled loosely as they walked. Flat on the floor lay an empty gold frame, a thin ragged strip of canvas along its perimeter. The velvet rope on its stand had been upended and one end was stiff with some sort of paste. On the wall a picture wire dangled naked and forlorn where the portrait had hung. The lone window stood closed but unlocked and when William crossed to it he could just make out soot smudges on the inner sill.

Is Breck finished in here?

Aye. Shore bit down hard on the stem of his pipe but did not trouble to light it.

William walked in a wide approach to the picture frame and crouched down beside it. Tell me about this night watchman, he said. He lowered his face until his eyes were level with the back of the frame.

Name's Owen Archer, Shore said. A retired soldier, served in India for years. Swears he heard nothing, saw nothing. Blackwell's inclined to believe him.

A job like this usually has a man on the inside.

You think I should bring him in?

Probably. William furrowed his brow. The painting was cut carefully from its frame. Whoever did this knew what they were doing. And they didn't want to damage the painting. That means either they mean to sell it, which is unlikely, or to keep it for themselves, which would require a queer sort of passion, or else—

Or else what?

Or else they obviously mean to honour the terms of the letter. To return it undamaged.

Shore grunted. Looks pretty damaged to me.

The thief came in and out through the window, as Breck suspects, William said. That means he's agile, and strong. But also small. He would have needed someone to stand lookout below but this would be a small job, a professional job. You'll be looking for a slight man, a professional criminal, who is clever enough to have avoided being implicated. Most likely he has a heavy-set and tall accomplice who could help him scale the wall. The letter was deposited Saturday evening or on Sunday, most likely the former. Which means either this thief or one of his accomplices was present at the party. By invitation, one presumes, to arouse no undue suspicion. Breck thinks he's come over from America. Sound like anyone we know?

Shore gave him a look. Sounds a little bit like you, he said.

William smiled a wolfish smile. If I were the thief, I'd want the perfect alibi. And what better than to have been seen at Farquhar's own residence that night? But there's something he wasn't counting on.

What?

Fingerprints.

Breck said he didn't leave any trace.

William withdrew the letter from his pocket with great care and held it out by one corner. This is his mistake. Have Dr. Breck dust this.

Shore stared at him in amazement. Why would he leave his fingerprints on that? If he were so damned careful with the rest?

The letter was deposited before our little demonstration, John. The theft was executed after. When he left this, he didn't have to worry about his fingerprints yet.

Shore stared at him. He shook his head. You and your bloody Edward Shade, he muttered. You think everything comes back to him.

Everything does, said William.

THIRTY-SEVEN

Foole woke early and lay with his eyes open in the darkness, listening.

Somewhere above him Charlotte slept. Her warm skin soft under sheets. The knowledge of it burned inside him like a slow-breathing ember and after a while he shifted onto his side, the mattress creaking under his elbow. He drew the blankets tight in a huddle and he stared at the shapes of the furniture.

He had never imagined her like this. The haunted weariness around her eyes, as if she were squinting at him from some small point very far away. The hair hanging in strangled ropes over her eyes. A slash of light at her throat like a knife. And then her voice. He had stared at her as the night coalesced coldly in her hair and poured into her eyes and then he had looked down and seen her small traveller's case standing at her feet and felt Mrs. Sykes's hand on his arm and had stepped aside.

He remembered Mrs. Sykes bundling her into a blanket, clicking her tongue the while, giving Fludd a strange unreadable look. Come now, love, she was saying, let's get you in out of that weather. Molly had already dissolved back into the stairwell, only the whites of her eyes visible.

You were dead, Foole had said. I saw your body.

Charlotte looked at him, uncertain. She pulled off her gloves, finger by finger, and rested a cold hand against his cheek as if in answer.

———

He could feel it still, the pressure of that hand. He ran his fingers lightly over his face as if her touch had left some trace on him. After a moment he rose from the bedsheets, he danced across the freezing floorboards, he dipped his fingers in the basin on his washstand. He rubbed at his face and throat, he splashed his armpits, he shivered. Despite his exhaustion a quiet triumph was building in him, something delicious and impossible and sacrosanct. Somewhere overhead Charlotte lay dreaming, somewhere Charlotte breathed.

He opened his wardrobe soundlessly. The looking glass on the interior door flared like open water, flared and then darkened. Foole dressed quickly and went out past the landing and down.

He knew Mrs. Sykes would be awake, already stirring the ashes in the kitchen. But the candles in their sconces had not been lit, the parlour was cold. He passed through into the Emporium and he saw a light underneath a door and these rooms were warmer but when he went in to greet his housekeeper he stopped in the doorway surprised.

I thought you'd be sleeping, he said.

Charlotte turned at the fire, her hands held out before her. The deep purple lines under her eyes, the skin at her mouth drawn and grey. I couldn't sleep, she said. I haven't been sleeping much.

He did not know what to say.

I lit the fire. I hope I did not overstep—

But she did not finish and her words drifted away and she lowered her face. He shut the door, he approached slowly, as if entering a dream. She wore a pale green dress he had seen on Hettie and the sleeves were short at the wrists. Her skin was ethereal and white and with her black hair loose she looked a visitant from some other world. Watching her he had all at once the uneasy sense that a stranger stood inside her, peering back at him with a sinister and vicious intent. But then her features shifted and he saw the girl he had known and he understood. Inside him lurked just such a stranger also.

What is it? she said. The glint of her eyes watching his.

He swallowed. I just thought, well. It's been so long.

A faint smile. You got old too, she said.

He blushed and looked away.

The fire burned on. They said nothing for a time, unfamiliar, uneasy. Foole stood flexing his hands on the back of the reading chair and after a time Charlotte rose and drifted across to a tall shelf, her pale fingers moving soundlessly over the objects there. The whorled stone of an ammonite. A set of salt-rusted leather journals. A wooden crate filled with coins dug from the earthworks at Nantes.

I spoke to Gabriel and Rose, he said at last. They think you're dead. I had Mr. Fludd into half the flash houses in London, making inquiries. No one seemed to know much. Gabriel heard a rumour Pinkerton had birked you. I thought it might be an old grudge. He looked up. I tracked down the Saracen.

She looked back over the scoop of a shoulder. Cooper?

I found him at the Lascar's.

She took this in, surprised, perhaps, that he had learned of her arrangements with the man.

There isn't much of him left, Foole added. He paused. I'm sorry.

Cooper was dead years ago, she said in a flat voice. He just didn't know it. She reached up with two hands and smoothed and twisted her dark hair over one shoulder and she said, We had our differences. But I wouldn't have wished black pudding on him. He'd have cut his own throat if he'd known he'd end up like that.

But there was no kindness in her tone and Foole noticed the set of her mouth and wondered at how the years had hardened her. The logs cracked in the grate, a soft rapid popping, a shirr of ashes blown upward. Foole felt his hands tighten on the back of the chair. He stared at her and forced the pity he felt into a small hard knot in his heart. He said, Where have you been, Charlotte?

She looked away, her face reluctant.

I thought you were dead. You must have known I was here.

I heard you were looking. Yes.

You've been in London then.

She nodded.

And yet you never contacted me. You never sent word.

She turned, hands clasped before her. Why would I contact you? You've been arm in arm with William Pinkerton. I saw your Mr. Fludd with him, outside a coffee house in Haymarket.

Pinkerton was hunting your killer, he said softly.

My killer.

Your killer. Yes.

She stepped forward and stood beside her chair and said, But William Pinkerton knows I didn't die.

Foole studied her, the play of firelight along her arm, her throat.

He saw me. Last month. He followed me in the street. Why else would I have been in hiding all this time?

He could think of many reasons but he did not voice them. He told himself her secrets were hers by right and it was not his place to interrogate them and he pinched his eyes shut as if to convince himself. Molly and Japheth will have questions, he said instead.

And you? You must have questions also?

He shrugged. It isn't my business.

It might be.

Well.

What is it.

The detective you mentioned in your letter. In December. That was Pinkerton?

Yes.

What did he want? How did he find you?

She ran an abrupt hand over her throat. I didn't know who he was. An American detective, in London? He could have followed me for months, I'd not have suspected.

How did you sight him?

I thought it was chance. It wasn't.

He let you.

He let me. He tipped his hat and held my eye in the Underground one day. Then he tailed me across half of London and I couldn't shake him. The next day he came to my door and pressed the buzzer and left. He did that every morning for a week. He knew I was inside, he knew I wouldn't open the door to him. I thought it over and started to get cross and the next time he came I invited him inside to tea. He declined. That was when he told me his name. He left me his card.

What did he want?

Charlotte gave him a long level look as if expecting him to answer his own query. Lowered her eyes. She said, He'd followed me for weeks. At first it was nothing, a nuisance. It complicated my intentions for greasing my uncle from Millbank, true, but nothing more. Then it grew threatening. Watching my house at night. Footprints on the carpets when I came home. Once I was standing at the footway of Potter Street and someone pushed me into the traffic and I was nearly run down. It was him.

Foole did not think that sounded like William Pinkerton. But then he knew, too, the nature of that man and how mercurial it could be. He said, That was when you sent me the letter.

That was when I wrote you, yes.

I got your letter on Christmas Eve.

She said nothing.

I never expected to hear from you. After your uncle was arrested, I'd hoped to. For years, I hoped. I didn't think it would happen.

She wet her lips, she started to say something and then stopped. What was between us, she said instead. I have always cherished it.

But—

It's in the past.

He nodded, feeling a quick sharp pain.

You are not who you were either, Adam.

He nodded.

I was married, she said.

I'd heard, yes. He cleared his throat, he paused. You were married? Not still?

I waited for you, she said abruptly, a bitterness creeping in. Did you know? I waited months. I lived in my uncle's lodgings in Whitechapel for six months, until the rent was due. You had the address. You could have written. You did not.

He nodded unhappily, he stared into the fire, remembering. I was young. I was angry.

You were foolish.

He smiled vaguely. That too.

I thought I'd been mistaken in you. I thought my uncle was right. There was something in her expression both plaintive and miserable and then it was gone.

Right about what?

Charlotte gave him a long quiet look. She said, Three weeks after I'd returned, a visitor arrived at my uncle's door. I recognized him at once. It was the French merchant from our hotel in Port Elizabeth. He had been informing on us, watching us. My uncle knew all about us. I remember he called me into his study. The Frenchman said you'd arranged a buyer to meet you in Brindisi. He said you'd already cheated us, that before your journey north you'd established for a transfer of funds to a private bank in Venice. He said you'd confided all this to a man at a campfire in the veld. Her eyes watched his as if for some sign, some recognition. My uncle left for Brindisi in a fury. He did not allow me to go. He was gone six weeks. And when he came back, well. The inspectors were waiting for him on the pier. I did not ever see him free again.

I was sick in Brindisi, Charlotte. I was in a fever.

In prison he said you'd threatened us. He had a letter, written in your hand, justifying your claim to the diamonds and denying me. His left hand was in bandages. He said you'd attacked him with a knife in an alley near the port.

That never happened.

No?

For god's sake. Foole shook his head, he turned away, he
turned back. I had nothing, no money, nothing. I couldn't even
walk. Martin betrayed me. He took the diamonds and left me.

I know.

I couldn't make sense of it. Why would he do it? Why
cross me?

For love, she said simply.

Foole paused and studied her. He was not sure of her
meaning. I visited him a few weeks ago, he said. In the Tench. I
wanted to tell him about you, about what had happened. Foole
cleared his throat. He told me there'd been a child.

She was quiet.

I didn't know, he said. If I had known it then, that you were—

Her eyes weighed him a moment. Did he tell you it was
yours? Is that what my uncle said?

Wasn't it?

No.

Foole felt his face darken.

I was pregnant two years after Port Elizabeth, Adam, she
said. It wasn't yours. She stood unmoving, her white hands
clasped before her, hair in a curtain fall over her cheek. He
wasn't yours, she said again.

He, Foole murmured. You had a son.

Her own voice came low, soft. Does it appall you to hear
this? It was like the poor thing just gave up. I was afraid from
the very moment I held him. He never made a sound, not for
two days. She looked at him. I have made my peace with it.

Foole swallowed.

He looked like his father. David was a forksman and a grifter.
David Aldergate. Daring, quick, strong. You'd have liked him. I
don't know that love was a part of it but we made an effective
team. What else was I to do? We left London for Kent in the
autumn where he started a grift, using me as the lure. I'd been
recently widowed, had lost my inheritance to relatives in
Scotland, David was my loyal manservant, worried for my safety
and for the child's. There was a baroness living in that vicinity

who was known to have lost her own grandchild due to similar circumstances. It went well at first and when the baby came the baroness stepped in and brought us onto her estate and we lived for a while in comfort. She believed our account.

Foole could hear the street waking beyond the windows. A peddler crying hoarsely.

It went well and then it didn't, as always happened. We had to flee in the night and David had a trunk of the old woman's silver strapped to our carriage and we rode fast. The carriage went off the road, we were stranded, it was the middle of winter. The baby—

Died. And David died the next year in a road accident in Newcastle. I think he never forgave himself. Our marriage was ashes by then. Charlotte breathed quietly and said nothing for a long while and then she said, I grew ill after Kent. I wanted to die too.

He stared at her. It felt all at once as if no time had passed, as if a hole had opened in their lives and they had slipped through to the intimacy they had known before, but awash now in sadness.

She held out her wrists to him and he could see the white cross-hatching of old scars.

I have lost too much, she said simply. I do not wish to lose any more.

Foole nodded.

The Tench is closing, Adam. They mean to send my uncle to Portsmouth. To the hulks there. He'll die. He'll rot in them and die and I shall never see him again. She made some small gesture with her hand. I did not want to ask it of you. Gabriel thought you might be willing.

Foole stared at the fire. I came to London for you. Not for your uncle.

It is the same thing.

He frowned.

He's to be transported Wednesday. I have a guard who will arrange a miscount at a roadhouse in Heyshott. In Chichester. I'll be there to spirit him away.

Wednesday.

Three days from now. Yes. She frowned as if watching for some betrayal in him. This wasn't how I'd arranged it, she said. My uncle wasn't due to be transported until the spring.

But you'll attempt it regardless.

I must.

She met his eye. There was no recrimination in it, no bitterness, only a long languid sadness. He felt again that sense of a second Charlotte, a shadow figure glancing sidelong from under her hair. She curled her fingers over the back of the sofa, stood very still, and after a moment she said, Pinkerton kept asking about someone, a magsman he was hunting. Some man Shade. Edward Shade.

The clock ticked in the gloom. A log shifted on the fire and a soft hiss of sparks burst in the grate and was drawn up into the blackness.

It's you, isn't it? she said. It's you he was looking for. You are this Edward Shade.

Why would you think that?

Tell me I'm mistaken.

A quick incredulous smile. A weak daylight was creeping across the far shelves, creeping towards them. He could hear in the house above them Molly and Fludd, waking, stamping about.

Adam?

Edward Shade's been dead a long time, he said at last. And the dead don't come back.

She shook her head at that.

I did, she said.

THIRTY-EIGHT

T alk of the dead and hear them choke.

      Blackwell came to the hotel the next morning. It was Tuesday. William was standing at a window fastening his cufflinks when he saw the inspector unfold bat-like down from a four-wheeler in the street below. The man held his hat out before him and he wiped at its crest with a sleeve then stared abruptly up at William. The sheen of glass concealed him but still he stepped back in alarm. He had heard nothing further from Scotland Yard about the stolen painting and supposed Blackwell had come with some word. But he had not come about that.

The woman from the Thames? William said to him in surprise. He left the door standing open and turned away, speaking over one shoulder. You've finished your inquiries then.

Yes sir. It's the man I told you about. The publican.

William wrestled into his frock coat, adjusted his collar with his thick scarred fingers. And not Charlotte Reckitt.

No sir. Blackwell's voice was low, urgent. If you'd care to fetch your hat, sir—

John mentioned you might come by.

And now Blackwell smiled a shy smile. It was a strange sight and all at once the funereal visage William had come to know dissolved and in its place was the face of a still-young man, an anxious, tired, excited young man. William reached over the inspector's brushed bowler and took his own hat down from its peg and he held it upside down in his big hands as if it were very fragile, as if the nothing it held was rare and of great worth.

Show me, he said.

They rode slowly through the crush of traffic in an open hansom with a wool blanket heavy with damp shared between them and the smell of the wet reminded William of riding single file in the rain through the hills outside Santa Fe with a rifle strapped to his saddle. The streets were filled with carts and skeletal horses with heads low and labourers with great piles of goods on their backs and women in rags and shawls hauling barrows of laundry. A miserable crush of hogs shouldered its way around them, snorting. As they went Blackwell told him what he had learned.

Her name was Ellen Shorter and she had been barmaid and then wife to a tavern keeper in a northwest district of London. The tavern was named the Baker's Dwarf and despite his name the man Shorter had not founded it but had bought it out of receivership some twelve years ago. He was past forty by Blackwell's best reckoning and the wife twenty-nine last April. Two children stillborn, a boy dead of fever at six months. Black hair, black eyes, she spoke a passable French from her mother's family in Brighton which had kept her popular with a certain class of Continental customers. By all accounts a friendly woman and attractive.

William ran his hand over the back of his neck. What do you mean friendly?

Friendly, sir. With the working men.

She was a prostitute?

No sir.

She was a flirt.

Blackwell looked uncomfortable. Shorter himself is considered by everyone a gentle giant, he said. A very big man, sir. But no one I spoke to ever heard of him getting into a temper or raising a hand to anyone. He's known by the art students nearby as a soft touch for a bottle or a hot meal.

But?

But one student, sir, a James McKinnon. Saw Shorter once mad as a hornet. It seems he had received a letter by mistake, addressed to his wife, and in this letter were certain inappropriate details. I understand he opened the letter in front of Mr. McKinnon.

A love letter.

An assignation, sir.

Isn't that the same thing?

Sometimes.

So he's a gentle giant except where his wife is concerned. And where's his wife now?

Visiting a sick aunt in France.

William frowned. I see.

It seems she left rather abruptly, sir.

Mm.

No one has heard from her in six weeks. Though Shorter insists she has written him several times.

And the letters?

Burned accidentally. Misplaced. Eaten by stray cats.

What about the good doctor's blind insects? Is there a cellar?

I couldn't say, sir. Not yet at least.

William was shaking his head. Is that it? A wife visiting sick relatives and a man with a temper?

Blackwell frowned. He said a constable had met Shorter during his investigations and the man had expressed no interest at all in the ruse of the inheritance. He said the tavern keeper had looked at the sketch and said he had never seen the woman. But several customers identified her as Ellen Shorter. All of this struck the constable as curious but there were several other leads to pursue and at the time they were still seeking Charlotte Reckitt. He said yesterday a witness had come forward with information about a possible suspect for the theft of the Farquhar painting, a man complaining of a pocket watch stolen on an American liner just after the New Year. And that after interviewing the witness he had happened to pass by another interrogation of an elderly man reporting his missing daughter. Blackwell wiped at his nose with a red handkerchief and William recognized it as his own. The inspector told him this elderly man had come into the city from Brighton and that his daughter was missing and that her husband claimed she had travelled to France to visit sick relatives.

William was no longer listening. Wait, he said. This man with the pocket watch, this witness to the Farquhar heist—

Sir?

From the passenger liner. Who was he? What did he see?

A doctor from Liverpool, sir. He said he had a pocket watch stolen from him while on board and that he encountered the thief at Mr. Farquhar's gallery shortly before the theft. He seemed quite insistent about it.

That's all, nothing useful? What did the man look like?

The doctor?

The thief.

Blackwell cleared his throat. He claimed he was a gentleman travelling over from Boston with his young daughter. A smaller man, white hair, well-groomed, piercing eyes.

William smiled. He watched a waggon inch up alongside them, its high wet wheel spitting mud. Did anyone else talk to him?

I filed a report, sir. But it seemed a rather unreliable account.

And this man from Brighton. This would be Ellen Shorter's father, I guess?

Blackwell nodded. He told William the curious thing was that this man had heard nothing of any sick relatives himself. He believed his daughter had come into some trouble. He said he did not like the husband nor trust him.

And you were already investigating Shorter?

Yes sir.

Fair bit of luck there. William set a hand on the rail of the hansom as it jounced over the granite setts. What does Shorter say to all this?

I had a constable in to talk to him. He says his wife was estranged from her father. She'd told the man nothing for years. He says his father-in-law is in debt to him for several hundred pounds.

Sure. Whose elbows are the more frayed.

I beg your pardon, sir?

Doesn't matter. He waved a hand. Tell me something. How much of this is gut feeling, Blackwell?

Gut feeling, sir?

Instinct. Yes.

Blackwell bristled. It's detective work, sir. Logic.

William smiled, turned away. Two-thirds of this job is done when you're not thinking about anything, Inspector. It's your gut tells you what's what. The trick is learning to trust it.

The Baker's Dwarf was an ancient tavern at the edge of Edgware Road directly across the field from where the grisly torso was found. It had been built in the eighteenth century, Blackwell told him, as an overnight house for travellers into London to change horses. That was in an age of highwaymen when London was confined to its own limits and nightfall set the hours of a man's living. Now the city had devoured its outliers and what had once been an outpost was a casual drinking house for labourers coming off shift.

There were fewer people in the streets there at that hour. The Dwarf was a crooked free-standing tavern with rooms to let above and an ancient faded sign hanging on its chains over the lintel. A weak gas lamp was burning even during the daylight hours but it shed no light and William shivered and turned up the collar of his coat against the chill. The air was grey with a weak mist.

Is it warmer inside, do you think? William muttered.

I fear not, sir.

They stamped the cold from their boots and shut the door with a bang and made their way across to the bar. There were figures huddled at tables nursing their pints and two languid whores blinking sleepily from a corner and William and

Blackwell shook the weather from their sleeves and took off their hats and William called for whiskey and the narrow door to the kitchen swung wide and out came the proprietor Shorter himself.

William looked at his face and looked at his eyes and he knew him at once for a killer. It was nothing he could have articulated had he been asked. A faint crackling in the skin as the man emerged, a kind of red darkness in the eyelids.

Shorter was enormous, thick-necked, his blue eyes bulging from their sockets as he made his way towards them. There was a power to his movements but he was slow and heavy. William had ridden out with his father once against a grizzly that had been killing stock and the man Shorter had something of that creature's loose rippling power in his shoulders. He was bearded and his voice was loud as a prophet's calling them to account.

What'll it be then? he boomed. And set both broad palms down on the counter and smiled.

William smiled back. The man loomed a full head taller than him but he had struck down men half as big again in blacker days. Whiskey, he said again. The finest you have.

American, eh? Shorter reached down under the counter and drew out a dusty bottle and two glasses upended between his knuckles. Ye never tippled a whiskey until ye tasted some of this.

William glanced deliberately around the room. Where's the wife?

What?

The missus.

Shorter's smile faltered. Do ye know her?

William held up a hand. Not as such, he said. We came through here this time last year and she was awful nice to us.

Where you lads from then? Shorter asked. He had not uncorked the bottle and now he leaned across and drew out an ale and cut the foam and slid the pint across to a man in coveralls with his head down on the brass railing of the bar.

Florida.

The both of ye?

William glanced at Blackwell, glanced back. Yes.

Shorter chuckled. He don't look like a Yankee.

He's a Canadian.

An what brings you through to England?

William shrugged. Oh, business. Pleasure.

Which one is it?

William laughed. That depends. What class of bottle you keep here?

The bottle was standing yet between them. Shorter set both stout hands on the bar and took a deep breath and his chest thickened and widened and the seams of his coat stretched. His nostrils flared as he smiled. This here's the finest whiskey in any city establishment what don't require you to pay for membership. Down out of the Hebrides, it is.

William let his eye pass across it and then the other bottles ranged behind the bar.

I'd not lie to ye.

William glanced at Blackwell, smiled at Shorter. You don't have anything a little more expensive?

Ye won't try this?

William lifted his eyebrows.

Shorter's smile went very tight. We might just could have, he said. It'll cost ye.

William reached into his pocket and set a five-pound note on the bar.

The both of ye has the thirst? Shorter looked at Blackwell and smiled his flushed wide smile. Don't he have a tongue in his head?

He likes to do his talking with a glass in front of him, said William.

The three of them stood in silence for a moment, Blackwell smiling.

At last Shorter rooted a thumb around in one nostril and sniffed sharply. All right then, he said. Come on an I'll show it to ye. She takes all kinds, this world, she do. Betts, he shouted.

A haggard old woman appeared at the kitchen door. What?

You watch the front awhile. I'll be to takin these gents down for a peek at the queer.

Down to where?

He gestured with his thumb. Down below.

Down to where, you say?

He waved a hand at her, turned away. He had withdrawn from under the counter a greasy lantern and now took it across to the cinder fire and opened its glass door and lit the wick and shut it again carefully. They followed him down through a small passage behind the bar. The stairs were ancient, and made of wood, and rattled dangerously under their weight. Shorter led the way, his huge back and hairy neck blocking their sight. William felt a tension run through him, a kind of electricity, like the feeling in his skin when he would stand in the wheat fields as a boy and watch a lightning storm roll in.

The cellar stank of damp and sawdust and night soil and William squinted as they came down. The ceiling was low, the rough floor hewn from rock and the lantern glinted and shivered off slime on the walls. Ranged along two walls were rows of barrels and cords of firewood and along a third leaned a shelf of bottles all staggered and askew. William tried to catch Blackwell's eye but the inspector was following Shorter across to the dusty corner bottles. The floor near the stairs was covered in sawdust from a chopping block but the dust looked strangely deep and evenly distributed and covered the floor some full five feet from the block itself. William drew a crescent in the sawdust with his heel.

There were bloodstains soaked into the floor.

What happened here? he said.

Shorter straightened from where he had been kneeling among the bottles and laughed. Bloody butchers' strike, he said. He turned back nonchalantly.

William walked over to the chopping block and lifted up the axe. He could see even in the bad light a faint matting of dried blood and hair. You use an axe for that?

Now Shorter got to his feet and wiped his free hand on his apron. The other hand with knuckles whitening gripped a bottle by its throat. Sometimes I do, he said.

I believe we'd like to ask you a few questions, sir, Blackwell said.

Shorter shook his head. Funny accent for a Canadian, he said.

Yes, said William. He was still holding the axe.

Where did you say your wife was, sir?

Shorter gave the smaller inspector a quick fierce glance but then his eyes settled on William.

Ye mean to kill me? he said. Whatever he's to payin ye I'll double it.

Put down the bottle, said William.

We're not here to harm you, sir. Blackwell took a step forward. I'm Detective Inspector Blackwell, of the Yard. This is my associate.

The hell ye are.

Put down the bottle, William said again.

What's happened to your wife, sir? Blackwell said quietly.

Shorter's face had gone grey and the muscles in his big shoulders were cording and bunching and William thought for an uneasy moment that the man would need to be struck down. But it was not rage but regret which made the man tremble. He stared at the bottle in his hands as if he did not know it and then he set it carefully down on the floor and he stood with his head bowed and his long greasy hair fallen forward.

Mr. Shorter, sir. Would you like to tell us about it?

I never meant nothin to happen to her, he said in a whisper.

I understand, sir.

It weren't planned. He looked up. He had started to tremble. She were goin to leave me.

Yes.

I caught her at it red-handed, like. I known somethin was wrong and made some excuse to go out for an errand on a Monday night. Then I come back in, quiet. Caught her upstairs in the bar with her bags all packed for Gravesend. She were dressed in a man's suit and she was a-meanin to rendezvous with some bastard painter. Had cut her hair off an the like.

What happened, sir?

Shorter put out a big hand and rested it on the shelf of bottles and the glass rolled and clinked under his weight. I hit her. I never meant it to hurt her. I hit her with a open hand, I swear to god. But her eyes just rolled up in her head and she fell down dead right on the floor. Shorter glanced up at William who stood yet with the axe at his side. I brung her down here and tied her up an poked her a couple a times to see if she were goin to wake up. I thought she might be tryin to trick me, see. She were clever like that. But she were dead. I didn't know what to do.

So you cut her into pieces, William said.

The man's heavy eyes shut fast and he swayed on his feet but he said nothing.

What happened to the painter, sir?

Michael Witten, Shorter said softly. I went looking for the bastard, I did.

And?

An I cut his throat while he was sleepin.

Where is he now?

Shorter stared glassily at them. Somewheres in the river, he murmured. I'd do it a second time if he was to rise right up out of the grave an walk down them stairs, so help me god I would.

We'll need to put some restraints on you, sir, Blackwell said calmly.

Shorter nodded.

The inspector took from his pocket the ancient wrist shackles and adjusted their screws and set them on the big man's wrists and the tavern keeper made no effort to resist.

William scowled. Except your wife didn't die from being struck, he said. She was poisoned.

Poisoned?

The chloroform.

The man blinked, turned a heel in the sawdust.

It wasn't all quite so accidental and unplanned as you say, was it?

I loved her, Shorter said.

Fine way of showing it, William said angrily. He started kicking through the mess of the cellar. There isn't enough blood here for that kind of cutting up, he said.

Mr. Shorter, sir? Blackwell said.

But the tavern keeper was staring down at his shackled hands and said nothing.

And then William found it. A small locked door under the stairs. He broke it open and found a narrow shaft that once must have held firewood and at the bottom he could see a loose rope and a pair of men's shoes. The walls of the shaft were black with blood.

Shorter, William said. He turned back and crossed the cellar and sat on an upturned crate facing the enormous man. Did Ellen confess to her affair?

He looked up. She never did, he said. She were too mighty clever for that.

And did Witten confess before he died?

Shorter's face twisted. I never give him the chance, he spat.

But there was no fight in the man and he did not struggle against them. William stamped up out of the cellar and called out a guinea to the first man who returned with a constable and went back down to find Blackwell lighting a pipe for the tavern keeper. The three of them made their heavy way back up the stairs and stood in the kitchen among the grimy pots and the knives and a roasting pig and waited. When a constable arrived William gave Blackwell a long weary look and then went out and he was surprised to hear Blackwell come out behind him. The street was cold, the air damp. William pulled on his gloves. The door banged shut behind them.

Let me ask you something, he said. What are the chances of someone else being involved?

Someone else, sir?

A confederate. Someone with a motive. Someone linked to the flash.

In this? Blackwell was studying him with his hooded eyes. I don't see how, sir. If you mean to suggest the letter from Mr. Witten was false—

William rubbed at his eyes. Ellen Shorter might just as easily have been running from her husband without any lover being involved.

And the letter, sir?

William frowned. There was something in it that troubled him but it might only be the ordinary shabby mystery of any killing. It was a thing he could not get used to. The faded wooden sign creaked on its chains over the doorway. Never mind it, he said reluctantly, and nodded at the young inspector. You did fine work here, Blackwell.

Blackwell flushed. Thank you, sir.

But William had already turned away. He was thinking of Shade and other kinds of jealousy and of the strange elusive bond between the thief and his own father. Love is a quiet and quicksilver thing and best left unjudged, Margaret liked to say. He had a sudden memory of her, one elbow propped on the lining of a carriage door, her head cradled in her palm as she peered sidelong at him and smiled. A waft of gardenias. Where had that been? He closed his eyes and rubbed at his temples and knew he had been too long from home.

Shall I fetch you a cab, sir? Blackwell said.

He stared at the inspector as if he had forgotten the man's presence and then he shook his head. No, he said. Thanks. I'll find my own way.

And lowered his hat and drew on his gloves and walked back through the narrow stone streets alone, towards the city, a man descending.

THIRTY-NINE

J ust don't you ask me to trust her, Molly said at breakfast
that first day.

Running a bitten thumb under red-rimmed eyes,
scowling. An egg was gleaming in its shell before her, her spoon
ablaze with light like some offering of grace.

Aye, Fludd grunted later on the stairs. Wrapping his huge
hand over the balustrade and lowering his voice. Molly ain't
wrong bout her, Mr. Adam. That sort is like to steal the bleedin
shoes off your feet, they is.

To both he had listened in silence and studied them with
hooded eyes and scratched at his whiskers and turned away. For
some strange dark fascination had bloomed again in him. He
brooded and weighed Charlotte's intention to free her uncle
from the prison transport in Chichester but he could not think
his way through it. She had asked for his help and he had wanted
to say no but had not. He knew whatever he had shared with
her would of course never be again as it was. Meanwhile Fludd
knuckled his beard, glowered blackly, and Molly stamped from
room to room in displeasure. Charlotte kept apart.

O-ho, Molly muttered at that. Too good for us is she.

Fludd lifted an eyebrow, pointedly.

Foole himself reeled, light-headed. When he knew where
Charlotte was he avoided her and when he did not he drifted
from room to room, floor to floor, seeking her out. He did not
defend her to his companions but neither did he attack her and

this reticence was mistaken by Molly for weakness, by Fludd for strength. Foole, unfocused, knew it to be neither. In the afternoon he felt a presence at his back and then her fingers were resting on his neck, on his throat, and he heard her murmur, I forgot how your skin smells. Like river water. But when he turned she was not there. That night as he went upstairs with a candle guttering before him he found her on the landing grey and indistinct, like an apparition, and when he held the flame high he saw she had been crying. He did not breathe. She stepped forward, and took his free hand, and held it to her breast. Her fingers like ice. The hot wax dripping and singeing his other wrist.

When he tried to kiss her she pulled away, she glared at him inexplicably, she disappeared into the gloom.

The next day was Monday. Foole and Molly and Fludd sat in the backroom of the Emporium, poring over the dailies, working through the details of their plan. Saturday's heist had made the front page of most London papers and the public outcry was magnificent. Some blamed the Irish, some the French, an editorial in the *London World* hinted at George Farquhar's own involvement. There was speculation as to the painting's true value and the nation's claim to the precious artwork. The auction date was postponed. Subscribers wrote letters with advice to the police as to how to trace the painting. Others described suspicious persons seen at the docks, at the train stations. Foole read with impatience, the red drapes drawn thickly over the daylight, the gaslights burning low. Fludd lost interest, picked idly through armfuls of wool batting in an open crate. Then he spat dust from his beard and reached with both hands into the box and withdrew, very carefully, a polished wooden mask. Strands of human hair twisting from its forehead, the scoop of its interior stained dark as if with blood.

Now this could be useful, he snorted. What do you reckon it is? A disguise?

The mask leering its twisted leer, dozens of tiny human teeth embedded in circles around the eye sockets. Ancient coins of some Spanish minting knotted and clattering from the jawline. A gruesome thing, a frightening thing, ugly.

Fludd held it to his face, peered through its slitted sockets. His muffled voice. An how do me face look now?

Much improved, Molly laughed.

Fludd pulled it away, looked at Foole. Well? he said. Anything to make us reconsider?

The exchange? No. Foole rotated his wrist, hearing the joint crack. Farquhar should be encouraged by all of the publicity. It should guarantee him a strong sale in his auction. The letter instructed him that Gabriel would be in contact. He'll wait for it. We'll move on Friday.

Pluckin a picture, Molly muttered. Not so much as a finger on his whole bloody palace full of diamonds, but the picture? Sure.

Foole held up a hand. Gabriel will write to Farquhar on Thursday with details. Expect the man at eleven o'clock, Billingsgate, as arranged. It will be for you, Molly, to meet with him. You'll work the open, Japheth and I will work the close. You know him by sight?

Poncey bugger like him? I don't expect a challenge.

An the peelers? Fludd said. Billingsgate Stairs like to be crawlin with them. You don't trust him to come alone?

Foole shook his head. He won't involve the police unduly. I expect some few to be there, for safety. Farquhar is a man of some importance. But he wants his painting, he won't risk losing it. And constables on the embankment won't trouble us any.

Aye. Fludd leaned forward, sawed at his beard with the back of his hand. Because of the river. You engaged the steamers, kid?

Molly nodded. They're just waiting on the second payment. She glanced from Foole to Fludd and back again. You sure the peelers won't be able to follow?

Unless they swim like fish.

Well I don't swim like no fish, Molly said abruptly. I swim like a bloody anchor.

Best not to fall in the drink then, Fludd grinned.

Adam—

You'll be fine, Molly. There won't be any complications.

We can tie a rope to you, Fludd suggested.

Molly furrowed her brow. An you two? You all set then yourselves, for your part?

Japheth?

Aye. There's a farrier up Albert Courts what rents out his old growler. I'll see to him in the morning. You finished with your mouldin, Mr. Adam?

Foole nodded. I will be. There's one last thing. Mrs. Sykes has procured a second residence for us, in Newington. It seems the owners are out of England for the year. It'll do fine for us. We'll need to relocate there at once. Mrs. Sykes and Hettie will close up the Emporium and stay on here.

Fludd looked at Molly. Because bloody Pinkerton come by here.

Yes.

You really reckon he's such a problem? With *The Emma* an all? I don't see how he could know it were us, Mr. Adam. There won't even be no charges laid, if Farquhar holds true.

We just need to keep our heads low for a few more days. I don't mean to invite complications, by allowing William Pinkerton to visit at his leisure.

An what do you aim to do with her ladyship? Molly said sarcastically.

Her ladyship.

Aye.

By that you mean Charlotte.

I weren't talkin bout Jappy.

You joke, Fludd said. But I make a pretty piece in a girdle.

Foole was looking at Molly, her eyes small and glinting weirdly in the gaslit sconces. Charlotte is not a part of this, he said softly. We don't bring her into it. Tell her nothing.

Molly set her jaw. You mean to leave her here then? she pressed. With Mrs. Sykes?

Not exactly.

Fludd was picking at some seam of dirt in his palm, rubbing it out with the ball of one thumb as if to erase his fate. He met Foole's eye. What Molly's sayin is, it's a question of trust. We don't neither of us suppose it were just coincidence, Pinkerton bein in London, an Charlotte writin you to take on a job. She's a Reckitt, Mr. Adam. You'd be wise to take that serious, like.

They all three sat enshrouded in a troubled silence and then Foole rose with his walking stick and opened the door and leaned into the hallway and called loudly for Charlotte. He banged twice on the banister and the sound rattled up through the house. He turned back and left the door standing open. Charlotte has somewhere to get to, he said. I don't mean Newington. I want you to hear it from her.

Molly was on her feet.

Easy kid, Fludd said.

Charlotte appeared in the doorway, then came in, pausing just inside the door and casting a quick unreadable look at Foole. She clasped her hands before her and her knuckles turned white and she regarded the three of them. What is this? she said.

Tell them what you told me, Foole said. What you mean to do.

She did not hesitate. My uncle is in Millbank, she said. I mean to follow his transport when he is moved to Portsmouth, on Wednesday. I mean to help him escape. I've asked Adam to help me.

For a long moment no one spoke.

That's a part of it you failed to mention, like, said Fludd slowly.

It's a bloody joke, Molly said. Tell us you told her no.

Charlotte was staring at Foole with a steady dark hopeful eye and Foole looked away, embarrassed. He's her uncle, Japheth, he said. I don't expect you to understand.

You said yes, Fludd interrupted. It was not a question.

Foole nodded.

It's like to be dangerous.

Yes.

You mean to do it alone? To break that old bastard out?

Not alone, Foole said. Charlotte and I'll do it together.

Bugger that, Adam, Molly muttered. Don't do it.

Fludd enfolded a hand over the girl's shoulder.

Foole fixed his bright eyes on her. I won't be gone more than a night, Molly. You and Japheth will continue with our work in the meantime. I'll be back to see it through.

Molly scowled. An if you're not?

Fludd rose up wrathful and elemental and smelling of the city's alleys and he glared down at Foole in silence and then he pressed past towards the door. Molly, he called over one shoulder. Come on, kid. We've heard enough.

Molly gave Foole a sullen glower. You got to ask yourself what's important, she said.

And then she too swept past and was gone.

The room was quiet. Foole grimaced and stared down at the opened crate, the mess of batting strewn from its opening like a spill of innards, the mask grinning face up from the floor. He could hear Molly's angry footsteps overhead, then the low shuddering tread of Fludd behind her. A door banged somewhere in the house.

Will you do it then? Charlotte said from behind him. Have you decided?

Foole turned, studied her.

The child doesn't approve.

Molly's like a daughter to me. I don't require her approval.

Mm.

What.

Maybe she's not mistaken, Adam. No good can come of this.

Of what?

Charlotte glided forward. Us.

Foole stiffened but did not move away. I need to ask you something. When you wrote me the letter—

Yes?

He forced himself to meet her eye. Did you already think I was Shade? Did you think I was the man Pinkerton wanted when you brought me into this?

Charlotte paused. You are asking if I lured you here, to Pinkerton?

I am.

She said nothing and all at once Foole felt strangely, obscurely, ashamed. Then she turned without speaking and went to the door. When she looked back her eyes were slitted and hurt. If you think me capable of that, she began. But she did not finish.

It was, he would reflect later, a most impressive performance.

On Tuesday Fludd rented the farrier's battered old growler and piled it with their trunks and travelling cases and he and Molly rode south in their heavy coats towards Newington. Foole stood with Mrs. Sykes at the parlour window and watched them go. In the mid-morning he took Charlotte by hansom to collect a list of items needed for their pursuit of her uncle. They bought tickets for the Portsmouth stage due to depart at four o'clock the following morning, Mr. and Mrs. Balderdash, yes, B-A-L-D-E, ah, I see, sir, thank you. They drifted through the shops, her hand resting lightly on his wrist, his cane clicking as they went. Parcels were wrapped, sent on ahead to Half Moon Street. They strolled among the crowds on the Strand their breath visible in the chill and they ridiculed the theatre posters in St. Martin's Lane and all the while Foole kept his eyes low but he saw neither police nor Pinkerton. In the early afternoon they went down to the Thames and walked the Embankment under the leafless trees and Foole had the eerie sensation that he was living a borrowed life. He thought of how he might have lived, had things been otherwise, had the ordinary creep of time not stretched on.

At Blackfriars Bridge they paused in the span and Charlotte stared down at the Thames swirling thickly below and at the barges passing under them and Foole felt a shiver go through him. The day was dark, the afternoon was dark.

Is this the place? he asked. Is this where you jumped?

She was quiet.

You're all secrets, he said.

She looked reprovingly at him. The traffic crossing the bridge was loud, the shouts of men in heavy scarves over the backs of horses, a drove of pigs rattling angrily on to the slaughteryards. The stone railing under his glove gave off a low thrum.

You have no faith in people, she said.

I'd have had faith in our son. He had not meant to say it and he looked up at her in surprise. Forgive me.

Her thin eyebrows sharpened. My son, she said, is dead.

Yes.

He died in Kent.

They were quiet then. Some figure bundled in rags had run to the railing farther down the bridge, was hurling a packet of papers into the river. Foole watched the scatter of pages, the slow spread of sheets in the water as they sank from view. A man in a blue frock coat was hollering.

Charlotte shook her head. She said, I came from over there. It was night. William Pinkerton was behind me and not stopping. It was like being charged by a bull. I knew as soon as I'd turned into the traffic here that I'd made a mistake. I climbed over the rail, there, I stood on the parapet. And then I just let go. Her face was far away, her eyes staring down at the freezing river below. I thought I'd die, she said. I couldn't feel anything. And I just kept thinking of my baby. She had lowered her voice so that Foole had to strain to hear her. There was a river near where our carriage overturned, she said. I remember we walked down to it and I bundled him up and set him in a little basket. The river was high. I lost sight of him at once. I kept thinking about that.

Foole shifted his feet. The papers long since lost to the waters, the fuliginous river muscling brutally past.

We were trapped on that road for three nights, she whispered.

It was a terrible place. The river high and in flood and me with nothing in my arms.

Foole was shaking his head and he stared a hard stare at the murky Thames and he gripped the stone railing and he thought of the Confederate carriage he had nearly drowned in twenty years before, the black water in his lungs, the desperate soldier kicking at him for purchase. He thought of Allan Pinkerton, in silhouette, watching him ride southward to his death.

Charlotte put a small gloved hand on his sleeve. Something went through him, a shiver. What is done out of love, must be judged through love, she said. You said that to me once.

His eyes drifted down to her gloved wrist, the crescent of skin visible between the kidskin and her cuff.

You don't remember?

I'd sooner remove a man's hands than let him cut me twice, he said, his eyes clear. I don't care the reason. He ran the tip of his tongue along his eye teeth. A knot of birds lifted from the far embankment like a shudder in the air. The sky darkened, the river deepened, bruising. Steamer ferries with small fires burning on their decks were paddling the waters downriver.

We should go, he said. Tomorrow will come early. There's much still to do.

But he was watching her as he spoke and she looked up at him and there was in her face a sadness he had not seen there before.

You have changed, she said.

FORTY

I n the morning the city loomed, soot-stained, teeming. William left his hotel and wended his way through narrow cobbled lanes wreathed in fog and came out into the roar of men and horses and carriages sliding on the icy setts under railway arches and through all this he walked with his hat low and his gloved fists at his sides. He was thinking all the while on Ellen Shorter's husband. That man's love had first destroyed itself and then destroyed her leaving nothingness and loss in its place. William had lived his life among such men and still he did not know what it was in a person that led to such brutality. He did not believe men were made for violence and yet somehow savagery was ever near at hand. In you as in any, he thought. As he waited for a break in the traffic he glimpsed, distorted, in a glass shop display, his own reflection dark and faceless and rippling among the clerks surrounding like a creature out of nightmare. He looked away.

It was Wednesday. He walked as far as Half Moon Street and there he paused and stared up at the Emporium. He could see at once that Foole, Shade, was gone. The curtains drawn, the chimneys cold and dead. He had not noticed before the ragged brickwork, its cinder bricks standing out from the facade, like footholds for climbing.

He set a gloved hand on the iron gate, glanced back along the street. Margaret would have told him there is no living in regret. You make the choices in the moment and then you live with them. When the front door opened William turned, surprised.

It was Foole's housekeeper. A stout powerful woman with a shawl wrapped tight at her shoulders and a bonnet askew. Hard, intelligent eyes.

The master's not at home, she called. Whatever it is you're wantin.

William stepped forward. Do you expect him back soon?

A pause, her face squashing in concentration. You. You was by the house two weeks back.

William paused. Yes.

You was mighty rough with the wee one.

He opened the gate and came through and approached. That was a misunderstanding, he said, and I do regret it. I'm an acquaintance of Mr. Foole's. Is the child here? Could I tell her so myself?

She's gone out of the country too. We're just to shuttering the house now, we are.

He climbed the steps and stood towering over her and he could see her knuckles white in the cold where she gripped her shawl. Behind her through the open door he glimpsed the elegant interior, a dust sheet already drawn up over a pier table in the foyer. A ghost of a girl with a cleaning brush in one hand peered at him from the parlour doorway and when he met her eye she startled and vanished.

When do you expect Mr. Foole to return?

I wouldn't know that, now. Commerce bein commerce, an all.

More than a week though. If you're closing up the house.

Aye.

More than a month?

She screwed up one eye, glared. It's the modern world. Keeps a poor man from sittin by his own fire.

There must be some forwarding address. If I left a message—

Wouldn't reach him. Not for lord knows how long.

He gave her a look. What about Mr. Fludd? Is he here?

Now look, she said sharply. My girl and me we got a week's worth of work to get through in a day. You be off now, Mr. Pinkerton.

He looked up in surprise and met her gaze and then he stepped closer.

Aye, I know you, she scowled, sidling back. And I know your kind too.

And what kind is that? he said softly.

Her lips tightened. You disappointed the master something awful. Ought to be ashamed, way you carry on. Persecuting a good man like that.

And she turned and shut the door firmly and after a moment William heard the bolts rasp into place and though he had not moved he had the eerie feeling he had passed a threshold there was no returning from. He looked at his shoes, uneasy, he stared out at the street.

In the sky a great brown drift of fog thickened and slid past.

But Foole was not gone yet. Whatever that housekeeper claimed. This he knew with the same cold certainty that told him the elegant thief had been the architect behind the *Emma* heist. At a restaurant in a deserted square he sat at a window and while he ate he withdrew from his coat the old photograph of his father's operatives in Cumberland. The blurred boyish figure of Shade visible there. He stared at the boy. Then he stared at his father, bearded, savage, fierce, one hand creeping into his frock coat as if towards a weapon. How unlikely, he thought, that the boy he'd trained and the son he'd raised would someday stalk each other in a foreign city, haunted by separate griefs. He set the photograph aside and looked out at the February cold.

In the afternoon he made his way to Scotland Yard and found Shore in his shirt sleeves, hat off, head cradled on his desk, snoring. William had come noisily in and he stared at the man in surprise, spotted red skin visible through his hair.

William, Shore muttered. Lifting his face and rubbing at his whiskered cheeks with open palms, grimacing sleepily.

I didn't mean to wake you.

Come in. Shut the door, for god's sake.

William shut the door and stood turning his hat in his fingers. Rough morning?

Rough night. Some lunatic's been hammering away at the whores south of Ludgate. Starting to upset the honest folk. He scraped at a nostril with a thumbnail, snorted. Never mind it. You've seen the papers? George Farquhar calls in here near every day. Just can't sit still.

Well. It must be trying for him.

Trying for him? Shore grunted. You have no notion the pressure I'm under. George Farquhar dines regularly with Lord Hattersby. He keeps the counsel of half Parliament. This is not a man I'd like to see ruined, not on my watch.

William frowned in sympathy.

No word yet from the thief, Shore added. I expect that should come through in the next day or two. We're to meet at Mr. Farquhar's residence when that happens. Shore raised his eyes, paused. Your presence has been requested.

Mine.

Aye. Seems Farquhar wants to hire you. To ensure his safety or some such.

He's decided to go along with the exchange then.

Never doubted he would, man like that. Shore wrestled into his frock coat, set his hat on his head. I'm sorry about it, William.

So there'll be no charges laid.

Aye. And no legal grounds to collar the bastards that did this. Seems your rogue's file on Mr. Shade will have to wait awhile yet. But Shore's face as he said this was drawn and gentle and disappointed on William's behalf and there was no trace of mockery in it. Mr. Blackwell informs me you had some success in closing that Charlotte Reckitt case, he said.

Well. It wasn't her.

No.

William rubbed at his old knee injury, starting to ache. It's strange, he said, and smiled a faint smile. There's no evidence she's even dead. Maybe she'll resurface, maybe she'll prove my lead back to Shade after all. Imagine that. He looked up. Unless Farquhar were to change his mind.

I'd think not. He means to negotiate.

On whose advice?

He wants his property returned, William. I can understand it.

Edward Shade did this, John. I'm sure of it.

Doesn't matter. You can't move on a man without cause.

I'll find cause.

Not in London you won't. Must I say it again? Last thing I need is some notorious American detective turned vigilante.

William paused. He looked at Shore, at the man's long calculating glower, and all at once something clicked into place. What is it? he said. Did Breck finish dusting the letter?

Shore's eyes shrank to small points of light. All this time, he said, I thought you were chasing a ghost. You and your father. He took out his pipe and lit it. He nudged the box of tobacco towards William and the two men sat in a slow white wreath of smoke. Aye, they're a match, Shore said at last. The fingerprints belong to your Edward Shade.

Son of a bitch, William muttered. I knew it.

But you can't do a thing with it, William.

He looked up and met the other's eye.

Not legally I can't, he said.

FORTY-ONE

The Portsmouth stage rattled south into the red of the rising sun and Foole and Charlotte sat stained by its glow, the red light slatted over their faces, their huddled shoulders, their gloves shuddering on the blankets in their laps. A freezing wind whistled through the cracked and broken panes and carried on the wind were the voices of the driver and the young passenger riding crow's seat. The driver was an older man with thick brown mutton chops and a green scarf double-wrapped at his throat and his gloves had been sliced at the fingers. In the half dark of the inn yard where the stage began the driver had stood blowing into his fingers and studying his customers coolly and he had not helped load the trunks to the roof but had climbed up after and lashed them fast.

Charlotte seemed disconsolate. She stared out at the passing fields, saying little, her small mouth down-turned, while the farmhouses with white smoke rising from their chimneys slid past, the long sinuous hedgerows marking the grazing land. Foole watched her from the corner of his eye but did not disturb her. He felt a slow bloom of sadness coming up in him but could not account for it.

The only other passenger was an elderly man with wire-rimmed spectacles and an unfashionable silk hat and he smiled and nodded when he caught Foole's eye.

A fine thing, getting up out of the smoke, he said. To Portsmouth, is it?

Foole shook his head. Chichester. My wife's sister. She's ailing, I fear.

Ah, the man said, withdrawing slightly, glancing at Charlotte, glancing back. A shame, that. You wouldn't be from thereabouts yourself, though.

No.

I allowed maybe you weren't. On account of your— And the man waved a hand back and forth in front of his face.

My what.

The man blinked behind his spectacles, uncertain. Why, your complexion, he said.

They rattled along in silence then for a time and then the man said, Had a sister myself once. Funny little teeth. We used to call her Peggers, on account of them. Well. All in the past, now. The elderly man leaned forward over his leather satchel. She had three little ones, all dead inside of a year. Fourth one took her with it. He clicked his tongue, remembering. A poor affair, that was.

Foole glanced out the window.

What ails your sister-in-law?

Disease, he said blackly.

A shame, the man said again. And so young too, I wager.

The stage rattled and banged and clattered on. Foole tried to fix his gaze on the passing scenery and thereby discourage the man from further conversation. By noon the stage had arrived in Guildford and Foole and Charlotte got down at the local inn and stood in the yard with their two modest trunks standing under the cover of the front entrance and Charlotte went inside for a bite to eat and Foole followed. The only course on offer was a bowl of beef stew thick with onions and carrots and Foole ate heartily but Charlotte set her spoon aside, her face pale, and did not eat. After lunch they walked out past the chicken yard until they reached a small stable at the end of the lane and Charlotte went inside and asked for Hadfield Crooke.

That isn't his real name, Foole said with a smile. It can't be.

She smiled vaguely.

A short clean-shaven man with a birthmark covering half his neck came out, still struggling into his frock coat. How can I be of help, then? he said.

Mr. Crooke?

Aye.

We wrote ahead, Charlotte said. We were told a carriage was for hire.

The man grunted. One surely is, ma'am.

But what he presented to them was not a carriage but an open waggon with an ancient ship-ribbed mare attached and Foole took one disgusted look at the condition of its wheels and turned to go.

Suit yourself, the man Crooke said. But you'll find no other. Folks round here don't hire out what they need theirselves.

Foole tipped his hat. We'll find another. Charlotte?

But Charlotte had walked over to the shaggy mare, set a hand on its flank. Pay the man, she said. We'll take this one.

They loaded their trunks into the bed of the waggon and set off by early afternoon on the Midhurst road. The going was slow in places with the churned mud frozen into ragged crests in the ruts. They were in West Sussex, in the middle of the western Weald, and passed alongside stands of oak and rolling hills marked with medieval boundary stones and all of it blue and gloomy where a cold winter mist hung low to the ground. Swirling up around the creaking of their waggon's wheels then coalescing and closing up in their wake as if they had never been.

At Midhurst they got down into the biting chill and unhitched and fed the miserable creature in the yard of an inn. The ground was barren, snowless, hard. In the common room they called for a glass of porter and two hot ciders and stood with their hands to the fire, speaking to no one. Then they harnessed their mare and climbed back up and crossed the River Rother and rode the three miles south into Heyshott. The village looked gloomy, deserted. They passed St. James's Church and its spindly tombstones and the small unfenced green where a lone dog trotted past and they drew up outside the Unicorn pub. Both Charlotte and Foole took note of the ebony carriage next to the stables, with its royal insignia and its barred windows and its twin lanterns already lit in the failing light. That would be the prisoners' transport.

Charlotte rummaged in her trunk and took out a thick wool coat and a pair of men's breeches and stiff new boots and stuffed them all into a long satchel and then they went inside. They took a table at the back of the room. The pub was crowded, smoky, a low orange wood fire burning in the grate and Foole looked at Charlotte but she seemed distant, watchful, cold. The prisoners were not, of course, among them.

I don't see him, Foole said.

Charlotte did not answer but got to her feet and stood waiting and after a moment a guard in a red coat and brass buckler and wearing a truncheon at his hip came over to their table. He held a half-full tankard in one fist and he nodded soberly to the two of them.

You lot down from London, then? he said pleasantly.

Charlotte studied him with a cold eye. Sit, Mr. Bailey, do, she said.

I allowed it was you, the man said, lowering his voice. We're just to changing the horses now.

Charlotte had taken from inside her coat a small felt pouch and it clinked as she set it on the table. That marks the rest of it, she said.

Bailey glanced uneasily about, snatched it up, pocketed it.

Where is he? she said.

A sly grin. Bein seen to. There's seventeen of them in the links. Got to be fed the old pease-pottage, a little somethin to wash it down with, quick step to shit-shed. He tipped his hat. Beggin your pardon.

How will you manage it?

Oh, run him to the tunny last. How much do he know? He won't start hollerin up a piece will he? When neither answered

Bailey shrugged. Well I'll manage the count when we're back loaded. Shouldn't be noticed until we get to Portsmouth. He gave Charlotte a quick fierce look. And that's my work in full then.

Foole frowned. How soon until you depart?

Bailey shrugged. Quarter of an hour all told. Less. I'm already out the door. You lot don't leave much margin for error, do you? I was thinking maybe you got cold feet.

It was a slow road in, Charlotte said. Just get him to the privy, Mr. Bailey. We'll see to the rest.

They waited ten minutes and then got up and went out into the cold and walked around the outside of the pub and stood at the corner as the afternoon daylight faded and they watched the guard Bailey frogmarch the prisoners one by one to the outhouse and take them back. They could hear the other two guards barking orders and the heavy rattle of chains and lastly they saw Bailey lead a frail old man out to the privy and enter it with him and the door shut behind them. A minute passed, two. Then Bailey came out alone and slipped back towards the transport and climbed up inside to start locking the leg irons into place.

Wait, Foole said. He set a hand on Charlotte's arm.

She looked at him.

Wait, he said again. I'll go first.

The thick doors of the transport waggon shut, were locked, double-locked, and then the two guards climbed up front and one climbed into the perch at the back of the waggon and the horses were snapped into motion and the transport rolled out at speed.

He pulled away from Charlotte and crossed the pale clay yard and banged open the door of the rickety wooden privy and there sat Martin Reckitt, frail, confused, blinking in his brown prison issue. He stared up in astonishment.

You, he said. This is your doing?

Foole held the door open a crack for light to see by. The privy was narrow, its walls awash in filth and a powerful reek of ancient shit and urine. Martin Reckitt looked grey, his skin bleached of colour, his eyes pale, the only colour the sore red rims around them and the rashes on his throat and the backs of his hands. Foole could see nothing of the dangerous man he had met at Millbank, only a befuddled and miserable creature. He crouched, he studied the chains at the man's ankles. He knew the locks, double Frobishers now thirty years out of date. They would not be difficult to spring.

What are you doing? the old man said. What is this?

How much were you told?

Reckitt's head shuddered on his neck, imperceptible, old.

Kill me quickly, the old man hissed. If you have the nerve for it.

But just then the door was pulled from Foole's grasp and he turned in sudden fury but it was only Charlotte, pressing in behind him, and he looked back in time to see Martin Reckitt, open-mouthed, sight his living niece in the flesh. The privy latticed in shadow and light, the three of them crowded inside.

Martin Reckitt trembled, he leaned unsteadily towards her. And then he embraced her.

Lord God in heaven, all that is Holy, he murmured. My Lord my God. He turned his face in wonder to Foole and Foole could smell the black stink of the old man's breath. How is this possible?

His hands trembling.

We haven't the time, Charlotte said abruptly, pulling back. Adam. The chains.

He made his way back out and collected his small black pouch of picking tools from his trunk and he glanced quickly around him and then returned to the privy. He kneeled in the filth of the floor next to the open hole and he worried away at the fetters and had them off in minutes and he kicked the chains into the pit with a splash.

Charlotte had opened her satchel and pulled out the clothes and Foole began to help the old man undress. They kept elbowing up against the cold walls and the wood there was slick with some foul matter. The old man's skin was streaked with grime, a welt of sores in bloom on his belly and his thighs.

Charlotte, the old man said, unashamed. My little Charlotte.

Later, Foole said sharply. We need to be gone now.

The old man pale and eerie in the early gloaming did not look at Foole, might not have even heard.

Charlotte herself was staring with anguish at her uncle as if at a stranger and then she saw Foole watching and her face closed over and she pushed at the door and was gone.

They rode out of the roadhouse yard crowded onto the box of the waggon and the tired thin mare straining at her harness and the darkness already descending in the east. A line of bright grey sky almost white in its shining was visible above the western horizon and even as they rode out of Heyshott into the Weald it started to fade and go down.

Martin sat in the middle, frail, shivering, his face turned towards Charlotte. No one spoke. Foole could not gauge the old man's expression but he could see the deep frown at Charlotte's eye where she strained not to look back at him. The shadow road unscrolled before them. Foole did not know what was in Charlotte but he knew it was not joy, not relief.

At last they could go no farther and they drew the waggon roughly off the road into a stand of oaks and walked some thirty paces farther on and found the remains of an old firepit. Blackened stones, the charred remains of some feral creature. In the twilight Foole collected dead branches and scooped an armful of hay from the back of the waggon and set about lighting a fire. With a sudden whoosh the straw caught and flared and bloomed up into flame. He stepped back, waved the sparks from his face with his hat.

It's still got the wet in it, he said. There won't be much heat.

Martin said nothing. Foole could not see Charlotte and supposed she had gone back to the waggon to collect some food.

At least there's light, he muttered.

There is always a light, Martin said quietly, if only we cared to see it.

Foole crouched on his haunches, stirred a branch deeper into the fire.

We imagine we stand at the centre of the story but we do not, Martin said, peering up at Foole. His eyes reflected the firelight. I see that now. It is not your story, Adam Foole, that you find yourself in. Nor is it mine. It belongs to the Lord and the Lord only and He will tell it as He will.

Foole saw in the old man's ravaged face the weight of his solitary bitterness and he understood something had twisted inside the man that could not be sorted out. It was not madness, not exactly, but a kind of warping all the same. He looked up. The last of the day's light had slipped away.

We'll need to find something to eat, he said after a time. How hungry are you?

The old man seemed not to hear. He was seated on a wind-fallen tree staring into the fire, sloe-eyed, his head trembling on its thin stalk of a neck. It is not my flesh that hungers, he said. I have no words, no words for this, and he held out his claw-like hands to the fire. That is a terrible thing, Adam Foole. To have lived by words and to lose them at such a moment.

Foole looked at him. What moment would that be?

But the old man did not answer.

When Charlotte emerged out of the darkness behind her uncle she appeared like a grey ghost her face bloodless and she wrapped one slender arm around the old man's forehead and snapped his head back and the other hand inserted a blade under the carotid artery and punched it forward. A black spray of blood crossed the mossy earth and then a sheet of it poured downward out of his throat and over his frock coat and his knees. He gave out a strangled groan and his eyes rolled back in his head and he pitched forward into the dirt.

Foole was on his feet. Charlotte, he cried. Jesus.

She stood breathing and she looked up at him in horror and then she started to shake.

The old man lay face down, his blood steaming out into the frozen earth.

She said nothing. She stood with the dagger still clutched in her hand.

Foole stepped back out of the firelight. All at once he understood. You meant this, he said. All this time. This was your intent.

She stared through Foole not seeing him and then she came to and gave a small shiver and turned away.

He watched her gather her belongings and stuff them into a small satchel and he followed her down to the hired waggon. She unhobbled the horse and backed it slowly into its harness.

She paused. He could see her breath in the cold. Five years ago a man approached me in a pub in Lambeth. He thought I was a whore. He said I was the spitting image of a woman he'd once fancied. Turned out that was my mother.

Foole stood shivering in the cold night. The fire was burning in the trees beyond.

He told me an account of my father. Said he was a clever man, a good man, fell afoul of very bad people. Said they killed him, ruined my mother. Killed her too, in their way. I went to the old neighbourhood where we'd lived, found others who remembered them. Remembered me. I heard from several the name of the man who did it. There was no mistaking it.

Martin.

She nodded. She was starting to shake in earnest now and her eyes looked wild. He did it, Adam, she whispered. He killed my father. He had my mother and me run out of our lodgings. When he came for me in the workhouse it wasn't mercy. It was revenge.

You could have left him to rot. You could have left him to die in Portsmouth.

Would you? Would you have done so?

Foole pursed his lips. He thought of his own father, he thought of Mrs. Shade. He thought of Allan Pinkerton's fatherly hand gripping his shoulder. Where will you go now? he said. What will you do?

I don't want you to remember me like this, she said. You must think me a villain.

I don't.

You will.

Her body was trembling violently now.

Wait, he said. He went back and dragged his trunk down the slope and threw it up onto the bed of the waggon. In the lamplight he opened the lid and took out a heavy blanket and a bag of salt crackers and his black pouch of lock-picking tools and then he shut the lid and stepped away.

You could come with me, she said.

But he could not. He shook his head. He studied her shocked face in the faint light, thinking how it was something he would not see again, thinking it was a face he had not ever really seen. Not truly.

She did not ask him twice. She gathered the reins and turned the horse. As she rode off the single orange lantern swayed and flickered and was gradually lost to view. If she glanced back he did not see it.

FORTY-TWO

William and Shore were let into George Farquhar's upstairs study by a man with fishy lips and bad teeth and the placid cowlike eyes of a born swindler. This man was Farquhar's butler and William paused and took his measure and then pushed past. The house, palatial and dazzling by gaslight, in the day appeared cold and marbled and forbidding, the polished white columns of the stairwell shining with their own luminescence.

Farquhar rose from his antique desk and came to meet them: immaculate in a black high-cut suit, a green vest, his slender face both anxious and haughty. Well, sir? And what does Scotland Yard propose to do? He did not extend his hand.

Mr. Farquhar, sir. You remember Mr. Pinkerton.

Of course. Your entertainment on Saturday left quite an impression on my wife, sir. On her and me both.

The study was long, narrow, with deep cherrywood panels in the ceiling and a lacquered oak mantel over the fireplace that gleamed like oil. On the man's desk stood a tall silver candlestick, branched and ornately carved, inscribed with symbols and all of it wreathed by a silver vine clambering over its seven branches. It looked, to William's eye, strange and beautiful and exotic.

You admire it, sir? Farquhar said, catching his gaze. It is a menorah, out of Russia. A Jewish ritual object. Lovely, is it not? I mean to display it downstairs in the great hall. It is very rare.

The rabbis don't mind you having it? William asked.

Farquhar smiled gravely, as if at a witticism. He said, My wife is unwell, sir, or she should be here to welcome you herself. I have been urging her to travel to our house in Yorkshire. Half the household has already been sent on ahead. I cannot think what keeps her here.

Perhaps when she is feeling more herself, sir.

Perhaps. This affair has upset her so. Have you seen the newspapers, Mr. Shore? Have you seen what they write about me?

You mustn't mind the gossips, sir.

They claim I am involved, man. They say I have orchestrated this entire affair. Why? Why, to drum up publicity.

William grunted. He took off his hat and laid it on the desk and he sat wearily in one of the armchairs, propriety be damned. He said, Mr. Shore tells me you don't wish to prosecute the thief.

Thieves, corrected Shore. Be assured, this will prove a crew.

Farquhar shook his head. I care little for their situation. It is *The Emma* that concerns me. I would like it returned, Mr. Pinkerton. And I should not care to find my ten thousand pounds taken, without being assured of such an outcome.

Shore was still standing, uneasy, and only now when Farquhar returned to his desk and sat did the chief too take a seat. It is my job to ensure that does not happen, sir, he said.

It was your job, sir, to prevent such misfortune from happening at all. Are the streets not safe anymore? I am frankly amazed you would come to our city, Mr. Pinkerton, riddled as it is with such crime. You must think us all barbarians.

It's never the city, Mr. Farquhar. It's always the people.

The city, sir, makes the people.

Shore cleared his throat, withdrew a small notebook and pencil. If you'd care to tell us what you've heard, sir. Did you say ten thousand? Am I to understand the thieves have been in touch?

Farquhar nodded gravely. They demand ten thousand pounds, divided equally between notes and open bonds, sir. Yes. A letter was delivered to me this morning, from their solicitor. He carefully shifted the silver menorah to one side of the desk and then he gave Shore a hard look. Is it not rather strange, sir, that they should retain legal representation? Does it not make them vulnerable?

Vulnerable?

Why, could you not find them through this man, this— Farquhar rose abruptly, crossed the room, snatched a sheet of paper from a cigar table and scanned it—this Gabriel Utterson?

Utterson, William muttered.

Shore gave him a quick look. Gabriel Utterson's somewhat notorious, Mr. Farquhar. A clever fellow. Not an ethical bone in his body. The problem, sir, is that his actions here are perfectly legal. Everyone is entitled to legal counsel. And unless you agree to press charges, there is no legal ground for the Yard to get involved.

Mr. Pinkerton, Farquhar said, hooking a thumb into his waistcoat pocket and turning one foot out and cocking his knee. At the recommendation of one of my oldest friends, Mr. Busby, I have decided I would like to hire you, sir. I understand your terms are rather—

Henry Busby? William interrupted. Our results for him were less than satisfactory.

He was most impressed by your methods, sir.

William did not know what the gallerist might know of the Busby blackmail letters but it could not be much. Henry Busby had been blackmailed for lewd sexual acts and in the end every evidence turned up by the Pinkerton operatives suggested that the man, wealthy, unmarried, eccentric, had been blackmailing himself. The case had been abandoned.

Farquhar steepled his fingers before him. Shall we discuss the matter of payment, sir?

Fifty dollars a day, plus expenses, William said at once. It's standard and non-negotiable. In this matter it should prove modest enough. We'll complete the paperwork at a later date.

You accept then, sir?

I must remind you the Pinkertons are not police, Mr. Farquhar, said Shore.

Farquhar gave the chief a withering look. Let me be clear. I wish to hire Mr. Pinkerton to ensure the safe return of *The Emma*. I do not wish to prosecute the men responsible. I have no interest in revenge.

William grimaced. Maybe you should.

I beg your pardon?

You give these men what they want, it makes you a more attractive target. For the next time.

Tomorrow shall be the last time, Farquhar said gravely. This will not happen again.

Tomorrow?

The letter stipulated tomorrow, sir? Shore rubbed at his whiskers. That is rather immediate.

Farquhar passed across the letter from Utterson and the chief inspector scanned its contents.

These are unusually organized thieves, Shore said. One typically waits weeks or even months to hear from them. I wonder at the speed of this. He glanced up. You will need to act quickly to collect the ransom, sir. I would suggest you do not attend to your bank alone. I can send a man with you.

William took the letter from Shore. So you don't yet know where the exchange will take place. Is that correct?

It is indeed, sir. The solicitor will send the details tomorrow morning. I am to wait for them here.

Shore nodded. As soon as you hear, come by the Yard. We shall establish our final details then.

How is this to work, gentlemen? the gallerist said uneasily.

It's simple, William said. You do what they ask. You take the money to them where they ask for it, hand it over, the thieves will then deliver the painting to you. It's all on their terms.

And I am expected to just trust them, sir? To have faith in their honesty, that they will present me with *The Emma*?

William gave the man a long level look. Yes, he said. You are.

FORTY-THREE

Martin Reckitt lay with his face white against the earth and in the moonlight Foole sat staring at it, bereft. He ate the salt crackers slowly. Something had broken in him and would not be repaired. For ten years he had dreamed of Charlotte, carried her daguerreotype, weighed her in his heart and found her measure and all that time he had been wrong. Had not known her in the least. At last he rose and slid on his heels down a low wet slope of grass to a stand of oaks at the bottom and he huddled against a fallen tree but he did not sleep. He could not shake the eerie feeling that he was not alone. At dawn he rose and studied the sky and then retraced his steps and stood over the cold corpse and stared at it again and then he took from the dead man's pockets a billfold Charlotte had given him and he left that place forever.

It was four miles into the town of Midhurst through wet fields and he waited in the local square with his shoes sopping for the post office to open and he followed the clerk inside and purchased a ticket home. He did not care that his actions must look suspicious. The London & South Western punched through Midhurst at 10:15 every day and Foole the lone passenger on the platform climbed wearily aboard and the ticket agent hollered the all-clear and the engine huffed and steamed back up to speed. He rode the line through to Waterloo Station and so returned to London, silent, dark, alone.

———

He said nothing of the killing to Fludd or Molly.

As he came up through the mustard-brown fog at Penton Place Fludd opened the door and stood glowering. The house Mrs. Sykes had located for them looked cold, its owners gone for the season, the neighbours down on their luck and unlikely to take an interest. The street had been fashionable once or at the least had been wealthy but that age was long past and in the fog the houses looked now cold, soot-stained and desolate.

You look like you slept in the open, Fludd grunted. Or failed to. Is that a twig in your hair?

Slamming the door and locking it behind them.

Foole stripped off his frock coat, damp yet at the collar and wrists, and looked about and then hung it on the hat stand in the corner. I could use a bite, he said. What do we have?

What do we have what's warm? Nothin but a bit of porridge. Fludd stepped back, ran his knuckles through his beard. We never known if you was comin back alone, Mr. Adam.

Foole blew out his cheeks. As you can see, he said.

Everythin go all right then?

He shrugged, not wanting to talk about it. Tell me how we fare, he said instead. Is the cart hired? Have we heard from Gabriel?

Go on, where's the flit then? Molly announced, coming out from the parlour. She was wearing boots laced with mud and tracking prints across the carpet. She paused when she saw Foole's expression.

Charlotte ain't come back, Fludd said. It's like Mr. Adam told us.

Done what you set out to, is it? Martin Reckitt's clear of the clink?

Something like that.

But the child seemed to sense his distress and gave him a strange look and this in itself, this gentleness, made Foole suddenly fierce. He thought of Charlotte's face in the firelight the night before. She had not betrayed him perhaps but neither had she been forthright. He thought of her standing with him that night on Blackfriars. She had tried to warn him that her ends were not his to know but he had not wanted to hear it. He looked up and saw Fludd and Molly, pity in their eyes.

He scowled. We have much to do. Where is my trunk? You did not leave it at Half Moon Street?

Fludd gestured to the stairs.

I never trusted her, Adam, said Molly. I never did.

It doesn't matter.

An if she comes back here? said Fludd.

She won't.

But if she do?

We won't see her again, Foole said angrily. Any of us.

He had brooded over what had happened with Charlotte all the long grey train journey back into London. The worst was that he had not seen it coming. He had understood she was different from how she had been and he had recognized something, some trace or hint or warning in her, but he had failed to realize its import. She had murdered her uncle out of a vengeance that Foole too could understand. Had killed him and walked away from it and who was he to condemn her for it. He thought of Allan Pinkerton and felt a great black ache in his heart.

He left Fludd and Molly below and climbed the stairs tiredly and entered a small bedroom at the top of the house and there was a ladder standing down through the ceiling and this he climbed into the attic. A small narrow bed, Foole's travelling case standing open upon it. A green trunk with clothes in disarray. Papers and dossiers stacked against one wall. A porcelain washstand stood in a corner with a towel folded over it and Foole washed the mud and road grease from his face and hands and he washed the back of his neck and dried himself with a towel and when he turned around he saw Fludd standing at the ladder.

What is it, he said, less kindly than he meant it.

He had some idea of the run of the giant's thinking and he did not think he would like it. But it was not about Charlotte Reckitt.

Your bloody Molly, Fludd said instead. Guess who rode the bloody carriage into a worksite off Lambeth Road yesterday an knocked over a ladder holdin a sheet of iron so the whole bloody slice of it come down on me like an axe? Cleaved the damned horse in two, it did. Near took off me own bleedin head.

It weren't that bad, Molly's voice piped up from below.

Me arse it weren't.

Foole stared hard at Fludd filling the trap door. What he wanted was to rest. Must we discuss this now? Can it not wait?

But then Molly was shrugging her way up the ladder and poked her head through and said, half grinning, There were a bloomin rat the size of a ham climbin my leg. What would you do?

Foole laid himself down on the cot, still dressed, he folded a hand over his eyes. What are you saying? he said slowly.

Our horse is dead.

The beast you hired?

Aye.

He raised his head. Do we have another?

Fludd looked at Molly. She studied with great interest a grease mark on the wall.

Find us one, Foole said. Before tomorrow.

Aye.

Molly, he said. You go see Mr. Appleby Barr. Tell him we'll have some business to clear with him tomorrow afternoon. I think he's been patient enough. He rubbed at his eyes with the back of his wrist and then he said, Japheth. Wait. On second thought hire us a new waggon too. Something clearly marked, noticeable. A labourer's cart. Wasn't there an outfit outside Waterloo Station the flash used to frequent?

Old Monkey Abbott's, Fludd said. Aye, I know the place.

But Foole did not rest. In the afternoon he stripped down to his shirt sleeves and went into the scullery at the back of the house and heated a pot of water and went to the kitchen and stoked the fire there until it reached a high blaze. The heat was ferocious. He unwrapped the wax impressions of the gallerist's keys from the strips of oilskin where he had kept them. There were seven impressions in total. He was cautious and slow at his work and he poured and cooled and heated again what was needed using the strange contained furnace that he had erected. He was alone in the house with Fludd seeing to their transport and Molly arranging a meeting with Appleby Barr for the following day and he would pause often and stoke the fire and listen to the house over its roar. Then he would wipe at his brow and again tug on the heavy fireproof mitts and fumble with the astrolabe of molten metal. He did not finish until late into the evening and when he looked up he saw Molly in the doorway hands on her forehead and sweat cooling on her throat and he did not know how long she had been there. A rawness was in him that had nothing to do with the next day's events.

Is he prepared then? he said at last. Mr. Barr will see us?

Aye.

Good.

An the picture's all safe an swaddled like a babe in a basket.

Foole nodded, exhausted.

Gabriel sent a message. Farquhar knows what we want. All's in place. Or will be. Molly nodded at the elaborate alchemical apparatus set up behind him. An you? she said. You an Jappy all set then for your part?

I guess so.

How do you aim to manage it, while I'm on the river?

Foole lifted his eyebrows. Manage what? he said innocently.

Molly smiled.

FORTY-FOUR

Then it was Friday. William woke early and washed his chest and arms in cold water and the water foamed black with soot. He dressed in the darkness and stood at his window smoking with his hands clasped behind him. In the street below a ship-ribbed horse trotted ghostlike through the emptiness without handler or rein and vanished like an omen into the mists. William watched the hole in the fog where it had gone close slowly over. After a minute a crossing sweeper emerged and worked his slow way across the setts. Then two clerks hurried past. The fog thinned.

It was the day of the exchange. At eight o'clock he slung his chesterfield over one arm and set his silk hat on his head and went down through the lobby to the cab stand on the corner. He had eaten no breakfast and was not hungry. He caught a hansom to Scotland Yard feeling a stillness coming over him and it was a thing he had felt before and he knew by this that something that day would go wrong.

The Yard felt drab, sombre, miserable in its greyness. He nodded to the desk sergeant and flexed his wrists to get the blood moving and signed his name with stiff fingers. At Shore's office he stopped and glanced uneasily down the passage and started to knock but then just turned the handle and went in.

You're late, Shore said with a grunt.

Pushing with both palms on the desk, lumbering to his feet. A plate of cold chicken at his elbow. The drapes drawn wide, the pane beaded with condensation. Did you breakfast?

Is that an offer?

Shore gave him a sidelong grin. Aye. But I'll have to take it out of your docket.

William took off his hat, ran his fingers through his hair to smooth it. Where's Farquhar? I'll want to go over the details.

Shore shrugged. Blackwell's with him at Gilly's across the way. I'll take you down. You ready for this?

Is he?

George Farquhar will prove tougher than you suppose. Shore took a key from his pocket and unlocked the bottom drawer of his desk and withdrew a revolver and a box of ammunition. He said, Blackwell did a fine job on that tavern killer. You and Blackwell both. I signed the report on the matter yesterday morning. My superiors are pleased. He unclicked the cartridge from the weapon and loaded it and replaced it and then he slid the revolver across his desk. The poor girl, he said as he worked, meeting William's eye. Thirty years and I'm still surprised how a case can turn out.

I'm sure that's true.

You joke. But I'm not ashamed to say it.

I'm sure that's true too. He nodded at the weapon. What's that for?

For you. For protection.

William withdrew his own loaded Colt from his coat pocket and cradled it in his open palm for Shore to see and the chief inspector grinned a quick wolfish grin around the stem of his pipe. William bloody Pinkerton, he said, shaking his head. London just isn't safe with you in it.

Or out of it.

Shore paused. There's something else. Martin Reckitt was found murdered yesterday.

Murdered?

Aye.

William could feel the blood slow in him and he opened and closed his hands and after a moment he shook his head. How?

Botched escape maybe. An argument. Doesn't much matter. The bastard was being transported out to the hulks in Portsmouth and disappeared during a miscount. Seems all of the other prisoners were accounted for. Shore gave him a gruff frown. Farmer from Heyshott brought the body up out of the woods in a barrow-cart. Throat was cut. There was a woman from out of town sighted at the pub where the miscount took place. Shore passed across a telegram to William and William looked at the description there and then he looked up.

It's Charlotte Reckitt, he said in surprise.

Aye. Explain that one to me.

William sat in his heavy chesterfield with mud dried to a crust on the front and he stared at his hat and set it on his knee. I have no fucking idea, he said softly. You think she's been murdered too?

I think she was a part of it.

Killing her uncle?

Aye.

She's not a killer. I know killers.

Anyone can kill, William. It just takes the right circumstance.

He knew this was true but it was not his meaning and he said nothing and then he got to his feet. Farquhar would be waiting. He set his hat low on his head.

Shore paused with one arm in the sleeve of his frock coat. Thing of it is, London's not like other cities, he said. Not even like your New York. It's not a matter of us and them. Young ones like Mr. Blackwell don't understand that. Crime is how this city works. Some folk steal to stay alive. Other folk find employment replacing what gets stolen. Others sell the stolen goods back out and all this keeps the little folk alive. I know it. I was a part of it. I grew up in it. Shore held William's eye. But Reckitt wanted to burn all that. He had a black heart, that one. He was a crook through and through.

Reckitt said the same about you.

They always do, Shore said with a tired smile.

Shore led him down and outside into the dissipating mist of Great Scotland Yard Street and he ducked around the slow-moving

carts and crossed the street and entered a narrow wooden doorway under a red awning. Gilly's was a small dining-house with
private rooms in the back. Shore passed through a curtain and
along a stone-flagged passage and at the third door he paused.
You know negotiations like this don't usually much trouble me,
he said. Seems a rather civilized way to work a thing of value
back to its owner. But this Edward Shade's as like to do one
thing as another, when he sees you. You be careful.

I always am.

The hell you are. I've assigned Mr. Blackwell to assist. He'll
stay back and out of sight of course. But I'll not send you and
Mr. Farquhar in without protection. These aren't amateurs.

If it was bloodshed Shade wanted, he'd be doing this
differently, John.

Shore gave him a long pitying look as if he had spoken
foolishly and then opened the door. Blackwell was seated at a
table in his shirt sleeves. George Farquhar paced at the window,
smoking a cigar. He was dressed in a fine winter coat and a grey
hat and his eyes were ringed in shadow. He smoked fast, fidgeted.
Gripped in his left hand was a black leather satchel with silver
buckles.

Gentlemen, William said. Are we prepared?

Blackwell rose and cleared his throat. Mr. Shore, sir, Mr.
Pinkerton.

A damned nuisance, this, said Farquhar. His voice came
creaking and bent.

William wrestled out of his chesterfield and laid it across a
chair and crossed to the sidebar and poured out four glasses of
sherry. Sit, he said. We have much to discuss.

Farquhar peered at William with a questioning look but
came to the table and stubbed out his cigar and sat.

William gestured at the satchel. Is that the fee?

It is.

May I see it?

Farquhar reluctantly passed the satchel across. It is all there,
sir. I assure you.

He looked up and regarded the gallerist and then opened it. Stacks of bills, untraceable bonds. He proceeded to count them. When he was satisfied that the entire ten thousand pounds was present he looked at Blackwell and he looked at the gallerist and he sighed and said, Have you ever been in a situation like this before?

Why? Is there a problem with the amount?

William passed the satchel back. The amount's fine, he said. The difficult thing is keeping your head and understanding what this morning's about. It's about not having control. You don't get to ask the questions.

Mr. Farquhar, sir. Shore folded his red hands on the table before him. What Mr. Pinkerton means is that he's done these sorts of transactions dozens of times. You will have to trust him. Now there's no need to be anxious. You'll have Mr. Blackwell in plainclothes nearby at all times, to ensure your safety. But exchanges like this are always tense. One doesn't want to give anyone cause to cut out early.

Forgive me, said Farquhar gravely. But I should not want them to see a police inspector and believe I had betrayed them.

It's standard procedure, sir. They'll be expecting it.

And they won't see me, sir, Blackwell added. Unless they give cause to.

Farquhar glanced at William. Is it all right, sir, in your opinion?

William frowned. Everyone wants the same thing here. Including the thieves.

You mean the safe return of *The Emma*, sir.

Yes.

And not the apprehension of the criminals.

William paused. That's right.

Shore gave him a look. I trust that's the truth, William.

A cold February light was filtering in through the window, dust adrift in its slant. William folded his fists on the table before him. The low daylight was reflecting in the blacks of Shore's eyes, giving him a sinister look. The truth, he said quietly, yes.

Blackwell cleared his throat. Then shall we begin, gentlemen?

FORTY-FIVE

H e was still fixing his collar when Molly came to him
in his study, working an unpeeled orange in her hand.
She sat with a frown.

Gabriel sent a runner, she said. Says he'll be in place at
eleven o'clock.

Foole withdrew an oblong oak box from the bottom drawer
of his writing desk and began to sift through various delicate
disguises. At last he found a matted grey moustache and some
thorny eyebrows and he unstoppered a bottle of paste.

The liner don't depart Liverpool for six more days, she said.
I were thinkin maybe Devon be a fine quiet spot to lie low in.

No. Liverpool. Then we won't have to travel by rail and risk
being sighted.

She unscrewed a tube of paste, sniffed at it, wrinkled her nose.

Foole had removed a wrinkled plaster mask and was
softening its surface with a horsehair brush dipped in castor oil.
I sent Japheth to make arrangements and return with the cart.
We'll watch until you go down. You know which pier?

Aye. Billingsgate Stairs. Peeling back the orange with her
thumbnail in a long single corkscrew peel, holding it under her
nose. You're certain old Farquhar don't mean to caulk it up.

I'm certain.

And if he don't come alone?

He'd be a fool if he did. And George Farquhar is no fool.
Expect the pier to be crawling with peelers. He curled the edges

of the mask, the empty eye sockets, the mouth drooping in horror. Then he laid the empty mask down on the oilcloth and kneaded it as if it were dough. The exchange will take place downriver, he went on. Wait thirty minutes after the payment and then return. Be sure Gabriel counts the money twice. He should know to take his time, he's done this before. I expect there shouldn't be any complications, but—

I know. Don't trust Utterson.

Trust, Foole said, and made a face. It's not Gabriel I'm worried about. He's been paid well enough. How well can you swim?

No better now than last you asked. Unless floating counts.

Foole smiled. At the first sign of trouble I want you over the railing and floating as fast as you can for shore.

Molly split the orange, slid a quadrant into her mouth. What about you? she said, chewing.

Japheth and I will use the time to our advantage.

She grinned. Fine advantage.

Remember your real purpose in this, Molly.

O I'll keep the old bugger occupied. I heard his wife were so distraught she up an run off to the countryside.

To her estate there, yes.

She furrowed her brow. Chewed and chewed.

What is it.

She grunted. Pinkerton won't give us no grief?

Foole tilted his chin back and pressed the plaster to his skin with his eyelids crushed shut and he worked his fingers around his hairline and under his jaw and smoothed it into place. It felt cool, like a damp towel. He said, muffled, William Pinkerton will be eager to hear how the morning pans out, I'm certain. He never played the short game in his life. He'll want this exchange to proceed. If it doesn't he'll believe his chances of tracking us will be much slimmer.

Them peelers goin to get a good long look at Gabriel.

With his eyes still shut, his face still tilted back: And at you.

Pinkerton's already done that.

Foole cracked an eyelid. Gabriel's doing nothing illegal. There's no law against private transactions. It matters not at all if he's seen to be party to this. And you're just some poor miserable creature hired off the street to facilitate the rendezvous. He began to apply the moustache and eyebrows, the plaster crackling but not splitting. He ran a hand lightly along the sags and wrinkles around his eyes. How do I look?

Molly looked at him, all at once serious. You be careful, Adam.

I always am. Foole studied his reflection in the mirror for a moment feeling the old thrill he always felt to see a stranger's face staring back. As for Mr. Farquhar—

We leave him on the river. I know.

You leave him on the river. Yes. It wouldn't do to be followed. Foole unscrewed a jar of powder and dipped a moist finger into the makeup and rubbed it into the new skin.

Adam, she said.

He held her gaze in the mirror.

I were real sorry about your Charlotte. It not workin out, an all.

My Charlotte. He looked down at his hands. He did not know how much the child suspected but he knew she was no fool. As it turns out, he said, she was never mine after all.

FORTY-SIX

William gripped Farquhar's satchel to his chest. The streets were raucous, street sellers pouring north from London Bridge, touts running along behind the omnibuses hollering their fares hoarse. Farquhar carried kidskin gloves crumpled in one fist and the sharpened bones of his wrists stuck out from his coat sleeves. They had climbed down from the police brougham at the bottom of Threadneedle Street as instructed and William led Farquhar by the shoulder across the crowded thoroughfare in the light fog breathing in the yellow sulphur and the putrid smell of the garbage and watching the tired horses stumble past. He stood under the statue of Cornwallis, glaring.

He saw no sign of Shade.

A small urchin in an outsized red cap and a grimy face appeared before them biting at its nails. Spare a copper, mister?

Off with you, Farquhar barked.

William paused. The creature was looking him up and down with interest. You wasn't supposed to come, it said. Then it turned to the gallerist. You'd be Mr. Farter, I expect?

I beg your pardon?

The creature gave an exasperated look. Well, come on. You don't get nothin for lollin about. Leave the ape here.

When the gallerist did not move William said, I expect this is Mr. Shade's accomplice. We'll need to go with her.

Farquhar studied the creature in disgust. This?

What was you expectin, the bloody Queen?

All right, said William, stepping forward. Lead on.

But the urchin only scowled. My instructions was to bring this one alone.

Nobody moved. For a long moment the creature stared at William as if considering and then shrugged and started off. They were led down towards the river through a maze of mews and stables and back alleys until they came to a roiling mass of passengers and clerks all pressed in a crush towards a high stone wharf. William saw over the heads of the crowd a sign for the London Bridge Steam Wharf and he kept close to Farquhar and turned his shoulder and began to muscle his way forward. The crowd parted like the sea. Then they were squeezing into a covered passage plastered with advertisements for *Collins' Wonder Soap* and *McMullen's Hair Tonic* and the *Starr Brothers' Magic Portraits off Coomb's Court*. The density of the crowd and the noise would all work to Shade's advantage, William knew.

Where's your master? he demanded. Is he meeting us here?

But the urchin ignored him.

They descended a set of rickety wooden stairs so steep William felt his heels almost give out on him and he had to turn his feet sideways to keep upright. At the small wooden floating dock in the shadow of the bridge the Thames looked black and foamy and cold. There were wooden booths with great signs stating PAY HERE and men shouting for customers but the urchin ducked aside and started walking fast under the bridge on a narrow wooden boardwalk.

The span arched high overhead, birds arcing and vanishing in the cathedral-like gloom. Empty steamer ferries were shooting the high waters between the pillars near enough for a man to jump aboard and the weak daylight filtered down through the stone arches like drifting smoke and it seemed all at once a different city, a different time.

The urchin led them on to a ramshackle dock filled with barkers shouting out destinations and lines of clerks waiting for the passenger ferries. It was Billingsgate Stairs. Shade was nowhere in sight. In the foam and frenzy of steamers pulling into their slips and casting off there was a solitary hired steamer with a red hull and a squat captain in a frock coat standing at its cabled railing watching them. The deck lifted, fell in the swells. William could very clearly read the vessel's name, *Goliath*, whited out at the waterline. And then he understood. The exchange would take place on the river.

The river? Farquhar said, slowing. We are to travel the river?

What's wrong with the river?

Farquhar met William's gaze. I was on the *Cricket* when it exploded at the Adelphi, sir. I have not taken passage on a steamer since.

The *Cricket* what blowed up? the urchin said. It gave the gallerist a queer grin, ran a knuckle under its nose. You ain't going to like today then.

William caught the creature's arm. I know you, he said. How do I know you?

It shook itself free. But all at once he recognized her. It was the girl he had accosted outside Foole's Emporium in Piccadilly.

He must have betrayed something in his face for the girl met his eye boldly, she bared her teeth.

I know you too, Mr. Pinkerton, she said, unsmiling.

They cast off and moved swiftly out into the current and downriver. There were many other ships on the river, dark barges drifting cautiously through the fog. They steered clear of most and the captain did not speak other than to grunt some greeting to the urchin but neither did the captain take his eyes off William as they went. He was a bullish man with peat-brown whiskers and an enormous black silk hat perched crazily on his head and he seemed to William a man for hire and not a part of Shade's retinue. William had his Colt in his pocket and the heavy satchel under his left arm and he wondered that he had not been searched for weapons. At last the steamer slowed and the captain hove to and held his wheel fast and the strong pull of the Thames turned their bow slowly and then William saw through the mist the second boat approaching.

It was a steam-powered launch not unlike their hired steamer but with a tapered bow and a green hull. The figure standing at its railing with his hands crossed behind his back was dressed in a long fur-lined greatcoat open to the wind and underneath he wore a white suit and a white hat like some madman out of the tropics and not at all fit for the cold London weather. No one spoke. William glanced across at the child but she was peering across the deep waters, the fog tendrilling there low and thin and fast.

Farquhar stiffened at his elbow. Is that him? Is that the man I am to meet?

William watched but said nothing.

You two, the urchin barked. You stand there and wait.

William could see a second silhouette farther back on the launch. Appearing and then vanishing in the fog. He slipped one hand into the pocket of his chesterfield and felt for his revolver. Then the launch was in the clear and slowing and turning lengthwise to come up alongside them and William could see the deck clearly. Two men, one in the wheelhouse. And the man in white was not Shade. Stout, his whiskers wild and leonine and crowning his red face like a banker's, one hand held up in greeting. It was Gabriel Utterson.

Mr. Pinkerton, Farquhar murmured. That is the man's proxy, yes?

He glowered.

Mr. Pinkerton.

He shook himself, glanced away. That's his solicitor. Yes.

Farquhar studied William's face with an anxious expression. You were expecting some other? Is anything the matter?

William watched the urchin swipe her red cap from her head, stuff it inside her coat. She scrambled over the railing and perched above the freezing waters as the launch neared. He took his hand off the revolver in his pocket. He had been naive, thinking Shade would appear.

It's fine, he muttered. Let's get this over with.

Gabriel Utterson hailed them from the railing of the launch. His captain had tamped the boiler and the vessel had slowed and drifted sideways and then come in close.

I trust you have not come empty-handed, gentlemen, Utterson shouted across.

William held the satchel high.

Utterson nodded. I'll examine the contents, please, he called.

William gave the satchel to the urchin on the outside of the railing and she turned swinging it in one hand and took two swift steps and leaped across the gap. The boats rocked and shifted and drew apart and drew close.

William casually withdrew his revolver.

Where is the painting? Farquhar hissed at him. I do not see it, sir.

Patience, Mr. Farquhar.

What if it is a trick?

William gave the gallerist a grim look. In my experience, he said, crooks are usually the least dishonest of the bunch. It's not in their interest to deceive you, sir. This is how they make their living. Be patient.

Farquhar gave an uneasy glance at the fog creeping in and blowing past. A collier slid wraithlike through the mist.

Utterson kneeled in the folds of his heavy coat and he took off his gloves and unbuckled the satchel. No one spoke. The decks rolled gently in the current. At last the man rose one knee at a time with a stiffness and he grimaced to Molly and buckled the satchel tight. The launch powered up and a cloud of white steam belched from its stack and Farquhar sucked in his breath.

Easy, William said.

And then the launch drew in close and Utterson clambered over the railing and leaned one tentative foot out and hooked himself onto the steamer's deck. William stepped forward, clasped his hand, hauled the stout solicitor across the gap.

Dear god, he gasped. A damned foolish location for a business meeting. He smoothed his collar, the thick sleeves of his greatcoat. Mr. Pinkerton, sir. I was not informed you would be present. And this must be Mr. Farquhar. A pleasure, sir, even under such circumstances.

Such circumstances, sir, Farquhar said coldly, are of your own devising.

Utterson held a hand to his heart. Please do not imagine I condone this sort of behaviour. I act to ensure everyone's honest compliance, sir. I take no side in the matter, I assure you. And I have no vested interest in its outcome.

Except if we get crossed, said William.

Sir?

If that girl disappears with the money, you'll be held responsible.

Ah. Utterson smiled tightly. By whom, I wonder?

By me.

Farquhar ran a gloved finger under his chin. Mr. Utterson, I am not accustomed to waiting. My painting?

Shortly, sir, shortly. Utterson turned and gave a stiff wave and the urchin cried some word to the captain and the launch began to pull away into the mist.

She is leaving with the bonds, Mr. Pinkerton, Farquhar barked sharply. He strode to the railing, gripped it fiercely.

William set his hand on the gallerist's elbow. Patience, he said. She'll be back. They won't have come to the meeting with the painting. They're not so trusting as that.

But we are expected to be?

William shrugged.

Ten minutes passed, twenty. At thirty minutes Farquhar started to pace the deck in a temper, at the turning of the first hour he ceased pacing and settled himself under the stacks where the heat of the engine could be felt. The river grew colder. They waited in silence and William began to fear he had been misled but when he studied Utterson's expression it seemed bored, unconcerned.

At last through the mist they heard the launch approaching and then it came into view. The urchin was standing at the bow clutching a long painter's tube in one elbow, the strap looped at her wrist.

Your painting, sir, Utterson said wearily.

They were all three cold. As the launch drew up alongside the urchin leaned back and pitched the tube overhand across the water and Utterson caught at it and dropped it and it clattered rolling on the deck and banged up against the wheelhouse.

Farquhar seized it up in a panic.

My god, he swore. What is wrong with that creature?

Utterson glared across at the urchin. I couldn't say, sir. A most foolish display.

The steamer was drifting lazily to port. Their captain stood at his wheelhouse, arms folded, silk hat rakishly atilt, smoking quietly. William could hear the low distant thrum of river traffic in the fog. Farquhar had already unstoppered the tube and drawn the oilcloth bundle carefully clear and cracked open the roll. He unrolled only as much as the top edge of the painting and he ran a soft finger along the cracks.

Well, sir? Utterson stood over the gallerist, rubbing his hands for heat. Are you satisfied? Can we get off this blasted river?

The gallerist met William's eye. It is *The Emma*, Mr. Pinkerton. I can't know the condition until we return to a proper location. But it is she.

It will prove undamaged, sir, I am certain of it.

Farquhar was cautiously rolling the oilskin tight and sliding it all back into the leather painter's tube. Who are these men? he said with a sudden fierce dignity. Mr. Utterson, you keep very poor company, sir. I should be ashamed.

But Utterson only shrugged, unoffended. I serve the interests of the law, sir. That is all.

William turned in time to see the girl's launch pull away and gather speed and disappear upriver into the mist. He stood, brooding. And then he strode sharply past the two men and leaned in at the wheelhouse and told the captain to follow the launch.

The captain took the pipe in his fist, looked at him. Follow it? And the river in traffic? he said dubiously. I were paid to deliver ye downcurrent. He had the powerful forearms of a sailor and the thick tattooed neck of a pugilist but William stood half again his weight and he wrapped a hand over the captain's lapels.

Follow that boat, he said again. This is police business.

Ye ain't police. But there was uncertainty in the man's eye.

Mr. Pinkerton, Utterson called sharply. I must advise against whatever it is you are intending. My clients were forthright and direct with you. You would do well to respect that. Captain, please proceed with your instructions.

The captain was looking angrily at William.

William withdrew his Colt from his pocket and cocked the hammer and pressed it against the captain's forehead. No one spoke.

Aye, said the captain, very still. We'll follow her.

William uncocked the hammer and lowered the weapon.

The captain stamped twice on the trap door of the boiler and the steamer lurched and started to catch speed and the deck rolled and rose cresting and fell in the spray. The launch was gone in the fog and the river traffic and William did not know if it could be overtaken. They were moving at speed and the hull smacked and jounced over the chop. He did not see the green hull of the launch. The wind was bitingly cold and William felt the wings of his chesterfield crackling out behind him and he leaned into the rise and drop of the planks under him to hold his balance. Out of the corner of one eye he glimpsed Utterson, shifting his weight, starting to approach, and William half turned and raised his revolver. He could see Farquhar's face in the lee of the stack, lean, grey. Eyes closed, the painting in its tube crushed to his chest.

You stay back, William hollered. The wind sucking the words from his lips.

Utterson froze. Tried to raise his hands on the rolling deck. What is it you mean to do, sir?

William did not reply but turned back, staring into the fog at the passing vessels. Colliers with men clambering over their piles, ferries crammed with clerks, scows stacked with crates. One hand fixed to the railing to steady himself. And then the captain slowed and pointed and William glimpsed the small green stern of the launch ahead.

Don't overtake them, he called. Keep us a distance back.

The urchin's launch drew in close to a rickety pier on the north bank below London Bridge and William watched her leap nimbly ashore before the vessel had even moored and then she was gone under the span in the crowds. He walked slowly the length of the deck and gripped the cables staring all the while at the space where she had vanished and as they drew near he looped a leg over the railing. He'd be damned if he would let her escape. She was his one lead to Shade.

Mr. Pinkerton, sir, Farquhar called. He got unsteadily to his feet. You cannot mean to leave me here, sir. I hired you to ensure the safe return of *The Emma*.

You have your painting.

It has not yet been returned, sir. Not to safety.

It's safe enough. William paused, glared at the solicitor. Mr. Utterson here has been hired to facilitate the exchange. It is in his interest to make sure no harm comes to you or to the painting. It is his reputation at stake here.

The captain's face lifted from behind his wheel. *The Emma*, he said. That ain't that painting what was stolen an in all the dailies, now, is it?

William frowned. Mr. Blackwell will be along shortly, I don't doubt, he said. Make your own way or wait for his arrival, Mr. Farquhar. Either should suffice. He gave Utterson a black look. I'll hold you responsible, sir, should any misfortune befall this gentleman. Captain, he called.

The burly man peered at him.

William tipped his hat. Thank you, sir.

And then the pier was within reach and he hurled himself across the closing gap and rolled to his feet and snatched up his hat and pressed through the crowds after the girl.

FORTY-SEVEN

Foole had stood silhouetted high in the cold of the stone overpass watching Farquhar and Pinkerton climb down from their brougham into the crowd. He wore a frayed wool labourer's suit and he stood with his weight twisted over one leg like a man arthritic and long worn down by the world and he let the minutes pass. The itch and curl of the plaster worried away at the skin under his collar and he raised two ruined fingers, smoothed the beard glued to his chin. Though he would be visible against the sky should Pinkerton look his way the detective did not lift his face. He watched Molly approach and then she was leading them down towards Billingsgate Stairs and Foole turned and walked briskly back across the span. Fludd was waiting in a stained apron, running a hand over the mare's flanks, murmuring. They were reined up in a filthy court and neither spoke but instead climbed aboard the bench seat and Fludd clicked the reins and the waggon creaked slowly out into the morning traffic.

The clock? Fludd grunted.

Past eleven. Gives us an hour in the clear.

You seen to the butler, then.

Called away this morning on sudden family business. A sister facing imminent eviction.

Fludd smiled. Nice. An the cook? Them two cleanin girls?

Gone to the country with the mistress.

Fludd cracked the reins in impatience and the mare lurched

and leaned into her harness. The peeling slat boards of the waggon rattling as they went. The going was slow and they did not reach Farquhar's residence until half past the hour and Fludd was careful to pull sidelong to the bollards out front. On the gate of the waggon was painted *Abbott's Carting & Movers* in bold red letters. From the back Fludd lifted out an enormous wood crate, empty. FRAGILE stamped on the side.

Foole took up several empty dun sacks. He pushed his cap back on his head, squinched up one eye. All righty, he said in a rough accent. Let's get this here delivery done, eh, ye moke.

Fludd grunted in disgust.

Oi. Ye don't like me accent?

Is that what that is?

Foole grinned. The morning was bright, clear, there were ladies walking the footway escorted by men in silk hats and Foole and Fludd tipped their caps as they passed. They walked boldly up to the tall front doors and set down their loads and Foole withdrew the forged keys on their ring and calmly tried each in the lock until the fourth took and he turned it twice and then the heavy oak doors to George Farquhar's mansion swung open, and the two men glanced back once, picked up their empty crate and sacks, and walked in.

The house was still. They knew what they hunted but stood in the gloom listening all the same. No footfall, no movement. Foole had explained the floor plans to Fludd as he had traced them on the night of the dinner and the two men moved now as one, sliding silently towards the staircase. Farquhar would be somewhere down the Thames by now, Foole knew, Pinkerton with him.

At the base of the stairs they parted. Fludd went ahead into the depths of the house with his empty crate held out before him in search of silver plate and valuables from the dining room. Foole ascended the stairs. He went at once to the gentleman's bedroom and opened the drawers and riffled through and scooped out the man's cufflinks and examined each in the weak light and placed them one by one into a sack. Farquhar had a fine collection of gold and silver pocket watches and Foole took these as well. He found a small safe in the man's wardrobe and he tried the various keys until he found the right one and inside he discovered a large amount of cash and securities. He took all of it. He was quick, silent, to the point. There were packets of private correspondence and these he did not disturb.

He paused in the upper hall and admired a small watercolour of the Thames and considered removing it from its bracket but then thought otherwise. He passed on into the man's study and there he searched the man's desk but he did not find the letter he had left. He checked the pockets of the man's several coats but it was gone. He frowned, he stood with a hand on his head and turned slowly. Out of pique he took a gold-plated writing set and a fine crystal paperweight and a rare early copy of Shakespeare from the seventeenth century and then he slipped back out into the hall.

Eleven minutes had passed.

Inside Farquhar's wife's bedchamber he paused, hand still on the door, feeling all at once uneasy. The room was dim, heavily furnished, a great oak four-poster with its drapes drawn looming in the centre of the carpet. He did not know why the curtains of an unoccupied bed would be drawn. But the feeling passed and the room still stood silent and he went in and crossed to the far wall and started going through the bureau. It was then he heard it: a soft sigh, a creak of the mattress.

A grey hand parted the curtains of the bed and the slow sleep-rumpled figure of Mrs. Farquhar emerged.

Foole froze. He melted back into the shadows, dark, wrathful. Her grey hair looked wild, her cheeks smudged with the night's makeup. She turned her face, coughed sharply, spat some substance into the carpet at her feet. Then sat, rolling her shoulders, opening and closing her mouth.

Foole did not dare breathe.

But she did not look his way. After a moment she groaned and eased her feet into a pair of velvet slippers and got up and picked a robe from her bedside chair and went out. Foole stood in the suddenly empty bedchamber shaking in disbelief and clutching his half-filled sacks and then he followed her to the door.

She was descending the stairs, old, stiff, miserable.

He thought of Fludd below, filling his crate, and he thought to follow and warn him but then changed his mind and slipped back into the old woman's bedchamber. The giant had a gift for such work and would handle himself. Foole found nothing of value in the bureau and he glanced anxiously at the door but heard nothing and then he opened an ancient creaking wardrobe and there it was. A second safe. The same key opened it as had opened her husband's and Foole shook his head, amazed. Inside were two shelves, each filled with large jewellery boxes, heavy, and Foole opened the lid of the first and for a sudden impossible moment crouched there, dazzled. Nine, ten, twelve necklaces. Cut diamonds of every carat shining with a luminescence that burned up out of the stones themselves and filled the room with light. The pieces were exquisite. He shut the lid and slipped the box into the sack and did not trouble to open the others but took them all. Shut the safe, shut the wardrobe, hurried out into the hall.

The old lady still had not returned.

He moved cautiously to the landing in the dimness. He did not know if Fludd had found her yet and he leaned out over the railing and there he saw, in the gloom, the huge silent figure of Fludd with his back pressed to a pillar in the great hall, wary. He could just make out the old lady in her pale robe emerging from the back hall with an enamel tray in her hands, a pitcher of water and a plate of cold chicken on the tray, and he watched the woman approach. She would need to turn at the pillar and would pass the giant where he hid and Foole tried to catch his companion's eye to warn him but could not.

The old lady came nearer.

Foole feared what Fludd must do should she find him and he had just set his sacks down and readied himself to leap the railing when Fludd, liquid, noiseless, poured around the pillar at the very moment she turned, keeping himself concealed, a shadow, a wraith, and the old lady glided unaware past.

Then she was ascending the stairs and Foole hid behind a potted fern and watched her go back to her bedchamber and he lifted the sacks silently into his arms to keep them from tinkling and slipped noiselessly, step by step, down the carpeted stairs.

Fludd was waiting with the full crate in his arms and he gave Foole a long angry glower and then the two thieves slipped outside, into the frenzy of the noon street, simple labourers, one a feeble-minded giant in an apron, the other an old man worn by the world, eager to be gone.

FORTY-EIGHT

William came at a run up the crooked stairs from London Bridge Pier, the nailed wood slats rattling under his weight, the clerks and passengers roughed up against the railing as he went. He did not see the girl. She had conducted herself with great coolness and professionalism that morning and he understood whatever else that she was no hired amateur in this but some valued part of Shade's crew. He pushed across to an iron gas lamp on a stone pedestal and half climbed its length and scanned the roar of bridge traffic pouring north into King William Street but she had vanished into the mist, his last trace back to Shade. A crossing sweep chuckled at him, face blacked, shoeless in the cold.

Fine day for it, sir, he grinned.

William looked at him, looked away. And there, out across the span of the bridge, he saw the girl.

Crossing over into Southwark, red hat doffed, small shoulders hunched. She walked fast, ducking around the crush of carts, the leather satchel gripped tight.

He dropped back to the ground and started to run. He would slow every twenty paces and hoist himself up onto the railing of the bridge and find her again. At last he had caught up to her and he kept himself some thirty feet back just at the edge of the drifting fog and he followed her down off London Bridge and into the industrial chaos of Borough High Street.

The traffic was rougher there, the men all in leather aprons or stained woollens. The girl glanced back the way she had come then ducked into a small sweet shop. William drew his hat low, waited in a doorway across the street. After ten minutes a man in an ill-fitting coat came out wiping his hands on his trousers and made his way down the block to a cab stand and unhooked the nosebag from his mare and climbed up into the driver's perch of his carriage. Then the girl came out. She kept her head low with her cap obscuring her eyes and went straight to the carriage and climbed in.

William understood too late what was happening and he swore and started across the street at a run. But the carriage was already pulling out and he reached the cab stand out of breath and set a hand on the first hansom in line and called out for the driver.

Aye sir, and where is it you're bound to then? A young man slid lazily out from under a shelter. He was eating an apple.

William gestured at the carriage disappearing in the traffic. I need to follow that carriage. You can manage that?

The driver peered after the carriage. What, that four-wheeler there? Aye, I'd say so, he said, cocking his hat back on his head. Be a shilling or two extra for the trouble, though.

Don't lose it and I'll pay you double.

Double it is, sir. Up you get.

William hauled himself forcefully up and the driver hooked a foot on the stem-pole and scrambled onto his perch and the hansom took off at a wild jouncing pace. William gripped the leather handle and leaned forward louring at the shapes in the fog. He was thinking of his father's Shade. In that Cumberland photograph he had seen no indication of love. Nothing fierce nor unyielding nor to be dreaded. Still he felt a rage rising in him and he sat with his fists bunched before him as the cab rattled sharply on.

The girl's carriage halted at a small public square at the junction of Newington Butts. Unwashed children lurked on the steps and a knife-grinder's cart stood forlorn at an open gate. William's cab clattered past and reined up some twenty feet beyond at a wholesale grocer's yard off Kennington Park Road. He swung down with the air cold on his face and he crushed a five-pound note into the driver's hand.

It's too much, sir, the man called in astonishment.

But William was already striding away. The girl herself did not slow but turned purposefully at Penton Place. It was a shabby terrace in that south London district with houses set hard up against the footways and a roadway filled with mud as if it had once been set and then the stones taken again up. He passed maids in heavy coats and delivery men coaxing their waggons along the ruts and junk men hauling their carts by hand. A stink hung in the air from the sperm-oil works nearby and he could not get the taste of it from his nostrils. His Colt Navy swung in his pocket heavy as a stone in a stocking and he set one hand on it to check its swing. Something about the street felt wrong.

At last the girl turned and entered a house on the left. A strangled flower bed lay walled in and dying under the front steps and there were rusting hinges where a gate must once have hung. On either side stood the melancholy darkened houses of the dispossessed with undressed windows and faded To Let signs propped against their panes. In the back stood a railway cutting with the trains rattling noisily past trailing clouds of smoke.

He did not stop but walked slowly on. A pale face appeared at the parlour window then vanished, the drapes swaying back into stillness. He did not know if Shade was inside or not and he walked with his face averted until he was out of sight and then doubled back and slid into a shadowed alcove facing the house.

He smoothed his moustaches with his fingers. He checked his gun.

He waited.

FORTY-NINE

Fludd heaved the crate up onto the bed of the waggon with a bang and climbed unsteadily aboard after it and shoved it farther up against the rear slats. Foole crouched, tied off the twin sacks, got up into the driver's bench. Neither man spoke. But both tipped their caps to any lady who passed and Fludd whistled pleasantly while unhooking the mare's nosebag and then he hauled himself up behind the reins.

They rode slowly and kept to the thoroughfares and were soon lost in the chaos and they made their way south towards the Strand and then they were crossing the Thames under a louring sky while the river traffic slid by underneath.

There were plumes of brown smoke ahead in the haze of Southwark where the factories churned night and day and they drove east until they reached the Booth Brothers' Factory gates and there they slowed and came to a halt some twenty paces past. Appleby Barr kept a small shabby office in the rear of the second floor and Foole intended to offer him the entire haul to settle his debts and establish credit and he would take only a small fee in exchange. The ten thousand pounds from the painting's negotiation would take care of their needs for some time. As he turned to get down Fludd put a hand on his arm. It felt heavy, hot.

We ought to be careful, Mr. Adam. The bugger's like to be watched hisself.

Foole nodded. He has two peelers who stand at the gates taking the measure of anyone who goes inside.

On his payroll?

I'm sure. But with peelers, who can say.

You can't know his intentions neither.

Foole paused, studied Fludd's face. Barr has nothing to gain by complicating his relationship with me, Foole said softly. I'm not anxious in that regard. Wait here.

He got down and crossed the street examining the faces of the indigent there until he found a particular creature folded upon its haunches. Crouched against the lee of an inner court, in rags twice its size.

Geoffrey, he murmured.

The waif cast a mistrustful eye.

Foole withdrew a guinea from his waistcoat pocket and shuffled over and held it out in a trembling palm. Go on, he said. Take it.

Why, Mr. Foole, sir, the waif whispered in astonishment. And snatched it quickly up. I been here all mornin like you said to, sir. I seen him go in.

Was he alone?

Never had no grippers with him, if that's your meaning.

Foole crouched, ancient with pain.

It don't hardly look like you at all, Mr. Foole, the boy said in wonder. If I can say so.

There's another guinea for you if you do one last thing, Foole said.

Aye, sir.

Those two peelers just inside, that you told me about. I want you to call them away down the street in five minutes. Tell them there's been a carriage overturned. Tell them it looks like a lady is injured. Can you do that for me?

Eyes like slits. A tooth out in front. Five minutes?

Foole gestured to the public clock face on the market building opposite. You can count the time, Geoffrey?

A sudden quick grin through the filth. Aye for a guinea I can, sir.

———

Back at the waggon Foole stood with one hand on the footboard
and the other on his hip. Fludd was studying the open iron gates
of the factory, the yard beyond where barrels swung suspended
in nets and stacks of tall crates were just visible. A man in shirt
sleeves and a leather apron came to the street and stared west
and removed his cap and ran a hand through his hair and then
went back inside. Foole knew that yard well, the solid iron
doors to the factory beyond, the orphans creeping barefoot
among the machinery and sweeping out the corners and the
suspended catwalks with the overseers stalking back and forth.
Barr had taken the place from the three Booth brothers four
years earlier in exchange for a debt and established a front for
his activities and he arrived at his office three days a week
promptly and sat at his desk going through his ledgers and
taking meetings like any good industrialist. There would be
men with knives and clubs and others with pistols at the doors
and the base of the stairs.

Ten minutes, said Foole. Then go on inside.

You ain't comin?

He shook his head. I'll meet you in Newington. Give me
an hour.

You got somewhere more important to be?

Something like that.

The giant leaned creaking down. Go on, he muttered,
incredulous. You ain't serious, like?

There's someone I need to say goodbye to, Foole said. An
old friend I don't expect to see again. He met his companion's
eye. Mr. Barr's expecting us, Japheth. I've known the man years,
he's in the red.

He don't worry me.

Foole went around back and climbed into the bed of the
waggon and opened the crate and sifted through the contents.
You did fine, he said, there's plenty here. He withdrew, at last,
a long ornate seven-branched candlestick made of silver. Ran
his fingers over the weird symbols at its base, the vined
scrollwork in delicate detail flowering the length of the stalks.

Glanced around then slid it under the wing of his coat and buttoned himself back up and jumped down.

A price on the lot of it then? Fludd said dubiously. You want I should drive the bargain?

Fence it for what you can, Foole said, but don't drive it. Whatever we lose in the turnover we gain in good grace. There's no losing here.

And he reached up and took the man's hand and then went off in search of a cab. Some twenty feet away he paused and turned back, a strange feeling in him. Fludd was seated in the waggon, shaggy head upraised, fixed and unmoving like a warning from a world that was no longer, about a world that was to come.

FIFTY

William had not waited thirty minutes when an old man in a scuffed black suit walked up Penton Place and stepped lightly across a puddle and made his way down towards the terrace house. William knew him at once, even in disguise.

He waited but he saw no curtain stir, no light go on. No one else came or went. He had seen no sign of the manservant, Fludd. That man had lived a life of brutality and violence but Shade was the more dangerous by half. After a moment William detached himself from the shadow and crossed the street cautiously and went up the steps and banged on the front door with an open hand.

Shade, he shouted. Shade!

He kicked at the frame with his boot. When there was no sound from within he stepped back and glared up at the facade. The house stood dark and closed.

He stood calmly in the front walk and held his Colt out before him and methodically dialed through its loaded chambers knowing they would be watching him and knowing Shade would see the seriousness in him. Then he turned and lazily lifted one elbow and punched in the glass of the sidelight and reached in and unlocked the door.

He paused then, listening. Glanced back at the street. At last, his fists bared, he stepped inside.

In the gloom he stood letting his eyes adjust, listening as the grandfather clock clicked down through its registers and the timbers of the house creaked around him. Shards of glass crunched under his feet like frost. The parlour doors stood open. He could make out a mahogany table stained the colour of blood, an empty birdcage, stairs rising into shadow.

Edward, he called up. I've come to talk.

Stillness and gloom. He held his Colt low at his side.

Show yourself, he shouted.

There was the bang of a door closing and William started to move. But something slid flashing past the corner of his eye and he turned and saw the child emerging from the darkness and the child's low quick hand and then he saw the fireplace poker. He moved before he could stop himself and had the girl by the throat and his hand reached in a crushing grip from ear to ear and he knocked the poker aside and threw the girl backward. She lay crumpled against the wall amid a shatter of debris and her limbs did not look right but her chest was moving. He glanced down at a line of blood welling up from his hand and closed his fist upon it.

And then he heard a low grunt from the front steps outside, and turned.

It was the manservant Fludd. He came roaring in out of the grey noon light elemental with rage and a long knife upraised in one fist and William took an unsteady step back but could not find his footing on the broken glass and he lifted his gun and he fired.

FIFTY-ONE

Foole heard the crack and shatter of glass in the foyer below and for an impossible moment thought he had imagined it. He was alone in the house but for Molly. He had just peeled the disguise from his face and was wiping with a moist towel at the strings of glue on his skin when Pinkerton had started shouting for Shade in the street below. Foole knew no lawful charges had been laid and that meant the detective was acting outside the law and not bounded by its rules and the knowledge of it made him, for the first time, afraid.

He went at once to the open suitcase and took out his old revolver. It was scarred and notched but he had kept it in good working order since the days of his suffering in Virginia. He checked its chamber, clicked it shut, slipped it into the waistband of his trousers. He picked up the leather satchel with the gallerist's bonds inside. Then he ran for the servants' stairs.

On the first-floor landing he felt something give in his knee and he sucked in his breath but did not slow nor did he make a sound. He paused breathing silently and stared in the gloom but heard nothing and then he saw Molly materialize at the door of the kitchen.

Adam, she hissed. Go. Now.

She turned from him, ducked away. He paused, one hand on the balustrade, the other fumbling his old revolver, the satchel tucked under his elbow. He found her again lurking wraithlike at the door to the hall, listening intensely towards the front of the house.

Edward, a voice bellowed. I've come to talk.

We need to go, Molly, he said softly. He could not make out her eyes.

Show yourself, Pinkerton was hollering.

He ain't interested in no one except you, she whispered. Go on. I'll slow him down some an then make myself scarce.

Foole shook his head. But he understood the truth in it and that the child had the steady swift hand of a creature of the streets and that she had never been a stranger to violence. He put a hand on her arm. You know where I'll be.

She nodded angrily at the dark scullery beyond. Bloody go, she said.

When he turned back he caught a glimpse of Molly, pale and ethereal in the gloom, flowing through the kitchen towards the front of the house with a barbed iron poker in one fist. And then he heard the detective huffing and stamping in the hall like a bull and he was opening the scullery door and stumbling out into the cold.

When the gunshot sounded he slowed at the high edge of the railway cutting and he started to go back but then he stopped. The pain in his knee was savage. He did not hear a second shot. He was standing with his coat open unsure what to do and the fog moving around him and he fumbled with the satchel and took out the revolver and checked its chambers and stared back through the haze and thought he glimpsed, for just a moment, a silhouette staggering out of the scullery door, into the garden. Lifting its face, peering up at him.

And then the fog closed in and the figure, whatever it was, dissolved again away.

FIFTY-TWO

William could not find his footing and he lifted his gun and fired but the bullet passed harmlessly to one side. Then the giant's huge arm came down.

It came down swatting the Colt from William's hand as if striking down a wasp. Both gun and knife cracked against the floor, skittered off into the darkness. His forearm and elbow were ringing like steel hammered flat and he swung around and tried to avoid the giant's grip but he could not do so. The man took him in both his arms as if he were beloved, he lifted him from the earth.

He could feel the great slow power of the giant's embrace and his vertebrae popped one by one and he could not breathe. A blackness was creeping in at the edges of his vision and he crushed his eyes shut and opened them, a ringing in his ears. He could smell the vinegar stink of the giant's sweat and the man's coarse beard scraped against his nose in some demented kind of nuzzle and he could feel the man's breath hot in his eyes. He thought of Margaret and of his daughters in their spring garden in Chicago among the cherry blossoms and he bared his teeth and he bit with all his strength into the giant's face and the blood was hot and he came away with a piece of the man's cheek in his mouth. The man shuddered but did not let go. William drove his forehead mightily down upon the giant's face and felt the man's nose split like ripe fruit, both of their faces streaming with blood, and then he was free.

He slithered to the floor, gasping.

The giant was on his knees also, cradling his face and shaking his head from side to side. William got unsteadily to his feet. Swayed. Picked up the iron poker where the girl had dropped it and dragged it scraping over the floorboards and lifted his hand and swung.

He stayed only long enough to watch the giant fall. When he stumbled out the back door and into the garden he saw the figure silhouetted in the fog at the top of the railway embankment and he knew it would be Shade. Then the fog closed in and he stumbled into a run. At the back of the garden he found a gate, a series of in-cut steps beyond. He went up gasping and wiping with his sleeve at the blood drenching his moustaches and his chin, his face dripping like some ghoul just risen, his right arm dangling useless at his side.

At the top of the stairs he found himself on a high stone wall and he could see into the cutting below. He glanced swiftly along the railway ties where they stretched sleekly out of the earth towards the city itself like an incision but could see no sign of Shade. The stones were slick underfoot and covered here and there in patches of tall grey weeds bending up through the cracks and William stumbled on at that eerie height with the backs of the terrace houses in the fog beyond half concealed and the strangeness of that space as if he were moving through the backstage of some theatrical production.

Then he saw Shade.

The thief was not running. He stood favouring one leg and faced William as he approached and the revolver in his hand looked light, warm, as if it were a part of him, some smooth extension of his wrist and not iron but flesh. He raised this part of himself and held it out in a kind of offering of violence and William went very still.

Are you alone? Shade called.

William said nothing. He was standing some ten paces away and knew he could not bridge that distance.

Go back to Chicago, Shade called. This is finished.

The hell it is.

William.

He took a step forward, bloodied palms raised. Tell me about my father, he shouted. What happened between you?

The cold fog drifted around them, pressing in and pulling apart like a thing alive. Slowly Shade turned his face aside and peered down into the shadows of the cutting below as if listening for a train and after a moment William could feel it also. The low thrumming in the stone underfoot as if the earth itself were set trembling. The distant roar, the far whoosh and in-suck of air.

Edward, he called. He ran a bloodied wrist over his forehead. Whose blood is that?

That weapon still levelled at his heart. The train grew louder.

William stared down at his wrist as if only just seeing it and then he looked up in surprise. I didn't kill them, he shouted. Fludd or the girl. Neither of them.

Shade said something but the roar of the train drowned out his words and then he shook his head and shouted angrily, This isn't how your father would have wanted it.

I'm not doing this for him.

Shade hollered, Your whole life has been for him.

And then the train roared up out of the earth black and aflame in a whirlwind of smoke and fury and Shade gave him a strange regretful look and limped to the edge of the cutting. The smoke boiling up around him, the air crackling his clothing into silhouette and curling up around the satchel and its ten thousand pounds and knocking his hat from his head.

Wait, William cried.

The thief glanced back once but William could not see his face and then he turned and stepped casually out into the maelstrom and vanished.

There was neither blood nor carnage. No long drag of a body, no stain or smear on the tracks. Only the man's hat caught in a tangle of weeds where it had been sucked over. William climbed down and retrieved it and stood with it in his hands staring at the suddenly vacant cutting around him. He could feel the cold crumpling of his shirt where the blood had dried. After a short while he climbed back out and saw the swing of a bull's-eye lantern in the fog, its beam startling and sliding over the slick stones and crossing and sliding again away. That was a young helmeted constable called in by neighbours who had heard gunshots. A runner was sent, John Shore descended, the vacant terrace house was gone over but no trace of Shade's destination was found.

So he's gone, Shore said. Standing at the precipice of the embankment, banging his hat against his thigh. Edward Shade's gone.

William closed his eyes, opened his eyes. And then he was missing Margaret with a passion that left him gutted and trembling.

I guess so, he said. I guess he is.

In the end everyone would come to grief, he knew. No one would be spared. There were the dead in his own country too. The following morning he went out to the steamship offices on the lower Strand and purchased a one-way ticket to New York set to depart in ten days' time and when he stepped back out into the street he was struck all at once by the stark desolate beauty of the city. The clerk who had sold him his ticket had upgraded him from second class at a reduced rate and William had set his gloved fist on the counter and studied the young man and then nodded and thanked him. Over the Thames the winter sky was very blue, very cold. He rubbed his hands, walked briskly. Sat an hour in a café at a table near the steamed-over windows studying a railway timetable, planning a route north. He had ten days before sailing and thought he might go to Glasgow. He wanted away from London.

At noon he went into a haberdasher's off Piccadilly and purchased several elaborate hats in the French style for his wife and daughters. They had enormous soft brims and slouching ostrich feathers and he filled out his address in Chicago and instructed the sales clerk to pack them with care. For his brother he purchased a leather-bound set of Dickens. He wrote to Margaret, he wrote to Robert. He sent several telegrams with details of his arrival in New York. He returned to his hotel and slept a dreamless sleep and woke in the evening refreshed. His old steamer trunk he packed slowly as if to fill his hours and his folded shirts he tied with twine and the package with Edward Shade's measurements and fingerprints he laid between the clothes. He locked the trunk and left the key standing in it, pointing at him like a finger. No he did not believe the thief dead. That night he shaved using hot water from his bath and he dried his face with a clean towel. He wiped his hand across the mirror and stared at his worn face, unsatisfied.

The next morning was Sunday and it brought a knock at the door. He opened it in his shirt sleeves and saw John Shore bareheaded picking at his hat and the chief glanced up and said, There's something you should know.

Shouldn't you be at church?

Shore smiled tiredly. He handed across a small slip of paper with an address scrawled upon it in brown ink.

William glanced at it. What's this?

It's in the southwest. Out past Sands End. I had Mr. Blackwell make some inquiries.

William stood perplexed and neither man spoke for a long moment and then Shore said, gruffly, It seems she isn't dead after all.

And he gripped William's shoulder and there was kindness in it and even a little pity and then he set his hat back on his head and went.

He did not go to Scotland. That afternoon he took passage on a crowded passenger steamer at Waterloo Pier and journeyed upriver through the noise and he disembarked at Pimlico Pier watching the sky for rain. There he hired an ancient rowboat oared by an old man with a single yellow tooth standing up from his lower gums. The man's accent was thick and William could not understand him. They rowed slowly on west, passing under the dripping arches of Battersea Bridge and wending uneasily in the shallows past the low-set colliers moored at the mouth of Chelsea Basin where the gasworks lay. The sky darkened. A stretch of meagre brown meadow came into view on the north bank and the old man in his oilskin rowed in silence his eyes on William's face. The river traffic thinned. At last they reached Broomhouse Dock and William got out his legs stiff and he set off walking up the lane past the estates there until he reached Fulham Road. The air was crisp, clean, trees and fenced-in fields lining the roads. He turned north again towards Walham Green and it started to rain and he drew his hat low but did not seek shelter. The rain was not heavy. He had to stop and ask directions as he could see no street signs but at last he found the low stone walls of Westminster Cemetery and her small cottage set within sight of the fields of the dead.

He scraped his shoes on the iron scraper, stamped them twice for good measure. Then he knocked and waited what seemed a long time while the rain dripped from the eaves. A bolt rasped in its draw. The door opened.

Standing there was an old woman, leaning stoutly in her rags like a melted candle. One gnarled hand trembled on the edge of the door. William was shaking his head and staring and she was squinting back from the fog of her failing eyesight like a woman confronting a ghost.

You don't got no sense at all, do you? she said at last. And waved a gruff hand, her voice dry. She kept clearing her throat and flaring her nostrils as if struggling for breath, some low flicker of something in her cloudy eyes.

Sally Porter, he said. Holding his hat in his hands, water streaming down his face. Sally Porter.

The cottage was small but warm for a wood fire burned in the grate. On the mantel fastened in its own wax and leaning at a crazy angle stood the stub of a red candle. William sat in his wet clothes on a dirty sofa. There was no carpet over the bare planks and the boards were coming loose in their nails and creaked under his weight. It was a square room and he saw at a glance the stained wallpaper some twenty years out of fashion and under it in places the crumbling plaster. She shuffled slowly at her tasks and her hands shook and she kept her eyes downcast. He did not take off his coat. On the table in the corner stood an elegant, seven-branched silver candlestick with a vine carved into its stalks. He did not need to look closer to know its origin.

I ain't goin to ask how you found me, she said.

He shrugged. John Shore.

Ha. That John Shore never tracked nothin in his life.

But now that he had come he felt an overwhelming sadness and suddenly wished he had not found her. He gestured half-heartedly with his hat and said, It's nicer than the last. I like the candlestick. Is it Jewish?

She grunted. We put some money aside.

I got your letter.

I know you did.

What happened to California?

Sally gave him a quick sharp look. She sat in a high-backed rocking chair and a white cat unfurled from under the window and padded over to her and leaped into her lap. She combed her knuckles through the cat's fur. It all felt suddenly mean and heavy to William, the shock of seeing her beginning to dissipate. He said, directly: Edward Shade is gone.

She inclined her head yes. Her face was hard, there was no apology in it.

I came here to ask for the truth, Sally.

I know you did.

His lips were dry, his tongue thick as cotton webbing in his mouth. He was thinking about her letter and Edward Shade and struggling to put it together but something was not right and he could not do so. Will you tell me about it? he said gently. Will you tell me how it happened?

You ain't likely to understand it, she said. But she paused and some uncertainty twisted in her face and then she said, He always was a good boy. Or near enough to one, Billy. Like you was. An he grown up to be a fine man despite it all.

You can't mean Shade.

All right.

You've been in contact with him all this time?

Not like you mean it.

He shook his head. Shade betrayed my father, he said softly. He lied to him, humiliated him. My father trusted you.

Stop all that now. Ain't no understandin a cat by skinnin it.

He watched the old woman's cat lift its face and stare into the corner then rise like smoke and vanish into the gloom. He got to his feet, crossed to the dirty window. He felt huge, and dark, a wrath rising. What would Ben have said? he muttered.

Sally looked away. Her gnarled hands locked and rigid in her lap like twists of driftwood.

Then William understood. Ben was a part of it too? You and Ben both? Lying to my father all these years.

Don't you talk like that.

And to me. You must have been terrified. You must have thought I was there to—

No.

And all that in the letter, the things you sent me. He gave those to you. Shade did.

Billy.

I was such a fool, he said bitterly.

You ain't goin to understand it. You father he loved that poor boy like he were a son to him. Like he were you or Robert either one. I reckon it were his worst grief. I ain't sayin it to hurt you.

The hell he did.

She gave him a long slow measured look and it seemed to William he was being seen through, stared into, as if she had lost one kind of vision for some other, a way of seeing that would cut her off from this world of the human and the hidden. She said, My Mister Porter found him, six years ago now. He were workin deliveries an followed some dipper not hardly more than a child up out of Bermondsey and she led him right down to a park an who do you reckon was standin there but Edward hisself. Edward didn't hardly hesitate. Just walked right up to Ben an put his arms round him and give him a hug like to take the life out of him.

He knew he was being hunted.

I reckon he known it for always. You father, bless his heart, he was wantin for somethin, some notion of rightness, I reckon you know that better than most.

Something turned over in William's stomach, some foreboding.

After the war ended Edward went up to Chicago to find him, Sally said. She was peering in his direction with her vague eyes and when he said nothing she said, You father he done just returned from the Mireau Gang Murder out of Texas. Young Edward broke into you father's study with a knife and a pistol.

He did not interrupt but still she raised a hand as if to stay his questions. Edward waited for you father with the express purpose of shooting him dead, she said. Nodding and nodding as she spoke. That boy was all of eighteen years old and he carried nothin but murder in his heart. He sat behind you father's desk an he listened to you folks talk out in the hallway. He known what had been done, see. He'd had four years to think it through and he come to the conclusion that you father sent Ignatius Spaar into Richmond to tie up his loose ends. He supposed you father and General McClellan come under scrutiny and no further embarrassments after Lewis and Scully and poor Timothy Webster was to be risked. He were just cleanin house, is how he put it.

Sally worked her lips as if rubbing some oil into them and then she lifted her face. The one thing young Edward weren't never able to understand was just how the Confederate Secret Service got to him so quick. They was there outside his door almost before Spaar come at him. He fought off Spaar and killed him in the fight and they was in the room quick as sugar on a finger.

She took a long slow rattling breath and then she sat a moment in the gathering gloom as if she had lost the thread and then she nodded in his direction. Spaar done turned, she said. An assassination, is what it was. But who had ordered it?

Not my father.

Or not only him, Sally said quietly. Truth was, Spaar was taken by the Confederates his second day in Richmond and made a deal for his life. O he had Confederate fingers in his pocket, no mistake. And if he'd succeeded, if he'd killed Edward? Then the Confederates would have taken him into custody just the same and hanged him just the same. Like they done to Webster.

Why would they do that?

She shrugged. Everyone was betraying everybody.

Except my father.

Except you father. And Edward.

A log collapsed in the hearth. William scoffed. How do you know all this?

But she didn't answer. Instead she said, Young Edward didn't know none of this either when he gone to you father's study that night. He meant to kill you father dead and when you father come in and seen Edward he knowed it also. He told me once, he said, the boy's eyes wasn't even human that night. It frightened him, it did. They didn't light no candles but the one, they sat in the near darkness, the house goin about its ordinary nighttime business, the maid goin up and down them stairs. But now Edward didn't shoot. There were somethin in you father's face that give him pause. What do you suppose that was?

William sat quiet, listening. The rain had stopped.

You father he was crying. That were what stayed Edward's hand. He made no sound but he were crying and Edward tried to hold on to his spite and he told him what he'd come to do and what he held you father accountable for. You father just looked at young Edward and said that was okay except he didn't want you mother to find his body. Then he said he'd searched for Edward after the war and did the boy know about it. He said he'd resigned from the service in sixty-two in part because the government had refused to negotiate Edward's release. He said ever man has something he has to do in his life to learn what he is capable of and to understand the past can't be altered none nor corrected and he said if killing him could not be avoided then it were best it were done quickly and Edward got himself gone. And then he did one thing that left the boy more confused than ever. He stood up and he come round the desk and he pulled him towards him and he held him.

Shade never shot at him.

Edward said he always figured you father wanted him to.

They sat like that a long moment.

Why didn't you tell me about this before? he asked. Why did you lie to me?

Some truths ain't ours to do with as we'd wish, Billy. You got to let some things go, if you goin to find happiness. You father he ain't never understood this.

My father.

Now you listen, she said sharply. I loved you father. An my Mister Porter did too. Weren't nothin we wouldn't of done for him. That's God's own truth.

He looked at her without anger but she flinched all the same. He pulled his wet hat low and went to the door and started to go but then he paused. Where is he? he said. Where did he go?

I ain't never known that, she said gruffly.

Where is he, Sally?

She wet her cracked lips, glared across at him. Don't you leave here pretending like I ain't got no notion of how things was. You father could be right mean and difficult and about as forgiving as a hole in a boat. I known how it was between you. I ain't the one tryin to forget it. Her voice was creaking and she fell silent then as if out of breath. A shadow like a great wing passed over the far wall.

Where is he? he said a third time.

Aw now, Billy, she said. Her face twisted into a mask of grief. He's gone on ahead to Argentina. He's gone. You best to let it lie.

Argentina, he said. He looked at her as if for the last time. Is there more?

She peered up at him through milky eyes. Not that I can tell to you.

He opened the door of the cottage, his back to her. You should thank god my father's dead, he said. You'd have broke his damn heart.

There was only one liner leaving direct for Buenos Aires and it did not depart Liverpool until that Saturday. All week William slept late and ate heavily and settled his affairs at Scotland Yard and said nothing of Sally's information to Shore or Blackwell. His anger again cooled. He turned over Sally's account in his mind trying to make sense of it but he could not do so. On Friday evening he took an overnight train to Liverpool and in the morning walked out of the railway station and down to the riverfront pier with a red sun low in the sky at his back. He descended a rattling wood quay. Walked through a crowd of strangers weeping into their hands, his own gloved fists curled like great brown spiders. The pain in his ribs was at last beginning to subside. The dark liner loomed at its moorings and he walked its length. On board was a coffin holding a young actress bound for New York but this meant nothing to him. He waded through the curious and the grieving a head taller than most and his tall silk hat taller yet. He wore black like a figure out of nightmare and his eyes were cold and his moustaches thick and no man who met his eye held it for long. He spoke to no one, he carried no luggage, he trudged up the gangway with his thick shoulders turned and he went through and in. It was the last day of February, 1885.

He was thinking about the minutiae of a life. What a person was and was not. He was not given by nature to philosophical problems and felt largely that the thing in front of him was mostly what it looked like, and felt like, though this too, he knew, was a kind of philosophy. He had wept for his father after the funeral but it had been a strange furtive kind of grief and what he felt now, pressing past the figures with their waving handkerchiefs and their clutter of luggage, was not the same but something very close.

He made his way below decks in the first-class area to the second largest of the staterooms and fumbled in his pockets but they were empty and when he tried the door he found it unlocked.

There were several trunks and suitcases on the floor beside the bedding alcove. They had not yet been stowed for the passage and he glanced at them and then glanced away. He could hear ladies laughing in the hallway beyond and he shut the door with a clang and walked to the small sofa under the porthole. He sat, he stood, he paced. On the narrow desk was a morning edition looking unread and William picked it up and studied the headlines. It was seven days old and the front page was covered with articles about the stolen painting's return and notions about the men responsible and the motives behind it. William had heard rumours that Farquhar had engineered the entire thing for the publicity. One politician had suggested the Russians were responsible. The world of men was, he thought, ridiculous. Then there was a low scraping at the door and then the handle punched down and Edward Shade stepped through.

He saw William at once but only nodded and took off his hat and smoothed down his white hair. If he was astonished to see the detective he gave no sign. He smiled a wry smile and crossed to the cupboard of the stateroom and returned with a bottle of port and two glasses hung upside down from between his knuckles.

I was hoping you would show, he said.

Upending the glasses with a clink on the desk and unstoppering the bottle.

William smiled cautiously.

We never said a proper farewell. Isn't it strange, how some things come full circle?

There were gulls crying in the morning sky outside and William watched Shade pass across a glass then sit with his legs crossed at the knee.

You're alone? Shade said.

William inclined his head.

Shade shrugged but there was a weariness to it. My excellent Mr. Fludd is here with me somewhere. As you will have gathered. A little bored and looking for excitement.

His face?

Well. His career on the stage will be ruined.

William furrowed his brow. And the girl?

Molly.

She's all right?

She doesn't take a knock without wanting to give one back.

William nodded. I didn't come here to do violence, he said.

I should be disappointed if you had. The thief was wearing a fine striped suit cut for warmer weather. He sipped his port and William watched the morning light flare and fracture in the cut glass but he himself did not drink and he held the delicate glass between his thick fingers feeling rough and tired. His eyes were sore.

Shade waited.

At last William shifted in his seat and let his frock coat fall open to reveal the Colt at his side and he ran his tongue along his gums and grimaced and said, I brought you something.

Shade furrowed his brow. He was holding his walking stick loose across his knees as if to ward off some sudden movement.

William fumbled in his frock coat and withdrew the folded photograph from Sally Porter. He opened it and studied the muddy camp at Cumberland, the operatives in their cool horror, his younger father chewing on his cigar, his hard Scottish eyes black as obsidian. The blur of the bad capture of the boy Shade had been. He passed it across and Shade took it and stared at it and then he murmured, That was another lifetime.

It wasn't.

Shade looked up, his eyes glinting in the shadow. I loved your father, he said quietly. But I was never his son.

That's right. You weren't.

Shade sighed, he set the photograph on the side table. You've been to see Sally then.

I've seen her, yes.

Shade regarded him carefully. Sipped his drink, said nothing.

William cleared his throat. Here's what I don't understand, he said. Here's what I haven't stopped puzzling over, not since I talked to her. My father hired the Porters to find you. Why would he send operatives you had known and would recognize? Why send two Negroes into London, for god's sake?

He trusted them.

He didn't trust anyone. But he loved them, and I believe they loved him. Yet when they found you, they didn't report you and even began to work for you. They were my father's oldest associates, he had helped smuggle them to freedom, they had stood by him during the war, but still they ended up working for you.

Shade said nothing. His luminous eyes brilliant. A wry smile, soft as velvet, soft as a handshake in the dark.

They protected your secret, William pressed.

What can I confess to? I'm a charming man.

Not that charming.

Shade shrugged. I paid them well.

They never cared about money.

Everyone cares about money.

William shook his head but ignored this and he said, instead, My father left no file. No reports. Nothing that could be traced back to you.

Because the Porters destroyed them.

He never risked his only copy of anything. He kept reports of his childhood medical exams, for god's sake. He kept dental records on his horses.

Shade studied him. What are you saying, William?

William leaned forward and set his glass of port, untouched, on the low steel table. The liquid wobbled into equilibrium. I'm saying you've been played, he said.

A fold of darkness between Shade's eyes, a crease of a frown.

All this time you thought you had him deceived—

Because I did, Shade said with a low ferocity. He never caught up to me.

He knew you were alive.

Yes.

And exactly where to find you.

Shade smiled a quick incredulous smile.

All these years you've been hiding from him. All this time. And you never realized it. He didn't hire Sally and Ben to find you. He hired them to watch out for you.

That's ridiculous.

You and your famous luck, William went on. Escaping the police in Montreal just before the Pinkertons arrived. Avoiding prison in Boston and New York. Somehow getting out of the trains before they were searched, crossing the Atlantic how many times without being recognized. You never wondered about it? You never thought it unlikely?

William rose wearily, he put on his hat and ran a finger along the brim, he pulled on his gloves. The ship's horn sounded three times, like a warning out of a dream. The daylight darkened imperceptibly. He had crossed to the door of the stateroom and he paused now with his hand on the door and his great bulk looming. He looked back at the thief and was surprised to feel a kind of sadness. He looked at the smaller man's beautiful eyes and wondered at the love his father must have held for the man. The clean manicured hands, the fold of his pinstriped trousers. A crescent of morning light crossed his cheekbones and whiskers.

I didn't come to say goodbye, he said with a frown. I came because I wanted you to know.

Shade stared at him. The glass of port was very still in his hand. Know what? he said.

Outside the cold waters ran red in the red light. There were gulls crying and wheeling in the sky and their shadows rippled and cut across the surface of the river.

William smiled a sly smile.

That I can find you, he said.

Epilogue

1913

OREGON

When does a life begin its decline.

His wife had been dead now nearly eighteen years. He thought of that sometimes with a faded sorrow. His younger daughter had nearly died in an automobile accident in 1905 and the elder had married and moved away. He still wrote both long letters even now though his handwriting had deteriorated to a scrawl and he sometimes burned with a longing to see them again which he felt like a physical pain. It would overwhelm him and leave him gasping. When his brother died in August of 1907 he knew at last he was truly alone. He slept less and less and then he slept too much. His hair greyed and he cut off his moustaches and he changed the cut of his suits to weather the times. His office in Chicago was dark with leather and mahogany and paintings of long-dead thoroughbreds and it began to feel like a room preserved. As the years passed there were fewer and fewer dossiers on his desk each night and slowly he began to slip from the office earlier and earlier in the day. He became a man revered. At banquets he sat in the place of honour. When he rode down to the stables of an evening he still wore his Colt Navy but the chambers now were empty. Shadows lengthened under the oaks. Stars came out. He walked at first slowly and then with a cane and then the heaviness of his flesh began to leave him and his weakened shoulders started to ache. Some black thing was growing in a cavity behind his spine and he felt it like a bruise when he lay down at night and he knew it would one day kill him. In 1896 Shore retired from the Yard haunted yet by the murders in Whitechapel and in 1898 he was hired as Pinkerton's London agent. John Shore of the indomitable health, ruddy-faced, strong even at sixty, who would not live to see the new century. Somewhere he heard Adam Foole had died a pauper in Genoa in 1893, somewhere he heard Foole had been sentenced to a life of hard labour in Marseilles. That last was in 1896 and he did not believe it. That was the year Japheth Fludd was photographed after a knife fight in Cathay holding his stomach in his hands. The Agency grew bigger. There were invitations to speak in public and the newspapers came to love him. It seemed a world had passed almost overnight into a kind of legend and its survivors few as they were lived now like artifacts of that lost era. The years moved fast, the ocean grew smaller. He marvelled at airplanes with the hunger of a younger man. But he hated the telephone and regarded automobiles with the eye of a skittish horse and he missed the open country. It had been fourteen years since he had last heard the name Edward Shade and that he had whispered to himself. Fourteen years.

How did he live? He washed his hands carefully in cold water. He ate little. He stopped drinking.

He lived.

He was recuperating in northern California when his San Francisco office received the telephone call. An Oregon sheriff described the holdup and the man responsible and the style of it seemed an echo from an earlier life. A man wearing heavy spurs and the outsized and dusty rawhide of another age had walked clinking into a bank in Portland on a Monday afternoon and demanded cash. He was very old and had drawn with difficulty a huge ancient revolver from under his coat and had needed both thumbs to cock the hammer. His hands shook so bad the teller had feared being shot in error. The man was dark and small-boned and shrivelled from the sun and he had very bright very clear eyes.

I reckon it must be old Bill Miner, the sheriff had said into the telephone. There was a buzz and a click and then a silence. Then he said, If you could send someone up. We heard reports of a camp up in the hills out back of a logging outfit. It's probably him.

It was the detail about the eyes that decided him. He journeyed north by special train all that night and was standing in the empty street in Portland as the sun rose the following morning with his nurse at his side holding a blanket around his shoulders. By nine o'clock they were driving into the mountains. A sunlight fell dappled through the high alpine trees and the old detective rode with one hand clutching the edge of the door as the automobile rattled and jounced over the ruts in the road. It was a logging road and dragged clear by rolls of timber and they drove slowly. He was thinking of the different kinds of sunlight and how some carry a sadness in them the way certain wines will do. There was in that high alpine light something that made him think of his earliest years with Margaret when the future seemed a single fixed thing they moved towards together. He was lonely, he was resigned. His heart, he knew, was an unswept room and would remain so until his death.

There were two men with him one a sheriff and both were younger by four decades at least. His nurse slept in the back seat beside him with a red wool shawl draped around her shoulders and her knees half parted and her head lolling side to side as they passed under the pines. Slats of shadow, slats of sunlight. This was her world, their world. A world of telephones and automobiles and streetcars. A world of barbed wire and moving pictures. The first time he had seen a moving picture it was of Butch Cassidy being pursued by Pinkerton men and he had felt sick and made his slow way up through the smoke to the exit in disgust. His kind was like the horse. There was no open anywhere left for the running now.

At the edge of a meadow the sheriff parked the automobile and he listened to the engine rattle out and fall still. The sudden quiet in the trees surrounding made him wipe at his eyes. Then the second man gestured at a thin line of smoke rising above the trees and the sheriff nodded. There were low tangled white flowers in the meadow like clover and their boots made no sound as they walked. He leaned on his cane. He felt no need to keep up. The nurse he had left asleep in her seat and he followed the men across the meadow then up through the sparse pines feeling the soft give of the needles underfoot. He was wearing his Colt as he had always done but it was holstered now and he clutched instead in one claw-like fist a folder of Agency documents and clippings. He wore a three-piece suit and a narrow blue tie. He moved very slow.

Miner had been making coffee. When they found him he was sprawled out on the edge of a wind-fallen log with his hands folded at his belly and he looked to be dead. His grey face upturned and mouth aghast. After a few minutes he awoke and wiped at a line of spittle on his chin and peered about blinking in confusion then sat up and began raking through the coals with a whittled stick. A battered tin coffee pot sat balanced on three rocks. He seemed not to have noticed the three men standing at the edge of his camp.

William felt a sudden great affection for the outlaw. The old crook had held up his first stagecoach in 1866. He had robbed the famous Del Norte Colorado and crawled on his belly away from the vigilantes who were stringing his partner up by the throat. It was said he had invented the expression *Hands up!* and that in 1881 he had organized a small outfit of men to knock down trains in Oregon and California. He had escaped from prison that year by scaling the walls barefoot and a trail of bloodied footprints led the guards to a flat stone in the river and no farther. In 1901 he had slipped from two Pinkerton agents over the border to Canada only to be picked up in 1906 by the Royal North-West Mounted and tried and sentenced to life. He had escaped one month later. He was ninety-one years old.

The sheriff tipped his hat back with his thumb. Morning, he said.

Miner glanced up in alarm, watery eyes squinting. Who's that? he demanded. Show yourselves.

The sheriff held his hands out before him and stepped forward. His badge catching the light. It's all right, he said. Just doing some camping, are we?

Miner said nothing.

Aw now, we're just being friendly.

You boys best be getting along, Miner said.

You wouldn't be interested in us, Bill, the second man said. We're not worth the robbing.

Miner glared at them. Who you boys with? he demanded. What outfit you got?

No one's with anyone anymore, Bill, William said. He felt so tired. He said, There are no outfits. All that's finished now. It's been over for fifteen years.

Miner furrowed his brow suspiciously. I know you, he said.

The sheriff had set his thumb on the revolver in his belt but he did not look as if he had any expectation of drawing. He said, You know why we're here, Mr. Miner. We've come to get the twelve thousand dollars back and to bring you in for the robbery of the Northern Securities Bank in Portland.

Miner grinned. His head was trembling and when he took off his hat he was bald as a tortoise and his scalp looked liverspotted and old. A ring of grime encircled his skull like war paint. Portland, Portland, he said. Isn't that in Arizona? I just come up here for the camping, Sheriff. There ain't no law against that now.

William smiled despite himself. You didn't rob the Northern Securities?

No, sir. I never did.

You didn't escape from a jail in Vancouver seven years back?

No I did not.

There isn't a bag of money and securities somewhere in this camp if we go looking for it?

Miner worked his gums and frowned. What's here is all my own property. You take any of it and that's called robbery.

William shrugged tiredly and looked at the sheriff then opened the folder and passed it across to Miner. Photographs, trial transcripts, testimonies from long-forgotten stagecoach robberies. Then he passed across a copy of eyewitness accounts of the recent holdup. The outlaw squinted and shook. He could see the man's ancient fingers trembling.

Son of a bitch, Miner said. Look at this. Look at how handsome I was.

Can you read? William asked.

I got my letters.

What's it say?

Miner did not answer. He closed the dossier with care. Can I get a copy of this? he said.

Nobody had drawn a weapon.

You know, Miner said wearily. I'm getting too damned old for this line of work.

Later, collecting up the remnants of the old man's camp. Kicking through the few rags and pans then stuffing all of it into heavy evidence satchels brought along for the purpose. William stopped a moment and took off his hat and stared out at the trees surrounding. He said, I came all this way. He shook his head in disbelief. He said, It was just old Bill Miner after all.

The sheriff was sifting through the ashes of the fire with a stick and he lifted a scorched tin can that had twisted from the heat then let it fall.

Who were you expecting? he said.

He said it casually and William looked at the younger man and his dark eyes were set deep in his weathered face and he felt all at once his years. He was listening to the silence brush against the fir needles and feeling the cold mountain air on his face and hands. It was a good place. In the meadow below their strange new automobile crouched on its wheels like a great black spider. There was a nurse down there wearing a shawl the colour of blood, and an ancient outlaw, and a man of the new breed with neither face nor name. He put his hat back on his head with shaking fingers.

After a moment the sheriff asked it again. Who did you think you'd find?

Who did I think I'd find?

The sheriff met his eye. What were you looking for, Mr. Pinkerton?

The trees around them were very quiet. He felt a wind on his neck.

What was I looking for, he muttered.

He was the oldest son.

His eyes were failing. His hair had greyed then thinned and he had cut off his moustaches with a razor in cold water one winter afternoon in a hotel room in Gainesville, Georgia. His wife had been dead then half as many years as their marriage had lasted and the pain of it had become a part of him like a badly set bone. He would walk down to her grave on Sunday mornings and clear the dead flowers and fill the porcelain vase with cold clear water then stand reading the inscription and thinking nothing at all. He slept. He did not sleep. He slept.

He closed his eyes and he saw. A quarter century had passed and still he closed his eyes and saw. Darkness like a fog pouring over frozen cobblestones. The creak of chains sawing from hooks in alleys, eyes in the shadows stagnant and brown as smoke. He could smell the rot around him. A clatter of iron-shod hooves on stone, crowds of men wending between the omnibuses in silk hats and black cloaks and whiskers. He was walking. He was walking with his powerful shoulders set low and his fists like blocks of tackle and it was dusk, it was night, he could just make out the silhouette standing under the gaslight waiting. The face was turned away but it did not matter, he knew that one well. The battered trunk at his feet, as if preparing for a journey.

That one had always been waiting. That one would always be.

AUTHOR'S NOTE

While several incidents described in these pages can be traced to real places, and real events, this story is a work of fiction. Its characters, both real and imagined, are creations of the author. The gaslit London of its pages never existed.

There are many excellent nonfiction accounts of the early Pinkerton Agency, the Civil War, and the lives of criminals in Victorian London.

This is not one of them.

ACKNOWLEDGMENTS

Thanks are due, first, to the magnificent Jonathan Galassi, for his gentle, judicious eye and critical acumen; also to Jo Stewart, Jeff Seroy, Rodrigo Corral, Lottchen Shivers, and everyone at FSG. I am grateful to Juliet Mabey for her grace, enthusiasm and publishing dazzle; also to James Magniac, the talented James Jones, and everyone at Oneworld. I feel deeply lucky for the care and consideration of Kristin Cochrane, Anita Chong, Marion Garner, Aoife Walsh, Kelly Hill (for her gorgeous design), John Sweet, Shaun Oakey, Sharon Klein, Trish Kells, and everyone at M&S. Trident Media has made everything happen, especially Claire Roberts and the stalwart Alexa Stark. John Baker, Jeff Mireau, and the steadfast Jacqueline Baker discussed and improved multiple drafts from the beginning. Ellen Levine, my agent and friend, has been the quiet tidal force behind everything and there would, quite simply, be no novel without her.

Throughout the editing of this novel Ellen Seligman was a voice of passion and fire. Her intelligence, excitement and insight made themselves felt on every page. She is irreplaceable.

Above all, always, I owe this life to Esi: my love, my friend, my first and truest reader.

The text of *By Gaslight* has been set in Goudy, (often referred to as Goudy Oldstyle) a face designed in 1915 for the American Type Founders by the prolific typographer Frederic W. Goudy. Used with equal success in both text and display sizes, Goudy remains one of the most popular typefaces ever produced. It is best recognized by the diamond-shaped dots on punctuation; the upturned "ear" of the g; and the elegant base curve of the caps E and L.